T0110646

MORE PRAISE FOR RHYS BOWEN'S
USA TODAY BESTSELLING ROYAL SPYNESS MYSTERIES

Heirs and Graces

"It's the perfect fix between seasons for *Downton Abbey* addicts."
—Deborah Crombie, *New York Times* bestselling author of
The Sound of Broken Glass

The Twelve Clues of Christmas

"*The Twelve Clues of Christmas* is yet another brilliant novel from Rhys Bowen. . . . Like all of Rhys's books, this is so much more than a murder mystery. It's part love story, part social commentary, part fun and part down-right terrifying. And completely riveting. I adore this book and can hardly wait to give it to all my family and friends for Christmas! For all who love the season, and a great murder mystery, this book is perfect."
—Louise Penny, author of *The Beautiful Mystery*

"Bowen's sixth whodunit featuring the irrepressible Lady Georgiana Rannoch . . . may be her best yet . . . Bowen blends zany humor with fair-play detection as well as any author of traditional mysteries."
—*Publishers Weekly* (starred review)

"Hilarious adventure . . . What an absolute delight! With a witty and clever plot, it's clear that Agatha Christie is alive and kicking and what's more, she's funny!"
—Hannah Dennison, author of *Thieves!* a Vicky Hill Exclusive! Mystery

"The sixth in Bowen's delightful Royal Spyness mysteries set in the 1930s . . . gives readers a blueprint for an old-fashioned English Christmas, complete with traditional recipes, games, drinks, and homicides."
—*Kirkus Reviews*

"A delightful diversion even after the Christmas season is over . . . *The Twelve Clues of Christmas* is a bonbon, a delicious treat. You'll read it with a smile on your face from beginning to end."
—*Gumshoe Review*

continued . . .

Naughty in Nice

"Georgie's latest adventure is charming and lighthearted as ever, though the 1930s setting carries ominous hints of the future." —*Kirkus Reviews*

"Whimsical . . . Bowen successfully melds a whodunit with comedy as few contemporary writers can." —*Publishers Weekly*

"Don't miss a trip to the French Riviera when Lady Georgiana (*Royal Blood*) is sent by the queen on a new secret mission. Add a dash of Coco Chanel and a murder or two—how can you pass up the fifth treat in this delectable series?" —*Library Journal*

Royal Blood

"A wedding in Transylvania . . . Wonderful characters . . . [A] delight." —Charlaine Harris, #1 *New York Times* bestselling author of the Sookie Stackhouse novels

"Bowen keeps the mystery light and humorous, but the discerning reader will note the social problems underlying Georgie's breezy narrative." —*Booklist*

"Agatha winner Bowen successfully mixes Wodehousian farce with a whodunit plot . . . [She] once again demonstrates her mastery of the light, romantic mystery." —*Publishers Weekly*

Royal Blush

"Bowen's winning third Royal Spyness whodunit . . . will please fans of romantic, humorous historicals . . . Bowen, who's won both Agatha and Anthony awards, puts a fresh slant on it." —*Publishers Weekly*

"As in previous entries in the series, Georgiana makes a superb sleuth, but much of the fun comes in the contrast between impoverished Georgie and the royal life of which—financial circumstances notwithstanding—she is still a part." —*Booklist*

"As usual, Georgie's high spirits and the author's frothy prose are utterly captivating."
—*The Denver Post*

A Royal Pain

"A delectable mystery with vibrant characters and a bit of romance, Bowen's latest is a rollicking good read."
—*Booklist*

"A pre–World War II mystery with a touch of romance that adds another winner to Bowen's accomplishments."
—*Kirkus Reviews*

Her Royal Spyness

"An insightful blend of old-fashioned whodunit, clever satire and drawing room comedy of errors . . . A feisty new heroine to delight a legion of Anglophile readers."
—Jacqueline Winspear, author of the Maisie Dobbs novels

"A smashing romp."
—*Booklist* (starred review)

"This merry first in a new cozy series from Agatha winner Bowen introduces a delightful heroine—her madcap antics are certain to leave the reader eager for the next installment . . . Quirky characters . . . add to the fun."
—*Publishers Weekly*

"Delightfully naïve, charming and quite smart, Georgie is a breath of fresh air."
—*Library Journal*

PRAISE FOR RHYS BOWEN'S
CONSTABLE EVANS AND MOLLY MURPHY MYSTERIES

"It's always a delight to discover a new book from the pen of Rhys Bowen."
—*The Tampa Tribune*

"Entertaining."
—*Detroit Free Press*

continued . . .

"A series that shows no signs of growing stale." —*The Denver Post*

"It's hard not to be charmed by this young immigrant woman."
—*Pittsburgh Post-Gazette*

"A sweet and sunny read." —*San Francisco Sunday Examiner & Chronicle*

"Maybe Evan can wait, but I'm already impatient for his next adventure."
—Margaret Maron, author of *The Buzzard Table*

"Pitch-perfect." —Laura Lippman, author of *And When She Was Good*

"Quiet humor . . . A jewel of a story." —*Publishers Weekly*

"Impeccable sense of timing . . . Outstanding."
—*Library Journal* (starred review)

A Royal Threesome

RHYS BOWEN

BERKLEY PRIME CRIME, NEW YORK

THE BERKLEY PUBLISHING GROUP
Published by the Penguin Group
Penguin Group (USA) LLC
375 Hudson Street, New York, New York 10014

USA • Canada • UK • Ireland • Australia • New Zealand • India • South Africa • China

penguin.com
A Penguin Random House Company

A ROYAL THREESOME

Her Royal Spyness by Rhys Bowen copyright © 2007 by Janet Quin-Harkin.
A Royal Pain by Rhys Bowen copyright © 2008 by Janet Quin-Harkin.
Royal Flush by Rhys Bowen copyright © 2009 by Janet Quin-Harkin.
The Edgar® name is a registered service mark of the Mystery Writers of America, Inc.
Penguin supports copyright. Copyright fuels creativity, encourages diverse voices,
promotes free speech, and creates a vibrant culture. Thank you for buying an authorized
edition of this book and for complying with copyright laws by not reproducing, scanning,
or distributing any part of it in any form without permission. You are supporting writers
and allowing Penguin to continue to publish books for every reader.

Berkley Prime Crime Books are published by The Berkley Publishing Group.
BERKLEY® PRIME CRIME and the PRIME CRIME logo are trademarks of
Penguin Group (USA) LLC.

Library of Congress Cataloging-in-Publication Data

Bowen, Rhys.
A Royal threesome / Rhys Bowen.
pages cm.—(A Royal Spyness mystery)
ISBN 978-0-425-26991-6 (pbk.)
1. Aristocracy (Social class)—Fiction. 2. London (England)—History—20th century—Fiction.
I. Bowen, Rhys. Royal Spyness. II. Bowen, Rhys. Royal pain. III. Title.
PR6052.O848R73 2014
823'.914—dc23
2013041933

PUBLISHING HISTORY
Berkley Prime Crime trade paperback edition / February 2014

Cover illustration by Laurence Whiteley.
Cover design by Rita Frangie.

This is a work of fiction. Names, characters, places, and incidents either are the product
of the author's imagination or are used fictitiously, and any resemblance to actual persons,
living or dead, business establishments, events, or locales is entirely coincidental.

147028622

Contents

Her Royal Spyness

Notes and Acknowledgments

This is a work of fiction. While some real historical personages make cameo appearances in this book, Georgie and her friends and family exist only in the head of the writer. I have tried to ensure that royal personages do nothing out of character and accurately play themselves.

I would like to thank those who provided valuable input and gentle criticism: fellow mystery writers Jane Finnis and Jacqueline Winspear; my husband, John (who knows what's what about who's who); my daughters Clare and Jane; and my cheering section, my wonderful agents Meg and Kelly.

Thanks also to Marisa Young for lending her name to an English debutante.

Chapter 1

There are two disadvantages to being a minor royal.

First, one is expected to behave as befits a member of the ruling family, without being given the means to do so. One is expected to kiss babies, open fetes, put in an appearance at Balmoral (suitably kilted), and carry trains at weddings. Ordinary means of employment are frowned upon. One is not, for example, allowed to work on the cosmetics counter at Harrods, as I was about to find out.

When I venture to point out the unfairness of this, I am reminded of the second item on my list. Apparently the only acceptable destiny for a young female member of the house of Windsor is to marry into another of the royal houses that still seem to litter Europe, even though there are precious few reigning monarchs these days. It seems that even a very minor Windsor like myself is a desirable commodity for those wishing a tenuous alliance with Britain at this unsettled time. I am constantly being reminded that it is my duty to make a good match with some half-lunatic, buck-toothed, chinless, spineless, and utterly awful European royal, thus cementing ties with a potential enemy. My cousin Alex did this, poor thing. I have learned from her tragic example.

I suppose I should introduce myself before I venture any further. I am

Victoria Georgiana Charlotte Eugenie, daughter of the Duke of Glen Garry and Rannoch—known to my friends as Georgie. My grandmother was the least attractive of Queen Victoria's daughters, who consequently never managed to snare a Romanov or a Kaiser, for which I am truly grateful and I expect she was too. Instead she was hitched to a dreary Scottish baron who was bribed with a dukedom for taking her off the old queen's hands. In due time she dutifully produced my father, the second duke, before succumbing to the sort of diseases brought on by inbreeding and too much fresh air. I never knew her. I never met my fearsome Scottish grandfather either, although the servants claim that his ghost haunts Castle Rannoch, playing the bagpipes on the ramparts (which in itself is strange as he couldn't play the bagpipes in life). By the time I was born at Castle Rannoch, the family seat even less comfortable than Balmoral, my father had become the second duke and was busy working his way through the family fortune.

My father in turn had done his duty and married the daughter of a frightfully correct English earl. She gave birth to my brother, looked around at her utterly bleak Highland surroundings, and promptly died. Having secured an heir, my father then did the unthinkable and married an actress—my mother. Young men like his uncle Bertie, later King Edward VII, were allowed, even encouraged, to have dalliances with actresses, but never to marry them. However, since Mother was Church of England and came from a respectable, if humble, British family at a time when the storm clouds of the Great War were brewing in Europe, the marriage was accepted. Mother was presented to Queen Mary, who declared her remarkably civilized for someone from Essex.

The marriage didn't last, however. Even those with less zip and zest than my mother could not tolerate Castle Rannoch for long. The moan of the wind through the vast chimneys, coupled with the tartan wallpaper in the loo, had the effect of producing almost instant depression or even insanity. It's amazing, really, that she stuck it out for as long as she did. I think the idea of being a duchess appealed to her in principle. It was only when she realized that being married to a duke meant spending half the year in Scotland that she decided to bolt. I was two at the time. Her first bolt was with an Argentinian polo player. Many more bolts have followed, of course. The French racing driver, so tragically killed in Monte Carlo, the American film producer, the dashing explorer, and most recently, I understand, a German industrialist. I see her from time to time, when she flits through London.

Each time there is more makeup and more exotic and expensive hats as she tries desperately to cling on to those youthful looks that made men fight over her. We kiss, cheek to cheek, and talk about the weather, clothing, and my marriage prospects. It's like having tea with a stranger.

Luckily I had a kind nanny, so my upbringing at Castle Rannoch was lonely but not too terrible. Occasionally I was whisked away to stay with my mother, when she was married to someone suitable in a healthy part of the world, but she wasn't really cut out for motherhood and rarely stayed in one place for long, so that Castle Rannoch became my anchor, known and trusted, even if it was gloomy and lonely. My half brother, Hamish (usually known as Binky), was sent away to the sort of boarding school where cold showers and runs at dawn are the norm, designed to mold future leaders of the empire, so I hardly knew him either. Nor my father, really. After my mother's much publicized bolt he sort of lost heart and wafted around the watering holes of Europe, losing more and more money at the tables in Nice and Monte Carlo until the infamous stock market crash of '29. When he learned that he'd lost what remained of his fortune, he went up onto the moors and shot himself with his grouse gun, although how he managed to do it has always been the object of speculation, my father never having been a particularly good shot.

I remember trying to feel a sense of loss when the news was delivered to me in Switzerland. I only had the vaguest image in my brain of what he looked like. I missed the concept of having a father, knowing he was there for protection and advice when really needed. It was alarming to realize that at nineteen, I was essentially on my own.

So Binky became third duke, married a dull young woman of impeccable pedigree, and inherited Castle Rannoch. I, meanwhile, had been shipped off to finishing school in Switzerland, where I was having a spiffing time mixing with the naughty daughters of the rich and famous. We learned passably good French and precious little else except how to give dinner parties, play the piano, and walk with good posture. Extracurricular activities included smoking behind the gardener's shed and climbing over the wall to meet with ski instructors in the local tavern.

Luckily some wealthier members of the family chipped in for my education and allowed me to stay there until I was presented at court and had my season. For those of you who might not know, every young woman of good family has her season—a series of dances, parties, and other sporting events, during which she comes out into society and is presented at court. It's a polite way of advertising "Here she is, chaps. Now for God's sake somebody marry her and take her off our hands."

"Season" is actually a rather grand word for a series of dismal dances, culminating in a ball at Castle Rannoch during the grouse season, to which the young men came to shoot and by evening were all too tired to dance. Few of them knew the Highland dances that were expected at Castle Rannoch anyway, and the bagpipes echoing at dawn from the north turret made several young men realize they had pressing engagements in London that couldn't wait. Needless to say, no suitable proposal was forthcoming and so, at the age of twenty-one, I found myself stuck at Castle Rannoch with no idea what I was going to do for the rest of my life.

Chapter 2

CASTLE RANNOCH
MONDAY, APRIL 18, 1932

I wonder how many people have had life-changing experiences while on the loo? I should point out that the bathrooms at Castle Rannoch are not the small cubicles one finds in ordinary homes. They are vast, cavernous places with high ceilings, tartan wallpaper, and plumbing that hisses, groans, clanks, and have been known to cause more than one heart attack, as well as such instant fits of insanity that one guest leaped from an open bathroom window into the moat. I should add that the windows are always open. It's a Castle Rannoch tradition.

Castle Rannoch is not the most delightful spot at the best of times. It lies beneath an impressive black crag, at the head of a black loch, protected from the worst of gales by a stand of dark and gloomy pine forest. Even the poet Wordsworth, invited here during his ramblings, could find nothing to say about it, except for a couplet scribbled on a sheet of paper found in the wastepaper basket.

From dreadful heights to lakeside drear
Abandon hope all ye who enter here

And this was not the best of times. It was April and the rest of the world was full of daffodils, blossoms, and Easter bonnets. At Castle Rannoch it was snowing—not that delightful powdery stuff you get in Switzerland but wet, heavy, slushy snow that sticks to the clothing and freezes one in seconds. I hadn't been out for days. My brother, Binky, having been conditioned to do so at school, insisted on taking his morning walks around the estate and arrived home looking like the abominable snowman—sending his son Hector, affectionately known as Podge, screaming for Nanny.

It was the sort of weather for curling up with a good book beside a roaring fire. Unfortunately my sister-in-law, Hilda, usually known as Fig, was trying to economize and only allowed one log on the fire at a time. This was surely a false economy, as I had pointed out on several occasions. Trees were being felled by gales on a daily basis. But Fig had a bee in her bonnet about economizing. Times were hard everywhere and we had to set a good example to the lower classes. This example included porridge for breakfast instead of bacon and eggs and even baked beans as the savory after dinner one night. *Life is dreary,* I wrote in my diary. I was spending a lot of time writing in my diary these days. I knew I should be doing something. I was itching to do something, but as my sister-in-law reminded me constantly, a member of the royal family, however minor, has a duty not to let the family down. Her look implied that I was liable to become pregnant or dance naked on the lawn if I went out to Woolworths unchaperoned. My duty apparently was to wait until a suitable match was made for me. Not a happy thought.

How long I would have patiently awaited my doom, I can't really say, if I hadn't been sitting on the loo one April afternoon, trying to avoid the worst of the driving snow that was blowing in upon me by holding up a copy of *Horse and Hound.* Over the moan of the wind, I became aware of voices. Owing to the eccentric nature of the plumbing at Castle Rannoch, installed many centuries after the castle was built, it was possible to overhear conversations floating up from many floors below. This phenomenon probably contributed to the delusions and fits that overcame even the sanest of our guests. I was born to it and had used it to my advantage all my life, overhearing many a thing that had not been meant for my ears. To an outsider, however, lost in contemplation on the loo, and staring in horror alternately at the dark crags outside the window and the tartan wallpaper within, echoing voices booming hollow from the pipes were enough to push them over the edge.

"The queen wants us to do what?" This was enough to make me perk

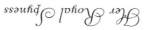

up and pay attention. I was always keen for gossip about our royal kin, and Fig had given a horrified shriek, quite unlike her.

"It's only for a weekend, Fig."

"Binky, I do wish these horrid common Americanisms were not creeping into your conversation. Next thing we know you'll be teaching Podge to say 'mirror' instead of 'looking glass' and 'serviette' instead of 'napkin.'"

"God forbid, Fig. It's just that the word 'weekend' does seem to sum it up quite nicely, doesn't it? I mean, what other word do we have for Friday, Saturday, and Sunday?"

"It implies that we are slaves to a week's labor, which we aren't. But don't try to change the subject. I think it's damned cheek on the part of HM."

"She's only trying to help. Something has to be done for Georgie."

Now I was truly attentive.

"I agree she can't spend the rest of her life moping around here and doing crossword puzzles." Fig's sharp voice echoed alarmingly, making one of the pipes hum. "But then on the other hand, she could prove useful with little Podge. It would mean we wouldn't have to hire a governess for him before he goes to prep school. I suppose they must have taught her something at that ridiculously expensive establishment in Switzerland."

"You can't use my sister as an unpaid governess, Fig."

"Everybody has to pull their weight these days, Binky, and quite frankly she's not doing anything else, is she?"

"What do you expect her to do, draw pints behind the local bar?"

"Don't be ridiculous. I want to see your sister happily settled as much as you do. But being told I have to invite a prince here for a house party, in the hopes of foisting him upon Georgiana—really, that is too much, even for HM."

Now I positively had my ear pressed against the pipes. The only prince that came to mind was my cousin David, the Prince of Wales. He was certainly a good catch, to whom I certainly wouldn't say no. It's true he was a good deal older than I, and not quite as tall either, but he was witty and a splendid dancer. And kind too. I'd even be prepared to wear flat-heeled shoes for the rest of my life.

"I would say it was a great deal of expense wasted on a hopeless cause."

Fig's sharp voice again.

"I wouldn't call Georgie a hopeless cause. She's a splendid-looking girl."

A little tall for the average chap, maybe, a little gawky still, but healthy, good bones, not stupid. A damned sight brainier than I, if the truth be known. She'll make a great wife for the right fellow."

"She's turned down everyone we've found for her so far. What makes you think she'll be interested in this Siegfried?"

"Because he's a prince, and heir to the throne."

"What throne? They murdered their last king."

"There is talk of reinstatement of the royal family in the near future. Siegfried is next in line."

"The royal family won't last long enough for him to succeed. They'll all be murdered again."

"Enough of this, Fig. And we don't need to mention any of this to Georgie either. Her Majesty has requested and one does not turn down a request from HM. A simple little house party, that's all. For Prince Siegfried and some of his English acquaintances. Enough young men so that Georgie doesn't get wind of our plans for her right away."

"That's an expensive proposition, Binky. You know how much these young men drink. We can't even offer them a shoot at this time of year. Nor a hunt. What are we going to do with them all day? I don't suppose this Siegfried will want to climb a mountain."

"We'll manage it somehow. After all, I am the head of the family. It is up to me to see my sister settled."

"She's your half sister. Let her mother find her somebody. God knows she has enough castoffs of her own, and most of them millionaires."

"Now you're being catty, Fig. Please reply to HM telling her we will be delighted to arrange the house party in the near future."

The speakers drifted out of range. I stood there at the bathroom window, impervious to the snow blowing in on me. Prince Siegfried of Romania, of all people. I had met him while I was a pupil at Les Oiseaux, my finishing school in Switzerland. He had struck me as a cold fish with staring eyes, a limp handshake, and a look that indicated a perpetual bad smell under his nose. When he was introduced to me, he had clicked his heels and murmured, "*Enchanté.*" The way he said it made me feel that I should be the one having the honor bestowed upon me, not the other way around. I didn't suspect he'd be any more enchanted to see me again.

"The time has come for action!" I shouted into the storm. I was no

longer a minor. I was able to go where I wanted without a chaperon, to make
my own decisions and to choose my own life. It wasn't as if I were either
the heir or the spare. I was only thirty-fourth in line to the throne. Being a
mere woman, I could never inherit the dukedom or Castle Rannoch even
if Binky had not produced a son. I was not going to sit around one minute
longer waiting for the future to come to me. I was going out into the world
to choose my own destiny.

I slammed the loo door and strode down the corridor to my room, where
I surprised my maid, hanging up freshly ironed blouses.

"Can you find my trunk in the attic, please, Maggie?" I said. "And pack
clothes suitable for city wear. I'm going to London."

I waited until Binky and Fig were taking tea in the great hall, then I
breezed in. Actually it wasn't hard to breeze anywhere at Castle Rannoch,
since there was usually a howling gale racing along the corridors, making
the tapestries flap. Binky was standing with his back to the fire, thus blocking the heat from the one log from reaching the rest of the room. Fig's nose
was blue enough to match her blood and I noticed she was cradling
the teapot in her hands, rather than let Ferguson, the parlormaid, do the
pouring.

"Ah, Georgie, there you are," Binky said heartily. "Had a good day?
Beastly out. I don't suppose you went for a ride?"

"I wouldn't be so cruel to my horse," I said. I lifted the silver lid over
one of the dishes. "Toast," I said in disappointment. "No crumpets, I see."

"Economy, Georgiana," Fig said. "We can't eat crumpets if the rest of
the world can't afford them. It wouldn't be right. Heaven knows we can
barely afford them ourselves any longer. It would be margarine if we hadn't
a dairy herd."

I noticed she was spreading a generous amount of Fortnum's black cur-
rant jam onto her toast, but wisely said nothing. Instead I waited until she
had taken a mouthful before I said, "I'm popping down to London for a
while, if that's all right with you."

"To London? When?" Fig asked, her sharp little eyes glowering at me.

"Tomorrow, I thought. If we're not snowed in."

"Tomorrow?" Binky asked. "This is a bit sudden, isn't it?"

"Yes, why haven't you mentioned it before?" Fig seconded.

"I only found out myself today," I said, concentrating on spreading butter on toast. "One of my dearest school chums is getting married and she wants me there to help her with the wedding preparations. And since I'm not doing anything useful up here, I thought I should answer her call of distress. Baxter will be able to drive me to the station in the motorcar, won't he?"

I had invented this story on the way downstairs. I was rather proud of it.

"This is most inconvenient, Georgie," Binky said.

"Inconvenient? Why?" I turned innocent eyes upon him.

"Well, you see, it's like this—" He turned to Fig for inspiration, then went on, "We were planning a little house party. Getting some young people up here for you. We realize that it must be boring to be stuck up here with an old married couple like us and no dances or fun."

I went over to him and gave him a kiss on the cheek. "You are an old dear, Binky, thinking of me like that. But I couldn't possibly allow you to spend money on me. I'm not a child. I realize how frightfully right money is these days and I know you had to pay those awful death duties on the estate."

I could see Binky was in an absolute agony of indecision. He knew that Her Majesty would expect her request to be obeyed, and now I was about to bolt. He couldn't tell me why he wanted me to stay because it was supposed to be a secret. It was quite the most amusing thing that had happened in ages.

"So now you don't have to worry about me," I said. "I'll be mixing with young people in London and helping out a friend and getting on with my life. I may use Rannoch House as my base, may I not?"

I saw a quick glance pass between Fig and Binky.

"Rannoch House?" Fig said. "You want to open up Rannoch House, just for yourself?"

"Not really open it up," I said. "I'd only be using my bedroom."

"We can't spare a servant to go with you," Fig said. "We're down to the bare minimum as it is. Binky could scarcely summon up enough beaters for the last shoot. And Maggie would never leave her invalid mother to go to London with you."

"It's all right," I said. "I shan't want to take a servant with me. I shan't even turn on the central heating."

"But if you're going to help this girl with her wedding, won't you be staying with her?" Fig asked.

"Eventually, yes. But she hasn't arrived from the Continent yet."

"A continental, is she, this girl? Not English?" Fig looked horrified.

"We're not English," I said. "At least Binky and I aren't. We're part Scottish with a good admixture of German."

"Let me amend that to British then. You were brought up to be British. That's where the big difference lies. This girl is foreign, is she?"

I was dying to invent a mysterious Russian countess, but it was too cold for the brain to react quickly. "She's been living abroad," I said. "For the sake of her health. She's rather delicate."

"Then I wonder some poor chap wants to marry her," Binky said heartily. "Sounds as if she won't be much good at producing an heir."

"He loves her, Binky," I said, defending my fictitious heroine. "Some people do marry for love, you know."

"Yes, but not in our class," Binky said easily. "We do our duty. We marry someone suitable."

"I like to think that love may come into it a little, Binky," Fig said in a frosty tone.

"If one strikes it lucky, Fig. Like you and I."

He wasn't as stupid as he seemed, I decided. He was without guile, a man of simple needs, simple pleasures, but definitely not stupid.

Fig actually managed a smile. "Will you need to have your tiara brought up from the vault?" she asked, going back to practical matters now.

"I don't think it's a tiara sort of wedding," I said.

"Not St. Margaret's then?"

"No, it's to be a small affair. I told you the bride was delicate."

"Then I wonder she needs help in preparing for it. Anyone can arrange a simple wedding." Fig took another large bite of toast and jam.

"Fig, she has asked for help and I am responding," I said. "I'm just in the way up here and who knows, I may even meet somebody in London."

"Yes, but what will you do for servants?"

"I'll hire a local girl to look after me."

"Make sure you check her references thoroughly," Fig said. "Those London girls can't be trusted. And keep the silver locked away."

"I'm not likely to need the silver," I said. "I'm only going to use it as a place to sleep for a few nights."

"Well, I suppose if you must go, you must. But we'll miss you dreadfully, won't we, Binky?"

Binky went to say something, then thought better of it. "I'll miss you, old thing," he said. It was quite the nicest thing he had ever said to me.

I SAT LOOKING out of the train window as we sped southward, watching winter melting into glorious spring. There were new white lambs in fields, the first primroses on the embankments. My excitement grew as we neared London. I was on my own, truly on my own, for the first time in my life. For the first time I'd be making my own decisions, planning my own future—doing something. At this point I had no idea what I should be doing, but I reminded myself that it was the 1930s. Young ladies were allowed to do no more than embroider, play piano, and paint watercolors. And London was a big city, teeming with opportunities for a bright young person like myself.

The bubble of enthusiasm had burst by the time I reached Rannoch House. It had started to rain just outside London and by the time we came into King's Cross Station it was coming down in buckets. There were sorry-looking men lining up for a soup kitchen along Euston Road and beggars at every corner. I stepped out of the cab and let myself into a house as cold and dreary as Castle Rannoch had been. Rannoch House is on the north side of Belgrave Square. I remembered it as a place of bustle and laughter, always people coming and going to theaters, dinner parties, or on shopping expeditions. Now it lay shrouded in dust sheets, colder than the grave, and empty. The realization crept over me that this was the first time in my entire life that I had been all alone in a house. I looked back at the front door, half afraid and half excited. Was I stupid to have come alone to London? How was I going to cope on my own?

I'll feel better after a nice bath and a cup of tea, I thought. I went up to my bedroom. The fireplace was empty, the fire unlaid. What I needed was a fire to cheer me up, but I had no idea how one set about laying a fire. In truth I had never seen a fire laid, or lit. One awoke to a merrily crackling fire, never having seen the maid who slipped into the room at six o'clock to light it. Fig expected me to hire a maid of all work, but I had no money to do so. So I was going to have to learn to do things for myself. But I really didn't think I could face learning how to light a fire at this moment. I was tired, travel weary, and cold. I went through to the bathroom and started to run a bath. There was a good six inches of water in it before I realized that both taps were running cold water. The boiler had obviously been turned off and I had no idea what a boiler looked like or how I might get it going. I began to seriously question the folly of my rapid departure. Had I waited and planned better, I could surely have secured an invitation from someone who lived in a warm and comfortable house with servants to run my bath and make my tea.

Now in the depths of gloom, I went downstairs again and braved the door that led below stairs, to the servants' part of the house. I remembered going down there as a small child, sitting on a stool while Mrs. McPherson, our cook, let me scrape out the cake bowl or cut out gingerbread men. The big, half-underground kitchen was spotless, cold, and empty. I found a kettle and I even found a tinderbox and a spill to light the gas. Feeling very proud of myself I boiled some water. I even located a tea caddy. Of course that was when I realized that there was no milk, nor was there likely to be unless I contacted the milkman. Milk arrived on doorsteps. That much I knew. I rooted around in the larder and discovered a jar of Bovril. I made myself a cup of hot Bovril instead with some Jacob's cream crackers and went to bed. *Things are bound to be brighter in the morning,* I wrote in my diary. *I have taken the first steps in a new and exciting adventure. At least I am free of my family for the first time in my life.*

Chapter 3

RANNOCH HOUSE
BELGRAVE SQUARE
LONDON
FRIDAY, APRIL 22, 1932

Even the most minor member of the royal family is not supposed to arrive at Buckingham Palace on foot. The proper mode of entry is at the very least a Rolls-Royce motor or, in the case of reduced circumstances, a Bentley or Daimler. Ideally a state coach drawn by a team of perfectly matched horses, although not many of us run to coaches these days. The sight of one female person slinking across the forecourt on foot would definitely have my esteemed relative-by-marriage, Her Royal Majesty and Empress of India, Queen Mary, raise an eyebrow. Well, probably not actually raise the eyebrow, because personages of royal blood are trained not to react, even to the greatest of improprieties. Were a native in some dark corner of the colonies to strip off his loincloth and dance, waggling his you-know-what with gay abandon, not so much as an eyebrow twitch would be permitted. The only appropriate reaction would be polite clapping when the dance was over.

This sort of control is drummed into us at an early age, very much as one trains a gun dog not to react to the sound of a shot fired at close range or a police horse to a rapid movement in the crowd. Miss MacAlister, the governess who preceded my finishing school in Switzerland, used to chant to me, like a litany: A lady is always in control of herself. A lady is always in control of her emotions. A lady is always in control of her expression. A lady is always in control of her body. And indeed it is rumored that some royal personages can dispense with visiting strange water closets for days on end. I wouldn't be crass enough to betray which royal personages can achieve this feat.

Fortunately there are other ways into Buckingham Palace, preferable to facing those formidable gilt-tipped gates and then crossing that vast expanse of forecourt under the watchful eye of those impossibly tall, bear-skinned guards and possibly Her Majesty herself. If you go around to the left, heading in the direction of Victoria Station, you can enter through the Ambassador's Court and the visitors' entrance. Even more desirable, if you follow the high brick wall along that road, you will come across a discreet black door in the wall. I gather it was used by my father's uncle Bertie, who had a short but happy reign as King Edward VII, when he wished to visit the more shady of his lady friends. I expect my cousin David, the current Prince of Wales, has used it from time to time when staying with his parents. I was certainly making use of it today.

Let me say that I am not in the habit of visiting the palace from choice. One does not drop in for afternoon tea and a chat, even if they are relatives. I had been summoned, two days after my arrival in London. My esteemed relative the queen possessed one of the best underground intelligence networks in the country. I didn't think that Fig would have contacted her, but she had found out somehow. A letter had arrived, on palace writing paper, from Her Majesty's private secretary, Sir Giles Ponsonby-Smythe, indicating that Her Majesty would be delighted if I would take tea with her. Which was why I was slinking up the Buckingham Palace Road on a Friday afternoon. One does not refuse HM.

Of course I was more than a little curious to know why I was being summoned. In fact it crossed my mind that HM might sit me down to tea and then produce Prince Siegfried and a convenient Archbishop of Canterbury to perform the wedding ceremony on the spot. In truth I felt as Anne Boleyn must have done when Henry VIII asked her to drop in for a flagon of ale, and not to wear anything with a high neckline.

I didn't remember seeing my exalted relatives since my presentation as a debutante—an occasion I won't forget in a hurry, and I'm sure they haven't either. I am one of those people whose limbs don't always obey them in times of crisis. My gown with its long train, not to mention three ridiculously tall ostrich feathers bobbing in a hair ornament, was a recipe for

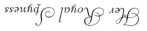

disaster. I had entered the throne room on cue, heard the booming announcement—"Lady Victoria Georgiana Charlotte Eugenie of Glen Garry and Rannoch!"—and executed the perfect curtsy, as practiced a million times at deb school. However, when I tried to stand up, it seems that my high heel had somehow caught itself in the train. I tried to move, but was tethered by my own heel spike. I tugged, gracefully, conscious of those royal eyes on me. Nothing happened. I felt perspiration trickling down my bare back. (Yes, I know ladies don't sweat, but something was trickling down my back.) I tugged harder. The heel came free and I was catapulted farther into the throne room as if I had been shot from a cannon at the very moment I should have been backing out of the royal presence. Even Her Majesty had looked mildly astonished, but nothing was said, on the occasion or subsequently. I wondered if it would come up over crumpets.

I made a successful entry along a narrow hallway that skirted the palace kitchens, and was making my way along the lower corridor, past various household offices, startling maids and footmen along the way, until in turn I was startled by a horrified voice exclaiming, "You, girl. Where do you think you are going?"

I turned to see an austere old gentleman bearing down on me.

"I don't know you," he said accusingly.

"I am Lady Georgiana, His Majesty's cousin," I said. "I am here to take tea with Her Majesty. I am expected."

There are some advantages to being a minor royal. The old man turned beetroot red.

"My lady, I do apologize. I can't think why I wasn't informed of your arrival. Her Majesty is awaiting you in the yellow sitting room. This way, please."

He led me up a side staircase to the *piano nobile*, which has nothing to do with the musical instrument but is the floor on which most of the royal life of the palace takes place. The yellow sitting room is in the southeast corner, with windows looking down the Mall to Admiralty Arch and also out over the start of Buckingham Palace Road. A great vantage point, in fact. As a room, however, it has never appealed to me. It is furnished largely with objects brought from the Royal Pavilion at Brighton, collected by King George IV at a time when chinoiserie was the height of fashion. Lots of dragons, chrysanthemums, and bright painted porcelain. I found it a little too flowery and garish for my taste.

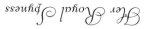

"Lady Georgiana, ma'am," my stuffy friend said in a low voice.

Her Majesty wasn't at the table in the window, but standing, peering into one of the glass cases that adorned the walls. She looked up briefly as I came in.

"Ah, Georgiana. I didn't see you arrive. Did you take a cab?"

"I walked, ma'am." I should explain that royals are always ma'ams and sirs, even to their closest relatives. I went over to plant the dutiful kiss on the cheek, plus execute a curtsy. The order of these two actions requires the most delicate timing. In spite of a lifetime of practice I always managed to bump my nose on the royal cheek as I stood up from the curtsy.

Her Majesty straightened up. "Thank you, Soames. Tea in fifteen minutes."

The elderly man backed out, closing the double doors. Her Majesty had gone back to peering into the glass case. "Tell me, Georgiana," she said, "am I right in thinking that your late father had a fine collection of Ming? I'm sure I remember discussing it with him."

"He collected lots of things, ma'am, but I'm afraid I wouldn't know one pot from another."

"That's too bad. You must come to the palace more often and let me educate you. One finds such solace in collecting beautiful objects."

I didn't point out that one needs money to collect beautiful objects and I was currently a pauper.

The queen still didn't look up from the glass case. "Your brother, the current duke, I suppose has little interest in objets d'art and antiques?" she asked casually. "He was raised to be like his grandfather—huntin', shootin', fishin'—the typical country squire."

"That's certainly true, ma'am."

"So it's possible that any number of Ming vases might still be lying around Castle Rannoch—unappreciated?"

There was the slightest of quivers in her voice and I suddenly understood where this conversation was going. She wanted to get her hands on items she lacked in her own collection. She confirmed this by saying, oh so casually, "I wondered if, next time you were home, you could take a look around. There is a smaller vase just like this one that would fit so well in this display. And if your brother isn't really interested . . ."

You want me to pinch it for you, I was dying to say. Her Majesty had an absolute passion for antiques and if she had not been Queen of England and Empress of India, she might have been one of the most skillful hagglers in the history of the antiques trade. Of course she possessed a trump card nobody else held. If she expressed admiration for any object, protocol demanded that it be presented to her. Most noble families hid the good stuff when a royal visit was imminent.

"I won't be going back to Castle Rannoch often anymore, ma'am," I said tactfully. "Now that the house has passed to Hamish and he is married, it isn't really my home."

"A great pity," she said. "But surely you'll pay a visit when you come to stay with us at Balmoral this summer. You will be coming to Balmoral, I take it?"

"Thank you, ma'am. I'll be delighted."

How could one refuse? When one was invited to Balmoral, one went. And the dreaded invitation fell on one or another of us relations every summer. Every summer we tried to come up with suitable excuses as to why we couldn't be there. These ranged from yachting on the Med to making a visit to the colonies. It is rumored that one female relative actually managed to have a baby during the Balmoral season each year, although I think this was being a little excessive. It really wasn't that bad for one brought up at Castle Rannoch. The tartan wallpaper, tartan carpets, the bagpipes at dawn, and the chill wind blasting in through open windows only reminded me of home. Others found it hard to endure, however.

"Then we may go over to Glenrannoch together. Such a pretty drive, I always think." She ushered me away from the glass cases and over to a small tea table. I must remind myself to write to Binky to warn him to lock up the best china and silver this summer I decided. "In fact, I rather suspect that my son David might have it in mind to persuade your brother to invite a certain woman to stay at Castle Rannoch this summer. David knows perfectly well that she would not be welcome at Balmoral, and Castle Rannoch is conveniently close by." She touched my arm as I pulled out a chair for her to sit down. "And I use the word 'woman' advisedly, because she certainly is no lady," she whispered. "An American adventuress, twice married already." She sighed as she took a seat. "Why he can't find someone suitable and settle down I simply can't understand. He's not getting younger and I would like to see him settled before he has to take the throne. Why can't he marry someone like you, for example? You'd do very well."

"I'd have no objection," I said. "But I'm afraid he sees me as a little girl still. He likes sophisticated older women."

"He likes tarts," Her Majesty said coldly. She glanced up as the doors opened and an array of tea trays was carried in. "Ah, tarts," she repeated, just in case her comment should have reached the ears of the servants.

One by one the dishes were placed on the table. Tiny finger sandwiches with cress poking out of them, cake stands dotted with miniature éclairs and strawberry tarts. It was enough to bring tears to the eyes of one who had been living under Fig's austerity all winter and for the past two days on toast and baked beans. The tears were not of joy, however. I had been to enough royal functions in my life to know the protocol. The guest only eats what Her Majesty eats. And Her Majesty was not likely to take more than a slice or two of brown bread. I sighed, waited for her to take brown bread, then took a slice myself.

"I thought I might employ you as my spy," she said, as tea was poured.

"This summer at Castle Rannoch, you mean?"

"I must find out the truth before that, Georgiana," she said. "I only hear rumors. I want a firsthand account from somebody I can trust. I understand that David has persuaded Lord and Lady Mountjoy to give a house party and May ball and to include this woman and her husband—"

"Her husband?" I knew one should never interrupt the queen. It just slipped out.

She nodded with understanding. "Such behavior may well be considered acceptable in America. She is apparently still living with her husband. He, poor creature, is dragged around to provide respectability and to dispel rumors. Of course one can never dispel rumors. It has been all we can do to keep the press mute on the subject and if David becomes more brazen in his pursuit of her, then I don't think we'll be able to suppress the rumors much longer. I say his pursuit of her, but frankly I believe it to be the other way around. I suspect that this woman is relentlessly pursuing him. You know what he's like, Georgiana. An innocent at heart, easily flattered, easily seduced." She put down the slice of brown bread and leaned a little closer to me. "I need to know the truth, Georgiana. I need to know whether this is a mere flirtation for this woman, or whether she has serious designs on my son. My worst fear is that, like all Americans, she is fascinated with royalty and dreams of being Queen of England."

"Surely not, ma'am. A divorced woman? That's impossible."

"Let us hope it is impossible. The only solution is for the king to go on living until David becomes too old to be desirable as a catch. But I fear my husband's health is failing. Never the same after the Great War. The strain was too much for him."

I nodded with sympathy. "You said you wanted me to be your spy?"

"I do indeed. The house party at the Mountjoys' should give you ample opportunity to observe this woman and David together."

"Unfortunately I haven't been invited," I said.

"But you came out with the Mountjoys' daughter, didn't you?"

"I did, ma'am."

"There you are, then. I'll let it be known that you are currently in London and would like to renew your acquaintanceship with the Mountjoy girl." (She pronounced it "gell.") "People don't usually turn down my suggestions. And you need to be out in society if you're ever going to find yourself a husband." She looked up at me sharply. "So tell me, what are you planning to do with yourself in London?"

"I've only just arrived, ma'am. I haven't yet decided what I'll be doing."

"That's not good at all. With whom will you be staying?"

"At the moment I'm at Rannoch House," I said.

The royal eyebrow went up. "Alone in the London house? Unchaperoned?"

"I am over twenty-one, ma'am. I have come out."

She shook her head. "In my day a young woman was chaperoned until the day she was married. Otherwise a future husband could not be sure whether or not he was getting—umm—soiled goods, so to speak. No proposals on the horizon?"

"No proposals, ma'am."

"Dear me. I wonder why." She eyed me critically, as if I were one of her art objects. "You're not unattractive and at least half your pedigree is impeccable. I can think of several young men who would be suitable. King Alexander of Yugoslavia has a son, hasn't he? No, maybe that part of the world is a little too brutal and Slavic. What about the Greek royal family? That delightful little blond boy? But I'm afraid he's too young, even for you. Of course, there's always young Siegfried, one of the Hohenzollern-Sigmaringens of Romania. He's a relative of mine. Good stock."

Ah, yes, Siegfried. She couldn't resist bringing him into the conversation. I had to squash this idea once and for all.

"I've met Prince Siegfried several times, ma'am. He didn't seem much interested in me."

She sighed. "This was all so much simpler in my day. A marriage was arranged and we got on with it. I was originally intended to marry His Majesty's brother, the Duke of Clarence, but he died suddenly. When it was suggested that I marry His Majesty instead, I acquiesced without a fuss. We have certainly been happy enough, and your great-grandmother adored Prince Albert, as we all know. Perhaps I'll see what I can do."

"This is the 1930s, ma'am," I ventured. "I'm sure I'll meet someone eventually, now that I'm living in London."

"That's what I'm afraid of, Georgiana. Your father was not known for making the most sensible of choices, was he? However, I don't doubt you'll be married one day; one hopes to somebody suitable. You'll need to learn how to run a great house and act as ambassador for your country, and heaven knows you've had no mother to show you the ropes. How is your mother these days? Do you ever see her?"

"When she flits through London sometimes," I said.

"And who is her latest beau, may one ask?" She nodded to the maid who was offering slices of lemon for the china tea.

"A German industrialist, the last time I heard," I said, "but that was a couple of months ago."

I caught the briefest of twinkles in the royal eye. My austere relative might look starchy and forbidding, but deep down she did have a sense of humor.

"I shall take the matter in hand myself, Georgiana," Her Majesty said. "It's not good for young girls to be idle and unchaperoned. Too many temptations in the big city. I'd take you on as one of my own ladies-in-waiting, but I already have a full complement at the moment. Let me think. It's possible that Princess Beatrice could use another lady-in-waiting, although she doesn't go out as much as she used to. Yes, that might do splendidly. I shall speak to her about it."

"Princess Beatrice, ma'am?" My voice quivered a little.

"You must have met her. The old queen's only surviving daughter. The king's aunt. Your great-aunt, Georgiana. She has a charming house in the country, and a place in London too, I believe, although she rarely comes to town anymore."

Tea came to an end. I was dismissed. And doomed. If I couldn't come up with some brilliant form of employment in the near future, I was about to be lady-in-waiting to Queen Victoria's only surviving daughter, who didn't get out and about much anymore.

Chapter 4

I came out of Buckingham Palace in deep gloom. Actually the gloom had been deepening ever since my season ended and I realized that I was facing life ahead with no funds and no prospects. Now it seemed that I was to be locked in the country estate of an elderly princess while my royal kin found a suitable husband for me. The only spark of excitement in my dreary future would be the challenge to spy on my cousin David and his latest "woman."

I was in distinct need of cheering up, so I boarded the district line train to visit my favorite person. Gradually city sprawl gave way to Essex countryside. I disembarked at Upminster Bridge and soon I was walking along a row of modest semidetached homes on Glanville Drive, their pocket handkerchief–sized gardens decorated liberally with gnomes and birdbaths. I knocked at the door of Number 22, heard a muffled grunt, "I'm coming, I'm coming," and then a Cockney face peered around the half-open door. The face was perky, beaky, and wrinkled like an old prune. It took a second to register who I was and then lit up in a huge grin.

"Well, blow me down with a feather," he said, flinging the door wide open. "This is a turnip for the books. I didn't expect to see you in a month of Sundays. How are you, my love? Come and give your old granddad a kiss."

I suppose I should have mentioned that while one of my grandparents was Queen Victoria's daughter, my only living grandparent was a retired

Cockney policeman who lived in a semidetached in Essex with gnomes in the front garden.

His stubbly face was scratchy on my cheek as he planted a kiss and he smelled of carbolic soap. I hugged him fiercely. "I'm well, thanks, Granddad. How are you?"

"Can't complain. The old chest ain't what it was, but at my age that's what you expect, isn't it? Come on in. I've got the kettle on and a nice bit of seedy cake, made by the old bat next door. She keeps sending round food, in the hopes of showing me what a good cook she is and what a good catch she'd make."

"And would she make a good catch?" I asked. "You have been living on your own for a long while now."

"I'm used to my own company. Don't need no meddling old woman in my life. Come on in and take a pew, ducks. You are a sight for sore eyes."

He beamed at me again. "So what brings you to this neck of the woods? In need of a good meal, by the look of it. You're all skin and bones."

"As a matter of fact, I am in need of a good meal," I said. "I've just come from the palace, where tea consisted of two slices of brown bread."

"Well, I can certainly do better than that. What about a couple of poached eggs on toasted cheese and then some of that cake?"

"Perfect." I sighed happily.

"I bet you didn't tell that lot at the palace where you were coming afterward." He bustled around the meticulously neat little kitchen, breaking two eggs into the poacher. "They wouldn't have liked that. When you were a little girl, they used to intercept the letters we sent you."

"Surely not."

"Oh, yes. They didn't want no contact with us poor folk. Of course, if your mum had stuck around to do her duty and bring you up proper, we'd have been invited to stay or she could have brought you to see us. But she was off haunting herself somewhere. We often worried about you, poor little mite, stuck in that big drafty place all alone."

"I did have Nanny. And Miss MacAlister."

He beamed again. He had the sort of smile that lit up his whole face. "And you turned out a treat. I'll have to admit that. Look at you. The proper young lady. I bet you've got the boyfriends lined up and fighting for you, haven't yer?"

"Not exactly," I said. "In fact I'm rather at a loose end, not quite sure

what to do with myself. My brother's not giving me an allowance any longer, you see. He claims abject poverty."

"The dirty rotter. Do you want me to come up and give him a piece of
my mind?"

"No, thanks, Granddad. There's nothing you could do. I think they are
genuinely hard up, and I'm only a half sister, after all. He told me I was
welcome to stay on at Castle Rannoch, but having to amuse little Podge
and help Fig with her knitting was really too dreadful. So I bolted, just like
my mother. Only not as successfully. I'm camping out in the London house.
Binky is letting me live there for the moment but it's freezing cold without
the central heating on and I have no servant to look after me. I don't suppose you could show me how to light a fire, could you?"

My grandfather looked at me, then started laughing, a wheezy laugh
that turned into a nasty cough. "Oh, you're a proper treat, you are. Teach
you how to light a fire? Bless your little heart, I'll come up to Belgravia and
light your fire for you, if that's what you want. Or you can always come and
camp with me." His eyes twinkled with glee at the thought of this. "Can
you imagine their faces if they knew that the thirty-fourth in line to the
throne was living in a semidetached in Hornchurch?"

I laughed too. "Wouldn't that be fun? I might just take you up on it,
except that it would only make the queen speed up with her arrangements
to ship me to some royal aunt as a lady-in-waiting. She thinks I need training in how to run a great house."

"Well, I expect you do."

"I'd die of boredom, Granddad. You can't imagine how dreary it is,
after all the excitement of a season, all those coming-out parties and balls,
and now I've no idea what to do next."

The kettle started to whistle and he made the tea. "Get yourself a job,"
he said.

"A job?"

"You're a bright girl. You've been well educated. What's to stop you?"

"I don't think they'd approve."

"They're not supporting you, are they? And they don't own you. It's not
like you're taking public money to carry out royal duties. You go out and
have fun, my girl. Find out what you'd really like to do with your life."

"I'm sorely tempted," I said. "Girls are doing all kinds of jobs these days,
aren't they?"

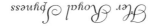

"Of course they are. Only don't go on the stage like your mum. She was a nice girl, properly brought up, until she got those stars in her eyes and went on the stage."

"She certainly made a success of it, didn't she? Bags of money and married a duke?"

"Yes, but at what price, ducks? At what price? Sold her soul. That's what she did. Now she's clinging on to those good looks for dear life, dreading the day that no man is interested in her anymore."

"She bought you this house, didn't she?"

"I'm not saying she hasn't been generous. I'm just saying it changed her whole personality. Now it's like talking to a stranger."

"I agree," I said, "but then I never really knew her. I gather she's with a German industrial baron now."

"Ruddy German," he muttered. "Pardon my language, love, but just talking about them gets my goat. And that new chap, that Hitler. He's up to no good, I can tell you. He'll want watching, you mark my words."

"He may be a good thing for them. Help get the country back on its feet again," I suggested.

He scowled. "That country deserves to stay where it is. It don't need no encouragement. You didn't serve in the trenches."

"Neither did you," I reminded him.

"No, but your uncle Jimmy did. Only eighteen he was and he never came home."

I hadn't even known I had an uncle Jimmy. Nobody had ever told me.

"I'm sorry," I said. "It was a horrible war. Let's pray there will never be another one."

"There won't, as long as the old king stays alive. If he kicks the bucket, all bets are off."

He put a large plate of food in front of me and for a while I was silent.

"Blimey," he said. "You can certainly knock that back. You been starving yourself?"

"Living on baked beans," I confessed. "I haven't found a grocer's shop yet in Belgravia. Everyone has things delivered. And frankly I don't have any money."

"Then you'd better come down here and have Sunday dinner with me. I expect I could manage a roast and two veg—got lovely cabbages in the back garden, and of course later in the summer there will be beans. Can't do any better than that, even at your fancy posh restaurants in the West End."

"I'd love to, Granddad," I said and I realized that he needed me as much as I needed him at the moment. He was lonely too.

"I don't like the thought of you living in that big house all on your own," he said, shaking his head. "Some funny types up in the Smoke these days. Not quite right in the head after the war. Don't you go opening the door to any strangers, you hear? I've a good mind to get out my old uniform and patrol up and down outside your front door."

I laughed. "I'd like to see that. I've never seen you in uniform." I knew that my grandfather had been a policeman once, but he'd given it up long ago. He gave a wheezy laugh. "I'd like to see it too. My jacket would never button up around my middle these days, and my old feet would never hold up in those boots. But I still don't like the thought of you trying to survive in that big place on your own."

"I'll be fine, Granddad." I patted his hand. "So teach me how to light a fire. Teach me how to do the washing up. I need to know everything."

"Lighting a fire starts with going down the coal'ole," he said.

"The coal'ole?"

"Yes, you know. They pour in the coal from a manhole on the street and you shovel it out through a little door at the bottom. I'm sure you'll find that's the way it's done at your place. But it's usually dark and dirty and there are bound to be spiders. I can't see you wanting to do that."

"If it's a choice between getting dirty and freezing, I'll choose getting dirty."

He turned to look back at me. "I must say I like your spunk. Just like your mother. She'd let nothing stand in her way either." He broke off with another fit of noisy coughing.

"That cough sounds terrible," I said. "Have you been to a doctor?"

"On and off all winter," he said.

"And what does he say it is?"

"Bronchitis, love. All this smoke in the air and the winter fogs are bad for me. He says I should give myself a nice holiday at the seaside."

"Good idea."

He sighed. "It takes money to go on holiday, sweetheart. Right now I'm not exactly flush. All those doctor visits last winter. And the price of coal going up. I'm trying to live off the little bit I've got put by."

"You're not getting a police pension?"

"A very small one. I wasn't on the force long enough, see. Got meself involved in a little bit of a fracas, coshed over the head, and then I started getting dizzy spells, so that was that."

"Then ask Mother to help you out. I'm sure she's got plenty."

His face hardened. "I'm not taking German money. I'd rather starve first."

"I'm sure she has money of her own. She's been with an awful lot of rich men in her time."

"She might have managed to put a bit away, but she'll need that for herself when her looks finally go and she's on her own. Besides, she was good enough to buy your grandma and me this house. She don't owe me nothing. And I'm not asking anyone for charity."

I noticed as I carried my plate across to the sink that the kitchen did look bare. An awful thought struck me that he had given me his last two eggs.

"I'll get a job, Granddad," I said. "And I'll learn to cook and then you can come to dine with me at Rannoch House."

That started him laughing again. "I'll believe it when I see it," he said.

I felt terrible as I rode the train back to London. My grandfather needed money badly and I couldn't help him. Now I'd have to get a job in a hurry. It seemed that it wasn't as easy to escape from family as I had thought.

It was a bright, warm evening and I was loath to go back to that dreary, empty house with the furniture covered in dust sheets and rooms that never warmed up enough to be comfortable. I got off at South Kensington and started to walk up the Brompton Road. Knightsbridge was still bustling with elegant couples on their way to an evening's entertainment. You'd never know that there was a depression and that a good portion of the world was lining up for a bowl of soup. Having grown up in such privileged circles, I'd only just become aware of the terrible injustices in the world and they worried me. If I'd been a lady with a comfortable private income, I'd have volunteered at those soup kitchens. However, I was now also one of the unemployed poor. I might be needing that bread and soup myself. Of course, I realized that it was different for me. I only had to agree to go and live with an elderly prin-cess and I'd be dining well and drinking the best wines, without a care in the world. Except that now the thought was creeping into my consciousness that one should be doing something worthwhile. One should be doing care.

I paused as I passed Harrod's windows. All those stylish dresses and shoes! My only attempts at keeping up with the latest fashion had been dur-ing my season, when I had received a meager clothing allowance, studied magazines to see what the bright young things about town were wearing this season, and then had the gamekeeper's wife run me up copies. Mrs. MacTa-vish was good with her needle but they were poor imitations at best. Oh, to have the money to sail into Harrods and choose an outfit, just like that!

I was lost in reverie when a taxi pulled up at the curb, a door slammed, and a voice exclaimed, "Georgie! It is you. I thought I spotted you and I made the taxi driver stop. What a surprise. I didn't know you were in town."

There before me, looking dazzlingly glamorous, was my former school-friend Belinda Warburton-Stoke. She was wearing an emerald green satin opera cape—the kind where the sides are joined together to make the sleeves, thus making most people look like penguins. Her hair was styled in a sleek black cap with a jaunty hair ornament on one side, complete with ridiculous ostrich feather that bobbed as she ran toward me.

We rushed to embrace. "How lovely to see you, Belinda. You're looking fabulous. I would have hardly recognized you."

"One has to keep up appearances or the customers won't come."

"Customers?"

"My dear, haven't you heard? I've started my own business. I'm a fash-ion designer."

"Are you? How is it going?"

"Frightfully well. They are positively fighting to have the chance to wear my creations."

"How wonderful for you. I'm envious."

"Well, I had to do something. I didn't have a royal destiny, like you."

"My royal destiny doesn't seem too promising at the moment."

She pulled out some coins to pay the taxi driver, then linked arms with me and started to march me up the Brompton Road. "So what are you doing in town?"

"I bolted, taking after my mother, I suppose. I couldn't stand Scotland a minute longer."

"Nobody can, darling. Those awful loos with the tartan wallpaper! I have a permanent migraine when I'm there. Were you on your way some-where? Because if not, come back and have a drink at my place."

"You're living near here?"

"Right next to the park. Terribly avant-garde. I've bought myself a dear little mews cottage and done it up and I'm living there alone with just my maid. Mother is furious, but I am twenty-one and I've come into my own money so there's not much she can do, is there?"

I allowed myself to be swept up Brompton Road, along Knightsbridge, and into a cobbled back alley where the former mews were now apparently transformed into living quarters. Belinda's cottage looked quaint on the outside but inside was completely modern—all white walls, streamlined, Bakelite and chrome with a cubist painting on the wall, possibly even a Picasso. She sat me on a hard purple chair, then went across to a generously stocked sideboard. "Let me make you one of my cocktails. I'm famous for them, you know."

With that she poured dangerous amounts from any number of bottles into a shaker, finished them off with something bright green, then poured the shaken result into a glass and dropped in a couple of maraschino cherries. "Get that down you and you'll feel wonderful," she said. She took a seat opposite me and crossed her legs, revealing a long expanse of silk stocking and just a hint of gray silk petticoat.

The first sip took my breath away. I tried not to cough as I looked up and smiled. "Very interesting," I said. "I don't have much opportunity to drink cocktails."

"Do you remember those awful experiments creating cocktails in the dorm at Les Oiseaux?" Belinda laughed as she took a long drink from her own glass. "It's a wonder we didn't knock ourselves out."

"We almost did. Remember that French girl, Monique? She was sick all night."

"So she was," Belinda's smile faded. "It already seems so long ago, like a dream, doesn't it?"

"Yes, it does," I agreed. "A beautiful dream."

She looked at me sharply. "So do I gather that life isn't too wonderful for you at the moment?"

"Life is pretty bloody, if you really want to know," I said. The cocktail was obviously already having an effect. "Bloody" wasn't a word I habitually used. "If I don't come up with something to do with myself soon, I'll be shipped out to a stately home in the country until the royal kin come up with some awful foreign prince for me to marry."

"Could be worse. There are some frightfully good-looking foreign princes. And it might be nice to be a queen someday. Think of all those lovely tiaras."

I scowled. "In case you haven't remembered, there are precious few kingdoms left in Europe. And royal families seem to be a disposable commodity. What's more, the suitable young men I have met have been so dull that assassination actually seems preferable than a long life with them."

"Dear me," Belinda said. "We are in a blue mood, aren't we? So your sex life must be pretty dismal at the moment."

"Belinda!"

"Oh, I'm sorry. I've shocked you. The set I mix with now has no qualms about discussing their sex lives. And why not? It's healthy to talk about sex."

"I don't mind talking about it really," I said, although in truth I found myself squirming with embarrassment. "God knows we used to talk about it all the time at school."

"But doing is so much better than talking, don't you agree?" She smiled like a cat with cream. Then she looked horrified. "You're not still a virgin?"

"Afraid so."

"It's no longer required of a potential princess, is it? Don't tell me they still send an archbishop and the lord chancellor to check personally before the marriage can be consummated."

I started to laugh. "I assure you I'm not saving myself from choice. I'd be perfectly happy to rip my clothes off and roll in the hay just as soon as I find the right man."

"So none of the young men we encountered during our season gave you hot pants for them?"

"Belinda, your language!"

"I've been mingling with Americans. Such fun. So naughty."

"If you want to know, the young men I have encountered have all been insufferably dull. And from my limited experience of groping and gasping in the backseats of taxies, I think sex must be overrated anyway."

"Oh, trust me, you'll like it," Belinda smiled again. "It is quite delish, with the right man, of course."

"Anyway, there is no point in talking about it, because I'm not likely to get in much practice, unless it's with gamekeepers like Lady Chatterley. I'm being banished to the country to be the lady-in-waiting to an aged relative."

"They can't banish you. Don't go."

"I can't stay in London indefinitely. I've nothing to live on."

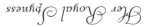
"Then get a job."

"Of course I'd love to get a job, but I suspect it won't be as easy as that. You've seen men queuing up for work. Half the world is looking for non-existent jobs at the moment."

"Oh, the jobs are there for the right people. You just have to find your niche in life. Find a need and fill it. Look at me. I'm having a whale of a time—nightclubs, all the social life I could wish for, my picture in *Vogue.*"

"Yes, but you obviously have a talent for dress design. I've no idea what I could possibly do. Our schooling equipped us only for marriage. I can speak passable French, play the piano, and I know where to seat an archbishop at table. This hardly makes me employable, does it?"

"Of course it does, darling. All those nouveau riche middle-class snobs will positively snap you up, just to boast about you."

I stared at her in horror. "But I couldn't let them know who I really was. It would get back to the palace and I'd be whisked away to marry a prince in Outer Mongolia before I had time to catch my breath."

"You don't have to tell them who you are. One look at you and anyone can see you are top drawer. So get out there and have some fun."

"And earn some money, more to the point."

"Darling, are you stony broke? What about all the rich relatives?"

"Money comes with strings in my family. If I go as a lady-in-waiting, I'll obviously get an allowance. If I agree to marry Prince Siegfried, I'm sure they'll come up with a wonderful trousseau."

"Prince Siegfried? The one we met at Les Oiseaux? The one we called Fishface?"

"The very same."

"Darling, how frightful. Of course you couldn't possibly marry him. Apart from the fact that Romania's monarchy is in a bit of disarray at the moment. Exile can be remarkably dreary."

"I'm not sure that I want to marry any prince," I said. "I'd rather build a career of my own, like you're doing. I just wish I had some talent."

She eyed me critically, just as the queen had done. "You're tall. You could be a model. I have connections."

I shook my head. "Oh, no. Not a model. Not walking up and down in front of people. Remember the debutante fiasco."

She giggled. "Oh, yes. Maybe not a model then. But you'll find something. Secretary to a film star?"

"I can't take shorthand or type."

She leaned across and patted my knee. "We'll find something for you. What about Harrods? It's on the doorstep and it would be a good place to start."

"Working behind the counter at a department store?" I sounded shocked.

"Darling, I'm not suggesting you work as a belly dancer in the casbah. It's a perfectly respectable department store. I shop there all the time."

"I suppose it might be fun. But they wouldn't take me on with no experience, would they?"

"They would if someone who was a well-known society figure and woman-about-town wrote you a fabulous letter of recommendation."

"Who are you suggesting?"

"Me, you idiot." Belinda laughed. "When I've finished my letter, nobody would dare turn you down."

She took out pen and writing paper and started to write. "What name will you use?" she asked.

"Florence Kincaid," I said after a moment's thought.

"Who on earth is Florence Kincaid?"

"She was a doll my mother brought me back from Paris when I was little. Mother wanted me to call her Fifi La Rue, but I decided that Florence Kincaid sounded nicer."

"You'd probably be offered more interesting jobs if you called yourself Fifi La Rue," Belinda said with a wicked smile. She sucked on the end of her pen. "Now, let me see. Miss Florence Kincaid has been in my employ for two years as my assistant in the organization of charity fashion shows. She is of impeccable character and breeding, shows great initiative, poise, charm, and business sense, and has been a joy to work with. I release her with profound reluctance, realizing that I can no longer offer the scope that her kind of talent and ambition needs to blossom. How does that sound?"

"Fabulous," I said. "You are wasted as a fashion designer. You should become a writer."

"Now, I'll write it out neatly and you can take it round to Harrods in the morning," she said. "And now that I know you're living on my doorstep, we must get together more often. I'll introduce you to some naughty men-about-town. They'll show you what you've been missing."

That sounded like an interesting proposition. I had yet to meet any really naughty young men. The only ones who had verged on the naughty

were the ski instructors who frequented the inn across the street from Les Oiseaux and our interaction with them was limited to throwing notes out of the windows or, on a couple of occasions, drinking a glass of mulled wine with their arms around our shoulders. The young Englishmen were revoltingly proper, maybe because our chaperons lurked in the background. If they took one outside for a stroll and tried a quick and hopeful grope, one stern rebuke would make them gush out apologies. "So sorry. Damned bad form. Can't think what came over me. Won't happen again, I promise."

Now I was twenty-one. I had no chaperon and I was dying to see what naughty young men had to offer. From what I had heard, I was somewhat confused about sex. It sounded rather horrid, and yet Belinda obviously enjoyed it—and my mother had done it with oodles of men on at least five different continents. It was, as Belinda had said, about time I found out what I had been missing.

Chapter 5

I woke the next morning determined to take Belinda up on her other suggestion—the one for gainful employment. Armed with Belinda's glowing recommendation, I sat facing the head of personnel at Harrods. He was eyeing me suspiciously and waved the letter in my direction. "If you had indeed proved so satisfactory, why did you leave this position?"

"The Honorable Belinda Warburton-Stoke is going through a difficult period, as one does when setting up a new business, and had to give up charity events for the time being."

"I see." He examined me critically, as several other people had done in the past twenty-four hours. "You're well enough spoken and you've been well educated, that is obvious. You say your name is Florence Kincaid? Well, Miss Kincaid, don't you have family connections? I'm wondering why you would want a job like this. Not just for fun, I hope, when so many poor souls are on the brink of starvation."

"Oh, indeed not, sir. You see, my father died some years ago. My brother has inherited the property and his new wife doesn't want to have me there any longer. I'm as much in need of a job as anyone else."

"I see." He frowned at me. "Kincaid. That wouldn't be the Worcester Kincaids, would it?"

"No, it wouldn't."

We stared at each other for a while, then my impatience got the better of me. "If you have no position vacant, please inform me immediately, so that I can take my skills to Selfridges."

"To Selfridges?" He looked horrified. "My dear young lady, you need no skills at Selfridges. I'll take you on trial. Miss Fairweather could use some help on the cosmetics counter. Follow me."

And so I was handed a smock in an unflattering salmony pink that made me, with my Celtic reddish blond hair and freckles, look like a large cooked prawn, and installed in cosmetics, under the disapproving glare of Miss Fairweather—who eyed me with a more superior stare than I had ever seen coming from one of my austere relatives.

"No experience at all? She's had no retail experience? I don't know how I'm ever supposed to find the time to train her." She sighed. She spoke with the kind of ultraposh upper-class accent developed by those of humble birth who want to conceal this fact.

"I'm a quick learner," I said.

She sniffed this time. Frankly I thought she was a poor choice to put in charge of cosmetics, as no amount of cream, powder, or rouge would make that face look either soft, appealing, or glamorous. It would be like powdering granite.

"Very well, I suppose you'll have to do," she said. She gave me a rapid tour of our products and what they were supposed to do. Until now I had thought that cosmetics consisted of cold cream, a brushing of the lips with Natural Rose, and powdering one's nose with baby powder or those handy *papiers poudrés*. Now I was amazed to see the selection of powders and creams—and the prices too. Some women obviously still had money in this depression.

"If a customer asks you for advice, come to me," Miss Fairweather said. "You have no experience, remember."

I murmured humble acquiescence. She moved to the other side of the counter like a ship in full sail. Customers started arriving. I called Miss Fairweather when necessary and I was just feeling that I was getting the hang of it and it wouldn't be too odious a job after all when a voice said imperiously, "I need a jar of my very special face cream that you always keep hidden away, just for me."

I looked up and found myself face-to-face with my mother. I'm not sure who was the more horrified.

"Good God, Georgie, what on earth are you doing here?" she demanded.

"Trying to earn an honest living like everybody else."

"Don't be ridiculous, darling. You weren't raised to be a shopgirl. Now take off that horrible smock at once. It makes you look like a prawn. And let's go and have some coffee at Fortnum's."

She still had that china-doll look that had made her the darling of the London stage, but the eyelashes were definitely too long to be real and there were circles of rouge on both cheeks. Her hair was black this time and she was wearing a pillar box red jacket of obvious Parisian design and a matching jaunty red beret. Around her neck was a silver fox, complete with beady-eyed head. I had to admit that the effect was still stunning.

"Would you please go away," I hissed at her.

"Don't tell me to go away," my mother hissed back. "Is that any way to talk to your mother, who hasn't seen you in months?"

"Mummy, you'll get me dismissed. Please just go away."

"I certainly won't go away," my mother said in her clear voice that had charmed audiences in the London theaters before my father snapped her up. "I have come to buy face cream and face cream I shall have."

A floorwalker appeared miraculously at her side. "Is there some problem, madam?"

"Yes, this young person doesn't seem to be able or willing to help me," my mother said, wafting a distressed hand in his direction. "All I need is some face cream. That shouldn't be too difficult, should it?"

"Of course not, madam. I'll have our senior assistant assist you as soon as she is finished with her customer. And you, girl. Fetch a chair and a cup of tea for madam."

"Very well, sir," I said. "I was perfectly willing to help madam,"—I put emphasis on the word—"but she wasn't able to tell me the brand of face cream she needed."

"Don't answer back, girl," he snapped at me.

Seething with annoyance, I went to get my mother a chair and a cup of tea. She accepted both with a smirk. "I need cheering up, Georgie," she said. "I am quite desolate. You heard about poor Hubie, of course?"

"Hubie?"

"Sir Hubert Anstruther. My third husband, or was it my fourth? I know we were definitely married because he was the straightlaced type who wouldn't countenance living in sin."

"Oh, Sir Hubert. I remember him." I did too, with a warm kind of glow.

He was one of the few husbands who had actually wanted me around and I still had fond memories of the time I spent at his house when I was about five. He was a big bear of a man who laughed a lot and had taught me how to climb trees, ride to hounds, and swim across his ornamental lake. I was brokenhearted when my mother left him and moved on to pastures new. I had rarely seen him since, but I received the occasional postcard from exotic parts of the world and he sent me a most generous check for my twenty-first.

"He's had an awful accident, darling. You know he's an explorer and mountaineer. Well, apparently he's just had a terrible fall in the Alps. Swept away by an avalanche, I believe. They don't expect him to live."

"How horrible." Instant feelings of guilt that I hadn't been to see him recently, or even written anything more than thank-you letters.

"I know. I've been devastated ever since I heard. I adored that man. Worshipped him. In fact I believe he was the only man I truly loved." She paused. "Well, apart from dear old Monty, of course, and that gorgeous Argentine boy."

She shrugged, making the silver fox around her neck twitch in a horribly lifelike way. "Hubert was very fond of you too. In fact he wanted to adopt you, but your father wouldn't hear of it. But I believe you're still mentioned in his will. If he does die, and they say his injuries are absolutely frightful, you won't have to work behind shop counters anymore. What do the royals think about this, anyway?"

"They don't know," I said, "and you are not to tell them."

"Darling, I wouldn't dream of telling them anything, but I really can't come to London never knowing when I'm going to be served by my own daughter. It just isn't on. In fact . . ."

She looked up with a charming smile as Miss Fairweather approached. "I am so sorry to keep you waiting like this, your ladyship. It is still your ladyship, isn't it?"

"No, I'm afraid not. Just plain Mrs. Clegg these days—I believe I am still legally married to Homer Clegg. What an awful name to be stuck with but Homer is one of these straightlaced Texan oil millionaires and he doesn't believe in divorce, unfortunately. Now, my needs are very simple today. Just a jar of that very special face cream you always keep hidden away for me."

"The one we import specially from Paris, madam, in the crystal jar with the cherubs on it?"

"That's the one. You are an angel to remember." My mother gave her

brilliant smile and even the stern-faced Miss Fairweather flushed coyly. I could see how my mother had made so many conquests in her life. As Miss Fairweather went to hunt out the face cream, my mother straightened her hat in the mirror on the counter. "Poor Hubert's ward must be quite crushed by the news too," she said, without looking up at me. "He worshipped his guardian too, poor little chap. So if you happen to bump into him, do be kind to him, won't you? Tristram Haubois." (She pronounced it "Hote-boys," naturally. It is the done thing to anglicize any French name when possible.) "You two were great chums when you were five years old. I remember you stripped off your clothes together and went romping in the foun-tains, Hubie did laugh."

At least I had had some illicit adventures with the opposite sex in my life, even if I was too young to remember them.

"Mother, about Granddad," I said in a low voice, not wanting to miss this opportunity. "He's not very well. I think you should go and see him—"

"I'd love to, darling, but I'm catching the boat train back to Cologne this afternoon. Max will be pining. Tell him next time we're over, all right?"

The cream was brought, packaged, and charged to my mother's account. She was escorted out with much bowing and gushing. I watched her go, feeling that annoyance I always felt after any encounter with my mother—so many things I wanted to say and never a chance to say them. Then the floorwalker and Miss Fairweather returned to the counter, muttering together. She gave me a frosty stare and a sniff as she went around to her side.

"And you, girl, take off that smock," the floorwalker said.

"Take off my smock?"

"You are dismissed. I heard the tone of voice you used to one of our best customers. And Miss Fairweather claims she even heard you telling the customer to go away. You may have ruined Harrods's reputation forever. Go now. Turn in your smock and be gone."

I couldn't defend myself without revealing myself as a liar and a fraud. I went. My experiment with gainful employment had lasted all of five hours.

It was about two o'clock when I came out into a glorious spring after-noon. The sun was shining, the birds in Kensington Gardens were chirping, and I had four shillings I had earned in my pocket.

I wandered aimlessly through the afternoon crowds, not wanting to go home, not knowing what to do next. It was Saturday and the streets were packed with those who had a half day off work. I'd never get a job in another store now, I decided miserably. I'd probably never get another job anywhere and I'd die of starvation. My feet started hurting me and I felt almost dizzy with hunger. I realized they hadn't even given me a lunch break. I stopped and looked around me. I didn't know much about restaurants. People I knew didn't pay to go out to eat. They ate at home, unless they were invited to dine with a friend or neighbor. When we had been in London for my season we had eaten supper at the various balls. I had been taken to tea at the Ritz by a friend's aunt, but I could hardly go to the Ritz with four shillings in my pocket. I knew Fortnum and Mason, and the Café Royal, and that was about the extent of my restaurant knowledge.

I realized I had walked until the Kensington Road had become Kensington High Street. I recognized Barkers and knew that it would have a tearoom, but I had determined never to set foot in a department store again. In the end I went into a dismal Lyons, ordered a pot of tea and a scone, and sat feeling sorry for myself. At least I'd eat well as lady-in-waiting to a princess. At least I would be addressed politely and wouldn't have to put up with people like Miss Fairweather and that floorwalker. And I wouldn't risk bumping into my mother.

I looked up as a shadow hovered over me. It was a dark-haired young man, slightly unkempt, but not at all unattractive, and he was grinning at me.

"My goodness, it is you," he said in a voice that bore traces of an Irish brogue. "I couldn't believe my eyes as I walked past and saw you in the window. That's never her ladyship, I said to myself, so I had to come in to see." He pulled out the chair opposite me and sat without being invited to do so, still studying me with amused interest. "So what are you doing, seeing how the other half lives?"

He had unruly dark curls and blue eyes that flashed dangerously. In fact he so unnerved me that I resorted to type. "I'm sorry, I don't believe we've been introduced," I said. "And I don't speak to strange men."

At that he threw back his head and laughed. "Oh, that's a good one. Strange men. I like that. Do you not recall dancing with me at a hunt ball at Badminton a couple of years ago? Obviously not. I'm mortally wounded. I usually make a far greater impression on a girl I've held in my arms." He held out his hand. "Darcy O'Mara. Or should I say the Honorable Darcy O'Mara, since you obviously care about such things. My father is Lord

Kilhenny, a peerage that goes back far longer than your own admirable family."

I took his hand. "How do you do?" I said tentatively, because in truth I was sure I'd have remembered meeting him and especially being in close contact in his arms. "Are you sure you're not mistaking me for someone else?"

"Lady Georgiana, is it not? Daughter of the late duke, sister to the boring Binky?"

"Yes, but . . . " I stammered. "How can I possibly not remember dancing with you?"

"Obviously you had more desirable partners that night."

"I assure you I didn't," I said hotly. "All the young men I remember were as dull as ditchwater. They only wanted to talk about hunting."

"There's nothing wrong with hunting," Darcy O'Mara said, "in its place. But there are many preferable occupations when in the presence of a young woman."

He looked at me so frankly that I blushed and was furious with myself. "If you'll excuse me, I'd like to drink my tea before it gets cold." I looked down at the grayish, unappetizing liquid.

"Don't let me stop you," he said, waving expansively. "Go ahead, if you think you'll survive the experience without being poisoned. They lose a customer a day here, you know. Just whip them quietly out the back entrance and go on as if nothing has happened."

"They do not!" I had to laugh.

He smiled too. "That's better. I've never seen such a grim face as you were making earlier. What's wrong? Have you been dumped by a deceiver?"

"No, nothing like that. It's just that life is insufferably gloomy at the moment." And I heard myself telling him about the room in the cold house, the embarrassment at Harrods, and the prospect of banishment to the country. "So you see," I concluded, "I've not much to look cheerful about at the moment."

He eyed me steadily, then he said, "Tell me, do you have a posh frock with you?"

"Posh as in dressing for dinner posh, or as in going to church posh?"

"As in attending a wedding posh."

I laughed again, a little uneasily this time. "Are you suggesting we run off and get married to cheer me up?"

"Good Lord, no. I'm a wild Irish boy. It will take a lot to tame me and drag me to the altar. So do you have a suitable outfit within reach?"

"Yes, as a matter of fact I do."

"Good. Go and put it on and meet me at Hyde Park Corner in an hour."

"Do you mind telling me what this is all about?"

He touched his finger to his nose. "You'll see," he said. "A damned sight better than tea and scones at Lyons anyway. Are you going to do it?"

I looked at him for a moment, then sighed. "What have I got to lose?"

Those roguish eyes flashed again. "I don't know," he said. "What have you?"

⁂

YOU ARE QUITE, quite mad, I said to myself several times as I washed, dressed, and attempted to tame my hair into the sleekness required by fashion. Going out on a whim with a strange man about whom you know nothing. He could be the worst sort of imposter. He could be running a profitable white slave ring, pretending to know young girls and luring them to their doom. I stopped what I was doing, rushed down to the library, and pulled out a copy of Burke's Irish Peerage. There it was all right: Thaddeus Alexander O'Mara, Lord Kilhenny, sixteenth baron, etc. Having issue: William Darcy Byrne . . .

So a real Darcy O'Mara did exist. And it was midafternoon. And the streets were crowded. And I wouldn't let him take me to a low-down dive or sleazy hotel. And he was awfully good-looking. As he said, what had I got to lose?

Chapter 6

RANNOCH HOUSE
SATURDAY, APRIL 23, 1932

I almost didn't recognize Darcy O'Mara as he came toward me on Park Lane. He was wearing a full morning suit, his wild curls had been tamed, and he looked remarkably presentable. The quick once-over glance he gave me told me that he thought I also passed muster.

"My lady." He gave me a very proper bow.

"Mr. O'Mara." I inclined my head to reciprocate the greeting. (One never calls anybody honorable, even if they are.)

"Please forgive me," he said, "but was I correct in addressing you as 'my lady' and not 'your royal highness'? I'm never quite sure of the rules when it comes to dukes."

I laughed. "Only the male children of royal dukes can use the HRH." I said. "I, being a mere female, and my father not being a royal duke, even though of royal blood, am simply 'my lady.' But just plain Georgie will do."

"Not at all plain Georgie. It was good of you to come. I assure you won't regret it." He took my elbow and steered me through the crowd. "Now let's get out of here. We look like a couple of peacocks in the hen coop."

"Do you mind telling me where we're going?"

"Grosvenor House."

"Really? If you're taking me to dine, isn't it a little early, and if you're taking me to tea, aren't we overdressed?"

"I'm taking you to a wedding, as I promised."

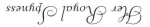

"A wedding?"

"Well, the reception part of it."

"But I haven't been invited."

"That's all right," he said calmly as we started down Park Lane, "neither have I."

I wrenched my arm free of him. "What? Are you out of your mind? We can't go to a wedding reception to which we haven't been invited."

"Oh, it's all right," he said. "I do it all the time. Works like a charm."

I eyed him suspiciously. He was grinning again. "How else would I get a decent meal once a week?"

"Let me get this straight. You intend to gate-crash a wedding at Grosvenor House?"

"Oh, yes. As I told you, there's never a problem. If you look right and you speak with the right accent and you know how to behave, everyone takes it for granted you are a legitimate guest. The groom's side thinks the bride's must have invited you and vice versa. You, being absolutely top drawer—they'll be proud and happy to have you there. Raises the tone of the whole occasion. Afterward they can say to each other, 'I hope you noticed we had a member of the royal family present.'"

"Just a distant relative, Darcy."

"Nonetheless, a catch. They'll be thrilled, you'll see."

I pulled away from him. "I really can't do this. It's not right."

"Are you backing out because it's not right or because you're afraid of getting caught?" he asked.

I glared at him. "I was brought up to behave properly, which may not have been the case in the wilds of Ireland."

"You're scared. You're afraid there's going to be a scene."

"I am not. I just don't think it's the right thing to do."

"Stealing their food by false pretense, you mean? As if anyone who can afford a wedding reception at Grosvenor House would notice if anyone took a couple of illegal slices of cold salmon." He took my hand. "Come on, Georgie. Don't back out on me now. And don't say you're not interested. Anyone who was attempting to eat one of Lyons's scones is obviously in need of a good meal."

"It's just that . . ." I began, conscious of his hand holding mine. "If I'm caught there might be a frightful stink."

"If they notice you and realize that they didn't invite you, they'll only feel mortified that they left you off the list and glad that you came."

"Well . . ."

"Look at me. Do you want smoked salmon and champagne or to go home to baked beans?"

"Well, if you put it that way, lead on, Macduff."

He laughed and took my arm. "That's the ticket," he said and swept me along Park Lane.

"If you're really Lord Kilhenny's son," I asked, my courage returning, "why do you need to gate-crash other people's weddings?"

"Same story as your own," he said. "The family's penniless. Father invested heavily in America, lost it all in '29; then there was a fire in his racing stables. Lost all that too. Had to sell the property and when I turned twenty-one he told me there was nothing for me so I'd have to make my own way. I'm making it the best I can. Ah, here we are."

I glanced up at that formidable red and white brick building on Park Lane as Darcy swept me up the steps under the colonnade and into the front entrance of Grosvenor House Hotel.

The doorman saluted as he opened the door. "You're here for the wedding reception, sir? To your right, in the blue ballroom."

I was whisked across the foyer and suddenly found myself in a queue for the reception line. I was expecting doom to fall at any moment, when the bride and groom would look at each other. I could hear them saying loudly, "But I didn't invite her, did you?" Luckily brides and grooms must be in a state of shock on such occasions. The bride's mother murmured, "So kind of you to come." The bride and groom were momentarily involved with the person ahead of us and Darcy took the opportunity to steer me toward a passing tray of champagne.

After a few minutes of feeling that my heart was going to leap into my mouth, expecting at any second to feel that hand on my shoulder, that voice barking, "She's a gate-crasher, please have her escorted from the premises," I started to relax and look around me. It certainly was very pleasant. The event was not being held in the grand ballroom, to which I had been for a ball during my season; it was in a smaller room, big enough for only two hundred or so, and now richly decorated with early spring flowers—the scent was heavenly. At the far end was a long, white-clothed table on which I could glimpse the many tiers of a cake. In one corner an orchestra (composed, as they so often are, of elderly men) was playing Strauss waltzes. I took a hot vol-au-vent from a passing tray and began to enjoy myself.

Darcy had been quite right. If you behave as if you should be there, then nobody questions it. People who half recognized me drifted up and there were several conversations along the lines of, "So, have you known old Roly long?"

"Can't say I know him well at all."

"Oh, so you're one of Primrose's lot then. Stunning girl!"

"You see how easy it is?" Darcy whispered. "The only difficulty arises when there is a sit-down banquet with assigned places at the table."

"What on earth do you do then?" I asked, the panic returning as I looked around to detect evidence of an adjoining dining room.

"I make my apologies for having to catch a train and I melt away before it starts. But this one is only nibbles and cake. I checked first. I usually do."

"You're amazing."

He laughed. "We Irish have learned to live by our wits after centuries of being occupied by you English."

"If you don't mind, I happen to be Scottish. Well, one-quarter Scottish anyway."

"Ah, but it was your great-grandmother who went around subjugating half the world. Empress of all I survey, and all that. You must have that quality somewhere in your makeup."

"I've never had a chance to subjugate anybody yet, so I can't really say," I confessed, "but I'm frequently amused and she never was, apparently. At least not after Albert died. In fact, given my grim list of ancestors, I'd say I'm pretty normal."

"I'd say you turned out pretty damned well, for someone who is more than half English," he said and, to my annoyance, I blushed again.

"I think I'll go and try some of that crab," I said and turned away, only to bump into a familiar face.

"Darling!" Belinda cried excitedly, "I had no idea you were coming to this bash. Why didn't you tell me? We could have taken a cab together. What fun, isn't it? Who'd have thought that Primrose would settle down with someone like Roly?"

"Primrose?" I glanced across the room to glimpse the bride's back, hidden beneath a long veil around which everybody was cautiously stepping.

"The bride, darling. Primrose Asquey d'Asquey. She was at school with us, don't you remember? Well, for one term anyway. She was expelled for giving the new girls a lecture on how to use the Dutch cap."

We looked at each other and started to laugh.

"I do remember," I said.

"And now she's marrying Roland Aston-Poley. Military family. Which means she's gone from being Primrose Asquey d'Asquey to being Primrose Roly Poley. Not a happy choice, if you ask me."

I laughed with her.

"So you're part of Roly's brigade then," she said. "I didn't realize you had army connections."

"Not really." I started to blush again, then grabbed her arm and dragged her out of the main crush of guests. "Actually I'm here with an extraordinary chap. Darcy O'Mara. Do you know him?"

"Can't say that I do. Point him out to me."

"Over there by that flower arrangement."

"I say. Not bad. You can introduce me anytime you want to. Tell me all about him."

"That's just it," I whispered. "I'm not really sure if he's who he claims to be or a confidence trickster."

"Has he asked you to lend him money?"

"No."

"Then he's probably all right. Who does he say he is?"

"Lord Kilhenny's son. Irish baron."

"There's a million of them. I wouldn't doubt it for a moment. So he's the one who knows Roly?"

I leaned even closer. "He doesn't know either of them. We're gate-crashers. Apparently he does this sort of thing often, just to get a free meal. It's shocking, isn't it? I can't believe I'm doing this."

To my horror, she started to laugh. When she had controlled her mirth, she leaned toward me. "I'll let you into a little secret. I'm doing exactly the same thing. I wasn't invited either."

"Belinda! How could you?"

"Easily. Exactly the same way you could. My face is sort of familiar. I'm seen at Ascot and the opera, so nobody ever questions whether I was invited or not. It works wonderfully."

"But you said you were doing so well in your career."

She made a face. "Not all that well, actually. It's tough to start up a business, especially if you want to design clothes for the fashionable set. They never want to pay, you see. They gush over the dress I've designed for them and tell me they positively adore it and I'm the cleverest person they've ever met. Then they wear it to the opera and when I remind them they haven't paid, they point out that they have been advertising my dress just by wearing it and I should be grateful. I'm sometimes owed several hundred pounds, and the fabrics are not cheap."

"How awful for you."

"It's difficult," she agreed, "because if I make a fuss and upset one of them, she'll tell the rest of her set and they'll drop me like a hot potato."

I did see that this was likely to happen. "So what are you going to do? You can't keep financing their new clothes forever."

"I'm hoping for the big break, I suppose. If one of the royal family—or one of the Prince of Wales's lady friends—decides she likes my dresses, then everyone in the world will want them. That's where you could be most helpful, you know. If you are going to be mingling with your royal cousin and his set, I'll lend you one of my designs to wear and you can gush about me."

"I wouldn't guarantee that my cousin's women would pay up any quicker than your current clients," I said. "But I don't mind trying for you. Especially if it allows me to wear a slinky new dress."

"Splendid!" Belinda beamed at me.

"I'm sorry you're going through such a tough time," I said.

"Oh, there are a few honest ones among them—mostly old money, you know. Properly brought up, like you. It's those dreadful nouveau riche women who try to wriggle out of paying. I could name one society belle who looked me straight in the eye and insisted she had already paid, when she knew as well as I did that she hadn't. They're just not like us, darling."

I squeezed her arm. "At least you are out and about in society. You're bound to meet a rich and handsome man and then your money worries will be over."

"So will you, darling. So will you." She glanced across the room. "I take it that handsome Irish peer's son does not come with a fortune?"

"Penniless," I said.

"Dear me. Not a wise choice then, in spite of his looks. Although after last night's little conversation about sex lives, he might be just the one to . . ."

"Belinda!" I hissed as Darcy was making in our direction. "I've only just met him and I have no intention—"

"We never have, darling. That's just the problem. We never have." Belinda turned to meet Darcy with an angelic smile.

The afternoon went on. Smoked salmon came around, and shrimp and sausage rolls and savory éclairs. My spirits began to rise with the champagne intake until I was actually enjoying myself. Darcy had vanished into the crowd and I was standing alone when I noticed a potted palm tree swaying by itself as if in a strong wind. Since no wind is allowed to blow through ballrooms at Grosvenor House I was intrigued. I made my way to the corner and peered around the palm tree. A vision in alarming royal purple satin stood there, holding on to the palm tree as it swayed. What's more, I recognized her. It was another old school chum, Marisa Pauncefoot-Young, daughter of the Earl of Malmsbury.

"Marisa," I hissed.

She attempted to focus on me. "Oh, hello, Georgie. What are you doing here?"

"More to the point, what exactly are you doing—dancing with a palm tree?"

"No, I came over all dizzy so I thought I'd retire to a quiet corner, but the damned tree won't stay still."

"Marisa," I said severely, "you're drunk."

"I fear so." She sighed. "It was all Primrose's fault. She insisted on having a very boozy breakfast to pluck up courage before the ceremony and then I got rather depressed all of a sudden and champagne does have a wonderful way of lifting the spirits, doesn't it?"

I took her arm. "Come on, come with me. We'll find somewhere to sit and get you some black coffee."

I led her out of the ballroom and found two gilt chairs in a hallway. Then I hailed a passing waiter. "Lady Marisa isn't feeling well," I whispered. "Do you think you could rustle up some black coffee for her?"

Black coffee appeared instantly. Marisa sipped and shuddered alternately. "Why can't I ever be a happy drunk?" she demanded. "One too many and my legs won't hold me up any longer. This is very sweet of you, Georgie. I didn't even know you were coming."

"Neither did I until the last moment," I said truthfully. "So tell me, why were you so depressed?"

"Look at me." She made a dramatic gesture at herself. "I look as if I've been swallowed by a particularly unpleasant variety of boa constrictor."

She wasn't wrong. The dress was long, tight, and purple. Since Marisa has no figure to speak of and is almost six feet tall, the effect was something like a shiny purple drainpipe.

"And I thought Primrose was my friend," she said. "I was flattered when she invited me to be bridesmaid, but now I see that she only did it because we are cousins and she had to, so she made damn sure that I wouldn't outshine her going up the aisle. Actually I could hardly totter up the aisle, due to the tight skirt. And it was so dark in St. Margaret's that I bet I looked like a floating head with a couple of disembodied arms on either side clutching this hideous bouquet. I'm not going to forgive her in a hurry."

She sighed and drained the last of the black coffee. "And then I got here and I thought at least being bridesmaid usually has its perks. You know, a quick kiss and cuddle with an usher behind the potted palms. But look at them—not a single grab and grope among the lot of them. Most of them are Roly's older brothers, and they've all brought their wives along. And the others are not that way inclined—daisy boys, you know."

"You mean pansy boys," I said.

"Do I? Well, you know what I'm getting at, don't you? So not the teeniest bit of titillation all afternoon. No wonder I turned to drink. It was good of you to rescue me."

"Not at all. What are school friends for?"

"We did have fun at Les Oiseaux, didn't we? I still miss it sometimes, and all the old friends. I haven't seen you in ages. What have you been doing with yourself?"

"Oh, this and that," I said. "I'm newly arrived in town and I'm hunting for a suitable job."

"Lucky you. I do envy you. I'm stuck at home with Mummy. She hasn't been too well, you know, and she won't hear of my going off to London alone. How I'm ever going to meet a potential husband, I can't think. The season was a hopeless failure, wasn't it? All those dreadful clodhopping country types who held us as if we were sacks of potatoes. At least Mummy is talking about taking a place in Nice for the rest of the spring. I certainly wouldn't say no to a French count. They have those wonderful droopy come-to-bed eyes."

She looked up as a burst of applause came from the ballroom.

"Oh, dear. They've started the speeches. I should be there, I suppose, when Whiffy proposes a toast to the bridesmaids."

"Do you think you can stand without swaying now?"

"I'll try."

I helped her to her feet and she tottered uncertainly back into the ball-room. I slipped into the back of the crowd, which now clustered around the podium with the cake.

The cake was cut and distributed. Speeches began. I was also beginning to feel the effects of three glasses of champagne on a relatively empty stomach. There is nothing worse than speeches about someone you don't know, made by someone you don't know. How my royal kin manage to sit there, day after day, and look interested through one deadly dull speech after another inspires my highest admiration. I looked for Darcy but couldn't see him, so I prowled the back of the crowd, hoping to find a chair I might sit on unobtrusively. The only chairs were occupied by elderly ladies and an extremely ancient colonel with a wooden leg. Then I thought I spotted the back of Darcy's head and I moved back into the crowd again.

"My lords, ladies, and gentlemen, pray raise your glasses for the loyal toast," the toastmaster boomed out.

I accepted another glass of champagne from a passing tray. As I was raising it, my elbow was jogged violently and the champagne splashed up into my face and down my front. Before I could do any more than gasp I heard a voice saying, "I'm most frightfully sorry. Here, let me get you a napkin." Like many young men of our class, he could not, or would not, say the letter *r* and pronounced it "fwightfully."

He reached across to a nearby table and handed me a piece of linen.

"That's a tray cloth," I said.

"I'm so sorry," he said again. "It's all I could find."

I dabbed at my face with the tray cloth and was now able to focus on him. He was tall and slim, like an overgrown schoolboy who is wearing his big brother's morning suit. An attempt had been made to slick down his dark brown hair but it still flopped in boyish fashion across his forehead and his earnest brown eyes were now pleading with me in a way that reminded me of a spaniel I once had.

"I've ruined your lovely dress. I really am the most clumsy ox," he went on as he watched me dry myself off. "I'm absolutely hopeless at events like this. The moment I put on a morning suit or a dinner jacket, I am positively guaranteed to spill something, trip over my shoelaces, or generally make an utter fool of myself. I'm thinking of becoming a hermit and living in a cave somewhere on a mountaintop. In Scotland, maybe."

I had to laugh at that. "I don't think you'll find the food is as good," I pointed out. "And I think you'd find a Scottish cave incredibly cold and drafty. Trust me, I know whereof I speak."

"You do have a point." He observed me and then said, "I say, I think I know who you are."

This was not good. It was bound to happen, I suppose. Just in case things got awkward, I tried to spot Darcy in the crowd. However, I was completely unprepared for what the young man said next: "I believe that you and I are related."

I went through a quick mental list of cousins, second cousins, and second cousins once removed.

"Really?" I said.

"Well, sort of related. At least, not actually related, but your mother was once married to my guardian, and we played together when we were little. I'm Tristram Hautbois, Sir Hubert Anstruther's ward."

All I could think was what terrible twist of fate had christened somebody Tristram who could not say his *r*s properly. He pronounced it "Twistwam."

"We ran through the fountains naked, apparently," I said.

His face lit up. "You remember it too? We thought we'd get into frightful trouble, because a lot of important people had been invited to tea on the lawns, but my guardian thought it was frightfully funny." His face became solemn again. "You've heard what's happened, I suppose. Poor old Sir Hubert's had a terrible accident. He's in a coma in a Swiss hospital. They don't expect him to live."

"I only heard about it this morning," I said. "I'm very sorry. I remember him as such a nice man."

"Oh, he was. One of the best. So good to me, you know, even though I was only a distant relative. My mother was his mother's cousin. You knew his mother was French, I suppose. Well, my parents were killed in the Great War and he took frightful risks coming over to France to rescue me. He has raised me as if I were his own son. I owe him a huge debt of gratitude that I'll never be able to repay now."

"So you're actually French, not English?"

"I am, but I'm afraid my mastery of the language is no better than the average schoolboy's. I can just about manage '*la plume de ma tante*' and all that. Shameful, really, but I was only two years old when I was brought to Eynsleigh. It's a lovely house, isn't it? One of the prettiest in England. Do you remember it well?"

"Hardly at all. I have a vague memory of the lawns and those fountains, and wasn't there a fat little pony?"

"Squibbs. You tried to make him jump over a log and he bucked you off."

"So he did."

We looked at each other and smiled. I had thought him the usual run-of-the-mill mindless twit until now, but the smile lit up his whole face and made him look quite appealing.

"So what will happen to the house if Sir Hubert dies?" I asked.

"Sold, I expect. He has no children of his own to inherit. I am the closest he has to a son, but he never officially adopted me, unfortunately."

"What are you doing with yourself now?"

"I've just come down from Oxford and Sir Hubert arranged for me to be articled to a solicitor in Bromley in Kent, of all places. I'm not sure that I'm cut out for the law, but my guardian wanted me to have a stable profession, so I suppose I've got to stick with it. Frankly I'd much rather be off on adventures and expeditions like him."

"A little more dangerous," I pointed out.

"But not boring. How about you?"

"I've just arrived in London and I'm not sure what I'm going to be doing with myself. It's not quite as easy for me to just go out and get a job."

"No, I suppose it wouldn't be," he said. "Look, now that you're in London, maybe we can do some exploring together. I happen to know the city quite well and I'd be delighted to show you around."

"I'd like that," I said. "I'm staying at the family home. Rannoch House on Belgrave Square."

"And I'm in digs in Bromley," he said. "A slight difference."

Another young man in a morning coat approached. "Buck up, old thing," he said to Tristram. "We need all the groomsmen outside toot sweet. We've got to sabotage the car before they drive away."

"Oh, right. Coming." Tristram gave me an apologetic smile. "Duty calls," he said. "I do hope we meet again soon."

At that moment Darcy appeared. "Are you ready to go, Georgie? The bride and groom are about to leave and I thought . . . " He broke off when he saw I was standing beside Tristram. "Oh, I'm sorry. I didn't mean to interrupt. How are you, Hautbois?"

"Pretty fair. And yourself, O'Mara?"

"Can't complain. Will you excuse us? I have to take Georgie home."

"I turn into a pumpkin at six o'clock," I attempted to joke.

"I look forward to seeing you again, Lady Georgiana," Tristram said formally.

As Darcy turned away and attempted to fight his way through the crowd to the door, Tristram grabbed my arm. "Watch out for O'Mara," he whispered. "He's a bit of a cad. Not quite trustworthy."

Chapter 7

RANNOCH HOUSE
SATURDAY, APRIL 23, 1932

We came out to a mild April evening. The setting sun was streaming across the park.

"There," Darcy said, taking my arm to help me down the steps. "That wasn't so bad, was it? You survived perfectly well and you're considerably better fed and wined than you were a couple of hours ago. In fact there are now nice healthy roses to your cheeks."

"I suppose so," I said, "but I don't think I plan on doing it again. Too hair-raising. There were people who knew me."

"Like that twerp Hautbois?" Darcy said scathingly.

"You know Tristram, then?"

"I can't say I actually socialize with him these days. We were at school together. At least, I was a couple of years above him. He snitched to the masters and got me a beating once."

"For doing what?"

"Trying to take something from him, I believe," he said. "Sniveling little brute that he was."

"He seems quite pleasant now," I said.

"Has he asked to see you again?"

"He's offered to show me around London."

"Has he now."

With a thrill I realized that he might be jealous. I grinned.

"So how on earth do you know him?" Darcy went on. "He can't have been one of your partners at those dreary deb balls, surely?"

"We were practically related once. My mother was married to his guardian. We used to—to play together." Somehow I couldn't use the word "naked" with Darcy.

"I'd imagine you are probably practically related to a good many people on several continents," he said and raised an eyebrow.

"I think my mother only actually married the first few bolts," I said. "In those days she was conventional enough to still believe she should marry them. Now she just—"

"Lives in sin?" Again that challenging smile that did something to my insides.

"As you say."

"That would never work for me," he said. "As a Catholic, I'd be damned to hell if I kept marrying and divorcing. The church considers marriage sacred and divorce a mortal sin."

"And if you kept living in sin with somebody?"

He grinned. "I think the church would prefer that, given the options."

I glanced up at him as we waited to cross Park Lane. Penniless, Irish, and a Catholic too. Quite unsuitable in every way. If I were still being chaperoned, I'd have been bundled into the nearest cab and whisked away instantly.

"I'll see you home," he said, taking my arm again when I teetered as we crossed the street.

"I'm perfectly capable of finding my own way home in broad daylight," I said, although I had to admit that my legs weren't exactly steady after all that champagne and with the heady prospect of his walking beside me.

"I'm sure you are, but wouldn't you rather have my company to enjoy this lovely evening? Were I currently in funds, I'd have arranged a horse-drawn carriage and we'd clip-clop slowly along the leafy avenues. As it is, we can still walk across the park."

"All right, then," I said, rather ungraciously. Twenty-one years of strict upbringing were shouting that I should have no more to do with a man whom I had been warned was a cad and unreliable, as well as being penniless and a Catholic. But when had I ever had such a tempting chance to stroll through the park with someone so devastatingly handsome?

There is nothing as lovely as a London park in springtime. Daffodils among the trees, new green emerging on those spreading chestnuts, elegantly turned-out horses crossing from the riding stable toward Rotten Row, and courting couples strolling hand in hand or sitting rather too close to each other on the benches. I stole a glance at Darcy. He was striding out, looking relaxed and enjoying the scene. I knew I should be making conversation at this moment. At all those training sessions at Les Oiseaux, when we had to dine with each of the mistresses in turn, it was drummed into us that it was a mortal sin to allow a silence to descend upon a dinner party.

"Do you actually live in London?" I asked Darcy.

"At the moment. I'm sleeping at a friend's place in Chelsea while he's on his yacht in the Med."

"That sounds awfully glamorous. Have you been to the Med yourself?"

"Oh, yes. Many times. Never in April though. Not smooth enough. I'm a rotten sailor."

I tried to form the question I was dying to ask him. "So do you have some kind of profession? I mean, if you have to gate-crash functions to get a good meal and your father has cut you off without a penny, how do you survive?"

He looked down at me and grinned. "I live by my wits, my girl. That's what I do. And it's not a bad life. People invite me to make upon even number at dinner parties. I'm awfully well house-trained. I never spill soup on my dinner jacket. They invite me to dance with their daughters at hunt balls. Of course they don't all know what I've told you about being penniless. I'm Lord Kilhenny's son. They think I'm a good catch."

"You will be Lord Kilhenny one day, won't you?"

He laughed. "My old man is likely to live forever, just to spite me. He and I have never been the greatest of pals."

"And what about your mother? Is she still living?"

"Died in the flu epidemic," he said. "So did my little brothers. I was away at school so I survived. The conditions were so brutal there, the food so bad, that even the influenza bugs didn't think it worth visiting." He smiled, then the smile faded. "I think my father blames me for living."

"But you'll have to do something with yourself someday. You can't go on sneaking in to eat at other people's functions."

"I expect I'll marry a rich heiress, probably an American, and live happily ever after in Kentucky."

"Would you like that?"

"Good horses in Kentucky," he said. "I like horses, don't you?"

"Adore them. I even adore hunting."

He nodded. "It's in the blood. Nothing we can do about it. That's the one thing I regret, the destruction of our racing stable. We had some of the finest thoroughbreds in Europe at one time." He stopped as if the idea had just struck him. "We must go to Ascot together. I know how to pick winners. If you come with me, you'll win yourself a tidy amount."

"If I can win myself a tidy amount, why don't you win tidy amounts for yourself and thus not be quite so penniless?"

He grinned. "And who says I don't win myself very tidy amounts from time to time? It's a great way to keep my head above water. I can't do it too often, though, or I'd find myself in trouble with the bookmakers."

I looked up and saw to my regret that we were approaching Hyde Park Corner and Belgrave Square lay just on the other side.

It was one of those rare spring evenings that holds the promise of summer. The sun was about to set and the whole of Hyde Park was glowing. I turned to savor the scene.

"Don't let's go indoors yet. It's lovely to be outside. I'm afraid I was brought up to be a country girl. I hate looking out of my window at chimneys and rooftops."

"I feel the same way," Darcy said. "You should see the views from Kilhenny Castle—all those lovely green hills and the sea sparkling in the distance. Can't beat it anywhere in the world."

"Have you been around the world?" I asked.

"Most of it. I went to Australia once."

"Did you?"

"Yes, my father suggested I try to make my fortune there."

"And?"

"Not the right sort of place for me. They're all plebs, all mates together. They actually enjoy roughing it and going to a loo in the backyard. Oh, and they actually expect one to work by the sweat of one's brow. I'm afraid I was made for civilization." He found a bench and sank onto it, patting the seat beside him. "Good view from here."

I sat beside him, conscious of the closeness and warmth of his leg against mine.

"So tell me," he said. "What do you plan to do with yourself now that Harrods is no more?"

"I'll have to look for another job," I said, "but I rather fear that Her Majesty is making her own plans. At the moment it is a choice between marrying a ghastly foreign prince or becoming lady-in-waiting to a great-aunt, Queen Victoria's last surviving daughter, in the depths of the countryside where the height of entertainment will be holding her knitting wool or playing rummy."

"So, tell me"—he looked at me with interest—"how many people actually stand between you and the throne?"

"I'm thirty-fourth in line, I believe," I said. "Unless somebody's had a baby in the meantime and pushed me further back."

"Thirty-fourth, eh?"

"I hope you're not thinking of marrying me in the hopes of gaining the crown of England one day!"

He laughed. "That would be a trump card for the Irish, wouldn't it? King of England, or rather Prince Consort of England."

I laughed too. "I used to do that when I was small—lie in bed and work out ways to kill off all those ahead of me in the line of succession. Now I'm grown up, you couldn't pay me enough to be queen. Well, actually that's a lie. If my cousin David proposed, I'd probably accept."

"The Prince of Wales? You think he's a good catch?"

I looked surprised. "Yes, don't you?"

"He's a mama's boy," Darcy said scornfully. "Haven't you noticed? He's looking for a mummy. He doesn't want a wife."

"I think you're wrong. He's just waiting to find a suitable one."

"Well, this latest flame won't be suitable," Darcy said.

"Have you met her?"

"Oh, yes."

"And?"

"Not suitable. Charming enough, but definitely an older woman and far too worldly-wise. They'd never let her be queen."

"Do you think she wants to be?"

"Well, as of now she's still married to someone else, so it's probably a moot point," he said. "But I shouldn't keep your own hopes up. Your cousin David is never going to pick you as his consort. And frankly, you'd soon tire of him."

"Why? I think he's most amusing, and he's a topping dancer."

"He's a lightweight," Darcy said. "No substance to him. A moth flitting around, trying to find out what to do with himself. He'll make a rotten king."

"I think he'll step up when the time comes," I said huffily. "We have all been brought up with duty thrust down our throats. I'm sure David will do his one day."

"I hope you're right."

"Anyway," I whispered confidentially, "I've been asked to spy on her." I realized as I said it that too much champagne had loosened my tongue and I should not be confiding things like this to strangers, but by the time I had processed this information, it was too late.

"To spy on her? By whom?" Darcy was clearly interested.

"The queen. I'm supposed to attend a house party to which the prince and his lady friend have both been invited, then report back to HM."

"You'll probably have nothing good to say about her." Darcy grinned. "Men universally find her delightful and women universally find something catty to say about her."

"I'm sure I shall be very fair in my assessment," I said. "I am not prone to cattiness."

"That's one of the things I think I might like about you," Darcy said. "And there are others." He looked around. The sun had gone down and it had become instantly chilly. "Best get you home before you freeze in your posh frock."

I had to agree that I was now feeling the cold, especially since the champagne down my front hadn't quite dried yet. And no maid to sponge away the stains. What was I going to do about that?

He took my hand and dragged me across the traffic at Hyde Park Corner.

"Well, here I am," I said unnecessarily as I stood outside my front door and fumbled in my purse for the key. As usual in moments of stress, my fingers weren't obeying very well. "Thank you for a lovely afternoon."

"Don't thank me, thank the Asquey d'Asqueys. They paid for it. Aren't you going to invite me in?"

"I don't think I'd better. I'm living alone, you see."

"And you're not even allowed to have a young man in for a cup of tea? I didn't realize the royal rules were still so strict."

"It's not royal rules." I laughed nervously. "It's just that—I'm afraid none of the rooms fit for entertaining are open. And I have no servants yet. I'm just sort of camping out in one bedroom and the kitchen, where my culinary talents don't stretch beyond baked beans and tea. I did take cooking classes at school, but all useless items like petit fours that I never could master."

"I prefer petit fives myself," he said, making me smile.

"I never learned to make those either."

I glanced into the gloomy interior of the front hall and then back at
Darcy. The thought of being alone with him was tempting. Twenty-one
years of training won out. "Thank you for a lovely afternoon," I said again,
and held out my hand. "Good-bye then."

"Good-bye then?" He gave me the most appealing little lost boy look.
I almost melted. But not quite. "Look, Darcy, I would love to invite you in,
but it is getting late, and . . . you do understand, don't you?"

"Turned out alone into the snow. How cruel." He pulled a tragic face.

"You said five minutes ago that it was a lovely afternoon."

"Ah well," he said. "I can see you're not going to be moved whatever I
say. Twenty-one years of royal upbringing. Never mind, there will be other
occasions." He took my hand, brought it to his lips, and this time he kissed
it, sending a shiver all the way up my arm.

"If you like, I'll take you to a party at the Café de Paris next week," he
said casually, releasing my hand again.

"Are you crashing this one too?"

"Of course. It's given by Americans. They just love British nobility.
When they hear you are related to the royal family, they'll be kissing your
feet and plying you with cocktails and inviting you to stay on their ranches.
Will you come?"

"I expect so."

"I can't remember which day, offhand. I'll let you know."

"All right," I said. I lingered, feeling awkward. "Thank you again."

"The pleasure was all mine." He made that somehow sound sinful. I
fled into the house before he caught me blushing again. As I closed the door
behind me and stood in that cold, dark front hall with its black-and-white
checked floor and dark embossed walls, a disturbing thought came into my
mind. It occurred to me that Darcy might now be using me to gate-crash
even more events. Perhaps I was now a guaranteed entry ticket to places he
had been barred from before.

Indignation rose up for a second. I didn't like the thought of being
flattered and used, or being flirted with as if he really meant it. But then I
had to agree that it was more fun than the humdrum life I had been leading
recently. Certainly better than doing crossword puzzles at Castle Rannoch
or sitting in the subterranean kitchen eating baked beans. As I had said
earlier, what had I got to lose?

Chapter 8

I was about to go upstairs to take off my posh frock, as Darcy called it, when I noticed some letters were stuck in the box. Hardly anybody knew I was in town yet so letters were a novelty. There were two of them. I recognized my sister-in-law's writing on one of the envelopes, and the Glen Garry and Rannoch crest (two eagles, trying to disembowel each other over a craggy mountaintop), so I opened the other one first. It was the predicted invitation. Lady Mountjoy would be so delighted if Lady Georgiana could join them at their country estate for a house party and a masked fancy dress ball.

There were a couple of postscripts. The first a formal one: *Please bring fancy dress costumes with you as there is nowhere in the neighborhood that rents out such things.*

And the second, less formal: *Imogen will be so delighted to see you again.*

Imogen Mountjoy was among the dullest, stodgiest girls in the world. She and I had scarcely exchanged more than two words during our season, and those were both about hunting, so I truthfully couldn't imagine her being delighted at the thought of seeing me, but it was a kind gesture and I resolved to RSVP as soon as I had read the missive from Fig.

Dear Georgiana,

Binky has just informed me that he has to pop up to town on Monday on a matter of urgent and unforeseen business. With the world in its current sorry state and everybody being asked to economize, I thought it seemed silly and wasteful to go to the expense of sending staff in an advance party to open up the house when you are already there. Since you are living "grace and favor" as it were, I hope it won't be too much to ask to have Binky's bedroom and study aired out for him, and maybe just the little morning room for him to read the newspapers. (You have ordered the Times, *I hope.)*

I'm sure he'll be dining at his club so you don't have to worry too much about the food side of things. I expect the house will be quite chilly. Maybe you could have a fire going in Binky's bedroom on the day he arrives. Oh, and a hot water bottle in his bed too.

Your loving sister-in-law, Hilda

She always was known for her stuffy formality. Nobody ever called her by her real name. And I could see why. A more ridiculous name for a duchess I have never heard. If I had been called Hilda, I would have drowned myself in the nursery bathtub rather than grow up saddled with such a burden.

I stared at the letter for a moment. "What cheek," I said out loud and it was echoed back from the high ceiling of the hallway. *Not only are they no longer supporting me, but now they're treating me like a servant. Perhaps she forgets that I'm here all alone, without a maid, even. Does she want me to dust and make beds and light fires myself?* Then I realized that it probably had never occurred to Hilda that I was living here without servants. She obviously expected that I had hired a maid by now.

After I had calmed down, I supposed it wasn't such an unreasonable request. I was able-bodied enough to take off a few dust sheets and even run a carpet sweeper over a floor or two, wasn't I? I had grown up never having to make my own bed, never having got myself a glass of water until I went to school, but I was capable of doing both. I was making splendid progress really. I hadn't actually attempted to light a fire yet, of course, even though Granddad had given me the most basic instruction the previous day. It was the thought of that coal'ole, as he called it—the dreaded coal cellar replete with spiders—that put me off. But it would have to be tackled sometime. With all those ancestors who fought at Bannock Burn and Waterloo and every battle in between, I should have inherited enough spunk to face a coal cellar. Tomorrow was Sunday, when I was expected for lunch with my grandfather. I'd have him take me through the complete fire-lighting experience. Never let it be said that a Rannoch was defeated by anything!

ON SUNDAY MORNING I was up, bright and early, ready to tackle my task. I put on an apron I found hanging in a cupboard below stairs and I tied a scarf around my hair. It was actually quite fun to whip off dust sheets and shake them out of the window. I was dancing around with the feather duster when there was a knock at the front door. I didn't stop to think about the way I was dressed as I opened it and found Belinda on the doorstep.

"Is her ladyship at home to callers?" she asked, then she started as she recognized me. "Georgie! What on earth? Are you auditioning for the role of Cinderella?"

"What? Oh, this." I glanced down at the feather duster. "On the orders of my dear sister-in-law. She wants me to get the house ready for the arrival of my dear brother, the duke, tomorrow. Come on in." I led her down the hallway and up the stairs to the morning room. The windows were open and a fresh breeze stirred the lace curtains.

"Do sit down," I said. "The seat has been newly dusted."

She looked at me as if I had turned into a new and dangerous creature. "Surely she didn't mean that you were to take it upon yourself personally to clean the house?"

"I'm afraid that's exactly what she did mean. Do take a seat."

"What was she thinking?" Belinda sat.

"I think the word for my sister-in-law is frugal, at best. She didn't want to pay for the extra train tickets to send down the servants ahead of Binky. She reminded me of my grace and favor status, thereby suggesting that I owed Her Grace a favor."

"What nerve," Belinda exclaimed.

"My own sentiments exactly, but she obviously assumes I've hired a maid by now. She gave me a long lecture on the untrustworthiness of Londoners and how I should check all references."

"Why didn't you bring a maid with you?"

"Fig wouldn't release one of ours and frankly I couldn't afford to pay her anyway. But, you know, it's not too bad. In fact it's been quite fun. I'm getting rather good at it. It must be that humble ancestry on my mother's side coming out but one gets quite a satisfaction from polishing things."

Then suddenly it was as if I was hit with a flash of divine inspiration. "Wait," I said. "I've just had a marvelous idea—I wanted a paying job, didn't I? I could do this for other people and be paid for it."

"Georgie! I'm all for standing on your own feet, but there are limits. A member of the house of Windsor acting as a char lady? My dear, think of the stink there would be when it was found out."

"They don't need to know it's actually me, do they?" I gave a couple of whisks with the feather duster as I warmed up to the idea. "I can call myself Coronet Domestics and nobody need ever know that I, and I alone, am Coronet Domestics. It's better than starving, anyway."

"What about the lady-in-waiting thing? How does one turn down the request of a queen?"

"Very cautiously," I said. "But luckily nothing in the palace happens overnight. By the time HM has it arranged, I shall tell her that I am fully occupied and financially stable."

"Well, good luck then, I suppose," Belinda said. "You wouldn't find me cleaning lavatories."

"Oh, dear," I said, coming down to earth with a bump. "I hadn't counted on lavatories. I was thinking more a quick whisk with my handy duster. That much I can handle."

She laughed. "I fear you may have a rude awakening. Some people are absolute pigs, you know." She leaned back against the velvet upholstery and crossed her legs in a move that must have been practiced and designed to drive young men wild. It had no such effect on me except to elicit a wave of envy over her silk stockings.

"So how did you enjoy your outing with the attractive Mr. O'Mara?" she asked.

"He is quite dashing, isn't he?"

"What a pity he's penniless. Not exactly the escort you need at this stage of your life."

"Maybe we go together well," I said.

"You've tried, have you?" Belinda asked.

"Tried what?"

"Going together."

"We've only just met, Belinda. Although he did kiss my hand on the doorstep and suggest that I invite him inside."

"Did he? How terribly un-British."

"I have to confess I did enjoy the hand-kissing part and I almost relented and let him into the house."

She nodded. "He's Irish, of course. They are a wild race, but more fun, one has to admit, than the English. Heaven knows Englishmen have no idea at all about the gentle art of seduction. The best most of them can manage is to slap you on the behind and ask if you fancy a spot of the old rumpy-pumpy."

I nodded. "That does sum up my experience so far."

"There you are then. So he may well be the one."

"To settle down with? We'd starve."

"Not to settle down with." She shook her head at my stupidity. "To rid you of the burden around your neck. Your virginity, I mean."

"Belinda! Really!"

She laughed at my red face. "Someone has to before you turn into a sour old maid. My father always says that once women turn twenty-four, they are beyond redemption, so you've only got a year or so." She looked at me, expecting an answer, but I was still lost for words. Discussing my virginity did not come easily to me. "You are seeing him again?" she asked.

"He's taking me to a party at the Café de Paris next week."

"Oh, my dear. Very swank."

"Gate-crashing again, I'm afraid. He says it's given by Americans and they'll fall over backward to have a member of the royal family present, even if it's a minor one."

"He's absolutely right. When is it?" She produced a small diary from her bag.

"Belinda, you're as bad as he is."

"Maybe we're kindred spirits. You should keep us apart. I think I might rather fancy him myself, although I'd never step on the toes of an old school chum. And being penniless does limit the desirability. I do have horribly expensive tastes." She jumped up and grabbed the feather duster from me. "I almost forgot what I came for. I bumped into another old school chum at the wedding yesterday. Sophia, that round little Hungarian countess. Didn't you see her?"

"No, I didn't. There were so many people and I was attempting to lie low."

"Well, anyway, she invited me to a little party on a houseboat in Chelsea this afternoon and I asked if I could bring you. I tried to find you, but you'd vanished."

"Darcy and I melted away before the party dispersed."

"So will you come to the party on the houseboat?"

"It does sound rather fun. Oh, wait a minute. No, I'm afraid I can't come after all. I've just remembered that I promised to have Sunday lunch with my grandfather. In fact"—I glanced at my watch—"I have to run and get changed instantly."

"Your nonroyal grandfather, I take it?"

"The other one is long dead, so that would have to be a séance and no lunch."

"And your living one? Don't I remember that your family discouraged any communication with him? Why was that?"

"He's a Cockney, Belinda, but he's an old dear, quite the nicest person I know. I just wish I could do more for him. He's not exactly in funds at the moment and he needs a good holiday by the sea." I brightened up again. "So maybe my housecleaning experiment will be so successful that I can send him on his holiday and all will be well."

Belinda eyed me suspiciously. "I am not normally one to look on the dark side of things, but I think you are courting disaster, my sweet. If news of your new career choice ever made it back to the palace, I fear you'd be married off to the frightful Siegfried and locked away in a castle in Romania before you could say Ivor Novello."

"This is a free country, Belinda. I am twenty-one years old and nobody's ward and I'm not next in line to the throne and frankly I don't give a hoot what they think!"

"Well said, old thing." She applauded. "Come on then, let me help you compose your advertisement before you depart."

"All right." I went over to the writing desk and took out pen and paper. "Do you think the *Times* is preferable to the *Tattler* in attracting the right clientele?"

"Do both. Some women never read a newspaper but always look at the *Tattler* to see if they are in it."

"I'll bite the bullet and pay for both then. I hope a commission comes along quickly or I'll be standing in a bread line myself in a week or so."

"It's a pity you can't come to the party with me this afternoon. Sophia is a robust girl in that typically middle-European way, so I'm sure food will feature prominently. And she mixes with all kinds of delightful bohemians—writers and painters, that kind of thing."

"I wish I could, but I'm sure food will figure prominently at my grand-father's too. He's promised me a roast and two veg. So what shall we say in this advertisement?"

"You have to make it quite clear that you are not interested in scrubbing their loos, just light dusting and opening their houses up for them. How about: 'Coming to London but want to leave your staff at the country seat?'"

I scribbled away. "Oh, that's good. Then we could say Coronet Domestics Agency will air out your house and make it ready for your arrival."

"And you have to give an endorsement from someone of status."

"How can I do that? I can hardly ask Fig to recommend me and she's the only one for whom I've ever cleaned a house so far."

"You endorse yourself, you chump. As used by Lady Victoria Georgiana, sister of the Duke of Glen Garry and Rannoch."

I started laughing. "Belinda, you are positively brilliant."

"I know," she said modestly.

☙

LUNCH WAS A huge success—lovely leg of lamb, crispy roast potatoes and cabbage from Granddad's back garden, followed by baked apple and custard. I felt the occasional pang of guilt as I wondered whether he could really afford to eat in this way, but he was taking such obvious pleasure from watching me eat, that I let myself enjoy every bite.

"After lunch," I said, "you really must teach me how to light a fire. I'm not joking. My brother will be arriving tomorrow and I've been instructed to have a fire lit in his bedroom."

"Well, blow me down. Of all the cheek," he said. "What do they think you are—a skivvy? I'm going to give that brother of yours a piece of my mind."

"Oh, it's not Binky," I said. "He's actually quite a dear. Very vague, of course, never notices anything. And not very bright. But essentially a kind person. And it is my fault partly, I suppose. My sister-in-law took it for granted that I'd be hiring staff as soon as I got to London. I should have made it quite clear that I couldn't afford to do so. Stupid pride."

My grandfather shook his head. "I told you, my love. If you want to light a fire, you'll have to go down the coal cellar."

"If I must, I must," I said. "I'm sure plenty of servants have been down into the coal cellar and survived. What then?"

He talked me through it, from the newspaper to the right way to lay the sticks and then the coal on top, and all about opening dampers. It sounded daunting.

"I wish I could come up and do it for you," he said. "But I don't think your brother would take kindly to my being in the house."

"I wish you could come up and live with me for a while," I said. "Not to look after me, but to keep me company."

He looked at me with wise dark eyes. "Ah, but that would never work, would it? We live in different worlds, ducks. You'd want me to sleep above stairs in your house and I wouldn't feel right doing that, but then I wouldn't feel right sleeping below stairs, like a servant either. No, it's better this way. I welcome your visits, but then you go back to your world and I stay in mine."

I looked back longingly as I walked up Glanville Drive past the gnomes.

Chapter 9

RANNOCH HOUSE
SUNDAY, APRIL 24, 1932

When I arrived back at Rannoch House I changed into my servant garb, tied up my hair, and ventured downstairs until I located the dreaded coal hole. As Granddad had predicted, it was awful—a dark opening in the outside well, only a couple of feet high. I couldn't find a shovel and I wasn't going to reach my arm into that dark unknown. Who knows what was lurking in there? I went back into the kitchen and discovered a large ladle and a towel hanging on a rack. Then I used the ladle to scrape out bits of coal, one at a time, then picked them up with the towel to put into the coal scuttle. By this method it took a good half hour to fill the scuttle but at least I didn't touch any spiders and my hands remained clean. Finally I staggered upstairs with it, with new admiration and respect for my maid, Maggie, who obviously had to do this chore every single morning.

I experimented with lighting a fire in my own room and by the end of the evening I had a very smoky room, but a crackling blaze going. I was quite proud of myself. Binky's bedroom was ready for him, with clean sheets and windows opened. I laid a fire in his grate and went to bed satisfied.

On Monday morning I went into the *Times* office and placed an advertisement for the front page. I provided a post office box to reply to, as I didn't think Binky would take kindly to requests for a char lady coming to Rannoch House. Then I went to the *Tattler* and repeated the process.

I had just returned home when there was a knock at the front door. I went to answer it and found a strange man on the doorstep. He was a sinister-looking figure, dressed from head to toe in black—long black overcoat and broad-brimmed black hat tilted forward so that it was hard to see his eyes. What I could see of his face I didn't like. He might have been good-looking once, but he had one of those faces that has started to sag. And it had the pasty pallor of one who is not often in the fresh air. Nobody at Castle Rannoch ever had such a complexion. At least the biting wind produced the rosiest of cheeks.

"I am 'ere to see zee duke," he said in what sounded like a French accent. "You will inform him immediately that Gaston de Mauxville has arrived."

"I'm sorry but the duke hasn't arrived himself yet," I said. "I don't expect him until this afternoon."

"Most inconvenient," he said, slapping one black leather glove against the palm of his other hand.

"He's expecting you, is he?"

"Of course. I shall come in and wait." He attempted to push past me.

"I'm afraid you won't," I said, taking an instant dislike to the man's arrogant manner. "I don't know you. I suggest you come back later."

"Why, you impudent girl. I'll have you dismissed." He raised a glove and I thought for a moment he was going to strike me. "Do you know to whom you are speaking?"

"More to the point, do you know to whom you are speaking?" I said, giving him my most frosty stare. "I am the duke's sister, Lady Georgiana."

At this his bluster subsided, but he continued to splutter.

"But you open the door like a 'ousemaid. Most irregular, most embarrassing."

"I'm sorry," I said, "but the staff are still in Scotland, I am in the house alone, and I'm sure you would agree that my brother would not want me to entertain a strange man, unchaperoned."

"Very well," he said. "You will inform your brother that I expect to see him the moment he arrives. I am staying at Claridge's."

"I'll inform him, but I don't know of his plans," I said. "Do you have a card?"

"Somewhere," he said, patting various pockets, "but in this instance a card will not be necessary, I believe."

He turned as if to leave, then looked back suddenly. "This is the only property you own apart from Castle Rannoch?"

"Yes," I said. "I don't own it. My brother does."

"Naturally. And Castle Rannoch—what is it like?"

"Cold and drafty," I said.

"Most inconvenient, but it can't be helped. And the estate—it produces a good income?"

"I have no idea what kind of income the estate produces," I said, "and if I knew, I should not be discussing it with a stranger. Forgive me, but I have things I must attend to."

With that I closed the door. Horrible man. Just who did he think he was?

Binky arrived around four, also rather flustered as he had traveled without a manservant.

"I couldn't find a porter and had to carry my own bag across the station," he said grouchily. "I'm so glad to find you still here. I thought you'd be off helping with some wedding or other."

"That's not for a couple of weeks," I said, glad he had reminded me of the story I had concocted to facilitate my escape. "And I gather the bride's house is packed full of relatives, so I'll be staying on here, if that's all right."

He nodded absentmindedly. "I'm quite frazzled, Georgie. A good soak in the tub and then tea and crumpets should revive me, I think."

"You still take cold baths, do you?" I asked.

"Cold baths? I had to have them every day at school, of course, but not lately by choice."

"Well, that's the only choice at the moment," I said, secretly rather enjoying it. "The boiler has not been lit."

"Why on earth not?"

"Because I have been here alone, dear brother, and your wife did not give me permission to turn on the boiler, even if I had any idea how to perform such a feat. I have been heating a pan of water to wash in the mornings, and I'm afraid you'll just have to do the same."

"That's a dashed unpleasant blow to a chap after he's come all the way from Scotland on a beastly cold train." He broke off, as my words had finally penetrated. "Here all alone, you say? No servants or anything?"

"Just me," I said. "Fig wouldn't lend me any of your staff and I have no money to hire staff of my own, as you very well should know, since you were the one who cut off my allowance on my twenty-first birthday."

He went red. "Look here, Georgie. You make me sound like an ogre. I really didn't want to but, dash it all, I just haven't the income to support you for the rest of your life. You're supposed to marry, you know, and let some other poor blighter take care of you."

"Thank you for those kind words," I said.

"So what you're saying is, in effect, that there is nobody here to run my bath, nobody to make me tea and crumpets, nothing?"

"I can make you tea and toast, which is almost as good as crumpets, as your wife pointed out."

"You know how to make things? Georgie—you're a bloody genius."

I had to laugh. "I hardly think that tea and toast constitute genius," I said, "but I have learned a thing or two in the past week. You'll find a fire going in your bedroom, laid and lit by me."

I turned to lead the way up the stairs, opening his bedroom door with a flourish.

"How on earth did you manage that?"

"My grandfather showed me how to do it."

"Your grandfather? He was here?"

"Don't worry. He wasn't here. I went to visit him."

"Out in Essex?" He sounded as if I had made the journey by camel, across the Gobi Desert.

"Binky, contrary to popular belief, people have made it to Essex and back and lived to tell the tale," I said. I ushered him into his bedroom and waited for him to compliment me on my fire and the sparkling clean state of the place. Being a man, he wasn't impressed by either, but started to unpack his overnight bag.

"By the way, you had a visitor this morning," I said. "A most unpleasant fat Frenchman called Gaston something. Extremely arrogant. Where on earth did you meet him?"

Binky's face had turned pale. "I've never actually met him yet. We have only corresponded," he said, "but he is the reason I have come to London now, in the hopes of sorting things out."

"Sorting what things out?"

Binky stood there, clutching his pajamas. "I suppose you have a right to know. I haven't even told Fig yet. I dare not tell Fig. I don't know how I'll ever tell Fig, but she'll have to know eventually."

"Know what?" I demanded.

He sank to the bed. "That man, Gaston de Mauxville. Apparently he is some kind of professional gambler, and apparently he used to play cards with

Father in Monte Carlo. I suppose you've guessed that Father wasn't a very good gambler. Apparently he lost what was left of the family fortune at those tables. And now apparently he lost even more than the family fortune."

"Would you stop saying 'apparently,'" I snapped. "If this is all hearsay, I'm not interested."

"Oh, it's more than hearsay." Binky gave a big sigh. "Apparently—no, *actually*, this bounder de Mauxville claims that Father bet Castle Rannoch in a card game, and lost."

"Father lost our family home? To that horrible rude, flabby foreigner?" I heard myself screeching in most unladylike tones.

"Apparently."

"I don't believe it. The man is a confidence trickster."

"The man claims he has a watertight document in his possession. He is going to present it to me today."

"It would never hold up in a British court, Binky."

"I'm due to see the family solicitors tomorrow, but de Mauxville claims that the document has been witnessed and notarized in France and will stand up in any court in the world."

"How awful, Binky." We stared at each other in horror. "No wonder he was asking about Castle Rannoch this morning. I'm so glad I told him it was cold and drafty. If only I'd known I'd have said it was haunted too. You don't think he really wants to live there?"

"I think what he really wants is for me to buy him off."

"Can you afford to buy him off?"

"Absolutely not. You know we're flat broke, Georgie. What with Father losing in Monte Carlo and then saddling me with the death duties when he shot himself—" He looked up hopefully. "That's it. I shall challenge him to a duel. If he's a man of honor, he'll accept. We'll fight for Castle Rannoch, man to man."

I went over and put a hand on his shoulder. "Binky, my sweet, I hate to remind you, but apart from Father you are without doubt the worst shot in the civilized world. You have never managed to hit a grouse, a deer, a duck, or anything that moves."

"De Mauxville won't move. He'll be standing there. And he's a big target. I can't actually miss."

"He will undoubtedly fire first and he's probably the best shot in all of France. I don't want a dead brother as well as no family home."

Binky sank his head into his hands. "What are we going to do, Georgie?"

I patted his shoulder. "We'll fight it. We'll find some way. At very worst we'll take him up to Scotland to show him his new home and he'll get pneumonia within the week. And if he doesn't, I'll take him up the crag to show him the view over the whole estate and push him off!"

"Georgie!" Binky looked shocked and then laughed.

"All's fair in love and war," I said, "and this is war."

⁂

BINKY DIDN'T RETURN home until late that evening. I had waited up for him, impatient to know how he had fared with the horrible Gaston de Mauxville. When I heard the front door slam, I ran downstairs in time to see Binky trudging wearily up toward me.

"Well?" I said.

He sighed. "I met with the fellow. An absolute cad, I'm sure, but I fear the document is genuine. It certainly looked like Father's handwriting to me, and it's been witnessed and sealed too. The rotter wouldn't let the original out of his possession, but he's given me a copy to show our solicitor in the morning. Frankly I'm not too hopeful."

"Why don't you call his bluff, Binky? Tell him he can have Castle Rannoch. Tell him you're glad to get rid of it. He wouldn't last a week there."

"But that wouldn't work at all," he said. "He's not interested in living in the place. He's going to sell it—turn it into a school or a golfing hotel."

"A school maybe," I said. "It would take considerable improvements before anyone would actually pay to stay there."

"It's no laughing matter, Georgie," Binky snapped. "It's our home, damn it. It's been in the family for eight hundred years. I'm not just handing it over to some Continental gambler."

"Then what are we going to do?"

He shrugged. "You're the bright one. I hoped you might come up with a brilliant idea to save us."

"I've already thought of pushing him off the mountain. Pushing him out of the train on the way north, maybe?" I smiled at him. "I'm sorry, Binky. I wish I could think of something. Let's hope the solicitors will know a legal way out of this in the morning."

He nodded. "I'm going straight to bed," he said. "I'm exhausted. Oh, and just a simple breakfast in the morning, I think. A few kidneys, and maybe some bacon, and the usual toast, marmalade, coffee."

"Binky!" I stopped him. "I've told you we have no servants. I can manage a boiled egg, toast, and tea. That's it."

His face fell. "Dash it all, Georgie. You can't expect a chap to face the world fortified only by a boiled egg."

"As soon as I get a job I'll engage a servant who will cook you all the kidneys and bacon you want," I said, "but in the meantime you should be grateful for a sister who is willing to cook for you."

Binky stared at me. "What did you just say? Get a job? A job?"

"I'm planning to stay on in London and make my own way in life. How else do you think I'm going to support myself?"

"I say, Georgie. People like us don't get jobs. It's just not done."

"If Castle Rannoch goes to de Mauxville, you may have to face finding a job yourself or starving."

He looked utterly horrified. "Don't say that. What on earth could I do? I'd be hopeless. I'm all right pottering about the estate and all that. I've got a reasonably good seat on a horse, but apart from that I'm an utter failure."

"You'd find something if you had to support your family," I said. "You could always become a butler to rich Americans. They'd be tickled pink to have a duke waiting on them."

"Don't even say that in jest," he groaned. "The whole thing is just too dreadful to contemplate."

I took his arm. "Go to bed," I said. "Things may look better in the morning."

"I hope so," he said. "You're my rock, Georgie. An absolute brick. I'm counting on you."

I came to London to escape from my family, I thought as I made my way to my own bedroom. But it seemed that escape was not as easy as I had thought. For an instant marrying Prince Siegfried didn't seem such a bad option after all.

$\mathcal{C}$hapter 10

In the morning I insisted on going with Binky to our solicitors'. After all, it was my family home too. I wasn't about to give it away without a darned good fight. Messrs. Prendergast, Prendergast, Prendergast, and Soapes were in chambers just off Lincoln's Inn. Binky and I arrived early so that we could speak with them before the dreaded Gaston arrived. We were informed that Young Mr. Prendergast would be delighted to see us and ushered into a wood-paneled room in which a man of at least eighty sat. I found myself wondering, if this was Young Mr. Prendergast, what Old Mr. Prendergast might look like. I was already so tense that I started to giggle. Binky turned and glared at me, but I couldn't stop.

"I'm sorry," Binky said to Young Mr. Prendergast, "the shock has been too much for her."

"I quite understand," the old man said kindly. "It has been a shock to all of us. We at Prendergast, Prendergast, Prendergast, and Soapes have represented your family for the past two centuries. I would hate to see Castle Rannoch fall into the wrong hands. May I see the offending document?"

"This is just a copy. The bounder wouldn't let the original out of his hands." Binky handed it to him.

The old man clucked as he studied it. "Dear me. Dear me," he said. "Of course, the first step will be to have a handwriting expert study the original to make sure it is not a forgery. We have your father's handwritten will and signature on file here. Then I shall need to consult an expert on international law, but I rather fear that this will have to be contested in the French courts—an expensive and frustrating proposition."

"Have we no other avenues open to us?" I asked. "No other options?"

"We could try to prove that your father was not of sound mind when he signed the document. That, I fear, would be our best hope. We would need to bring in character witnesses to prove that he had been acting strangely and irrationally, maybe a doctor to testify that insanity ran in the family—"

"Wait a minute," I interrupted. "I'm not having my father ridiculed in a court of law. And I'm not having any hints of insanity in the family either."

Mr. Prendergast sighed. "It may come down to that or losing your home," he said.

Binky and I emerged in deep gloom after an hour or so with the solicitor. De Mauxville had agreed to meet with a handwriting expert. He seemed so confident that I couldn't help thinking that the document was indeed genuine and that Castle Rannoch was on its way to becoming a golfing hotel for rich Americans.

It was only when Binky was reading the *Times* in the cab on the way back to our house that I remembered my advertisement. I glanced at the front page and there it was. Now all I had to do was to await my first reply. In spite of the awful gravity of our situation, I couldn't help feeling the teeniest bit excited.

I didn't have to wait long. The first response arrived the next day. It was from a Mrs. Bantry-Bynge, who had a house on the crescent beside Regent's Park. She had to come up to London unexpectedly for a dress fitting on Thursday, and finding my advertisement was a godsend, as her household staff were becoming frail and elderly and no longer traveled well. She would be traveling alone and dining with friends. All she needed was a place to lay her head that night.

Essentially she just wanted clean linens on the bed, everything given a good dusting, and a fire laid in the bedroom grate. It sounded easy enough. I went into a public telephone booth and dialed the number she had given me, confirming that I would have everything in perfect order before she arrived in the evening. She sounded delighted and told me that the key could be obtained from the housekeeper of the house next door. She asked me to return the following morning after her stay, bundle the sheets into a laundry bag, and deposit them with the same housekeeper when I returned the key. Then she asked me what my fee would be. I hadn't really thought that one through.

"The agency charges two guineas," I said.

"Two guineas?" She sounded shocked.

"It is a specialized service, madam, and we have to make sure our staff is the finest."

"Of course you do."

"And it's probably cheaper than bringing your staff up from Hampshire."

"Of course it is. Very well, I'll leave the money in an envelope you'll find when you come to strip the bed in the morning."

I hung up the phone with a big smile of satisfaction on my face.

Now there was just the question of what I was going to wear. I went below stairs and rummaged in the servants' cupboard until I found a suitable black housemaid's dress and white apron. I even added a jaunty little white cap for style. I couldn't be seen leaving Belgrave Square wearing it, of course.

I was creeping downstairs in my maid's uniform, trying not to wake Binky, when suddenly he called to me from the library.

"Georgie, old thing, would you come in here? I thought I'd do a little research into the history of Castle Rannoch," he said. "I thought that maybe there might be something in our family history or documents granting us peerage that states that the Glenrannoch property can never be bequeathed away from the family."

"Good idea," I said, standing in shadow on the stairs so that Binky wouldn't notice what I was wearing.

"And it's frightfully chilly in here, so I wondered, since you're a wizard at lighting fires, whether you'd get me a small blaze going in here."

"Sorry, old thing, but I have an appointment," I said. "I'm just dashing out the door. You'll have to find a scarf and gloves, I'm afraid, until I get back."

"Confound it, Georgie, how can I be expected to turn pages with gloves on? Can't you be a teeny bit late?" He poked his head around the door, sounding petulant. "Aren't women supposed to be late for everything? I know Fig always is. Spends hours doing things to her eyebrows, I believe, but you always look—" He broke off when he saw me. "Why are you wearing that extraordinary garb? It looks like something the servants would wear."

"It's for a silly hen party, Binky," I said breathlessly. "We're all to come dressed as maids. One of these prewedding things, you know."

"Oh, right. Oh, yes, I see." He nodded. "Oh, all right then. Off you go. Have a good time and all that."

I grabbed my overcoat to cover the maid's uniform and fled. Outside the house I heaved a sigh of relief. That was a close one. I hadn't thought of the problems that could be caused by having to avoid people I knew.

I did say a silent prayer, as I approached the house on Regent's Park Crescent where I was to pick up the key, that nobody would recognize me. Luckily Regent's Park is not quite as top drawer as Belgravia or Mayfair. Not likely to be frequented by my family and acquaintances. However, I did look around as I went up the steps and knocked on the adjoining front door. The maid looked me up and down with a look of utter disapproval, and didn't invite me in while she summoned the housekeeper. The housekeeper opened her mouth in horror when she saw me standing there.

"What on earth were you doing, ringing the front doorbell as if you were company?" she demanded. "In this household servants use the tradesmen's entrance."

"I'm sorry," I muttered. "I didn't see where it was."

"Down the steps at the side, same as every house," she said, still looking at me with disdain. "No good comes of getting ideas above your station, my girl, even if you do work for one of those fancy domestic agencies."

She regarded me in the most patronizing manner.

"I hope you'll do a good job for Mrs. Bantry," she said. She spoke in that quaite, quaite exaggeratedly posh accent so often affected by the lower classes when they want to sound educated. "She has a lot of lovely things in that house. Quaite the world traveler, she and her husband, the colonel. You are from a locally hired firm, I believe."

"That's right," I said.

"I hope she's had your references checked."

"We come highly recommended by the Lady Georgiana, sister of the Duke of Glen Garry and Rannoch," I said, humbly surveying the milk bottles on the step.

"Oh, well, in that case . . . " She let the rest of the sentence dangle in midair. "That's almost as good as royalty, isn't it? I saw her once at a party, you know. A lovely young thing. Quite as pretty as her mother, who was a former actress, you know."

"Oh, yes," I said, deciding on the spot that her eyesight was probably defective.

"It's my belief that the Prince of Wales should look no further," she said, confidentially now. "It's about time he took a bride, and a good English one is what we'd all like. Not one of these foreigners, especially not a German."

Since my ancestry was a quarter Scottish and had a good admixture of German, I stayed silent.

"Thank you for the key," I said. "I'll return it tomorrow after I've straightened up the place."

"Good girl." She smiled at me in almost a kindly fashion now. "I like it when girls are well spoken. It's all very well to make an effort to better yourself. Just don't get those ideas above your station."

"No, madam," I said, and beat a hasty retreat.

I climbed the steps to the Bantry-Bynge house triumphant, with the key in my hand. First test accomplished. I turned the key and the door swung open. Second test, ditto. I stepped inside and savored the quiet of a sleeping house. A quick tour revealed that this job would be a piece of cake. The reception rooms lay swathed in dust sheets. I went up the stairs and located Mrs. B-B's bedroom easily enough. It was all pink and white and frothy with garlands of roses on the wallpaper. Expensive perfume lingered. Very much a lady's room. I wondered how often the colonel was invited in. I set to work, opening the windows and letting in the good, fresh air, whisking off dust sheets and shaking them out of the window. There were lots of little ornaments and crystal jars around so I was extra careful with my dusting, knowing my tendency to clumsiness. Then I found that they had a vacuum cleaner. I had never used one before but it looked like fun—and a lot less work than pushing a carpet sweeper up and down. I turned it on. It promptly raced across the carpet with me holding on for dear life and started sucking up the lace curtains. Finally I managed to turn it off before the whole curtain rod came down. Fortunately I also managed to rescue the curtain, which survived with only a slight chewing in one corner. After that I decided that the carpet sweeper might just be safer.

Then I found the linen closet and made up the bed. The sheets were trimmed with lace and smelled of roses. Finally I went down to the coal cellar, which was properly equipped with tongs and shovel this time, and laid the bedroom fire. A few weeks ago this would have been a task beyond my wildest imagination.

I was just putting the finishing touches to the room when the front doorbell rang. I had intended to be out and gone before Mrs. B-B herself showed up, but then she wouldn't be ringing her own doorbell, would she?

I went down and opened it. A rather dashing man stood there, his hair parted in the middle and slicked down, a neat line of mustache on his upper lip. He was wearing a blue blazer and flannels, carrying a bouquet of freesia, and had a silver-tipped cane tucked under one arm.

"Hello," he said, giving me a smile that showed too many white and even teeth. "Are you a new maid? I didn't think she usually brought servants with her."

"No, sir. I'm employed by a domestic service. Mrs. Bantry-Bynge hired me to open up the house and get a bedroom ready for her."

"Did she, by jove. Excellent idea." He attempted to come inside.

"I'm sorry, sir, but she hasn't arrived yet," I said, blocking his path.

"That's all right. I expect I'll find something to amuse myself," he said. This time he pushed past me and took off his gloves in the hallway. "I'm Boy, by the way, and you are . . . ?"

"Maggie, sir," I said, my own maid's name being the first thing that came into my head.

"Maggie, eh?" He came rather too close to me and put a finger under my chin. "Lively little Maggie, eh? Good show. So you've been getting a bedroom ready, have you?"

"Yes, sir." I didn't like the way he was looking at me. Leering would be closer, actually.

"Why don't you show me what a good job you've been doing? I hope you have done a good job, because if not, I may just have to give you a good spanking."

His finger that had been under my chin was now tracing its way down my throat. For a second I was too shocked to react but before it reached anything crucial I leaped away. It took all my self-control not to behave as I would normally and tell him what I thought of him. In my head I was screaming that maids do not stamp on toes, kick in shins, or employ any other known method of self-defense without being dismissed on the spot. "I'll just put these flowers in water for you, sir," I said. "They look as if they are about to wilt."

Then I fled in the direction of the kitchen. I had heard whispered stories about men having their way with servants, but it had never crossed my mind that this might be a hazard of my new profession. I was still in the kitchen when I heard voices and came back to find a woman in the front hall. She was on the chubby side with peroxide blond hair set in neat little waves, a lot of face makeup, and an expensive-looking fur draped around her neck. She was also surrounded by an aura of perfume. Mrs. Bantry-Bynge had arrived. Saved by the bell, I thought.

Mrs. Bantry-Bynge looked decidedly flustered. "Oh, you're still here. I hadn't realized. I thought—you see, I came up by an earlier train," she gushed. "And I see my—cousin—has arrived to drive me around in his motor. Isn't that nice? How kind of you, Boy."

I gave what I hoped would pass as a suitable bobbed curtsy. "I'm all finished, madam," I muttered. "Just about to go."

"Splendid. That's wonderful. I do hope Boy has not been—getting in your way." The look she gave implied that he had got in the way of a great many females.

"Oh, no, madam," I said. "I have just been putting these flowers he brought you in water."

She took the vase from me and buried her face in them. "Freesias. How divine. You know I adore freesias. You are so sweet to me."

She peeped at him seductively over the top of the flowers. Then she remembered I was still there.

"Thank you. You may go now. I've told your employer that the money will be on the bedside table when you return to strip the bed and tidy up the room tomorrow."

"Yes, madam. I'll just get my coat and I'll be off then."

I was rather worried that she might notice the coat was cashmere, but then perhaps she'd think it was a hand-me-down from a very kind former employer. As it was, she and Boy only had eyes for each other as I tiptoed past them. When I returned in the morning, the rumpled state of the bed gave me to think that a visit to the dressmaker had not featured in the trip to London at all.

Chapter 11

My next assignment, which came in the afternoon post that day, was not going to be as simple as Mrs. Bantry-Bynge's. It was from none other than Lady Featherstonehaugh (pronounced "Fanshaw," to the uninitiated), the parent of one Roderick Featherstonehaugh, usually known as Whiffy, with whom I had danced at debutante balls and who had been best man at last week's wedding. They were coming up to town for a few days, arriving on Sunday, bringing staff with them, but would like the place aired out and dusted first, fires laid ready to be lit and hot water bottles placed in Sir William and Lady Featherstonehaugh's bedrooms. Their son, Roderick, might be joining them if he could get time off from his regiment, but this was unlikely. I was remarkably glad that it was unlikely. I had no wish to bump into Whiffy when I was in full cleaning mode. Bumping into Binky had been bad enough, but he was easy to fool. I couldn't think how I'd explain myself away to someone stiff and correct like Whiffy Featherstonehaugh. Regent's Park was one thing. I could pass there without being recognized, but I knew practically everyone who lived in Eaton Place.

Binky moped around the house, sunk in gloom, and I couldn't think of anything to cheer him up. Because, frankly, the news was not reassuring. The document was deemed to be genuine and Binky started questioning whether it would be too-too awful to claim that Father had been off his rocker for years. "He did always have that rubber duck in his bathtub, didn't he?" he demanded. "That's not normal, is it? And remember when he took up Eastern meditation and stood on his head?"

"Lots of people stand on their heads," I said. "And it is well known that all aristocrats are eccentric."

"I'm not eccentric," Binky said hotly.

"Binky, you go around the estate talking to the trees. I've heard you."

"Well, that's just common sense. Things grow better when you talk to them."

"I rest my case," I said. "And you'd have to prove that Father was practically foaming at the mouth before the court would say he was too incompetent to sign that document."

"He did foam at the mouth once," Binky said hopefully.

"When he swallowed that piece of soap on a bet."

Binky sighed.

He was normally such a cheery soul and I hated to see him like this, but I couldn't think of anything I could do. It even crossed my mind that I might borrow a vampish dress from Belinda and try to seduce de Mauxville, thus obtaining the document from him in the heat of passion. But frankly I didn't think I'd be very good at it.

Friday morning I set out for Eaton Place, my black servant's uniform disguised under my cashmere coat, my cap tucked into my pocket to be put on at the last minute. I scurried down into the tradesmen's entrance and put on my cap before I turned the key I had been given and let myself in.

I stood in a cavernous entry hall, decorated with the heads of hunted African beasts and the odd ceremonial spear. Once inside, my enthusiasm waned. The house was even bigger than our London place and it was full of objects brought back from generations of army postings around the world. I'm sure some of them were valuable and even attractive in their own way, but they were on every surface—curved daggers, ebony masks, statues, jade elephants, carved ivory goddesses—all highly breakable, by the look of them. There were walls full of paintings, mostly of great battles. There were regimental flags, glass-topped tables full of medals, and swords of all kinds of shapes hanging everywhere. The Featherstonehaughs had clearly been a military family of distinction for generations—which explained why Whiffy was in the Guards. There was enough to keep me dusting all day. I went from room to room, wondering if they needed all the large formal rooms on the ground floor opened up, or whether the pretty little drawing room on the first floor would do just as well for a short visit.

There was a vast fireplace at the far end of a ballroom-sized main reception room and I said a silent prayer of thanks that they hadn't wanted that one laid. On every wall there were crossed swords, shields, even suits of armor. It seemed that the Featherstonehaughs had been killing people successfully for quite a few generations.

I went upstairs and was relieved to find the bedrooms were not equally full of artifacts, in fact were rather austere. I was about to start on the bedrooms when I heard a tap dripping in a bathroom. I looked inside and was not thrilled with what I saw. The bathtub had a disgusting black line around it. There were several towels dropped in a heap on the floor and the loo was also not the cleanest. That dripping tap in the basin had left a trail of lime. If this is how they leave their house, I thought, then they don't deserve a good cleaning. Then it occurred to me that someone might actually have been living in the house, and that someone might be Whiffy. I crept from room to room until I was satisfied I was in the house alone.

Then my pride and conscience got the better of me. I didn't want them to think I did shoddy work. I set to attacking that disgusting bathroom. I picked up the towels and disposed of them into a laundry hamper. I scrubbed at the basin; I even got down on my knees and attacked the ring around the bathtub. But as for sticking my hand down someone else's lavatory . . . there were limits, after all. In the end I found a brush hanging up behind a door. I tied a cloth around this and, standing suitably far away and averting my eyes, I gave the toilet bowl a quick going-over. Afterward I hurriedly dropped the offending cloth into the nearest rubbish bin and hung up the bath brush as if nothing had happened. It was only as I replaced it on its hook that it occurred to me that it was probably hung there to scrub the hard-to-reach parts of someone's back. Oh, dear. They need never know what it had been used for, I decided.

And of course I realized at that very moment that we upper classes are open to all kinds of fiendish tricks with which our servants can vent their anger and frustration. I'd heard once about a butler who peed into the soup. I wondered what the servants did at Castle Rannoch. The motto is obviously always to treat servants as one would wish to be treated. The golden rule does make a lot of sense.

Feeling more satisfied now, I started in the back bedrooms and removed the dust covers very carefully. I swept. I even went down to the coal cellar and I laid fires. That went smoothly enough, although I was out of breath after carrying a full coal scuttle upstairs several times. Then I came to the main bedroom, looking out onto Eaton Place.

This room was dominated by a giant four-poster bed, the sort that Queen Elizabeth had obviously slept in on her way north. It was a ghastly affair with faded velvet curtains. The rest of the room was no more conducive to a good night's sleep. On one wall was a hideous mask with tusks, on another a print of a battle scene. As I went to shake out the satin quilt that covered the bed, I misjudged its weight. It flew up, knocking that mask off the wall. Almost as if in slow motion, I watched the mask fall and, in its turn, knock a small statue off the mantelpiece. I flung myself across the room to grab it, but I was too late. It hit the fender with a neat clunk and broke in half. I stared at it in horror.

"Stay calm," I told myself. "It's just one small statue in a house full of ornaments."

I picked up the two pieces. It looked like some kind of Chinese goddess with several arms, one of which had now snapped off at the shoulder. Luckily it was a clean break. I stuffed both pieces into my apron pocket. I'd take it away, have it repaired, and then slip it back into the house later. Hopefully nobody would notice. I could bring up another, similar piece from downstairs to replace it until I could return it.

I had just heaved a sigh of relief when I froze. Was I now oversensitive, or had I heard footsteps down below? I stood, holding my breath, until I heard the unmistakable creak of a stair or floorboard. Someone was definitely in the house with me. Nothing to get alarmed about, I told myself. It was broad daylight in a fashionable London square. I'd only have to open the window and shout for help and any number of maids, chauffeurs, and delivery boys would hear me. Remembering how Mrs. Bantry-Bynge and her friend Boy had arrived earlier than originally planned, I presumed it was a member of the Featherstonehaughs' entourage. I just prayed it wasn't Whiffy.

There was a big wardrobe in the bedroom and I was tempted to hide. Then the voice of reason won out. Since servants were supposed to be not seen and not heard, I decided I shouldn't announce my presence. A servant would just go on with her work, no matter what was happening around her in the household.

The footsteps came closer. It was hard to keep making that bed without turning around. In the end I just had to peek.

I jumped a mile as Darcy O'Mara stepped in through the bedroom door. "Holy mother of God, what an impressive bed," he said. "This certainly rivals the Princess and the Pea, doesn't it?"

"Darcy, what are you doing here?" I demanded. "You almost gave me a heart attack."

"I thought I saw you crossing Belgrave Square earlier, looking rather furtive, so I decided to follow you. I watched you go in the tradesmen's entrance of the Featherstonehaughs' house when I knew they were still in the country. And I was intrigued. Being of a curious nature I wanted to know what the hell you were doing in someone else's empty house. I waited. You didn't reemerge, so I came to take a look for myself. You didn't lock the door after you, naughty girl."

"All right," I said. "You've discovered my guilty secret."

"Your secret pleasure is to go around making other people's beds? Sigmund Freud would find that interesting."

"No, silly. I've started a new career. I'm running a domestic service to get people's houses ready for them when they want to come to London and save them the expense of sending staff in advance."

"Brilliant notion," he said. "Where is the rest of your team?"

"It's just me so far," I said.

He burst out laughing. "You're doing the housecleaning yourself?"

"I don't see what's so funny about that."

"And when have you ever cleaned a house? I bet you've been polishing the floors with the stuff they use to clean the silver."

"I didn't say I was doing the spring cleaning," I retorted. "My service offers to air out and dust off a few rooms. Make ready the house, that's all. I can run the carpet sweeper, put clean sheets on the beds, and do a good dust."

"I'm impressed—but I bet your family wouldn't be."

"We'll just make sure they don't know. If I start doing well enough, I can hire a staff to do the actual work."

"Very enterprising of you. I wish you luck." His gaze strayed back to the bed, now in half-made disarray. "My, but that is a fine-looking bed," he said. He gave the mattress an experimental push to test the springiness. "Who knows what notable historical characters might have had a romp on

this bed? Henry the Eighth, do you think? Nell Gywnne and King Charlie?"
Then he looked up at me.

He was standing very close, so close that I found it unnerving, especially given the subject matter of the conversation and the way he was looking at me.

I moved away. "I don't think the Featherstonehaughs would approve if they arrived early and found a strange man in their house, bothering the servants."

He smiled, his eyes flashing a challenge. "Oh, so you're getting bothered by me, are you?"

"Not at all," I said haughtily. "I am being paid to do some work and you are keeping me from carrying out my duties, that's all."

He was still smiling. "I see," he said. "Very well, I'll go. I can tell when my presence is not wanted. Although I can name a long list of girls who would have found the chance to be alone in such surroundings with an attractive man like myself too good to turn down."

I realized with a pang of regret that I may have given the impression that I wasn't at all interested, which wasn't exactly true.

"You said something about taking me to a party this week?" I said as he turned away. "At the Café de Paris? With Americans?"

"It turned out not to be suitable for you after all." He was looking away from me, and it came to me that he had taken someone else in my place.

"What were they, drug fiends?"

"Journalists. And you can bet they'd just love a scoop on a real royal personage gate-crashing their party."

"Oh, I see." Now I didn't know whether he was genuinely concerned for my welfare or had just decided that I was too straightlaced and boring to be bothering with anymore. He must have noticed my face fall.

"Don't worry about it. The world is full of parties. You haven't seen the last of me, I promise you that," he said. He put a finger under my chin, drew me toward him, and brushed my lips with the lightest of kisses. Then he was gone.

And I stood there, watching the dust motes dance in the morning sunlight, half wishing for what might have been.

⚜

I HAD FINISHED the bedrooms and finally plucked up courage to attack that drawing room. There was no way I was going to take out those Persian rugs and beat them, the way any good servant would have done. I ran a sweeper over them and then started to sweep the dust off that vast parquet floor. I was down on my hands and knees, sweeping the area around the drawing room fireplace, when I heard men's voices. Before I could do anything sensible such as hide behind the nearest suit of armor, the voices came closer. I kept my head down and brushed away furiously, praying that they wouldn't come in here, or at least not pay any attention to me.

"So your parents are arriving today?" One of the voices floated toward me, echoing from all that marble in the foyer, even though he was speaking softly.

"Today or tomorrow. Not sure. Better stay away, just in case, or I'll have the mater going on at me again. You know what she's like."

"So when will I see you?"

The voices had reached the open doorway on the far side of the living room. Out of the corner of my eye I recognized the stiff, upright bearing of the son of the house, the Hon. Roderick (Whiffy) Featherstonehaugh, and behind him, in shadow, another tall and lanky young man. I turned my back to them and kept sweeping, hoping to build up a cloud of dust around me. The sounds of my brush hitting against the brass fender must have startled them.

There was a pause and then Whiffy said, *"Pas devant la bonne."*

This was the standard phrase for times when something was about to be discussed not suitable for servants' ears. It means, "Not in front of the maid," for those of you who are not conversant with French.

"What?" the other man asked, then obviously spotted me. "Oh *oui*, I see. *Je vois.*" Then he continued in atrocious French. *"Alors. Lundi soir, comme d'habitude?"* (Meaning, "Monday night as usual?")

"Bien sûr, mon vieux. Mais croyez vous que vous pouvez vous absenter?" ("But do you think you'll be able to get away?") Whiffy's French was marginally better, but still with a ghastly English accent. Really, what do they teach these boys at Eton?

"J'espère que oui." ("I hope so.") Then the speaker reverted to English as they headed out of the room again. "I'll let you know how it goes. I think you may be wunning a fwightful wisk."

I froze with my brush in midair. The other speaker had been Tristram Hautbois. I heard their voices disappearing down the hallway, but I had no idea which room they had gone into. It took all my self-control to finish my sweeping, gather up my cleaning paraphernalia, and deposit it in the broom cupboard before escaping through the servants' entrance.

My heart was thumping wildly as I crossed Eaton Place. This scheme of mine was madness. Already, on my second day of work, it had led to two embarrassing encounters. Next time I couldn't count on being so lucky and getting away unscathed. I felt my cheeks glowing pink at my choice of words.

Getting away unscathed—that was precisely what had happened to me in the bedroom. If Darcy had decided to force his attentions upon me, as the older generation so quaintly worded it, I'm not sure I would have been strong-minded enough to have resisted him.

A fierce wind sprang up as I crossed Eaton Place and I held my coat around me as I hurried home, looking forward to a cup of tea—no, make that a brandy—to calm my rattled nerves. It had been quite a morning. I let myself into Rannoch House and stood in the marble-tiled hallway.

"Binky," I called. "Are you home? I am in desperate need of a glass of brandy. Do you have the key to the liquor cabinet?"

There was no answer. I felt the emptiness of the house pressing down on me. It wasn't usually the brightest of places but today it felt positively chilly. I shivered and went upstairs to take off my maid's uniform. As I passed the bathroom on the second floor I heard a loud drip, drip, drip. Then I saw a trickle of water, coming out from under the bathroom door.

Really, Binky was just too hopeless, I decided. He must have decided to have another attempt at a bath and had forgotten to turn the tap off properly. I threw open the bathroom door and stopped short, my mouth open in alarm. The bathtub was full to overflowing, and occupied. For a moment I thought it was Binky lying there.

"Frightfully sorry, " I muttered, then I took a second look.

A fully clothed man was lying submerged in the bath, not moving, his face under the water and his eyes wide open, staring upward. What's more, I recognized him. It was Gaston de Mauxville.

Chapter 12

I had never actually seen a dead body before and I stared at him in fascination. He can't really be dead, I told myself. It's some kind of macabre French joke, or he's trying to frighten me. Or maybe he's sleeping. But his eyes were open and staring vacantly at the ceiling. I tugged experimentally on a black-patented toe that was sticking out of the water. He sloshed around a bit, sending more water onto the floor, but his expression didn't change. That's when I admitted what I had known all along. Gaston de Mauxville was lying dead in my bathtub.

A cold dread seized me. Binky had been in the house earlier. Had the same madman also murdered him? "Binky!" I shouted, running out of the bathroom. "Binky, are you all right?"

I searched his bedroom, the study, the morning room. No sign of him. Then panic really overtook me and I pictured his body hidden under one of the dust sheets, so I ran from room to room, tearing them off, looking in wardrobes, under beds. I even went down to the servants' quarters and poked around there. There was no trace of him, not even in the coal 'ole. I went back into his bedroom, and I noticed his clothes were gone. A terrible suspicion began to take shape. I remembered Binky's brave assertion that he would challenge de Mauxville to a duel. Could he possibly have killed de Mauxville? Then I shook my head firmly. Binky was brought up to be the honorable sort. He'd mentioned challenging de Mauxville to a duel. I could picture any kind of fair play and may the better man win, although I thought it hardly likely that Binky would turn out to be the better man in any kind of combat. But drowning somebody in a bathtub? Binky would never resort to such demeaning behavior, even to his worst enemy, and even if he were strong enough to hold a large chap like de Mauxville under the water long enough to drown.

I went back to the bathroom, half hoping that the body might have disappeared. But he still lay there, eyes staring upward, black overcoat bobbing in the water. I had no idea what to do next, but an extraordinary idea came to me: the document. Maybe he carried it on his person. Fighting back waves of revulsion, I reached into his pockets and extracted a soggy envelope. I was in luck. It contained the document. I proceeded to tear it into little pieces and flushed it down the lavatory. I was immediately appalled by what I had done, of course, but it was too late to retrieve it. At least the police would find no incriminating evidence on him when they arrived.

I paced up and down the second-floor landing, trying to put my thoughts in order. I knew I ought to summon the police, but I hesitated to do so. Our nemesis was lying dead in our bath, and any policeman would leap to the conclusion that one of us must have killed him. I didn't think I could persuade the police to believe that a stranger had chosen our bathtub, out of the whole of London, in which to commit suicide.

But I had just destroyed the incriminating evidence, hadn't I? So who knew, apart from us, that he was our nemesis? Oh, blast and damnation. Our solicitors, of course. They even held a copy of the document and I didn't think they'd be easily persuaded to hand it over, or destroy it, even given their two hundred years of loyalty to our family. And I also didn't think I could persuade them not to mention our association with de Mauxville when the news of his death was made public.

I peeped into the bathroom again. Absurd thoughts were now flashing through my head. Would it be possible for Binky and me to remove the body and drop it into the Thames when nobody was looking? One drowning would appear pretty much like another. But it all seemed rather daunting: de Mauxville was heavy in life, for one thing, and for another, we had no loyal servants or means of transportation in London. I could hardly see us hiring a taxi and propping the body between us while saying, "The Embankment, my good man, and make it a deserted stretch of river." And even if it could be accomplished, it would somehow be letting down generations of fierce Scotsmen whose motto had been Death Before Dishonor. I'm not so sure about the Hanoverian ancestors. I think they could be quite devious when they wanted to.

I was still in midthought when the doorbell rang. I nearly jumped out of my skin. Should I answer it? What if it was only Binky, who was quite likely to have forgotten his key? Whoever it was, they might only come back if the door wasn't answered now. I would just have to get rid of them. I shuddered at that particular choice of words. Not the best in current circumstances. I started down the two flights of stairs, was just about to open the front door, and suddenly realized I was still wearing my maid's uniform. I grabbed my coat from the hall rack and slipped it on, wrapping it tightly around me. Then I opened the door.

"Oh, hello, may I speak to Lady—oh, my gosh, Georgie, it's you."

Tristram Hautbois stood there, his dark hair flopping boyishly over his forehead, beaming at me.

"Tristram. Oh. What a surprise," I stammered.

"Sorry to show up unexpectedly like this," he said, still with that expectant smile on his face, "but the old boy at the solicitors I work for sent me to deliver some papers to an address just around the corner and I thought it seemed too tempting not to see where you lived and say hello. It feels like ages since I saw you last."

Since I had seen him less than an hour ago, I didn't know what to say to this. Obviously he didn't associate the kneeling sweeper in black uniform with me. I pulled the coat more tightly around me.

"Were you just going out?" he asked.

"No, just got home. Haven't had time to take off my coat yet," I said.

"Are you under the weather?"

"No, why?"

"It's not that cold out today," he said. "In fact it's quite mild. I'm not even wearing an overcoat and here you are, all bundled up."

"The house is always so chilly with these high ceilings." I could hear myself babbling and tried to regain my composure.

"What a piece of luck that my timing was so good then, wasn't it?" he said. "I hope you don't mind my showing up on your doorstep like this. So this is Rannoch House. I must say it's pretty impressive. I'd love you to show me around. I understand that your father was something of a collector and you've some fine paintings."

"I'd be happy to show you around, Tristram, but now isn't the best of times," I said, cutting off the end of his sentence.

His face fell. He had the most schoolboyish of faces, his joy or despair clearly showing for all to see.

"I thought you might be pleased to see me," he said in a small voice.

"I am pleased to see you," I said, "and any other time I'd be delighted to invite you in, but I'm in the house alone, and you know what my royal relatives would say if I entertained a man, unchaperoned, even in the middle of the day, so I'm afraid . . ."

"I do understand," he said, nodding earnestly. "But don't the servants count as chaperons?"

"No servants either," I said. "I'm living here alone at the moment until I can hire a maid."

"Gosh, that's awfully daring of you," he said. "So modern."

"I'm not trying to be modern and daring," I said. "Simply lack of funds. I have to find a way to support myself."

"Then we're in the same boat." He beamed again. Truly he had a most endearing smile. "Abandoned and fighting the cruel world."

"Not exactly," I said. "Not like those poor wretches on the bread lines."

"Well, no," he admitted.

"And at least you have gainful employment. When you've finished your articles you'll have a profession. I, on the other hand, am qualified only for marriage and I'm only qualified for that by my pedigree. My family is determined to marry me off to some awful foreign prince who is bound to be assassinated within the year."

"You could always marry me," he said, pronouncing it, of course "mawwy."

I laughed. "What, and trade a freezing and empty house for a bedsitter in Bromley? It's a sweet offer, Tristram, but I hardly think you're in a position to support a wife, nor will be for some time."

"I may be," he said. "If I come into my guardian's fortune . . ."

"What a horrid thing to say," I snapped, my nerves close to breaking point by this time. "You almost sound as if you're hoping Sir Hubert dies."

"Not hoping. Good Lord, no," he stammered. "Nothing's further from the truth. I worship the old boy. He couldn't have been kinder to me. But I'm only going by what the quacks have said and they have impressed upon me that the outcome is not likely to be good. Bad head injuries, you know. In a coma."

"So sad," I said. "If it's head injuries, then I'd rather he died. Such an energetic man could never be a lifelong invalid."

"My sentiments exactly," Tristram agreed. "So I'm trying to hope for the best, but prepared to accept the worst."

Suddenly I couldn't stand there chatting a second longer without exploding. "Look, Tristram, I am most pleased to see you, but I have to go now. I'm . . . meeting someone for tea and I have to change."

"Another time, maybe? At the weekend? I had promised to show you London, had I not?"

"Yes, you had. And I'm looking forward to it, but I'm not sure what I'll be doing on Saturday and Sunday." (I can't use the word "weekend," even in moments of stress.) "My brother is in town, you know. I may have family matters to attend to."

"Your brother? I don't believe I've met him."

"You probably wouldn't have. He's my half brother, actually, and he would have been away at school when I came to stay with my mother at Sir Hubert's."

"Where did he go to school?"

"Gairlachan. That formidable place in the Highlands."

"With the cross-country runs and cold showers at dawn? Just like the Spartan boys. The weak die and the strong become empire builders."

"That's the one."

"Sir Hubert threatened to send me there if I didn't pull my socks up, but he settled for Downside instead, since Mama was a Catholic and he wanted to honor her wishes. I must say I was relieved. Those monks like their creature comforts."

"That's where you were at school with Darcy?"

"O'Mara, you mean?" His face clouded. "Yes, he was a couple of years above me but we were in the same house." He leaned closer to me, even though we were the only two people on a deserted pavement. "Look, Georgie, I meant what I said the other day. He's a bad egg, you know. Untrustworthy, just like a typical Irishman. Shake hands and then stab you in the back as soon as you turn away." He paused and looked at me. "You're not—er, involved with him, are you?"

"He's just a casual acquaintance," I said, half wanting to lie and watch Tristram's face when I said that we were lovers. "We met at a hunt ball, apparently, and then at that wedding. That is the sum total of our acquaintanceship." I didn't mention the unsettling little scene in the Featherstonehaughs' bedroom.

Relief flooded his boyish features. "That's good, only I wouldn't like to see a nice girl like you ending up with her heart broken, or worse."

"Thank you, but I have no intention of anybody breaking my heart," I said, my hand already itching to close that front door. "I must go now, Tristram. Please excuse me."

"So may I see you again soon? Maybe I could take you to lunch somewhere? Nothing too fancy, I'm afraid, but I know some good cheap Italian places. You know, spaghetti Bolognese and a glass of red plonk for one and sixpence."

"Thank you," I said. "I'm sorry about today, but I really must go. Now." With that I turned and fled into the house. Once I'd closed the door, I stood for some time, leaning against the solid coldness of the oak while my heart regained its normal pace.

Chapter 13

At least that little interlude had helped me get my thoughts into order. First I must find Binky, I decided. Before I summoned the police, I had to know for certain that he had no part in the killing of de Mauxville, and the most likely place to find him would be his club. He had been taking his meals there since coming to London and it was where he felt comfortable. I tried to think positively: maybe his disappearance had nothing whatever to do with the body. Perhaps he had finally decided that it would be easier to take a room at his club and avoid walking home after dinner and several brandies.

He might have mentioned it to me, I thought angrily. Typical Binky.

I dialed the telephone exchange and asked to be connected to Brooks, which had been my grandfather's club, my father's, and was now Binky's.

"May I help you?" said a quavering old voice.

"Could you please tell me if Lord Rannoch is currently in residence?" I asked.

"I'm afraid not, madam."

"You mean he's not in residence or you can't tell me whether he is or isn't?"

"Precisely, madam."

"I am Lady Georgiana Rannoch, the duke's sister, and I wish to speak to him on a matter of great urgency. Now, could you tell me whether he is in residence?"

"I'm afraid not, my lady." The voice was unperturbed and it was quite clear that the old man was prepared to die rather than disclose the whereabouts of a club member to one of the opposite sex. There was nothing for it but to go there myself.

I went upstairs and changed out of the maid's uniform, trying not to look at the bathroom door as I went past. The fact that Binky's clothes had gone presumably meant that he wasn't intending to come back. And I could only conclude the worst—that he had seen the body and panicked. Now I just hoped he wasn't somewhere spilling the beans.

I took pen and paper and wrote him a note, in case he returned before I did. *Binky. There is a corpse in the upstairs bathtub. Don't do anything until I return. Above all, don't telephone the police. We need to talk about what we should do. Love, Georgie.*

I set off at a brisk pace up Picadilly to St. James's Street, home of the oldest London clubs, went up the austere steps of Brooks, and rapped on the front door. It was opened by an extremely ancient hall porter with watery blue eyes, fine white baby hair, and a perpetual tremor.

"I'm sorry, madam. This is a gentlemen's club," he said, giving me a look of such horror that one might think I was standing on the doorstep dressed as Lady Godiva.

"I know it's a gentlemen's club," I said calmly. "I am Lady Georgiana Rannoch and I telephoned a few minutes ago. I need to know immediately whether my brother, the duke, is on the club premises. If he is, I wish to speak to him on a matter of great urgency."

I was doing quite a good imitation of my esteemed great-grandmother—the Empress of India, not the one who had sold fish in the East End, although I gather she had a commanding presence and was also good at getting her own way.

The hall porter quivered but did not budge. "It is against club policy to reveal which members are in residence, m'lady. If you care to write His Grace a message I will see that it is delivered to him, should he appear in the club at any time."

I stared at the porter, wondering what would happen if I pushed past him and took a quick look at the guest book. He was definitely smaller and frailer than I. Then I decided that such unforgivably boorish behavior would get back to HM within the hour and by the end of the week I'd be a lady-in-waiting in deepest Gloucestershire. I wrote my note to Binky and sensed the smug look on the hall porter's face as he took it from me.

Now I had no idea what to do next. Really it was too bad of Binky to have vanished into thin air at a moment like this. I stood at the edge of Green Park, feeling warm spring sunshine on me, watching nannies pushing their little charges for an outing in the fresh air, and found it hard to believe that all around me life was going on as normal. It came to me that I had never been truly alone in my life before. A feeling of utter desolation swept over me. I was alone, unprotected, abandoned in the big city. To my horror I felt tears welling up in my eyes. What on earth had made me bolt to London without any sensible preparations? If only I'd stayed in Scotland, I'd never have found myself in this mess. I had the strongest urge to pack my bags and catch the next train home—which, of course, I realized was exactly what Binky must have done. It's that built-in homing instinct common to generations of Rannochs who crawled back to Castle Rannoch, wounded and exhausted after the latest skirmish against the English/Vikings/Danes/Romans/Picts or whomever they were fighting at the time. I was now absolutely sure that Binky had gone home, but there wasn't much I could do about it. Even if he had fled on discovering the body, he would be on a Scotland-bound train for hours yet, and then he'd have to make his way to Glenrannoch, which meant he probably wouldn't arrive home until sometime tonight.

I pulled out my handkerchief and surreptitiously dabbed my eyes, utterly ashamed of this weak behavior. A lady never showed her feelings in public, according to my governess. And a Rannoch certainly didn't crumble at the first small hurdle in her life. I reminded myself of my ancestor Robert Bruce Rannoch, whose right arm had been hacked off in the battle of Bannockburn and had promptly transferred his sword to his left hand and gone on fighting. We Rannochs did not give in. If Binky had let down the family by running away, I wasn't about to do the same. I would take action, and immediately.

I started to walk back to Rannoch House, trying to decide what to do next. I couldn't leave the body in the bath indefinitely. I had no idea when bodies started decomposing but I had no wish to find out. And I certainly wasn't going to sleep in a house with a body floating yards away. I heard a clock strike four and my stomach reminded me that it was teatime and I hadn't even had lunch. I realized that all my life I had been guided, protected, cocooned by nannies, governesses, servants, chaperons. Other people of my age had learned to think for themselves. I had never had to make a major decision for myself. In fact the first important decision I had made was to run away from Castle Rannoch. That one hadn't turned out too wonderfully so far.

I needed help, and swiftly, but I had no idea to whom I could turn in this hour of need. Certainly not to my kin at the palace. Then the vision of food made me think of my grandfather—the live one, not the ghost who played bagpipes. He was such an obvious choice that a great sense of relief swept over me. He'd know what to do. I was just about to find the nearest underground station when I stopped short: he had, after all, been a policeman. He would be horrified that I hadn't called the police immediately and would make me do so. And then, of course, I'd have to explain why I had fled to Essex rather than reporting a murder right away.

So not my grandfather then. What I needed at this moment was someone to talk to. I realized that making the right decision at this moment was vital. A problem shared is a problem halved, as my nanny used to say. I almost wished I had let Tristram come in when he had appeared on my doorstep and shown him the body in the bath. He was, after all, practically a relative. Not that he'd have had the slightest idea what to do about my current predicament (he'd probably have fainted on the spot), but at least I'd have shared my problem with someone.

Apart from Tristram, whom did I know in London? There was Darcy, who might well know how to make a corpse disappear. But I wasn't sure that I completely trusted Darcy, and anyway, I had no idea where he lived. Then I remembered Belinda. She had been wonderful in a crisis at school, like that time we had caught the potting shed on fire.

Belinda was just the sort of person I needed at this moment. I set off for her little mews cottage at top speed, uttering a silent prayer that she would be home. I was quite out of breath and feeling horribly hot in my tweed suit by the time I got there, the day having turned out warmer than I had expected. (Of course I could never admit that I was hot. Another thing that my governess used to say was that the words "hot," "lot," and "got" were not part of a lady's vocabulary.) I rapped on the door, which was opened by her maid.

"Miss Belinda is resting and not to be disturbed," she said.

"It's an emergency," I said. "I simply have to talk to your mistress right away. Please go and wake her."

"I can't do that, miss," the maid said, looking as imperturbable as that wretched hall porter at Brooks's. "She gave strict instructions that she was not to be disturbed come hell or high water."

I had had enough of being rebuffed by loyal retainers for one afternoon.

"This is both hell and high water," I said. "A matter of life and death, in fact. If you don't go and wake her, I shall do so myself. Kindly tell her that Lady Georgiana is here on a matter of great urgency."

The girl looked frightened, although whether it was of me or of waking her mistress, I wasn't sure. "Very good, miss, I mean your ladyship," she stammered. "Although she's going to be awful cross, because she didn't get 'ome until three this morning and she's due out again tonight."

She turned reluctantly from the front door and dragged her feet toward the staircase. But at that moment a dramatic figure appeared at the top of the stairs. She was wearing a scarlet Japanese kimono and a mask, pushed up just above her eyes, and she stood in dramatic film star pose, one wrist raised to her temple.

"What is all this racket, Florrie?" she asked. "Didn't I tell you I wasn't to be disturbed?"

"It's me, Belinda," I said. "I have to speak to you."

She raised the mask a little higher. Bleary eyes focused on me.

"Georgie," she said.

"I'm sorry to wake you but it's a real crisis and I couldn't think of anyone else I could turn to." To my horror my voice trembled at the end of this sentence.

Belinda started to grope her way down the stairs in a good imitation of Lady Macbeth in her sleepwalking scene. "Make us some tea, please, Florrie," she said. "I suppose you'd better sit down, Georgie." She collapsed onto the sofa. "God, I feel like hell," she muttered. "Those cocktails must have been lethal and I did have an awful lot of them."

"I'm sorry to be disturbing you like this," I repeated. "I really am. I wouldn't have come if I could have thought of anywhere else to go."

"Sit down and tell Aunt Belinda everything." She patted the sofa beside her.

I sat. "She can't overhear us, can she?" I muttered. "This is strictly for your ears only."

"The kitchen's at the back. So go on. Spill the beans."

"I'm in awful trouble, Belinda," I blurted out.

Her perfectly plucked eyebrows shot up in surprise. "It was only just over a week ago that you expressed interest in losing your virginity. You can't possibly be pregnant already!"

"No, it's nothing like that," I said. "There is a body in my bathtub."

"A dead body, you mean?"

"That's exactly what I mean."

Belinda was now wide awake. She perched on the edge of the sofa, and leaned in closer. "My dear, how absolutely fascinating. Anyone you know?"

"Actually, yes. He was an awful Frenchman called de Mauxville, who was trying to claim ownership of Castle Rannoch."

"A long-lost relative, then?"

"Good Lord, no. Nothing to do with us. He won the house from Father in a card game, or so he was trying to claim."

"And now he's lying dead in your bath. Have you called the police yet?"

"No, I didn't want to do that until I could find Binky and now he's vanished, so I don't know if he had anything to do with it or not."

"It won't look good—you both have an awfully good motive for killing him, after all."

"I know that."

"So what are you planning to do—dispose of the body somehow? Does Rannoch House have a back garden? Flower beds?"

"Belinda! I couldn't bury him in the back garden—it simply isn't done."

"It would be the simplest solution, Georgie."

"No, it wouldn't. For one thing he's rather large and I don't think even two of us could drag him out to the garden successfully. For another, someone is bound to be looking out of a window and see us, and then I'd be in worse trouble than I am now. At least at this moment I can face the police with true innocence. And don't forget that the Rannoch family motto is Death Before Dishonor."

"I bet you'd have done it if he'd been a small man and you'd had a wilderness behind the house," Belinda said, grinning.

I had to smile too. "Maybe I would."

"Who else would know that this de Mauxville had come to claim Castle Rannoch?"

"Our solicitors, unfortunately. Apart from them, I couldn't say."

She sat frowning for a moment. Then she said, "I think your best approach is to play your trump card."

"Trump card?"

"Your royal connection, my dear. You summon the police, acting with righteous indignation. You have just found a body in your bathtub. You have no idea who he is or how he got there. Kindly have it removed instantly. Think of your great-grandmother. The lower classes are always in awe of anything royal."

"And if they ask me if I know him? I can't tell a lie."

"Be suitably vague. You think he came to the house once to see your brother. Of course you were never personally introduced to him, so officially you don't know him."

"That's true enough. I never was introduced." I sighed.

She patted my knee. "You do have a good alibi, don't you?"

"Me? Not one I can divulge to them. I was cleaning somebody's house. I can't let anyone know about that."

"No, of course you can't. Oh, dear, then we'd better give you one. Let's see. You and I went shopping at Harrods together in the morning and then we lunched together at my place, and arrived, together, at Rannoch House. You went up to change and discovered the body, after which we summoned the police immediately."

I looked at her with admiration. "Belinda—you'd do that for me?"

"Of course. Think of what we went through together at Les Oiseaux. I'll never forget all those times you covered for me when I was in a pickle. That time I got locked out and had to climb up the ivy—"

I smiled. "Oh, yes. I remember."

"There you are, then. We'll have some tea. I'll get dressed and we'll go to face the music."

Chapter 14

"There he is." I pushed open the bathroom door and pointed dramatically at the body, which hadn't moved since I'd seen him last.

Belinda went over and eyed him critically. "What a nasty-looking man. Was he equally unpleasant in life?"

"Worse," I said.

"Then you have obviously done society a favor. The world is less one horrid person."

"I had nothing to do with his death, Belinda, and I'm sure Binky didn't either. We've just provided the bath."

She peered closely at him, utterly unsqueamish about the revolting spectacle. "So how did he get into your bath, do you think?"

"I have no idea. I went out to do my domestic duties, leaving Binky in the house. I came home to find the front door unlocked, water all over the floor, and this man lying here."

"And what does Binky say about it?"

"I'm afraid he's done a quick getaway back to Scotland."

"How frightfully unchivalrous of him—leaving you to face the music. You don't think this is his doing, then?"

I weighed it in my mind. "I really don't think so," I said at last. "I simply can't picture Binky drowning someone in a bathtub. He's too clumsy, for one thing. He'd have slipped on the soap or something. And if he had made up his mind to do away with de Mauxville, he would hardly have left him lying in our own bathtub, would he?"

"It's certainly not the brightest thing to have done," she said, "but your brother was never noted for his high intellect, was he?"

"Even Binky couldn't be that stupid, surely." I heard the note of uncertainty creep into my voice. "Anyway, I suspect he's on a train heading north at the moment. I'm waiting for him to arrive home in Scotland, so that I can telephone him and find out the truth. But in the meantime, what should I do? We can't just leave de Mauxville lying there."

Belinda shrugged. "If you don't want to try burying him in the back garden, which I personally think is an excellent idea, you'll simply have to call the police."

"I suppose so," I agreed. "After all, why should I be afraid? I am innocent. I have nothing to hide—"

"Apart from the small fact that you dress up as a maid and go to scrub other people's lavatories," Belinda reminded me.

"Well, apart from that."

"Don't worry. I'm here at your side," Belinda said. "It would take a formidable policeman to get the better of the two of us."

I managed a weak smile. "All right. I'll do it."

I went downstairs to the telephone, then we waited, perched side by side on the stairs, staring at the front door, listening to a clock ticking somewhere in the emptiness of the house.

"Who do you think could have done it?" Belinda asked at last. "What was he doing here in the first place?"

"I suppose he must have come to see Binky."

"But if Binky didn't kill him, who did?"

I shrugged. "Someone else. A stranger, I suppose."

She shook her head. "You want the police to believe that a complete stranger broke into your house while you were out and drowned somebody in your bathtub? That would take a great deal of nerve and planning, Georgiana, as well as a great deal of luck."

"I know. It hardly seems feasible, does it? I mean, who could possibly know that de Mauxville was coming here? Hardly anybody even knew we were in London. And surely de Mauxville can't have many acquaintances here."

She stared thoughtfully at the chandelier. "This de Mauxville," she said, "is he one of us, or strictly NOCD?" (Which, in case you don't know, is shorthand for "not our class, dear.")

"I really couldn't say. He was rather rude, but then I know plenty of rude peers and I expect you do too."

"Do you know where he was staying?"

"Claridge's."

"That does imply money but no club."

"He's French, Belinda. Would a Frenchman belong to a London club?"

"If he had London connections and made frequent trips across the Channel, he would. So staying at Claridge's implies that he doesn't know people here and doesn't come here often."

"Not very helpful," I said.

"You need to find out all about him. If you found him unpleasant, he may have annoyed any number of people who were just waiting to drown him in somebody's bath. So find out what he does when he comes to England—when he's not trying to get his hands on your castle, I mean."

"I agree, but how?"

"I know an awful lot of people," she said. "Including people who spend half the year on the Continent. People who frequent the casinos in Nice and Monte Carlo. I could ask questions for you."

"Belinda—would you really? You are an absolute brick."

"I shall find it rather fun, actually. Belinda Warburton-Stoke, girl detective."

In spite of the tension, I had to laugh. "Girl detective," I echoed.

"I'm sure I shall be better at it than the dreary, plodding policeman they are bound to send to investigate."

As if on cue there was a thunderous knocking at the front door. I shot Belinda a look and went down to open it. Several blue uniforms were standing on the front steps and in their midst was one fawn raincoat and trilby. Beneath the trilby was a tired-looking face—a sort of fawn-colored, washed-out face with an expression that indicated life was always unutterably awful, and a fawn mustache that matched the raincoat. The trilby was raised halfheartedly.

"Good evening, miss. Inspector Harry Sugg. I understand that somebody at this address reported a dead body on the premises."

"That is correct. Won't you come in, Inspector?"

He was regarding me suspiciously. "I take it there really is a dead body and this isn't one of those pranks that you bright young people seem to find so amusing—like stealing policemen's helmets?"

"I can assure you there is a body and it's not at all amusing," I said.

I turned and led the way back into the house. Belinda had stood up and was waiting halfway up the stairs. The trilby was raised to her. "Good evening, madam. Are you the owner of this establishment?"

"No, she's not," I said shortly. "This is Rannoch House, owned by the duke."

"What duke would that be, miss?" he asked, taking out a notepad and pencil.

"The Duke of Glen Garry and Rannoch," I said. "My brother. I am Lady Georgiana Rannoch, great-granddaughter to the late Queen Victoria, cousin to His Majesty. This is my friend Belinda Warburton-Stoke."

He didn't seem particularly impressed—not bowing and scraping as Belinda had suggested.

"How do you do, miss?" He nodded to her. "All right then. Supposing you show me this body."

"This way," I said. I realized I had taken an instant and completely irrational dislike to him. I led him up the first flight of stairs, across the landing, and then up the second flight. I noticed he was puffing a little by the time we got to the top. Not used to climbing Scottish crags, obviously.

"He's in the bath," I said.

He still looked as if he wasn't taking me seriously and was dying to prove me an idiot. "In the bath, eh? Are you sure that one of your friends didn't have a drop too much and is now sleeping it off?"

"I doubt it. He's underwater, for one thing. See for yourself." I pushed open the bathroom door. He stepped inside, then visibly recoiled.

"I do see what you mean," he said. "Yes, he's definitely dead, all right. Rogers! In here! You better get on the blower to headquarters and tell them we'll want the fingerprint kit, the camera with the flash, the lot."

He stepped out of the bathroom and turned to me. "This is nasty. Very nasty indeed. Unless he decided to end his own life, it looks very much as if someone ended it for him."

"Why would he choose to end his own life in Lady Georgiana's bathtub?" Belinda said.

"And if he were going to do so, he wouldn't have worn his overcoat," I added.

"Unless he found the water a trifle chilly, or he wanted it to weigh him down," Belinda said, with the faintest of twinkles in her eyes. I could tell she was finding this rather fun, but then she wasn't the prime suspect. I found myself wondering if those of royal blood still had the privilege of being hanged with a silken cord, then decided that having my neck irritated by coarse hemp would be the least of my worries.

Inspector Sugg looked around, as if seeking inspiration. "Is there somewhere we can sit down and talk while I wait for my team to get here?"

"The morning room is opened up," I said. "It's this way."

"The morning room," he echoed. I wondered if he was playing with the word, or thought I had meant "mourning." He followed me back down the stairs. We sat. I was wondering what the protocol was at this juncture and whether I should offer to serve tea. Since I had no servant and did not want to put myself into that role in front of the inspector, I declined.

"Right, let's get to business," he said. "Who was it found the body?"

"I did," I said.

"And I was right behind her at the time," Belinda added for good measure.

"What time was that, miss?"

I was obviously still going to be "miss" to him even though I had told him that I was the duke's sister. Perhaps he'd never learned to use "my lady" or even "your ladyship." Perhaps he was a socialist of the most egalitarian brand. Perhaps he was just plain thick. I decided not to let it rankle.

"We had been shopping together all morning, then we had a spot of lunch together, and came back here about fifteen minutes ago," I said, repeating our carefully rehearsed plan. "I went upstairs to change, saw water on the floor, opened the bathroom door, and found the body."

"Did you touch anything?"

"I started to rescue him, until I realized he was dead," I said. "I had never seen a dead body before so it was rather a shock."

"And who is he?"

"I'm not really sure," I said. I couldn't make myself tell an outright lie. "I believe I've seen him before, but I certainly was never introduced to him. An acquaintance of my brother, perhaps."

"Your brother, the duke?"

"That's right."

"And he is where?"

"In Scotland, I believe, at the family seat."

"So what was his friend doing here then?"

That one I could answer. "He wasn't my brother's friend, I can assure you. And I have absolutely no idea what he was doing here. He certainly wasn't here when I left the house this morning and when I returned he was lying dead in our bath."

"So who else was in the house?" The inspector chewed at his pencil—a nasty habit that Nanny had cured me of at four.

I hesitated, just for a second. "Nobody," I said.

Then I simply couldn't leave it at that. "My brother had been in London on business, but he had been staying mainly at his club."

"When did he leave London?"

"I couldn't tell you. He is a rather vague person and doesn't communicate his plans to me."

"And what about servants? Where were they today?"

"We have no servants down here," I said. "The family residence is in Scotland. I came down alone. My Scottish maid didn't want to leave her invalid mother and I haven't had time to hire a local maid yet. I'm really only using this as a pied-à-terre, until I settle my future plans."

"So you are, essentially, living in the house alone?"

"That's right."

"So let me get this straight: you left the house this morning, spent the day with your friend here, came back this afternoon to find a body in your bathtub—someone you don't even recognize. And you have no idea who let him in or what he was doing here?"

"That is correct."

"And a little hard to believe, wouldn't you say?"

"I agree, it seems completely impossible, Inspector," I said, "but it's the truth. I can only conclude that there is some kind of sick-minded madman running around London."

"You simply can't stay in this house alone any longer, Georgie," Belinda interrupted. "Pack some things and you can sleep on my sofa."

The inspector now turned his attention to her, which was, perhaps, what she wanted.

"Miss Warburton-Stoke, did you say?"

"That's right." She flashed him a dazzling smile.

"And your address is . . . ?"

"I live in a dinky little mews cottage. Three Seville Mews. Just a stone's throw away in Knightsbridge, actually."

"And you were with your chum when she discovered the body?"

"I was with Lady Georgiana, yes," she said. "At least, she went upstairs to change while I waited downstairs. I came when I heard her scream."

"Have you seen the body, miss?"

"I certainly have. Horrid-looking man, I'd say. He didn't even look as if he'd shaved today."

"And you'd never seen him before?"

"Absolutely not. Never seen him in my life. And believe me, Inspector, I'd remember a nasty face like that."

The inspector got to his feet. "Very well, then. I suppose that's all for now. But I shall need to speak to your brother, the duke, you know. How can I reach him in Scotland?"

I didn't want the police talking to Binky before I had a chance for my own little chat with him. "As I said, I'm not quite sure where he is at present. You could always try his club, in case he hasn't left London."

"I thought you just said he was in Scotland."

"I said I wasn't sure of his whereabouts and assumed he'd gone home. If you like, I'll try friends and family in Scotland for you, although the telephone is not in the widest use up there. It is rather remote."

"Don't worry, miss. We'll find him, all right."

Belinda took my arm. "Inspector, we really should let Lady Georgiana have a cup of tea. She's obviously in shock. I mean, who wouldn't be if they found a dead man in their house?"

He nodded. "I suppose you've both had a bit of a shock. Off you go and have a cup of tea and a lie-down then. I know where to find you if I need you. And in the meantime if that brother of yours turns up, tell him we need to speak to him right away. Is that clear?"

"Oh, absolutely, Inspector," I said.

"Off you go, then. I'll have men working at the house for some time, I expect." He tried to chivvy us to the front door.

"It will be well supervised, I hope," I said. "There are many valuable objects in this house. I wouldn't want to risk their getting stolen or damaged."

"Don't worry, miss. Your house will be in good hands. There will be a constable on guard outside until this little matter is cleared up. Now off you go."

"Her ladyship needs to collect some belongings before she goes. She can't leave without so much as a toothbrush."

"Very well," he said. "Rogers, go with the young lady and keep an eye on her. We don't want her mucking about with valuable evidence."

I stomped up the stairs, fuming with indignation, threw various illogical articles into a bag, and then realized something. "My toothbrush, soap, and flannel are in that bathroom," I said.

"I don't think you can touch anything in there," the constable said, looking worried.

"I don't think I'd want to use any of them again after this," I replied.

"Darling, I'm sure we can go to my chemist and buy you a new toothbrush," Belinda soothed. "Let's just go. This place is beginning to depress me."

"Got what you need, then?" The inspector halfheartedly raised his hat as we left.

"What a horrid man," Belinda said as soon as the door closed. "I wouldn't mind seeing him floating in a bathtub."

Chapter 15

BELINDA WARBURTON-STOKE'S MEWS COTTAGE
3 SEVILLE MEWS
KNIGHTSBRIDGE
LONDON
STILL FRIDAY

As soon as we reached Belinda's mews cottage, I asked to use her telephone and called Castle Rannoch. The call was answered, as usual, by Hamilton, the butler.

"Hello? Castle Rannoch here. His Grace's butler speaking." Our elderly butler has never learned to be comfortable with telephones.

"Hello, Hamilton, this is Lady Georgiana," I shouted, because the line was particularly bad and Hamilton has been growing increasingly deaf.

"I'm afraid her ladyship is not in residence at the moment," came the soft Scottish voice.

"Hamilton, this is Lady Georgiana. I am telephoning from London," I positively shouted into the phone. "I wish to leave a message for His Grace."

"I believe His Grace is somewhere out on the estate at the moment," he replied in his calm Scottish voice.

"Don't be ridiculous, Hamilton. You know perfectly well that he's not on the estate. He could not possibly be in Scotland yet unless he has developed wings. Please tell him to telephone me the moment he gets home. It is vitally important and he will be in serious trouble if he doesn't do so. Now let me give you the number at which I can be reached."

It took a good deal of yelling and spelling before he had successfully noted the number. I put down the phone in annoyance. "He's already persuaded our butler to lie for him."

"My dear, I think you should consider the fact that your brother may well be guilty," Belinda said. "Come and have a cup of tea. You'll feel better."

When I took the teacup I found, to my horror, that my hand was shaking. This had been a most vexing day.

A troubled night on Belinda's sofa followed. Belinda herself disappeared to yet another party. She generously invited me to come with her but I was in no mood for parties and had nothing to wear. Also I was waiting for Binky's phone call. The maid went home for the night and I tried to sleep. The sofa was modern, streamlined, and devilishly uncomfortable. So I lay awake, staring into the darkness, feeling scared and empty. I couldn't believe that Binky was guilty, but I also couldn't imagine how a stranger could end up in our bathtub dead unless Binky had had a hand in it. I couldn't wait to speak to him, to know he was all right and not guilty. If only he could have left me some kind of note before he disappeared. If only . . .

I sat up, now horribly wide awake. A note. I had left a note for Binky on his bed, a note in which I had mentioned the corpse in the bath and told him not to telephone the police. I could hardly have left anything more incriminating and the police must have found it by now. I wondered if the constable was stationed outside Rannoch House all night, or if I had any hope of sneaking in to retrieve it, on the unlikely chance that it hadn't yet been discovered. I realized that it would possibly make the police even more suspicious of me if I was caught breaking into my house at night, but it was a risk I had to take. There was just a chance they hadn't done a thorough search yet and the note was still there. I got up and put on my dress and coat over my pajamas, then I stuck some paper into the latch to make sure it would open again (one of the few useful pieces of education I had acquired at Les Oiseaux) and crept out into the night.

The city streets were deserted, apart from a constable on his beat, who eyed me suspiciously.

"Are you all right, miss?" he asked.

"Oh, yes, thank you," I replied. "Just going home from a party."

"You shouldn't be out this late alone," he said.

"I only live around the corner," I lied. He let me go on my way, but I could tell he wasn't happy about it. The farther I went, the more I agreed with him. I heard the sound of Big Ben striking midnight, borne across the city on the breeze. It was cold and I wrapped my coat around me. Belgrave Square slumbered in darkness; so did Rannoch House. No sign of a constable. I went up the steps and put my key in the lock. The front door swung open. I stepped inside, fumbling for the light switch. The hall light threw long shadows up the staircase and I considered, for the first time, that the body might still be lying in the bathtub. I usually pride myself on my sang-froid: when I was three my brother and some friends home for the school holidays had lowered me into the disused well in the courtyard at Castle Rannoch in an attempt to discover whether it was bottomless, as reputed. Fortunately for me, it was not. And once I had sat on the battlements all night in the hope of seeing my grandfather's ghost playing the bagpipes. But the thought of de Mauxville rising from the bathtub to exact revenge was so overwhelmingly disgusting that I could hardly make my feet go up the stairs.

I reached the first landing, then turned on the light and started up the second flight. I let out a little squeak and almost lost my footing as an ominous shadow reared over me, arm raised. It took my heart a couple of minutes to start beating again, before I realized that it was only the statue of an avenging angel that had been banished to the second-floor landing after Binky had chipped its nose with a cricket bat. I felt very foolish and chided myself as I continued up the stairs. Someone had cleaned the water from the floor. The bathroom door was shut. I tiptoed across the landing to Binky's bedroom at the front of the house. The note was no longer on the bed. I hoped that it might have fallen onto the floor and knelt down to look under the bed. I recoiled in horror as my knee touched a wet patch, and stood up again, my heart beating wildly. I made myself kneel and examine the patch and decided that it was nothing more than water. That could be easily enough explained—Binky had come into his room dripping wet from his bath and left a wet towel on the floor. I went carefully around the room, looking for clues, but found nothing.

I was just about to leave when I was sure I heard a heavy tread on the stairs. I couldn't help remembering that someone had committed a murder in this house earlier today. If Binky had indeed had nothing to do with the crime, then a perfect stranger had found a way into our house and lured de Mauxville to his death. Maybe he had returned. I looked around the room, wondering if I should try to hide in a wardrobe. Then I decided that nothing would be worse than waiting to be discovered and helplessly trapped.

At least this way I had an element of surprise and might be able to push past him down the stairs. I went out onto the landing, then gave a gasp of horror as a tall figure loomed ahead of me.

The tall figure gave a similar gasp and almost fell back down the stairs. As he did so, I noticed the blue uniform.

"Are you all right, Constable?" I ran to assist him.

"Lawks, miss, you didn't half give me a turn," he said, recovering himself enough to put his hand to his heart. "I didn't think no one was in the place. What on earth are you doing here?"

"I live here, Constable. It's my home," I said.

"But there's been a crime committed. There didn't ought to be nobody in the house."

"I realize that. I'm spending the night with friends but I remembered that I had left my headache powders at home, and I can't sleep when I have one of my headaches." I was rather pleased with the brilliance of this spur-of-the-moment explanation.

"And so you come back on your own at night?" he asked incredulously. "Didn't your host have no aspirins in the house?"

"My doctor makes me up very special headache powders," I said. "They are the only thing that will work, I'm afraid, and I simply couldn't face a sleepless night after what I'd been through today."

He nodded. "So have you found them?"

I realized the light in Binky's room was shining out across the landing. "I thought I must have lent them to my brother when he was here last," I said, "but they don't seem to be in his room."

"They might have been removed as evidence," he said knowingly.

"Evidence? The man was drowned."

"Ah, but what's to say he wasn't rendered unconscious with a drug first and then put in the bathtub?" He looked rather smug, I thought.

"I can assure you that my mild headache powders wouldn't kill a mouse. Now, if you don't mind, I'm going back to bed. It will have to be aspirin after all. I presume you will be staying here and keeping an eye on things? I was quite surprised to find the house unattended when I arrived."

I had obviously hit a nerve. He flushed. "Sorry, miss. Just had to pop to the nearest police station to relieve the call of nature."

I almost said, "Well, don't let it happen again." My look implied it as I made a majestic descent, worthy of my great-grandmother, down the staircase.

I hurried back to Belinda's, let myself in, and tried to sleep. I wasn't any more successful than I had been before. The police had the note I had left for Binky. They had presumably felt the wet patch on his floor and might well have decided that he had soaked his clothing in trying to drown the victim. And another thought crept into my mind: the murderer hadn't just wanted to kill de Mauxville. He had wanted to punish us as well.

At last I suppose I must have drifted off to sleep because I shot awake at the sound of a door closing. Belinda was making a poor attempt to tiptoe quietly across the parquet floor. She looked across at me and noticed my eyes were open.

"Oh, you're awake," she said. "Sorry. There's no way to close that door quietly." She came across and perched on the sofa beside me. "God, what a night. I swear every new cocktail is more lethal than the one before. They were making something called Black Stallions—I don't know what was in them but, God, did they pack a punch. I'm going to have a frightful hangover in the morning."

"Do you want me to help you make some black coffee now?" I asked, having no clue how one made black coffee.

"No, thank you. Bed is what I need. Bed alone, I mean. I was offered plenty of the accompanied kind, but turned them all down. I didn't want you to wake up all alone."

"That's very kind of you," I said. "Almost beyond the call of duty."

"To be honest, they weren't that desirable," she admitted with a grin. "I could tell they were going to be the 'fancy a spot of the old rumpy-pumpy?' kind. You know, a quick poke and over in five seconds. Honestly, public schools are doing Englishmen a great disservice by not providing elementary lessons in lovemaking. If I were in charge, I'd have employed a school prostitute, preferably French, to teach the boys how to do it properly."

"Belinda, you are terrible." I couldn't help laughing. "And what about a male equivalent for the girls' schools?"

"We had it, darling. Those delicious ski instructors we used to meet at the inn."

"They didn't, did they? All I got was a quick kiss behind the woodshed. Not even so much as a grope."

"Primrose Asquey d'Asquey reputedly used to have it on a regular basis with Stefan. Remember the big blond one?"

"The same Primrose who was wearing white for her wedding the other day?"

Belinda laughed. "Darling, if only true virgins were allowed a white wedding, church organists would die of starvation. I must see if I can line up a suitable foreigner for you. A Frenchman would be ideal. I gather they can keep one in ecstasy for hours."

"At the moment I don't think I'd be anxious to meet any more Frenchmen," I said. "The dead one in my bathtub is bad enough."

"Oh, and speaking of the dead one, I asked a few discreet questions on your behalf. And several people had come across your horrid de Mauxville in Monte Carlo. Nobody had anything good to say about him. Apparently he's one of those fringe dwellers, one gathers—seemed to have connections, but nobody was sure to whom. Always playing at the high-stakes tables—oh, and one person suggested that he was not above a spot of blackmail."

"Blackmail?"

She nodded.

I sat up now. "If that were true, and somebody had had enough of being blackmailed, then killing him would be the answer."

"Exactly what I thought."

"But why in our bathtub?"

"Two reasons: one, because it would not make the murderer the obvious suspect; and two, because somebody had a grudge against you or your brother."

"That's ridiculous," I said. "Nobody knows me, and who could have a grudge against Binky? He's the most inoffensive chap in the world. Not a mean bone in his body."

"Against your family, then? A feud of long standing? Even someone who was antiroyal and thinks that by striking at you they are somehow harming the royal family?"

"That's also ridiculous," I said. "We are so far removed from the line of succession that nobody would care if we were all wiped out in a Scottish avalanche."

Belinda shrugged. "I can't wait to hear what your brother has to say on this. I'm afraid he still has by far the best motive."

"I agree. He does. I hope he's really on his way home to Scotland and that the murderer hasn't disposed of him too."

Belinda yawned. "Sorry, old thing, but I simply have to go to bed. My legs won't hold me up for another second." She patted my hand. "I'm sure everything will be all right, you know. This is England, home of fair play and justice for all—or is that America?" She shrugged and then tottered gamely up the stairs.

I tried to get back to sleep again, but only succeeded in dozing fitfully. I was woken by the shrill ring of the telephone at first light. I leaped up, trying to grab it before it woke Belinda.

"Trunk call from Scotland for Lady Georgiana Rannoch," came the woman's voice on the line, with much crackling.

"Binky?" I demanded.

"Oh, hello there, Georgie, old thing. I hope I didn't wake you." He sounded positively cheerful.

"I was waiting for you to ring me last night, Binky. I stayed awake."

"Didn't get in until midnight. Didn't think I should disturb you at that hour."

He sounded so normal, not at all worried, that my anxiety exploded. "You are absolutely impossible! You run away and leave me here alone and now you are talking to me as if you haven't a care in the world. I take it you did see the body in the bathtub before you made your rapid departure?"

"Careful, old thing. *Pas devant la opérateur.*" (His French always was abysmal. She was feminine.)

"What? Oh, I see, yes. You did see a certain object, in the *salle de bain*? And you recognized it?"

"Of course I did. Why do you think I decided to clear out in a hurry?"

"And left me to face the music alone?"

"Don't be silly. Nobody would suspect you. There's no way a slip of a girl like you could lug a *grand homme* into *le bain*."

"And how do you think it will make you look if they find out? It's just not on, Binky," I snapped, feeling close to tears. "It's not how a Rannoch behaves. Think of your ancestor who rode fearlessly into the guns at the charge of the Light Brigade. He didn't even consider running away, with cannons to the right of him, cannons to the left of him. I will not allow you to let down the family name in this way. I expect you back in London immediately. If you hurry you can catch the ten o'clock from Edinburgh."

"Oh, look here—couldn't you just say that—"

"No, I certainly couldn't," I shouted down the hollow crackling line with my own voice echoing back at me. "And what's more, if you don't come back right away, I'll tell them you did it."

I put the phone down with a certain amount of satisfaction. At least I was learning to assert myself. Good practice for saying no to the queen and Prince Siegfried.

Chapter 16

Now that Binky was presumably wending his way back to London, I felt a little better. Belinda's maid arrived about seven and bustled about making so much noise that I had to get up in self-defense. Belinda herself did not appear until after ten, looking pale and wan in her silk kimono.

"No more Black Stallions ever," she groaned, feeling her way to the table and reaching out for the cup of tea the maid placed in front of her. "I seem to remember hearing the telephone. Was that your brother?"

"Yes, and I've told him to come back to London immediately," I said. "I was very firm."

"Good for you. But in the meantime we should start our sleuthing."

"Should we? Doing what?"

"Darling, if your brother didn't drown de Mauxville, then somebody else did. We need to find out who."

"Won't the police be doing that?"

"Policemen are notoriously dense. That inspector has probably leaped to the conclusion that your brother is guilty and thus will look no further."

"But that's awful."

"So it will be up to you, Georgie."

"But what can I do?"

Belinda shrugged. "Start by asking people around the square. Someone might have noticed de Mauxville arriving, possibly with a stranger. Or a stranger trying to get into your house."

"That's true."

"And we could ring up Claridge's and ask them who left messages for de Mauxville or visited him."

"They are not likely to tell me that," I said.

"Pretend to be a relative from France. Distraught. Desperate to find him. Family crisis, you know. Use your feminine wiles."

"I suppose so," I said hesitantly.

"Do it now. Go on." She pointed to the telephone. "With any luck the police haven't grilled everybody yet."

"All right." I got up and went over to the instrument, picking it up gingerly.

" 'Allo," I said in pseudo-French when I was connected to the Claridge's operator. "Zis is Mademoiselle de Mauxville. I believe zat my bruzzer stay wiz you, *n'est-ce pas?* De Mauxville?"

"Yes, that's right. Monsieur de Mauxville has been staying with us."

"Would you please put me through to him?" I asked, the French accent already slipping.

"I'm afraid that—that is, he was not in his room last night, Mademoiselle de Mauxville."

"Ooh la la. Terrible. Out on zee town again, I fear. Could you tell me, please, has he had any messages?" (I made it rhyme with "massages.") "Did somebody give 'im zee message from me yesterday? I am desperate to contact 'im and he doesn't call me."

"A message was delivered to his room yesterday, but I couldn't say who it was from. I show no message from you, mademoiselle."

" 'Ow is zis possible?" I demanded. "I telephone from Paris in zee morning."

"Maybe your message was passed along verbally," the switchboard girl suggested.

"And has he had any visitors? I need to know if my cousin has encountered him on a matter of family business."

"I'm afraid I don't know that. You'd have to ask at reception and I don't think they'd be at liberty to tell you. Now, if you'd give me your address and telephone number, mademoiselle, someone will probably want to contact you about your brother in the near future."

"My address?" My brain raced. "I am unfortunately touring wiz friends at zee moment. I will telephone you again tomorrow and in the meantime, please tell my bruzzer zat I must speak wiz him."

I put down the phone. "I think they must know," I said. "She wanted my address in France. But a message was delivered to him yesterday, and he may have had a visitor."

"Did she describe the visitor?"

"She wouldn't say."

"You may have to go there and question the staff. They'd probably tell you."

Telephoning was one thing. Grilling the staff at Claridge's was quite another. Besides, my picture was well enough known that I was likely to be recognized, which would only make things worse for Binky and me.

"I suppose I could go and question people around the square," I said. "Will you come with me?"

"It does sound like fun," she said, "but I have a client coming to my dress salon at two. Tell you what—I'll do your sleuthing with you if you'll come to my salon with me and model clothes for the client."

"Me? Model clothes?" I started to laugh.

"Oh, be a brick, Georgie. Usually I have to model them myself and it would be so much easier, and so much better for my prestige, if I could just sit there chatting with the client while someone else modeled them. It's what they do at all the big houses—and I really need this sale. I think this one might actually pay cash for once."

"But, Belinda, I fear I'd be more of a hindrance than a help," I said. "Remember the debutante disaster. Remember when I was Juliet in the school play and I fell off the balcony. I am not known for my grace."

"It's not as if you have to walk down a runway, darling. Just open the curtains and stand there. Anyone could do it, and you are tall and slim. And your red hair will go so nicely with the purple."

"Oh, dear. All right," I said.

It took Belinda a good two hours to breakfast, bathe, and get dressed, so that it was noon by the time we made our way back to Belgrave Square. This time there were two police cars parked outside Rannoch House, a constable standing on guard, and—horror of horrors—gentlemen of the press, complete with cameras. I grabbed Belinda's arm.

"I can't be seen here. My picture would be in all the papers."

"You're quite right," Belinda said. "You go back to my place and I'll have to do it for you."

"But they might accost you," I said.

"I'll take that risk," she said with an enigmatic smile. "Brave dress designer fights to clear chum's name." The grin broadened. "A little publicity might be just what my business needs."

"Belinda, you will be careful, won't you? Don't say anything about our knowing de Mauxville, or that you're asking questions to try and prove our innocence."

"My dear, I shall be the soul of discretion, as always," she said. "See you in a jiffy."

Reluctantly I left her to her task—as I now remembered that she hadn't always been the soul of discretion at school—and went back to wait nervously at her mews cottage. Time ticked by and finally she arrived back at one thirty, looking smug. "I was only accosted by one reporter. I pretended I had just heard the news and come to hold your hand through the crisis. I was absolutely devastated to find you weren't there. I was awfully good."

"But did you find out anything?"

"One of the gardeners in the square saw your brother arrive on foot and then depart in a taxi. He couldn't tell what time but around the lunch hour, as he was sitting down with his cheese and pickle sandwiches at the time. A chauffeur at the corner house saw a dark-haired man in an overcoat going up the steps of Rannoch House."

"That would be de Mauxville. So he was alone?"

"One gathers so."

"So we now know that my brother and de Mauxville did not arrive together, also that de Mauxville didn't arrive at the same time as anyone else. That must mean that someone was there to let him into the house. Anything else?"

"The only other people the chauffeur remembered seeing were the window cleaners, working their way around the square."

"Window cleaners!" I said excitedly. "Absolutely perfect. A window cleaner could slip into the house through an open window, slip out again, and it wouldn't matter if he looked wet and bedraggled."

Belinda nodded. "You don't happen to know what firm of window cleaners is employed on the square, do you?"

"I don't. One doesn't notice window cleaners, unless they peer in one's bedroom when one is still in bed."

"I'll slip back to the square on our way to my salon. I'm sure to encounter a servant who will know. Then we can ring them up and find out who was working this morning."

"Good idea." I was feeling positively hopeful.

But by the time we reached the square, more press had arrived and there was not a servant to be seen. Reluctantly we had to continue to Belinda's salon. She glanced at her watch as we came to Hyde Park Corner.

"Damn, we're going to be late if we don't hurry."

"Should we hail a cab?" I asked.

"No need. It's just off Curzon Street."

"Mayfair? You pay to have your workshop in Mayfair?"

"Well, it's not exactly a workshop," Belinda threw back at me as she dodged between a bus, a taxi, and an elderly Rolls. "I have a little woman in Whitechapel who does the actual sewing for me, but Mayfair is where I meet my clients."

"Isn't the rent frightfully expensive?"

"Darling, the right sort of people wouldn't come if it was in Fulham or Putney," she said breezily. "Besides, my uncle owns practically the whole block. It's a dinky little place but just big enough for little *moi*. You'll love it."

Belinda had not been exaggerating. The place consisted of one room, carpeted, with a sofa and low glass table. A big gilt mirror had pride of place. Pictures of Belinda's creations and famous people wearing them hung on the walls. A couple of lovely bolts of silk were flung carelessly in a corner and the far end was blocked off by velvet curtains.

"You pop behind the curtains, darling, and change into the purple evening dress. It's an American lady and you know how impressed they are by royalty and it has that lovely coronationy feel. What's more, I'm sure I can make her come up with the cash in advance. I just hope she's not too large—that dress would make a large person look like a beached whale."

I pulled back the curtains and found a long purple dress hanging there.

"I've seen this dress before, surely," I said. "Didn't Marisa wear it at Primrose's wedding?"

"Similar, but not the same," Belinda said frostily. "I saw the idea and copied it. I expect Marisa paid a fortune for hers in Paris. I'm not above stealing other designers' ideas."

"Belinda!"

"Nobody need know," she said. "The wedding is over. The dresses will never be worn again and I'm sure no American ladies were present."

"Maybe they gate-crashed like us," I suggested.

"If they did, they can't afford my creations," Belinda said smugly. "Hurry up, she'll be here in a second."

I retreated behind the curtains and started to get undressed. It was dark and cramped with hardly enough room to move my arms. I heard a tap on the door when I was standing in my underclothes, wondering whether to put the dress on over my head or to step into it. I hastily stepped into it as I heard strident American tones echoing through the small room.

"People have been mentioning your name and I thought I'd just pop by, as I need something stunning for some upcoming functions. It has to be the very height of fashion, mind you. Important people will be present."

"I think I have something you're going to love," Belinda said at her most condescendingly British. "I have to tell you that royalty have worn my creations."

"Oh, my dear, I won't hold that against you, but please never use that as a selling point again. I immediately picture the dowdy duchess, looking like a Christmas pudding with a tiara on top, or that awful straight-backed queen of yours, looking as if her corset were made of reinforced steel and two sizes too tight."

It was all I could do to stay behind the curtain. The dowdy duchess she was referring to had to be Elizabeth of York, who was delightful, amusing, a fellow Scot whom I absolutely adored, and the queen was—well, she was the queen. Enough said.

"I'll tell you what I want, honey," the American woman went on. "I want an outfit suitable to be worn for cocktails at a smart nightclub—maybe for dancing afterward. Something avant-garde that will make all heads turn in my direction."

"I have the very thing," Belinda said. "One moment while I get my girl to model it for you."

She darted behind the curtain. "Quick. Out of the purple and into that black and white." She almost flung it at me, and disappeared again. I wriggled out of the purple, then tried to put on the black and white creation. In that confined darkness it was hard to see which way to attack it. Tentatively I stepped into it and started to wriggle it upward.

"Hurry up in there. We can't keep the customer waiting," Belinda called.

I struggled manfully. It was black satin with a long, very tight skirt, so tight I could hardly pull it over my thighs and hips. The upper part of the dress had something resembling a white waiter's dicky in the front that buttoned around the throat, and a low back.

"Aren't you ready yet?" Belinda called.

I left one button at the neck undone, hoping that wisps of hair would cover it, and came out. I could hardly walk and had to take teeny, tottering steps. Surely this wouldn't be practical for dancing and nightclubs. She'd never make it down the steps, for one thing. As I walked I noticed something flapping beside me, like a train, but at the side, not behind. Really, it was the strangest garment I had ever seen. The customer obviously thought so too.

"What in heaven's name?" she declared. "Honey, I have more derriere than she does. I'd never fit into something like that. And she looks as if she's about to fall over any second." This as I made a grab for the curtain and almost knocked over the potted palm.

Belinda had leaped up. "Wait, that's not right," she said. Then she shrieked. "It's supposed to be trousers, Georgie. You've got two legs crammed into one."

The American woman gave a shrill laugh. "What a dope," she said. "What you need is a new model, preferably French."

She had risen to her feet. Belinda leaped to her side. "You see, I didn't warn her. She'd never seen—"

The woman cut her off. "If you can't even get good help, honey, I don't hold out much hope for the end product." And she swept out, slamming the door behind her.

"What a rude woman," I said. "Do you have to put up with that sort of thing all the time?"

Belinda nodded. "It's the price one pays," she said. "But honestly, Georgie—who else but you would have tried to cram yourself into one trouser leg?"

"I had no time," I said. "And I warned you I was accident-prone."

She started to laugh. "You did, and you are. Oh, my poor sweet, take a look at yourself. I must say you look absolutely ridiculous."

I laughed for the first time in days.

$\mathcal{C}$hapter 17

It took quite a while to extract me from the trouser leg without ripping the seams.

"She'd have looked stupid in it anyway," Belinda said, glancing in the direction of the door. "Too old and too short."

"Who was she anyway?" I asked.

"The name's Simpson, I believe."

"Mrs. Simpson?"

"You know her?"

"My dear, she's the Prince of Wales's latest flame, the one I have to spy on at the house party next weekend."

"Spy? For whom?"

"The queen. She thinks David is becoming too interested in this Simpson person."

"Is she divorced, then? I gathered there was still a husband in tow."

"There is. Poor chap is dragged around for respectability's sake."

"I must say your family does exhibit awful taste in women," she commented. "Look at the old king and then your mother probably wasn't a suitable choice either."

"My mother was a darned sight more suitable than that woman," I said.

"I nearly burst out from behind the curtains and bopped her when she started insulting the family." I glanced up at the clock across the street. "Oh, Lord, is that the time? I have to go to the station to meet Binky. I want to make sure I speak to him before the police quiz him."

"All right then, off you go," Belinda said. "I'll tidy up in here, then I've another party tonight. I presume you'd like to stay with me again?"

"It's very kind of you. But if Binky wants to stay at the house and we are allowed to, I should keep him company there. I don't want him to feel all alone."

We parted ways. I paused for a cup of tea and a toasted tea cake, then had to fight the rush hour traffic when I made my way to King's Cross in time to meet Binky's train. I came out of the tube to hear the newsboys shouting, "Read all about it. Body in duke's bath."

Heavens, Binky would have a fit. I'd have to try and whisk him through the station without his noticing any of this. The express pulled in on time at five forty-five. I stood behind the barrier, watching anxiously. For a moment I thought he hadn't caught the train, but then I saw him, striding out in front of a porter who carried his ridiculously small overnight bag with some distaste.

"Quick, let's get a taxi." I grabbed his arm as he stepped through the barrier.

"Georgie, stop grabbing me. What's the rush?"

Suddenly a voice shouted, "There he is. That's the duke. He's the one," and people began to congregate around us. A flashbulb went off. Binky looked at me with utter panic in his eyes. I grabbed the overnight case from the porter, took Binky's hand and dragged him through the crowd, then shoved him into an arriving taxi, much to the annoyance of those waiting patiently in line.

"What on earth was that?" Binky asked, wiping the sweat from his brow with a monogrammed handkerchief.

"That, dear brother, is the London press. They've found out about the body. They've been camped outside the house all day."

"Oh, Lord. Well, that settles it. I'm going to my club. I'll not put up with that kind of rubbish." He tapped the glass. "Take us to Brooks, driver."

"What about me?" I demanded. "Did it occur to you that I can't go to your club?"

"What? Well, of course you can't. No women allowed."

"I'm currently sleeping on a friend's sofa, but it's dashed uncomfortable," I said.

"Look, Georgie, maybe you should go on home."

"I've told you, there are reporters camped out in the square."

"No, I meant home to Scotland, out of the way of all this unpleasantness," he said. "It would be the safest thing to do. Book a sleeper on tonight's Flying Scotsman."

"I'm not leaving you in the lurch," I said, thinking that any amount of policemen was preferable to being marooned alone with Fig. "And I think the police would be highly suspicious if I suddenly vanished, the way they are currently suspicious about your vanishing act."

"Oh, dear, are they? When I realized who was floating there, I thought they'd immediately assume that I did it, and then I thought if I'm up in Scotland, they can't suspect me, so I made a beeline for King's Cross and off I went."

"And left me to be their number one suspect!" I said indignantly.

"Don't be silly. They can't possibly suspect you. You're a mere slip of a girl. You wouldn't have the strength to drown a big chap like de Mauxville."

"Not alone. I could have had an accomplice."

"Oh, I suppose so. Didn't think of that. I must admit it did cross my mind that you might have arranged to do him in. After all, you were the one who talked about pushing him off the crag." He paused, then asked, "You didn't tell the police anything, did you?"

"I have nothing to tell them, Binky. I don't know what happened. All I know is that you were there in the morning and when I came back in the afternoon there was a body in our bathtub and you had vanished. In fact, since I seem to be involved in this, whether I like it or not, I wouldn't mind knowing the truth."

"I'm completely in the dark myself, old bean," he said.

"So you didn't arrange to meet with de Mauxville at the house?"

"Certainly not. Actually, it was the rummest thing—my club telephoned to say that some chap wanted to meet me there, right away. I went to the club but nobody there seemed to have any interest in me at all. I came home, went upstairs, wondered where I had left my comb, wandered into the bathroom, and saw someone lying in the bathtub. I tried to get him out; got rather wet and realized he was dead. I also realized who he was and I might not be the brightest chap in the world, but I realized the ramifications."

"So somebody lured you out of the house, brought de Mauxville there, and killed him," I said.

"Must have done."

"What did the person sound like?"

"I don't know. A bit muffled actually. He said it was the club calling and I assumed it was one of the hall porters. They've only got half their teeth and they are not always easy to understand."

"So it was an English voice?"

"What? Oh, definitely English, yes. Oh, I see. You're saying that it wasn't actually a club employee who called me. It was an imposter. What a perfectly despicable thing to do. So someone else must have wanted de Mauxville dead—but why arrange it at our house?"

"To implicate you, or us."

"Who on earth would want to do that?" He stared out of the cab window as we waited on the corner of Baker Street. I looked across at the place where 221B should have been, and wished it had been real. A good detective was exactly what I needed at this moment.

"Do you think they've discovered the letter yet?" Binky asked in a small voice.

"I happen to have destroyed the original. It was the first thing I thought of. I went through his pockets, found it, and flushed it down the lav."

"Georgie, you're brilliant!"

"Not quite brilliant enough. I'd forgotten that our solicitors still have a copy and there may be other copies lying around."

"Oh, cripes. Hadn't thought of that. It won't look too good for us if the police find a copy, will it?"

"It won't look too good for you, Binky. You're the one who fled the scene of the crime. You're the one who possesses the strength to have drowned him."

"Oh, come on, old bean. You know I don't go around drowning people, not even rotters like de Mauxville. You don't think you could tell the police that I left town before all this happened?"

"No, I couldn't. I'm not lying for you, Binky. And besides, all sorts of people will know exactly when you left—porters and taxi drivers and ticket collectors. People do notice when a duke travels, you know."

"Do they? Oh, blast. What do you think I should do?"

"Unfortunately you were seen coming back to Rannoch House and then departing again in a taxi, so you can't claim that you'd been at your club or already left. I suppose you could say that you never went upstairs—you were catching the midday train for Scotland—you came home only to pick up your suitcase in the front hall. That might work."

"They won't believe it, will they?" He sighed. "And they'd find out about the letter and I'll be doomed."

I patted his hand. "We'll sort this thing out one way or another. Everyone who knows you can testify that you're not the violent type."

"Too bad it's Saturday. We'll have to wait until Monday to go to our solicitors'."

"Do you think we can persuade them not to mention the letter?"

"I've no idea." Binky ran his hands through his unruly mop of hair. "This is a nightmare, Georgie. I don't see any way out of it."

"We'll have to find out who really did it," I said. "Now think, Binky. When you left the house, did you lock the door after you?"

"Not sure. I'm not very good at locking doors, because there are always servants around."

"So the murderer could have walked up the front steps and entered the house with no problem. Did you notice anybody in the square when you left?"

"Can't say I did. The usual—chauffeurs hanging around, nannies pushing prams. I believe I said good morning to that old colonel from the corner house."

"What about window cleaners?" I asked. "Were the windows being cleaned when you were there?"

"I don't notice window cleaners. I mean, one doesn't, does one."

"Do you happen to know what firm we employ?"

"No idea. Mrs. McGregor is the one who pays the bills. She'd have it in her housekeeping journal, but that's probably with her in Scotland."

"We must find out," I said. "It may be important."

"Window cleaners? Do you think they saw something?"

"I mean that the murderer could have disguised himself as a window cleaner to gain access to the house."

"Oh, I see. You know, you're dashed clever, Georgie. What a pity you're the one with the brains. I'm sure you'd have made a splendid go of Castle Rannoch."

"I'm afraid I'll need every ounce of brainpower that I possess to get us out of this mess."

He nodded gloomy agreement.

The taxi pulled up outside the imposing entrance of Brooks's. The doddering porter hobbled down the steps to take Binky's bag.

"Welcome back, your lordship," he said. "May I offer my commiserations in such a distressing time. We have been gravely concerned for your safety. The police have been here asking for you more than once."

"Thank you, Tomlinson. Don't worry. It will all soon be sorted out." He gave me a valiant smile and followed the old man into the building. I was left standing on the pavement alone.

Chapter 18

I waited for Binky to reappear but he didn't. Really, men are too hopeless. Wrapped up in themselves from the day they are born. I put it down to a public school education. It would serve him right if he was arrested, I thought, then immediately regretted it. Anyone who had gone straight from the rigors of Gairlachan school to Brooks club couldn't be expected to know any better.

I stood on the pavement outside Brooks, watching a parade of taxies and Rolls-Royces go past as the fashionable set headed out to evening functions, and I wondered what to do next. Belinda was going out for the evening. Rannoch House was teeming with police and reporters. I was beginning to feel rather lost and abandoned, when there was the sound of a siren and a police car pulled up beside me. Out of it stepped Inspector Sugg. He tipped his hat to me.

"Evening, miss. I understand that your brother has just arrived back in town."

"That's correct, Inspector. He's just gone into his club."

"I'd like a word with him, if I may, before he settles down for the evening," he said and strode up to the front door.

Good luck, I thought, and expected him to be repelled from that bastion as I had been. But in no time at all Binky appeared, with Inspector Sugg following on his heels.

"We're just on our way to Scotland Yard for a little chat," the inspector said. "This way, if you please, sir."

"It's 'Your Grace,' " Binky said.

"What?"

"One addresses a duke as 'Your Grace.' "

"Does one?" Inspector Sugg was clearly not impressed. "I haven't had the pleasure of arresting too many dukes in my career. Into the backseat, if you don't mind."

Binky shot me a frightened glance. "Aren't you coming along too?"

"I didn't think you needed me," I said, still rankled by his lack of sensibility.

"Good Lord, yes. Of course I need you."

"It might be useful to have you there too, miss," Sugg said. "Certain facts have come to light . . ."

He knows about the letter, I thought.

Binky stood aside to help me into the car. "Oh, and for the record, Sergeant, my sister is 'her ladyship.' "

"Is she, now? And I'm 'Inspector,' not 'Sergeant.' "

"Are you really?" Binky gave the smallest of smiles. "Fancy that."

Sometimes I think he's not as dense as he makes himself out to be.

We set off, mercifully without the bell ringing. But it was an odd feeling when we passed through the gate of New Scotland Yard. Visions of my ancestors going to the Tower flashed through my mind, even though I knew that Scotland Yard had no dungeons and no chopping block. We were escorted up a flight of stairs and into a drab little room that looked out onto a courtyard and smelled of stale smoke. The inspector pulled out a chair for me on the far side of a desk. I sat. Binky sat. The inspector surveyed us, looking rather pleased with himself, I thought.

"We've been searching for you, Your Grace," he said, stressing the last two words. "Looking all over."

"Nothing hard about finding me," Binky said. "I was at home in Scotland. I went back yesterday and it's damned inconvenient to have to turn around because some fellow drowned himself in my bathtub."

"Not drowned himself, sir. I imagine that someone helped him. So was he a friend of yours?"

"I really can't tell you that, Inspector, since I haven't had a chance to look at the blighter."

I glanced at Binky. That good old Rannoch and royal blood certainly comes through in moments of crisis. He sounded quite "we are not amused."

"You mean to tell me you didn't see the body in your bathtub?"

"Absolutely. Rather. That's precisely what I mean."

I glanced at him. He was sounding a little too emphatic.

The policeman obviously thought so too. "If you hadn't seen him in the bathtub, sir, how did you know he was a blighter?"

"Anyone who has the nerve to die in my bath without my permission has to be a blighter, Inspector," Binky said. "If you must know, the first I knew about it was when my sister telephoned me with the news."

"If I tell you the gentleman's name was Gaston de Mauxville, does that ring a bell?"

"De Mauxville? Yes. I know that name." Again he was sounding too hearty.

"I believe he was an acquaintance of our late father, wasn't he?" I cut in.

"De Mauxville. Yes. I met him once or twice."

"Recently?"

"Not that recently."

"I see. So would it surprise you to know that a note was found in that gentleman's hotel room inviting him to speak with you on a matter of great urgency at eleven o'clock yesterday at your London address?"

"Not only would it surprise me but I can tell you that I wrote no such note," Binky said in his best ducal tones. Again our great-grandmother would have been proud.

"I happen to have the note here." The inspector opened a folder and pushed a sheet of paper in front of us. "This was delivered by hand to Claridge's yesterday morning and taken up to Monsieur" (he pronounced it "Mon-sewer") "de Mauxville's room."

Binky and I looked at it.

"Certainly a forgery," Binky said.

"And how can you tell that, sir?"

"For one thing, I only write on paper embossed with my crest. This is cheap stuff that one would buy in Woolworths."

"And for another," I said, "it's signed 'Hamish, Duke of Rannoch.' My brother signs letters just plain 'Rannoch' to social equals, and if he were to include his full title, it would be 'Duke of Glen Garry and Rannoch.' "

"And what's more, it's not my handwriting," Binky said. "Close, I'll agree. Someone has tried to imitate my style, but I cross my *t*s differently."

"So you are maintaining that this note was not sent by you."

"Precisely."

"So what happened when the gentleman showed up on your front door-step?"

"I have no idea. I wasn't home. Let me see. Where was I?"

"You were planning to go home to Scotland, Binky," I reminded him.

"That's right. I had packed my bags ready to leave when I received a telephone call asking me to come to my club on a matter of urgency. Naturally I went straightaway and found that no such message had been sent. I chewed the fat with a couple of friends and then came back to Rannoch House in time to pick up my bag from the front hall and take a taxi to the station." It did rather sound as if he were rattling off his lines, the way one does in a school play.

"How very convenient, sir."

"It's 'Your Grace.' "

"As you say, sir." He looked from my brother to me. "You know what I think? I think the two of you are in this together. Why would a duke and his sister come to London alone, leaving all their servants behind, if it was not for something underhanded?"

"I've already told you that I left my maid behind and hadn't had enough time to hire a new one," I said, "and my brother was only down on business for a couple of days. He took his meals at his club."

"But who dressed him?" The inspector was smirking now. "Don't you upper-class folks all need valets to help you dress?"

"When one has been to a school like Gairlachan one has learned to stand on one's own feet," Binky said frostily.

"Besides," I said, "what possible motive could the duke and I have in wanting to kill a strange Frenchman?"

"Plenty of motives come to mind, your ladyship." These last words dripped with sarcasm. "This man was known to be a gambler. He was seen in one of the city's most notorious gambling haunts this week. Maybe your brother had run up gambling debts that he couldn't afford to repay. . . ."

"My dear man," Binky spluttered, rising to his feet. "I can barely afford to keep my place in Scotland running. It takes every penny of my meager income to feed my cattle and my staff. We don't heat the place. We live with incredible frugality. I assure you I have never gambled in my life!"

"All right, sir. As yet nobody has accused you of anything. We're merely putting together pieces of the puzzle. I think that's all for now. But I expect we'll want to speak to you again. Will you be staying at your house—without servants?"

"I'll be at my club," Binky said, "and Lady Georgiana, I believe, is staying with friends."

"We'll be in touch, sir." The inspector got to his feet. "Thank you both for coming in."

The interview was at an end.

"I thought that went rather well, don't you?" Binky said as we came out of Scotland Yard.

Rather well? This was rather like our ancestor, Bonnie Prince Charlie, saying that he thought the battle of Culloden went rather well. I wondered whether the men of our family line were unbridled optimists or just plain thick.

⁂

THE NEXT MORNING I awoke, with a definite crick in my neck, to see Belinda tiptoeing across the room.

"You're up early," I said drowsily.

"Darling, I haven't been to bed yet—or should one correct that to I haven't been to my own bed yet."

"So I take it the selection of males was preferable to last night's?"

"Absolutely, darling."

"Are you going to elaborate?"

"That would not be discreet. Suffice it to say that it was heavenly."

"And will you be seeing him again?"

"One never knows." Again a dreamy smile as she made for the stairs. "I am now going to sleep. Please do not wake me, even if a body turns up in my own bathtub."

She reached the bottom step then turned back to me. "There's going to be a fabulous party on a boat this evening. A real boat with a motor this time. We're going to take a picnic down the Thames to Greenwich, and you're invited, of course."

"Oh, I don't think—" I began but she cut me off.

"Georgie, after what you've been through, you need some fun. Let your hair down. Besides, there are certain people who will be most disappointed if you don't show up."

"What people?"

A beatific smile. She put a red-nailed finger to her lips. "Ah, that would be telling. We'll be taking a cab at five. See you then. Night night."

And she was gone, leaving me wondering which people hoped to see me. Probably thrill-seekers wanting to get the gory details on a murder story, I thought angrily. I wouldn't go. But then a ride down the Thames and a picnic in a park did sound heavenly. How long had it been since I'd truly had fun?

Until then I had already decided what I was going to do: I was going to ask help of the only person who could be of use to me—my grandfather. It was a glorious May Day with the sun shining down, the trees in blossom, the birds chirping madly, and pigeons whirling in flocks. The sort of day when one is glad to be alive, in fact. I caught the train to Upminster Bridge and walked back up the hill to Granddad's house. He looked half pleased, half startled when he opened the door and saw me standing there.

"Well, blow me down," he said. " 'Ello, my love. I've been worried sick about you. I read it in the papers this morning. I was thinking of going to the telephone kiosk and ringing you up."

"It wouldn't have done any good. I'm not at Rannoch House at the moment. It's swarming with police and reporters."

"Of course, it would be. It would be," he said. "Well, don't just stand there. Come in. Come in. What a terrible thing to have happened. What was it? He'd drunk too much?"

"No, I'm afraid he was murdered," I said. "But neither Binky nor I has a clue as to who could have done it. That's why I came down to see you. You used to be in the police force."

"Ah, yes, but just on the beat, ducks. 'Umble copper plodding his beat, that's what I was."

"But you must have been part of criminal investigations. You know how these things work."

He shrugged. "I don't see what I can do. Nice cup of Rosie Lee?" he asked, using the Cockney tradition of rhyming slang.

"Yes, please." I sat at his tiny kitchen table. "Granddad, I'm worried about Binky. He's the obvious suspect and the fact that he fled to Scotland on discovering the body won't help him."

"Does your brother have close ties with the murdered man?"

"Unfortunately one close tie." And I told him about the letter.

"Oh, dear me. Dearie me. That's not good, is it?" he said. "And you're sure your brother is telling you the truth?"

"Positive. I know Binky. When he lies his ears turn red."

Granddad picked up the shrieking kettle and poured the water into the teapot. "It seems to me you need to find out who else knew this chap was coming over to London. Who else he planned to meet while he was here."

"How would we do that?"

"Where was he staying?"

"Claridge's."

"Well, that makes it easier than a private house. Good hotels know everything about their guests—who visits them, where they ask a taxi to take them. We can go to Claridge's and ask a few questions. We can also take a look at his room."

"What would be the point of that? Wouldn't the police have searched it thoroughly?"

"You'd be surprised at what the police don't consider important."

"But it's two days now since he was murdered. Won't they have removed his things and cleaned out his room?"

"Possibly, but in my experience they don't rush these things, especially over the weekend. They'll want to make sure they haven't missed anything. And after the police have released his effects, they'd have to be stored somewhere until they have orders to ship them to a next of kin."

I shook my head, feeling as if I were about to face a horrible exam. "Even if his things are still in his room, who would let us in? They'd think it highly suspicious if I asked to go in there."

He looked at me, head tilted to one side in the cheeky Cockney way. "Who said anything about asking?"

"You mean break into his room?"

"Or find a way to get in. . . ."

"I can get my hands on a maid's uniform," I said, cautiously. "Nobody ever notices maids, do they?"

"That's the ticket."

"But, Granddad, it's still breaking and entering."

"Better than swinging on the end of a rope, my dear. As an ex-member of the force I shouldn't be encouraging this sort of thing, but it seems to me that you and your brother are in big trouble and desperate means are called for. I'll come along and have a little chat with the doorman and the bellboys. Some of them may still remember me from the time when I was on the beat."

"That would be brilliant," I said. "And another thing. I need to find out if real window cleaners were working in the square on Friday, and if so, who they were. I'd ask myself, but with all those reporters . . ."

"Think no more about it, my love. That much I can do for you. And I'd ask you to stay for lunch but I promised I'd go over to the widow next door. She kept on inviting me and I kept on refusing, and then I thought, Why not? What's wrong with a bit of company?"

"What's wrong indeed," I said. I reached across the table and took his hand. "Can she cook?"

"Not as good as your grandma, but she ain't bad. She ain't bad at all."

"Enjoy your lunch, Granddad."

He looked almost bashful. "She can't be after my money," he said with a wheezy laugh, "so it must be my good looks. Shall I meet you tomorrow, then? I'll find out about your window cleaners and then we'll go to Claridge's."

"All right," I said, feeling my stomach twisting itself into a knot. Posing as a maid to get into a person's room was serious business. If I was caught, I might well harm Binky's cause rather than help it.

Chapter 19

Belinda roused herself shortly before five o'clock and came downstairs looking stunning in red trousers and a black riding jacket. This immediately reminded me that I had nothing to wear, even if I could get into Rannoch House, which didn't seem likely. I lamented this to Belinda, who immediately opened up her wardrobe and fixed me up with a spiffing yachting outfit consisting of white skirt and blue blazer with white trim. It even came with a jaunty little sailor's cap. The result, when I looked in the mirror, was quite satisfying.

"Are you sure you don't want to wear this?" I asked Belinda.

"Good Lord, no. It's not exactly the height of fashion, darling. You can get away with it, of course, but if I were to be seen in it at Cowes, bang would go my reputation."

I thought privately that her reputation had probably gone bang already.

"Off we go, then," she said, slipping her arm through mine.

"Belinda, I'm very grateful for everything you're doing for me," I said.

"Darling, think nothing of it. I would have been expelled from Les Oiseaux many times over if you hadn't rescued me. And you are certainly in need of a friend at the moment."

I couldn't have agreed more. We took a taxi to the boat dock at Westminster pier, even though I suspect that neither of us had money to waste on taxis. But one had to arrive properly, as Belinda put it, and so we did.

The boat/ship/yacht currently tied up at the pier was large and sleek, bigger than any cabin cruiser I had seen—a sort of junior transatlantic liner. An awning had been erected on the rear deck (Is that called the poop? I'm not up in nautical terms). A gramophone was playing and couples were already dancing some kind of hop. I was so enthralled with the scene on board that I almost caught my foot in a rope lying across the top of the steps and would have sprawled forward if Belinda hadn't caught me.

"Careful," she said. "You don't want to arrive headfirst. Now go down the ladder backward and watch your footing. I really don't want to have to fish you out of the Thames."

"I'll try hard," I said. "Do you think I'll ever outgrow my clumsiness?"

"Probably not," Belinda replied with a grin. "If deportment classes, gym at Les Oiseaux, and climbing those crags in Scotland haven't cured you, I'd say you were destined to be clumsy for life."

I lowered myself down the ladder carefully. I hadn't reached the bottom step when hands came around my waist and lifted me to the deck.

"Well, look who's here," said a familiar voice and there was Darcy, looking devastating in a white open-necked shirt and rolled up sailor's trousers. "I'm glad Belinda persuaded you to come."

"So am I," I stammered, because his hands were still around my waist. To my annoyance I found myself blushing.

"Aren't you going to give me a hand, Darcy?" Belinda asked. Darcy let go of me.

"If you wish, although I thought you were capable of doing most things remarkably well."

There was something in the quick glance that passed between them that I couldn't interpret. It did cross my mind that his might have been the bed she shared last night. I was surprised at the rush of jealousy I felt. But then, I reasoned, why would she have insisted that I come this afternoon if she wanted him for herself?

"Come and meet our host," Belinda said, dragging me away. "Eduardo, this is my good friend Georgiana Rannoch. Georgie, may I present Eduaro Carrera from Argentina."

I found myself looking at a most suave gentleman, maybe in his late twenties, dark sleek hair, Ronald Coleman mustache, dressed impeccably in blazer and flannels.

"Señor Carrera." I held out my hand and he brought it to his lips.

"Delighted to welcome you on board my little tub, Lady Georgiana," he said in perfect English without trace of a foreign accent.

"Little tub!" I laughed. "Did you sail it all the way from Argentina?"

"No, I regret it was just from the Isle of Wight. Although she is supposed to be up to an Atlantic crossing. I have not been back to Argentina since my parents sent me to Eton. Obviously I'll have to go back sometime to take over the family business, but until then I make the most of the delights Europe has to offer." He let his gaze linger first on me then on Belinda in a most suggestive way. "Let me find you some champagne."

Belinda nudged me as he moved off. "See what I mean about charming foreigners? Any Englishman you meet would say, 'What-ho, old thing,' and start talking about the cricket or at most the hunting."

"He is rather dashing," I said.

"His mother's Argentine English. Between the two families they own half of Argentina. Not a bad catch at all."

"Are you angling yourself or are you telling me to cast my line?" I whispered.

She smiled. "Haven't decided yet, so feel free. My theory is always that all is fair in love and war." Again I wondered if she was referring to Darcy.

"So where did you meet Darcy?" I couldn't help asking. "Was it at the party last night?"

"What?" She appeared distracted. "Darcy? Oh, yes. He was there. He may be a little too wicked for you, Georgie, but I can tell you that he's certainly still interested. He asked a million questions."

"About what?"

"Oh, this and that. Of course everyone was speculating about the murder. They were all on your side, by the way. Nobody in the room could believe that Binky could drown anyone in a bathtub."

"Did they have any theories on who might have done the drowning?"

"None at all. But I can tell you that de Mauxville was not the most popular man in the world. Everyone agreed that he cheated at cards and did not behave like a gentleman. So I think it's safe to say he had his share of enemies."

"No suggestion as to who they might be?"

"If you mean did anyone own up to the murder, the answer is no. The murderer could be quite outside of our set. If de Mauxville has criminal connections it could be a falling-out of thieves."

"Goodness, I hadn't thought of that," I said. "But we'd have no way of checking up on criminals."

"Everyone got a glass in their hands?" Eduardo called. "Right-o. Take a seat and hold on tight so that we can cast off."

"Let's sit here, on the side, so that we'll get the heavenly breeze in our faces," Belinda said, hoisting herself up onto the rim of the boat with her feet on the teak seat. I followed suit. "I'm sure we'll be going very fast, if I know Eduardo. He also drives racing cars, and he flies."

"Like Peter Pan?"

She laughed. "A plane, darling. A dear, dinky little plane. He's promised to take me up sometime."

As if on cue a motor roared to life, making the whole boat throb with power.

"Ready to cast off," Eduardo shouted as someone rushed to release the ropes that held the ship fast to the jetty. Suddenly we took off with such force that I was thrown backward. I made a futile grab at the smooth side of the boat as I went flying off into the ice-cold water. Around me the water was churning madly and the thrashing of propellers boomed through my ears. Gasping, I fought my way to the surface. I'm a strong swimmer and wasn't particularly scared until I realized I was being dragged along. Something was wound tightly around my ankle and I couldn't reach it because of the speed at which I was being dragged. I fought to keep my head above water long enough to scream, but I couldn't without getting a mouthful of water. Surely someone must have seen what had happened. I had been surrounded by people. Belinda had been sitting right beside me. I waved my arms frantically. Then there was a splash, strong arms came around me, and the motor was mercifully cut. I was dragged back to the ship and hauled back on board. Everyone was making a big fuss of me, while I sat there, gasping and coughing like a landed fish.

"Are you all right?" Darcy asked, and I saw from his wet state that he had been one of those who dived in to save me.

"I think so," I said. "More shocked than anything."

"You're lucky you didn't bash your head on the side as you went in," another voice said and I looked up to see the stiff, upright form of Whiffy Featherstonehaugh. "Because then you'd just have gone under and we might never have noticed you."

I shivered. Whiffy patted my shoulder awkwardly. "Anyway, my dear

Georgie, I regret to inform you that there are no fish big enough in the Thames to warrant using you as bait," he said. The typical Englishman's way of offering sympathy. I noticed he was not wet.

Eduardo appeared with a blanket in one hand and a brandy in the other. "I'm so frightfully sorry," he said. "I can't think how that happened."

"It's just Georgie," Belinda said, helping to put the blanket around my shoulders. "Things seem to happen to her. Accident-prone, you know."

"Then I'll watch out for albatrosses on the voyage," Eduardo said. "Come down to the cabin and I'll find some dry clothes for you."

"So you have to almost drown a girl before you can lure her to your cabin these days, eh, Eduardo?" someone asked.

Everyone was making light of the episode, the way people do after they have had a fright. Belinda went down below with me and helped me into Eduardo's striped fisherman's jersey and a pair of baggy trousers about five sizes too big for me.

"Honestly, Georgie," she said, laughing and looking worried at the same time, "who else but you could fall off a boat with her foot tangled in a rope?"

"I can't imagine how it happened," I said. "The beastly thing was absolutely knotted fast around my ankle. I tried to get it off but I couldn't."

"I'm going to watch over you like a hawk for the rest of the trip," she said. "Now come back on deck and let's see if we can dry out your clothes."

"They are your clothes and I'm afraid they are rather the worse for being in Thames water," I said. "It tasted foul."

Darcy was waiting as I came out of the cabin. "Are you sure you're all right?" he said. "My God, you look like a drowned rat. Are you sure you wouldn't rather I took you home?"

I had to admit that I wasn't feeling too well. I must have swallowed gallons of Thames water and I was still shivering, probably with delayed shock.

"If you really don't mind," I said. "It might be best. But I don't want to spoil your afternoon."

"I am also, as you might notice, pretty darned wet," he said, "and Eduardo didn't offer to take me to his cabin and dry me off."

I laughed.

"That's better," he said. "You looked as if you were about to pass out a minute ago. Come on, let's see if Eduardo knows how to back this thing up."

A few minutes later we were moored, once again, at the jetty.

"Watch out for ropes this time," Belinda called after me. "See you tonight."

Darcy hailed a taxi.

"Belgrave Square, isn't it? What's the number?" he asked.

"I can't go home," I said dismally. "The police may still be there and anyway the house is surrounded by reporters and the morbidly curious."

"Then where are we going?"

"I've been sleeping on Belinda's sofa," I said. "I do have a change of clothes there and I can wash out the clothes she lent me before they are stained forever with this Thames water."

"You want to go back to Belinda's place?"

"I can't think where else to go right now," I said, and my voice wobbled. "The problem is that it's her maid's day off and I only know how to cook baked beans and I was so looking forward to a lovely picnic."

"I tell you what," Darcy said. "Why don't we go back to my place? Don't look like that. I promise to behave like a gentleman and there is good wine in the cellar and I know a great place to have a picnic. And I am about to catch pneumonia myself and you wouldn't want that, would you, especially after I dived into that awful water to rescue you."

"How can I refuse," I said. "And it does sound a lot better than baked beans."

The taxi now whisked us in the direction of Chelsea and stopped outside a pretty little blue and white shuttered house. "Here we are," he said.

Darcy opened the front door and ushered me through to a tiny living room. No heads or shields on the walls, no portraits of ancestors, just a couple of good modern paintings and comfortable sofas. This is how ordinary people live, I thought with a pang of envy, and I pictured myself living in a house like this with Darcy, doing the cooking and cleaning myself, and . . .

"Give me a second to go and change," he said. "If you want to rinse out those wet clothes there's a sink in the scullery."

Thanks to living alone at Rannoch House, I now knew where a scullery was to be found and went through a small, neat kitchen to the room beyond. Here I ran the sink full of water (hot water, oh, the bliss of it; I almost jumped in with the clothes) and plunged the clothes into it. When they came out, I did notice that the white skirt had now become light blue, but hoped it might go away when the garment dried. I opened the door to find a place to hang them and found myself beside the Thames. I was in a small, pretty garden with a tiny lawn and a tree that had just burst into leaf. Beyond was a jetty. I stood there entranced until I was found by Darcy.

"Now you've seen how the plebs live," he said. "Not bad, eh?"

"It's lovely," I said, "but didn't you say you were borrowing it?"

"Absolutely. I can't afford this kind of place. It belongs to a distant cousin of mine who chooses to spend his summers on the Med in his yacht. Fortunately I have cousins all over Europe, thanks to the Catholics' view on birth control. Stay here and I'll bring out the wine and whatever food I can rustle up."

Soon we were sitting on deck chairs in that little garden with cold white wine, ripe cheeses, crusty bread, and grapes. It was a warm evening and the setting sun glowed on the old brick of the walls. For a while I ate and drank in silence.

"This is heaven," I said. "Hooray for all your cousins."

"Speaking of cousins," Darcy said, "I gather that poor old Hubert Anstruther is not expected to last much longer. In a coma, so they say."

"Do you know him?"

"Went climbing a couple of times with him in the Alps. Didn't strike me as the kind of fellow that would let himself be swept away by an avalanche."

"Tristram is devastated," I said. "Sir Hubert was his guardian, you know."

"Hmph," was all he said to this.

"And neither Sir Hubert nor Tristram is my relative," I added. "My mother was married to Sir Hubert many husbands ago, which made Tristram and me almost related once, that's all."

"I see." There was a long pause while Darcy poured us another glass of wine. "So are you seeing much of that blighter Hautbois?"

"Darcy, I do believe you're jealous."

"Just keeping a protective eye on you, that's all."

I decided to strike back. "So I gather you were at a party with Belinda last night."

"Belinda? Yes, she was at the party. What a grand girl she is—heaps of fun. Not an inhibition in sight."

"She told me you might be too wild for me." I paused. "I wondered how she knew that."

"Did you, now? That would be telling."

He grinned at my obvious discomfort, then he leaned closer to me. "Are you going to let me kiss you tonight? Even though I'm wild?"

"You did promise to behave like a gentleman, remember."

"So I did. Here, let me fill that wineglass for you."

"Are you attempting to get me drunk so that you can have your way with me?" I asked, my own inhibitions miraculously melting with the first glasses of wine.

"I don't believe in that approach myself. I like my women to be fully aware of what they are doing so that they get the maximum enjoyment from it." His eyes, over his raised wineglass, were flirting with me. I was very conscious of those melting inhibitions.

I made an attempt to stand up. "It's getting rather cold out here, isn't it? Don't you think we should go inside?"

"Good idea." He picked up our glasses and the wine bottle, which was now miraculously empty, and went ahead of me into the house. I followed with the remains of the food. I was just setting it down in the kitchen when his arms came around my waist.

"Darcy!"

"I always think it's better to take 'em by surprise," he whispered, and started kissing the side of my neck in a way that made me go weak at the knees. I turned to face him and his lips moved to meet mine. I had been kissed plenty of times before, behind the potted palms at deb balls, in the backseats of taxies on the way home. There had even been a bit of groping thrown in, but nothing had made me feel like this. My arms came around his neck and I was kissing him back. Somehow my body seemed to know how to respond. I felt giddy with desire.

"Ow," I said as I was somehow backed into a cooker knob.

"Kitchens are damned uncomfortable places, aren't they?" He was laughing. "Come on, let's go and take in the sunset from upstairs. It's the most glorious view across the Thames."

He took my hand and started to lead me up the stairs. I floated behind him, half in a dream. The bedroom was bathed in a glorious rosy sunset and the waters of the Thames below sparkled like magic. Swans were swimming past, their white feathers tinged with pink.

"This is heavenly," I said again.

"I promise you it will be even more heavenly," he said and started kissing me again. Somehow we seemed to be sitting on the bed. But that was when the little alarm bells started going off in my head. I hardly knew him, after all. And it was just possible that he had spent last night with Belinda. Was that what I wanted for myself—a man who flitted from girl to girl, from one encounter to the next? And another thought alarmed me even more. Was I following in my mother's footsteps? Would I be starting down that long road that she took, moving from one man to the next with no home, no stability?

I sat up and took hold of Darcy's hands. "No, Darcy. I'm not ready for this," I said. "I'm not another Belinda."

"But I promise you'd like it," he said. The way he was looking at me almost melted my resolve again. I rather thought I might like it myself.

"I'm sure I would, but I'd regret it afterward. And with all that's going on in my life right now, this would not be the right time. Besides, I want to wait for a man who really loves me."

"How do you know I don't love you?"

"Today, maybe, but can you guarantee tomorrow?"

"Oh, come on, Georgie. Let go of that awful royal training. Life's for having fun. And who knows how it might turn out."

"I'm sorry," I said. "I should never have led you on. You did promise to behave like a gentleman."

"As for that"—he had such a wicked grin—"your relative King Edward was a perfect gentleman but by God he bedded half the females in his kingdom."

He took a look at my face and stood up with a sigh. "All right, then. Come on. I'll call a cab to take you home."

$\mathcal{C}$hapter 20

When I arrived back at Belinda's place that night, with more than a modicum of regret, I found a note from Binky, instructing me to meet him at our solicitors' office at ten o'clock. This could prove to be awkward if it went on too long, as I had arranged to meet my grandfather at lunchtime. To be on the safe side, I went into Rannoch House early in the morning to pick up the maid's uniform. This was a wise move as there was no sign of either police or journalists outside at that hour. The house felt very strange and horribly cold, although all traces of the body had been removed from the bath. But I found myself tiptoeing past the bathroom door under the watchful eye of that avenging statue.

As I took the maid's uniform out of my wardrobe, I heard something chink. I put my hand into the apron pocket and there was the figurine I had broken at the Featherstonehaughs'. So much had happened since, that I had completely forgotten about it. Oh, dear. Now I'd have to think of a way to have it mended and sneak it back. I just hoped they hadn't noticed it was missing among all those swords and gods and whatnots. I shoved it into the top drawer of my dressing table and put the maid's uniform into a carrier bag. I'd have to find a loo to change in somewhere along the way.

I was just leaving the house when the telephone rang.

"Georgie?" a male voice asked.

For a second I thought it was Binky, but before I could answer he went on to say, "It's Tristram. Sorry to ring you at this hour. Did I wake you?"

"Wake me? Tristram, I've been up for hours. Actually I'm staying with a friend and I just stopped at Rannoch House to pick up some things before I have to meet my brother at the solicitors'. You've heard the news presumably?"

"I saw it in the papers. I couldn't believe my eyes. What a rum do. Your brother's not the sort who goes around bumping off people, is he?"

"Absolutely not."

"So who could it have been? I was talking to Whiffy on the phone last night and we just couldn't imagine why someone would leave a body at Rannoch House. Do you think it was a poor sort of joke?"

"I've no idea, Tristram," I said.

"Rotten luck on you, anyway."

"Yes. It has been pretty rotten."

"And Whiffy tells me that you had a nasty accident yesterday. Fell off a boat and nearly drowned, so he says."

"Yes, things don't seem to be going too swimmingly at the moment," I said, trying to think how I could end this conversation politely.

"And Whiffy said you went off with that O'Mara fellow."

"Yes, Darcy was kind enough to escort me home," I said.

"I ballywell hope he behaved like a gentleman," Tristram said.

A smile twitched across my lips. "Tristram, I believe you're jealous of Darcy."

"Jealous. Good Lord, no. I'm just worried about you, old thing. And I make no bones about it: I don't trust that O'Mara. Nothing good ever came out of Ireland."

"Whiskey," I said, "and Guinness."

"What? Oh, rather. But you know what I mean."

"Tristram, Darcy is a peer of the realm and he behaved like one," I said firmly, thinking of the extraordinary ways I had known peers to behave. Before he could answer this I said briskly, "But I really have to run. I'm going to be late."

"Oh, right. I just wanted to offer my services, you know. See if there's anything I can do."

"It's sweet of you, but there's nothing, really."

"I suppose your brother is taking good care of you."

"My brother is at his club."

"Weally? If you wanted me to come and stand guard at night, I'd be happy to."

I had to chuckle at the thought of Tristram standing guard. "Thank you, but I'll probably continue to stay with my friend for a while."

"Good idea. Quite a relief to have someone keep an eye on you. I don't suppose you'd like to meet me later, so that I can take you for a bite to eat and cheer you up?"

"Thank you. You're very kind, but I don't think I'm in the mood for eating and I've no idea how long this will take."

"Right-o, then. I'll check in from time to time and see how you're getting along. Whiffy and I both want to help if we can. Toodle-oo, then. Keep your pecker up, old thing."

I hung up and hurried out to meet Binky. I was rather intrigued to know whether we might see Old Mr. Prendergast today and how he might look, until I was informed that he had been dead for ten years. Young Mr. Prendergast tut-tutted and sighed as he sat surveying us. "A bad business, Your Grace. A nasty business indeed."

"I give you my word my sister and I had nothing to do with it," Binky said.

"My firm has handled the legal affairs of your family for generations," the old man said. "Your word is enough for me."

"But you can see how bad it looks for us."

"I can indeed. Most unfortunate."

"We were wondering," Binky said, "whether you would have to tell the police about the letter—if they haven't yet found out about it. Because, I mean to say, that would really put the cat among the pigeons, so to speak."

"That is indeed a difficult ethical decision, Your Grace. Our loyalty to our clients versus withholding information in a criminal case. I should, of course, be obliged to answer any question truthfully, should the police choose to question me. That would include revealing the document. However, as to whether I feel it incumbent upon myself to volunteer information to the police that might incriminate my client—a client who has given me his word that he is innocent—then I think that I feel no such obligation."

Binky got to his feet and shook the old man's hand. I could hear the bones creaking.

"I think that went rather well," Binky exclaimed as we came out. "Care to go for a spot of lunch with me somewhere? Claridge's, maybe?"

"Claridge's?" It came out as a squeak. "I'd love to, but unfortunately I'm meeting my grandfather today. Remember he was in the police once. I'm hoping he'll have some advice for us and maybe still know some men at Scotland Yard."

"Spiffing. Super idea."

"And anyway I hear the food's not up to much at Claridge's these days," I added for good measure, just in case he decided he was going to take his luncheon there without me.

"You don't say? I always thought Claridge's was the tops," Binky said. "Oh, well. Might as well eat at the club and save money, then. Where will I find you, Georgie? And how long do you think I'm supposed to hang around down here? It's costing a fortune to stay at the club, you know. Those whiskey and sodas don't come cheap."

"You'll have to ask the police when it's all right for you to go home," I said. "And as to where you can find me, I'm thinking of moving back into the house. I was there this morning and the police have gone. So has the body."

"That's dashed brave of you, old bean. I don't think I could stomach it, somehow. And they do make one so blinking comfortable at the club."

With that we parted company, he into a taxicab and me down the steps of the underground at Goodge Street Station. I went one stop, then changed at Tottenham Court Road. I suppose I could have walked to Holborn and thus not had to change but it had started to rain and I had no wish to appear like a drowned rat.

I had ridden the underground so seldom in my life that I was always somewhat bewildered by the various passages and escalators leading from one line to the next. Tottenham Court Road was a hub of activity, with people running in all directions. Everybody seemed to be in a frightful hurry. I took the escalator down to the Northern Line, getting buffeted by people trying to push past me on the right. At last I found the right platform and stood at the front, waiting for the train. More and more people streamed onto the platform behind me. At last there came the rumbling of an approaching train. A wind came rushing ahead of it from the tunnel. Just as it appeared I was shoved hard from behind in the middle of my back. I lost my footing and went pitching forward toward the electric rails. It all happened so quickly. I hadn't even time to scream. Hands reached out and grabbed me and I was yanked back onto the platform again, just as the train thundered past me.

"Phew, that was a close one, miss," a large laborer said, as he stood me on my feet again. "I thought you was a goner then." He looked positively green.

"So did I," I said. "Someone pushed me."

I looked around. People were already streaming past us onto the train as if we didn't exist.

"They're always in so much of a bloomin' hurry, I'm surprised there aren't more accidents," my workman friend said. "There's too many people in London these days. That's the trouble. And those what's got motorcars can't afford to run them no more, what with the price of petrol."

"You saved my life. Thank you very much," I said.

"Don't mention it, miss. Probably wise not to stand too near the edge next time," he said. "You've only got to have one person stumble or shove behind you and you're off the edge, under a train."

"You're right," I said. "I'll be more careful."

I completed the journey, glad for once that Belinda wasn't with me. She'd definitely have something to say about my clumsiness getting out of hand. Although this time it hadn't been my clumsiness. I had been at the wrong place at the wrong time.

My fingers still trembled as I changed into my maid's uniform in the lady's lavatory at Charing Cross Station, but by the time I reached Claridge's, I had calmed down. It was lucky it was raining, as I could conceal my uniform under my mackintosh. As I approached Claridge's, I saw my grandfather's familiar form waiting for me.

"Hello, my ducks. How are you holding up, then?"

"All right," I said. "Apart from nearly being pushed under a train."

I saw the worried look cross his face. "When was this?"

"On my way from my solicitors'. I was at the front of a crowded platform and the crowd must have surged forward at the approach of a train. I was almost pushed in front of it."

"You want to be more careful, my love. London's a dangerous place," he said.

"I will be in future."

He looked at me for a moment, head cocked on one side, then he said, "Oh, well, I suppose we had better get on with what we came to do."

"Have you had a chance to speak to anybody yet?"

He touched the side of his nose. "Hasn't lost his touch, your old grand-dad. Still got what it takes. Knows how to butter 'em up. I went to your posh square first and I can tell you that there weren't no window cleaners working that day."

"So if somebody saw a window cleaner . . ."

"It was someone up to no good."

"Exactly what I thought. I wonder if they could describe him, or them?"

"Nobody notices tradesmen, my love."

"The same as nobody notices maids," I said. "I'm wearing my maid's uniform, but I have to find out which room and I have no idea how I can possibly get into it."

"As for that, it was room 317. And what's more, it ain't been cleaned out yet. Seems that the gentleman paid a week in advance and so they didn't like to shift his things without instructions."

"How did you manage to find out all that?"

He grinned. "Alf the doorman still remembered me."

"Granddad, you're a genius."

"See, your old granddad does still have his uses." He beamed at me.

"Anything else you can tell me?"

"Your Monsieur de Mauxville went out every night gambling—to Crockford's and to other places less savory. And he had a visitor. A dark-haired young man. Posh."

"Anything else?"

"Not yet. I thought I'd have a chat with the bellboys and you could ask the other maids on that floor."

"All right," I said. Now that it was about to happen, I was terrified. Breaking and entering were serious enough, but they would also make me look guilty in the eyes of Inspector Sugg. "How can I possibly get up the stairs without being noticed? People might recognize me."

"Fire escape. There always has to be a safe way out of a hotel."

"Here I go, then. You wouldn't like to come with me, I suppose?"

"I'd do a lot for you, my sweet, but not this. I'm an ex-policeman and a nobody. The law would treat me very differently from you, if we're caught. I've no wish to spend the rest of my days in Wormwood Scrubs."

"I'm not too anxious to do so either," I said and he laughed.

"Wormwood Scrubs is a men's prison. But they'd let you off, being who you are and knowing you were just trying to help your brother."

I nodded. "I sincerely hope so. Wish me luck, then," I said. "I'll meet you back here in an hour."

I made it up the fire escape staircase with no problem, left my mack rolled up in a corner, put on my maid's cap, and came out onto the third floor. Then, of course, it occurred to me that I had no way to get into the room. I clearly hadn't thought this thing through properly. I wandered down the hall, trying the door handles, until a voice behind me made me jump out of my skin.

"Hey, you, what are you doing?"

I turned around to see a fresh-faced Irish girl in a maid's uniform quite unlike my own. I decided to change my story rather rapidly.

"My mistress was staying here last night and her diamond earring must have fallen off while she was asleep. She doesn't usually go to bed with earrings on, but she got in so late. So she's asked me to retrieve it. But nobody answers the door so the master must have also left by now."

"What room was it?"

"Three seventeen."

She looked at me queerly. "Three seventeen was that French gentleman who was murdered," she said.

"Murdered? Here?"

"Don't you ever read the papers? Not here. In some duke's bathtub. Anyway, the police came and gave his room a good going-over."

"Did they find anything?"

"How would I know? They'd not have told me, would they?"

"So did you have to pack up all his things?"

"Not yet. They're still in there, as far as I know, and the police have given orders that no one is to go in."

"How terrible that he got killed. Was he a nice man?"

"Quite the opposite. Rude and ungrateful, from what I saw. He snapped his fingers and shouted at me because I'd moved the papers on his desk."

"What kind of papers?"

"Nothing special. Just some magazines he'd been reading. You'd have thought I'd been snooping." She brushed down her uniform. "Anyway, I can't stand here chatting. I have to get back to work."

"And I have to find that earring or risk getting my head bitten off. My memory's hopeless. Could it have been 217? Any idea where Lord and Lady . . . " I let the rest of the sentence hang, hoping she'd take the bait. She did.

"Lady Furness? That was 313."

"Oh, thank heavens. I'd never have heard the last of it if I returned home without her earring. Do you think you could let me in?"

"I suppose so, but I really ought to—"

"Look, Lady Furness is lunching with a friend in the restaurant downstairs. Do you want me to go and find her to tell you that it's all right for me to go in there?"

She looked at me long and hard, then she said, "No, I suppose it can't do no harm, can it? But the bed's already been stripped. If it hasn't been found yet, chances are it's not going to be."

"A little diamond could have fallen down the back of the bed and nobody would notice it," I said. "Anyway, I've been commanded to search and search I'd better, or else. You should see her when she gets rattled."

She grinned at me then. "Go on, then, in you go and make sure you shut the door firmly behind you. I don't want to get in trouble for leaving a door open."

"Oh, definitely. I'll make sure I shut it," I said. "I'll even keep it shut while I'm searching."

She opened the door. I went inside and shut it behind me. I wasn't quite sure what use it was being in room 313, but it was better than nothing. I opened the window and saw that there was a broad ledge running around the outside. If the window of 317 was not latched tightly, it was possible I might get in that way. I climbed out gingerly onto the ledge. It was certainly a long way down. I could see the parade of bright red buses passing below me along the Strand. And that broad ledge didn't seem so broad any longer. I didn't have the nerve to stand up. I started to crawl slowly along the ledge. I passed 315 successfully and reached 317. It was hard to get any purchase on the window frame from my precarious position, but at last I felt it give a little.

I managed to raise it, then crawled inside and stood, breathing very hard, on the carpet of the deserted room. As the maid had said, the room had been stripped since de Mauxville left. No sheets, no towels. There were still papers on the desk in a neat pile. I went through them but found only a three-day-old copy of the *Times*, and some sporting magazines. His wastebasket had been emptied. No telltale marks on the blotting paper. I looked under his bed but the floor was spotless. I opened the chest of drawers but they only contained some rather gray undergarments and a pair of socks in need of darning. The handkerchiefs, however, were embroidered with a crest. Then I went through his wardrobe. A dinner suit was hanging there, and a couple of clean white shirts. I tried the pockets of the dinner jacket and found nothing. But when I put it back on the hanger, it just didn't hang correctly. Gentlemen's suits should be tailored to perfection and not droop. I tried pockets again and found that the lining was torn on one inside pocket. I traced down the tear in the lining and brought out a roll of paper. I let out a gasp when I saw what it was: a tight roll of banknotes—five pound notes, hundreds of them—well, maybe not hundreds but a big fat wad of them. I stood there staring at the money. To someone like me, who had been penniless most of her life, it represented a fortune. Who would know if I took it? The words echoed through my head. Ill-gotten gains of a dead man—surely nobody would ever find out. But then my ancestors, both sides of them, triumphed. Death Before Dishonor.

I was about to put them back when I realized I might be handling evidence and I was busily leaving my fingerprints all over them, and all over the room! I couldn't believe my stupidity. I didn't know whether the police could test things like money for fingerprints, but I wasn't going to take a chance. Hastily I wiped the roll with my apron and put it back. Then I went around the room, wiping every surface I had touched.

There was a notepad beside the telephone. It appeared unused, but as the light struck it I could tell that there was an imprint on the top sheet as if the writer had pressed too hard as he wrote. I went over to the window and held the sheet up.

It said, *R—10:30!*

I wondered if the police had torn off that top sheet. Even the least intelligent policeman would be able to deduce that *R* meant "Rannoch." Things didn't look good for Binky unless I could find out where these large sums of money came from.

The room revealed no more secrets and I made my way back onto the ledge, carefully closing the window behind me. I started to crawl back. I had just reached the window of number 315 when I heard voices in the room. I froze. To my horror I heard someone say, "Isn't it stuffy in here?" and there came the sound of the window being opened. I scrambled to my feet and stood to one side of the window, pressing myself against the drain-pipe, holding on for dear life. A young sandy-haired man looked out. I heard him say, "There, are you satisfied now?" and he moved away again. Now I had to risk crossing an open window or going back into 317 and risk being seen coming out.

I decided on the latter. As I tried to kneel down again the drain-pipe moved with me. It started to come away from the wall. I clawed at the stonework on the building and grabbed on to it. I suppose I must have screamed because a voice behind me asked, "What the devil are you doing?" and it was the young man with the sandy hair peering out of the window.

"Sorry, sir. I dropped my feather duster out onto the ledge when I was shaking it," I said. "And when I climbed out to get it, I couldn't get back in again."

"My dear girl. A feather duster isn't worth risking your life for," he said. "Here. Give me your hand and come inside here." He helped me step down into his room.

"Thank you, sir. You're most kind," I said in what I hoped was an Irish accent.

He reached into his waistcoat pocket and drew out a sovereign. "Here, that should buy you a new feather duster so that you don't get into trouble."

"Oh, no, sir. I couldn't."

"Take it. I've had rather a successful week, as it happens." He forced it into my hand.

"Thank you, sir. Very generous of you."

I nodded to the young woman who appeared from the bathroom and made a hurried exit. There was no sign of the Irish maid.

I hummed to myself as I put on my mack and made my way down the stairs. A sovereign for my pains. Maybe I should think of working in a hotel!

Chapter 21

My grandfather was waiting for me, standing under the awning while the rain came down. Unfortunately he had nothing much to report. I told him about the five-pound notes and suggested that he should call the police with an anonymous tip about de Mauxville's gaming. I felt the least I could do was treat him to lunch, and almost had to drag him to Lyons Corner House. I tried to be jolly and bright but he looked worried and preoccupied the whole time. When we parted company he looked at me long and hard. "Take care of yourself, won't you, and if you'd rather come and stay with me, then you know you're more than welcome."

I smiled at him. "That's sweet of you, Granddad, but I have to stay in town to keep an eye on Binky, and to find out things."

"I suppose so," he said with a sigh. "But watch out for yourself."

"Don't worry about me. I'll be fine," I said with more bravado than I felt. I looked back once and saw him standing there, watching me.

When Belinda did her Lady Macbeth routine down the stairs about two o'clock, I told her of my decision to move back to Rannoch House.

"Georgie, are you sure?" she asked.

"I went back this morning. All traces of the body have been removed and it seems silly to go on sleeping on your sofa when I have a perfectly good bed of my own."

"I think it's awfully brave of you," she said, but I could tell she was relieved.

"I do have one teeny favor to ask," I said. "Do you think you would mind keeping me company tonight? I'm not sure how hard it will be and I'd really appreciate knowing you were there with me for the first night at least."

"You want me to stay at Rannoch House?" I could see she was struggling. Then she said, "Of course. Why not? It's about time I had an early night with no parties. I saw bags starting to form under my eyes when I looked in the mirror."

So that evening, after the press and any gawkers had gone home, we made our way up the steps and into the house.

"This place has always struck me as creepy at the best of times," Belinda said. "It's always so cold and damp."

"Compared to Castle Rannoch it's a furnace," I said, laughing uneasily because I too found it cold and damp. I was about to suggest that we go back to Belinda's comfortable mews again, until I reminded myself that a Rannoch never runs away from danger. We undressed and prepared for bed, then I went downstairs and poured us both a Scotch to bolster our spirits. We sat on my bed, talking about anything rather than turning the light out.

"My dear, I'm dying to hear the details on last night," Belinda said. "I almost woke you when I got home. You did have a lovely smile on your face so I could only conclude that Mr. O'Mara had revealed to you the mysteries of life and love."

"He wanted to."

"But you didn't?"

"It wasn't that I didn't. As a matter of fact I did. Very much."

"Then why didn't you?"

"I just couldn't go through with it. I realized that he wasn't suitable husband material and I had this horrible vision of ending up like my mother."

"But she's had plenty of husbands."

"But I want somebody who's going to love me and stick with me for the rest of my life."

"Darling, how terribly old-fashioned. And someone has to relieve you of this frightful burden you carry. Who better than Darcy?"

"You can recommend him, can you?"

She looked at me and gave a delightful peal of laughter. "Oh, so that was it! You thought that Darcy and I—and you didn't want to tread on my toes. Aren't you sweet."

I didn't like to mention that I didn't want shop-soiled goods.

At that moment a great blast of wind came down the chimney. The storm had been building all day and we looked at each other in alarm.

"You don't think his ghost is lingering here, wanting vengeance, do you?" Belinda asked.

"Castle Rannoch is full of ghosts. I'm used to them."

"Really? Have you ever actually seen one?"

"Sort of. You know, when you are aware of something out of the corner of your eye."

"Does it really go awfully cold before they appear?"

"You can't tell at Castle Rannoch."

There was a clattering noise on the street below.

"What was that?" Belinda asked nervously.

I went to the window. "I can't see from here," I said.

"It sounded as if it was close. Maybe in your basement area."

"It's probably only a cat or a rubbish bin blown over. But we can go down and see."

"Are you mad? A killer has been in this house."

"Belinda, there are two of us, and we'll take something to hit him with. The house is full of weapons. Take your pick."

"All right." She didn't sound all right at all, but suddenly I felt very angry. My whole life had been turned upside down. My brother was suspected of a crime and I wanted this over. I stamped down the stairs, grabbing an assegai that a family member had brought back from the Boer War.

We made our way down to the kitchen, not turning on the light to warn whoever it was. Halfway across the kitchen floor a shadow of a man outside the window was thrown across the room and we leaped into each other's arms.

"Enough stupid bravery. Call the police," Belinda hissed and I couldn't help but agree with her. We crept to the phone and called the police, then waited clinging on to each other as if we were in a storm-tossed ocean. At last I thought I heard shouts and a scuffle and then a thunderous knock at our front door. I opened it a crack and saw with relief two constables standing there.

"We've caught someone snooping around your house, my lady," one of them said. I recognized him as the constable from the other night.

"Good work, Constable. It may be the man who broke in and killed the Frenchman. Where is he?"

"Bring him over here into the light, Tom," my constable instructed.

A fellow constable appeared, forcing in front of him a man in a raincoat. I looked at him and let out a shout. "Granddad! What are you doing here?"

"You know this man, my lady?"

"It's my grandfather."

He released Granddad. "Sorry, sir, only the young lady called us to say she heard noises outside."

"No offense, Constable. My granddaughter had no idea that I'd be here."

"I'm glad you are here now," I said. The constables departed and Granddad came inside. We all poured ourselves another Scotch to calm our nerves and sat in the morning room.

"What were you doing here?" I asked. "You scared us to death when we saw your shadow outside."

He looked sheepish. "I was worried about you, so I decided to come and keep an eye on you. Just in case."

"You think I'm in danger?"

He nodded. "Listen, my love. I've lived in London all my life and I can only think of one or two accidents on the tube lines. People don't fall off platforms very easily."

"What do you mean?"

"I mean that somebody might be trying to kill you."

"Kill me—why?"

"I've no idea, but it did cross my mind that the person who murdered that Frenchie might have thought he was killing your brother."

"Oh, surely not." Even as I said it I realized that they were about the same build.

"Well, I for one am glad that your grandfather is here," Belinda said, getting up and yawning. "Let's make a bed up for him and we can all get some sleep."

※

I LAY LISTENING to the storm blustering outside, the rain peppering the windows, the wind howling down the chimney. Given the perpetual gales at Castle Rannoch I should have been immune to a mild London storm, but this night I was so tense that I jumped at every noise. I tried to tell myself that, now Belinda was sleeping beside me, now my grandfather was here, everything was all right. But he had injected a new and alarming facet into this nightmare: the suggestion that someone was trying to kill me. Also that someone might have mistaken de Mauxville for Binky. I racked my brains but I had no idea who or why. We weren't the sort of people who had enemies. We were too far from the throne to warrant bumping us off. We were well behaved to the point of being boring.

I relived that moment on the tube platform, trying to remember if I had seen any vaguely familiar face in the crowd, but the whole thing was just one big blur. One thing was very clear, however: but for that giant of a workman standing on the platform beside me, I should be dead by now.

Then I realized something else: the accident on the boat the night before. I sat up in bed, every muscle tense. It had been no accident. I might be clumsy, but how could a rope have wound itself so tightly around my ankle that I couldn't undo the knot, unless somebody had deliberately tied that rope? I realized that I had been sitting on the side of the boat, with loads of other people standing and sitting around me. We'd all been having a good time and truthfully I would probably not have noticed if someone had eased a rope around my ankle and then given me a shove at the right moment. Someone I knew, then. One of my own set. I felt cold all over.

"Belinda," I whispered and nudged the shape beside me.

"Mmmm," she grunted, already deeply asleep.

"Belinda, wake up. I need to know who was on that boat."

"Wha . . . boat?"

"The one I fell off. Belinda, wake up, do. I need to know exactly who was on that boat. You were there the whole time."

She turned over, grunting, and half opened her eyes. "The usual crowd," she said, "and some friends of Eduardo. I didn't know them all."

"Tell me who you did know. People who knew me."

"I really don't know who knew you. Whiffy Featherstonehaugh, for one. And Daffy Potts was there, and Marisa, the girl who got so drunk at the wedding. Apart from that I can't really say. Now can I go back to sleep?" And she did.

I lay listening to her breathing. Whiffy Featherstonehaugh. Wasn't he the one who had helped Eduardo with the ropes, climbing on board at the last minute with a rope in his hand? But what kind of grudge could he possibly have against Binky or me? I did remember that he hadn't been wet when he spoke to me. He had not dived in to save me.

$\mathcal{C}$hapter 22

I woke with a start as a hand touched me.

"It's all right, my love. Only me," came my grandfather's calm voice, "but you're wanted on the telephone."

Sun was streaming in through the window. The storm had blown itself out during the night. I got up and slipped on my dressing gown, then I padded downstairs to the front hall.

"Hello?"

"Georgie, it's me, Binky," came the voice. "I'm at Scotland Yard. They've arrested me."

"Arrested you? They're mad. They have no evidence. They are just clutching at straws. What do you want me to do?"

"For one thing get in touch with Prendergast. I tried phoning but there's nobody in their office yet."

"Don't worry, Binky. I'll come to Scotland Yard immediately and get things sorted out. It's that bumbling Inspector Sugg. He can't see an inch past his face. We'll have you out of there in no time at all."

"I hope so." Binky sounded desperate. "I jolly well hope so. I mean, hell's bells, Georgie. This shouldn't happen to a chap. It's humiliating, that's what it is—being dragged in like a common criminal. They've even taken away my Conway-Stewart fountain pen with the gold nib that I got for my twenty-first. Apparently they thought I might want to stab myself with it.

And I shudder to think what Fig will say when she finds out. In fact, hanging sounds rather preferable to facing her."

I had to smile in spite of the gravity of the situation. "Hang on, Binky, and don't say anything until our solicitor is with you. I'm coming over right away."

I rushed upstairs and threw on a smart town suit—the sort of thing I'd use for opening bazaars. One had to look the part today. Then I wrote out a message for Young Mr. Prendergast and asked my grandfather to telephone his office on the stroke of nine thirty. I managed to drink a few sips from the cup of tea Granddad pressed on me then hailed the nearest taxi for Scotland Yard, which I entered like a ship in full sail.

"I am Lady Georgiana Rannoch. I have come to see my brother," I said.

"I'm afraid that's not possible," I was told by a burly sergeant. "He's being interviewed as we speak. If you'd care to take a seat and wait?"

"I wish to speak with Inspector Sugg's superior officer immediately," I said. "It is vitally important."

"I'll see what I can do, your ladyship," the sergeant said.

I sat and waited in a grim hallway. After what seemed like hours I heard the brisk tap of shoes on the floor and a man came toward me. He was wearing a well-tailored suit, crisp white shirt, and a striped tie. I couldn't immediately identify the school but I wasn't going to hold that against him at this point.

"Lady Georgiana?" he said. He sounded as if he'd been to the right sort of school.

I got to my feet. "That's right."

"I'm Chief Inspector Burnall." He held out his hand to me. "Sorry to keep you waiting. If you'd like to come this way?" He led me up a flight of stairs and into a spartan office.

"Please do take a seat."

"Chief Inspector," I said, "I understand that my brother has been arrested. This is absolutely ridiculous. I do hope you can instruct your junior officers to let him go immediately."

"I'm afraid I can't do that, my lady."

"Why not?"

"Because we have enough evidence in our possession to believe that your brother was the most likely person to have murdered Mr. de Mauxville."

"I have one word for you, Chief Inspector. Balderdash. All you have is a note purporting to come from my brother, which is an obvious forgery. There must be fingerprints on it. You can analyze the handwriting."

"We have done so. There are no fingerprints but de Mauxville's, and it is not at all clear that the handwriting is forged. I agree there are some vital differences from the way your brother forms some of his letters, but that could have been done to make the note appear like a forgery."

"And my brother has already told you that he would never write to anyone on writing paper that did not bear the family crest, unless he was at his club at the time, in which case it would bear the club crest."

"Again he could have deliberately substituted substandard notepaper, to make this very argument."

With the use of the word "notepaper," my opinion of him went down. Not the right sort of school then. "I have to tell you, Chief Inspector, that my brother has never been known for his quick wit or his brainpower. He would never have thought through such complicated details. Besides, what possible motive could he have had for killing a man he hardly knew? Without a motive, surely you have no case."

He looked at me long and hard. He had the most piercing blue eyes and I found it hard to hold his gaze. "We happen to think he had the strongest of motives, my lady. He was fighting to preserve his home."

He must have noticed my face fall.

"Of which I am sure you were fully aware. Or maybe you were in on it too. We'll be looking into that, but you do seem to have an alibi for the day in question, if your friend can be trusted."

"May one ask how you came about this knowledge?" I asked.

"Pure luck. The handwriting expert we took the writing samples to was the same woman who had been asked to verify your father's handwriting. Of course she was delighted to show us her copy of de Mauxville's document. Maybe your brother thought that with his royal connections, he was above the law. But I can assure you that the law is the same for a duke or a pauper. We think he killed Gaston de Mauxville and if he did, then he will hang for it."

"I trust you are still considering other leads, or have you decided that my brother makes a good sitting duck?" I tried to sound calm and in control although my mouth was so dry it was hard to form the words.

"If we find any other credible leads, we will pursue them," he said calmly.

"I have been asking around and I understand that this de Mauxville was a known gambler, also a known blackmailer. Did it occur to you that someone he had been blackmailing had finally had enough?"

He nodded. "Yes, that did occur to us. We found a wad of five-pound notes in his suit pocket. And it did cross our minds that he might also have been blackmailing your brother."

I had to laugh at this. "I'm sorry, Chief Inspector, but one person in the world you couldn't blackmail is my brother. Hamish has led an impeccable life to the point of being utterly boring. No affairs, no debts, no bad habits at all. So find somebody with a more interesting lifestyle, and you'll have your killer."

"I admire your loyalty, Lady Georgiana. I assure you that we will be looking into all possibilities and your brother will get a fair trial."

"Before you hang him," I said bitterly and made a sweeping exit.

I left Scotland Yard in deep gloom. What could I possibly do to save Binky? I hardly knew my own way around London. We would have to rely on a solicitor who should have retired to Worthing or Bournemouth years ago.

As I passed the post office, I realized that I had completely forgotten about my new business enterprise. I hardly felt in the mood to clean houses at the moment, but I would need money if I was to go running around London in taxies on Binky's behalf. So I went inside and was handed two letters. The first was from a Mrs. Baxter of Dullwich who wanted extra staff for her daughter's twenty-first birthday party. Since I could only supply a staff of one, I thought that assignment highly unlikely.

The next was from Mrs. Asquey d'Asquey, mother of the bride at the Grosvenor House wedding. Her daughter (now Primrose Roly Poley) was due home from her honeymoon in Italy on the seventh and she wanted to surprise her by having her new house opened up, clean and welcoming, with windows open and fresh flowers everywhere. I was tempted to accept. The money was desperately needed, but the risk was just too great. I had no guarantee that Primrose's mother would not be sailing in and out with her arms full of fresh flowers, reorganizing Primrose's furniture, if my suspicions were correct. She might not have noticed me at the wedding, when everyone is in a state of shock, but she'd certainly recognize me if I was dusting her bedroom. Reluctantly I'd have too many prior assignments this week to meet her needs.

I came home to the most heavenly smell of cooking. My grandfather was making a steak and kidney pudding. What's more, the boiler was now working and the house was delightfully warm in a quite un-Rannoch-like way. Belinda had already escaped to the comfort of her own house, declaring that one night of excitement was all she could take, so Granddad and I sat together, debating what could be done for Binky. Neither of us could come up with any good suggestions.

At four o'clock Fig telephoned. She was coming to London the next day to be at her husband's side. Would I make sure her bedroom and dressing room were ready for her? A fire would be nice as she'd be tired from the journey. She blamed me, she went on to say. How could I possibly let Binky get into such a mess? Now she supposed she'd have to sort it out. For a moment I actually pitied the policemen at Scotland Yard. I couldn't wait to see the meeting between Fig and Harry Sugg. If the situation hadn't been so grim, I would have chuckled.

The next morning I was in the midst of dusting her dressing room when there was a knock at the front door. Granddad, who had now turned himself into butler as well as cook, came back to report that there was a policeman to see me. A Chief Inspector Burnall.

"Show him into the morning room," I said with a sigh and hastily removed the scarf I had been wearing for my cleaning duties.

The chief inspector was looking impeccably groomed and very distinguished and I was horribly aware that I was wearing an old skirt in which the tweed had bottomed over the years. He rose to meet me and greeted me with a polite bow.

"Your ladyship. I'm sorry to disturb you again. I see you now have your butler in residence."

His smug look indicated that we'd had no servants in the house only while we killed de Mauxville.

"That is not our butler. It's my grandfather. He's come to keep an eye on me since he thinks my life might be in danger."

"Your grandfather. Well, I'm damned."

"So what brings you here this morning? Good news, I hope. You've found the real killer?"

"I'm afraid to disappoint you in that, my lady. In fact I come on a quite different matter today. One of great delicacy."

"Really?" I couldn't think what he could be talking about. "I suppose you'd better take a seat."

We sat.

"You are familiar with the home of Sir William Featherstonehaugh on Eaton Place?"

"Of course I am. Roderick Featherstonehaugh was one of my dancing partners when I came out."

"I regret to inform you that several items of considerable value were found to be missing from that house when Lady Featherstonehaugh arrived last weekend."

"How terrible." I could feel my heart thumping and hoped he couldn't actually hear it.

"It transpires that Lady Featherstonehaugh hired a domestic agency to open up the house for her. Coronet Domestics, I believe the name is. And following up on the advertisement in the *Times*, it appears that Coronet Domestics is owned by none other than yourself, Lady Georgiana. Is that correct?"

"That is correct."

"Interesting. May I ask if you have any input in the day-to-day running of this service or are you merely the titular head?"

"No, I am involved."

"I see. So I would be grateful if you would supply me with the names of the staff members who were working at Lady Featherstonehaugh's that day. I trust you have checked all their references thoroughly before you employed them?"

I swallowed hard, trying to think of a plausible lie, but couldn't come up with one.

"This is strictly between ourselves, Chief Inspector," I said. "I'd appreciate it if it didn't go any further than necessary."

"Go on."

"The truth is that I am Coronet Domestics. As yet I have no staff."

He couldn't have looked more shocked if I had told him that I danced naked on the tables at the Pink Pussycat. "You clean other people's houses? Yourself?"

"Strange though that may sound, I do it out of necessity. My allowance has been cut off and I need to survive on my own. This seemed a good way to start."

"I must say, I take my hat off to you," he said. "Right. Well, this should make it much simpler. I am going to read you a description of the objects and maybe you can tell me whether you noticed them while you were doing your domestic duties.

"A Georgian silver coffeepot. A large silver salver. Two miniatures of the Moghul school from India. A small Chinese figurine of the Goddess of Mercy."

"I can answer that one," I said. "I broke an arm off, accidentally. I took it with me, planning to have it repaired and replace it. I didn't think it would be noticed among so many knickknacks."

"Apparently it's eighth century."

"Gosh, is it?" I swallowed hard. "As to the other things. I remember dusting a glass-topped table full of miniatures, but I don't think any were missing, or I'd have noticed the gaps. And I really can't remember seeing a silver coffeepot or a salver."

I noticed he was looking around the room, as if he expected to see the coffeepot hidden behind the ormolu clock.

"You did say you were short of funds, my lady. Maybe the temptation was just too great."

I felt a Great-grandmother impersonation coming on. "Chief Inspector, did you ever steal anything?"

He smiled. "Scrumping apples from a nearby orchard when I was a small boy."

"When I was three I took one of Cook's shortbread biscuits from the rack where they were cooling. They had just come out of the oven and were still hot. I burned my mouth. I have never taken anything since. But you are most welcome to search this house if you choose."

"I take your word for it. Besides, a pawnbroker or jeweler would remember someone like you coming into his shop."

"You're confident the items will show up at a pawnshop or jeweler's?"

"Unless the thief is a pro, then they'd be handed over to a proper fence. But we've got our spies working that aspect as well. One of the items will appear somewhere before long, you'll see."

"You don't think the thief is a professional?"

"Not worth his while. If he gained access to the house, why limit himself to a few items when there was plenty of more valuable stuff there for the taking? This was someone who seized the opportunity to grab a few things. So let me ask you—were you alone in the house the whole time?"

I opened my mouth but no sound would come out. I couldn't tell him about Darcy's visit without getting myself into deep trouble. Because Darcy would say that he had come to visit me and then the Featherstonehaughs would know that I'd been cleaning their house and it would be all around London in two seconds and at the palace in three.

"Not all the time," I said carefully, trying to avoid a complete lie. "The Featherstonehaughs' son came in at one stage with one of his friends."

"And saw you?"

"He didn't recognize me. I was on my hands and knees at the time and I made sure I didn't look up. Besides, nobody looks twice at servants."

"When you left did you lock the front door?"

I considered this. "Yes, I think I heard the latch click behind me. I don't know if Roderick Featherstonehaugh was still in the house when I left. He might have been the one to have left the door open. As my brother said, when one is used to servants in the house, one doesn't think about locking doors."

Burnall rose to his feet. "Sorry to have troubled you again, my lady. If you happen to remember seeing any of those items, do get in touch, won't you? And the little Chinese figure—if you hurry up and get it repaired, I'll take it back to Lady Featherstonehaugh and I'll be suitably vague about where we located it."

"Very kind of you, Chief Inspector."

"The least I could do, my lady."

My grandfather was waiting in the front hall with the inspector's hat. He inclined his head to me and departed. I went upstairs again to finish Fig's room. Having specks of dust pointed out to me would be the last thing I could stand at the moment. In fact I was so wound up I felt as if I might snap. More than anything I was furious with myself for being so naïve. Darcy had just been using me. Why else would he have sought out my company after he found out that I was as penniless as he? I wasn't the sort of fun-loving, nightclubbing girl he liked. I ran downstairs and put on my coat.

"I'm going out," I shouted to my grandfather and took a cab to Chelsea.

Darcy looked as if he had just got out of bed. He was barefoot, in a toweling robe, and he hadn't shaved and his hair was tousled. I tried not to register how very attractive that looked. His eyes lit up when he saw me on the doorstep.

"Well, what a surprise this is. Good morning to you, my lovely. Have you come back to continue from where we left off the other night?"

"I've come back to tell you that you are a despicable rat and I never want to see you again and you're very lucky that I didn't give your name to the police."

Those alarming blue eyes opened wide. "Whoa, now. What is it that I can possibly have done to produce such a tirade from those genteel lips?"

"You know perfectly well what you've done," I said. "I have been a complete fool to think you might actually be interested in me. You were using me, weren't you? You pretended you came to the Featherstonehaughs' to see me, when you really wanted an excuse to get inside their house and help yourself to their valuables."

He frowned. "Their valuables?"

"Oh, come on, I'm not that stupid, Darcy. You tiptoe into the house, pretend to flirt with me, and then, miraculously, several valuable items go missing."

"And you think I took them?"

"You told me yourself that you are penniless and you live by your wits. I imagine your lifestyle with the nightclubs and the women is rather expensive to maintain. And who would notice an odd piece of Georgian silver missing? You're just damned lucky that I didn't tell the police, but now I'm their obvious suspect. It's bad enough that they think Binky and I murdered de Mauxville. Now they also think I do burglaries on the side. So if you really are anything of a gentleman, you'll return those items immediately and go and confess."

"So that's what you think of me—that I'm a thief?"

"Don't play the innocent with me. I've been stupidly naïve over too many things. Why else would you pretend to be interested in me after you found out I had no money? I certainly couldn't offer the delights of a Belinda Warburton-Stoke."

With that I fled before I started to cry. He didn't attempt to come after me.

Chapter 23

I was overcome with gloom. Fig had arrived and made it clear that she didn't appreciate having my grandfather in the house. She'd found fault with everything, including the fact that the house was too warm and it was an unheard-of expense to run a boiler for one person. Grandfather beat a hasty retreat, telling me I was welcome to stay with him, and I was left alone with Fig and her maid. I don't think I had ever felt more wretched. What else can possibly go wrong? I wondered.

I didn't have long to wait. Fig's maid handed me a letter that had just been hand-delivered from the palace. Her Majesty would like to see me immediately. Strangely enough, Fig was quite put out by it. "How is it that Her Majesty wants to see you?" she demanded.

"I am a relative," I replied, rubbing in the fact that she wasn't.

"Perhaps I should go with you," she said. "Her Majesty is of the old school and would not like the thought of an unmarried woman going around without a chaperon."

"Kind of you, but no, thanks," I said. "I am not likely to be accosted going up Constitution Hill."

"What can she possibly want?" Fig went on. "If she wanted to speak to anybody about poor Binky's current situation, she'd speak to me."

"I have no idea," I said.

Actually I did have an idea. I suspected that she'd found out about

Coronet Domestics and I was about to be dispatched to darkest Gloucestershire to hold knitting wool and walk Pekinese dogs. I put on my one
smart black-and-white suit and this time I presented myself at the correct
visitors' entrance on the left of the main forecourt, having successfully
negotiated the bearskins on guard. I was escorted upstairs and around to
the rear wing of the palace, to the queen's private study, overlooking the
gardens. It was a simple, peaceful room, perfectly mirroring Her Majesty's
personality. The only adornments were some lovely pieces of Wedgwood
and a small marquetry table. One wouldn't speculate how or where they
were acquired.

Her Majesty was sitting, straight-backed and severe, at her writing desk,
with spectacles perched on her nose, and she looked up as I was announced.

"Ah, Georgiana, my dear. Do come and sit down. A bad business." She
shook her head, then turned her face for the obligatory cheek kiss and curtsy.
"I was most distressed when I heard the news."

"I'm sorry, ma'am." I perched on the striped Regency chair opposite her.

"It's not your fault," she said curtly. "You can't always be watching that
fool of a brother. I take it he is innocent?"

I heaved an enormous sigh of relief. She hadn't heard about my domestic adventures, then. "Of course he's innocent, ma'am. You know Binky—
can you imagine him drowning somebody in a bath?"

"Frankly, no. Shooting somebody by accident, perhaps." She shook her
head again. "So what's being done for him, that's what I want to know."

"His solicitor has been notified. His wife has arrived and is currently
tackling the police."

"Then if they are his entire defense team, I don't hold out much hope
for a happy outcome," she said. "I'd like to help but the king says we must
not intervene. We must be seen to have complete faith in our country's legal
system and not pull rank just because it's a family member."

"I quite understand, ma'am."

She peered at me over her glasses. "I'm counting on you, Georgiana.
Your brother is a decent sort of fellow, but not overly endowed with brains,
I fear. You, on the other hand, have always had more than your share of wit
and intelligence. Use them on your brother's behalf or I'm afraid he'll end
up confessing to a crime he didn't commit."

This was all too true. "I am doing what I can, Your Majesty, but it's not
easy."

"I'm sure it's not. This French person who drowned—do you have any idea who might have wanted to drown him in your bathtub?"

"He was a known gambler and blackmailer, ma'am. I suspect somebody took the opportunity to get out of a debt to him, but I don't know how I could find out who that was. I have no idea about gambling dens."

"Of course you haven't. But it must also have been somebody who knew your family—on equal terms, so to speak. You don't risk drowning somebody in a peer's bathtub if you are a laborer or a bank clerk."

I nodded. "One of our set, then."

"It must have been somebody who had at least passable knowledge of the workings of Rannoch House. Someone who knew your brother reasonably well, I'd say. Do you know which of his friends has visited the house on a regular basis?"

"I'm afraid I have no idea, ma'am. I've rarely been in London apart from my season, and have hardly stayed at Rannoch House since my father died. But from what I know of my brother, he doesn't come to London unless he has to. He much prefers pottering around his estate."

"As did his grandfather," the queen said. "The old queen had to practically issue a royal command to make him bring his wife to court to visit her mother. So you don't know which of your brother's friends is currently in London?"

"I'm afraid I don't even know who his friends are. If he meets them it would be at his club."

"Perhaps you could make discreet inquiries at his club, then. Brooks, isn't it?"

"Easier said than done, ma'am. Have you ever tried to persuade a gentlemen's club to tell you who is currently in residence?"

"I can't say I ever had to, not having the wandering kind of husband, but I'm sure my predecessor, Queen Alexandra, had to do so on a regular basis. But this may be one area in which the palace can help. I will ask the king to have his private secretary visit Brooks on our behalf. I believe he's a member. I hardly think they will refuse him the information, and if they do, he can always take a look at the membership book, can't he?"

"That's a splendid idea, ma'am."

"And in the meantime, keep watch. The murderer may want to know how the investigation is going. He may be enjoying your brother's current humiliation. They say murderers are vain fellows."

"I'll do my best, ma'am."

She nodded. "Well, let's see what Sir Julian can unearth for us, shall we? We should know something by the time you return from Sussex on Monday."

Sussex? I racked my brains to think of any royal relatives who lived in that county. Her Majesty frowned. "Don't tell me you have forgotten about the small assignment I gave you—the house party at Lady Mountjoy's."

"Oh, of course. The house party. The Prince of Wales. So much has happened in the past few days that it had slipped my mind."

"But you do still plan to attend? In spite of the current unhappy circumstances?"

"If Your Majesty wants me to, I'll be happy to oblige."

"Of course I want you to, and a few days in the country will do you good, and whisk you away from the scrutiny of the gutter press. Everything I hear about this woman is repugnant to me. I must know the truth, Georgiana, before the king and I attempt to nip any hint of romance in the bud."

"I have met her already," I said.

She removed the spectacles and leaned closer. "You have?"

"Yes, she came to my friend's clothing design salon."

"And?"

"She was horribly unpleasant. I couldn't stand her."

"Ah. Just as I thought. Well, by the end of this house party I hope she'll have laid out enough rope to hang herself. Oh, dear, not a good metaphor, given the current situation. Come to tea on Monday. I should be back from opening a mother and baby clinic in the East End by three. Shall we say four o'clock? Then we can exchange news."

"Very good, ma'am." I got to my feet.

"I'll ring for Heslop to escort you out. Until Monday, then. And don't forget—you are my eyes and ears. I am relying on you to be my spy."

⚜

THE MOMENT I got home, Fig peppered me with questions.

"Her Majesty has a plan to rescue Binky, does she?"

"Yes, she's going to disguise the king as Robin Hood and have him swing into Scotland Yard from Big Ben."

"Don't be facetious, Georgiana. Honestly, your manners have become appalling these days. I told Binky it was a waste of money to send you to that awful and expensive school."

"If you must know, Fig, it wasn't anything to do with Binky. It was something to do with the house party she wants me to attend on Friday."

I could see right away that this really upset her. "A house party? Her Majesty is inviting *you* to house parties these days?"

"Not inviting me. Sending me on her behalf," I said, enjoying every moment of this.

Fig's face was positively puce. "You are now representing Her Majesty at an official function? You, with a mother who was only a chorus girl?"

"Never a chorus girl, Fig. An actress. Maybe she thinks I've inherited my mother's talent for being friendly and gracious in public. Not everybody has that quality, you know."

"I just don't understand it," Fig muttered. "Your poor brother about to face the hangman's noose and Her Majesty sends you off to enjoy yourself in the country. I am obviously the only one who is going to stick by poor Binky." She put a lace handkerchief to her face and stalked out of the room in a huff. It was the only moment I had enjoyed in quite a long time.

But she was right. I really should be doing something constructive for Binky. If only someone could pay a visit to the gambling clubs de Mauxville had visited. Maybe something significant had happened there—he had cheated someone or he had collected blackmail money. Granddad had mentioned Crockford's, but I couldn't go to a place like that, could I? It needed someone with social ease and brilliance, part of that racy set. . . . Of course!

I set off for Belinda's place right away. She was awake and dressed, sitting at her kitchen table with a pad and pencil in front of her.

"Don't disturb me. I'm designing a new gown," she said. "I've actually got a commission. Some owner of a motorcar factory is going to be made a peer and his wife wants the kind of dress that the aristocracy wears. And she's going to pay me proper money for it too."

"I'm happy for you, but I wondered if you had any plans for tonight."

"Tonight, why?"

"I want you to go to Crockford's with me."

"Crockford's? Are you taking up gambling now? Out of your league, my dear. They cater to the gambling elite—very high stakes."

"I don't want to gamble, but the doorman at Claridge's said that de

Mauxville frequented the place. I want to know who he met there and whether anything important happened—an argument, maybe."

"I'd like to help, but I'm afraid I have other plans tonight," she said.

I took a deep breath. "Then could you lend me a vampish outfit and I'll go on my own."

"Georgie, you have to be a member. They'd never let you in."

"I'll think of something. I'll claim to be meeting someone there. It's just important that I don't look like me or they'll recognize me. Please, Belinda? Someone has to do it, and my sister-in-law certainly can't."

She looked up at me, sighed, and stood up. "Oh, very well. I still think this is doomed to failure, but I suppose I could find something suitable to lend you."

She took me upstairs, tried various dresses on me, and finally settled on long, black, and slinky with a red ruched cape.

"And if anyone asks you who designed it, you can hand them my card."

She then found a black cap with feathers to hide my untameable hair and showed me the cosmetics on her dressing table to make up my face. The result that evening was startling. Surely nobody would recognize the sultry young woman with the bright red lips and long black eyelashes?

I stayed at Belinda's place, leaving Fig to forage for her own supper, then at nine o'clock I paid out more hard-earned money on a cab and off I went, quaking in my boots—although I wasn't actually wearing boots but Belinda's high-heeled shoes, one size too big for me.

Crockford's was one of London's oldest and swankest gambling clubs, on St. James's Street, only a stone's throw from Brooks's. As my cab pulled up, chauffeurs were assisting other gamblers from their Rolls-Royces and Bentleys. They greeted each other merrily and sailed in past the uniformed doorman. I did not.

"Can I help you, miss?" He stepped out in front of me.

"I'm supposed to be meeting my cousin here, but I don't see him." I pretended to look around. "He said nine o'clock and it's already past nine. Do you think he could have gone inside without me?"

"Who is your cousin, miss?"

Obviously I couldn't use the name of any of my real cousins. "Roland Aston-Poley," I said, complimenting myself on my quick thinking. At least I knew he was in Italy on his honeymoon.

"I don't believe I've seen Mr. Aston-Poley tonight," the doorman said, "but if you'll step inside, I'll have one of the gentlemen look after you."

He led me in through the door into a gracious foyer. Through an archway I glimpsed a scene of sparkling elegance—the wink of chandeliers and diamonds, the clatter of chips, the rattle of the roulette wheel, excited voices, laughter, clapping. For a moment I wished I were the kind of person who had the means to frequent places like this. Then I reminded myself that my father had been that kind of person, and my father had shot himself.

A swarthy little man in a dinner jacket came up to us. There were muttered words between him and the doorman. The small man shot sideways glances I didn't much care for in my direction.

"Mr. Aston-Poley, you say?" He peered in through the doors. "I don't believe he's arrived yet, Miss . . . ?" He waited for me to supply my name. I didn't. "If you'd care to take a seat, I will go and check for you."

I sat on a gilt and satin chair. The doorman went back to his door. More members arrived. I watched them sign the book on a side table. The moment I was alone I jumped up and went over to the book. I started to turn back the pages. De Mauxville had been killed last Friday, so I would need dates before that. . . . I hadn't expected so many attendees each night. I was astounded at how many people had a suitable income to gamble here. But I spotted one name I recognized: Roderick Featherstonehaugh had been here on several occasions. And then another name I hadn't expected to see: the Hon. Darcy O'Mara had been here too.

Two men strolled past me, both smoking cigars. "I lost ten grand the other night," one said in an American accent, "but if the oil keeps on pumping, who's complaining?" and they both laughed.

My heart was beating so loudly I felt as if it must be reverberating around that foyer.

"I'm sorry, miss." I jumped at the voice close behind me. The dark little man had come back. "But your cousin doesn't appear to be here. I have just checked the *salle prive*. Are you sure you have the correct date?"

"Oh, dear, maybe I've made a mistake," I said. "Was he here last night?"

He turned back the pages, allowing me to peek over his shoulder. "Not last night, or the night before. It doesn't appear that he has been here at all this week. Not since last Saturday."

"Last Saturday?" The words blurted out.

He nodded. So it appeared that Primrose Asquey d'Asquey, now Roly Poly, had been honeymooning alone, at least for part of the time. No wonder her mother felt that she needed cheering up.

"I'm sorry we couldn't help you." The little man was now ushering me toward the front door. "If he does come in later, whom shall I say was waiting for him?"

I tried to come up with a name, then I had a brain wave and produced a card. "Belinda Warburton-Stoke," I said.

His expression changed to one of hostility and suspicion. "Is this some kind of schoolgirl prank?" he demanded.

"What do you mean?"

"That you are most certainly not Miss Warburton-Stoke. That young lady is well known to us here. Good night to you."

I was deposited outside with my cheeks burning. Why hadn't Belinda mentioned that she frequented Crockford's? How could she afford to frequent Crockford's? And what else had she neglected to tell me?

Chapter 24

Fortunately Belinda was out for the evening when I returned the garments to her. I went home to find that Fig had gone to bed and I curled up in my own bed, feeling thoroughly miserable. It seemed there was nobody I could trust anymore and in the darkness my suspicions ran riot. It was Belinda who had sat beside me on that boat. I seemed to remember that she had bent to straighten her stocking at some point. Could she have tied that rope around my ankle? But why?

In the morning I found that Fig had turned the boiler down to a level at which lukewarm water came out of the hot taps. Not that I fancied having a bath any longer anyway. I looked forward to a few days of luxury—extravagant meals, warm house, amusing guests, and all I had to do for once was keep an eye on a certain American woman. I took the invitation from my mantelpiece and was reminded that there was to be a fancy dress ball. I had neither time nor money to hire an expensive outfit at the moment so I hacked at the skirt of the maid's uniform I had been wearing until it came up above my knee, found a white frilly apron, and decided to go as a French maid. Ooh la la.

I tried on the outfit and was rather pleased with my task when the doorbell rang. I answered it without thinking and found Tristram standing there. He opened his mouth in surprise. "Oh, I say, it's you, Georgie. I thought you'd got a new maid."

"I'd never hire anyone who wore her skirts this length," I said, laughing. "It's for a fancy dress ball. I'm a French maid. What do you think?"

"Rather fetching," he said. "But you need fishnet stockings and high heels to complete the picture."

"Good idea. I'll go out and buy a pair today."

"It's for the Mountjoys' do, I suppose."

"You know about the Mountjoys' house party?"

"Rather. I've been invited too."

"I didn't realize you knew the Mountjoys."

"It's obvious, really, with their place only a stone's throw from Eynsleigh. I used to play with the Mountjoy sons."

"The Mountjoys have sons?" This weekend might turn out to be quite promising after all.

"Both away, so I gather. Robert is in India and Richard is at Dartmouth." (These came out as "Wobert" and "Wichard," naturally.) "Navy family, you know. I came to ask you if you'd like a wide down to their place tomorrow. I've managed to borrow a car."

"How very kind of you. Thank you very much. I was wondering how I'd get there."

He beamed, as if I'd just given him a present. "That's splendid, then. About ten all right for you? I'm afraid it's only a little runabout. Couldn't rustle up a Rolls." (Which of course sounded like "wustle up a Wolls.")

"Perfect. Thank you again."

"Maybe we could stroll over to Eynsleigh together and relive old times."

"As long as you don't want me to run through any fountains with you."

He laughed. "Oh, goodness me, no. How embarrassing." His face grew serious. "I thought I should call on you because I realized you must be fwightfully upset about your brother. What an awful thing to have happened."

"Yes, it is pretty shocking," I said. "Binky's innocent, of course, but it's not going to be easy to prove. The police seem to be sure that he's guilty."

"The police are idiots," he said. "They always get it wrong. Look, I don't have to be back in the office for an hour or so. I could do what I promised and show you around London a bit, to cheer you up."

"It's very sweet of you, Tristram, but frankly I don't think I'd take anything in today. I've just too much on my mind. Some happier time, maybe."

"Quite understand. Beastly rotten luck, I say. But how about a cup of coffee? I'm sure there must be a café somewhere nearby and I'd certainly like a cup before I have to go back to work."

"There are plenty along Knightsbridge, including a Lyons."

"Oh, I don't think we have to descend to a Lyons. Let's go and see, shall we?—After you change your clothes."

"Oh, yes." I smiled, glancing down at my outfit. "Do come in and wait in the morning room. It's the only room that's suitable for guests at the moment." I led him up the stairs to the first floor. "Take a seat. I won't be long. Oh, and my sister-in-law is in residence, so don't be surprised if a strange woman wants to know who you are."

I changed quickly and came down to find Tristram sitting with such a strained expression on his face that I knew he had encountered Fig.

"Your sister-in-law is a bit of a stickler, isn't she?" he muttered as we left the house. "She said she had no idea you'd been entertaining gentleman callers unchaperoned and that was no way to behave when they'd been so generous in letting you stay in the house. She positively glared at me as if I were Don Juan. I mean to say, do I look like Don Juan?"

"Oh, dear," I said. "More trouble. I can't wait to get away tomorrow and go to a place of peace, quiet, and jollity."

"Me too," he said. "I can't tell you how utterly dreary it is working in that office. Filing, copying lists, more filing. I'm sure if Sir Hubert had realized what it was like he'd never have sentenced me to be articled there. He'd never have stuck it for two minutes. He'd have gone mad with boredom."

"How is he?" I asked. "Is there any news?"

He bit his lip, like a little boy. "No change. Still in a coma. I'd really like to go over to be with him, but there's nothing I could do, even if I could afford the fare. One feels so helpless."

"I'm really sorry."

"He's the only person I have in the world. Still, these things happen, I suppose. Let's talk about more cheerful subjects. We'll have a rattling good time at that fancy dress ball. Will you dance with me?"

"Of course, if you can bear my standard of dancing."

"Mine too. We'll both say 'ow' in unison."

"What are you going as?" I asked.

"Lady Mountjoy said she has some costumes we can borrow. I thought

I'd take her up on her kind offer. I don't really have the time or money to visit the costume shops in the West End. She mentioned a highwayman and I must say that rather caught my fancy. Swashbuckling, don't you know."

We laughed as we reached the busy thoroughfare of Knightsbridge. We soon found a quiet little café and ordered coffee. A large woman was seated at the next table. Her face was too obviously made up, and a fox fur grinned at us from around her neck. She smiled and nodded to us as we sat down.

"Lovely day, isn't it? Just the right sort of day for young people like you to go walking in the park. I'm just off to Harrods myself, although they are not what they were, are they? Catering to the masses nowadays, I always say." She broke off as the waitress put a cup in front of her, and then gave us our coffees. "Ta, love," she said, "and don't forget the cream slice, will you? I must have my cream slice to keep up my strength."

"I'll get it for you," the waitress said.

Tristram glanced at me and grinned.

"Sugar?" Tristram dropped a lump into his coffee, then offered me the bowl.

"No, thanks. Don't take it."

I felt a tap on my back. "Excuse me, miss, but could I borrow your sugar? There doesn't seem to be any on my table. Really, standards are getting so lax these days, aren't they?"

I took the bowl from Tristram and handed it to her, noticing that her pudgy hands were covered in rings. She dropped several lumps into a coffee cup then handed the bowl back to me, looking up expectantly as the cream slice arrived. I had scarcely turned back to my own coffee when I heard choking noises. I looked around. The fat lady was turning almost purple, her hands waving in the air in panic.

"She's choking." Tristram leaped up and began slapping her on the back. The waitress heard the commotion and rushed out to help. But it was no good. The woman's choking turned to a gurgle and she collapsed onto her plate.

"Get help, quickly!" Tristram shouted. I stood there in a state of shock as the waitress ran out screaming.

"Can't we do something?" I demanded. "Try and remove what's choking her."

"Whatever she swallowed is too far down or it would have come up by now. I'm scared I'd only wedge it more firmly if I tried anything." Tristram looked ashen white. "How awfully horrible. Shall I take you home?"

"We should stay until help gets here," I said, "even though I don't see what we could do."

"I'm afraid she asked for it," he said. "Did you see the way she was cramming that cake into her mouth?"

Help arrived in the shape of a policeman and a doctor who had happened to be passing. The doctor set to work instantly, then took her pulse.

"I'm afraid there's nothing we can do," he said. "She's dead."

We gave our statements to the policeman and tiptoed home. Tristram had to go back to work and I tried to pack for the house party. Fig was off somewhere, probably annoying Scotland Yard again. I wandered around the empty house, trying to shake off a feeling of dread that just wouldn't go away. If this had been my first brush with death, it would have been different. But within one week to have found a body in my bath, been dragged off a boat, then almost pushed under a train made this death almost too much of a coincidence. A disturbing thought crept into my head that the same killer had been aiming for me once again.

The sugar bowl—the woman had asked to borrow the sugar and I had handed her our bowl. Was it possible that someone had poisoned the sugar? The only person who could have done that was Tristram. I shook my head. That was impossible. He hadn't touched the sugar bowl until he took a lump himself and then offered it to me. He couldn't have known in advance where we were going because I had been the one that suggested Knightsbridge and chose the coffeehouse. And as far as I knew, Tristram hadn't been on the boat last Sunday.

Then I remembered something that made me feel cold all over. That first meeting with Darcy in Lyons. He had made a joke about being poisoned by their tea and how they carried out the dead customers. And Darcy had been on the boat last Sunday. I was very glad that I was getting away from all this to the safety of the country. Roll on tomorrow.

$\mathcal{C}$hapter 25

I wasn't sure what to believe anymore. Yesterday's incident could be no more than a greedy woman choking to death, and yet it had happened after I handed her my sugar bowl. I was now almost ready to believe that there was a clever conspiracy against my brother and me. Perhaps Darcy and Belinda, maybe even Whiffy Featherstonehaugh were all in it together. It was just possible that Tristram was part of it too, although I didn't think he had been on the boat on Sunday. The only thing I couldn't come up with was a motive. Why would anybody want to kill me?

So it was with some apprehension when I climbed into the little two-seater beside Tristram and watched him strap my suitcase to the boot. He caught me looking and gave me a jaunty smile. How ridiculous to suspect him, I thought. But it was just as ridiculous to suspect Belinda or Whiffy. I didn't want to suspect Darcy either, but with him I couldn't be sure. At any rate Tristram would have two hands on the wheel, all the way to the Mountjoys'.

Fig had decided that traveling alone with a young man, especially one she had never heard of until this moment, was quite unsuitable. I practically had to wrestle the telephone from her grasp as she attempted to call a cab to take me to Victoria Station.

"Fig, I am over twenty-one and you and Binky have made it very clear that I am no longer your responsibility," I snapped. "If you wish to reinstate my allowance and pay for my household staff, then you can start trying to order me around. If not, then my activities and choice of companions are none of your business."

"I have never been spoken to like that before in my life," she spluttered.

"Then it's about time."

"I must say that your lack of breeding on your mother's side comes out now," she sniffed. "I've no doubt it will be one unsuitable young man after another, just like her."

I gave her a serene smile. "Ah, but think of the fun she's had doing it."

She couldn't come up with an answer to that one.

So now we were puttering merrily along. City gave way to leafy suburbs as we joined the Portsmouth Road. Then suburbs turned into true countryside with spreading chestnuts and oak trees in fields, horses looking over gates. I felt the weight of the last days gradually lifting. Tristram chatted merrily. We stopped at a bakery to buy some sausage rolls and Chelsea buns and then we puttered up one flank of the Hog's Back and pulled off at the top to admire the view. As we sat on the verge beside the road eating our impromptu picnic, I gave a contented sigh.

"It's good to be out in the country again, isn't it?"

"Absolutely. Do you dislike the city as much as I do?"

"I don't dislike it, in fact it could be rather fun if one had money, but I'm a country girl at heart. I need to ride and walk along the loch and feel the wind blowing in my face."

He stared at me for a long while before saying, "You know, Georgie, I wasn't joking the other day. You could always marry me. I know I don't have much now, but one day I'll be very comfortably off. Perhaps we could live at Eynsleigh and get those fountains going again."

"You really are sweet, Tris." I patted his hand. "But I already told you that I plan to marry for love. You feel more like a brother to me. And I won't ever marry for convenience."

"All right. I understand. Still, a fellow can always hope to make you change your mind, can't he?"

I got to my feet. "It's pretty here, isn't it? I wonder if there is a view through the trees."

I started walking down a little path. It was amazing how quickly the car and the road vanished and I was in the middle of the wood. Birds called from the trees, a squirrel raced in front of my feet. I'd been an outdoor girl all my life. Suddenly I sensed that the wood had gone quiet. It felt tense, as if every-thing were listening and watching. I looked around me uneasily. I was only a few yards from the car. I couldn't be in any danger, could I? Then I remem-bered a crowded tube platform. I turned and hurried back to the road.

"Ah, here she is," said a hearty voice. "We wondered where you'd got to."

Another car had parked beside us, this one driven by Whiffy Feather-stonehaugh and containing Marisa Pauncefoot-Young and Belinda, who were now spreading out their own picnic mat on the grass.

"Where are you heading for?" I asked and was greeted with merry laughter.

"Same as you, silly. We're the rest of the house party."

"Come and sit down." Whiffy patted the mat beside him. "Marisa's mum has rustled up some spiffing food from Fortnum's."

I sat and joined them in a far better picnic than our own, but I couldn't really enjoy the cold pheasant or the Melton Mowbray pies or Stilton, because I couldn't shake off the thought that the very people I was trying to avoid were now going to be with me in the country.

We set off again. I stared at their Armstrong Siddeley as it drove ahead of us. Could it possibly be my Celtic sixth sense that made me feel uneasy the moment they arrived?

This was all so ridiculous. These were people I had known for most of my life. I told myself that I was overreacting. All those accidents this past week had been accidents, nothing more sinister. I had read more into them because of the body in the bath and because I was alone and out of my ele-ment. I was now going to have a few days of ease and fun and try to forget what had happened to poor Binky and me.

The more powerful Armstrong Siddeley left us behind and we puttered along leafy byways. At last Tristram slowed the car and pointed. "There, through the trees. That's Eynsleigh. Do you remember it?"

I looked down a long graceful driveway lined with plane trees. Beyond was a rambling Tudor mansion in red and white brick. Happy memories stirred. I had ridden up that driveway on a fat little pony called Squibs. And Sir Hubert had made me a tree house.

"I can understand why you love it so much," I said. "I remember it as a very happy place."

We drove on and were soon approaching yet another lovely house. This one was Farlows, home of the Mountjoys. It was Georgian, with elegant lines, its balustrade crowned with classical marble statues. There was a colonnade of more statues along the driveway.

"Quite an impressive showing, don't you think?" Tristram said. "There is obviously money in the arms game. There's always a war somewhere. Even the statues look violent, don't they? Even more alarming than that fierce angel at your place."

We passed an ornamental lake with fountains playing and came to a halt beside a flight of marble steps, leading to the front door. Liveried servants came out immediately, murmuring, "Welcome, m'lady," as they whisked away my luggage. At the top of the steps I was received by the butler. "Good afternoon, my lady. May I be permitted to say how sorry I was to read of His Grace's current plight. Lady Mountjoy is awaiting you in the long gallery if you'd care to take tea."

I was back in a world where I knew the rules. I followed the butler through to the long gallery, where Whiffy and his party were already attacking the crumpets with Imogen Mountjoy. Several older people were seated together. I recognized Whiffy's parents among them. Lady Mountjoy stood up and came to greet me.

"My dear, so good of you to come at such an unsettling time. We all feel for your poor, dear brother. Such a travesty. Let us hope they get to the bottom of it rapidly. Come and meet Imogen and our American guests."

Imogen pretended to be thrilled. "Georgie. How lovely," she said. We kissed the air somewhere near each other's cheeks. I glanced around, expecting to see Mrs. Simpson, but the Americans turned out to be a Mr. and Mrs. Wilton J. Weinberger.

"I understand your brother is the Dook we've been reading about," he said as he shook my hand.

"And these are our neighbors, Colonel and Mrs. Bantry-Bynge." Lady Mountjoy whisked me away before I could be interrogated on this subject. I had wondered why the woman had seemed vaguely familiar. I felt my face flushing and awaited doom. Colonel Bantry-Bynge shook my hand. "How de doo," he said heartily.

Mrs. Bantry-Bynge also took my hand. "Delighted to make your acquaintance, your ladyship." And gave a little curtsy. Her eyes were lowered and I had no way of knowing whether she recognized me as her former maid or not. If she did, she was obviously not going to say anything, given that I knew what I knew. I stood with the group, exchanging a few pleasantries on "your delightful British countryside and how disappointed Willy is that he couldn't try the hunting," then I was mercifully dragged away by Imogen to see pictures of her recent trip to Florence.

"Is this the sum total of male dance partners?" I whispered to her. "Whiffy and Tristram?"

She made a face. "I know. It's grim, isn't it. But Mummy says it's not really a young person's weekend and it all is for the prince and his pals, but she is trying to come up with a couple more men who are not old fogies in time for the ball tomorrow. Whiffy's not a bad dancing partner but Tristram is guaranteed to step on one's toes. He's hopeless, isn't he? I used to hate it when he was brought over to play with us. He was always breaking one's toys or falling out of trees and getting us into trouble."

"Imogen, why don't you show your friends to their rooms," Lady Mount-joy suggested. "I'm sure you young people have masses to talk about."

"Good idea. Come on, then." She led us up the stairs, marching in unladylike fashion. "Anything to get away from those awful people," she said, glancing back down the curved staircase. "Thank God it's not hunting season or that Wilton person would have ruined our horses. Utterly dreary so far, don't you think? I mean, one had hopes about the Prince of Wales, but one gathers that he has other interests."

"Who will be arriving with her own husband," Belinda said, laughing.

"Really?" Marisa looked fascinated.

"Absolutely. The poor thing is dragged around like a dog on a leash."

Marisa made a face. "Just don't let me drink too much and make a fool of myself in front of HRH. You know what I'm like."

We reached the first landing—a grand affair with marble busts in niches and a noble corridor going off in both directions. "You're down here, Georgie," Imogen said. "You get the royal treatment in the best bedrooms, along with HRH. The rest of us are up another floor, slumming it."

"I hope certain other guests will also be on this floor," Belinda whispered, "or there will be a lot of creeping up and down stairs during the night."

"I'm not sure it's reached the creeping-up-and-down stage yet," Imogen said. "But I can tell you that a certain married couple has been given rooms on this floor, only on the other side of the great staircase, so it will still be a long hike, and cold feet on the marble floor." Imogen giggled. "If you hear a shriek, Georgie, that's what it will be—cold feet."

My room was at the far end of the corridor. It was quite delightful, with bay windows overlooking the lake and the park. My clothes had already been unpacked and put away.

"Did you bring your maid or do you want me to send one down to dress you?" Imogen asked.

"My maid's still in Scotland, but I've learned to dress myself," I said.

"Have you? Clever you."

"My maid's arriving by train," Belinda said. "You can borrow her if you like."

I could sense the strain between Belinda and myself and didn't know if it all came from me. I noticed she hadn't been her normal friendly self.

"We'll leave you to change then, while I take these two to their humble abodes up above," Imogen said. "Cocktails at seven. Have a nice rest first." At the doorway she turned back. "Oh, and there's a little staircase right beside your room, which actually leads into the long gallery, where we'll be having cocktails."

Left alone, I lay on my bed, but couldn't relax. I got up and paced around the room. From my window I spotted Whiffy Featherstonehaugh striding out away from the house. At one point he looked up at the house and then hurried on. I watched him, my thoughts churning. Someone I had known for most of my life—a Guards officer, a little stiff and stuffy, perhaps, but surely not a murderer. But he was also a frequent visitor at Crockford's, at times when de Mauxville had been there. And . . . I remembered one thing more . . . the impression on the pad beside the telephone in de Mauxville's room: *R—10:30.* Whiffy's name was Roderick. Somehow I had to confront him this weekend. I had to find out the truth. I was fed up with living with danger.

I put such thoughts aside and applied myself to the task of getting dressed for dinner. For once I had to look respectable. I had brought a cream silk dress with burgundy sleeves that complemented my coloring rather well and had enough shape to it to prevent me from looking like a beanpole. I ventured a little rouge to my cheeks, a dash of lipstick to my lips, and put my twenty-first birthday pearls around my neck. I was rather proud of doing the whole thing without help. Thus adorned, I went to meet and mingle. My end of the corridor was unlit and I descended the little spiral staircase with caution. One step. Two. Suddenly I lost my footing, pitched forward, and hurtled downward. There was no banister and my hands slid off smooth walls. I suppose it all happened quickly but it was almost as if I were flying downward in slow motion. I saw a suit of armor looming up ahead of me only an instant before I collided with it. I noticed that its ax was raised and I raised my own arms to defend myself. There was a crash, a clatter, and I found myself sitting with bits of armor raining down around me.

Instantly people came running up from below.

"Georgie, are you all right?"

Worried faces stared at me as I was helped to my feet. I brushed myself down and appeared not to have suffered any major damage, apart from some scrapes to my arms and a laddered stocking.

"I should have warned you about that staircase," Lady Mountjoy was saying. "The lighting is poor. I've spoken to William about it."

"Honestly, Georgie," Belinda said, attempting to laugh it off, "I swear you'd find something to trip over in the middle of a large polished floor. Oh, your poor arm. Lucky you weren't wearing long gloves or you would have ruined them. Let's go back to your room and get it cleaned up. And you've laddered your stockings. Do you want another pair?"

Everyone was being very kind. I let them minister to me and noticed how carefully they led me downstairs again.

"Here she is, safe and sound." Lady Mountjoy sounded relieved. "Come and be presented to His Royal Highness." She led me over to where my cousin David was standing with Lord Mountjoy and a couple of stiff young men who were obviously HRH's equerries.

"What-ho, Georgie," David said before Lady Mountjoy could do any presenting. "Been fighting suits of armor, so I hear."

"Just an unlucky tumble, sir," Lady Mountjoy said, before I could answer. "But all is well. A glass of champagne, or would you rather have a cocktail, Georgiana?"

"She needs a brandy after that scare," Lord Mountjoy said and one was brought to me. I didn't like to admit that I don't enjoy brandy and was grateful to have something to sip. Because it was going to take a lot to calm my nerves at the moment. As I was being ministered to upstairs, I picked something from my skirt. It was a piece of strong black thread. I couldn't think how it got there until it dawned on me that somebody could have strung it across the top of those steps—someone who knew that I would probably be the only person who used them tonight. My attacker was indeed in the house with me.

$\mathcal{C}$hapter 26

I had no time to think, however, as I was led away to meet the women. I spotted Mrs. Simpson instantly. She was dressed in a trouser outfit rather like the one I had modeled so disastrously, and was holding court on the most comfortable sofa, currently giving what sounded like an impression of the Duke of York's stutter. We were duly introduced.

"I think I've seen you somewhere before, haven't I?" she drawled, eyeing me critically.

"It's possible," I said, trying to sound disinterested and remembering all the rude things she had said.

"Let's see, now. You're the one whose mother was an 'actress' who snagged a duke, right?" She made the word sound as if it were a euphemism for something less reputable.

"She was indeed," I said. "If you get a chance to meet her, then maybe she could give you some pointers on how to act like a princess." I smiled sweetly. There was gentle tittering but she looked daggers at me. As I excused myself and walked on I heard her say loudly, "That poor girl, so tall and gawkish still. If she marries at all, she'll probably have to settle for some brute of a farmer."

"Who will be considerably better in bed than anything she has at the moment," said a voice in my ear and there was my mother, looking stunning in peacock blue, complete with a ruff of peacock feathers. "And what's all this nonsense about Binky? If he killed anybody I'd have expected it to be Fig."

"It's not funny, Mother. He could be hanged."

"They don't hang dukes, darling. He'd be let off by reason of insanity. Everyone knows the upper classes are batty."

"But he didn't do it."

"Of course he didn't. He's just not the violent type. He used to throw up every time the hounds got at the fox."

"What are you doing here anyway?" I asked, for once delighted to see her.

"Max has business connections with Lord Mountjoy. They're in the armaments game together, and he also hunts with HRH, so here we are," she said. "Come and meet Max. His English is atrocious, I'm afraid."

"And you don't speak German, do you? So how do you manage?"

She laughed, that delightful, infectious laugh that had filled theaters. "My darling, one doesn't always need to talk."

She slipped her arm through mine and led me over to a stocky but imposing blond-haired man, who was deep in conversation with the prince and Lord Mountjoy.

"Ya, de vild boar," we heard him say. "Bang bang."

"See what I mean?" my mother whispered. "A definite deficiency there. But the sex is heavenly."

The mention of sex reminded me of a pressing question. "I wonder who is supposed to escort me in to dinner tonight? I do hope it won't be Lord Mountjoy. I hate having to make polite conversation to older people."

"I gather he's escorting that awful American woman," my mother whispered. "Just as if she were officially with you know who. Poor old Mr. S, whom you'll notice skulking in the background over there, will be forced to make his own way in at the end of the procession. Damned bad form, I call it."

"Then it looks as if I'll be stuck with either Whiffy Featherstonehaugh or Tristram. Hardly scintillating conversation."

"Poor little Tristram. How's he holding up?"

"All right, I suppose. He asked me to marry him."

She laughed. "That's awful. Almost like incest. You had the same nanny, for God's sake. Still, I suppose he might be a good catch if poor old Hubie does die."

"Mother, he's very sweet, but can you imagine being married to him?"

"Frankly, no. But I thought Lady Mountjoy had said that they'd invited a partner for you."

At that moment the double doors opened, and the butler stepped into the room and announced, "His Serene Highness, Prince Siegfried of Romania."

Siegfried, his pale blond hair slicked down, his military evening jacket adorned with more orders and medals than any general's, strode into the room, marched up to Lady Mountjoy, clicked his heels, and bowed. "So kind," he said. From her he went over to the Prince of Wales and clicked his heels again. They exchanged words in German and then Siegfried was brought over to me.

"I believe you already know Lady Georgiana, Your Highness?"

"Naturally. We meet again at last." He bent to kiss my hand with those large, cold fish-lips. "You have been well, I trust?"

I was seething. The crafty old thing, I thought. She didn't want me to spy on David at all. She planned this so that I would be thrust together with Siegfried again. She knew I'd wriggled out of the encounter in Scotland and she simply wasn't going to let me escape. Well, you could lead a horse to water, but you can't make her marry anyone she loathes.

I had, however, been well brought up. I was polite and attentive as Siegfried talked about himself. "I had brilliant skiing this winter. Where do you ski these days? I myself am a magnificent skier. I know no fear."

The dinner gong sounded and we formed up to parade into the dining room. I, of course, was paired with Siegfried, right behind the prince and Lady Mountjoy. We took our places and my eyes strayed around the table. Who had been devious enough to tie that black thread across those stairs? It was a miracle I was still alive. If I had landed slightly differently, that ax would have come crashing down on me or I'd have broken my neck. I stared at Whiffy then Tristram. Neither one was what I'd call a live wire when it came to brains. But Belinda—she had been one of the cleverest girls in school. I shook my head in disbelief. Why on earth would Belinda want me dead?

There was one place still vacant at table. The moment I noticed it the door opened again.

"The Honorable Darcy O'Mara," the butler announced and Darcy came in, looking dashing in his dinner suit.

"Mr. O'Mara," Lady Mountjoy said as he presented himself to her with apologies. "You managed it after all. I am so glad. Do sit down. They are only just serving the soup."

Darcy cast me the briefest of glances as he sat opposite me, then started talking to Marisa on his left. I felt that my cheeks were flaming. What was he doing here? Who had invited him and why?

Over the polite murmur of conversation I heard Mrs. Simpson's strident voice. "So let me get this straight. Does one now have to call you 'Frau' or 'your ladyship,' or are you simply 'Mrs.'?"

She was, of course, addressing my mother, who had unwisely been seated within firing range.

"Simply 'Mrs.,' " my mother said sweetly, "and how about you? Are you still married to anybody?"

There was a moment's frosty silence before the table went back to talk of the weather and the next day's game of golf.

"Tomorrow we shall go out riding, do you think?" Siegfried asked me. "Myself I ride magnificently. I am a magnificent horseman. I know no fear."

This couldn't be happening to me. I was trapped in a room with my mother, Mrs. Simpson, Fish-Lips, Darcy, and/or someone who was trying to kill me. How much worse could things get?

Somehow I survived dinner. The redeeming feature was the magnificent food. For one who had been living on baked beans, there was one heady course after the next—turtle soup followed by sole Veronique followed by squab followed by roast beef followed by charlotte russe followed by anchovies on toast. I was amazed at the amount I was able to eat, given my nervous state. And wine to accompany each course.

I noted that Mrs. Simpson picked at her food and cast glances in the direction of the prince, who was doing a lot of cow-eyed gazing in her direction.

"I'm afraid I have to eat like a sparrow these days or I put on weight," she commented to those around her. "You're so lucky. Germans like their women fat." This last remark addressed to my mother, of course.

"In which case I should eat up if I were you," my mother said, glancing at the prince whose royal ancestor included the Elector of Hanover and Prince Albert of Saxe-Coburg-Gotha. She was clearly enjoying herself. I was relieved when Lady Mountjoy indicated that the ladies should withdraw and we followed her into the drawing room where coffee awaited us. My mother and Mrs. Simpson, now already sworn enemies, were still exchanging the most deliciously honeyed barbs. I would have enjoyed observing this spectacle, but Belinda was sitting beside me, offering to put cream and sugar into my coffee. I declined both.

"But I thought you always claimed that black coffee at night kept you awake," she said.

I looked across at my mother. Could I count on her as an ally? As a mother she hadn't exactly fulfilled the role, but surely she'd want to protect her only child. The men arrived soon after.

"David, come and sit here." Mrs. Simpson patted the sofa beside her. There was an almost discernible gasp from the rest of the party. Princes are "sir" in public, even to their closest friends. His Highness just smiled and hurried to perch on the arm at her side. Mr. Simpson was nowhere in sight. Gone to play billiards, so I was told. Darcy settled himself between Marisa and Imogen and didn't once look in my direction.

"I gather you had a nasty tumble," Whiffy said. "The lighting is so poor in the corridors, isn't it? Old Tris tripped over a suit of armor on our floor. That's par for the course for him. Clumsy as an ox. Have you seen him, by the way?"

At that moment he appeared, in animated conversation with Prince Siegfried. They were both heading in my direction. I couldn't stand it a minute longer. I excused myself as soon as I was able, and went to my room. I went up the little staircase, looking carefully for clues. It was too dark to see much, but I knelt down and examined the third step, which was where I had taken the tumble. There was no sign of a nail from which a string could be tied, but there were telltale holes in the walls. My adversary thought he or she had removed the evidence, but one can't remove holes.

I went into my room and locked the door, but I couldn't sleep. Every house has a set of skeleton keys that my killer could acquire, but at least I'd be ready for him. I looked around for a suitable weapon, then took a warming pan off the wall and laid it beside me. At the first hint of anyone near my door, I'd be waiting, armed and ready to bash him over the head and scream the place down.

The hours ticked on. An owl hooted and somewhere in the park there was a scream, probably a fox taking a rabbit. Then I heard the floorboards outside my door creak. It was the slightest of sounds but I was up in an instant, warming pan in my hands, standing beside the door. I held my breath, waiting, but nothing happened. At last I could stand it no longer. I unlocked the door as quietly as possible, and looked out. A figure in a dark robe was creeping down the hall as if he or she didn't want to wake anyone. My first thought was the Prince of Wales, returning from a visit to Mrs. Simpson, or vice versa. But I could see that the person was taller than either the prince or the American woman. The form passed the prince's suite and kept on going. At last it paused outside a door, tapped very gently, then entered.

I crept down the hall, counting doors, trying to make sense of what I'd just seen. I passed the Prince of Wales's suite. The room had to be Prince Siegfried's. And from the outline of the figure against the light on the landing, it could be none other than Tristram. I hadn't even realized that Tristram knew the prince. So why was he visiting him in the middle of the night? Naïve as I was, I could only come to one conclusion. And this was someone who only yesterday had proposed marriage to me. Like everything else at the moment, it didn't add up.

Chapter 27

I finally managed to sleep after placing a chair back under my doorknob and awoke to hear that doorknob being rattled fiercely and then a loud tapping on my door. It was broad daylight. I opened the door to find the maid with my morning tea. It was a lovely day, she said, and the gentlemen were off to play golf. The American ladies were joining them. If I also wanted to, I'd have to hurry.

I had no intention of straying from my mother, Lady Mountjoy, and Marisa. There had to be safety in numbers. I dressed and came down to breakfast to find Belinda busy attacking the kidneys. "Lovely spread," she said. "One forgets how much one misses this sort of thing."

I smiled at her and went to the sideboard to help myself.

"You've been awfully quiet," she said. "Are you worrying about your brother?"

"No, I'm worrying about me." I looked her straight in the eye. "Someone's trying to kill me."

"Oh, Georgie, surely you're imagining things. You're the type of person who has accidents, you know that."

"But several accidents in one week? Even I am not that clumsy."

"Horrible, I agree, but accidents nonetheless."

"Only not last night," I said. "Someone strung black thread across the top of those stairs. I found a piece on my skirt."

"And nails in the wall?"

"No, but there were holes where nails could have been. My attacker must have removed them. He or she is obviously very sharp."

"He or she? Who do you think it could be, then?"

"I have no idea," I said, still staring at her. "Someone who is somehow linked to the death of de Mauxville. Tell me, was Tristram Hautbois on that boat on Sunday?"

"Tristram? No, he wasn't."

"Well, that shoots that theory, then."

Belinda got to her feet. "I really do think you're letting your imagination run riot," she said. "We're all your friends. We've known you for years."

"And haven't been quite straight with me."

"What do you mean?"

"That you didn't tell me you frequented Crockford's. You were well known to the staff there."

She looked at me and laughed. "You didn't ask. All right, I confess I do adore gambling. I'm actually rather good at it. It's what keeps my head above water, financially. And I rarely have to come up with the money for my own stake. Older men love to befriend a helpless and charming young woman." She dabbed at her mouth with a napkin. "Did you find out anything there?"

"Only that several people I know gamble more than they should."

"One needs some excitement in life, doesn't one?" Belinda said. She got up and left me alone at the breakfast table, still not knowing if she was a suspect or not.

My mother came in before I had finished and I latched on to her. Max was off golfing so she wasn't averse to some time with her daughter. She whisked me up to her room for some "girl time," as she called it, and made me try endless jars of cosmetics and various perfumes. I feigned interest while trying to think how to tell her that my life was in danger. Knowing her, she'd just tell me not to be silly and go on as if nothing had happened.

"What are you doing with yourself?" she asked. "Not still working at Harrods in that awful pink smock?"

"No, I got the sack, thanks to you."

"I got you the sack? Little *moi*?"

"They told me I was rude to a customer and I couldn't very well tell them that you were my mother."

She gave a great peal of laughter. "It's too, too funny, darling."

"Not if you need money to buy food, it's not. I'm not getting anything from Binky, you know."

"Poor Binky. He may not be in a position to give anyone anything again. Such an awful thing to have happened. How did that terrible de Mauxville man come to be in your house in the first place?"

"You know him, do you?"

"Of course. Everyone on the Riviera knows him. Odious man. Whoever drowned him did the world a service."

"Except that Binky is likely to be hanged for a crime he didn't commit unless I can find out who did it."

"Leave that kind of thing to the police, darling. I'm sure they'll sort it all out nicely. Don't worry about it. I want you to enjoy yourself—come out of your shell, start flirting a little more. It's time you snagged yourself a husband."

"Mother, I'll find myself a husband when the time is right."

"What about the Student Prince at dinner last night? You'd never find a man with more orders or medals."

"Or flabbier lips," I said. "He looks like a cod, Mother."

She laughed. "Yes, he does, rather. And deadly dull, I should imagine. Still, future queen isn't to be sniffed at."

"You tried duchess and you didn't stick with it for long."

"True enough." She looked at me critically. "You do need better clothes, now that you're out in society, that's obvious. I'll see if I can worm a little something out of Max. What a pity you're not my size. I'm always throwing away absolutely scrumptuous things that I can't wear because they are last year's. Of course, if poor Hubie actually dies, I'd imagine you'd be able to buy yourself a decent wardrobe, and a house to go with it."

I stared at her. "You said I was mentioned in his will, but—"

"Hubie is rich as Croesus, darling, and who else does he have to leave it to? Poor little Tristram will probably get his share, but I got the impression that Hubie wanted to make sure you were provided for."

"Really?"

"He was so fond of you. I probably should have stayed with him for your sake, but you know I couldn't take all those months with no sex while he was rafting up the Amazon or scaling some mountain." She pulled me to my feet. "Let's go for a walk, shall we? I haven't had a chance to explore the grounds yet."

"All right." A walk would be a good chance to tell her about my "accidents."

We went down the stairs, arm in arm. The house was remarkably quiet. It seemed that most of our party had gone to play golf. A blustery wind was blowing outside and my mother decided she had to return to the house to find a scarf for her hair or she'd look a fright. I waited outside the house, wondering about a lot of things. If I was going to inherit money from Sir Hubert's will, then Tristram did have a motive to want to marry me. But to kill me? That didn't make sense. He was due to receive his own share of the inheritance. Besides, he hadn't been on the boat, and I hadn't spotted him at that tube platform either. What's more, he seemed like the kind of person who would faint at the sight of blood. He had certainly looked as if he was about to faint when that woman choked to death beside us.

There was a sound above me. I started to look up. At the same time my mother's voice screamed, "Look out!" I jumped and one of the marble statues from the balustrade crashed to the ground beside me. Mother rushed down the steps to me, her face deathly white.

"Are you all right? What an awful thing to have happened! Of course, it's so windy today. That thing had probably been unstable for years. Thank God you're all right. Thank God I wasn't still standing beside you."

Servants ran out. Everyone was trying to comfort me. But I shook myself loose of them and ran into the house. I was tired of being a victim. I wasn't going to take it any longer. I rushed upstairs, one flight then the next. And bumped into Whiffy Featherstonehaugh, running down.

"You!" I shouted, blocking his way. "I should have known when you didn't jump in to try and save me on the boat. I can understand killing de Mauxville, but what have you got against Binky and me, eh? Come on, out with it!"

Whiffy swallowed hard, his Adam's apple jumping up and down, eyes darting nervously. "I'm afraid I haven't a clue what you're talking about."

"You've just been up on the roof, haven't you? Come on, don't deny it."

"The roof? Good Lord, no. What would I have been doing on the roof? The other fellows snapped up the good fancy dress costumes. Lady Mountjoy said there was another trunk of costumes up in the attic, but I couldn't find them."

"Good excuse," I said. "Quick thinking. You're obviously brighter than you make out. You must be, to have lured de Mauxville to our house and killed him. But why pick us?—that's what I want to know."

He was looking at me as if I were a new and dangerous species of animal.

"Look here, Georgie. I don't know what you're on about. I—I didn't kill de Mauxville. I had nothing to do with his death."

"You mean he wasn't blackmailing you?"

His jaw dropped. "How the devil did you know about that?"

I didn't like to say "lucky guess." It had suddenly come to me in a flash of inspiration as I noticed how tall and dark-haired and distinguished-looking he was. "They described you as visiting him at Claridge's, and I saw your name in the book at Crockford's, and de Mauxville had scribbled something about meeting 'R' on a pad."

"Oh, cripes. Then the police also know."

I was probably standing on a staircase with a killer. I wasn't stupid enough to admit that the police knew nothing. "I'm sure they do," I said. "Did you decide to kill him to end the blackmailing?"

"But I didn't kill him." He looked desperate now. "I can't say I'm not glad he's dead, but I swear I didn't do it."

"Was it gambling debts? Did you owe him money?"

"Not exactly." He looked away. "He found out about my visits to a certain club."

"Crockford's?"

"Oh, good Lord, no. Crockford's is acceptable. Half the Guards gamble."

"Then what?"

He was looking around him like a trapped animal. "I'd rather not say."

"A strip club, you mean?"

"Not exactly." He was looking at me as if I were rather dense. "Look, Georgie, it's really none of your business."

"It damned well is my business. My brother has been arrested for a murder he didn't commit. I'm in danger and so far you are the only one with a motive to want de Mauxville dead. I'm going straight downstairs to telephone the police. They'll get to the bottom of this."

"No, don't do that. For God's sake. I swear I didn't kill him, Georgie, but I can't let my family find out."

Suddenly light dawned. The conversation I had overheard at Whiffy's house . . . and last night Tristram tiptoeing down the hall to Prince Siegfried's room. "You're talking about clubs where boys go to meet boys, aren't you?" I said. "You and Tristram, you're both that way inclined."

He flushed bright scarlet. "So you see what it would be like if anyone found out. I'd be out of the Guards on my ear, and my family—well, my family would never forgive me. Military since Wellington, you know."

Another idea was forming in my head. "So how did you manage to pay off de Mauxville? Not on a Guards officer's pay."

"That was the problem. Where to get the money."

"So you took things from your family's London house?"

"Good God, Georgie—are you a blinking mind reader or something? Yes, I took the odd item, here and there. Pawned them, you know, outside of London. Always planned to get them back."

"And you don't know who killed de Mauxville?"

"No, but I'm bally glad they did. God bless them."

"And did you see anybody upstairs, when you were heading for the attic?"

"No. Can't say I did. But I'll come and look with you, if you like."

I hesitated. A strong Guards officer might not be a bad idea if I was to tackle a murderer, but I could also find myself trapped on the roof alone with him.

"We'll get the servants to search," I said and walked down the stairs with him.

The search revealed nobody hiding on the roof, but my attacker would have had plenty of time to sneak down while I was questioning Whiffy. Everyone but me seemed to think it was a horrible accident. I no longer felt safe anywhere and there was something I had to know. I slipped out of the house when no one was looking and walked the length of the driveway. Then, after half a mile or so, I followed the long drive to Sir Hubert's sprawling Tudor mansion.

The door was opened by a maid and the butler was summoned.

"I'm sorry but the master is not in residence," he said as he came to meet me. "I am Rogers, Sir Hubert's butler."

"I remember you, Rogers. I am Lady Georgiana and at one time I knew this house very well."

His face lit up. "Little Lady Georgiana. Well, I never. What a young lady you've grown into. Of course we've followed your progress in the newspapers. Cook cut out the pictures when you were presented at court. How kind of you to come and visit at such a sad time."

"I'm so sorry to hear about Sir Hubert," I said. "But I'm actually here on a very delicate matter and I hope you'll be able to help me."

"Please, come into the drawing room. Can I bring you a cup of coffee or a sherry, perhaps?"

"Nothing, thank you. It's about Sir Hubert's will. Something my mother said gave me to understand that I am mentioned in it. Now, I'm not after his money, I can assure you I'd much rather he lived, but strange things have been happening to my family, and it just occurred to me they may have something to do with this will. So I wondered if it was possible he kept a copy of his will on the premises?"

"I believe there is a copy in the safe," he said.

"Under normal circumstances I wouldn't dream of asking to see it, but I have reason to believe my life is in danger. Do you happen to know the combination?"

"I'm afraid I don't, my lady. That was the sort of thing that only the master knew."

"Oh, well, never mind." I sighed. "It was worth a try. Can you tell me who are Sir Hubert's solicitors?"

"Henty and Fyfe, in Tunbridge Wells," he said.

"Thank you, but they won't be available until Monday, will they?" I felt remarkably near to tears. "I hope that's not too late."

He cleared his throat. "As it happens, my lady, I know the contents of the will," he said, "because I was asked to witness it."

I looked up at him.

"There were small bequests to the staff, and a generous bequest to the Royal Geographical Society. The rest of the estate was divided into three parts: Master Tristram was to receive one-third, yourself one-third, and the final third was to go to Master Tristram's cousin, one of Sir Hubert's French relatives, called Gaston de Mauxville."

Chapter 28

I stared at him, trying to digest this. "I'm to be left a third of the estate? There must be some mistake," I stammered. "Sir Hubert hardly knew me. He hadn't seen me for years. . . ."

"Ah, but he remained very fond you, my lady." The butler smiled at me benevolently. "He wanted to adopt you once, you know."

"When I was an adorable child of five and liked to climb trees."

"He never lost interest in you, not even after your mother moved on to—" he finished that phrase discreetly with a cough. "And when your father died, he was most concerned. 'I don't like to think of that girl growing up without a penny to her name,' he said to me. He hinted it was clear your mother was never going to provide for you."

"How very kind of him," I muttered, almost moved to tears, "but surely Mr. Hautbois should have been left the lion's share of the estate. He is Sir Hubert's ward, after all."

"The master felt that too much money might not be in Mr. Tristram's best interests," the butler said dryly. "Nor Monsieur de Mauxville's, even though he was his sister's only child. Addicted to gambling apparently. Moved in shady circles."

I fought to retain my composure while the butler took me downstairs to meet Cook and then had to eat a slice of her famous Victoria sponge I had always adored as a child. All that time my thoughts were in utter turmoil. The will gave Tristram a motive for wanting both de Mauxville and myself out of the way, but I had no proof that he had done anything. On the contrary, Tristram's slight build against the stocky de Mauxville made it hard to believe that he had carried out that murder. Unless he had had an accomplice. I remembered the pally conversation at Whiffy's house when I had been cleaning floors and they hadn't known I could speak French. So it could have been a conspiracy, beneficial to both of them. Which meant I had two sources of danger, not one, waiting for me back at Farlows.

The obvious thing was to go to the police, even to summon Chief Inspector Burnall of Scotland Yard, but I realized that everything I would tell him was pure supposition. How clever my assailant had been. Every one of those attacks could be passed off as an accident. And as for killing de Mauxville, there was nothing that linked Tristram to that crime.

As I turned out onto the road another idea struck me. Maybe Tristram wasn't the killer at all. I hadn't found out who would inherit Sir Hubert's estate if both Tristram and I were dead. Whiffy had mentioned something about Tristram falling over a suit of armor the night before. What if there was another person lurking in the background, waiting for an opportunity to get rid of Tristram and me?

I had reached the impressive stone gateway leading to Farlows and hesitated. Was it really wise to go back there? Then I decided I wasn't going to run away. I had to know the truth. I glanced up at the colonnade of statues as I walked past. There was something about them. . . . I frowned, but it wouldn't come. As I reached the lake I met Marisa, Belinda, and Imogen out for a walk.

"Oh, there you are," Marisa called. "Everyone wondered where you'd got to. Poor Tristram was positively pining, wasn't he, Belinda? He pestered everyone, asking for you."

"I just went for a walk to see a house where I once stayed. Where is Tristram now?"

"I don't know," Marisa said. "But he seems awfully keen on you, Georgie. I think he's really sweet—like a little lost boy, isn't he, Belinda?"

Belinda shrugged. "If that sort appeals to you, Marisa."

"And where's everyone else?" I asked casually.

"Most of the golfers aren't back yet. Apparently Mrs. Simpson wanted to go shopping in Tunbridge Wells—as if anything will be open on a Saturday afternoon," Imogen said.

"It's just an excuse to be alone with the prince; you know that," Marisa added.

"The only person whose whereabouts are certain is your dear Prince Fishface," Belinda announced with a grin. "He fell off his horse trying to make it jump a gate. He jumped the gate, but the horse didn't. I gather he won't be joining us for dancing tonight."

In spite of everything, I had to laugh.

"So you'll be stuck getting your toes trodden on by Tristram after all"— Imogen slipped her arm through mine—"unless some of the neighbors come. It's always so much easier when my brothers are here."

We started walking toward the house, past the last of the long line of statues.

"I gather one of our statues nearly toppled down on you today," Imogen said. "What awful bad luck you're having, Georgie."

Suddenly I realized what had been worrying me. I realized that Tristram had given himself away. He had compared those statues to the vengeful angel at Rannoch House. But he could only have seen that statue if he had been upstairs on the second-floor landing, where the bathroom was.

Now at least I was sure of my adversary. I was lost in thought all the way back to the house, where Lady Mountjoy appeared to tell us that tea was being served and to eat heartily, as supper wouldn't be before ten. We followed her into the gallery and found my mother already tucking in. For a small, slim person she certainly had an appetite. Mrs. Bantry-Bynge was trying to chat with her, with little success. For someone who had been born a commoner, my mother was rather good at cutting dead anyone she considered common.

"If anyone needs a costume ironed, just let me know," Lady Mountjoy said. "You have all brought costumes, I hope. Those young men are always so helpless. Never bring anything with them. I had to throw together costumes this morning and then young Roderick complained that he didn't want to be an ancient Briton. Too bad, I told him. I had managed to put together a highwayman and an executioner for Tristram and Mr. O'Mara, but that was it, apart from the animal skins and the spear. I sent him up to hunt through the attic. You never know what you'll find up there."

So at least that much of Whiffy's story rang true. And I now knew that Darcy was going to be an executioner. He should be easy to pick out in that costume. I lingered over tea as long as I dared but neither Darcy nor Tristram appeared. When it was time to change, I suggested that the other girls might like to get ready in my room, since it was so spacious and had good mirrors. They agreed and that way I was guarded until it was time to go down to the ball.

They chatted excitedly, but I was a bundle of nerves. If I wanted to prove beyond doubt that Tristram was the murderer, I'd have to offer myself as bait. Only I'd need someone to keep an eye on me, who could later act as a witness.

"Listen, girls," I said, "whatever you say, I believe that someone in this house is trying to kill me. If you see me leaving the ballroom with any man, please come after us and keep an eye on me."

"And if we find you locked in passionate embrace with him? Do we stay and watch?" Belinda asked. She was still taking this as a joke, I could tell. I decided my only hope was Darcy. He was strong enough to tackle Tristram. But after the way I had treated him, had I any right to expect his help? I'd just have to throw myself on his mercy as soon as I got a chance to be alone with him.

I was still nervous as we made our way down the grand staircase, Belinda, Marisa, and I. A band was playing a lively two-step and more guests were arriving through the front doors. A footman stood at the bottom of the stairs with a tray, handing out masks to arriving guests who weren't wearing them. Marisa took some and handed them to us.

"Not that one," Belinda said. "It comes down to the mouth. I won't be able to eat any supper. The slim highwayman type will be better."

"There is a highwayman over there," Marisa whispered. "It must be Tristram. I didn't realize he had such good legs."

"I'm looking out for an executioner," I said. "Let me know when you see him."

"I hope you don't have a desire to follow your ancestors to the chopping block," Marisa said.

"It's Darcy O'Mara, you dope," Belinda said, giving me a knowing look.

I smiled and put my finger to my lips. The ballroom was filling up rapidly. We found a table and sat at it. Belinda was whisked away to dance almost instantly. Dressed as a harem dancer, she waggled her bottom seductively as she stepped onto the floor. Whiffy Featherstonehaugh approached us, looking very uncomfortable as an ancient Briton with animal skins draped around his shoulders. "Care to hop around the floor, old thing?" he said to me.

"Not now, thanks," I said. "Why don't you dance with Marisa?"

"Right-o. I'll try not to tread on toes," he said, taking her hand and leading her away. I sat and sipped at a glass of Pimm's. Everyone was having fun, dancing and laughing as if they hadn't a care in the world. I was conscious of the highwayman, standing at the far side of the ballroom, watching me. At least I was safe among so many people, surely. If only I could find Darcy.

At last I saw the executioner's black hood and ax moving among the crowd on the far side of the room. I got up and made my way toward him.

"Darcy?" I grabbed his sleeve. "I have to talk to you. I want to apologize and I really need your help. It's very important."

The band struck up the "Post Horn Gallop" and couples started charging around the room whooping loudly and shouting out "Tallyho!"

I took Darcy's arm. "Let's go outside. Please."

"All right," he muttered at last.

He allowed me to lead us out of the ballroom and onto the terrace at the back of the house.

"Well?" he asked.

"Darcy, I'm so sorry that I accused you," I said. "I thought—well, I thought that I couldn't trust you. I didn't know what to think. I mean, you did come into Whiffy's house that day and I couldn't believe it was just to see me. . . . And all those strange things going on. I didn't feel safe. And now I know who was behind them, only I need your help. We've got to catch him. We've got to get proof."

"Catch who?" Darcy whispered, even though we were alone.

I leaned closer. "Tristram. He was the one who killed de Mauxville and now he's trying to kill me."

"Really?" He was standing close beside me and before I knew what was happening, a black-gloved hand came over my mouth and I was being dragged backward into the shadows at the edge of the terrace.

I squirmed to glance up at that black-hooded face. The smile was not Darcy's. And too late I realized that he had said the word "really" with a *w*, not an *r*.

"That beggar O'Mara grabbed the highwayman outfit," he said as I flailed out at him. "But this worked out rather well, as it happens. I bagged his scarf."

I struggled to bite at his fingers, as the scarf came around my throat. I tried to thrash out at him, kick him, scratch his hands, but he had the advantage of being behind me. And he was much stronger than I had expected. Slowly and surely he was dragging me backward, away from the lights and safety, one hand still clamped over my mouth.

"When you're found floating in the lake, O'Mara's scarf will give him away," he whispered into my ear. "And nobody will ever suspect me." He gave the scarf a savage twist. I fought to breathe as he yanked me backward.

Blood was singing in my ears and spots were dancing in front of my eyes. If I didn't do something soon, it would be too late. What would be the last thing he'd expect of me? He'd expect me to try to pull away to break free of him. Instead, I mustered all of my failing strength and rammed my head backward into his face. It must have hurt him a lot because it certainly hurt me. He let out a yell of pain. He might have been stronger than I had expected, but he still didn't weigh much. He went down hard, with me on top of him.

"Damn you," he gasped and tightened his grip on the scarf again.

As I tried to get to my feet he yanked me down, growling like an animal as he twisted the scarf. With the last of my strength I raised myself up then rammed myself down onto him. My aim must have been good. He let out a yowl and for a second the scarf went limp. This time I scrambled off him and tried to get to my feet. He grabbed at me. I opened my mouth to yell for help but no sound would come out of my throat.

"And you pretended to play the innocent virgin," said a voice above us. "This is the wildest sex I've witnessed in years. You must teach me some of those moves next time we're together." And the masked highwayman stood there, holding out a hand to me. I staggered to my feet and stood gasping and coughing as he supported me.

"Tristram," I whispered. "Tried to kill me. Don't let him get away."

Tristram was also struggling to his feet. He started to run. Darcy brought him down in a flying rugby tackle. "You never were any good at rugger, were you, Hautbois?" he said, kneeling on Tristram's back and bringing his arm up behind him. "I always thought you were rotten. Lying, cheating, stealing, getting other fellows into trouble at school—that was you, wasn't it, Hautbois?"

Tristram cried out as Darcy rammed his face into the gravel with a good deal of satisfaction. "But killing? Why was he trying to kill you?"

"To get my part of an inheritance. He killed de Mauxville for the same reason," I managed to say, although my throat was still burning.

"I thought something strange was going on. Ever since you fell off that boat," Darcy said.

"Let me up. You're hurting me," Tristram whined. "I never meant to harm her. She's exaggerating. It was only fun."

"I saw the whole thing and it wasn't fun," Darcy said. He looked up as there were footsteps on the gravel behind us.

"What's going on here?" Lord Mountjoy demanded.

"Call the police," Darcy shouted to him. "I caught this fellow trying to kill Georgie."

"Tristram?" Whiffy exclaimed. "What the devil . . ."

"Get him off me, Whiffy. He's got it all wrong," Tristram yelled. "It was just a game. I didn't mean anything."

"Some game," I said. "You'd have let my brother hang for you."

"No, it wasn't me. I didn't kill de Mauxville. I didn't kill anyone."

"Yes, you did, and I can prove it," I said.

Tristram started to blubber as he was dragged to his feet.

Darcy put an arm around me as they led Tristram away. "Are you all right?"

"Much better now. Thank you for coming to my rescue."

"It looked as if you were doing rather well without me," he said. "I quite enjoyed watching."

"You mean you were standing there watching and didn't try to help?" I demanded indignantly.

"I had to make sure I could testify he was really trying to kill you," he said. "Quite a good little fighter, I have to say." He put his hands on my shoulders. "Don't look at me like that. I'd have intervened earlier if I'd seen you sneak out of the room. Belinda was doing a harem dance and I got distracted for a second. No, wait, Georgie. Come back here. . . ." He ran after me as I shook myself free and stalked away.

I strode out into the darkness until I stood at the balustrade overlooking the lake.

"Georgie!" Darcy said again.

"It's nothing to me what you and Belinda do," I said.

"Strangely enough I've done nothing more with Belinda than sit next to her at a roulette wheel. Not my type. Too easy. I like a challenge in life, personally." He slipped his arm around my shoulders.

"Darcy, if you'd come earlier you would have heard me apologizing. I thought you were dressed as the executioner, you see. I feel awful about the horrible things I said to you."

"I suppose it was a natural supposition."

I was very conscious of his arm, warm around my shoulder. "Why did you follow me into that house?"

"Mere curiosity and an opportunity to get you alone." He took a deep breath. "Look, Georgie. I've got a confession to make. After that wedding thing I got a tad drunk. I made a bet that I could lay you within a week."

"So when you took me back to your place, after the boat accident, you didn't really care about me at all. You were trying to win a stupid bet?"

He squeezed my shoulder more tightly. "No, that didn't cross my mind at all. When I pulled you out of that water, I realized that I really cared for you."

"But you still tried to get me into bed."

"Well, I'm only human and you were looking at me as if you fancied me. You do fancy me, don't you?"

"I might," I said, looking away. "If I felt sure that . . ."

"The bet's off," he said. He turned me toward him and kissed me full and hard on the mouth. His arms were crushing me. I felt as if I were melting into him and I didn't want it to stop. The hubbub that was still going on on the terrace faded into oblivion until there were just the two of us in the whole universe.

Later, when we walked back to the house together, our arms around each other, I asked him, "So who was the bet with?"

"Your friend Belinda," he said. "She said I'd be doing you a favor."

Chapter 29

It was almost morning by the time I finally fell into bed. I had spent the rest of the evening giving my statements to police. Chief Inspector Burnall arrived from Scotland Yard sometime during the night and I had to repeat everything. Finally Tristram was led away screaming and weeping disgracefully. Sir Hubert would have been mortified at his behavior. According to Darcy he'd been a rotten egg even at school, cheating on exams and getting Darcy blamed for something he had stolen.

I drove home with Whiffy, Belinda, and Marisa the next afternoon and arrived at Rannoch House just in time to witness Binky's triumphant return. A crowd had gathered outside on hearing the latest news and when Binky appeared from a police car, everyone cheered. Binky went quite pink and looked pleased.

"I can't thank you enough, old thing," he said when we were safely inside and he had poured us both a Scotch. "You saved my life, literally. I'll be in your debt forever."

I didn't like to suggest that he find a way to resume my allowance as a small thank-you gift.

"So how did they find out it was this blighter Hautbois who killed de Mauxville? Did he confess?" he asked. "I've only had the most sketchy news so far."

"He was caught trying to strangle me," I said, "which was lucky, as they'd have had no way to link him to de Mauxville's death. Or to those other attempts on my life."

"Attempts on your life?"

"Yes, Tristram tried diligently to push me off a tube platform, poison me, trip me down the stairs, and be squashed by a statue. I'm glad to say I survived them all." The one thing he hadn't done, so it seemed, was to push me off the boat. That really had been a freak accident, but it gave him the idea that it might be simple to get rid of me. "I was known to be accident-prone so nobody would ever have suspected," I said, with an involuntary shudder.

"So they'd no proof he was the murderer?"

"Actually now they have. An autopsy revealed there was cyanide in de Mauxville's system, and in the poor woman he killed accidentally."

"Killed accidentally?"

"He meant to poison me with a cyanide-laced sugar cube, but some woman took the sugar bowl from me and died instead."

Binky looked astonished. "A poisoned sugar cube? How did he know you'd take the right cube? Had he poisoned the entire bowl?"

"No, he was lucky as well as opportunistic. He had the cyanide in his pocket, waiting for a chance to use it. When the woman at the next table started speaking to me, I turned around just long enough for him to taint one cube. Then he made a show of taking a lump himself first, leaving the poisoned cube sitting on top."

"Well, I'm dashed," Binky said. "Smart cove, then."

"Very smart," I said. "He played the likeable dolt so well that no one ever suspected him."

"And all for money," Binky said with disgust.

"Money is quite a useful thing to have," I said. "You only notice how useful when you don't have enough."

"That's certainly true," Binky said. "Which reminds me. I had a brilliant idea when I was locked up with hours to think: we'll open up Castle Rannoch to the public. We'll bring rich Americans for a Highland hunting experience. Fig can do cream teas."

I started to laugh. "Fig? Can you see Fig serving cream teas to chara-bancs full of plebs?"

"Well, not exactly serve them herself. Preside over them. Meet the duchess, you know. . . . "

But I was still laughing. Tears streamed down my face as I laughed myself silly.

$\mathcal{C}hapter\ 30$

Buckingham Palace
Westminster
London
Later in May 1932

"Extraordinary," Her Majesty said. "From what one reads in the papers, one understands that this young man is a relative of Sir Hubert Anstruther."

"A distant relative, ma'am. Sir Hubert actually rescued him from France."

"French, then? And the man he killed was also a Frenchman, I believe. Well, that tidies it up nicely, doesn't it?" She looked at me over her Wedgwood teacup. "What one doesn't understand is why he picked Rannoch House to do the deed."

"He knew why de Mauxville was in London and realized that my brother and I would have a strong motive for murder."

"An intelligent young man, then." She took a thin slice of brown bread from the plate that was offered her. "I always feel it's such a pity when good brains are wasted." She looked up at me and nodded approvingly. "You seem to have made admirable use of your brains, Georgiana. Well done. I see that your brother was given a hero's welcome when he arrived back in Scotland."

I nodded. For some reason there was a lump in my throat. I hadn't realized how fond I was of Binky.

"And I haven't had a chance to ask you about the house party yet, with all of this sensationalism going on," the queen said. "I take it my son and that woman were both in attendance?"

"They were, ma'am."

"And?"

"I would say that His Highness is infatuated. He couldn't take his eyes off her."

"And is she equally infatuated with him?"

I thought before I answered. "I believe she likes the idea of having power over him. He's certainly already under her thumb."

"Oh, dear. Just as I feared. Let us hope this is another of his passing fancies or that she'll tire of him. I must speak to the king. This may be a good time to send David on a long tour of the colonies." She took another delicate bite of bread. I had just taken a second slice myself, in the hope that she wasn't counting.

"And what about you, Georgiana?" she asked. "What shall you be doing with yourself now that the excitement is over?"

"We've just had the good news that Sir Hubert has come out of his coma, and will be coming home," I said. "I thought I'd go down to Eynsleigh and keep him company. It will be an awful shock for him when he hears about Tristram."

"And it was all for nothing too," the queen said. "Sir Hubert is known for his strong constitution. I expect he'll now live for years."

"One hopes so, ma'am," I said, thinking that I'd have to go back to cleaning houses after all.

"Let me know when you return from Sir Hubert's," Her Majesty said. "I think I have another little assignment for you. . . ."

A Royal Pain

This book is dedicated to my three princesses:
Elizabeth, Meghan and Mary;
and to my princes: Sam and T. J.

Notes and Acknowledgments

This is a work of fiction. While several members of the British royal family appear as themselves in the book, there was no Princess Hannelore of Bavaria and no Lady Georgiana.

On a historical note: Europe at that time was in turmoil with communists and fascists vying for control of Germany, left bankrupt and dispirited after the first great war. In England communism was making strides among the working classes and left-wing intellectuals. At the other extreme Oswald Mosley was leading a group of extreme fascists called the Blackshirts. Skirmishes and bloody battles between the two were frequent in London.

A special acknowledgment to the Misses Hedley, Jensen, Reagan and Danika, of Sonoma, California, who make cameo appearances in this book.

And thanks, as always, to my splendid support group at home: Clare, Jane and John; as well as my equally splendid support group in New York: Meg, Kelly, Jackie and Catherine.

Chapter 1

RANNOCH HOUSE
BELGRAVE SQUARE
LONDON W.I.
MONDAY, JUNE 6, 1932

The alarm clock woke me this morning at the ungodly hour of eight. One of my nanny's favorite sayings was "Early to bed, early to rise, makes a man healthy, wealthy and wise." My father did both and look what happened to him. He died, penniless, at forty-nine.

In my experience there are only two good reasons to rise with the dawn: one is to go hunting and the other to catch the Flying Scotsman from Edinburgh to London. I was about to do neither. It wasn't the hunting season and I was already in London.

I fumbled for the alarm on the bedside table and battered it into silence.

"Court circular, June 6," I announced to a nonexistent audience as I stood up and pulled back the heavy velvet curtains. "Lady Georgiana Rannoch embarks on another hectic day of social whirl. Luncheon at the Savoy, tea at the Ritz, a visit to Scapparelli for a fitting of her latest ball gown, then dinner and dancing at the Dorchester—or none of the above," I added. To be honest it had been a long time since I had any events on my social calendar and my life had never been a mad social whirl. Almost twenty-two years old and not a single invitation sitting on my mantelpiece. The awful thought struck me that I should accept that I was over the hill and destined to be a spinster for life. Maybe all I had to look forward to was the queen's suggestion that I become lady-in-waiting to Queen Victoria's one surviving daughter—who is also my great-aunt and lives out in deepest Gloucestershire. Years ahead of walking the Pekinese and holding knitting wool danced before my eyes.

I suppose I should introduce myself before I go any further: I am Victoria Georgiana Charlotte Eugenie of Glen Garry and Rannoch, known to my friends as Georgie. I am of the house of Windsor, second cousin to King George V, thirty-fourth in line to the throne, and at this moment I was stony broke.

Oh, wait. There was another option for me. It was to marry Prince Siegfried of Romania, in the Hohenzollen-Sigmaringen line—for whom my private nickname was Fishface. That subject hadn't come up recently, thank God. Maybe other people had also found out that he has a predilection for boys.

It was clearly going to be one of those English summer days that makes one think of rides along leafy country lanes, picnics in the meadow with strawberries and cream, croquet and tea on the lawn. Even in central London birds were chirping madly. The sun was sparkling from the windows across the square. A gentle breeze was stirring the net curtains. The postman was whistling as he walked around the square. And what did I have before me?

"Oh, golly," I exclaimed as I suddenly remembered the reason for the alarm clock and leaped into action. I was expected at a residence on Park Lane. I washed, dressed smartly and went downstairs to make some tea and toast. You can see how wonderfully domesticated I'd become in two short months. When I bolted from our castle in Scotland back in April, I didn't even know how to boil water. Now I can manage baked beans and an egg. For the first time in my life I was living with no servants, having no money to pay them. My brother, the Duke of Glen Garry and Rannoch, usually known as Binky, had promised to send me a maid from our Scottish estate, but so far none had materialized. I suspect that no God-fearing, Presbyterian Scottish mother would let her daughter loose in the den of iniquity that London is perceived to be. As for paying for me to hire a maid locally—well, Binky is as broke as I. You see, when our father shot himself after the crash of '29, Binky inherited the estate and was saddled with the most horrendous death duties.

So I have managed thus far servantless, and frankly, I'm jolly proud of myself. The kettle boiled. I made my tea, slathered Cooper's Oxford marmalade on my toast (yes, I know I was supposed to be economizing but there are standards below which one just can't sink) and brushed away the crumbs hastily as I put on my coat. It was going to be too warm for any kind of jacket, but I couldn't risk anyone seeing what I was wearing as I walked through Belgravia—the frightfully upper-crust part of London just south of Hyde Park where our town house is situated.

A chauffeur waiting beside a Rolls saluted smartly to me as I passed. I held my coat tightly around me. I crossed Belgrave Square, walked up Grosvenor Cresent and paused to look longingly at the leafy expanse of Hyde Park before I braved the traffic across Hyde Park Corner. I heard the clip-clop of hooves and a pair of riders came out of Rotten Row. The girl was riding a splendid gray and was smartly turned out in a black bowler and well-cut hacking jacket. Her boots were positively gleaming with polish. I looked at her enviously. Had I stayed home in Scotland that could have been me. I used to ride every morning with my brother. I wondered if my sister-in-law, Fig, was riding my horse and ruining its mouth. She was inclined to be heavy-handed with the reins, and she weighed a good deal more than I. Then I noticed other people loitering on the corner. Not so well turned out, these men. They carried signs or sandwich boards: *I need a job. Will work for food. Not afraid of hard work.*

I had grown up sheltered from the harsh realities of the world. Now I was coming face-to-face with them on a daily basis. There was a depression going on and people were lining up for bread and soup. One man who stood beneath Wellington's Arch had a distinguished look to him, well-polished shoes, coat and tie. In fact he was wearing medals. *Wounded on Somme. Any kind of employment considered.* I could read in his face his desperation and his repugnance at having to do this and wished that I had the funds to hire him on the spot. But essentially I was in the same boat as most of them.

Then a policeman blew his whistle, traffic stopped and I sprinted across the street to Park Avenue. Number 59 was fairly modest by Park Lane standards—a typical Georgian house of the smart set, redbrick with white trim, with steps leading up to the front door and railings around the well that housed the servants' quarters below stairs. Not dissimilar to Rannoch House although our London place is a good deal larger and more imposing. Instead of going up to the front door, I went gingerly down the dark steps to the servants' area and located the key under a flowerpot. I let myself in to a dreadful dingy hallway in which the smell of cabbage lingered.

All right, so now you know my dreadful secret. I've been earning money by cleaning people's houses. My advertisement in the *Times* lists me as Coronet Domestics, as recommended by Lady Georgiana of Glen Garry and Rannoch. I don't do any proper heavy cleaning. No scrubbing of floors or, heaven forbid, lavatory bowls. I wouldn't have a clue where to begin. I undertake to open up the London houses for those who have been away at their country estates and don't want to go to the added expense and nuisance of sending their servants ahead of them to do this task. It involves whisking off dust sheets, making beds, sweeping and dusting. That much I can do without breaking anything too often—since another thing you should know about me is that I am prone to the occasional episode of clumsiness.

It is a job sometimes fraught with danger. The houses I work in are owned by people of my social set. I'd die of mortification if I bumped into a fellow debutante or, even worse, a dance partner, while on my hands and knees in a little white cap. So far only my best friend, Belinda Warburton-Stoke, and an unreliable rogue called Darcy O'Mara know about my secret. And the least said about him, the better.

Until I started this job, I had never given much thought to how the other half lives. My own recollections of going below stairs to visit the servants all centered around big warm kitchens with the scent of baking and being allowed to help roll out the dough and lick the spoon. I found the cleaning cupboard and helped myself to a bucket and cloths, feather duster, and a carpet sweeper. Thank heavens it was summer and no fires would be required in the bedrooms. Carrying coal up three flights of stairs was not my favorite occupation, nor was venturing into what my grandfather called the coal'ole to fill the scuttles. My grandfather? Oh, sorry. I suppose I hadn't mentioned him. My father was first cousin to King George, and Queen Victoria's grandson, but my mother was an actress from Essex. Her father still lives in Essex, in a little house with gnomes in the front garden. He's a genuine Cockney and a retired policeman. I absolutely adore him. He's the one person to whom I can say absolutely anything.

At the last second I remembered to retrieve my maid's cap from my coat pocket and jammed it over my unruly hair. Maids are never seen without their caps. I pushed open the baize door that led to the main part of the house and barreled into a great pile of luggage, which promptly fell over with a crash. Who on earth thought of piling luggage against the door to the servants' quarters? Before I could pick up the strewn suitcases there was a shout and an elderly woman dressed head to toe in black appeared from the nearest doorway, waving a stick at me. She was still wearing an old-fashioned bonnet tied under her chin and a traveling cloak. An awful thought struck me that I had mistaken the number, or written it down wrongly, and I was in the wrong house.

"What is happening?" she demanded in French. She glanced at my outfit. *"Vous êtes la bonne?"* Asking "Are you the maid?" in French was rather a strange way to greet a servant in London, where most servants have trouble with proper English. Fortunately I was educated in Switzerland and my French is quite good. I replied that I was indeed the maid, sent to open up the house by the domestic service, and I had been told that the occupants would not arrive until the next day.

"We came early," she said, still in French. "Jean-Claude drove us from Biarritz to Paris in the motorcar and we caught the overnight train."

"Jean-Claude is the chauffeur?" I asked.

"Jean-Claude is the Marquis de Chambourie," she said. "He is also a racing driver. We made the trip to Paris in six hours." Then she realized she was talking to a housemaid. "How is it that you speak passable French for an English person?" she asked.

I was tempted to say that I spoke jolly good French, but instead I mumbled something about traveling abroad with the family on the Côte D'Azur.

"Fraternizing with French sailors, I shouldn't be surprised," she muttered.

"And you, you are Madame's housekeeper?" I asked.

"I, my dear young woman, am the Dowager Countess Sophia of Liechtenstein," she said, and in case you're wondering why a countess of a German-speaking country was talking to me in French, I should point out that highborn ladies of her generation usually spoke French, no matter what their native tongue was. "My maid is attempting to make a bedroom ready for me," she continued with a wave of her hand up the stairs. "My housekeeper and the rest of my staff will arrive tomorrow by train as planned. Jean-Claude drives a two-seater motorcar. My maid had to perch on the luggage. I understand it was most disagreeable for her." She paused to scowl at me. "And it is most disagreeable for me to have nowhere to sit."

I wasn't quite sure of the protocol of the court of Liechtenstein and how one addressed a dowager countess of that land, but I've discovered that when in doubt, guess upward. "I'm sorry, Your Highness, but I was told to come today. Had I known that you had a relative who was a racing driver, I would have prepared the house yesterday." I tried not to grin as I said this.

She frowned at me, trying to ascertain whether I was being cheeky or not, I suspect. "Hmmph," was all she could manage.

"I will remove the covers from a comfortable chair for Your Highness," I said, going through into a large dark drawing room and whisking the cover off an armchair, sending a cloud of dust into the air. "Then I will make ready your bedroom first. I am sure the crossing was tiring and you need a rest."

"What I want is a good hot bath," she said.

Ah, that might be a slight problem, I thought. I had seen my grandfather lighting the boiler at Rannoch House but I had no personal experience of doing anything connected to boilers. Maybe the countess's maid was more familiar with such things.

Someone would have to be. I wondered how to say "boilers are not in my contract" in French.

"I will see what can be done," I said, bowed and backed out of the room. Then I grabbed my cleaning supplies and climbed the stairs. The maid looked about as old and bad-tempered as the countess, which was understandable if she'd had to ride all the way from Biarritz perched on top of the luggage. She had chosen the best bedroom, at the front of the house overlooking Hyde Park, and had already opened the windows and taken the dust covers off the furniture. I tried speaking to her in French, then English, but it seemed that she only spoke German. My German was not up to more than "I'd like a glass of mulled wine," and "Where is the ski lift?" So I pantomimed that I would make the bed. She looked dubious. We found sheets and made it between us. This was fortunate as she was most particular about folding the corners just so. She also rounded up about a dozen more blankets and eiderdowns from bedrooms on the same floor, as apparently the countess felt the cold in England. That much I could understand.

When finished the bed looked suitable for the Princess and the Pea.

After I had dusted and swept the floor under the maid's critical eye, I took her to the bathroom and turned on the taps. *"Heiss Bad für . . .* Countess," I said, stretching my German to its limit. Miraculously there was a loud whooomph and hot water came forth from one of those little geyser contraptions above the bath. I felt like a magician and marched downstairs triumphantly to tell the countess that her room was ready for her and she could have a bath anytime she wished.

As I came down the final flight of stairs, I could hear voices coming from the drawing room. I hadn't realized that yet another person was in the house. I hesitated at the top of the flight of stairs. At that moment I heard a man's voice saying, in heavily accented English, "Don't worry, Aunt. Allow me to assist you. I shall personally aid in the transportation of your luggage to your room if you feel it is too much for your maid. Although why you bring a maid who is not capable of the most basic chores, I simply cannot understand. If you choose to make life uncomfortable for yourself, it is your own fault." And a young man came out of the room. He was slim, pale, with ultra-upright carriage. His hair was almost white blond and slicked straight back, giving him a ghostly, skull-like appearance—Hamlet come to life. The expression on his face was utterly supercilious—as if he had detected a nasty smell under his nose, and he pursed his large codlike lips as he talked. I had recognized him instantly, of course. It was none other than Prince Siegfried, better known as Fishface—the man everyone expected me to marry.

Chapter 2

It took me a moment to react. I was rooted to the spot with horror and couldn't seem to make my body obey me when my brain was commanding me to run. Siegfried bent and picked up a hatbox and a ridiculously small train case and started up the stairs with them. I suppose if I had been capable of rational thought I could merely have dropped to my hands and knees and pretended to be sweeping. Aristocrats pay no attention to working domestics. But the sight of him had completely unnerved me, so I did what my mother had done so successfully, so many times and with so many men—I turned and bolted.

I raced up the second flight of stairs as Siegfried came up the first with remarkable agility. Not the countess's bedroom. At least I managed that degree of coherence. I opened a door at the rear of the landing and ran inside, shutting the door after me as quietly as possible. It was a back bedroom, one from which we had taken the extra quilts.

I heard Siegfried's footfalls on the landing. "This is the bedroom she has chosen?" I heard him saying. "No, no. This will not do at all. Too noisy. The traffic will keep her awake all night."

And to my horror I heard the footsteps coming in my direction. I looked around the room. It contained no real wardrobe, just a high gentleman's chest. We had taken the dust sheets off the chest and the bed. There was literally nowhere to hide.

I heard a door open close by. "No, no. Too impossibly ugly," I heard him say.

I rushed to the window and opened it. It was a long drop to the small garden below, but there was a drainpipe beside the window and a small tree that could be reached about ten feet down. I didn't wait a second longer. I hoisted myself out of the window and grabbed onto the drainpipe. It felt sturdy enough and I started to climb down. Thank heavens for my education at finishing school in Switzerland. The one thing I had learned to do, apart from speaking French and knowing where to seat a bishop at a dinner table, was to climb down drainpipes in order to meet ski instructors at the local tavern.

The maid's uniform was tight and cumbersome. The heavy skirts wrapped around my legs as I tried to shin down the drainpipe. I thought I heard something rip as I felt for a foothold. I heard Siegfried's voice, loud and clear in the room above. "*Mein Gott,* no, no, no. This place is a disaster. An utter disaster. Aunt! You have rented a disaster—and not even a garden to speak of."

I heard the voice come across to the window. I think I have mentioned that I am also inclined to be clumsy in moments of stress. My hands somehow slipped from the drainpipe and I fell. I felt branches scratching my face as I tumbled into the tree, uttering a loud squeak. I clutched the nearest branch and held on for dear life. The whole thing swayed alarmingly but I was safely among the leaves. I waited until the voice died away then lowered myself down to the ground, sprinted through the side gate, grabbed my coat from the servants' hallway and fled. I would have to telephone the countess and tell her that unfortunately the young maid I sent to the house had suddenly been taken ill. It seemed she had developed a violent reaction to dust.

I had only gone a few yards down Park Lane when somebody called my name. For an awful moment I thought Siegfried might have been looking out of a window and recognized me, but then I realized that he wouldn't be calling me Georgie. Only my friends called me that.

I turned around and there was my best friend, Belinda Warburton-Stoke, rushing toward me, arms open wide. She was an absolute vision in turquoise silk, trimmed with shocking pink and topped with cape sleeves that fluttered out in the breeze as she ran, making her seem to be flying. The whole ensemble was completed with a little pink feathered hat, perched wickedly over one eye.

"Darling, it *is* you," she said, embracing me in a cloud of expensive French perfume. "It's been simply ages. I've missed you terribly."

Belinda is completely different from me in every way. I'm tall, reddish-blondish with freckles. She's petite, dark haired with big brown eyes, sophisticated, elegant and very naughty. I shouldn't have been glad to see her, but I was.

"I wasn't the one who went jaunting off to the Med."

"My dear, if you were invited for two weeks on a yacht and the yacht was owned by a divine Frenchman, would you have refused?"

"Probably not," I said. "Was it as divine as you expected?"

"Divine but strange," she said. "I thought he had invited me because, you know, he fancied me. And since he's fabulously rich and a duke to boot, I thought I might be on to something. And you have to admit that Frenchmen do make divine lovers—so naughty and yet so romantic. Well, it turned out that he'd also invited not only his wife but his mistress and he dutifully visited alternate cabins on alternate nights. I was left to play gin rummy with his twelve-year-old daughter."

I chuckled. "And flirt with the sailors?"

"Darling, the sailors were all over forty and had paunches. Not a handsome brute among them. I came back positively sex starved, only to find all the desirable males had fled London for the country or the Continent. So seeing you is a positive ray of sunshine in my otherwise gloomy life. But darling Georgie"—she was now staring at me—"what have you been doing to yourself?"

"What does it look as if I've been doing?"

"Wrestling with a lion in the jungle?" She eyed me doubtfully. "Darling, you have a wicked scratch down one cheek, a smudge down the other, and you have leaves in your hair. Or was it a wild roll in the hay in the park? Do tell, I'm mad with curiosity and I'll be even madder with jealousy if it was the latter."

"I had to make a speedy exit because of a man," I said.

"The brute tried to attack you? In broad daylight?"

I started to laugh. "Nothing of the kind. I was earning my daily crust in the usual way, opening up a house for people arriving from the Continent, only the new occupants turned up a day early and one of them was none other than the dreaded Prince Siegfried."

"Fishface in person? How utterly frightful. What did he say when he saw you garbed as a maid? And more to the point, what did you say to him?"

"He didn't see me," I said. "I fled and had to climb down from an upstairs window. It's a good thing we became so adept at drainpipes at Les Oiseaux. Hence the scratches and the leaves in my hair. I fell into a tree. All in all a very trying morning."

"My poor sweet Georgie—what an ordeal. Come here." She removed the leaves from my hair, then took out a lace handkerchief from her handbag and dabbed at my cheek. A wave of Chanel floated over me. "That's a little better but you need cheering up. I know, let's go and have lunch somewhere. You choose."

I desperately wanted to have lunch with Belinda, but funds were horribly low at that moment. "There are some little cafés along Oxford Street, or one of the department stores?" I suggested. "They do ladies' lunches, don't they?"

Belinda looked as if I'd suggested eating jellied eels on the Old Kent Road. "A department store? Darling, such things are for old women who smell of mothballs and suburban housewives from Coulsden whose hubbies let the little woman come up to town for a day's shopping. People like you and I would cause too much of a stir if we appeared there—rather like letting in a peacock among a lot of hens. It would quite put them off their grilled sole. Now where should we go? The Dorchester would do at a pinch, I suppose. The Ritz is within walking distance, but I rather feel that all it does well is tea. The same goes for Brown's—nothing but old ladies in tweeds. There is no point in going to eat where one can't be seen by the right people. I suppose it will have to be the Savoy. At least one can be sure of getting decent food there—"

"Just a moment, Belinda." I cut her off in mid sentence. "I am still cleaning houses for a pittance. I simply couldn't afford the kind of place you're thinking of."

"My treat, darling," she said, waving a turquoise-gloved hand expansively. "That yacht did put into Monte Carlo for a night or two and you know how good I am at the tables. What's more, I've made a sale—someone has actually bought one of my creations, for cash."

"Belinda, that's wonderful. Do tell."

She linked arms with me and we started to walk back up Park Lane. "Well, you remember the purple dress—the one I tried to sell to that awful Mrs. Simpson because I thought it looked like an American's idea of royalty?"

"Of course," I said, blushing at the fiasco of my brief modeling career. I had been called upon to model that dress and . . . well, never mind.

"Well, darling, I met another American lady at Crockford's—yes, I admit it, gambling again, I'm afraid—and I told her I was an up-and-coming couturiere and I designed for royalty, and she came to my studio and bought the dress, just like that. She even paid for it on the spot and—" She broke off as a front door opened and a man came out, pausing at the top of the steps with a look of utter disdain on his face.

"It's Siegfried," I hissed. "He'll see me. Run."

It was too late. He looked in our direction as he came down the front steps. "Ah, Lady Georgiana. We meet again. What a pleasant surprise." His face didn't indicate that the surprise was in any way pleasant, but he did bow slightly.

I grabbed at my coat and held it tightly around me so that my maid's uniform didn't show. I was horribly conscious of the scratch on my cheek and my hair in disarray. I must have looked a fright. Not that I wanted Siegfried to find me attractive, but I do have my pride.

"Your Highness." I nodded regally. "May I present my friend Belinda Warburton-Stoke?"

"I believe we have had the pleasure before," he said, although the words didn't convey the same undertones as with most young men who had met Belinda. "In Switzerland, I believe."

"Of course," Belinda said. "How do you do, Your Highness. Are you visiting London for long?"

"My aunt has just arrived from the Continent, so of course I had to pay the required visit, although the house she has rented—what a disaster. Not fit for a dog."

"How terrible for you," I said.

"I shall endure it somehow," he said, his expression suggesting that he was about to spend the night in the dungeons of the Tower of London. "And where are you ladies off to?"

"We're going to lunch, at the Savoy," Belinda said.

"The Savoy. The food is not bad there. Maybe I shall join you."

"That would be lovely," Belinda said sweetly.

I dug my fingers into her forearm. I knew this was her idea of having fun. It certainly wasn't mine. I decided to play a trump card.

"How kind of you, Your Highness. We have so much to talk about. Have you been out riding recently—since your unfortunate accident, I mean?" I asked sweetly.

I saw a spasm of annoyance cross his face. "Ah," he said, "I have just remembered that I promised to meet a fellow at his club. So sorry. Another time maybe?" He clicked his heels together in that strangely European gesture, and jerked his head in a bow. "I bid you adieu. Lady Georgiana. Miss Warburton-Stoke." And he marched down Park Lane as quickly as his booted feet would carry him.

Chapter 3

Belinda looked at me and started to laugh. "What was that about?"

"He fell off his horse last time we were together, at that house party," I said, "after he had boasted how well he could ride. I had to say something to stop him from coming to lunch with us. What on earth were you thinking?"

Belinda's eyes were twinkling. "I know, it was rather naughty of me but I couldn't resist. You in your maid's uniform and Prince Siegfried at the Savoy—how utterly scrumptious."

"I thought you were supposed to be my friend," I said.

"I am, darling. I am. But you have to admit that it would have been a riot."

"It would have been my worst nightmare."

"Why should you care what the odious man thinks? I thought the whole idea was to make sure that he would rather fall on his sword than marry you."

"Because he is liable to report back to the palace, especially if he noticed I was dressed as a maid, and even more especially if he put two and two together and realized he'd just spotted me cleaning his house. And if the palace found out, I'd be shipped off to the country to be lady-in-waiting to Queen Victoria's one surviving daughter and spend the rest of my days surrounded by Pekinese and knitting wool."

"Oh, I suppose you do have a valid point there." Belinda tried not to smile. "Yes, that was rather insensitive of me. Come along, you'll feel better after a jolly good lunch at the Savoy." She started to drag me down Park Lane. "We'll take a cab."

"Belinda, I can't go to the Savoy dressed like this."

"No problem, darling." Belinda yanked me sideways into Curzon Street.

"My salon is only just around the corner. We'll just pop in there and I'll lend you something to wear."

"I couldn't possibly wear one of your dresses. What if I damaged it in some way? You know what I'm like. I'd be liable to spill something on it."

"Don't be silly. You'll be doing me a favor actually. You can be a walking advertisement for my designs when you mingle with your royal relatives. That would be a coup, wouldn't it? Couturiere by appointment to the royal family?"

"Not the culottes," I said hastily, my one modeling disaster dancing before my eyes. "Some normal kind of garment that I can wear without tripping over it or looking like an idiot."

Belinda gave her delightful bell-like laugh. "You are so sweet, Georgie."

"Sweet but clumsy," I said gloomily.

"I'm sure you'll grow out of your clumsiness someday."

"I hope so," I said. "It's not that I'm perpetually clumsy. It's just that I'm always clumsy at the wrong place and the wrong time, in front of the wrong people. It must have something to do with nerves, I suppose."

"Now why should you be nervous?" Belinda demanded. "You're just about the most eligible young woman in Britain, and you're quite attractive and you have that delightfully fresh and virginal quality to you—speaking of which, anything to report on that front?"

"My virginity, you mean?"

Two nannies, pushing prams, turned back to glare at us with looks of utter horror.

Belinda and I exchanged a grin. "This conversation should probably wait for somewhere a little less public," I said and bundled her into the doorway of the building that housed her salon. Once upstairs in her little room she had me try on several outfits before settling on a light brown georgette dress with a filmy gold short cape over it.

"Capes are so in fashion at the moment and it goes so well with your hair," she said, and it did. I felt like a different person as I stared at myself in her full-length mirror. No longer gawky but tall and elegant—until I came to my feet, that is. I was wearing sensible black lace-up maid's shoes.

"The shoes will have to go," she said. "We can pop into Russell and Bromley on the way."

"Belinda—I have no money. Don't you understand that?"

"The shoes have to complement the outfit," she said airily. "Besides, you can pay me back when you're queen of somewhere. You never know, you might end up with a maharaja who will weigh you in diamonds."

"And then lock me away in a harem. No, thank you. I think I'll settle for a less wealthy Englishman."

"So boring, darling. And so completely sexless." Belinda stepped out onto the street and hailed a taxicab, which screeched to a halt beside her. "Russell and Bromley first," she said, as if this were normal behavior. For her it was. For me it still made me feel like Cinderella.

It took Belinda half an hour to select a pair of gold pumps for me, then it was off to the Savoy. Belinda chattered merrily and I found my spirits lifting. The cab swung under the wonderfully modern streamlined portico of the Savoy and a doorman leaped forward to open the door for us. I swept inside, feeling sophisticated and glamorous, a woman of the world at last. At least until my cape, flowing out behind me as I entered, got caught in the revolving door. I was yanked backward, choking, and had to stand there, mortified, while the doormen extricated me and Belinda chuckled.

"Did you know that you design dangerous clothing?" I demanded as we went through to the grill. "That's twice now that one of your garments has tried to kill me."

Belinda was still laughing. "Normal people seem to have no trouble with them. Maybe they are secretly communist garments, sworn to destroy the house of Windsor."

"Then I definitely won't let you sell one to my cousins." I readjusted the cape so that the clip was no longer digging into my neck as we reached the entrance of the grill.

"You have a reservation, miss?" the maitre d' asked.

"I'm Belinda Warburton-Stoke and I'm here to lunch with Lady Georgiana Rannoch," Belinda said sweetly as money passed discreetly from her hand to his, "and I'm terribly afraid that we have no reservation . . . but I'm sure you'll be an absolute angel and find us a little corner somewhere. . . ."

"Welcome, my lady. This is indeed an honor." He bowed to me and escorted us to a delightful table for two. "I will send the chef out to give you his recommendations."

"I must say it is useful to have a name," I said as we were seated.

"You should make use of it more often. You could probably get credit anywhere you wanted, for example."

"Oh no, I'm not going into debt. You know our family motto—Death Before Dishonor."

"There's nothing dishonorable about debt," Belinda said. "Think of the death duties your brother was saddled with when your father shot himself."

"Ah, but he sold off half the estate, the family silver and our property in Sutherland to pay them off."

"How boringly noble of him. I'm glad I'm just landed gentry and not aristocracy. It comes with less weight of ancestors' expectations. My great-great-grandfather was in trade, of course. Your crowd would have nothing to do with him, even though he could buy the lot of 'em. Anyway, I quite enjoy the vices of the lower classes—and speaking of vices, you never did tell me . . ."

"About what?"

"Your virginity, darling. I do hope you have finally done something to rid yourself of it. Such a burden."

Unfortunately blushes really show on my fair skin.

"You have finally done it, haven't you?" she went on in her loud bell-like tones, eliciting fascinated stares from all the surrounding tables. "Don't tell me you haven't! Georgie, what's the matter with you? Especially when you have someone who is ready, willing and oh so very able."

The poor young man who was busy pouring water into our glasses almost dropped the jug.

"Belinda," I hissed.

"I take it that the rakish Darcy O'Mara is still in the picture?"

"He's not, actually."

"Oh no. What happened? You two seemed so awfully chummy last time I saw you."

"We didn't have a row or anything. It's just that he's disappeared. Not long after the infamous house party. He just didn't call anymore and I've no idea where he's gone."

"Didn't you go and look him up?"

"I couldn't do that. If he doesn't want me, then I'm not about to throw myself at him."

"I would. He's definitely one of the most interesting men in London. Let's face it, there are precious few of them, aren't there? I am positively dying of sexual frustration at the moment."

The chef, now standing at our table, pretended to be busy straightening the cutlery. Belinda ordered all sorts of yummy things—an endive salad with smoked salmon and grilled lamb chops accompanied by a wondrously smooth claret, followed by a bread and butter pudding to die for. We had just finished our pudding, and coffee had been brought to the table, when a braying laugh could be heard across the grill, a sort of "haw haw haw." A young man got up from the table in question, still shaking with merriment. "What a riot," he said and started to walk in our direction.

"Now you see what I mean about there being no interesting men in London," Belinda muttered. "This is the current flower of British manhood. Father owns a publishing house but he's utterly useless between the covers."

"I don't think I know him."

"Gussie Gormsley, darling," she said.

"Gussie Gormsley?"

"Augustus. Father is Lord Gormsley. I'm surprised he's not on your list of eligibles. Must be the publishing connection. No trade in the family and all that." She waved at him. "Gussie. Over here."

Gussie was a large, fair young man who would have made an ideal rugby forward. His face lit up with pleasure when he saw Belinda.

"What-ho, Belinda old bean," he said. "Long time no see."

"Just back from the Med, darling. Have you met my good friend Georgiana Rannoch?"

"Not Binky's sister? Good God."

"Why do you say good God?" I asked.

"I always thought—well, he'd always given us to think that you were a shy, retiring little thing, and here you are absolutely dripping with glam."

"Georgie is probably the most eligible woman in Britain," Belinda said, before I could stammer anything. "Men are positively fighting over her. Foreign princes, American millionaires."

"No wonder Binky kept you a secret," Gussie said. "I must introduce you to old Lunghi." He turned and waved back toward his table in the corner.

"Lunghi who?" Belinda asked.

"Lunghi Fotheringay, old bean." Of course he pronounced the second name "Fungy." One does.

"Lunghi Fungy? What a scream," Belinda said. "Why is he called Lunghi?"

"Just back from India, you know. Showed us a snapshot of himself with a bit of cloth wrapped around his loins and someone said, what do you call that, and he said a lunghi, and then we realized how funny it was. So Lunghi Fungy he became." He gestured again. "Over here, old man. Couple of delectable young fillies I want you to meet."

I felt myself blushing with all eyes in the Savoy on me, but Belinda turned on her brilliant smile as Mr. Fotheringay approached. He was slim, dark and serious looking. Not bad, in fact.

Introductions were made and then Gussie said, "Look here, there's going to be a bit of a shindig at our place next week. You two wouldn't like to come, would you?"

"Love to, if we're free," Belinda said. "Anyone interesting going to be there?"

"Apart from us, you mean?" the dark and brooding Lunghi asked, gazing at her seriously. It was quite clear in which of us his interest lay. "I can assure you we are the most fascinating men in London at the moment."

"Unfortunately that seems to be so," Belinda agreed. "London is singularly devoid of fascination at present. We'll take them up on it, then, shall we, Georgie?"

"Why not?" I replied, trying to indicate that such invitations were commonplace.

"See you there then. I'll pop invitations into the post so that it's official and all that. It's Arlington Street—that big modern white block of flats beside Green Park. St. James's Mansions. You'll know it by the sound of jazz emanating from it and by the disgruntled looks on the faces of the neighbors."

Belinda and I rose to leave. "There you are. Good things happen when you're with me," she said as she paid the bill without a second glance. "And he was certainly impressed with you, wasn't he?"

"With your outfit, more likely," I said. "But it could be fun."

"One of them might do, you know."

"For what?"

"Your virginity, darling. Really you are so dense sometimes."

"You said that Gussie was useless between the covers," I pointed out.

"For me. He might be all right for you. You won't expect too much."

"Thanks all the same," I said, "but I've decided to wait for love. I don't want to end up a bolter like my mother."

"Speak of the devil," Belinda said.

I looked up to see my mother entering the room.

She stood in the doorway of the Savoy Grill, pretending to be taking in the scene, but really waiting until everyone in the place had noticed her. I had to admit that she did look an absolute vision in flowing white silk with just enough touches of red to be startling. The cloche hat that framed her delicate face was white straw with red swirls woven into it. The maitre d' leaped forward. "Your Grace, how delightful," he muttered.

My mother hasn't been Her Grace since many husbands ago, but she smiled prettily and didn't correct him. "Hello, François. How lovely to see you again," she said in that melodious voice that had charmed audiences in theaters around the world before my father snapped her up. She started across the room and then she saw me. Those huge blue eyes flew open in surprise.

"Good heavens, Georgie. It is you! I hardly recognized you, darling. You look positively civilized for once. You must have found a rich lover."

"Hello, Mummy." We kissed, about an inch from each other's cheeks. "I didn't know you were in town. I thought you'd be in the Black Forest at this time of year."

"I came over to meet—a friend." There was something coy in her voice.

"So are you still with what's-his-name?"

"Max? Well, yes and no. He thinks so. But one does tire of not being able to chat occasionally. I mean the sex is still heavenly, but one does enjoy a good conversation and for some reason I simply can't learn German. And all Max likes to talk about is shooting things. So I have taken a quick flit over to London. Ah, there he is now." I saw a hand waving from a far corner of the restaurant. "Must fly, darling. Are you still at dreary old Rannoch House? We'll have tea or something. Ciao!"

And she was gone, leaving me with the usual disappointment and frustration and so many things left unsaid. You've probably guessed by now that as a mother she hasn't been too satisfactory. Belinda took my arm. "I don't know why you are adamant about not ending up like your mother. She does have a wardrobe to die for."

"But at what cost?" I said. "My grandfather thinks that she's sold her soul."

A taxicab was hailed for us. We climbed in. I stared out of the window and found that I was shivering. It wasn't just the meeting with my mother that had unnerved me. As we were getting into the taxi, I think I spotted Darcy O'Mara walking into the Savoy, with a tall, dark-haired girl on his arm.

Chapter 4

"You're very quiet," Belinda commented during the taxi ride home. "Did the food not agree with you?"

"No, the food was divine," I said. I took a deep breath. "You didn't happen to notice Darcy coming into the Savoy as we left, did you?"

"Darcy? No, I can't say I did."

"Then I may be imagining things," I said. "But I could swear it was he, and he had a young woman on his arm. A very attractive young woman."

"Ah well," Belinda said with a sigh. "Men like Darcy are not known for their spaniel-like devotion, and I'm sure he has healthy appetites."

"I suppose you're right," I said and sat for the rest of the cab ride in deepest gloom. It seemed that my stupid reticence had robbed me of my chance with Darcy. Did I really want him? I asked myself. He was Irish, Catholic, penniless, unreliable and in every way unsuitable, except that he was the son of a peer. But the image of him with another girl brought almost a physical pain to my heart.

What's more, those fleeting meetings with my mother always left me frustrated and depressed. So much I wanted to say to her and never a moment to say it. And now it seemed she might be moving on to yet another new man. It was the vision of ending up like her that had made me cautious about surrendering to someone like Darcy in the first place. I wasn't sure that I had inherited her flighty nature, but I was sure I had definitely inherited those stalwart Rannoch traits. And Death Before Dishonor was our family name!

I let myself into Rannoch House, still wearing Belinda's stylish outfit, my maid's uniform and the clompy shoes now in a Harrods carrier bag. I had tried to make her take back the clothes she had lent me, but she had insisted that it was going to be good advertising and all I had to do was to hand her card to anyone who complimented me. I suppose she was right in a way, although she obviously thought I saw my royal relatives more frequently than I really did. As far as I knew, the next time I would set eyes on the king and queen would be at Balmoral, whither I was summoned each summer, Castle Rannoch being but a stone's throw away. And at Balmoral it was strictly Highland dress.

I stepped into the gloom of the front hall and noticed a letter lying on the mat. I picked it up expectantly. Post was a rarity as hardly anybody knew I was in London. Then I saw what it was and almost dropped it. From the palace. Hand delivered.

I went cold all over. From Her Majesty's private secretary. *Her Majesty hopes that you will be able to take tea with her tomorrow, June 7th. She apologizes for the short notice but a matter of some urgency has arisen.*

My first thought, of course, was that Siegfried had recognized the maid's uniform and had promptly visited the palace to tell them the awful truth. I'd be sent to the country and—"Wait a minute," I said out loud. She might be Queen of England and Empress of India and all that, but she can't force me to do anything I don't want to. This isn't the Middle Ages. She can't have my head cut off or throw me into the Tower. I'm doing nothing wrong. I know that cleaning houses is a little beneath my station, but I'm earning an honest living. I'm not asking anybody to support me. I'm trying to make my way in the world at a difficult time. She should be proud of my enterprise.

Right. That's that, then. That's exactly what I'll tell her.

I felt much better after that. I marched upstairs and took off Belinda's creation. Then I sat at my desk and wrote out a bill, for half the agreed amount, to the Dowager Countess Sophia, with an explanation about the maid's sudden aversion to London dust.

RANNOCH HOUSE
TUESDAY, JUNE 7, 1932

Diary,
Lovely bright morning. Buck House today. Tea with queen. Not
    expecting much to eat. Really, royal protocol is too silly. May have

to distract HM and gobble down a quick cake this time. I wonder
what she wants. Nothing good, I fear. . . .

When I was dressing to go to tea at the palace, I wasn't feeling quite as
brave anymore. Her Majesty is a formidable woman. She is small and may
not appear too fierce at first glance, but remember my great-grandmother,
Queen Victoria. She was small and yet a whole empire trembled when she
raised an eyebrow. Queen Mary doesn't have quite that power, but one look
at that ramrod straight back and those cold blue eyes with their frank, appraising stare, can turn the strongest person to a jelly. And she doesn't like to
be crossed. I stared at the clothes in my wardrobe, trying to decide what
would make the best impression. Not too worldly, so definitely not Belinda's creation. I have some fairly smart formal dresses, but my summer day
clothes are sadly lacking. The dress I liked best was made of cotton. It needed
a proper ironing and I had not yet mastered the use of the iron. I ended up
with more creases than I started with, not to mention a scorch or two. And
now was not a good time to practice. In the end I opted for simplicity and
went with a navy suit and white blouse. Rather like a school uniform but at
least I looked neat, clean and proper. I topped it off with my white straw hat
(nothing like my mother's stylish little number) and white gloves, then off
I went.

It was a warm day and I was rather red in the face by the time I reached
the top of Constitution Hill. I dabbed at my face with my eau de cologne-
soaked hanky before I walked past those guardsmen. The visitors' entrance
is on the far side of the palace. At least a visitor like myself, arriving without
benefit of state coach or Rolls, can enter through a side gate. I crossed the
forecourt, feeling, as I always did, that eyes were watching me and that I'd
probably trip over a cobble.

I was received with great civility and ushered upstairs, the royal apart-
ments being one floor up. Luckily I didn't have to face the grand staircase
with its red carpet and statues, but was taken up a simple back stair to an
office that looked as if it could have been any London solicitor's. Here Her
Majesty's secretary was waiting for me. "Ah, Lady Georgiana. Please come
with me. Her Majesty is awaiting you in her private sitting room." He
seemed quite cheerful, jolly even. I was tempted to ask him if Her Majesty
had inquired about the train service to deepest Gloucestershire. But then

maybe she hadn't disclosed to him why she had summoned me. He may have known nothing about aunts with Pekinese dogs.

Thank heavens we're not Catholic, I thought. At least they can't lock me away in a convent until a suitable groom is found. That made me freeze halfway down the hall. What if I was ushered into the sitting room only to find Prince Siegfried and a priest awaiting me?

"In here, my lady," the secretary said. "Lady Georgiana, ma'am."

I took a deep breath and stepped inside. The queen was seated in a Chippendale armchair in front of a low table. Although she was no longer young, her complexion was flawless and smooth, with no sign of wrinkles. What's more, I suspected she didn't need the help of the various expensive preparations my mother used to hang on to her youthful looks.

Tea was already laid, including a delicious array of cakes on a two-tiered silver and glass cake stand. Her Majesty held out a hand to me. "Ah, Georgiana, my dear. How good of you to come."

As if one refused a queen.

"It was very kind of you to invite me, ma'am." I attempted the usual mixture of curtsy and kiss on the cheek and managed it this time without bumping my nose.

"Do sit down. Tea is all ready. China or Indian?"

"China, thank you."

The queen poured the tea herself. "And do help yourself to something to eat."

"After you, ma'am," I said dutifully, knowing full well that protocol demands that the guest only eats what the queen eats. Last time she had chosen one slice of brown bread.

"I really don't think I'm hungry today," she said, making my spirits fall even further. Did she realize what torture it was to sit and stare at strawberry tarts and éclairs and not be able to eat one?

I was about to say that I wasn't hungry either, when she leaned forward. "On second thought, those éclairs do look delicious, don't they? We'll forget about our figures for once, shall we?"

She was in a good mood. Why, I wondered. Was this a good-bye tea before she announced some awful fate for me?

"How have you been faring since I saw you last, Georgiana?" she asked, fixing me with that powerful stare.

I had been trying hard to take a bite of éclair without getting any cream on my upper lip. "Well, thank you, ma'am."

"So you stayed in London. You didn't go to the country after all, or home to Scotland."

"No, ma'am. I had been planning to keep Sir Hubert company when he returned home from the Swiss hospital, but he has decided to complete his recovery at a Swiss sanitarium and there was little point in going home to Scotland." (Sir Hubert was my favorite former stepfather and had been seriously injured during a mountaineering expedition in the Alps.)

"And are you fully occupied in London?"

"I keep myself busy. I have friends. I lunched at the Savoy yesterday."

"It's always good to be busy," she said. "However, I do hope that there is more to your life than luncheons at the Savoy."

Where was this leading? I wondered.

"At this time of crisis there is so much that needs to be done," she went on. "A young woman like yourself, as yet unencumbered with husband and children, could do so much good and set such a fine example. Helping out in soup kitchens, giving advice on sanitary conditions to mothers and babies in the East End, or even joining the health and beauty movement. All worthy causes, Georgiana. All worth devoting time and energy."

This wasn't going to be too bad then, I thought. She clearly expected me to stay in London if she was suggesting I help mothers and babies in the East End.

"Excellent suggestions, ma'am," I said.

"I am patron of several worthy charities. I will find out where your services would be most appreciated."

"Thank you." I really meant it. I would actually quite enjoy helping a charity to do good. And it would give me something else to do between house cleanings.

"We'll put that suggestion to one side for now," Her Majesty said, taking a sip of China tea, "because I am hoping to enlist you as a coconspirator in a little plan I am devising."

She gave me her frank stare, her clear, blue eyes holding mine for a long moment.

"I am desperately worried about my son, Georgiana."

"The Prince of Wales?" I asked.

"Naturally. My other sons are all proving satisfactory in their own ways.

At least they all seem to have a sense of royal duty in which David is hopelessly lacking. This American woman. From what I hear, his fascination for her shows no sign of abating. She has her claws into him and she is not going to let go. Of course at the moment the question of marriage cannot arise, because she is married to someone else, poor fool. But should she divorce him—well, you see what a predicament that would be."

"His Highness would never be allowed to marry a divorced woman, would he?"

"You say never allowed, but should he be king, who could stop him? He is then the titular head of the church. Henry the Eighth rewrote the rules to suit himself, didn't he?"

"I'm sure you're worrying needlessly, ma'am. The Prince of Wales might enjoy the playboy life at this moment but when he becomes king, he'll remember his duty to his country. It is inbred into all members of the family."

She reached across and patted my hand. "I do hope you are right, Georgiana. But I can't sit idly by and do nothing to save my son from ruin and our family from disgrace. It is time he married properly, and to a young woman who can give him children of the proper pedigree. A forty-year-old American simply won't do. To this end, I've come up with a little scheme."

She gave me that conspiratorial look again.

"Do you know the Bavarian royal family at all?"

"I have not met them, ma'am."

"Not related to us, of course, and unfortunately Roman Catholic. They are no longer officially the ruling family, but they do still enjoy considerable status and respect in that part of Germany. In fact there is a strong movement to restore the monarchy in Bavaria, thus making them strong allies against that ridiculous little upstart Herr Hitler."

"You are planning a match with a member of the Bavarian royal family, ma'am?"

She leaned closer to me, although we were the only two people in the room. "They have a daughter, Hannelore. A beauty by all reports. She is eighteen years old and has just left the convent where she has been educated for the past ten years. Should she have a chance to meet my son, what man could fail to be attracted to an eighteen-year-old virginal beauty? Surely she would make him forget about the Simpson woman and return to the path of duty."

I nodded. "But where do I come into this, ma'am?"

"Let me explain my little scheme, Georgiana. If David felt that he was being forced to meet Princess Hannelore, he would dig in his heels. He has always been stubborn, ever since he was a little boy, you know. But should he glimpse her, across the room, should it be hinted that she is promised to someone else—a lesser princeling—well, you know how much men enjoy the chase. So I've written to her parents and invited her to come to England—to bring her out into society and improve her English. And I have decided that she shouldn't stay with us at the palace." She looked up at me with that piercing stare. "I've decided she should stay with you."

"Me?" It was lucky I hadn't been sipping tea at the time. I should have spluttered all over the Chippendale. As it was, it came out as a squeak and I forgot to add the word "ma'am."

"What could be more pleasant for a young girl than to stay with someone her own age and of suitable rank? As you say, you mingle with friends. You dine at the Savoy. She will have a lovely time doing what young people do. Then, at the right intervals, we'll make sure that she attends the same functions as my son."

She went on talking easily. The blood was pounding through my head as I tried to come up with the words to say that there was no way I could entertain a young lady of royal blood in a house with no servants and in which I was living on baked beans.

"I may count on you, mayn't I, Georgiana?" she asked. "For the good of England?"

I opened my mouth. "Of course, ma'am," I said.

Chapter 5

I staggered out of Buck House as if in a dream. Well, nightmare, actually. In a few days from now a German princess was coming to stay at my house, when I had no servants and certainly no money to feed her. Queens never thought about little things like money. It probably never crossed her mind to inquire whether I had the funds to entertain a royal guest or whether I might like some help in that department. And even if she had promised me an allowance to help with the entertaining, that still neglected the fact that I had no maids, no butler, and worse still, no cook. Germans, I knew, liked their food. Baked beans and boiled eggs, which were the sum of my repertoire to date, simply would not do.

Why had I not spoken up and told the queen the truth? After the fact, it seemed quite silly that I had agreed to something so preposterous. But with those steely eyes on me, I simply didn't have the nerve to refuse her. In fact I had followed in the footsteps of countless antiques dealers who had never intended to let the queen walk off with one of their prized pieces and yet had found themselves graciously handing it over to her.

And now I had no idea what I was going to do next. I needed to talk to somebody, somebody wise who would see a way out of my predicament. Belinda would be no good. She'd think it was all a huge joke and be eagerly waiting to see how I handled it. But then she really couldn't imagine how penniless I was. She had come into a small private income on her twenty-first, which enabled her to buy a mews cottage and keep a maid. She also made money from her dress designs, to say nothing of her gambling winnings. To her, "broke" meant going without champagne for a few days.

Oh, God, I thought. What if this princess expects fine wines and caviar? What if she expects something other than baked beans and tea?

Then suddenly I had a brain wave. I knew the one person in the world to whom I could turn for help—my grandfather. Not the Scottish duke whose ghost now haunts the ramparts of Castle Rannoch (playing the bagpipes, if one is to believe the servants, although this does take a stretch of the imagination, as he couldn't play them in life). I'm talking of my nonroyal grandfather, the former policeman. I hurried to the nearest tube station and soon I was heading through the East End of London out to the eastern suburbs of Essex and a neat little semidetached house with gnomes in the front garden.

I went up his front path past a pocket handkerchief–sized lawn and two meticulously kept rose beds under the watchful eye of the gnomes and knocked on Granddad's front door. Nobody answered. This was an unexpected setback. It was six o'clock and I had felt sure that he couldn't afford to dine out. Fighting back my disappointment, I was about to go home. Then I remembered his mentioning the old lady who lived next door. "Old bat" was his actual term of description for her, but in a fond way. Maybe she might know where he had gone. A shiver of worry went through me. He hadn't been very well last winter and I hoped that he wasn't in hospital.

I knocked on the second front door and waited. Again no response. "Damn," I muttered, then glanced up to notice a net curtain twitching. So someone was there and watching me. As I turned to go, the front door opened. A large, round woman wearing a flowery pinny stood staring at me.

"Wot do you want?" she demanded.

"I came to visit my grandfather," I began. "I'm Georgiana Rannoch and I wondered if—"

She gave a great whoop of delight. "I know who you are. Blimey, what a turnup for the books. I never thought I'd have royalty on the doorstep. Am I supposed to curtsy or something?"

"Of course not," I said. "I just wondered if you knew where my grandfather might be. I came all the way to see him and—"

"Come on in, ducks," she said, almost hauling me inside. "I'll tell you where your granddad is. In my living room, having his tea, that's where he is. And you're more than welcome to join us. Plenty for all."

"That's very kind of you," I said.

"Don't mention it, love. Don't you mention it," she said expansively.

"I'm sorry, I don't know your name."

"It's 'uggins, love. Mrs. 'ettie 'uggins."

I thought that this was a rather unfortunate choice of name for someone who dropped aitches, but I smiled and held out my hand. "How do you do, Mrs. Huggins."

"Pleased to meet you, I'm sure, your 'ighness."

"I'm not a highness, just a lady, but Georgiana will do splendidly."

"You're a proper toff, miss, that's what you are," she said. She was halfway down the hall when my grandfather appeared.

"What's going on, Hettie?" he asked. Then he saw me and his face lit up. "Cor, strike me down. Ain't you a sight for sore eyes," he said. "Come and give your old grandfather a kiss."

I did so, enjoying the carbolic soap smell of his skin and the roughness of his cheek.

"I almost went home," I said, "but then I remembered your speaking of your next-door neighbor so I thought I'd just try, on the off chance. Then when Mrs. Huggins didn't answer her door to start with—"

"She's a bit jumpy right now," my grandfather said. "On account of the bailiffs."

"The bay leaves?" Images of Mediterranean casseroles swam into my head.

"That's right. She don't want nothing to do with them and they keep coming round."

I was rather confused by this statement. Why this irrational fear of bay leaves? Where did they keep coming around? In stews? In which case why couldn't she remove them?

"Bay leaves?" I asked. "What is so terrible about bay leaves?"

"They're trying to throw me out, that's what," Mrs. Huggins said. "Just because I fell a bit behind with the rent when I was poorly and had to pay the doctor."

Light finally dawned and I blushed at my stupidity. "Oh, bailiffs. Oh, I see."

"She don't own her house like I do," my grandfather said. "She weren't lucky enough to have a daughter who did right by her, were you, Hettie love?"

"I got four daughters and they all married rotters," she said. "It's me who's had to help them out, not the other way around."

"Any sons, Mrs. Huggins?" I asked before this conversation turned completely maudlin.

Her face went blank. "Three boys," she said. "All killed in the war. All three within a few days of each other."

"I'm so sorry."

"Yeah, well, there's not much we can do about it now, is there. Wishing won't bring them back. So I tries to muddle through as best I can. And enough of gloomy talk. Come on in and take a load off your feet, love."

She propelled me through into a tiny dining room. Not only did it have a table and four chairs in it, but armchairs on either side of a fireplace, and a sideboard with a radio on it.

"I hope you don't mind being in 'ere," she said. "We don't use the front parlor, except on special occasions. Sit down, ducks. Go on."

She motioned to a chair. I sat experiencing the feeling of unreality that always came over me in normal houses. I had grown up in a castle. I was used to rooms bigger than this whole house, corridors long enough to practice roller skating and great whistling drafts of cold air coming from chimneys large enough to roast an ox. A room like this reminded me of the play cottage that my cousins Elizabeth and Margaret had in their garden.

"I've just come from tea at the palace," I said as my thoughts returned to the royal family.

"The palace, well, I never." Mrs. Higgins looked at my grandfather with awe on her face. "I'm afraid you won't get nothing posh here, just good plain food."

I looked at the tea table. I had expected something similar—thin sliced bread, little cakes—but this was not tea as I knew it. Slices of ham and cold pork, half a pork pie, a wedge of cheese, a big crusty loaf, pickled onions and a dish of tomatoes graced the table, as well as a moist brown fruitcake and some little rock buns.

"This is some tea," I said.

"It's what we usually have, ain't it, Albert?"

My grandfather nodded. "We don't have no dinner at night, like the posh folks do. We have our dinner in the middle of the day and then this is what we have in the evening."

"It looks awfully good to me," I said and happily accepted the slices of ham he was putting onto my plate.

"So what brings you down Essex way?" my grandfather asked as we ate. "And don't tell me you was just passing."

"I came because I need your advice, Granddad," I said. "I'm in a bit of a pickle."

"Is there a young man involved?" he asked with a worried glance at Mrs. Huggins.

"No, nothing like that. It's just . . ." I looked up at Mrs. Huggins, sitting there all ears. I could hardly tell her why I had come but I couldn't drag him away without seeming rude. The matter was solved when he said, "You can say what you want in front of Hettie. She and I don't have no secrets, at least only the ones concerning my lady friends."

"Get away with you." Hettie chuckled and I realized that their relationship had progressed since I had last visited.

"It's like this, Granddad," I said, and related the whole conversation with the queen. "So I've no idea what to do next," I said. "I can't entertain a princess, but I dare not face the queen and tell her the truth either. She'd be so horrified that I'm slumming without servants that I know she'd send me off to the country to be some royal aunt's lady-in-waiting." My voice rose into a wail.

"All right, love. Don't get yourself into a two-and-eight about it."

"A what?"

"Two-and-eight. Cockney rhyming slang for a state. Haven't you never heard that before?"

"I can't say that I have."

"Well, she wouldn't, would she?" Mrs. Huggins demanded. "They don't use no rhyming slang at the palace."

Granddad smiled. "This wants a bit of thinking about," he said, scratching his chin. "How long is this foreign princess coming for?"

"I've no idea. The queen did mention that she'd want us to come to Sandringham and there are house parties that we should attend."

"So it might only be for a week or so?"

"Possibly."

"Because I was thinking," he said. "I know where I might be able to supply you with a cook and a butler."

"You do? Where?"

"Us," Granddad said, and burst out laughing. "Me and Mrs. Huggins. She's a fair enough cook and I could pass as a butler when needed."

"Granddad, I couldn't expect you to be my servant. It wouldn't seem right."

"Ah, but you'd be doing us a bit of a favor yourself, love," he said, with another glance at Mrs. Huggins. "You see it might be useful to be away from home if that bailiff is going to show up again with an eviction notice. He has to deliver it in person, don't he?"

"But I couldn't afford to pay you."

"Don't you worry about the money right now, my love," Granddad said. "We don't need paying, but you will need enough money to feed this young woman."

"She's probably going to expect the best," Mrs. Huggins agreed. "I'd say it was wrong of the queen to expect you to pay for this out of your own pocket."

"She just doesn't think of such things," I said. "The royal family never has to consider money. They don't even carry money with them."

"Nice for some," Mrs. Huggins said with a knowing nod to my grandfather.

Granddad scratched his chin. "I was thinking that you should write to your brother and ask him for some help. He owes you a big favor, after all."

"You're right, he does, but he's awfully hard up too."

"Then tell him you're bringing the princess home to Scotland. From what I know of your snooty sister-in-law, she'd do anything rather than have to entertain visiting royalty at her house."

"Granddad, that's a brilliant idea," I said, laughing. "Absolutely brilliant. And I'll remind Binky he promised to send me my maid as well. Oh, Lord, I'm sure the princess will expect someone to dress her."

"I ain't volunteering to dress no princesses," Mrs. Huggins said. "I wouldn't have no clue how them fancy clothes do up and my rough 'ands will probably scratch her delicate skin."

"If Binky sends my maid from Scotland as he promised, then she can wait on the princess," I said. "I've become quite used to doing without a maid myself."

"So when is this likely to start?"

"Within the next few days," I said. "Oh, dear. I'm not looking forward to it at all."

"Don't get yourself in a two-and-eight." Granddad patted my knee. "It will all work out. You'll see."

Chapter 6

Our butler up at Castle Rannoch has become hard of hearing recently. It took a good five minutes before I could make him understand that I did not want to speak to Lady Georgiana, but that I *was* Lady Georgiana. Eventually the telephone was grabbed by none other than my sister-in-law, Fig.

"Georgiana?" She sounded startled. "What's wrong now?"

"Why should something be wrong?"

"I trust you wouldn't be squandering money on a telephone call with the current telephone rates being so astronomically high, unless it were a real emergency," she said. "You are telephoning from Rannoch House, I take it?"

"I am, and it is something rather urgent." I took a deep breath. "I wondered whether you were going to be home for the next few weeks."

"Of course we're going to be home," she snapped. "Summer holidays are simply beyond our means these days. No longer can one think of jaunting off to the Med for the summer. I shall probably take little Podge to stay with his grandparents in Shropshire, but apart from that, it will strictly be a case of attempting to amuse ourselves at Castle Rannoch, however dreary that prospect may sound."

"That's good news, actually," I said, "because I am going to suggest a way to liven things up for you. I'm planning to bring a party of Germans to stay with you."

"Germans? With us? When?"

"The end of this week, I believe."

"You're going to bring a party of Germans to us this week?" Fig's usually impeccable upbringing showed definite cracks. A lady is brought up never to show her emotions. Fig's voice had become high and shrill. "How many Germans?"

"I'm not sure how big a retinue the princess will be bringing with her."

"Princess?" Now she was definitely rattled.

"Yes, it's all very simple really," I said. "I had tea at the palace yesterday and Her Majesty asked me if I'd be good enough to host a visiting Bavarian princess—"

"You? Why you?"

It irked Fig considerably that I was related to the king and she was not, especially since my mother was of humble birth and an actress to boot. The closest Fig ever came to royal chumminess was an evening or two at Balmoral.

"Her Majesty felt that the palace might be rather stuffy for a young girl and that she would have more fun with someone closer to her own age. I would have been happy to comply in normal circumstances and play host at Rannoch House, but as you know, I no longer have an allowance from my brother and thus can afford no staff, so I don't see how I can entertain anyone, especially a princess."

"Then why didn't you tell Her Majesty that?"

"Tell her that I'm living at the family home with no staff because my brother refuses to pay for them? How would that look, Fig? Think of the family name. The disgrace of it." Before she could answer this I went on brightly, "So that was when I came up with the brain wave. I'll just bring them all up to you in Scotland. They'll have a rattling good time. We can organize some house parties for them, and excursions to the sea, and then make up a shooting party when the season starts in August. You know how much Germans love shooting things."

"August?" Fig's voice had now risen at least an octave. "You are expecting them to stay until August?"

"I have no idea how long they plan to stay. One does not go into trivial details with Her Majesty."

"I am expected to feed a party of Germans until August? Georgiana, do you have any idea how much Germans eat?"

"I don't see any other alternative," I said, thoroughly enjoying this conversation so far.

"Tell the queen that you can't do it. Simple as that."

"One does not say no to the queen, Fig. And if I told her I couldn't do it, I'd have to explain why and there would be a horrible fuss. As I said, this could all be solved quite simply. I'd be quite happy to entertain the princess at Rannoch House, were I given the means to do so. Her Majesty did mention inviting us to Sandringham for part of the time, and of course there would be plenty of house parties to keep Her Highness entertained, so the expense shouldn't be too terrible. All Binky would have to do is to reinstate my allowance for a little while and send me down the maid he promised."

"Georgiana, if I didn't know you better, I'd say you were trying to blackmail me," Fig said coldly.

"Blackmail? Oh, good gracious, no. Nothing like that. I just wanted to remind you both that you do owe me a small debt of gratitude for what I did for Binky. Had I not uncovered the truth about who had really killed Gaston de Mauxville, I rather fear that Binky would be languishing in a jail cell. He could even have been hanged by now, leaving you to bring up little Podge and run the estate single-handedly. The use of one maid seems like a trifle in return."

There was a pause. I could hear Fig breathing. "We did ask your maid, Maggie," she said at last, "but as you know, she was reluctant to leave her mother, given her mother's current state of health. And there really isn't anybody else suitable. Mrs. Hanna, the laundress, has a daughter, but she is proving most unreliable. She slopped soup down Lady Branston's front the other day."

I almost commented that it would be hard to miss Lady Branston's front.

"If my allowance were reinstated, I could hire a temporary maid locally in London. My friend Belinda has a very suitable girl. I could use the same agency."

"But what about the rest of the staff?" Fig sounded desperate now. "You can't entertain a German princess with only one maid. Who will cook for you? Who will serve?"

"Ah, well, I do happen to know where I can borrow a temporary cook and butler—from friends who are going abroad, you know. So it's really only a maid, and the question of food. One does need to feed guests."

There was a long pause. "I must speak to Binky about this," Fig said. "Times are hard, Georgiana. I don't need to tell you that. I'm sure you pass bread lines in the city every day."

"I do, but I don't think you're exactly down to the level of queuing up for bread, are you, Fig?"

"No, but we jolly well have to live off the estate these days," she said hotly. "No more sending down to Fortnum's for the little treats that make life worth living. Binky has even given up his Gentlemen's Relish and you know how he adores it. No, it's simple, humble country food for us now."

"Too bad it's not hunting season," I said. "If it were, you could shoot enough deer to keep the Germans fed. I understand that they love venison."

"I'll talk to Binky," she said hastily. "I do understand that we shouldn't let down the family name to Her Majesty or to foreigners."

I replaced the mouthpiece with great satisfaction.

The next morning two letters arrived in the early post. One was from Binky, instructing me that he was having a modest amount transferred to my bank account, which was all he could spare at such short notice and such a difficult time, but which he hoped would prove enough to cover my temporary financial needs. Underneath Fig had added, *Make sure you double-check references for any staff you bring into OUR HOME and keep the silver locked up!!* The other letter was from the palace. Her Royal Highness Princess Hannelore would be arriving on Saturday's boat train. That gave me two days to turn my house into the sort of home fit for a princess, install my grandfather and Mrs. Huggins as butler and cook, and hire a maid for myself.

I sent for my grandfather and Mrs. Huggins then got to work immediately opening up the rest of the house. Since I moved in, I had been using my bedroom, the kitchen and the small morning room. The rest of the house remained shrouded in dust sheets. Now I went to work furiously dusting, sweeping floors and making beds. I got through with only minor mishaps. I did manage to knock the leg off a prancing horse statue, but I don't think it was Ming or anything and I found the glue to stick it back on again. Oh, and I dropped a sheet I was shaking out of the window onto a passing colonel. He wasn't too happy about it and threatened to report me to my mistress.

By the time Granddad arrived, I was exhausted. He and Mrs. Huggins toured the house without comment and I realized that they probably had no idea how much I had accomplished and thought that the house looked like this all the time. But then my grandfather stopped, his head on one side like a bird. "Don't tell me you made this bed up by yourself?"

"Of course I did. And cleaned the whole rest of the house too."

"Well, I never," Mrs. Huggins said. "And you a lady and all."

She looked rather dismayed when she saw the size of our kitchen, and even more dismayed when she saw the empty larder. I told her to make a list and stock up with food.

"I've no idea what a German princess would eat, ducks," she said. "And I can't make no foreign muck. No frog's legs and garlic and things."

"That's French," Granddad said. "Germans like their dumplings."

"You just cook what you are used to, Mrs. Huggins," I said. "I'm sure it will be perfect."

Secretly I was beginning to have serious doubts that it would be perfect. Granddad and Mrs. Huggins were lovely people, but what could they possibly know of the formality of court life? Then I reminded myself that the princess was straight from a convent. She probably had little idea of court life herself. Having settled in my butler and cook, I went to look for a maid. This was not going to be as easy as I had hoped. It seemed that all of the very best servants had fled to the country with their respective masters and mistresses. The agency promised to have some girls ready for me to interview by Monday or Tuesday—by which time they could have checked their references. When I asked if they might have someone who could fill in for the weekend, the refined lady behind the desk looked as if she were about to have a heart attack.

"Fill in?" she demanded. "For the weekend?" She winced as if each of these words were causing her pain. "I am afraid we do not handle that sort of thing." By that she implied that I had requested a stripper straight from the Casbah.

So that left me in a bit of a pickle. A princess, arriving from the Continent, would not expect to have to run her own bath, or hang up her own clothes. She probably wouldn't even know how to do either of those things. She wouldn't expect the cook to pop up from the kitchen and do it either. I needed a maid, and I needed one rapidly. I did the only thing I could think of and went posthaste to Belinda's little mews cottage in Knightsbridge.

"I need a big favor," I gasped as her maid showed me into the ultramodern sitting room with its low Scandinavian furniture and art deco mirrors.

"I wondered if I could possibly borrow your maid for the weekend." (Binky would have been horrified to hear me using such awful Americanisms as the word "weekend," but for once I had no choice.)

"Borrow my maid?" She looked stunned. "But darling, how could I possibly survive without my maid? I have to go to a party on Saturday night. Who would lay out my things? And she has Sundays off. No, I'm afraid that wouldn't work at all."

"Oh, dear," I said. "Then I'm doomed. I have a German princess arriving and only the most basic of staff."

"Last time I was at Rannoch House you had no staff at all, so things must be looking up," she said.

"I really have no staff this time—I've dragged my grandfather and his next-door neighbor up from Essex."

"Essex?" Her eyes opened wider. "You are expecting them to know how to wait on a princess?"

"It's better than nothing. The queen foisted this on me and I'm trying to do my best. Besides, the princess has just been let out of a convent. It can't be worse than that, can it?"

Belinda's face lit up. "How screamingly funny, darling."

"It's not funny at all, Belinda. It will probably be a disaster and I'll be banished to the country."

"But why is HM foisting a princess on you? Are they redecorating Buck House or something?"

"She, er, thinks the princess would have a better time with someone her own age," I said, not revealing the true reason, which was to hitch her up with the Prince of Wales. Belinda was part of the smart set and might well bump into the prince. And I didn't think she could be trusted not to spill the beans.

"I hope she's not expecting a good time with the bright young things," Belinda said, "because you don't exactly move in those circles, do you, darling?"

"If her family has taken the trouble to keep her shut away in a convent for most of her education, I rather suspect they'd like her to avoid the smart set," I said.

"Very wise. You have no idea what kind of thing is going on nowadays," Belinda said, crossing her long legs to reveal delicious white silk stockings. "The prince was at a party with another boy last night."

"The Prince of Wales?" I asked, horrified.

"No, no. He likes old hags, we know that. Prince George, I mean. The youngest son. They were passing around a snapshot of him wearing his Guardsman's helmet and nothing else."

She broke into giggles. I wondered if his mother knew anything of this, or whether he was one of the sons who was doing well in her eyes.

"I'd better go," I said. Somehow I couldn't bring myself to laugh. It was all becoming somewhat overwhelming.

"Don't forget Gussie and Lunghi's party next week, will you?" Belinda said as she escorted me to the door. "It should be tremendous fun. Gussie's father's got pots of money so I gather there will be a band and heaven knows what else."

"I don't know if I'll be able to go if I'm stuck with a princess," I said.

"Bring her along, darling. Open her eyes to what fun people we British are."

I didn't think Her Majesty would approve of the sort of parties Belinda thought were fun, and I walked home feeling as if I were about to sit for an exam for which I hadn't studied. I wondered if it would be too awful to come down with a sudden case of mumps, and thus foist the princess on to the palace instead.

Then, of course, that good old Rannoch blood won out. A Rannoch never retreats. I'd heard that often enough during my upbringing at Castle Rannoch. Who could forget Robert Bruce Rannoch, who, after his arm had been hacked off, picked up his sword with his other hand and went on fighting? I shouldn't retreat from a little thing like a visiting princess. With my head held high I marched to my destiny.

Chapter 7

Diary,
German princess due to arrive today.
Sense impending doom.

On the way to Victoria Station to meet the boat train, I nearly lost my nerve and had to give myself a severe talking to. She is a young girl, fresh from school, I told myself firmly. She will be enchanted with the big city, and with everything about London. She will be thrilled to be alone with such a young chaperon. All will be well. She'll only stay a few days and the queen will be pleased.

Thus encouraged by this little talk, I made my way across the station, past the hissing steam engines, the shouts and toots of whistles, to the platform on the far right where the boat trains come in. As that great fire-breathing monster pulled into the station, puffing heavily, something occurred to me. I had no idea what she looked like. I was told she was a pretty little thing, but that was about it. Would she look German? How exactly did Germans look? I had met plenty when I was at school in Switzerland but people of fashion usually dressed from Paris and were indistinguishable by race.

I stationed myself at a point where all those disembarking would have to pass me and waited. I approached several young women only to be met with suspicious glances when I asked if she was a princess. The platform cleared. She hadn't come. She's changed her mind and stayed home, I thought, and a great wave of relief swept through me. Then through the clearing smoke I saw a party of three women, standing together and waving arms as they negotiated with a porter. There was a stout elderly woman, a young girl and a third woman, plainly dressed, dark, sallow and severe-looking. The young girl was enchantingly pretty—very blond with long hair twisted into a braid around her head, and wearing a navy linen sailor suit. The elderly woman was wearing an unmistakably German cape—gray and edged with green braid, plus one of those little Tyrolean hats with a feather in the side.

I hurried up to them.

"Are you, by any chance, Princess Hannelore?" I asked, addressing the young one.

"*Ja*. This is Her Highness," the old woman said, bowing to the pretty girl in the sailor suit. "You are servant of Lady Georgiana of Rannoch?" She spat out the words with a strong German accent while giving me a critical stare. "We wait for you." (Of course, she said "Vee vait.") "You are late."

"I am Lady Georgiana. I have come personally to meet Her Highness."

The older lady recoiled and gave a bobbing curtsy. "*Ach, Verzeihung.* Forgive me. Most honored that you come to meet us in person. I am Baroness Rottenmeister, companion to Her Highness."

Oh, Lord. It had never occurred to me that there would be a companion! Of course there would. How dense of me. What king would send his daughter, newly released from the convent, across from the Continent without a chaperon?

"Baroness." I bowed in return. "How kind of you to bring the princess to visit us. Will you be staying long?"

"I stay wiz princess. She stay. I stay. She go. I go," she said.

Oh, golly. And I hadn't made up a second good bedroom. How and when was I going to do that without being noticed?

"May I present Her Royal Highness, Princess Maria Theresa Hannelore Wilhelmina Mathilda?" Baroness Rottenmeister gestured with a black-gloved hand. "Highness. I present Lady Georgiana of Glen Garry and Rannoch."

The pretty young girl held out her hand. "Hiya, doll," she said in a sweet, soft voice.

I was confused. Wasn't Huyerdahl a Norwegian name? What had it to do with German?

"Huyerdahl?" I repeated.

A big smile crossed her face. "Howya doin', doll?"

"Doll?"

The smile faded. "Is that not right? I speak real good modern English. I'm the bee's knees, no?"

"Highness, where did you learn this English?" I asked, still perplexed. "They taught it in the convent?"

She giggled wickedly. "The convent? No. In our village" (she said "willage") "is good cinema and they show many American films. We climb out of convent window at night and go see movies. I see all gangster films. George Raft, Paul Muni—you seen *Scarface*?"

"No, I'm afraid I haven't seen *Scarface*."

"Real good movie—lots of shooting. Bang bang, you're dead. I love gangsters. Is there much shooting in London?"

"I'm glad to say there is very little shooting in London," I said, trying not to smile because she looked so earnest.

"Gee. That's too bad," she said. "Only shooting in Chicago then?"

"I fear so. London is quite safe."

She sighed in disappointment.

"So where do you want me to shift this lot then?" the porter asked impatiently.

"Your chauffeur waits for us outside?" Baroness Rottenmeister asked.

"I have no chauffeur in London," I said. "We'll take a taxicab."

"A taxicab? *Gott im Himmel*."

"Taxicab. I like this." Hannelore looked excited. "My jewelcase, Irmgardt."

"I have not been presented to your friend," I said, nodding to the third woman of the party.

"Not friend. Zis is Her Highness's personal maid," Baroness Rottenmeister said coldly.

I beamed at her. She'd brought her own maid. Of course she'd brought her own maid. What normal person wouldn't? I was saved.

"Come. Vee go find taxicab," the baroness said imperiously and swept ahead of us.

Princess Hannelore sidled up to me. "Vee gonna ditch de old broad. Vee gonna have great time, you and me, babe, yeah?"

"Oh yes. Definitely." I smiled back.

When the taxi pulled up outside Rannoch House even Baroness Rottenmeister looked impressed. "*Ja,*" she said, nodding her thick neck. "Fine house. Is *gut.*"

Hannelore looked around excitedly. "Look," she whispered. A man was crossing Belgrave Square carrying a violin case. "He's a gangster."

"No, he's a violin player. He stands on the corner and earns pennies by playing the violin. I told you, there are no gangsters in London."

Hannelore took in the leafy square, a crisply starched nanny pushing a pram while a small girl beside her pushed an identical doll's pram. "I like London," she said, "even if no gangsters."

"Even if there were gangsters, I don't think you'd find them in Belgrave Square," I pointed out. "This is one of the most respectable addresses in London. Only a stone's throw from Buckingham Palace."

"Vee go meet king and queen soon?" Hannelore asked. "I'm real tickled to meet those old guys."

I could see some rapid English lessons would be needed before we met those "old guys."

I rang the doorbell, to alert my extensive staff that we had arrived. It was opened by my grandfather, wearing tails. I nearly fell over backward.

"Good afternoon, your ladyship." He bowed earnestly.

"Good afternoon, Spinks," I replied, trying not to grin. "This is Princess Hannelore with her companion, Baroness Rottenmeister, who will be staying here with us too, and her maid."

"Yer Highness. Baroness." Granddad bowed to them.

"Our trusty butler, Spinks," I said and as we entered I beheld a rotund figure in a smart blue uniform with starched white apron.

"And our housekeeper, Mrs. Huggins, my lady," Granddad said.

Mrs. Huggins dropped a curtsy. "Pleased to meet yer, I'm sure," she said.

"There are bags to be brought in from the taxi," I said, almost squirming with embarrassment. "Would you please take them straight up to the princess's bedroom. Oh, and we'll have to make up a bedroom for the baroness."

"Bob's yer uncle, me lady," Granddad said.

"Irmgardt, Mrs. Huggins will help make up a bedroom for you after you have helped with the bags," I said.

The maid stared at me blankly.

"She speaks no English," the baroness said. "She is a particularly stupid girl."

"Then please explain to her in German."

German instructions were rattled off. Irmgardt nodded dourly and went to retrieve the bags from the taxi.

"I go and see which bedroom I like," the baroness said. "I have many requirements. Must be quiet. Must not be too cold or too hot. Must be near bathroom." And before I could stop her, she stalked up the stairs.

Princess Hannelore looked at me. "She's a pain in the ass, right?"

Then she must have noticed that I looked shocked. "Highness, that's probably not an expression you should use," I said gently.

"Is bad word?" she asked innocently. "What is wrong about calling her a donkey?"

"It's not that sort of ass," I explained.

"Okey dokey," she said. "And we must be good pals. I am not Your Highness. My friends call me Hanni."

"Honey?" I asked because this was how she pronounced it.

"That's right."

"And I'm Georgie," I said. "Welcome to London."

"I know I'm gonna have a swell time," she said.

At that moment Baroness Rottenmeister came sweeping down the stairs again. "I choose room I vant," she said. "Quiet. Away from street. Your maid will make my bed for me."

"My maid?" I glanced out into the street where Mrs. Huggins and Granddad were wrestling with a mountain of cases. "I'm afraid she is not . . ."

"But she has already said she will do this for me right away. A sweet girl."

I looked up the stairs and almost fell over backward. Belinda was standing there, in a jaunty maid's uniform that looked as if it came straight out of a French farce. "All taken care of, your ladyship," she said in her best Cockney voice.

Chapter 8

By dinnertime my guests were installed in their rooms. They had taken hot baths (my grandfather having stoked the boiler up to full strength). The table was laid in the dining room with white linens and polished silver. Belinda had slipped away to go to her party, promising she'd try to come back the next day, if her hangover wasn't too terrible. Good smells were coming from the kitchen. It seemed as if this might work out after all.

"I hope your cook understands that I have a delicate stomach," Baroness Rottenmeister said as she came down to dinner. "I eat like a sparrow for the sake of my health."

Since she was of impressive girth, I privately questioned this remark. Hanni looked delightful in a pink evening gown trimmed with roses. I even began to feel hopeful that she would indeed catch the Prince of Wales's eye and all would be well with the future of the British monarchy. Maybe I'd be given a new title as a thank-you gift. Marchioness of Belgravia? And maybe it would come with property—my own estate, Lady of the Isle of somewhere or other. I'm sure there are still islands around Scotland waiting to be given away to the right person. With these happy thoughts I led my guests through to dinner.

"It's very cold in here," the baroness said. "Why is there no fire?"

"It's summertime. We never light fires after the first of May," I replied.

"I shall catch a chill," the baroness said. "I have a most delicate chest."

Her chest could in no way be described as delicate and she was wearing a fur wrap over her black evening gown. She also didn't appear to be concerned that her charge, Princess Hanni, was décolleté and wearing the lightest silk, from which she appeared to be suffering no ill effects.

Food arrived via the dumbwaiter. My grandfather served the plates.

"What is this?" The baroness poked experimentally with her fork.

"Steak and kidney pud," said Granddad. "Good old solid British grub."

"Steakandkidkneepood? Grub?" the baroness demanded. "Grub is word for insect, *ja?*"

"Cockney word for food, Yer Highness," my grandfather said.

"I do not think I shall like this," the baroness said, but she tried a small taste. "Not bad," she said, and promptly wolfed down everything on her plate.

When the pudding course arrived she looked puzzled. "There is no soup? No fish? No fowl? No salad? How am I supposed to keep my strength with so little to eat?"

"I live alone and have become used to eating simply," I said. "When we are invited to the palace to dine with the king and queen, I'm sure they will serve all of those courses."

"But until then I must suffer, I suppose," she said with dramatic resignation.

"I thought it tasted real swell," Hanni said. "Better than food at the convent. Nuns always make penance."

The dessert was placed in front of us. "And what is this now?" the baroness asked.

"Spotted dick and custard," Granddad said. "One of Mrs. Huggins's specialties."

"Spotted dick?" The baroness prodded it suspiciously. "You mean duck?"

"No, dick." Granddad caught my eye and winked.

"Duck I know. Dick I do not know," the baroness said.

I had to stare down at my plate for fear of laughing. "It's just a name," I said. "An old traditional name for a suet pudding."

"Suet? So bad for my digestion." But she ate it, clearing her plate before anyone else and not refusing seconds. "I suppose I have to eat something," she said with resignation. "Do all English noble families eat so simply?"

"There is a depression," I said. "We try to live simply when the ordinary people are having such a hard time."

"I see no point in being of noble birth if one can't eat well," she said. "We have so few privileges left."

"I like spotted dick," Hanni exclaimed. "And tomorrow you show me London and we go to parties and dance and have good time."

I thought that any good time might be severely restricted by Baroness Rottenmeister but wisely kept silent. Then, when the baroness excused herself for a few moments, Hanni hissed at me, "We have to get rid of pain in ass. She will not let me have good time. We should take her out."

"Take her out where?"

Hanni grinned. "You know. Take her out. Waste her. Bang bang. Curtains."

"Hanni, I don't think we're going to be able to waste the baroness, but I agree she's not going to make things pleasant for us."

"Then we must plan way to make her go home."

"How?"

"Make it not nice for her here. She likes to eat. Serve her very little food. And she likes to be warm. Open all windows. Make it cold. And she likes hot baths. Turn off hot water."

I looked at her in amazement. "For someone straight from the convent, you are quite devious," I said.

"What means devious?"

"Sneaky."

"Oh, like pulling a fast one," she said, beaming. "Yeah. Sure thing, baby."

"*Ach, dass ist gut.* You young ladies make friends. I like this," said the baroness as she reentered the room.

After coffee I escorted my guests up to bed. The baroness needed more blankets and complained that her room was damp and she was sure she saw a spider in the corner.

"I'm sorry. This house is very damp, even in summer," I said. "And I'm afraid there are often spiders. Although not many poisonous ones."

"Poisonous spiders? In London?"

"Only sometimes," I said.

And where was my maid to help her? she demanded. I explained that the maid had the night off.

"Night off? You allow servants out on Saturday night? Unheard of. In Germany our servants are there when we need them."

I finally got her settled in and popped in to see how Hanni was faring. She was sitting at her dressing table while her maid, Irmgardt, brushed out her long golden hair. Truly she looked like a princess from a fairy tale.

"Hanni, I'm going to have to watch you carefully," I said. "You may break a lot of hearts in London."

"What am I to break?" she asked with that lovely innocent smile.

"Hearts. Lots of Englishmen will fall in love with you."

"I hope so," she said. "I'm gonna be hot sexy dame. You can give me tips."

"I don't know about that." I laughed nervously. "I'm supposed to be keeping my eye on you. And I certainly don't know much about being hot and sexy."

"But you are not still wirgin?" she asked.

"Werging?"

"You are voman of vorld. Not wirgin."

"Oh," I said. "I see. Well, yes, I am still a virgin, I'm afraid."

"This is not good," she said, wagging a finger at me. "Young girl like me. Eighteen years old. Men like that I am virgin. But old like you, is not good. Men think there is something wrong with you."

"I'm not that old," I said. "I won't be twenty-two until August."

But she didn't look convinced. "We must do something for you. Pretty damned quick."

"You sound like my friend Belinda."

"Belinda? I like this Belinda. I will meet her soon?"

I couldn't say "You already have, hanging up the baroness's clothes." "I'm sure you will," I said instead. "She and I are great friends. But she really is a woman of the world. If you want to know anything, ask her."

"Maybe she will find me hot sexy guy?"

"Your Highness, I rather think that you'll be expected to save yourself for marriage," I said. "You'll be expected to make a good match with a prince."

"But princes are so dull, don't you think?" she asked.

This was not a good sign. She was supposed to fall hopelessly in love with the Prince of Wales.

"We have some awfully entertaining princes in England," I said. "You'll meet them soon."

In the middle of the night I woke up and lay there, wondering what had awoken me. Then I heard it again, the creak of a floorboard. One of my guests using the bathroom, I surmised, but I got up in case they couldn't find the light switch. I had just opened my door a few inches when I gasped: a dark figure was coming up the stairs from the ground floor. Before my heart started beating again, I recognized it was Irmgardt, Hanni's maid. She didn't notice me, but tiptoed right past and kept on going, up the next flight of stairs to the servants' quarters.

What had she been doing downstairs? I wondered. Obviously not fetching something for her mistress, or she would have brought it to her bedroom. I didn't notice anything in her hands but Fig's words about locking up the family silver did spring to mind. Surely a royal maid would have been well vetted before she was allowed to accompany a princess. Maybe she had just been looking for something as simple as a glass of water. I closed my door and went back to sleep.

Next morning I passed along Hanni's instructions to my grandfather and Mrs. Huggins. Cut back on the food and turn down the hot water. They were reluctant to do this. "What, and have them think I don't know how to cook proper?" Mrs. Huggins demanded. "I'm proud of my cooking, I am."

"And I don't want that old dragon coming after me because there's no hot water," Granddad said. "She's already waved her stick at me a couple of times."

"Tell her it's an old and eccentric boiler system in the house and it's unpredictable whether we have hot water or not. Tell her in England we are used to cold baths. My brother, the duke, takes them all the time."

"I hope you know what you're doing, ducks." Granddad shook his head. "You wouldn't want her complaining to the queen that you're not treating them proper."

"Oh, I don't think she'd do that," I said, but I wasn't sure. I rather had a feeling that this was a lost cause. Baroness Rottenmeister struck me as one of those noble creatures who will not flinch from her duty, however horrible it is. Rather like my ancestors, of course. Oh, God. I hope she doesn't have Rannoch blood!

SUNDAY, JUNE 12

Diary,
Pouring with rain today. Have no idea how to entertain visiting princess
    plus escort. Hanni seems nice enough and should be easy. Baroness
    will be another matter.

On Sunday morning the baroness, Irmgardt and Hanni had to go to mass. I sent them off in a taxicab. The baroness was horrified that I wouldn't be joining them. "In England we're all C of E," I said. "Church of England," I added when she clearly didn't understand. "The head of the church is the king, my cousin. We don't have to go every Sunday if we don't want to."

"You are relation of head of church? A nation of heathens," she said and crossed herself.

When they returned, Mrs. Huggins was about to cook bacon, eggs and kidneys for breakfast but I insisted on porridge.

"This is breakfast?" the baroness asked.

"Scottish breakfast. It's what we eat at home at Castle Rannoch."

She prodded it with her spoon. "And what goes with it?"

"Nothing. Just porridge. In Scotland we eat it with a little salt."

She sighed and pulled her shawl more closely around her. Luckily the weather was cooperating for once. The brief summery spell had been replaced by usual English summer weather. It was raining cats and dogs and was distinctly chilly. Even I looked longingly at the fireplace and almost relented about lighting fires. But I knew what was at stake and bravely sought out a woolly cardigan. There was no sign of Belinda all morning. I suspected that the party had not ended until the wee hours and rising early for her meant around eleven.

Mrs. Huggins absolutely insisted on cooking a roast for Sunday lunch. "I don't want them foreigners to think we don't do things proper in England," she said. "We always have a joint on a Sunday." But I did persuade her not to do too many roast potatoes to go with it, but a lot of greens. And for pudding something light. She suggested junket. Perfect.

The baroness ate her meat rapidly. "Good *Fleisch*," she said. "*Fleisch* is healthy." But I noticed she didn't attack the great mound of greens with the same enthusiasm, nor did she like the junket.

"Yoonkit?" she asked. "What means yoonkit?"

It had never been a favorite of mine. I always associated it with invalid food but I managed to give an impression of someone eating with gusto. After lunch it was too wet for a walk, so we sat in the cavernous drawing room while the wind whistled down the chimney. The baroness napped in an armchair. Hanni and I played rummy.

"Does nobody come to call? No visitors?" the baroness demanded, as she stirred during her nap. "Life in England is very dull."

"I think the rain is stopping." Hanni looked out of the window. "We go for walk. You show me London."

We left the baroness snoozing in her armchair.

"Let us walk through the beautiful park," Hanni suggested. "Very romantic place, no?"

So we walked through Hyde Park, where drops dripped on us from the horse chestnut trees and Rotten Row was sodden underfoot. The park was almost deserted until we came to Speakers' Corner. There a small crowd was gathered around a man standing on a packing case.

"The workers will rise up and take what is rightfully theirs," he was shouting, while around him other earnest young men were carrying signs saying, *Join the Communists. Make the world a better place. Down with monarchy. Equality for all. Up the workers.*

Hanni looked at them with interest. "They can say this and not be arrested?" she asked.

"This is called Speakers' Corner. You can say what you like here, however silly it is."

"You think communists are silly?" she asked.

"Don't you?"

"I think it would be nice if all people had money and houses and enough food."

"And you think the communists could deliver that? Look at the mess in Russia."

"I don't know," she said, then gave a little squeak as her glove dropped onto the wet ground. Instantly one of the young men lowered his sign and leaped for her glove.

"There you are, miss," he said, handing it back to her with a charming bow.

"Thank you very much." Hanni blushed prettily. "Your friend speaks very well," she told him.

He beamed at her. "Are you interested in coming to one of our meetings? We hold them at St. Mary's Hall in the East End. You'd be most welcome."

"You see. Communists are nice people, no?" Hanni whispered as he retrieved his sign. "He was handsome guy."

I had to agree he was handsome, even though he was wearing a threadbare tweed jacket and hand-knitted pullover. The interesting thing was that he spoke like a gentleman.

At that moment there was the tramp of boots and a group of young men wearing black shirts, adorned with an emblem of a lightning bolt, marched up to the communists.

"Go back to Russia where you belong," one of them shouted. "England for the English."

"We're as bloody English as you are, mate, and we've a right to speak here," the man shouted from his platform.

"You're a bunch of intellectual pansy boys. You're no bleedin' use to anybody," one of the blackshirts jeered and leaped up to push him from the platform. Suddenly a scuffle broke out around us. Hanni screamed. The young man she had spoken to tried to fight his way through the melee toward her, but he was punched by a large thuggish blackshirt. Suddenly a strong arm grabbed me around the waist and I found myself being propelled out of the skirmish. I looked up to protest and found myself staring at Darcy O'Mara.

"Over here, before things get ugly," he muttered and steered Hanni and me away into the park, just as the sound of police whistles could be heard.

"Those hooligans can't stop free speech in Britain. We'll show them the right way," someone was shouting as the police waded in to break up the fight.

I looked up at Darcy. "Thank you. You arrived at the right moment."

"Ah well, didn't you know I'm your guardian angel?" he asked with that wicked grin. "What on earth were you doing at a communist rally? Are you about to trade Castle Rannoch for a peasant's hovel?"

"We were only there by accident," I said. "We went for a Sunday afternoon stroll and Hanni wanted to know who was shouting."

Darcy's gaze turned to Hanni. "A friend of yours?" he asked. "I don't believe we've met."

"Highness, may I present the Honorable Darcy O'Mara, son and heir of Lord Kilhenny of Ireland. Darcy, this is Her Highess Princess Hannelore of Bavaria," I said. "She's staying with me at Rannoch House."

"Is she, by George." I saw his eyes light up. "Delighted to make your acquaintance, Your Highness." He gave a very proper bow, then lifted her outstretched hand to his lips. "I'd volunteer to escort you ladies back to Belgrave Square but unfortunately I'm already late for an appointment. I look forward to seeing you again soon, now that I'm back in London. Your Highness. My lady." Then he melted into the by-then considerable crowd.

"Wow, holy cow, hubba hubba, gee whiz. That was some guy," Hanni said. "Don't tell me he's your main squeeze!"

"My what?"

"Your honey. Your sugar. Isn't that right word?"

"In England we're a little less colorful with our language," I said.

"So you say it?"

"Boyfriend? Escort?"

"And is he?"

"Obviously not anymore," I said with a sigh.

Chapter 9

Monday morning—cold and blustery again. More porridge for breakfast. Mrs. Huggins wasn't particularly good at porridge and it was like gooey wallpaper paste. I ate mine with expressions of delight. I thought the baroness might be beginning to crack.

"When will king and queen invite us to palace?" she asked hopefully.

"I couldn't say," I said. "It depends how busy they are."

"Is most irregular that princess not received at palace by king," she said; then she added, "The food at palace is good?"

"They are also trying to eat simply," I replied, knowing that they were.

"And where is your maid?"

"I'm afraid she hasn't returned from visiting her mother."

"Servants in England have no idea of duty. You must dismiss her instantly and find a good reliable German girl," the baroness said, waving her stick at me.

At that moment the post arrived, bringing two letters. One was indeed from the palace, inviting us to dinner on Tuesday evening. The other had been forwarded from my post office box and was from a Mrs. Bantry-Bynge, one of my regular customers in the house-cleaning business. Every now and then Mrs. Bantry-Bynge abandoned Colonel Bantry-Bynge and popped up to town, apparently to see her dressmaker but really for a tryst with a frightful slimy man called Boy. I had been called upon to make up the bedroom for her on several occasions now. It was easy work and she paid generously. Buying my silence, Belinda called it.

But Mrs. Bantry-Bynge needed my services this Wednesday. She would be spending Wednesday night in town, dining with friends. Oh, bugger, I muttered. It is not a word that a lady ever says out loud, but one has been known to mutter it out of earshot in times of severe crisis. How on earth was I going to find an excuse to leave Hanni and the baroness for several hours? Maybe somebody at the palace dinner party might be persuaded to invite Hanni out for a spin in a Rolls, or maybe I could prevail on Belinda, wherever she was.

I was just showing my guests the dinner invitation to the palace when there was a knock on the front door and in swept Belinda herself, looking startling in a silver mack.

"My dears, it's raining cats and dogs out there," she said as my grandfather-turned-butler helped her off with the coat. "Positively miserable, so I thought I'd better come straight to you and cheer you up with good news."

"How kind of you," I said, "but you haven't met my guests."

I led her into the morning room and presented her.

"Miss Belinda Warburton-Stoke," I said. "A great pal of mine from school."

"How do you do." Belinda executed a graceful curtsy.

"How strange." The baroness stared at Belinda. "You bear a strong resemblance to somebody."

"I have relatives all over the place," Belinda said breezily. "How are you enjoying London so far?"

"So far it has been raining and we have sat alone in this house," the baroness said.

"Oh, dear. You'll be taking them out today, won't you, Georgie?"

"Yes, I thought maybe the National Gallery, since it's raining, or the peeresses' gallery at the House of Lords."

"Georgie, how positively gloomy for them. Take them shopping. Take them to Harrods or down Bond Street."

"Oh, *ja*. Let us go shopping." Hanni's face lit up. "This I like."

"All right," I said slowly, wondering if royal protocol would force me to buy things for the princess. "We'll go shopping."

Belinda opened her handbag. "Georgie, I came to see you because the invitation arrived this morning."

"Invitation?"

"To Gussie's party, darling. Here." She handed it to me. It was impressively large.

Augustus Gormsley and Edward Fotheringay invite you to an evening of merriment, mayhem and possible debauchery at St. James's Mansions, Wed., June 15th, 8.30 p.m.

This was most tiresome. I really wanted to go, but I shouldn't take a visiting princess to an evening of possible debauchery, and I could hardly go off and leave her.

"I don't think I can go," I said. "I mean, I couldn't leave Her Highness."

"Bring her along," Belinda said cheerily. "Give her a taste of the London smart set. I understand that a prince or two might be in attendance."

"I really don't think—," I began, but Hanni peered over my shoulder and gave a squeak of delight.

"Young men and dancing," she exclaimed. "Yes, this I should like."

"Good, then it's all settled then. Wednesday at eight," Belinda said. "I'll call for you. Must fly, darling. I'm working on a new design."

I escorted her out into the hall.

"You were running an awful risk," I hissed at her. "The old dragon almost recognized you."

"Nonsense, darling. One never recognizes servants. They are invisible."

"You were a scream, pretending to be my maid."

"I did a jolly good job too, I can tell you. And sorry about yesterday. I fully intended to come, but the truth was that I didn't get back to my own bed until five (he was divine, darling), and then I simply slept until five in the afternoon, when it was time to wake up for another party. So being a maid simply fell by the wayside."

"That's all right. The princess has a maid with her who has been press-ganged into looking after both of them. And Binky has sent me a little money to engage a new maid for myself and the agency is supposed to be rounding up suitable girls."

"Choose one who isn't talkative," Belinda said. "Nothing is worse than waking up in the morning to chatter, chatter when they bring in the tea. And then you never know to whom she will spill the beans about certain people who stayed the night. One does have a reputation of sorts, you know."

"That wouldn't apply to me," I replied. "My maid might die of boredom."

"Things will change, you'll see. You've only been here a couple of months. Once you're in with our set it will be party after party. And this little do of Gussie Gormsley's is just the thing. Everyone will be there, I can assure you."

"Are you sure I should bring the princess to a wild party?"

"Oh yes." Belinda grinned. "What better way to introduce her to life outside the convent? So until then"—she kissed my cheek—"toodlepip."

And she was gone, running down the front steps and out into the rain.

Baroness Rottenmeister insisted on coming with us to Harrods. I was rather reluctant to go there, as Harrods had been the site of one of the humiliations of my life. I had served behind the cosmetics counter for all of three hours before being sacked. But today I would be going as myself, accompanied by a princess and a baroness. I didn't anticipate any problems.

Hanni was like a small child in a toy shop the moment she entered the store. She danced from counter to counter uttering little squeaks of joy. "Oh, look. Rings. Necklaces. And lovely handbags. Oh, look, lipsticks." I had to admit that her vocabulary was quite impressive in this area and I wondered how she would have encountered English words like "cosmetics" at the convent. Maybe there were interludes between gang fights in those American movies. Maybe the gangsters' molls talked about their cosmetic preparations. We passed from accessories to the dress department.

"Oh, zat is a beautiful dress. I must try it on." Hanni was almost embracing it and a shop assistant was bearing down with a gleaming look in her eyes. "I have no sexy dress to wear to party. Just boring German dresses." She glanced at the tag. "It is only twenty-five pounds."

"That is the belt, madam," the assistant said, appearing miraculously behind her. "The dress is three hundred guineas."

"Three hundred. Is that much?" Hanni asked me innocently.

"Much," I said.

"I try anyway." She beamed at the assistant, while I tried to think of a way to tell her I had no money without general embarrassment. Perhaps the baroness had her checkbook with her.

"Is the young lady visiting from abroad?" the assistant asked me.

"She is Princess Hannelore of Bavaria," I said and noticed the woman's demeanor change instantly.

"Your Highness. What an honor. Let me bring you some other dresses to try on."

We spent a happy half hour, with Hanni looking more delightful in each successive dress and me feeling more ill at ease about who was expected to pay for them.

"I believe you've seen all our evening gowns now, Your Highness," the assistant said.

Hanni waved her arms expansively. "I will take them all," she said.

"No, you can't." The tension burst forth from me, louder than I had intended.

"Of course not," the assistant said, beaming at Hanni. "One would never expect you to have the inconvenience of carrying the dresses with you. We will have them delivered in the van this afternoon."

"Does the baroness have money from your father to pay for these dresses?" I asked.

"I do not." The baroness almost spat the words.

"Then I'm afraid you can't have them," I said.

"We will telephone my father." Hanni was pouting. "He will want me to have fashionable dress for meeting king and queen, not boring German dress."

"German dress is not boring," the baroness said, her face now beetroot red. "You should be proud to wear German dress. Come, Hannelore. We go now."

I gave the shop assistant a remorseful smile as Hanni was ushered out. We had almost reached the front entrance of the store when I felt a tap on my arm. It was a man in a frock coat and he was frowning. "Excuse me, madam, but were you intending to pay us now for the princess's purchase or should we send a bill?"

"Her purchase?" The dresses were surely still hanging in the fitting room.

"The handbag, madam." He indicated Hanni's arm, which was now tucked through the strap of a delightful white kid purse. "Fifty guineas."

"Your Highness?" I grabbed Hanni before she stepped out into the street. "I think you forgot to put back the handbag you were examining."

Hanni stared down at her arm in surprise. "Oh yes. So I did." And she handed it back to the floorwalker with a sweet smile. I sat in the taxi home watching Hanni as she pouted. Had she really forgotten the handbag or was she intending to sneak it out of the store?

"I must marry a rich man very soon," Hanni declared. "And so must you, Georgie. Will there be rich men at the party we go to?"

"Yes, I think there will."

"Good. Then we will each choose one." She paused, thoughtfully. "Will the beautiful man who saved us yesterday be there, do you think?"

"I don't think so," I said, hoping that he wouldn't. I had seen Darcy's eyes light up when he saw Hanni. "And men are not described as beautiful. They are handsome."

"He was beautiful," Hanni said wistfully.

I had to agree that he was. Probably the most beautiful man I was ever going to meet.

Chapter 10

That night Mrs. Huggins served toad in the hole and rice pudding. It was nursery food at its plainest and the baroness stared in horror when it was put before her.

"Toad in 'ole?" she asked, imitating Granddad's Cockney. "Toad? This is like frog, no? You bake frog in this pooding?"

"It's just a name," I said, although I was so tempted to let her think she was eating a baked toad. "We have a lot of quaint names for our food in English."

"I like toad in 'ole," Hanni said. "It tastes good."

And so it did. Like a lot of plain food, toad in the hole is delicious if well cooked, and I've always had a weakness for sausages.

"If is not frog, then what is it?" the baroness demanded of my grandfather.

"It's bangers, ducks," my grandfather said, smiling at Hanni. Those two had set up an immediate bond.

"You mean ducks that have been shot?" the baroness asked. "It does not taste like duck."

"Not ducks. Bangers," Grandfather said patiently.

"He means sausages. English sausages."

"But this is food for peasants," the baroness said.

"I like," Hanni muttered again.

The baroness went to bed early in a huff, muttering "no bathwater, no heat and toads to eat," all the way up the stairs.

I was still pondering how I was going to slip out to carry out my assignment with Mrs. Bantry-Bynge on Wednesday morning. Then, overnight, a brilliant idea struck me. I hadn't heard from the agency about my new maid.

I could claim I was going to interview candidates for the post. This brilliant scheme was frustrated by a telephone call while we were eating breakfast on Tuesday morning. It was the domestic agency; they had found a highly suitable person for the position if I might have the time to interview her.

"I'm afraid I must leave you to your own devices this morning," I said as I came back into the breakfast room. (It was kippers this time. The baroness complained about the bones.) "But I have to go and interview a new maid."

"What happened to your other maid?" the baroness asked. "Where has she gone? I thought she was good."

"Good, but unreliable," I said. "She went out on Saturday night and didn't turn up again. So I took your advice and decided I had to let her go."

She nodded. "*Gut.* One must be firm at all times with servants."

"So if you will excuse me, I need to interview her replacement. Maybe you would like to take a tour of the National Gallery. There are fine paintings there, I believe."

"It is raining too much," the baroness said. "And the princess needs to rest before our dinner at the palace. She must look her best."

"But I feel fine," Hanni complained. "I want to go see London. Meet people. Have a good time."

"The princess will rest," said the baroness. "She will write letters home."

"Okay." Hanni sighed.

I set off for the domestic agency feeling as if I were about to sit for a stiff examination. Hiring servants wasn't something I did every day—in fact I'd never done it before.

"I believe we have finally found a suitable maid for you, my lady." The woman at the desk was quite intimidating in her immaculate gray suit and white jabot. A cross between a hospital matron and school headmistress and with an air of more refinement than I could ever hope to achieve. She looked distinctly pleased with herself. "This is Mildred Poliver."

A woman in her forties rose to her feet and dropped a curtsy. "I am delighted to make your acquaintance, your ladyship. It would be an honor to serve you."

"I'm sure you'd like to ask Miss Poliver some questions," the headmistress lady said.

"Oh yes. Of course." I tried to sound efficient and breezy, as if I interviewed servants on a regular basis. "Um—what experience do you have, Miss Poliver?"

"I have been a leedy's maid for twenty-naine yahrs," she said in the sort of refined accent that those born to the lower classes seem to think sounds upper-class. "My last position was with Brigadier Sir Humphry Alderton. Do you know the Humphry Aldertons by any chance?"

"Not personally."

"A faine family. Very refained."

"So why did you leave?"

"They were returning to India and I had no wish to go to that country. I can't abide the heat, you see."

"I see."

"Mrs. Humphry Alderton gave me a glowing reference. It is here, should you wish to see it."

I glanced over it. *Mildred is a gem. Don't know what I'll do without her . . .*

"This looks quite satisfactory," I said.

"Miss Poliver would naturally expect a wage commensurate with her experience," the dragon said.

"How much did you receive at your last position?"

"Seventy-five pounds a year, all found. I require Thursday afternoons and Sunday evenings free."

"That sounds satisfactory," I said. I was sure the maids at home got nothing like seventy-five pounds a year. More like twenty. I was also calculating that Binky had given me one hundred pounds to cover the maid and the expenses of feeding our German visitors, and the baroness would soon prove expensive to feed. But then I didn't have to keep Mildred Poliver after my guests had gone. I could find some excuse to get rid of her. My honest nature won out of course.

"I should point out that the position may only be temporary."

"Temporary?"

"I am not sure how long I am remaining in London and I do have a personal maid at Castle Rannoch."

"As it happens, a temporary assignment would suit me to a tee," Mildred said. "I did so enjoy living in the country and I am not sure how I will like the hustle and bustle of London."

We shook hands and Mildred offered to start that very afternoon.

"That would suit me very well," I said. "We are expected for dinner at the palace tonight."

"The palace? Fancy." The two women exchanged impressed nods.

"Well, of course, your ladyship is related to the royal family, it stands to reason," Mildred said. I could see the wheels of her mind already working. She was going to enjoy boasting about the royal connection. She was probably even hoping that a royal relative might pop in for tea from time to time. I had actually taken an instant dislike to her but could find no way of rejecting her. It's only temporary, I told myself. A Rannoch can handle adversity.

Mildred set off to collect her things and I went home. With Mrs. Huggins's help I prepared a room for her, next to Irmgardt's, up under the eaves. It felt bitterly cold and damp up there and I understood for the first time why Irmgardt always looked so disgruntled. Could I possibly expect Mildred to be satisfied with such surroundings? Maybe she was used to adversity. But then maybe she would only stick it out for a few days, which would suit me well. She arrived not long after, bearing a pitifully small suitcase, and gushed over the impressive nature of Rannoch House's hallway. She was rather more quiet when I took her up three flights to her room.

"It's rather spartan," was all she managed.

"Of course we can make it more comfortable," I said rapidly. I couldn't understand why I was trying to please her. She was rather intimidating.

"And I should point out that my name is Mildred," she said. "I am never called Millie. Never."

"Of course not." I was apologizing again as if I had intended to be on chummy Millie–Georgie terms with her any moment.

I took her on a tour of the house. She approved of my bedroom, but not of the clothes draped over the backs of chairs. "I can tell your ladyship has been without a competent maid for a while," she said. "And the state of your clothes, my lady. Did your last maid not know how to use an iron?"

"Not very well," I said hastily. "Now, this room next to mine is currently occupied by my guest, Princess Hannelore of Bavaria."

"A princess here. Fancy." I rose in her estimation again.

"She has her own maid, called Irmgardt. We'll see if she's in here and I can introduce you, although she doesn't appear to speak anything but German."

I pushed open Hanni's bedroom door. There was no sign of Irmgardt. Hanni had obviously been writing letters. A piece of writing paper lay on her bedside table, on which someone had written in big letters *C.P.???* The envelope lay beside it. It bore a W.1. postmark. So Hanni did know someone else in London after all.

$\mathcal{C}hapter$ 11

Diary,
Buck House this evening. Oh, Lord, I hope Hanni doesn't do her
gangster impression! I hope everything goes smoothly. Maybe
the queen will be so enchanted with Hanni that she'll invite her
to stay at the palace instantly. . . .

It felt strange to have a maid dress me for the dinner at the palace. I had
become so used to fending for myself that I was embarrassed to stand there
like a dressmaker's dummy while Mildred fussed around me, powdering
my shoulders, hooking my dress, slipping my feet into my evening shoes
and then doing my hair. She despaired about the latter.

"May I suggest a good cut and a permanent wave, my lady? Waves are
fashionable these days."

"I'll consider it," I said lamely.

"And what jewelry has your ladyship selected for tonight?"

I hadn't even thought about jewelry. "I don't know. I have some nice
pearls."

"Pearls?" She sounded as if I had said a rude word. "Pearls are not worn
in the evening, unless, of course, they are exceptional pearls of great size
and history. Is your necklace of great size and history? Does it include other
precious stones?"

I had to admit that it didn't.

"May I suggest rubies, given the color of the dress," she said.

"I don't own rubies. I do have garnets."

"Garnets?" She actually looked pained.

In the end I handed her my jewel case and let her select. "The good stuff is at home in the vault," I said, trying to redeem myself. "My family worried about burglaries in London."

As I went downstairs to meet my guests I hated myself for letting her upset me. She was, after all, the servant and I the mistress. Why should I care if she thought my jewelry pathetic or my dresses crumpled?

Hanni looked stunning in an evening version of a German dirndl, the baroness fearsome in black with several strings of jet around her neck and a fierce black feathered concoction sticking out of her bun at the back of her head. As we rode to the palace in the taxicab, I gave Hanni a few last-minute warnings. "Please do not talk about gangsters or call Her Majesty a doll, babe or broad," I said.

"Okeydokey," she said happily. "I'll talk like London person now. Your butler, he help me."

This did not sound encouraging, but before I could do any more warning, we were turning in through the palace gate and pulled up in the courtyard. Liveried lackeys leaped forward to open the taxicab door and we climbed out. We were ushered into a brightly lit foyer. "Their Majesties are awaiting you upstairs," we were told.

"Bob's your uncle. We go up the apples and pears here," Hanni said loudly and brightly and started to ascend the broad marble stair decorated with gilt and statues.

"Maybe you shouldn't try to talk like a London person," I whispered.

"Apples and pears is not right?"

"Not for the palace. At least not for this palace. At the Hammersmith Palace it would be fine."

"Which palace?" she asked.

"Never mind. Just listen to what I say and try to use the same words."

At the entrance to the gallery we were announced and stepped into a room already full of people, most of whom I didn't know. The king and queen were standing at the far end, looking remarkably regal even though this was classed as an informal evening with no tiaras or sashes. The queen held out a white-gloved hand and greeted us warmly.

"Hannelore, my dear, we've so been wanting to meet you. How are you enjoying London so far?"

I held my breath, waiting for Hanni to answer in gangster or Cockney terms. Instead even she seemed a little awestruck. "I like very much," she said. "And I too am wanting to meet the lovely English queen and see the lovely palace."

"We must show you around on another occasion," the queen said.

"This I would like." Hanni beamed at them. So far so good.

"I do hope our sons are going to join us for dinner," the queen said. "I would so like you to meet them."

As if on cue the Prince of Wales sauntered up and gave his mother a peck on the cheek. He looked terribly dashing in his dinner jacket and black tie. (White tie and tails were reserved for formal occasions.)

"I'm glad you could come after all, David," the queen said.

"Just popped in but I can't stay long," he said. "I'm dining with friends."

"David, how tiresome. I particularly asked you to come and meet our guest from Germany. Princess Hannelore."

The prince nodded and spoke a few words in German to Hanni, who responded with a charming blush.

"I had hoped that my second son, the Duke of York, and his wife would be able to join us," the queen said, "but apparently one of their daughters is not well and they thought it wiser to stay home."

"He stays home because his daughter has the sniffles," David said with a derisive snort. "He positively wallows in domesticity these days. Hardly ever goes out. The devoted papa, you know."

"At least he has given me grandchildren," the queen said sotto voce as the prince turned away. "May I remind you that we don't have an heir yet."

"Don't start that again, for God's sake," the prince muttered back to her, then raised his voice. "In fact I think that's my cue to exit. Princess, Georgie, I bid you adieu for now." He nodded briefly to Hanni and me and disappeared into the crowd as the queen gave me a despairing look.

Hanni was taken around to be introduced to the guests by an elderly general who seemed rather smitten with her while I stood beside the queen.

"How are we ever to bring them together?" she asked me. "You must take her to the smart parties that David attends."

"I don't get invited to smart parties, ma'am," I said. I wasn't sure that the mayhem and debauchery of the following night should be mentioned. "And besides, if the Prince of Wales goes to a party, he is likely to be accompanied by the American lady."

"Woman," the queen corrected. "Certainly no lady. But I suppose you're right. She has him in her clutches and she's not going to let go. We'll have to think of something, Georgiana. You have a good brain. You come up with a plan."

"The Bavarian lassie is definitely charming," the king muttered to his wife as he drew close to her. "Did the boy seem interested?"

"Can't say that he did," she replied curtly.

"That boy will be the death of me," the king said as he moved off again.

As the royal couple greeted more guests, the baroness reappeared, beaming, with Hanni in tow. "I have found good friend here," she said. "Come. You must meet."

We were taken through the crowd.

"My good friend Dowager Countess Sophia," Baroness Rottenmeister said proudly, "and her nephew, Prince Siegfried."

I mumbled something and prayed for the dinner gong, or at least a large earthquake, while I waited for doom to fall. Any minute now she'd shriek, "But she came to clean my house!"

Apparently Belinda had been right and servants really are invisible, because she greeted me quite pleasantly. Siegfried chatted away in German to Hannelore, who insisted on answering him in her broken English. Hope rose in my heart. Maybe those two might make a match and I'd be off the hook. Knowing his predilection for boys, I didn't think it would be a very satisfying marriage for Hanni, but she didn't seem to possess many scruples. She probably wouldn't mind taking a lover or two.

Then the gong sounded and we were led in to dinner. I was seated next to Siegfried and had to listen to his account of how he had shot the world's largest wild boar in Bohemia. "As big as a bus with tusks as long as this," he exclaimed, almost knocking over a glass. As I nodded and muttered occasionally, Hanni's high, clear voice floated down the table to me. "*Ja*, I am liking the English food. The spotted dick and the bangers and the toad in the 'ole. They're the bee's knees."

She wasn't close enough to kick.

"How fascinating," said an elderly viscountess as she peered at Hanni through her lorgnette.

"Maybe in wintertime you come visit Romania and we go shoot wild boar," Siegfried was saying to me.

"Princess Hannelore likes shooting things," I said, bringing her into this conversation. "Don't you, Hanni?"

"Yeah, bang bang. Shooting is fun."

And they were off, discussing guns. Siegfried looked rather puzzled when Hanni mentioned machine guns and violin cases, and I had to explain that she was talking of a shoot-out in a gangster film. They seemed to be getting along splendidly. Unfortunately the queen wasn't equally delighted. As we ladies withdrew while the men passed the port and lit up cigars, she drew me to one side.

"Siegfried seemed to be paying her too much attention," she said. "We can't let that happen. You must show more enthusiasm for him, Georgiana. Men like to be flattered. And as for Hannelore, I'm counting on you to find a way to bring her and my son together."

She had just moved away to talk with another guest when the baroness came barreling down on me, still beaming. "Vonderful news," she said. "My kind friend the Dowager Countess Sophia has invited me to stay at her house. She has a good German chef and central heating and plenty of hot water. I shall take Hannelore and stay there."

Oh, dear. I didn't think the queen would approve of Hanni being under the same roof as Siegfried. My life seemed to be one continual stepping out of the frying pan and into the fire.

Chapter 12

Fortunately Hanni flatly refused to move to the dowager countess's house.

"But I like it with Georgie," she said. "The queen wishes I stay with Georgie."

"But Your Highness needs a chaperon," the baroness said. "What would your father say?"

"Georgie will be my chaperon. And Irmgardt will stay to look after me."

The baroness went to say something, looked hard at me, then closed her mouth again. I could tell she was torn between her duty to the princess and the good food and warmth that awaited at the dowager countess's house. Finally she nodded. "Very well. But you must not leave London without me and I insist that I accompany you to all official functions. Your father would expect it."

And so it was settled. Baroness Rottenmeister would move out the very next morning. I went to bed feeling optimistic for the first time in weeks. I awoke to a bump, a yelp and someone creeping around my room. I sat up, terrified. "Who's there?" I asked.

"Sorry, m'lady," said a voice from over near the window, and a curtain was drawn back, revealing Mildred. "I was bringing up your morning tea, but I'm not yet familiar with the layout of your furniture and I bumped into your dressing table. It won't happen again, I promise."

She came across to the bed and placed a tray on my bedside table. The tray contained a cup of tea with a biscuit beside it. "When should I run your ladyship's bath?" she asked.

I was beginning to see that this maid business might have some advantages. At home at Castle Rannoch we had never indulged in luxuries like tea in bed. I was contemplating lying there, reading the *Times* and sipping tea, when I remembered that I had a busy morning ahead of me: I had to see the baroness suitably transported to Park Lane and clean Mrs. Bantry-Bynge's house. How on earth was I going to manage that?

"And what are your ladyship's social engagements for today?" Mildred asked. "What outfit may I lay out for you?"

I could hardly say that I was going to sweep floors and wear a maid's uniform. "Oh, nothing special. A skirt and jersey. I can select them myself when I've had my bath."

"Certainly not, my lady. I am here to give service and service I shall give."

I sighed as she brought out a linen skirt and a silk blouse. Both had already been miraculously cleaned and pressed. Somehow, somewhere I was going to have to change from the clothes Mildred wanted me to wear into my uniform.

"You may run my bath now, Mildred," I said. "I have a morning visit I must pay"—then I remembered the happier news of the day—"and the baroness will be leaving us, so maybe you could assist Irmgardt with her packing."

I bathed, dressed and put my maid's uniform into a carrier bag, then I went downstairs to find my guests already at breakfast. In honor of the baroness's departure Mrs. Huggins had made bacon and kidneys and the baroness was devouring them as if she had been starving for months. "At last. Good *Fleisch,*" she said, smacking her lips.

I hoped the *Fleisch* wasn't so good that she had changed her mind about moving in with the dowager countess.

"I'm afraid I have to go out for a while this morning," I said. "I expect Hannelore would like to accompany you to Park Lane to make sure you are comfortably settled."

"Where do you go?" Hanni asked.

"Oh, just to visit a friend."

"I come with you," Hanni said firmly. "Is boring with old broads."

Oh, dear. "I'm afraid the friend I'm going to visit is very elderly herself," I said. "Bedridden, in fact, and not very well. I visit out of duty, once a month."

"I can come and make her happy," Hanni said. "Old women in bed like to see young smiling faces."

"Not this one. She only likes to see people she knows. Otherwise she becomes confused. And of course she has a rash, but I don't think it's catching." I heard a gasp from the baroness.

"Princess Hannelore will come with me," she said.

"Good idea." I heaved a sigh of relief. "I will call to escort you home in time for a rest before the party."

"I am thinking it is my duty to come to this party with Her Highness," the baroness said.

This day was turning into one complication after another.

"I'm afraid you would have a most disagreeable time," I said. "It will be young people and jazz music."

"Highly unsuitable," the baroness muttered. "I don't think her father would approve."

"My father wants me to meet young people," Hanni said.

"Young people of good family," I added. "And I promise to watch over the princess at all times."

The baroness snorted but I think was relieved to get out of an evening of jazz, not to mention debauchery. I offered my maid's services to help her pack, my butler to summon a cab and transport her luggage, and then I slipped down to the servants' quarters to change into my maid's uniform and slip out through the servants' entrance without being seen.

"So your little plan worked, did it?" my grandfather asked. "The old Kraut is off?"

"Yes, thank goodness. I told her you'd summon a cab and take down her luggage for her."

"Is she taking that maid, that Fireguard person, with her?" Mrs. Huggins poked her head around the kitchen door.

"No, Irmgardt is the princess's maid. She'll obviously be staying here," I said.

Mrs. Huggins sighed. "Gives me the willies, that one does. Drifting in and out like a black shadow, staring at you with a face that could curdle milk."

"She can't help her face, Mrs. Huggins, and she doesn't speak English, which must make it hard for her."

"I've tried teaching her English words but she don't seem too eager to learn. Thick as a plank, if you ask me. And downright unfriendly."

"I don't suppose the Germans think more kindly of us than we do of them," Granddad said. "But she won't even take her meals down here with us. Puts her food on a tray and then takes it up to her room. What with her and your Miss Lah-dee-dah . . ."

"Mildred, you mean?"

"Frightfully posh, she is. If she sticks her nose in the air any higher, she'll fall over backwards," Mrs. Huggins said.

I had to laugh. "Yes, she is rather annoying, isn't she? But it won't be for long, I promise. It's no easier for me, I can assure you. At least we're getting rid of the baroness. And I have to go out, I'm afraid."

I slipped into the downstairs cloakroom, changed into my maid's uniform and crept out of the tradesmen's entrance when no one was looking. I had to get through my assignment at Mrs. Bantry-Bynge's as early as possible. Mrs. B-B was not due until the afternoon, but I had once encountered her gentleman friend. He had been rather too friendly and I had no wish to fight him off again. I assumed that men such as he were not early risers so I hoped to complete my work unmolested. I took the bus to Regent's Park and had the whole thing done before noon, without any embarrassing encounters with men in blazers, then I went home to change out of my maid's uniform before I went to Park Lane to collect Hanni.

When I arrived home I was greeted by my grandfather.

"The princess isn't back yet, is she?" I asked.

He had a strange look on his face. "No," he said. "But there was a telephone call for her while you were out. It seems the piece of jewelry she saw this morning at Garrard's is ready to be delivered. They pointed out that they require C.O.D. for an item of that price. Apparently it's emeralds." He watched me wince. "That young lady needs watching," he said.

"You can say that again." I sighed. "Yesterday she tried to sneak a handbag out of Harrods. Now I suppose I'll have to explain to Garrard's that there has been a mistake. I just hope she didn't have it engraved."

"That's what happens if you keep girls locked away in a convent," Granddad said. "They go off the rails when they get out. If I were you, I'd let the queen know what you're going through, and ship Her Highness back to Germany. Nothing good ever did come out of that country!"

"Beethoven. Mendelssohn. Handel," I pointed out, "and Moselle wine. And I thought you'd taken a fancy to the princess."

"She seemed a nice enough little thing," he agreed. "But she still wants watching. She don't think like you and me."

I suffered an embarrassing interview at Garrard's, during which I had to hint that madness ran in the princess's family, then I went to Park Lane to bring Hanni home.

"But Siegfried escorted her back to your house immediately after luncheon," the baroness exclaimed. "I don't understand."

"She probably just went for a walk," I said. "It is a lovely day."

"That girl needs a good spanking," the baroness said. "I should not have let her out of my sight. Perhaps I should come back to your house after all. I am neglecting my duty."

"I'll go and find her right away and keep a closer watch on her," I said. "I'm sure there is nothing to worry about."

Of course I wasn't at all sure. I didn't mention the Garrard's episode. My grandfather was right. The sooner she was shipped back to Germany, the better.

I had no idea where to look for her and had visions of her rifling Harrods or buying up Bond Street at this very moment. I walked around aimlessly for a while then came home to find that Hanni had returned and was resting. She had fallen asleep and looked positively angelic. My opinion of her softened. She was, after all, a very young girl in the big city for the first time. She just didn't know the rules yet.

Chapter 13

Belinda called for us at eight. She was wearing the outfit she had made me model for Mrs. Simpson—black silk trousers with a white backless top. Stunning on her, of course—an utter disaster on me. I felt positively dowdy in my flowing taffeta panels made by our gamekeeper's wife. Hanni wore the same pale pink affair she had worn to dinner the first night. She looked the way a princess should look in fairy stories. I half expected to see her followed by dwarves.

We could hear the party in full swing as we pulled up in the taxicab outside St. James's Mansions. The deep thump thump of a jazz beat and the wail of saxophones floated down into the refined air of Arlington Street, making a pair of old gentlemen, on their way to their club, wave their canes and mutter about the youth of today and what they needed was a stint in the colonies or a good war in Africa. The flat was in one of the big modern blocks that overlook Green Park. We rode in the lift to the sixth floor and as the doors opened, we were hit by the full force of the sound. This was no gramophone recording. They had a full jazz band in there!

The front door was unlatched and Belinda didn't wait to be invited in. She went straight in and motioned for us to follow her. We stood in the square marble entrance hall, overwhelmed with the level of music. An archway led to the main living room. The lights were low and a smoky haze hung in the air, but I got an impression of white walls, low chrome furniture and highly modern paintings. At least I think they were paintings. To me they looked as if someone had hurled paint at a canvas and then jumped around on it. The carpet had been rolled back and the parquet floor was packed with gyrating couples. A colored jazz band took up most of the dining alcove. There was a bar in the hallway, with a steady procession of young people in the most fashionable evening clothes passing to and fro with cocktail glasses.

The only parties I had been to in my short and dull life had been the coming-out balls during my season, all taking place in well-lit and well-chaperoned ballrooms—at which the strongest concoctions had been punch with a hint of champagne. Apart from those there were the Christmas parties at Castle Rannoch with Scottish reels and bagpipes, plus the odd summons to Balmoral for the royal equivalent. But nothing like this. This was the sort of sinful, smart party I had dreamed of. And now I was here, I was overcome with awkwardness.

Belinda plunged right in, sailing up to the bar. "What are we making tonight, darlings?" she asked. "Can we manage a sidecar? Oh, and make it a double while you're about it, there's an angel."

She looked back at Hanni and me, still standing just inside the front door.

"Come on. What are you drinking?"

"I try some moonshine," Hanni said. "That is what Edward G. Robinson drinks."

"Hanni, this is England. Drinking is legal here. We don't need moonshine," I said.

At that moment the dance number ended and Gussie Gormsley came out of the drawing room, dabbing at his face with a red silk handkerchief. "My God, it's like a Turkish bath in there," he said. "A drink, my good man, and rapidly." Then he saw us and looked genuinely pleased. "Hello, Georgie, hello, Belinda. You came. Splendid. Hoping you would." Then his eyes moved to Hanni. "And who is this delightful creature?"

"This is Princess Hannelore of Bavaria," I said. "She's staying with me. I hope you don't mind that we brought her along."

"Not at all. Delighted. Most welcome, Princess."

"Call me Hanni," she said, graciously extending a hand to him.

"Hanni, this is one of our hosts, Augustus Gormsley," I said.

"Call me Gussie, everyone else does. And we're having a positively royal evening. Half the crowned heads of Europe will be here before the night is over. But where are my manners? You ladies need a drink before I introduce you."

He went up to the bar and handed us something pink with a cherry in it. "That will put hair on your chest," he said.

"But I do not wish hair on my chest," Hanni said, causing a general laugh.

"I'm sure your chest is absolutely beautiful the way it is," Gussie replied, studying it earnestly. "Come on in and meet people."

"It's awfully loud," Belinda said. "I'm surprised the police haven't shown up yet."

"Already been and gone, old thing," Gussie replied with a grin. "And we have the helmet to prove it. We did send the poor chap off with ten quid to keep him happy, however."

He took Hanni and me by the arm and steered us into the drawing room. "Look what I just found out in the hall," he called to Lunghi Fotheringay.

Introductions were made. Lunghi made a beeline for Hanni and steered her out to the balcony to see the view.

"He doesn't waste any time, does he?" Gussie said, looking a little disappointed. "Now, let's see. Who do you know?"

"I'm sure nobody," I said. "I don't exactly mix with the smart set."

"Nonsense," Gussie said. "I'm sure you know old Tubby, don't you? Tubby Tewkesbury? Everyone knows old Tubby."

A large, red-faced fellow turned at the sound of his name. That face lit up when he saw me. "What-ho, Georgie. Didn't expect to see you at a bash like this. In fact, I haven't seen you since you came out. Down in London for a while, are you?"

"I'm living here now. Attempting to make my own way in the world."

"Splendid. That is good news. Although you don't want to get mixed up with this lot. They'll lead you down the road to perdition, you know."

"Ah, but think of the fun she'll have along the way," Gussie said. "Come on, drink up."

The band struck up again and Tubby dragged me onto the dance floor. His gyrations were even more dangerous than those around us and I was lucky to come out of the dance with no black eyes or broken toes. "Another drink, I think," he said, as the sweat ran down his face. "Same for you, old thing?" and he took my glass for a refill before I could answer.

I stood alone, looking around the room, trying to recognize faces in the dark, and found myself looking directly at a face I knew only too well.

"Mother!" I exclaimed. "What are you doing here?"

"Having fun, darling, the same as you," she said. She was reclining in one of the low leather armchairs, a cigarette holder held nonchalantly in one hand, a cocktail glass in the other. "Dear Noel insisted on bringing me."

"Noel?"

"Noel Coward, darling. You must have heard of Noel. Everybody knows Noel. He writes the most divine plays and acts in them too. So talented. And he positively adores me."

"Mummy, so he was the man who was making you think of ditching Max?"

She laughed. "Oh no, no, no. He doesn't adore me in that way, I assure you, darling. But he's trying to persuade me to return to the stage. He wants to write a play especially for little *moi*. Isn't that touching?"

"Don't tell me you're actually thinking of returning to the stage?"

She looked coy. "Noel has been absolutely begging me. And I have to admit, it might be fun."

"You should take him up on his offer," I said. "You can't go on relying on men to support you for the rest of your life, you know."

She laughed, that wonderfully melodious peal that made heads turn throughout a room. "You are so sweet. If I were desperate I believe I'm still officially married to a deadly dull Texan millionaire and I could go and live on a ranch for the rest of my days. If not he, then several others are lining up for the position, you know. But as it happens, I'm not desperate. I do have a teeny bit tucked away for a rainy day, and that sweet little villa outside Cannes that Marc-Antoine gave me."

"Marc-Antoine?"

"The French racing driver who was so tragically killed at Monte Carlo. I truly believe I could have been happy with him for the rest of my life." An expression of grand tragedy covered her face, then the smile broke through again. "Well, maybe not. All those exhaust fumes. So bad for the complexion."

"So you're seriously considering going back on the stage?"

"I'm sorely tempted," she said. "But I can already hear the whispers: 'She started off as a duchess and it's been all downhill from there on.' "

"As if you worry what people say," I said. "There must have been a good deal of talk during your life."

She laughed again. "You're right. To hell with what people say. And speaking of what people say, you missed the grand entrance of the evening."

"Grand entrance and it wasn't yours?"

"The Prince of Wales, darling, with the dreadful American woman clinging to his arm."

"He brought her here with Mr. Simpson in tow?"

"He did indeed."

"The queen will be furious," I said. "Where are they now?"

My mother was positively gloating. "The spider-woman took one look at me and announced that the party wasn't her thing. 'You didn't tell me that the riffraff would be here, David,' she said and stalked out."

"Damned cheek."

"That's what I thought, considering I have legitimately been a duchess and she hasn't risen above the rank of American housewife. But they left and I stayed, which I consider a victory, darling." She sat up, suddenly alert. "Ah, there Noel is now, darling. Noel, have you brought me another drink, my sweet?"

The suave and elegant figure whom I recognized from the pages of countless magazines glided toward us with a glass in each hand and an ebony cigarette holder balanced between his fingers. "Your wish is my command, as you well know," he said. "Here's to us, darling, the two most beautiful and talented people in the room."

"And may I introduce my daughter, Georgiana?" My mother gestured to me.

"Don't be ridiculous, you are not old enough to have a daughter out of nappies."

"You are such a flatterer," she said. "You know I positively adore you."

"Not as much as I adore you."

I looked around to escape from this orgy of adoration and beat a tactful retreat toward the hallway. Hanni was standing surrounded by a group of young men.

"I like English parties," she said to me as I joined them.

Noel Coward reappeared, having apparently torn himself away from my mother. He eyed us both appraisingly. "What lusciously virginal apparitions," he said. "So ripe and absolutely begging to be deflowered instantly. I almost feel I should take up the challenge myself, if it wouldn't make a certain person insanely jealous."

I thought for a moment that he was referring to my mother, but I saw him glance across the hallway to where a man was leaning against the wall, watching him with a frown on his face. I reacted with surprise as I recognized the person. It was the king's youngest son, Prince George, currently an officer in the Guards. He noticed me at the same moment and came over to me.

"Georgiana. What a pleasant surprise." His hand firmly gripped my elbow and he steered me away. "For God's sake don't mention to my parents that you saw me here, will you? There would be a frightful row. You know what father is like."

"My lips are sealed, sir," I said.

"Splendid," he said. "Let me get you a drink."

I accompanied him to the bar. Noel Coward had now taken over at the piano. He was singing, in that peculiar clipped, bored voice of his, "It's a silly little ditty, and it really isn't pretty, but one really can't be witty all the time. . . ."

"I get another drink too." Hanni had appeared beside us at the bar. "I like cocktails." She pronounced it in the American manner—"cacktails."

"They are rather delicious, aren't they?" I agreed. They did seem to be slipping down remarkably easily.

"And so many sexy guys," she said. "The dark one. He said his name was Edward, but everyone is calling him Lunghi."

"It's a nickname, because he's just come back from India."

"India?"

"Yes, a lunghi is apparently what they wear there."

"Ah. He is sexy guy, don't you think?"

"Yes, I suppose he is." I looked around for him and then froze. Lunghi was now perched on the arm of my mother's chair and she was gazing up at him. As I watched, he took the cherry from his glass and placed it in my mother's mouth. I was wondering how to distract Hanni from this embarrassing scene but she had already given an excited little squeak. "And there is the man from the park."

Chapter 14

My heart leaped. I was sure she meant Darcy, but instead, standing in the doorway was the young man from the communist rally. He was not wearing threadbare clothes tonight, however, but a dinner jacket like everyone else. He looked positively civilized. Hanni rushed straight up to him. "Hiya, baby. What a kick to see you."

"Roberts just walked in," I heard Gussie say to Lunghi. "Did you invite him?"

"Had to, old chap. He's harmless enough, isn't he? Pretty much house-trained. Won't pee on the carpet."

"Yes, but, I mean to say . . . Roberts and the prince at the same party. Shows how broadminded we are, what?"

"Who exactly is this Roberts?" I asked Gussie. "Hanni and I saw him at a communist rally in Hyde Park."

"Doesn't surprise me at all. Terribly earnest is our Sidney. Good causes and rights for the masses and all that. Of course he came from the masses, so one can understand, I suppose."

"He's a GSB," Lunghi added, coming to stand beside us. "But a good enough chap, in his way."

"GSB?" I asked.

"Grammar School Boy," Gussie said, grinning. "He was at Cambridge with us, on a scholarship. Terribly bright. He got me through Greek."

"Hanni seems to like him," I commented as I saw them dancing together.

"I don't think the King of Bavaria would approve if his daughter went to live in a semidetached in Slough," Gussie muttered to me.

I laughed. "You're an awful snob."

Noel Coward's song finished to a burst of laughter and applause. Gussie took a long draw on his cigarette. "Born to it, my dear. Snobbery is in the blood, like hunting, as you very well know."

The band struck up another dance number and the floor filled with couples again. Tubby Tewkesbury stumbled past us clutching an empty glass. "Dying of thirst. Need refill," he muttered.

"Now, he'd make a good match for some poor girl," Gussie said. "Rolling in money, the Tewkesbury family. And of course he'll inherit Farringdons. You should snap him up."

I looked at the sweating back of Tubby's neck. "I don't think I could marry anybody just to inherit something."

"Plenty of girls do," he said. "Plenty of boys do it too. Money is a useful commodity, isn't it, Tubby, old bean?"

"What?" Tubby turned blurry eyes onto us and tried to focus.

"I said money comes in useful at times."

"Oh, rather." Tubby beamed. "If I were penniless, I'd never be invited to parties like this. No girl would dance with me. As it is I have a hard enough time . . . want to hop around again, Georgie? This one's a fox-trot, I think. I can manage that."

"All right."

He gave me a pathetically grateful smile. He was a nice enough boy. A lot of them were. So why couldn't I be practical and settle down as the Marchioness of Tewkesbury in that lovely old house?

In the middle of the dance I was aware of someone standing in the doorway, watching me. I looked around and Darcy was leaning nonchalantly against the doorpost, smoking a black cigarette while he studied me with amusement. I went on dancing, horribly conscious of Tubby's big, sweaty hand on my back, undoubtedly leaving a mark on the taffeta, and of his scary wiggles that passed for moving to the music. I forced myself to carry on chatting merrily and thanked him kindly when the dance was over.

"Now that's what I call charity," Darcy murmured, coming up behind me.

"He's a nice enough chap," I said. "And rich, and has a lovely family home. The ideal match for someone like me."

Darcy still looked amused. "You can't tell me you're seriously considering it?"

"I don't know. I could do worse. He has some redeeming qualities."

"Apart from the money and the house?"

"He's loyal, like a British bulldog. You can rely on someone like Tubby. He's not here today and gone tomorrow like some people." I gave him a meaningful stare.

"Ah, well, I'm sorry about that, but something came up unexpectedly and I've been out of town for a while." Darcy looked uncomfortable.

"Something with long dark hair and good legs. I saw her at the Savoy with you."

"Well, actually," he began but got no further as Hanni burst in, almost flinging herself upon Darcy.

"It is the kind man who saved my life in the park," she said. "I kept telling Georgie that I wanted to meet you again. Now my wish has been granted. I am so happy!"

She was gazing up at him with such open admiration that I thought that no man could resist. Darcy certainly couldn't. "I came to the party hoping to run into you again, Your Highness," he said. "What are you drinking?"

"Cocktails. I just love cocktails," she said. "The ones with cherries in them. You can get me another one. My glass is empty."

And off they went together. Lunghi Fotheringay had now taken over at the cocktail shaker. Interested though I was in observing how Hanni would handle flirting with the two young men she seemed to fancy at the same time, I was not going to stand in the hallway like a wallflower. I made my way back toward the dancing. There was no sign of Belinda anywhere, nor of my mother, Noel Coward or Prince George. The band was playing a lively syncopated number and couples were dancing wildly. I picked out Tubby leaping around shaking like a large jelly, then I noticed Hanni and Darcy come into the room and start dancing together. After a few moments the beat changed to a slower tempo and Hanni draped herself all over him. He didn't seem to be objecting.

Suddenly I felt horribly alone and out of place. What was I doing here? I didn't belong with the smart set and I certainly didn't want to stay and watch Hanni seducing Darcy, or vice versa. The effect of at least four cocktails was beginning to make itself felt. As I started to move toward the door, the whole room swung around alarmingly. This is terrible, I thought. I can't be drunk. I tried to walk in a controlled manner as I fought my way through the crowd and out to the balcony. There I leaned on the rail, taking great gulps of fresh air. Far below me Green Park stretched out in darkness, and the noise of the traffic along Piccadilly seemed muted and far away. It took me a while to realize I wasn't alone out there. Sidney Roberts, the earnest communist, was standing at the rail beside me, staring out into the night.

"Terribly stuffy in there, isn't it?" he said. "And loud too. Not really my thing at all but old Lunghi insisted that I come and he was dashed good to me at Cambridge, so I thought why not?" I could see that he had also been drinking quite a bit and had reached the maudlin phase. "Being a communist is a worthy cause, you know," he went on, more to himself than to me. "I mean, it's not right that people like Gussie and Lunghi can fritter a few thousand pounds on a party while the masses are out of work and starving, and one should do something to make the world a fair place. But the communists are so deadly dull. No parties. No laughter. Hardly any booze. And just occasionally one longs for fine wines and beautiful women."

"You're really one of us at heart," I said, laughing. "A true communist would be happy with a pint of bitter on Saturday nights."

"Oh, dear, do you think so?" He looked worried. "I'm not so sure. Even in Russia there are those who eat caviar. We just need a form of government that doesn't come from the ruling classes. Representation by the people and for the people."

"Isn't that what they have in America? I can't say it's working well there." He looked worried again.

"Besides, the British would never accept anything too extreme," I said. "And most people like things the way they are. The crofters on our estate love being part of the Rannoch family. They enjoy serving us."

"Has anyone actually asked them?" he demanded, then drained the rest of his glass.

"They could leave any time they wanted," I said hotly. "They could work in a factory in Glasgow."

"If there was any work for them."

"What's going on out here?" Gussie appeared with a drink in either hand. "Not interrupting a tryst, am I?"

"No, an argument about communism," I said.

"Too serious. No earnest talk allowed tonight. Strictly reserved for merriment and mayhem. What you need is another drink, old chap."

"Oh, no, thanks. I'm not much of a drinker," Sidney Roberts said. "I've already had enough."

"Nonsense. There is no such word as enough," Gussie said. "Go on. Take it. Down the hatch."

"I really shouldn't, but thanks all the same," Sidney said as Gussie tried to force it on him.

"If he doesn't want it, then I'll do him a favor and drink it for him." Tubby had come out onto the balcony. His face was now beetroot red and he was sweating profusely. Not a pretty sight, in fact. He grabbed the nearest glass from Gussie and drained it in one swig. "Ah, that's what I needed," he said. "Hair of the dog."

"I think you've had enough, old man," Gussie said. "You are seriously blotto."

"Not me. Cast-iron stomach. Never met a drink I didn't like," Tubby said with a distinctly slurred chuckle. Then he swayed, lost his balance and staggered backward.

"Look out!" Sidney shouted as there was a splintering sound and part of the railing collapsed.

As if in slow motion Tubby fell backward off the balcony—arms and legs spread like a starfish, his mouth and eyes opened wide with surprise—and disappeared into the night.

Chapter 15

For a second the three of us stood there, frozen with the horror of what had just happened.

"We must call an ambulance," I said, trying to make my legs obey me and walk back into the room.

"No bloody use calling an ambulance," Sidney said. "We're six floors up. The poor chap's a goner."

Gussie looked as if he might vomit any second. "How could that have happened?" he said. "How could it have happened?"

"He did weigh an awful lot," I said, "and he fell against the railing with all his weight."

"Oh, my God," Gussie said. "Poor old Tubby. Don't let them know in there what happened."

"They'll have to know. You'll have to call the police," I said.

"You saw it. It was an accident," Gussie said. "A horrible accident."

"Of course it was. You're not to blame."

"It's my party," Gussie said bleakly. "I shouldn't have let people out on the balcony drunk."

I took his arm and led him back inside.

"What's up?" Darcy grabbed my arm as I stumbled past. "Are you all right? Have you been drinking too much?"

"That chap I was dancing with," I whispered. "He just fell off the balcony. Gussie's gone to phone the police."

"Holy Mother. Then we'd better get Her Highness and yourself out of here while there is still time," Darcy said.

"But I should stay to answer questions," I said. "I saw him fall."

"You were out there alone with him?"

"No, Gussie was out there, and a chap called Sidney Roberts. It was horrible. He'd had far too much to drink. He staggered backward against the railing and it collapsed and he just went over."

"You're as white as a sheet." Darcy took my arm. "You need a good stiff brandy."

"Oh, no more alcohol, thank you. I've already drunk too much."

"All the more reason for spiriting you out of here. You don't want that to get back to the palace, do you?"

"No, but wouldn't it look odd if we fled?"

"Certainly not. You didn't push him, did you?"

"Of course not, but I know my duty . . ."

"Then you stay if you feel you must but someone should get the princess out of here. I'll take her home if you like."

"Oh no," I said. "I'm supposed to be chaperoning her. I wouldn't trust you to behave yourself. I've seen you looking at her."

"Just being friendly to foreigners." Darcy managed a grin. "Come on, let's go and find her before the police arrive."

We split up and looked around the flat. She wasn't in the main drawing room. I pushed open the door to the kitchen. It was as modern as the rest of the flat, with white painted cabinets and a large, impressive refrigerator. Several people were seated at the kitchen table and they looked up as I came in. Hanni was one of them. I went over and took her arm. "Hanni, we have to go home now. Come along quickly."

"I don't want to leave. I like it here. These nice guys are going to let me try what they are doing," Hanni said.

I stared at the table. It looked as if someone had spilled a line of flour across it.

"Get her out of here," Darcy hissed, taking Hanni by the arm.

"But I want to stay. I'm having fun," she complained loudly. It was clear that the drink was affecting her too.

"You wouldn't be having fun in prison, I assure you," Darcy said as he dragged her out of the door.

"What do you mean?" I whispered. "Why should Hanni go to prison?"

"My dear, you are a complete innocent, aren't you?" Darcy said. "They were sniffing cocaine in there. Hardly the sort of party the queen had in mind for her. And you can't afford to have your names plastered all over the front page of tomorrow's newspapers."

"Why would they put our names in the newspapers?" Hanni demanded.

I went to say something but saw Darcy's warning look.

"If the police raid the party," he said quickly. He steered a swaying Hanni toward the lift.

She was crying now. "I don't want to go home. I want to stay and drink cocktails," she was whimpering.

"What about Belinda?" I hadn't actually seen her since I arrived.

"Belinda can take care of herself, I guarantee," Darcy said. He bundled us into the lift, then quickly found us a cab.

"Are you not coming with us?" Hanni asked with obvious disappointment as Darcy gave the driver our address.

"No, I think I'd better go my own way," Darcy said. "I've a couple of things I should be doing. But I'm sure we'll meet again soon, Princess." He took her hand and kissed it, but his eyes met mine as his lips remained on her hand.

"I'll be seeing you soon," he said. "Take care of yourself, won't you?"

"That was fun," Hanni said as we drove off. "Why did we have to leave? I would have liked a police raid. Like Al Capone. Will the police have machine guns?"

"No," I said. "In England the police don't carry guns at all."

"How silly," she said. "How do they catch the crooks?"

"They blow a whistle and the crooks give themselves up," I replied, thinking that this did sound rather silly.

"But Mr. O'Mara says he will see us again soon. That is good news, no?"

"Yes, I suppose it is," I replied mechanically. I stared out of the window, watching the lights of Piccadilly flash past us. The shock of Tubby's death, mixed feelings about Darcy, combined with the effect of those cocktails, was just beginning to hit me. I felt that I might cry at any moment. I fled to my room as soon as we got home.

"Was it a good party, my lady?" Mildred rose from the shadows.

I leaped a mile. "Mildred, I didn't expect you to stay up so late. You didn't have to wait up for me."

"I always wait up to help my ladies undress," she said primly. I stood there and let her undress me like a little girl. She was just brushing out my hair when we heard raised voices from the next room. Mildred raised an eyebrow but said nothing.

"Will that be all, my lady?" she asked, putting the hairbrush back on my dressing table.

"Thank you, Mildred. It was good of you to stay up so late," I said.

As she opened my door to leave, Irmgardt came out of the princess's room next door and stomped past with a face like thunder. I suspected that the princess had revealed a little too much of what went on at the party. Suddenly I was overcome with tiredness. I got into bed, curled into a tight ball and tried to sleep.

THE NEXT MORNING'S *Times* had a small paragraph reporting the tragic death of Lord Tewkesbury's son, who plunged from a balcony after too much to drink at a Mayfair party. Fortunately the report didn't mention whose party, nor who had been on the guest list. I was still reading the *Times* in bed when my grandfather appeared at my door.

"There's a geezer downstairs what wants to see you," he said.

"What sort of geezer?"

"Says he's a policeman."

"Oh, Lord." I leaped out of bed and tried to put on my dressing gown. My head felt as if it were being hit with a large hammer. Oh, Lord, so this was a real hangover.

"Have you been doing something you shouldn't?" Granddad asked.

"No. I expect it's about the party last night. Some poor chap fell off the balcony. I saw it happen."

"That can't have been very nice for you. Drunk, was he?"

"Completely. Tell the policeman I'll be down immediately."

On my way out of my door I bumped into Mildred. "My lady, I should have been instructed to fetch you. It is quite unseemly for your butler to go into your room. Let me help you dress before you receive company."

"It's not company, Mildred. It's a policeman. And I'm respectably covered up, you know."

"A policeman?" She looked as if she might swoon.

"Nothing I've done." I dodged past her and went downstairs.

My grandfather had put the policeman in the morning room and given him a cup of tea. He rose as I entered and I was dismayed to see it was none other than Inspector Harry Sugg. I had encountered him once before and the memory was not a pleasant one.

"Ah, Lady Georgiana. We meet again," he said. "And again under tragic circumstances."

"Good morning, Inspector." I offered my hand and received a limp handshake, before sitting opposite him on an upright gilt chair. "Please forgive the attire. I wasn't expecting visitors this early."

"It is after nine o'clock." He repositioned himself on the sofa and crossed his legs. "The rest of the world has been out and working for hours."

The thought crossed my mind that he'd have got on like a house on fire with Sidney Roberts. They could have shared their communist sympathies.

"But then the rest of the world doesn't stay up at parties until all hours," he added.

Ah. So he did know I had attended the party last night. No point in denying it then.

"I imagine you're here to take my statement about the horrible accident."

"That's exactly why I'm here. It seems you made a quick getaway before the police arrived last night. Why exactly was that, miss?"

He still hadn't learned that one addressed the daughter of a duke as "my lady" and not "miss," but I had come to think it was deliberate in his case. I chose to ignore it.

"I should have thought it was perfectly obvious. I was extremely distressed by what I had seen. Kind friends put me in a taxi."

"And what had you seen?"

"Mr. Tewkesbury" (I couldn't remember his first name. I'd only ever known him as Tubby. And in my early morning fogged state I couldn't remember whether he was the Honorable Mr. or Viscount something) "fell from the balcony. I was out there. I saw the whole thing."

"Can you describe it for me?"

I went through the whole scene, relating word for word what had happened. When I had finished he nodded. "Well, that corresponds exactly with what Mr. Roberts told us. The other chap, Gormsley, must have been blotto by that time. He couldn't even remember who had been out on the balcony."

Dear Gussie, I thought warmly. Trying to protect me from involvement.

"There had been a lot of drinking going on," I agreed. "Poor Tubby was completely squiffy. That's why he fell over in the first place."

"And the balcony railings actually collapsed?"

"Yes. I heard them splintering. He was a big chap, you know."

"All the same, I presume they build railings to withstand big chaps leaning on them, and it is a new block."

I looked up. "What are you hinting?"

"Nothing at this stage. From what you and Mr. Roberts tell me, we can call it a horrible accident and close the books then?"

"Definitely," I said. "A horrible accident, that's exactly what it was."

"And you can swear that nobody gave him a shove?"

"A shove? Of course not. Why would anyone give him a shove?"

"Extremely rich young fellow, so I understand. People have been known to do a lot of things for money."

"The only person near him was Gussie Gormsley and he's also an extremely rich young fellow."

"There's also jealousy, over a woman?"

"Nobody would be jealous of Tubby," I said. "And besides, I saw the whole thing. Nobody touched him. He took a drink, lost his balance and fell."

The inspector rose to his feet again. "Well, that seems to be that then. Thank you for your time, your ladyship. There will obviously be an inquest in the case of unnatural death. You may be called upon to make a statement. We'll let you know when that will be."

"Certainly, Inspector," I said. "Glad to help."

I remembered to ring the bell to summon my grandfather.

"The inspector is leaving now," I said.

At the doorway Harry Sugg paused and looked back at me. "Strange, isn't it, that you've been involved in two deaths so close together."

"Not involved in either, Inspector," I said. "A witness, that's all. An innocent bystander, in the wrong place at the wrong time."

"If you say so, miss." He took the hat that Granddad had given him, tipped it to me then put it on his head. "Thank you for your time."

And he was gone. I got the impression that Inspector Sugg would dearly have loved it had I really been involved.

"Miserable-looking bloke he was," Grandfather said. "Did he want a statement from you about the party?"

"Yes. He wanted to make sure that Tubby wasn't pushed."

"You saw the whole thing, did you?"

"I did. It was just a horrible accident. Tubby was very drunk and very large."

I felt tears welling up again. I hardly knew Tubby, but he was a harmless fellow and he didn't deserve such a horrible fate.

"So silly, these young people, aren't they? Drink too much, drive too fast. Think they'll live forever. You'll be wanting your breakfast now, I expect."

"Oh, goodness. I don't feel like food at all," I said. "Some black coffee, please, and maybe some dry toast."

"Mrs. Huggins will be disappointed. She was looking forward to cooking real food now that the baroness has gone. What about the little lady? Is she up yet?"

"I haven't seen her yet. We got home very late. I expect she'll want to sleep in."

Granddad looked up the stairs then moved closer to me. "You want to watch that one," he said. "She may prove to be more trouble than she's worth."

"What do you mean by that?"

"Oh, don't get me wrong. She's a nice enough little thing. You can't help liking her, but there's something not quite right with her."

"What are you saying?"

"It's just a feeling I have. I've observed a lot of people in my time as a copper on the beat. Made plenty of arrests, and I think she's a wrong-un. Trying to pinch a handbag from 'arrods. Ordering herself jewels from Garrard's. Ordinary folk don't do things like that."

"Well, she is a princess, Granddad. And she is just out of the convent. She probably hasn't a clue about money and thinks that things she wants miraculously appear in front of her."

Granddad frowned. "I don't care who she is, princess or fishmonger's daughter, she should know right from wrong. And I tell you something else. I think I caught her using the telephone yesterday. I picked up the downstairs extension and I'm sure I heard a click, as if the upstairs receiver had been put down."

"Maybe she was just calling the baroness."

"If she was, why not ask your permission first? And why hang up when she thought someone was listening? She knows we don't speak Kraut."

"I don't mind if she uses the telephone."

"Your brother will mind if she's calling home to Germany," Granddad pointed out.

"Oh, golly, yes. Fig would be livid."

He leaned closer to me. "If I was you, I'd tell the queen you've bitten off more than you can chew with her and send her packing. They can decide at the palace what to do with her. If you don't, I get the feeling she'll lead you up the garden path."

At that moment the front doorbell rang again.

"Blimey, we are popular this morning, aren't we?" Granddad adjusted his tails and started toward the front door. "And you'd better get yourself out of sight. Standing in the hallway in your dressing gown—what will people think?"

I darted for the nearest doorway, then stopped when I recognized the voice.

"I know it's dashed early, but I had to talk to her ladyship before the police show up on her doorstep. Would you tell her it's Gussie? Gussie Gormsley."

I reappeared. "Hello, Gussie. I'm afraid you're too late. The police beat you to it."

"Well, that's a bally nuisance," he said. "I didn't like to wake you and I'd no idea they'd show up at the crack of dawn. No sense of propriety, those fellows. They were dashed rude last night too. Hinted to me that someone might have given poor Tubby a shove, or had been fiddling with the railings. 'Look here,' I told them, 'Tubby hadn't an enemy in the entire world. Everyone liked old Tubby.' I tried to keep you out of it, you know."

"I gathered that. Thank you for trying."

"Would have worked too, but that blasted idiot Roberts, with his lower-class morality, had to go and blurt out that you were on the balcony with us. Then, of course, they wanted to know why you'd done a bunk."

"Actually I wanted to stay, but Darcy thought I should get the princess away so that there was no making of an international incident."

"Oh, right. Good thinking. Darcy O'Mara, you mean?"

"Yes."

"Was he at the party last night?"

"Yes, he was."

"Didn't notice him. Don't think I invited him."

"He probably gate-crashed. He often does," I said.

"Friend of yours?"

"In a way."

He frowned. "Rum fellow. Irish, isn't he? Went to a Catholic school and Oxford, but we won't hold those against him. He plays a decent game of rugby. Father's an Irish peer, isn't he?"

"That's right."

"Don't think I'd quite trust the Irish," Gussie said. "I'd better be off, then."

"Thank you for coming," I said. "And for trying to protect me. It was very sweet of you."

"Not at all. Dashed awful thing to have happened, wasn't it? I can tell you I felt quite green myself. Poor old Tubby. I still can't quite believe it." He started to walk toward the front door, then turned back. "Look here, I gather that some fellows at my party were doing a little more than drinking, if you get my meaning. You saw them in the kitchen, didn't you? If the police question you again, I'd rather you conveniently forgot that. I'd hate to get the family name in the papers in any way mixed up with drugs."

"I understand," I said. "And frankly I had no idea what was going on. I thought they'd spilled flour on the table."

Gussie laughed. "That's a good one. I like you, Georgie. You're a great girl. I hope we can meet again soon. In happier circumstances, I mean."

"I hope so too."

"Is the princess staying with you long?" he asked wistfully.

So that was it. It wasn't me he wanted to meet again soon. It was Hanni.

Chapter 16

No sooner had Gussie departed than Hanni came down the stairs, looking fresh and bright and lovely. No sign of a hangover, and yet she had definitely consumed as many cocktails as I.

"Hello, Georgie. I'm not too late for breakfast, am I? I'm starving. Can we have proper English breakfast now that pain in ass is no longer here?"

"Hanni, that expression really isn't suitable. If you must say something you can say 'pain in the neck.' "

"Neck is better than ass?"

"Definitely. I'll tell Mrs. Huggins you want breakfast."

We went through into the breakfast room and I nibbled at a piece of buttered toast while Hanni attacked a huge plate of bacon, eggs, sausages, kidneys, the works.

"When can we go to another party?" Hanni asked between mouthfuls. "It was such fun. I like the music and the dancing and the cocktails were the bee's knees." She sighed happily. "And the sexy guys too. When can we go see Darcy again? I think he has the hot pants for me. He stayed beside me a long time last night. He wanted to know all about me—my home and the convent and my dreams for the future. He was really interested."

"I don't think you should take Darcy too seriously," I said.

"But he would make good match for me. He is Catholic. Good Irish family. My father would be happy."

"No, your father wouldn't be happy," I said, trying to keep my face calm. "His family is penniless, for one thing, and Darcy is not the type who settles down with one woman. He'll be tired of you by this time next week."

But as I said it, I couldn't help wondering. Did Darcy see the princess as a good bet for his future? Did he fancy himself as Prince of Bavaria with a handsome income for life? He was clearly opportunistic and he might not want to let such a catch as Hanni get away. The queen would be furious, I thought, and then a small voice in my head whispered that I wouldn't be too happy about it either.

"So where do we go today?" Hanni asked. "More shopping? I like London shops. Or lunch at the Savoy? Your friend Belinda said you met Gussie and Lunghi at lunch at the Savoy. I would like a place where I get good food and meet guys."

I began to think that Granddad was right. The princess was rapidly turning into more than I could handle. The small stipend from Binky certainly wouldn't cover outings like lunch at the Savoy and I couldn't risk letting Hanni loose in any more shops.

"You agreed to have lunch with Baroness Rottenmeister at the Park Lane house," I reminded her. "And this morning I think we should take in some British culture," I said. "I am supposed to be educating you. I'm taking you to the British Museum."

"Museum? But museums are full of old stuff. We have crummy old stuff in Germany. I like modern things."

"You may be a future queen," I said. "You need to know your history. British Museum and no arguing."

"Okay," Hanni said with a sigh.

I went upstairs to have my bath and get dressed. Mildred insisted on my wearing decent clothes, and a strand of pearls.

"I'm only going to a museum, Mildred," I said.

"It doesn't matter, my lady. You are a representative of your family and your class every time you set foot outside your front door. My previous ladies never went out unless they looked like aristocrats. The ordinary public expects it."

I sighed and let her attempt to brush my hair into fashionable waves. "And I'm sure you haven't forgotten, my lady, but I did request Thursday afternoons off."

"Oh, absolutely," I said with relief. "Go and enjoy yourself."

"I will indeed, my lady. I often take in a matinee of a show."

Feeling like a dowdy forty-year-old in my suit and pearls, I came out of my room and tapped on Hanni's door. "Ready to go?" I asked, pushing the door open.

Irmgardt looked up at me with her usual sullen blank expression. She was in the process of hanging up the princess's ball gown.

"Is the princess ready to go out?" I asked. "Princess? Downstairs?" I gestured.

She nodded. "*Ja.*"

Poor Hanni, I thought. I bet she didn't choose such a maid. Irmgardt was obviously an old family retainer who had been sent to keep an eye on Hanni by the palace. And she had given her little charge a good talking to the night before. I wondered if it would have any effect.

As I turned to leave, I glanced at the bedside table. There were some letters on it, including the strange sheet of paper with *C. P.* printed on it. And now somebody had slashed an angry red cross through the initials.

I stood staring at it. The angry red slash was quite out of character for Hanni. And I knew nobody called C.P. And anyway, her private mail was none of my business. I closed the door behind me and went downstairs.

⁂

HANNI ENJOYED RIDING on the top of a bus down Oxford Street. It was a lovely summery day, with a warm breeze in our faces, and the crowds below us looked happy and festive.

"Selfridges," Hanni exclaimed. "What is this?"

"Another department store, like Harrods."

"When can we go there?"

"One day, maybe," I said, and decided that I should write to the queen to find out how long I was to be saddled with the princess. It was about time someone else took over the responsibility.

I was glad when we reached the more sedate area of Bloomsbury and I led Hanni up the steps of the British Museum. She clearly wasn't interested in the Egyptian mummies or the Roman statues and wandered around mechanically with a bored expression on her face. I was tempted to give in and take her somewhere more fun like the zoo or a boat on the Serpentine.

We reached the Roman jewelry. "Look, Hanni," I said. "This should be more in your line. These fabulous emeralds."

I looked up from the glass case and she had gone.

The little minx, I thought. She's given me the slip. I had to catch her before it was too late. I hurried through one gallery after another, but the museum was a huge, rambling place. There were groups of schoolchildren to negotiate on the stairs, so many places she could hide, and I realized that my chances of finding her were slim.

"So she's run off," I told myself. She's eighteen years old and it's broad daylight. Why should I be so worried? The worst she'll do is to go shopping on Oxford Street. Yes, and try to shoplift again, and get arrested, I thought. And then what would the queen say?

Drat Hanni, I muttered, and was stomping down the main staircase when I saw her coming up toward me.

"I've been looking for you," she said. "I thought you went without me."

"No, we just mislaid each other," I replied, feeling guilty about my uncharitable thoughts. "But all is well. We've found each other."

"You're right. All is well," she said. "All is very well." She was glowing with excitement. "Something really good just happened. I met the guy from the party last night. Isn't that great?"

"Which guy?" I asked.

"You know, the serious one we met in the park. Sidney. He was here looking for an old book. He told me he works in a bookshop, you know. That is interesting, no?"

I should not have thought of Hanni as the bookshop type—nor the Sidney type. My first thought was that anyone working in a bookshop could not afford to feed and entertain Hanni. But I rapidly came to the conclusion that a bookshop was definitely healthier than parties and cocktails, not to mention cocaine. And he wasn't Darcy.

"Yes, that is interesting," I said. "Where is this bookshop?"

"He said it is in the old part of the city. It's an old, old bookshop. Sidney said the famous writer Charles Dickens used to visit it often. He has invited me to visit it too. He said it has much history. We can go, *ja?*"

"I don't see why not. It's definitely educational."

"Good, then we go tomorrow." Hanni nodded firmly. "Today is no use because Sidney will be here, studying boring old books all day."

"And you are expected at lunch with the baroness," I added.

She rolled her eyes. "Pain in neck," she said. Then her expression softened. "Sidney is nice boy, don't you think?"

"A little too serious for you, I'm afraid," I admitted.

"He is a communist," she said. "I never met a communist before. I thought they were all wild and fierce like in Russia, but he seems gentle."

"I'm sure he's a good person, and he is definitely idealistic. He likes the ideal of a communist society, but it would never work in reality."

"Why not?" She turned those innocent blue eyes on me.

"Because people are people. They are not willing to share equally. They always try to grab what they can. And they need to be led by those born to rule."

"I do not agree with this," she said. "Why should my father be a king, just because he was born to be king?"

"I suppose it does help if one is brought up to rule."

"Sidney is from lower classes, but he would make a good leader," she said.

I thought how easily she was swayed by a pair of earnest gray eyes. If she met a handsome fascist tomorrow, she'd be in favor of whatever it was he believed.

Hanni chatted excitedly all the way back to Park Lane. I found myself half hoping, half dreading that Prince Siegfried would be present at lunch and that Hanni would fall for him. At least he was suitable. Then I rationalized that she was acting like any typical eighteen-year-old straight from a girls' establishment. She wanted affirmation that she was attractive to young men—and at this moment it didn't matter if they were suitable young men or not.

Siegfried was not at lunch. The meal seemed to go on forever, with course after heavy course—the dowager countess's German cook producing dumplings and cream with everything. The baroness smacked her lips and wolfed down everything she was offered. I kept my head down, tried to say as little as possible and prayed with every moment that the dowager countess wouldn't suddenly realize she had seen me sweeping her floors.

I was glad when it was over.

"Now can we visit sexy guys?" Hanni asked. "We go and say hi to Darcy or to Gussie and Lunghi?"

"I hardly think the latter is appropriate," I said without thinking.

"Why?" Hanni turned innocent blue eyes on me.

"Because, er"—I remembered I hadn't told her the truth about what happened the night before—"one of the guests was taken ill and died." I hoped this half truth would suffice. "They are very upset about it," I added. "They won't want to entertain visitors."

"Darcy then? He could take me out to dinner tonight."

I was tempted to tell her the truth about Darcy's financial situation but instead I said, "Hanni, you must learn that a young lady should never be forward. It is not up to you to make the first move. You have to wait for a young man to ask you out."

"Why? This is silly," she said. "If I want to go on date with a young man, why can't I ask him?"

She did have a point. Maybe if I hadn't been so reticent with Darcy he might not have drifted into the arms of whoever the girl with the long dark hair was, and he would not have been flirting with Hanni last night. I remained firm, however, and decided to distract Hanni with a visit to the theater. I picked a light musical comedy by Sigmund Romberg, called *The Student Prince*. This was probably a mistake as it was all about a prince falling in love with a simple girl. In the end he renounces her for his duty. Hanni wept all the way home. "So sad," she kept on murmuring. "I would never give up the man I loved for my duty. Never."

Chapter 17

Diary,

Blustery day. White clouds, blue sky. It would have been a good day to go
   riding at home. Instead I have to take Hanni to meet a man at a
   bookshop. This chaperon business is tiring.

When she came down on Friday morning, I had visions of a repetition of
last night's play. Hanni was clearly excited about seeing Sidney again. "I
don't care if he is only a commoner," she kept saying. She ate sparingly at
breakfast and paced until it was time to leave the house. I was still not too
familiar with the geography of London and went downstairs to ask Granddad how I'd get to Wapping.

"Wapping, ducks?" he asked. "Now what would you be doing there?"

"Going to a bookshop."

"A bookshop in Wapping?" he said.

"That's right. It deals in old and rare books. Where is it?"

"Not the best area. Down by the river. Docklands. I wouldn't have
thought they went in for much reading there. Where is this place?"

"It's off Wapping High Street, near a pub called the Prospect of Whitby."

Granddad was still frowning. "I seem to remember that them communists hold meetings in a hall around there. You want to be careful, my
love. I hope you're not thinking of taking the princess to a place like that."

"She's the one who wants to go. She's met a young man . . . he's a communist and he works in this bookshop."

Granddad made a tut-tutting noise and shook his head. "She wants watching, that one."

"He's perfectly civilized for a communist, Granddad. He went to Cambridge and he seems terribly nice and earnest. And it is broad daylight."

Granddad sighed. "I suppose it is a weekday. People are working. They're not likely to have one of their punch-ups on a Friday morning. When they have their meetings, there's often a right brawl afterwards. The blackshirts and them go at it."

"I'm sure we'll be quite safe, and knowing Hanni, she'll be bored quite quickly in a bookshop."

"Just make sure you don't dress too posh," my grandfather warned, "and watch out for pickpockets and anyone who makes improper suggestions."

I passed on his advice to Hanni and we left the house in simple cotton skirts and white blouses—two young women on an outing to the city. We rode the tube to Tower Hill Station. I pointed out the Tower of London to Hanni, but she expressed little interest in London history, and dragged me forward like an impatient dog on a leash. It was a long, complicated walk to reach Wapping High Street. Roads twisted, turned and dead-ended between tall brick warehouses and docks. Exotic smells of spices, coffee and tea competed with the less savory odor of drains and the dank smell from the river. Barrows clattered past piled high with goods. Finally we came upon the high street. The bookshop was in a small alleyway off the busy street. It was still paved with cobblestones like a scene from an old painting. To complete the picture a beggar sat on the corner, rattling a couple of pennies in a tin cup in front of him. His sign read, *Lost leg in Great War. Spare a penny.* I felt awful and rummaged in my purse for sixpence, then changed my mind and gave him a shilling.

"God bless you, miss," he said.

There were only three shops in the alley. One was a cobbler (boots, shoes and umbrellas repaired like new!), another, halfway down on the left-hand side, was a Russian tearoom with a couple of sad-looking, down-at-heel men sitting in the window, conversing with dramatic gestures. The bookshop was at the dead end of the alley. Haslett's Bookshop. Established 1855. Specializing in Rare Books and Socialist Literature. An interesting combination since I suspected not too many communist workers collected first editions. Now that we had reached the door, Hanni hung back shyly and let me go inside first.

A doorbell jangled as the door closed behind us. The peculiar musty, dusty, moldy smell of old books permeated the air. Dust motes hung in a single shaft of sunlight. The rear of the shop dissolved into darkness, with mahogany shelves, crammed with books, towering up to a high ceiling. It was like stepping back in time. I almost expected an old Victorian gentleman with muttonchop whiskers and tails to come out to greet us. Instead the shop appeared to be deserted.

"Where can everyone be?" Hanni asked as we stood, taking in the silence. "Sidney said he would be here."

"Maybe he's somewhere in the back helping a customer," I suggested, peering past her into the dark interior.

"Let's go find him."

Hanni went ahead of me. The shop was like a rabbit warren, with passages between shelves twisting and turning. We passed dark little side aisles and negotiated boxes of pamphlets on labor unions and workers' rights. There was a Russian poster on the wall with happy, brave-looking workers building a bright future. Next to it was a shelf of first edition children's books. A delightful mixture. At last we came to a narrow stair twisting up to our right.

"Maybe they are upstairs," Hanni suggested. She started up the dark little stairway. I was about to follow her when I heard the bell jangling on the front door.

"My dear young lady, can I help you?" a voice called. Its owner was not unlike my vision of the Victorian gent—white whiskers, faded blue eyes, paisley waistcoat. Alas no tails, however. "I am so sorry." He continued, shuffling toward me. "I just stepped away for a moment. I had to hand-deliver a book. But my assistant should have been here to take care of you. I am Mr. Solomon, the shopkeeper. Now, how may I assist you?"

Hanni had already disappeared up the stairs. I returned to the old man.

"We were actually looking for your assistant, if you mean Mr. Roberts. He had promised to show us around your shop today."

"Mr. Roberts. A fine young man. A truly noble soul," he said. "Yes, he should be here somewhere. He's probably found a book that interests him and he's sitting somewhere, oblivious to the rest of the world. We'll go and seek him out, shall we?"

"My companion already went upstairs," I said.

"Yes, that's a likely place for him. He's writing a book on the history of the labor movement and we have a Russian section up there he's probably perusing. After you, my dear."

He motioned for me to go up the stairs ahead of him. They were steep and narrow and they turned two corners before we emerged at the upper level. This floor was even darker and mustier, with a lower ceiling and shelves stacked so closely together that one almost had to squeeze between them. Anemic electric lights hung here and there but did little to dispel the gloom.

"Hanni?" I called. "Where are you?"

There was no answer.

"Hanni? Mr. Roberts?"

At last a little voice said, "Over here. I'm over here."

I followed the voice to a side aisle. Hanni didn't look up or turn as we came toward her. Instead she stood like a statue, staring down at her hand with a look of utter surprise on her face. The hand held a long, slim knife, its blade coated in something dark and sticky. My gaze went beyond her to the white object on the floor. Sidney Roberts lay there on his back, his eyes open, his mouth frozen in a silent yell of surprise and pain. A dark stain was slowly spreading across the white front of his shirt.

Chapter 18

"My God, what have you done?" The old gentleman pushed past us to Sidney Roberts's body. "Sidney, my boy."

Hanni looked up at me with frightened eyes. "I found it on the floor," she said, holding out the knife to me. "I came around the corner and my foot kicked something. I bent to pick it up and . . . and I saw what it was. Then I saw Sidney lying there. I didn't do it."

"Of course you didn't," I said.

"Then who did?" Mr. Solomon demanded. He knelt beside Sidney and felt for a pulse.

"Is he . . . dead?" Hanni asked.

Solomon nodded. "I feel no pulse. But he's still warm. And the blood is still spreading. It can only just have happened."

"Then the murderer might still be in the shop." I glanced around uneasily. "Is there another way out?"

"No, there's only the front door."

"Then we should go downstairs immediately and call the police," I said. "He could be hiding anywhere. Come, Hanni."

She was still staring at the knife in her hand. "Here," she said and handed it to me.

"I don't want it!" My voice rose in repulsion as I felt the cold stickiness of the knife touch me. "Put it back on the ground where you found it. The police will want to know."

"I'm not sure where it was." She sounded as if she was about to cry. "It was about here, I think."

I replaced it on the floor and Mr. Solomon ushered us gallantly in front of him down the stairs.

"Alas, I have no telephone," he said. "I keep meaning to have one installed but my customers prefer to write to me."

"So where is the nearest telephone?" I demanded.

"I'm sure they have one at the accountant's opposite the tearoom. I'll go. You two young ladies should probably wait outside."

"But what if the murderer tries to make a break for it?" Hanni asked with a trembling voice. "We can't stop him."

"Of course you can't. Why don't you come with me to the accountant's if you feel safer. Or better still, wait in the tearoom." Mr. Solomon sounded as confused and upset as I felt.

"Yes, that's a good idea," I said. "We'll wait in the tearoom. Hanni looks as if she could do with a cup of tea." I rather felt as if I could do with a cup myself. I couldn't stop shivering.

We let the front door close behind us and followed Mr. Solomon over the cobbles. "Here's sixpence," I said to Hanni. "Get yourself a cup of tea. I'm going to see if I can find a constable before the murderer can escape."

"Don't leave me." Hanni grabbed my arm. "I'm scared. There are spots of blood on my dress, and look at my hands." And she started to cry.

I put my arms cautiously around her because I too had blood on me. "It's all right. I know it is utterly horrible, but don't cry. The police will be here soon and we'll be safe."

"Why would anybody want to kill Sidney?" she asked, brushing away tears. "He was nice, wasn't he?"

"Yes, very nice. You'll feel better after a cup of tea, and you'll be quite safe in the café," I said. "And I won't go far, I promise. See. You can keep an eye on Mr. Solomon from the window."

I watched her safely inside and then I ran back to Wapping High Street. I was just coming around the corner when I bumped into someone.

"Hold on, there, where's the fire?" he said, grabbing me by the shoulders. I went to fight him off until I realized it was Darcy.

"What are you doing here?" I stammered, almost wondering whether I was hallucinating.

"Keeping an eye on you. I called at your house and your butler told me where you had gone. He wasn't too happy about it, so I said I'd go after you to make sure you were all right."

"We're not all right." I heard my voice crack. "We've just found a man murdered. The bookshop owner is calling the police. I have to find a constable."

His hands tightened on my shoulders. "Murdered, you say? Where's the princess? You haven't left her alone, have you?"

"I left her in the tearoom. She was in shock."

"What on earth were you doing in a place like this anyway?"

"Hanni wanted to visit a chap she met at Gussie's party."

"I shouldn't have thought this was a likely location for any of Gussie's friends," Darcy said.

"His name was Sidney Roberts. I don't know if he's exactly a friend of Gussie. They were at Cambridge together. We also met him at the communist rally in the park, when you stepped in to rescue us."

"You say his name *was* . . . ? So that means that he . . ." Darcy looked at me inquiringly.

"Yes. He's the man lying dead upstairs in the bookshop. Somebody stabbed him."

"Holy Mother of God," Darcy muttered and almost went to cross himself. "And you and the princess found him?"

"Hanni did. She stumbled over the knife lying on the floor."

"You look as if you could do with a cup of tea too," Darcy said. "You're as white as a sheet."

I nooded. "It was awful, Darcy. All that blood and I touched the knife and . . ." I swallowed back a sob.

His arms came around me. "It's all right," he murmured, stroking my hair as if I were a little child. "You're safe now."

I closed my eyes, feeling the warmth and closeness of him, his chin against my hair, the roughness of his jacket on my cheek. I didn't want him to let go of me ever.

"Come on. We'd better get you that tea." He took my arm and led me to the tearoom. Hanni's eyes lit up when she saw him.

"It is Darcy! How did you find us here? You always come at the right moment to rescue us."

"That's me. Darcy O'Mara, guardian angel in disguise."

In the distance came the sound of a police whistle being blown and a constable came running down the alley. Mr. Solomon appeared from the office across the way, together with several interested clerks. When the constable heard that the murderer might well still be in the bookshop he was not too keen to go inside. He stood at the doorway of the tea shop with Mr. Solomon while Darcy took me to get a cup of tea. We didn't have to wait long. The incessant jangling bell of a police motorcar could be heard, echoing between high buildings. The noise caused several windows to open and brought more people into the alleyway.

The alleyway was just wide enough to accommodate a police motor. It came to a halt. Two plainclothes officers and two uniformed bobbies got out, pushing their way through the growing crowd. I returned to the door of the tea shop.

"Stand back, now. Go back to your business," one of the officers shouted. He saw the bobby standing guard at the doorway. "What have we got here then?"

"They say a man's been murdered and the murderer might still be in the building," the bobby said. "I didn't like to go in alone, sir, so I guarded the doorway to make sure he couldn't get out."

"Quite right," the plainclothes officer said. In spite of the warm day he was wearing the traditional fawn mack and trilby hat, pulled down low on his forehead. His face and mustache were fawn to match the raincoat. He had jowls that gave him a sad bulldog look. Worse still, I now recognized him. None other than Inspector Harry Sugg of Scotland Yard. He spotted me at the same moment and reacted similarly.

"Not you again. Don't tell me you've got something to do with this."

"Princess Hannelore was the one who found the body." I gestured an introduction to the princess inside the tea shop.

"Why on my shift?" he complained. His voice tended to whine at the best of times. "I'm not normally in this part of town. I just happened to be over this way, so they sent me. Are you making a hobby of finding dead bodies?"

"I don't actually enjoy the experience, Inspector," I said. "In fact I feel as if I might be sick at any moment. Someone was getting me a cup of tea."

"All right," Sugg agreed. "Drink your tea, but don't go anywhere. I'll have questions to ask you, and the princess." Hanni looked up at him, wide eyed, from the table at which she was sitting.

"Don't let any of them go anywhere, Collins," Sugg barked. "Stay out here and keep an eye on them. Foreman, James. Come with me."

They pushed past everyone and went into the bookshop. A little later they emerged again. "No sign of anyone in there," Sugg said as he came back into the tearoom. "Which of you is the bookshop owner?"

"I am." Mr. Solomon came forward.

"There didn't seem to be any other exits except for the front door."

"That is correct," Mr. Solomon said.

"You were the one who phoned the police?"

"I was indeed."

"And do you know the identity of the murder victim?"

"Of course I do. He is my assistant. His name is Sidney Roberts. As nice and respectable a young man as you could find. I don't understand how anybody got into my shop to kill him or why they'd do so."

Inspector Sugg turned to look at Hanni and me. "So this young lady found the body? Your full name is . . ."

"This is Her Royal Highness Princess Maria Theresa Hannelore of Bavaria," I said, adopting my most regal tones to make it very clear. "She is a guest of the king and queen. I am chaperoning her around London."

"And what's a visiting princess doing in a place like this, I'd like to know?"

"We met a young man at—the British Museum." I had been about to say "at a party" but I thought it wiser not to remind the police of the occasion of another dead body. "He told the princess about the bookshop where he worked. She accepted his invitation to be shown some rare old books."

Harry Sugg stared hard at me as if trying to gauge whether this sounded plausible or not.

"Does Her Highness speak English?" he asked.

"A little," I said before she could answer.

"So tell me, Yer Highness, how you found the body."

Hanni glanced at me for reassurance. "Lady Georgiana and I, we go to visit Sidney." I noticed she had picked up on my words and was speaking as if finding the right words in English was extremely hard for her. "We enter the bookshop. Nobody is there. We look. I find staircase. I go up the stairs in front of Georgie. It is very dark up there. I kick something with my foot. It is long and silver. I pick it up and it is sticky. I see it is horrible knife. And then I see the body lying there." She put her hand to her mouth to stifle a sob.

"And what did you do then?"

"Lady Georgiana and Mr. Solomon come immediately after me. Mr. Solomon sees that Sidney is dead and we go to call the police."

"How long do you think he had been dead, sir?" Inspector Sugg asked Mr. Solomon.

"Not long at all," Mr. Solomon said. "He was still warm. The bloodstain was still spreading. That's why we suspected the murderer might still be on the premises."

"So who else had been in the shop recently?"

"Nobody. Just myself and Mr. Roberts. A very slow morning. I left Mr. Roberts in charge and I went across the street to hand-deliver a book that had just come in. When I came back, these two young ladies were in the shop."

"Were you gone long?"

"Only a moment."

"And did you pass anybody in the alleyway?"

"The alleyway was deserted."

"Interesting." The inspector turned his attention back to Hanni and me. "Did you ladies pass anybody as you walked down the alleyway?"

"Nobody," I said. "Wait. There was a beggar sitting at the entrance to the alley, and then there were those two men sitting at the window of the tearoom. They haven't moved."

"Beggar, Foreman. Go and check on him and who he's seen," Sugg barked. "And James. Ask those geezers in the tea shop."

The crowd was steadily growing. Darcy handed me a teacup and I drank gratefully.

"If you don't mind my suggesting, Inspector," Darcy said, "but might it not be wise for me to escort these two young ladies home before the gentlemen of the press get here? This lady is a visiting foreign princess, after all. We don't want to cause an international incident, do we?"

I heard the whisper run through the crowd. Foreign princess. Some of them ran off to fetch their friends. Obviously this was going to be more interesting than the usual back-alley murder.

"And who might you be?" Sugg demanded, apparently not the least concerned about causing an international incident.

"O'Mara is the name," Darcy said with a certain swagger. "I am a friend of the young ladies."

"And I suppose you're also a prince or a duke?"

"Not at all. My father is Lord Kilhenny, Irish peer, if that's what you want to know, but I don't see what that has to do with anything."

"So were you here with the young ladies when they discovered the body?"

"No, I wasn't. I've only just arrived here myself."

"And what made you happen to be in the same, disreputable part of town? Pure coincidence?"

"Not at all," Darcy said again. "I called on Lady Georgiana and her butler told me where she had gone. He expressed concern, so I did the only decent thing and went to keep an eye on them."

"And exactly why did he express concern?" Sugg was still attacking like a bulldog, shaking and not letting go.

"Isn't that obvious, Inspector? Would you want your innocent daughters wandering through this part of London? These girls have been raised in seclusion. They have little experience of the seedier side of life in the big city."

Sugg stared at him, one eyebrow raised and a half smirk on his lips, then he said, "So you arrived on the scene exactly when?"

"Just before yourself. As I came around the corner into the alley, I met Lady Georgiana, running to find a police constable. She was extremely distressed. I brought her back to have a cup of tea. And now, if it's all right with you, I'd like to take her home. And the princess, naturally."

I was conscious of the growing crowd, swarming around us, staring with unabashed curiosity. It would only be moments before the first pressmen arrived. "You know where I live, Inspector," I said. "Her Highness is staying with me. If you have more questions for us, we'd be happy to answer them."

Harry Sugg looked from me to Hanni to Darcy and then back again. I think he was trying to decide whether he'd lose face by allowing us to go.

"If these ladies' faces appear on the front page of the newspapers in connection with an East End murder, the king and queen would not be pleased—you can see that, can't you?" Darcy said. "Added to which, they are both clearly suffering from shock."

"I'm not happy about this," Harry Sugg said. "Not at all happy, I can tell you. I know you young things and what you do for thrills. Stealing policemen's helmets, for one thing, and what goes on at your parties. Don't think I don't know about your thrills. Oh, I know right enough." His eyes didn't leave my face as he spoke, then he took a step closer to me so that I was conscious of that fawn mustache dancing up and down in front of my face. "Two bodies in one week. That's a little more than coincidence, wouldn't you say?"

"The other death was a horrible accident," I said. "I was there on the balcony when it happened. Nobody was near him. He fell. An awful accident."

"If you say so, my lady. I just find it strange, that's all. In the police force we are trained not to believe in coincidences. If something looks suspicious, it usually is. And if there's some kind of connection, trust me, I'm going to sniff it out."

"I assure you there is no connection between us and the murdered man, Inspector," I said coldly. "Now if you don't mind, I'd like you to take us home, Darcy, please."

Nobody stopped us as we walked out of the tea shop and forced our way through the crowd to Wapping High Street.

Nobody spoke much as we sat on the tube back to Hyde Park Corner. I had thought of getting a taxicab, but we couldn't find one in that part of the city and in the end it seemed simpler to take the underground. Even Hanni was unnaturally subdued and didn't attempt to flirt with Darcy once. Darcy escorted us all the way back from the station to Rannoch House.

"You'll be okay now, will you?" he asked.

I nodded. "Thank you for coming to look for us. If you hadn't been there, we'd probably have been off to prison in a Black Maria by now."

"Nonsense. You know how to stick up for yourself pretty well, I'd say."

"I'm very grateful. It is most kind of you to be concerned about us." I held out my hand. I've found that in moments of great duress, I revert to upbringing and become exceedingly proper.

A look of amusement flashed across Darcy's face. "You're dismissing the peasants, are you?"

"I'm sorry, but under the circumstances . . ."

Darcy took my hand and squeezed it. "I understand. Go and have a stiff drink. You'll feel better. You'll feel even better knowing that it's Binky's brandy you're drinking."

At that I managed a smile. As I went to withdraw my hand from his, his fingers closed around mine. "Georgie," he said. He opened his mouth to say more, but Hanni stepped between us. "I also thank you for saving us," she said, and wrapped her arms around his neck, depositing a big kiss on his cheek. I was so shocked I just stood there. Darcy extricated himself, giving me a half-embarrassed smile, and went on his way. I steered Hanni up the front steps.

"What will happen now?" Hanni asked. "I think that man did not believe us that we found poor Sidney dead."

"They certainly can't believe that one of us killed him. What possible motive could we have?" I asked, but even as I said it I saw that there might be motives that the police could unearth. I hadn't forgotten the cocaine at Gussie's party. And I had found Hanni sitting at the table in the kitchen with the cocaine users. What if Sidney were somehow involved with that? If he ran a cocaine ring, or he had not paid his drug debts—I had read that these people were ruthless. Maybe it was not for nothing that he worked in the East End of London, so close to the river. Perhaps the respectable bookshop was merely a front for less respectable activities. Perhaps this inquiry would open a whole can of worms. I felt quite sick as we went into the house.

My grandfather was waiting anxiously for us. I sent Hanni up to her room to lie down before lunch and then I went down to the kitchen, where he was polishing silver, and told him exactly what had happened. He listened with a concerned frown on his face.

"That's nasty, that is. Very nasty. Someone is killed at a party, then a few days later the princess meets someone she had met at that very party again, at the British Museum of all places, and he invites her to a bookstore in a shady part of London and you stumble upon him dead? It all sounds like too much of a coincidence to me."

"That's what the policeman in charge said. But it *was* a coincidence, Granddad. That's the awful thing. I know the first death was an accident. And why on earth would one of us want to kill poor Sidney Roberts? We both spoke with him at the party and he seemed a harmless, earnest kind of chap. Rather sweet, actually. Hanni must certainly have thought so. She seemed rather smitten with him. But we'd only met him on those two occasions. We knew nothing about him, really."

"If I was you, ducks, I'd get on the old blow piece to the palace right away. Let Her Majesty know what has happened and let her decide what to do with the princess." He put down the silver teapot he had been polishing. "I told you that one wanted watching, didn't I? Never did feel quite easy about her."

"Oh, but, Granddad, Hanni had nothing to do with this. She wanted to meet Sidney again because she is a little boy-mad, given her years in the convent. And he was very nice looking. And I think she was intrigued that he was a communist. But that's all."

"I'm not saying she stabbed the poor bloke or nothing. It was just a hunch I had about her. I've seen the type before. Where she goes, trouble follows. You'll be well rid of her, ducks."

"Oh, dear. I have to say that I agree with you. I'll go and telephone the palace right away."

"Have your lunch first." Granddad put an arm around my shoulders. "You look as if you've seen a ghost, you do. Nasty shock, I expect."

"Yes, it was. It was utterly horrible. And then the police and everything . . ." I didn't mean to cry but suddenly I could feel tears trickling down my cheeks.

"There, there. Don't cry, my love," Granddad said, and he enveloped me in a big bear hug. I stood there with my head on his shoulder, feeling the comforting firmness of his arms around me and realizing at the same time how strange this was. I believe it must have been the first time in my life that a relative actually hugged me and comforted me. Oh, to be sure, Nanny had hugged me when I had fallen down as a small child, but my parents had never been there. So this is what it is like for ordinary people, I thought. They care about each other. They comfort each other. I resolved there and then that I would be an ordinary mother to my children and hug them hard and often.

"I'm so glad you are here," I said.

"Me too, my love," he murmured, stroking my hair as if I were a little child. "Me too." Then he released me. "You'd better go and keep an eye on Her Highness before she gets into any more trouble."

"Oh, dear, yes, I suppose I had." I turned back to the stairs.

"Your cook's made one of her famous pork pies," Granddad called after me. "Known for her pork pies, 'ettie is."

I met Hanni coming down the stairs as I emerged through the baize door.

"Is lunch ready? I'm starving," she said, and in truth she looked as if she had just woken from a good night's sleep. She had changed out of the dress with blood on it and looked fresh and innocent. I stood looking at her for a moment, weighing in my mind what my grandfather had said. Was she indeed one of those people who seem to invite trouble, or had the last week been an unlucky one for both of us?

"It's almost ready," I said. "I see you've changed your clothes."

"I fear that dress will have to be thrown away," she said. "Irmgardt is working on it, but I do not think she will be able to remove the blood from the skirt."

"I should go up and wash and change," I said. "I'll be down in a few minutes."

I remembered with relief that Mildred was out for the afternoon. As I started to unbutton my dress I realized that I too still had traces of blood on my hands. I just stood there, looking down at them, fighting back the revulsion. Until recently I had never even seen a dead body. Now in the last few days I had watched two men die. I felt an overwhelming desire to rush to the station and catch the next train to Scotland. Castle Rannoch might be the most boring place on earth, it might contain Binky and Fig, but it was home. I knew the rules there. I felt secure. But there was the small matter of the princess. Surely the queen wouldn't expect her to go on staying with me after this.

I scrubbed my nails furiously and washed my hands in a way that would have been admired by my fellow Scot Lady Macbeth. Then I changed and went down to lunch. True to Granddad's predictions, Mrs. Huggins had made a delicious pork pie. Hanni tucked into it with gusto. "English food I like," she said.

I had to admit it looked wonderful, served cold with pickled beetroots, lettuce and pickled onions. But somehow I couldn't chew or swallow. I toyed with it, pushed it around on my plate, and only managed a couple of mouthfuls. When it was followed by jam roly-poly with custard, Hanni uttered squeaks of delight and fell upon it. It was a pudding of which I am particularly fond, but again after one or two spoonfuls I couldn't eat any more. I kept seeing the body lying on the floor with the blood soaking through his shirt, and I felt the cold stickiness of that bloody knife in my hands.

"You haven't eaten much," Granddad complained as he came to clear away. "That won't do."

"I'm sorry. I still feel a bit shaky," I said.

"Let me bring you a brandy," he said kindly.

I nodded. "Yes, that might be a good idea."

"I too like brandy," Hanni said brightly. "I too have the shock."

I didn't think she was showing it. She seemed to have bounced back with remarkable resilience, especially considering that this was a chap she was keen on. I thought for a second what I would feel like if it had been Darcy lying there. It was too painful even to contemplate.

Granddad returned with the brandies and coffee. Hanni and I sat chatting about anything but the morning's events, when Granddad appeared in the doorway.

"You have a visitor, my lady."

I rather feared it was a policeman. I stood up. "I'll come to the drawing room."

"No need to get up, darlings, it's only me," Belinda said, bursting in with her usual radiance and wafting hints of Chanel as she approached. "I simply had to come and apologize. My conscience was positively nagging at me."

"Apologize for what?" I asked.

"Why, for leaving you in the lurch at that boring party," she said. "The truth was that I was only there because I had my eye on some chap, so when I saw he had his eye on someone else—well, I decided to cut my losses and head for Crockford's and some productive gambling. Lucky I did, too, because not only did I win a couple of hundred pounds but I met the most divine Frenchman and one thing led to another and to put it bluntly, I've just surfaced from his hotel room. I do hope you managed to find your own way home with no problems."

I almost laughed at the irony of this statement. "Belinda, how do you do it?"

"Keep meeting men, you mean? Sex appeal, I suppose. Raw sex appeal."

"No, I don't mean that. I mean, how do you manage to skate over the surface of life, avoiding all the pitfalls?"

"What are you talking about?" She took off her dinky little straw hat and gloves and perched on a chair beside us.

"May I bring you some coffee, miss?" Granddad asked in his best formal manner.

"How kind." They exchanged a grin.

"You left the party before the poor man was killed?" Hanni asked.

She had obviously put two and two together from our conversations, proving that there wasn't much wrong with her English. "I wanted to find you but Darcy took us away," I said.

"Killed? What man was killed?" Belinda demanded sharply.

"Tubby Tewkesbury. He fell off the balcony."

"How utterly dreadful. Poor old Tubby. What an extraordinary thing to happen. I say, is that why a young man with a camera is standing in the square opposite Rannoch House?"

"Oh, gosh," I exclaimed. "Don't tell me the press is here already."

"Already? It doesn't usually take them days to sniff out a story, you know."

"She means the other man who was killed. Today. Not two hours ago," Hanni chimed in.

Belinda looked at me incredulously. "Another man? Where? When?"

"We went to visit a chap we met at the party and . . ." I told her the whole story. "It was all rather horrible, actually," I said. "I couldn't eat a bite of lunch."

"Of course you couldn't, darling," she said. "How utterly beastly for you. I must say, you do seem to be a bit of a body magnet this spring, don't you?"

"Don't joke about it, Belinda, please. The first one I didn't mind because he was such a horrible man, but these were two nice, decent boys and they didn't deserve this fate."

Belinda nodded. "I was going to invite you both to a show tonight, but given the circumstances . . ."

"I would like to see a show," Hanni said brightly. "I like London shows. I like the singing and the legs kicking up."

"Use your head, Hanni," I snapped. "If there is already one newspaper reporter standing outside the house, that means they know about this morning. Just think how bad it would look to picture you enjoying yourself at the theater."

Hanni pouted but didn't say anything.

"I'm off to the country tomorrow," Belinda said, "or I'd come and keep you company and fend off the press. I rather fear you're in for another bombardment like last time. Not very jolly for you, I'm afraid."

"Not at all jolly," I said. "The country sounds like a good idea. Maybe I'll suggest it to Her Majesty when I telephone her this afternoon."

"Between you and me, I rather wish I hadn't accepted the invitation now that I've met Louis, but one can't go back on one's word, can one?"

"No, one can't." I looked at her fondly, realizing how nice and solidly British she was in spite of her fast and loose lifestyle.

"So I should be going." She got up. "Ciao, darlings. Cheer up. At least it was someone you hardly knew."

"Don't forget your titfer," Hanni called after her.

Belinda looked back in utter surprise. "My what?"

"Your titfer. Tit for tat. That's how Londoners say hat, isn't it?"

Belinda picked up her hat from the seat. "You should definitely take her to the country before her vocabulary is irretrievably ruined," she said as she went out.

Chapter 20

After Belinda had gone, I suggested that Hanni pay a visit to the baroness, explain to her what had just happened, and ask her advice on how to proceed and what to tell her father. Hanni made a face. "She will be angry that I went to bad part of city. She will be angry that I went to meet boy."

"I can't help it. It must be done. You are a princess, Hanni. You've been away from royal life in a convent, but you have to realize that things have to be done in the correct manner. There is protocol to follow. Your father may wish you to return home immediately."

"Then I will say nothing to baroness. I do not wish to return home."

"Don't be silly," I snapped. "You don't want her to read it for herself in the newspapers, do you? There will be an awful fuss and you'll be in serious trouble."

"All right," she agreed with a dramatic sigh. "I go see old pain in neck."

As soon as she had gone, I put through a telephone call to the palace. I explained the events briefly to Her Majesty's private secretary. He informed me that Her Majesty was not at home, but he would inform her as soon as she returned.

I tried to rest but found it impossible. When I stood behind the net curtains in the drawing room I could see several men loitering across the street, leaning on the railings of the gardens, talking and smoking. One held a camera with a large flash attachment. Oh dear. I needed to take action immediately. I found the telephone number for the baroness, asked to speak to the princess and then instructed Hanni to be sure to take a taxi home. I would make sure one of us was on the lookout for her and she should run straight into the house without talking to anybody.

"The man try to talk to me when I go out," she said. "I tell him I am only the maid."

For all her naïveté and youth, Hanni was sharp when she needed to be. I wondered if I had misjudged her need to be protected in the big city. Then I remembered the incidents at Harrods and Garrard's. And my grandfather's comments. He was a wise old bird and had the experience of years on a city beat.

Hanni arrived home soon afterward and did exactly as I said, running up the steps from the taxi and in through the front door without pausing. "Do you have money for taxi man?" she asked me.

"I'll do it." My grandfather found some money and went out to pay the cabbie.

"So what did Baroness Rottenmeister say?" I asked.

"She was not there. She had gone out."

"So why didn't you stay until she returned?"

Hanni made a face. "I did not wish to see her."

"Did you at least leave her a note?"

Hanni stared at me defiantly. "She will be mad at us. She will want to take me home."

A huge feeling of relief swept over me. At least one good thing would have come from this horrid event. Hanni would go home. I'd be free of her. I could go back to my own, somewhat boring, life.

"I do not wish to go," she said firmly. "I like it here with you, Georgie. I like your butler and Mrs. 'uggins. I like that it is not formal and old-fashioned and full of rules. All my life has been rules, rules, rules."

I did see her point. I felt rather the same way about my upbringing. "I don't know what we're going to do, Hanni," I said. "It seems that the press has found out about us and they will hound us until they get a story. Trust me, I know. I have been through this before. I had to move in with Belinda last time."

"Last time?"

"A man was drowned in our bathtub," I said.

"So you know about dead bodies," she said happily.

"More than I care to."

"Then why don't we move in with Belinda," Hanni said. "I like Belinda.

She's hot sexy dame. She can teach me what to do with boys. The nuns taught us nothing. They said all things with men are sin. Even to think about them is sin."

"From what I've observed you have quite a good idea what to do with boys already," I said, remembering how she draped herself all over Darcy during a slow dance. "And remember you are a princess. It is rather expected that you will stay a virgin until you marry."

"Baloney," she said. An interesting expression that I hadn't heard before. I wasn't even sure whether it was a swear word or not.

"Anyway we are not going to stay with Belinda. She only has one bedroom. I had to sleep on the sofa, which was jolly uncomfortable."

"I'm hungry," Hanni complained. "Let's have tea. I like tea. It is a good meal. When I go home I shall make people have tea in Germany."

"I didn't think that royals had any power to make people do things any longer in Germany," I said, amused by the way she stuck out her little chin.

"This is true, but Herr Hitler, he will soon be our new leader and he likes me. He says I look like good healthy Aryan girl."

She did.

She smiled coyly. "So if I ask him please make everybody in Germany have teatime, he will say, *Jawohl, mein Schatz.*"

I laughed. "All right. Ring for the servants and ask if we can have tea a little early today," I said. "Tell Spinks we'll take it in the morning room. It's more pleasant in there."

We had just sat down to tea and I was in the process of being mother and pouring when Granddad appeared again.

"Sorry to trouble you, my lady," he said in a most formal tone, "but a man from Scotland Yard is here. He would like to speak with you and with Her Highness. I've shown him into the drawing room."

"Thank you, Spinks," I replied, in case the man from Scotland Yard could hear. "Is it Inspector Sugg again?"

"No, my lady. It's his superior this time. Here is his card." He came over and presented it to me.

"Chief Inspector Burnall," I said out loud, then lowered my voice. "He was the one who tried to send Binky to the gallows. And I haven't yet decided whether he is a gentleman or not. I don't recognize the school tie."

"I wouldn't hold that against him. The important question is whether he's a good copper or not."

"He wasn't very bright on the last occasion," I said, "but anything is preferable to the awful Sugg. There's nothing he'd like more than to have me convicted of something. I rather suspect he's a communist."

I got to my feet. "Sorry about this, Hanni, but we have to abandon our tea for now. I'm sure this is just a formality. Nothing to worry about."

With that I put on a bright face and walked into the drawing room with a confident stride. Chief Inspector Burnall was standing by the mantelpiece, examining the Spode figures. He turned as we came in, looking exactly as I had remembered him. He was a tall, erect figure of a man in a well-cut navy suit, unidentifiable school tie (or was it a regimental tie?), with dark hair graying at the temples, and a distinguished-looking face with a neat line of mustache, in the style of Clark Gable. He could equally have passed for an ex–Guards officer, a member of parliament, or a salesman at a gentlemen's clothing store.

"Lady Georgiana." He gave a small, correct bow. "I am sorry to trouble you again today."

"That's perfectly all right, Chief Inspector. This is Her Highness, the Princess of Bavaria. Highness, may I present Chief Inspector Burnall of Scotland Yard."

I just prayed she wouldn't say, "Hiya baby," or worse still, "Wotcha?"

She said nothing, but returned his bow with a gracious nod.

"Please be seated." I indicated the sofa and armchairs.

"I'm sure you realize, Lady Georgiana, that this was a very unfortunate incident that took place at the bookshop this morning."

"It is always tragic when someone dies," I said. "Especially someone so young and with such a promising future before him."

"Uh—quite." He paused, as if not quite sure how to proceed.

"I have been briefed on this matter by Inspector Sugg and I understand that you, Princess, discovered the body."

"I did," she said. "Because I went up the stairs ahead of Lady Georgiana."

"The victim was lying in one of the side alcoves where the lighting was very poor," Chief Inspector Burnall went on. "So I wonder how you happened to discover the body so soon after you went upstairs. You did say that you came upon it almost immediately, didn't you?"

"She discovered it because the knife was left lying on the floor. The princess kicked it, wondered what it was, and picked it up. Then she looked beyond and saw something lying there that proved to be the body."

"I'd prefer that the princess answer her own questions," the inspector said.

"I came right behind her," I said.

"And saw what?"

"I found her holding the knife, looking utterly shocked."

"Which brings us to an interesting question," Burnall said, looking hard at me. "Why did the killer drop the knife on the floor?"

"I suppose he had to leave in a hurry," I said. "I gather that Mr. Solomon only left the shop for a minute to deliver a book across the alleyway. If the killer had been in the shop, hiding, he would have seen this as an opportunity, rushed upstairs to catch Mr. Roberts unaware, then run out again before Mr. Solomon returned. Obviously he couldn't be seen running down a street with a bloody knife."

"Another interesting point," Burnall said. "The beggar who sat on the corner saw nobody running away just before you ladies arrived."

"Then the killer must have fled by another route."

"As far as we can tell, there is no other route," Burnall said. "It is a blind alley, of course. There is an attic, with a small window through which an athletic person could squeeze onto the roof tiles . . ."

"There you are, then," I said.

Burnall shook his head. "An athletic and daring person could then negotiate the steep pitch of the roof but would have to leap six feet across to a similar rooftop."

"So escape across the rooftops would have been possible," I said.

"Yes, but not probable. From the amount of dust in the attic, it would appear that the window has not been opened recently."

"Well, we saw nobody," I said. "And we saw and heard nothing when we came into the shop."

"And yet Mr. Solomon stated that the murder could have only taken place moments before."

"That's right," I said. "The stain on his white shirt was still spreading, and he was still warm."

"Which brings me to the next interesting question," Burnall said. "Exactly what you two young ladies were doing at the shop in the first place."

"We've already been through this once," I said, fighting to control my irritation. A lady never shows her emotions, as my governess chanted to me many times, but I'd already gone through enough today that they were horribly near the surface. "Her Highness ran into an acquaintance at the British Museum yesterday. He invited her to come and see the place where he worked."

"You had met him previously where?" Burnall asked.

"In the park and then at a party," Hanni said.

"How long have you been in England, Your Highness?"

Hanni wrinkled her delicate little nose. "One week."

"So in one week you've certainly seen plenty of action. You've been at a party where a man falls off a balcony. You've met a young man in the park, and again at the British Museum, and gone to his place of employment only to find him dying on the floor." He crossed his legs as he leaned closer to her. "I don't know about your country, but things in England usually tend to be a lot tamer than that."

"What means tamer?" Hanni asked.

"I mean that life goes on here at a sedate pace, with little violence or excitement. Is that not true, your ladyship?"

"Usually, yes."

"So how do you explain that this current outbreak of apparent gangsterism has coincided with the arrival of Her Highness?"

Oh, dear. I wish he hadn't said that. Until that moment it had never occurred to me to link together Hanni's love of American gangster films with any of the strange things that had happened to us. I ran through the various events of the week quickly in my mind. The fall from the balcony— Hanni had been nowhere in sight. And as for stabbing somebody—well, that was plain ridiculous. For one thing she wouldn't have had time. I came up the stairs right after her. And for another, she had looked absolutely shocked. And for a third, why would she want to stab a harmless young man she thought was attractive?

"You're not suggesting that Her Highness is a gangster in disguise, are you, Chief Inspector?" I asked.

He gave a nervous half laugh, half cough. "Good Lord, no. But you must admit it does seem a rum coincidence."

"I agree that it does, but a coincidence it is, I assure you. You can't for a moment think that either of us had anything to do with Mr. Roberts's murder."

"I have to pursue the facts, your ladyship," he said.

"Then I suggest you extract fingerprints from the weapon and go after the criminal whose fingerprints they match, rather than upsetting us."

"Ah," he said. "Now that is an interesting fact. There are only two sets of fingerprints on the weapon, and they are yours."

"That doesn't completely surprise me," I said. "If someone can slip in unnoticed, kill quickly and silently, then he is obviously a professional and as such would have worn gloves."

Burnall nodded. "Not a bad observation, because we do rather suspect that it was the work of a trained assassin. One quick thrust between the third and fourth ribs up into the heart, then the weapon is instantly withdrawn to allow the blood to flow freely. The poor chap probably didn't know what had hit him. Death would have been instantaneous."

Hanni gave a little gasp of horror. "Please don't," she said. "It is too awful. I can't stop thinking about it. Poor Sidney, lying on the floor, and all that blood."

"Do you need to go on with this?" I demanded. "You're upsetting the princess and I'm feeling a little queasy myself."

"Just a few more questions, and then I'll leave you in peace," he said. "I'm interested to know just why you were keen to visit this young man at the bookshop."

"It was Her Highness's wish to do this."

"And is Her Highness keen on books then?" His smile was close to a smirk. I found myself wondering whether policemen are hired for their annoying expressions or whether they develop them during the course of their employment.

"Her Highness was rather keen on the young man, I believe," I said, giving Hanni a reassuring smile. "He was very presentable and a thoroughly nice chap too."

"That being the case, why not meet him somewhere more suitable? A tearoom, or lunch in a more respectable part of the city."

"Had we known exactly where the bookstore was, I think we might have not chosen to visit him there," I said. "But I am not yet familiar with the various neighborhoods of the city."

"I ask the question," Burnall said slowly, "because of the nature of the bookshop. It may sell old books, but it is also an unofficial meeting place of those with strong leftist leanings. You might have seen the leaflets and the posters on the walls."

"We did," I said.

"And this Mr. Sidney Roberts. You say he was a thoroughly nice chap and yet it may surprise you to know that he was a card-carrying, fully paid up member of the Communist Party. An active member at that. He spent the last year organizing labor unions, strikes and marches as well as writing a regular column for the *Daily Worker*."

"We did know he was a communist," I said. "The first time we met him was at Speakers' Corner in Hyde Park. He was passing out communist leaflets."

"And you thought this was a noble cause? You were about to hand over your castle and go to live among the masses, were you?"

"Absolutely not," I said, giving him my best Queen Victoria stare. I was not her great-granddaughter for nothing. "As I said, it was Princess Hannelore who wanted to meet him again and her motives were based more on his appearance than his political beliefs."

"There will be an inquest, of course," Burnall said. "Which presents a tricky problem." He paused, staring at the princess. "Your Highness probably doesn't realize what a mess you have plunged us into. It can't have occurred to you that back at your home in Germany the communists and the fascists are deadly rivals. The fascists have won the power for now, but it could possibly still go either way. The communists are working hard to create an upheaval so that they can seize power."

"It's not as if we were planning to join the Communist Party, Chief Inspector," I said. "And anyway, I always understood that one of the benefits of living in England was that it was a free country, where one can express one's opinion, however silly and extreme, with no worries about recourse from the authorities. Is that no longer true?"

"Of course," he said. "But we are not concerned with England here. We are concerned with Germany. You must know that there is a delicate balance at the moment between the fascist far right and the communists. There is also a strong movement afoot in Bavaria to restore Her Highness's father to his throne, thus making him a force against the Nazis. When the news reaches Germany that the princess has been in cahoots with communists, I'm afraid the German regime will see this as a confrontation—an attempt to undermine the government. World wars have been started on less."

I laughed uneasily. "You're trying to tell us that Germany might declare war because the princess went to a communist bookshop to meet a young man?"

"Who was found dead. She may be implicated in the crime."

"Of course she's not implicated in the crime. This is ridiculous," I snapped.

"Georgie, does this man think that I was the one who killed Sidney?" Hanni asked in a frightened voice. "I do not know how to stab somebody, and I liked Sidney. I wanted a chance to talk with a young man, away from court, away from baroness, who always says no. At home there is always someone to tell me what I must do and what I must say. Here I thought I was free."

"There you have your answer, Chief Inspector," I said. "Her Highness has just emerged from an education in the convent. She is eighteen years old. Speaking to young men is a novelty to her. As for Mr. Roberts's killer, you said yourself that the fascists and communists are at each other's throats. We witnessed that in Hyde Park the other day. A horrid clash with the blackshirts. Maybe you should be looking for your murderer among their ranks."

"Trust me, we shall be leaving no stone unturned in our investigation, your ladyship," Burnall said. He stood up. "Thank you for your time. As I said, you will probably be required to give evidence at the inquest. Please do not think of leaving London. You will be notified when it will take place."

With that he gave a curt nod and rose to leave.

$\mathcal{C}$hapter 21

"This is not good, Georgie," Hanni said. "My father will get his knickers in a twist when he hears of it."

"His knickers in a twist? Where did you hear that?"

"Your cook. Mrs. Huggins. She said, 'Don't get your knickers in a twist' to your butler when he was upset. I like this expression. What means it exactly?"

"Something you don't want to know. One does not mention underwear in public, especially not in royal circles."

A flicker of enjoyment crossed Hanni's face. "Okeydokey," she said. "But my dad will still be angry. He will tell me to come straight home."

"I am going to see the queen," I said. "She'll decide what we should do next."

"Oh, swell. I like visits to palace. I will come with you."

"I rather think not, this time. It might be awkward as we discuss your future. You should go to Baroness Rottenmeister for now. I'll take you there myself."

"Everything has gone wrong," Hanni said.

"Now perhaps you see that your gangsters did not live such glamorous lives," I couldn't resist saying.

"I wish I had machine gun, then I'd shoot head off those horrible policemen," Hanni said.

"Hanni, for heaven's sake never let anyone hear you talking like that, even in fun," I said. "You are currently their only suspect in a murder."

"They can't pin the rap on me," she said.

"No more gangster talk. I absolutely forbid it," I said. "From now on you must act and sound like a princess at all times. You heard what the chief inspector said—wars have been started over less than this."

"I just make joke, Georgie," Hanni said, "because I am frightened."

"I'm a little frightened myself," I said. "But the police have gone now. We're home and we're safe and nothing else can go wrong tonight."

My grandfather tapped on the door before opening it. "Baroness Rottenmeister, my lady," he said in regal tones.

The baroness swept into the room like an avenging black angel, her cape streaming out behind her. If looks could kill, we'd have been sprawled on the carpet.

"What have you done, you silly girls?" she demanded in a booming voice. "The queen's private secretary telephoned me. He wanted to discuss this morning's tragedy. Naturally I knew no details because I wasn't there. And then I find out that a man has been killed and the police suspect Her Highness."

She glared at Hanni. "I leave you alone for two days. You beg me that you want to stay with Lady Georgiana. You tell me that she is responsible person and will take good care of you. And I believe you and think of my own comfort. Now I am deeply ashamed. My duty was at your side, even with the great inconveniences of living in this house. I should never have left you for one instant. I should have come to the party with you. I should have gone with you this morning and then none of this would have happened."

"The young man would still be lying dead, whether we had found him or not," I said. "And whether you had accompanied us or not."

"What do I care if this young man is dead or not?" The baroness was purple with rage by now. Obviously her governess had never told her that a lady is always in control of her emotions. "I care for the honor of your family. I care for the honor of Germany." Dramatic pause. "There is only one thing to do. I shall write to her father, asking for instructions, and I move back instantly to this house. I am willing to sacrifice my own comfort and happiness for the good of my royal family and my country."

Anyone would have thought she was being asked to undertake an expedition to the North Pole and live on seal blubber. Rannoch House really isn't that bad in summer.

"I am going to see Her Majesty as soon as she summons me," I said.

"She will decide the best course of action. It may be wiser if the princess goes home immediately."

"No way," Hanni said angrily.

"Hannelore, this has gone on long enough," the baroness said. "You must remember you are a princess and speak and act like one from now on. Go up to your room immediately and write a letter to your father, apologizing for your thoughtless actions." She lapsed into German at the end of this sentence, but I think that was the gist of it. Then she turned to me. "And you, Lady Georgiana, will be good enough to ask your cook to prepare a dinner that is kind to my digestion. Although with all this worry, I am sure I will not be able to swallow one mouthful."

I went down to Mrs. Huggins in the kitchen.

"Kind to her digestion?" she asked, hands on her broad hips. "I didn't notice much wrong with her digestion before. Knocked back everything she could lay her hands on, that one. A right pig, if you ask me. And in more ways than one. Ordering me and your granddad around as if she was the bleedin' Queen of England. 'You will do this and then you will do that.' I felt like telling her she was the foreigner here and London is my town and I don't let nobody speak to me like I'm dirt."

"Quite right, Mrs. Huggins," I said. "I know it's awful and I'm terribly grateful for everything. You've been an absolute brick. And your cooking has been splendid."

She blushed modestly. "Well, thank you kindly, your ladyship. Happy to do it, I'm sure. But can you tell me how much longer we're going to be expected to keep this up? Yer granddad is getting restless for his garden and his routine at home. He don't say nothing because he'd do anything in the world for you, but I can tell it's all getting his goat."

"Let's hope it's coming to an end, Mrs. Huggins," I said.

"It's not the housework and the cooking I mind," she went on. "I've never minded hard work in my life. Used to it, you see. But it's these people. Herself with the face like the back end of a bus, and that maid person, Fireguard or whatever her name is, creeping around, never saying a word, just staring at us when we speak good English to her. And then there's that Mildred what you hired. Right stuck up, she is. Coming down here and telling us how much better everything was in the posh houses she's been in. 'You can't get much posher than her ladyship,' I told her. 'Related to the royals. If there was another of them flu epidemics and the lot of them died off, she might find herself queen one day, and don't you forget it.' "

I smiled at her fondly. "Don't wish that on me," I said. "Besides, it would have to be an awfully large flu epidemic. I'm only thirty-forth in line to the throne."

"Anyway, what I'm saying is, we'll stick it out for you, but it better not be for much longer."

"I do understand, Mrs. Huggins," I said. "I feel rather the same way myself. The princess is a delightful person in many ways, but it's like looking after a naughty puppy. You never know what she's going to do next. And she doesn't have a clue about what is proper and what isn't."

I looked up guiltily as I heard footsteps but it was only my grandfather.

"So we've got the old dragon back here again, I see," he muttered. "I've just had to carry up her great pile of baggage. What on earth does she want all that stuff for? I've only ever seen her in black. And was she in a bad temper! Do this, and not like that. It was all I could do to hold my tongue. I tell you this, Georgie love, I'm not cut out to be nobody's servant. Never was."

"It really won't be for long now, Granddad. I've spoken with the palace and I've an audience with Her Majesty tomorrow."

"The sooner that lot is shipped back to Germany, the better, that's what I say," Mrs. Huggins muttered. "And good riddance to 'em."

"I have to confess I'll be relieved to see them go," I said. "But about dinner tonight. Could you possibly cook something that's kind to the baroness's digestion?"

"What about a nice set of pig's trotters?" she asked. I couldn't tell whether she was being funny or not, having never eaten the said part of the pig.

Before I could answer, my grandfather dug her in the ribs. "Give over, 'ettie," he said and Mrs. Huggins broke into wheezy chuckles. "Or a nice plate of jellied eels?" she went on.

"If she wants something nourishing, then how about liver and bacon?" Granddad said when her laughter had died down. "Nobody can complain about liver and bacon. About as nourishing as you can get, that is. And a milk pudding to follow?"

"Right you are," Mrs. Huggins said. "All right with you, me lady?"

"Perfect," I said.

As I went to walk upstairs to our part of the house, my grandfather followed me. "So what did the inspector want?" he asked quietly. "Just routine, was it?"

"Anything but routine." I sighed. "He seems to think we may have caused a major international incident. If the princess is linked to a communist plot of some kind and the German government is anticommunist and pro-fascist, they may see this as an affront. Trying to convert their princess to the opposition, so to speak."

"Bloody stupid," Granddad muttered, then looked up at me with a guilty expression on his face. "Pardon the swearing. It just slipped out. So they think this man's death is somehow linked to communist activities, do they?"

"He was an active member of the Communist Party."

"Well, I never. Your German princess certainly picks 'em, don't she? Where on earth did you meet a communist?"

"In Hyde Park, at Speakers' Corner, and then again at that party."

"The party where the bloke fell off the balcony?"

"That's the one."

"Dear me," he said. "Makes you wonder if there's a link between the two deaths, don't it?"

"There can't possibly be. I was standing there, Granddad. I saw Tubby stagger backward, very drunk, and fall through the railings. I saw it."

"And this Tubby bloke. Was he also a communist?"

I laughed. "Good Lord, no. His family owns half of Shropshire."

"If you say so, love. But I can tell you this. When I was on the force, I'd have had a good look at that party, who was there and what was going on. You'll probably find out that this killing has nothing to do with communism. Probably something much more everyday than that—the young man got himself mixed up with the wrong crowd, that's what I'd guess."

"Then let's hope the police find that out quickly," I said. "It would be a huge relief to me." I paused, then a thought struck me. "Is there anything you can do, Granddad? I know you've been off the force for a while, but you must still know people. And you used to work that part of London, didn't you? Couldn't you ask some questions and find out if there are any gang rumors going around?"

"I don't know about that," Granddad said. "It's been a long while, ducks, and I'm pretty much tied down waiting on those Deutschy ladies of yours."

"Yes, I know you are. But all may be well by tomorrow. The queen may decide to send them home straightaway, or she may bring them to the palace and we can all breathe again."

"Let's hope so, love," he said. "Let us hope so."

I went upstairs to change for dinner. I stood in my room listening to the sounds of the square outside my open windows. There were children playing in the central garden. I could hear their high little voices mingling with birdsong and the muted sounds of traffic. It all sounded so happy and normal and safe. And yet those newspaper reporters were still lingering by the railings, reminding me that nothing was normal and safe at all. Why did we have to time our visit to the bookstore so unluckily as to arrive at that critical moment? Moments earlier and perhaps we could have prevented Sidney from being killed. Moments later and someone else would have found the body.

I paused and considered this. Had the murderer timed his killing to coincide with our arrival, thus putting suspicion on us? What if he were a friend or acquaintance of Sidney Roberts and Sidney had confided to him that a foreign princess was going to be visiting him that morning? It would be the sort of thing one might brag about. Maybe Sidney had even mentioned it at the café and someone had overheard.

The beggar at the end of the alley hadn't seen anyone, either entering or leaving that street before us. What if the killer was already there, working in one of the adjacent buildings, maybe? All he'd have to do is to come into the bookshop when no one was looking, which would have been easy enough, then wait until he spotted us turning into the street before doing the deed and slipping out again and into the building next door. Nobody would have noticed, especially if he worked on the street and was habitually seen coming and going. We wouldn't have seen him because we were reading the signs on the various shops as we came. And if we had glimpsed him, we were looking for a bookshop, not a person. He would have still gone unnoticed.

That's what the police should be doing—questioning those who worked in the buildings around the bookshop. I should also suggest maybe that Granddad ask his own questions there. I could even go and ferret around myself if I could get rid of the princess and—wait a minute. What business was this of mine? It was up to the police to solve the crime. I had been an innocent bystander. I had absolutely nothing to worry about.

Then why was my stomach twisting itself into knots? I had the police hounding me, the baroness bullying me, and an imminent interview with the queen during which she'd probably tell me how extremely displeased with me she was. If I were sensible, I'd catch the next train to Scotland and leave them all to sort it out without me. But then a Rannoch never runs. This was another of the words of wisdom instilled in me at an early age by my nanny and then my governess. It went along with tales of Rannochs past who stood their ground when hordes of English charged at them, or hordes of Turks, French or Germans, depending on the battlefield. All the stories ended with the particular Rannoch being hacked to pieces, so were not exactly uplifting in their moral.

What would a Rannoch do now, I wondered. Allow herself to be bullied by a German baroness, a smirking policeman, or the Queen of England? If I had my trusty claymore, I'd dispatch the whole lot of them with a single stroke, I thought, and smiled to myself. It was about time I learned to stand up for myself and let these people know that a Rannoch cannot be bullied.

I jumped as there was a tap on my bedroom door.

"You're wanted on the telephone," my grandfather said in a low voice, because Mildred was hovering somewhere close by. "The palace."

Chapter 22

RANNOCH HOUSE
SATURDAY, JUNE 18, 1932

Diary,
Weather: gloomy. Overcast with the promise of rain.
Mood: equally gloomy. Due at palace immediately after breakfast.

I searched through the *Times* when Mildred brought it up to me. There was only a small paragraph. Police investigate Thames-side killing. The body of a young bookstore clerk was found stabbed in Haslett's Bookshop, off Wapping High Street, yesterday. Police are anxious to speak with anyone who was in the area about ten thirty.

No mention of us, thank heavens. Of course this was the *Times*. Who knows what the *Daily Mirror* might have said?

Breakfast was a somber affair. I found it hard to swallow anything. Even the baroness didn't go back for a second helping of bacon and eggs. We were all feeling the cloud of doom hanging over us. I couldn't wait to go to the palace and get it over with. I even let Mildred choose my outfit to wear to see the queen. She was very excited and proud to be doing so. "The palace— of course you'll want to look smart, but understated. This would definitely be an occasion for the pearls, my lady."

The fact that I let her put the pearls around my neck shows the height of tension. I've never voluntarily worn pearls in the daytime in my life. At ten past nine off I went, after obtaining reassurances from the baroness that she would not allow Princess Hannelore out of the house under any pretext, and from my grandfather the butler that he would not admit anybody. I tied a scarf around my head, hoping that nobody would recognize me, and hurried in the direction of Buckingham Palace.

I was tempted to make use of the secret entrance in the side wall and thus gain access through that lower corridor past the kitchens, but I decided that this was one occasion when I should do everything by the book, and give Her Majesty no reason to find fault. So I mustered my courage, crossed the Ambassadors' Court and rang the bell at the normal visitors' entrance. It was opened by the same distinguished old gentleman who had accosted me once before when I was sneaking along a hallway. I never did find out who he was or his official title, and I could hardly ask him now. For all I knew he was the official royal door opener, no more than a glorified page. But he certainly adopted the airs and graces of a higher position.

"Ah, Lady Georgiana, is it not?" He bowed a little. "Her Majesty is expecting you. May I escort you to her?" Without waiting for an answer he led me up a flight of stairs to the *piano nobile.* On this floor everything was on a grander scale: the carpet was lush, the walls were hung with tapestries and dotted with marble columns and statues, and the corridor went on forever. So did the old man's chatter.

"Unseasonably cold for June, so I understand, although I have not been outside myself today. Her Majesty always takes her turn about the gardens in the morning and did vouchsafe to her maid that it was 'a little nippy.' "

"Yes, it is somewhat chilly," I replied, wishing that the interminable walk down the corridor would soon come to an end.

At last, mercifully, because we had run out of talk about the weather and the English prospects for Wimbledon, he paused in front of a door, turned to me to make sure I was ready and then knocked.

"Lady Georgiana to see you, ma'am," he said.

We both stepped inside and bowed in unison.

Her Majesty was standing at the window, looking out onto the gardens. With one elegant hand resting on the tasseled velvet drapes, she looked as if she were posing for the next royal portrait. She turned to us and nodded gravely.

"Ah, Georgiana," she said. "Thank you, Reginald, you may leave us."

The old man backed out and closed the doors silently behind him.

"Come and sit down, Georgiana," Her Majesty said as she came across the room, indicating a straight-backed chair facing a brocade sofa. She chose the chair, so I perched on the edge of the sofa, facing her. She studied me for a long moment while I waited for the ax of doom to fall and for her to say, "We've decided to send you as lady-in-waiting to a distant relative in the Falkland Islands." Instead she sighed, then spoke.

"A bad business, this, Georgiana."

"It is, ma'am, and I'm sorry to have caused you embarrassment because of it. But I assure you that I had no idea that we were doing anything stupid or out of the ordinary when I took the princess to visit a bookshop. Had I known that it was in a less-than-desirable part of London or that it had any links to the Communist Party, I would not have agreed to it."

"This young man," the queen went on, "the one who was murdered. How exactly did you meet him?"

"We met him in Hyde Park, ma'am."

"In Hyde Park?" she said with exactly the same intonation with which Lady Bracknell delivered the famous line "A handbag?" in *The Importance of Being Earnest.* "Do you make it a habit of speaking to strange young men in parks?"

"Of course not, ma'am. Her Highness wanted to see Speakers' Corner and she fell into conversation with this young man who was handing out leaflets."

"Communist leaflets?"

"Yes, ma'am. But it was all perfectly harmless. He was well-spoken and seemed pleasant enough. Then we were surprised to meet him again at a friend's party."

"So he was one of your set, then?"

"I don't actually have a set. But as to whether he was of our class, he wasn't. I understood that he was from lowly origins and had gone to Cambridge on a scholarship, where he became friendly with some of the chaps at the party."

"So he frequented Mayfair parties but yet we are given to understand that he was involved with the communists?"

"Yes, I gather he was a keen socialist, very idealistic about improving the lot of the working people."

"A strange mixture, wouldn't you say?" she asked. "One wouldn't have thought that someone who felt so strongly about the lot of the working people would indulge in the extravagances of the rich."

"Very true, ma'am. In fact the host was surprised to see him at the party."

"The host being . . . ?"

"Augustus Gormsley, ma'am. And I believe Edward Fotheringay was also giving the party."

"Gormsley. That's the publishing family, isn't it?"

"That's right."

"Nothing communist about them." She chuckled. "The old man built himself the biggest monstrosity in Victorian England. Made Sandringham look like a peasant's cottage in comparison."

I smiled. "The champagne and cocktails were certainly flowing at the party," I said. I didn't mention the cocaine. I had no idea whether that flowed or not, or whether Gussie knew what was going on in his kitchen and was simply turning a blind eye to it.

"The question is, what are we going to do about it, Georgiana?" Her Majesty said. "We have sent word to the newspaper owners asking them to keep your names out of any reports for the moment and I am sure they will comply with this—except for the *Daily Worker,* of course. We have no influence over them whatsoever, but then nobody of consequence reads that paper, anyway. Unfortunately, as soon as there is an inquest, your names will be on the public record and there is not much we can do then. All highly embarrassing, of course. Especially when relations with Germany are always so fragile, and Germany itself is in such an unsettled state at the moment."

"Baroness Rottenmeister has already ordered Her Highness to write to her father, explaining that we had accepted what seemed like a polite invitation to see some rare books and we knew nothing of the place's communist connections. Also that we hardly knew the young man in question and it was pure chance that we timed our arrival so poorly."

The queen nodded. "I wonder whether I should telephone the King of Bavaria? I rather think the best approach, given the location that this awful thing took place, would be to say that you were doing charitable works among the poor."

"That might indeed be a wise approach," I said. "But I've already told the police that we went to the bookshop at the invitation of the young man."

"What was so intriguing about a bookshop, pray?"

"It wasn't the bookshop, ma'am. It was the young man in question. The princess was rather smitten with him, I believe."

"Oh, dear. Straight from the convent. Desperate to meet boys. So what do you think we should do now, Georgiana?"

I was taken aback by this. I had expected to be told what would happen, not to have my opinion sought.

"I was wondering whether we should not send the princess home right away, so that she doesn't have to endure the newspaper reporters and the inquest. Her father would surely not want to put her through those."

The queen gave a little sigh. "But then we would have no chance of achieving our objective, would we? We still haven't come up with a suitable occasion for David to have a chance to see her and chat with her informally. That boy is hopeless. I had planned to place him beside her at our little dinner the other evening, but then he ran out on us."

"We may have to give this up as a lost cause, ma'am. The Prince of Wales showed no flicker of interest in her during our brief conversation."

"The boy is a fool," she said. "How can any young man be more interested in a desiccated and vicious middle-aged American woman than in a sweet and lovely young girl?"

"I don't know how men's minds work, ma'am."

"I don't think this has anything to do with David's mind. I don't even think it has anything to do with lust. She has some uncanny hold over him. Maybe he'll grow tired of her before long, but I'd really like to nip it in the bud, while she still has a husband to return to. You'd think her husband would do something about it, wouldn't you? Give her a damned good hiding and take her home—that's what any red-blooded young Englishman would do."

I listened, nodding politely.

"No, I'd really like to give this one more chance, Georgiana," Her Majesty continued. "I have discussed the matter with the king and it occurs to me that I may have the solution as to how we could kill two birds with one stone, so to speak. I know that the Cromer-Strodes are currently entertaining people—do you know the Cromer-Strodes?"

"I have met their daughter, Fiona, but I've never been to their house."

"Dippings. A lovely house with some fine antiques, and a mere stone's throw from Sandringham in Norfolk."

I wondered how the Cromer-Strodes had managed to hang on to those fine antiques if they were but a stone's throw from a royal palace.

"The king and I are motoring up to Sandringham today. He has been working too hard recently and he's not at all well, Georgiana. So I have persuaded him to take a few days off and he does so love Sandringham. It's the only place where he's truly comfortable, I believe. We'll have to come back to London for the garden party next week, of course, but the journey is not too long and arduous."

"Garden party?"

"One of those ghastly invite-the-masses events. Well, not exactly the masses, but dreary people like the head of the dock board and the railways and various members of parliament. People who feel entitled to shake hands with us once a year. You must bring Princess Hannelore. It will be good for her to see a traditional aspect of English life. You could motor up from Sandringham with us."

"Thank you, ma'am. I'm sure she'd enjoy it."

"Let's hope the weather is favorable this time. Last year it was most unpleasant, standing with that hot sun on one's back."

She paused. I waited for her to continue. Her eyes were focused on the far wall. "Those Worcester pieces," she said, indicating some royal blue china that was displayed in a Chinese cabinet, "so lovely, aren't they? We have the rest of that collection at Sandringham. I believe there is a bowl in the same pattern but I haven't managed to unearth one yet. If you ever see one during your travels, do let me know. . . ."

So that you can swoop down and relieve them of it, I thought. Her Majesty was notorious for pursuing antiques with such a passion that she had absolutely no scruples about acquiring them through fair means or foul.

"You were talking about Sandringham, ma'am. Do I understand that you'd want us to accompany you?"

"No, no, I don't think that would be the best idea. You see, David has given us to understand that he'll be coming to Sandringham with us and we don't want him to think that he's being thrown together with the princess. That would have quite the wrong effect. But my spies tell me that the dreadful American woman has managed to have herself included in the house party at Dippings—Lord Cromer-Strode married an American, you know, which is obviously why David is suddenly so interested in Sandringham."

I nodded with understanding.

"So my thought was this: if Princess Hannelore and you join the house party at Dippings, then David will be able to make the comparison—the young beauty and the old hag."

I laughed. "She may be old, but she's certainly not a hag, ma'am. She has exquisite taste in clothes and she's quite vivacious."

"So you like her, do you?"

"I absolutely loathe her, but I am just trying to be fair."

The queen smiled. "So what do you say, Georgiana? Does this seem like the best solution? We remove the princess from the public eye in London, whisk her to the safety of Dippings, and let things take their course from there."

"It does seem like a good plan, ma'am," I said, relieved that once we reached Dippings, the Cromer-Strodes would be responsible for her, not I. "But the police did indicate that we were not to leave London before the inquest."

"Not leave London? Blessed cheek. Do they expect you to flee the coop like the criminal classes? I'll have my secretary let them know that the king and I have invited you both to be with us in the country, after your unfortunate experience. We will personally guarantee that you will be motored back to London for the inquest."

"Thank you, ma'am."

"I just hope they manage to get to the bottom of this sordid business as quickly as possible. If the whole thing is brought to a satisfactory conclusion before the date of the inquest, then you might not even have to appear in public. And the newspapers would certainly have nothing to write about."

"Let us hope so, ma'am."

She was looking at me with that steely, unwavering stare of hers again. "You could help, Georgiana."

"Help with what?"

"To solve this murder. You have a good sharp mind. And you did so splendidly when your brother was wrongly accused."

"I solved that case mainly by accident, ma'am, and because my own life was threatened."

"Nonsense, you're being too modest," the queen said. "I was most impressed; so was the king. I think you could get to the bottom of this sordid little matter more swiftly than the police."

"I really don't think the police would take kindly to my interfering. I don't see how I could poke around and ask questions without incurring their suspicions."

"Your grandfather was a member of the police force, was he not?"

"Yes, ma'am, but several years ago, and he was only an ordinary bobby."

"Nevertheless, he'll know where to ask questions and whom to ask. I can't believe it can be that difficult, but policemen seem to be so dense. And they are like terriers—once they get one idea into their heads, they shake it and shake it and can't let it go."

Another thought struck me. "Ma'am, how can I look into a murder in London if I'm stuck at a house in Norfolk?" I blurted out, not thinking that this was probably an impolite way to address a queen.

"Ask your grandfather to do the spadework for you. Then, when you have settled Princess Hannelore at Dippings, you can slip back to London. We'll make sure the Cromer-Strodes have a car at your disposal to take you to the station."

"You're most kind," I said, although I was thinking the opposite. How on earth did she expect me to solve a murder? Even with Granddad's help, it seemed impossible. I had no idea where to start. Did she really expect me to go snooping around the docklands, asking questions? But I reminded myself that she was the queen, and one did not say no.

Chapter 23

All the occupants of Rannoch House were waiting for me as I came in through the front door.

"Well?" Baroness Rottenmeister demanded.

"Am I to be sent home?" Hanni asked.

I saw my grandfather lurking near the baize door. I expect that Mrs. Huggins was listening on the other side of it.

"The queen has come up with an admirable solution. We are to go to a country estate called Dippings, owned by Lord and Lady Cromer-Strode. They are having some people to stay for a house party and it should be quite lively for the princess."

I saw Hanni's face fall and the baroness look disapproving.

"But the policeman said we must not leave London," Hanni reminded me. "I do not wish to leave London."

"And who are these people, the Cromer-Strodes? They are royalty?"

"Nobility," I said.

The baroness frowned. "It is insult to Her Highness that she does not stay with royal peoples. I will write to her father and say is insult."

"The queen thinks highly of them," I said. "And their estate is close to Sandringham, one of the royal palaces, where Their Majesties will also be staying next week."

Hanni looked brighter for some reason. "I like to see royal palaces. The queen does not yet show me around Buckingham Palace and she promised."

"You're invited to a royal garden party next week," I said. "You'll like that. Strawberries and cream on the lawn."

Hanni nodded. "Yes," she said emphatically. "This I shall like."

"When do we leave for this country house?" the baroness demanded.

"The queen is sending a car for us in an hour."

"An hour? We are expected to be ready in one hour?"

"The queen thinks it would be a good idea if we got away from London as quickly as possible."

"Hannelore, go and tell Irmgardt to pack immediately," the baroness said. "If the queen wishes it, we cannot refuse. I hope it is not damp and cold at Deepings, and that the food is not too English."

"I understand that it is a very fine house, and Lady Cromer-Strode is American."

"American?" Hanni perked up again, probably hoping to meet some gangsters in residence.

The baroness, however, was not convinced. "English. American. All the same. No idea how to cook good food."

They went upstairs to instruct Irmgardt to pack. I followed them to impart this news to Mildred, who seemed positively thrilled by it. "We're going to the country, my lady? And to Dippings, too. I've heard so many wonderful things about it. It is supposed to be quait, quait lovely."

Until that moment I hadn't quite realized that she'd expect to come along on this jaunt. How thick could I be? Of course I'd be expected to take my maid with me. I'd become too used to doing without servants.

"When do we leave, my lady?"

"Immediately, Mildred. The queen is sending a car for us."

At this she became quite flustered. "Then I must pack immediately. Where are your trunks kept? You will need all your dinner gowns, of course. It would never do to wear the same gown at dinner more than once."

"I don't think I have more than a couple of dinner gowns," I said.

But she went on, still in raptures, "And there is bound to be a formal occasion or a ball, and then there's your tennis outfit and is there possibly yachting nearby?"

I laughed. "I don't possess a yachting outfit, if that's what you mean. There may be boating on the Norfolk Broads."

"A wonderful opportunity for you, my lady." Mildred beamed at me. "There will no doubt be a good selection of suitable young men at the house party."

Oh no. Now even she was trying to marry me off. She hummed to herself as she started going through my wardrobe. She was obviously going to be in her element, probably the senior ranking maid, thanks to being attached to me, and she was going to relish every moment. Well, she was going to be disappointed when I had to return to London on the queen's business—unless I could sneak away without letting her know!

I left her humming and packing and went to find my grandfather below stairs.

"So it looks like Mrs. Huggins and me can scarper off home, don't it?" he said.

"I'm not sure when we'll be back in London. I'm sure it would be fine for you to spend the next few days at home, but could you possibly be ready to come back if we have to return to London?"

"I expect we can, although Mrs. 'uggins is getting a bit cheesed off."

"How can I contact you in a hurry?" I asked.

"You can always telephone the pub on the corner. The Queen's 'ead. They'll let me know, and we can be back in London in a jiffy if you needs us."

"I really appreciate this, Granddad. You've been wonderful."

"Get on with you." He grinned and ruffled my hair. "I can't say I'll be sorry to leave. Not that I don't enjoy your company, my love, but them other lot, I don't know how you put up with them."

"One does what one has to," I said. "And I couldn't have done it without you and Mrs. Huggins. You've been real bricks."

"So what happens now with the police investigation?" he asked. "Is it okay for you to go running off before the inquest?"

"The queen is vouching for us." I paused and took a deep breath. "There's one other thing. She'd like me to solve the case before the inquest."

"She'd what?" he boomed.

I smiled. "I know, it's ridiculous. I don't see how I can do anything without annoying the police and casting more suspicion upon myself."

"Added to which you'd be poking around some pretty nasty people. Someone wanted that young man dead badly enough to take a large risk."

"Her Majesty suggested that you could help me, Granddad."

"Me? I really don't see what I could do."

"You used to be a policeman in that area. You know people."

"I might still know a few old geezers around the docklands," Granddad conceded. "If anyone's going to ask the questions, I'd rather it was me than you. Ruddy cheek that queen of yours has got—wanting to send you into harm's way, just to avoid a royal scandal."

"Rather more than a scandal, the way they put it. More like a diplomatic crisis."

"Ruddy Germans. Nothing but trouble, they are. You'd have thought they'd learned their lesson in the war, wouldn't you? But no, this Hitler bloke comes along with his blasted Nazis and starts upsetting everything again."

"So will you find out what you can for me?" I asked. "When the princess is settled I'm supposed to come back to London to snoop around and solve this murder."

"You stay put in the country, ducks," he said. "I'll do my bit for you, but there's no way I'm letting you poke around communist haunts. I'm your grandfather and I'm telling you straight."

I looked at him and grinned. "Yes, Granddad," I said.

❋

EVERYONE WAS CHEERFUL as the car arrived for us. It was a large Rolls with a well-attired chauffeur.

"Now this is as it should be," Baroness Rottenmeister commented. "Suitable transportation for Her Highness."

We left Mildred and Irmgardt standing on the pavement beside a Matterhorn of luggage, awaiting a taxi. No royal car for them. They were going to have to shepherd that pile of cases by train. I found myself feeling sorry for them and realized, with some shame, that such things had never crossed my mind before. Servants and luggage arrived where they were supposed to be and if they had inconveniences, they were no concern of ours. I think we truly believed that their one purpose in life was to make sure our lives ran smoothly.

Our car made its way through the faceless northern suburbs until the city sprawl melted into glorious countryside. Having been confined to London for most of the spring I was unprepared for the riot of summer green—spreading oak trees, rich pastures, wheat and barley already tall and feathery in the fields. There is nothing as lush as the English countryside in summer.

The baroness dozed in the heat. Princess Hanni looked out of the window.

"England is very flat," she commented. "No mountains."

"You're looking at the flat part of England," I said. "In the north and west we have many mountains, although not as high as the Alps in Bavaria."

"In Bavaria we have high mountains with snow," she said. "The highest mountains in the world."

"Not exactly," I said. "The Himalayas are the highest mountains in the world. The Alps are only the highest mountains in Europe."

"In Bavaria we have the highest peaks," she said. "The Zugspitze and the Jungfrau."

"Mont Blanc in France is higher, I regret to tell you," I said with a smile.

"Ah, Mont Blanc," she said dismissively. Then she turned to me. "This place Dippings. Is it nice?"

"I expect so."

"Will there be young men there? We will dance?"

"I have no idea, Hanni."

"Do you think that Darcy will be there?"

I kept my face completely composed. "I shouldn't think so."

"Gee, that's too bad. I want to see him more. I think he likes me."

There was silence in the car while I tried not to think of Darcy, and especially Hanni with Darcy.

"This is strange name," she said at last. "What means Dippings?"

"I expect it means little dips in the flat countryside."

"It is crummy name. Shall we visit the king and queen at their house?"

"If they invite us."

"I am princess. They should invite me. It is not right that I do not stay at palace."

"The queen was thinking of you. She felt you would have more fun with people your own age."

"But I do not meet people my own age. Only you. I have not yet had date with fun and sexy guy." I had been thinking that I had cured the princess of speaking American gangster slang. Obviously I hadn't.

"One week, Hanni. You can't expect too much in one week."

"But you do not understand. Soon I go home and then I will not be permitted to speak with men. Only guys my family want me to marry. Nobody hot and sexy. And someone like the baroness will always be with me. How will I learn what sex is all about?"

"I'm sure you'll pick it up rather quickly," I said. "You already seem to have the main idea."

"What main idea?"

"Hanni, we went to a party. You danced. You flirted. I saw you."

"What means flirt?"

"You know. Flutter your eyelashes. Tease. Act as if you are interested in a boy."

"This I can do. This I like to do, yes," she said. "But you do not. This is not good, I think. It means boy does not know you like him."

Well, that was a definite slap in the face. Maybe what she said was true. Maybe Darcy had moved on because I hadn't shown that I liked him enough. But flirting does not come easily to someone brought up in a remote castle with tartan wallpaper in the bathrooms, bagpipes at dawn and men who wear kilts.

"I'll try harder in future," I reassured her.

"I have not yet kissed a boy," she went on. "Is this very pleasurable?"

"Oh yes, very, with the right boy."

"You have found right boy?" she asked. "You know a hot and sexy guy?"

I stared out of the window, watching a stream meander through a meadow while cattle stood in dappled shade. "Obviously not yet, or I'd be married."

"You want to be married?" she asked.

"Yes, I suppose so. It's what every woman wants. Don't you?"

"Not before I have known what it is to live my own life," she said, seriously for her. "I have things I want to do. Things that married women cannot do, especially not married queens and princesses. I have dreams."

"Such as what?" I asked, intrigued.

"Silly things. Go to the shops. Eat in a café." She turned abruptly away and stared out of the window.

Only the baroness's rhythmic rumblings broke our silence. I found myself thinking things over. Everything had been so confused for the past few days. First Tubby plunging to his death and then the horrible episode in the bookshop with poor Sidney Roberts lying there, blood spreading across his white shirt. Granddad seemed to think there had to be a connection. Personally I couldn't think what it was, unless it had something to with the cocaine I saw in Gussie's kitchen. I knew little about drugs but I had heard that they were bought and sold by ruthless people. If Tubby and Sidney had been involved with them, and perhaps had not paid their bills, then maybe they had been taught the ultimate lesson. But by whom?

The flatlands of East Anglia opened up before us—a landscape that seemed nearly all sky. White clouds hung like cotton wool, sending patches of shadow over the fields. In the distance a church spire betrayed the presence of a village among trees. We passed through Little Dippings, and then Much Dippings, a similar village with a cluster of thatched pink and white cottages around a church and pub (the Cromer-Strode Arms), before driving along a high brick wall and turning in at an impressive gateway. The first part of the estate was wild parkland, with lots of trees and what looked like rhododendrons, although they had already finished blooming. A pheasant took off with a clatter of wings. A small herd of ornamental deer moved away as they heard the car approaching. Then Hanni said, "Look. What kind of animal is that over there in those bushes? It is pink, but I do not think it is a pig."

I stared hard at the pink thing among the foliage. It seemed to have an awful lot of limbs. "I really don't know," I said, but then suddenly I did. It seemed to me that it was two people, without clothes, wrapped around each other in the grass and doing what I could only guess at. Our driver, on the other side of his glass partition, coughed discreetly and put his foot down on the accelerator. As the couple heard the approaching car, a head was raised in surprise. I caught a glimpse of a shocked face before we passed.

Chapter 24

Then we came around a bend and there was Dippings before us in all its glory. Like most houses in the area, it was built of red brick, which had mellowed over hundreds of years into a lovely muted rose pink. The Elizabethan chimneys were striped in white and red brick and a classical portico and flight of marble steps had been added to the front of the house in Georgian times. There was an ornamental pond with fountain playing in the forecourt. A flight of white doves wheeled overhead. All in all a most pleasing aspect. We drove between well-kept lawns and shaded drives until we came to a halt at those front steps.

The baroness stirred.

"We have arrived," Hanni said. The baroness hastily adjusted her hat as the door was opened by footmen.

"Welcome to Dippings, my lady," one of them said as he helped me out.

We had barely set foot on the gravel forecourt than a figure came flying down the steps to greet us. She was tall, angular and almost painfully thin. Her face was a perfect mask of makeup, from the plucked eyebrows to the startling red lips (though not executed quite as perfectly as my mother's). Her mauve dress had panels that flew out around her as she hurtled toward us, arms outstretched.

"Welcome, welcome to Dippings," she called in a southern American drawl. "You must be Lady Georgiana, and this is the princess. Welcome, Your Highness." She attempted a jerky bob of curtsy. "How lovely to have you here with us. I can't tell you how excited I was when the queen called and suggested you join our little gathering. I know you'll just love it here.

Everyone does. My husband is such a wonderful host. He always takes care of everyone so well and makes sure they have a good time. Come on in. Come on in."

Hanni and I glanced at each other, feeling somewhat breathless, as she went ahead back up the steps, still talking away. "We've quite a jolly little group here. Some young people your age. You probably know most of them, I'm sure, but my nieces are here from America. Such dear girls. You're going to love them, I just know it."

We entered a wood-paneled foyer, hung with family portraits and the occasional, obligatory pair of crossed swords and frayed standard from some long-ago battle.

"I'm afraid you're too late for lunch," she went on, "and tea won't be for another hour. But I expect you're starving. How about some sandwiches and lemonade out on the back lawn? Or do you want to see your rooms first? We've sent someone to meet the train with your luggage so you should be able to change as soon as it arrives."

She paused for breath. I realized she had asked about a dozen questions and hadn't waited for a single answer. I tried to remember what the choices had been.

"There's not much point in going up to our rooms before our maids and our luggage arrive," I said, "so some lemonade on the lawn would be lovely."

"I don't know where everyone else has got to," she said. "They may be playing tennis, although it's rather hot for it today, wouldn't you say? I expect Fiona is with her American cousins. You remember my daughter, Fiona, don't you? I know you two girls were at that fearfully expensive school together."

It's funny how outsiders always give themselves away as being "not one of us." People I knew would never consider whether a school was expensive or not. If it was the right school and the rest of the family had been there, one bit the bullet and paid for it somehow.

Lady Cromer-Strode (I presume it was she although there had never been proper introductions) now led us through a series of dark paneled rooms and galleries until we came to a charming drawing room with lots of low, comfortable armchairs and French doors opening onto lawns. Chairs and tables had been set up in the shade of an enormous copper beech in the middle of the lawn and several people were sitting there. They looked up as we came out onto the terrace and down the steps to the lawn.

"Here they are. They have arrived," Lady Cromer-Strode announced to the world.

The young men rose awkwardly from their deck chairs. It is never easy to get out of a deck chair gracefully. "Everybody, this is Lady Georgiana and Princess Hannelore. They're going to be joining our jolly little gathering. Won't that be fun?"

"And may I present Baroness Rottenmeister, who is accompanying the princess," I said, since she had been ignored by our hostess until now and was hovering behind us, looking decidedly out of sorts.

"What-ho, Georgie. Good to see you again." One of the young men revealed himself to be Gussie Gormsley. "And you, Your Highness."

"Please, call me Hanni. We are among friends," she said.

Fiona Cromer-Strode, large and pink, came to embrace me. She was carrying a tennis racquet and looked revoltingly hearty. "How absolutely lovely to see you again, Georgie. Doesn't it seem simply ages since we were at Les Oiseaux? Wasn't it simply ripping fun?"

"Yes, it was." Fiona and I had scarcely known each other at Les Oiseaux, but now I remembered she had always been annoying.

"This is my cousin Jensen Hedley," she said. "She's visiting from Baltimore. Her two sisters are away for the day, visiting Cambridge, but you'll meet them at dinner tonight."

The pale, elegant young American, wearing a dress that could only have come from Paris, smiled charmingly. "Gee, I've always wanted to meet a real princess," she said and shook Hanni's hand.

"I thought you were more interested in meeting a prince," Fiona teased.

"All the princes around here seem to be otherwise occupied," Jensen said and gave a quick glance over her shoulder.

Mrs. Simpson was lounging in the shade behind us, wearing white shorts and a bright red halter top and apparently reading a magazine. She hadn't bothered to move when we arrived. Now she felt eyes on her and looked up.

"Why, it's the actress's daughter," she said, in feigned surprise. "Fancy seeing you here."

"The queen suggested it so that she could keep an eye on us from

Sandringham," I said. "We are apparently close to Sandringham, as you probably know." I smiled sweetly.

Her eyes narrowed, then focused on Hanni. "And who is the pretty little blond girl?"

"Her Royal Highness Princess Hannelore of Bavaria," I said, stiffly. "Highness, this lady is Mrs. Simpson, also visiting from America."

"I love America." Hanni was beaming. "Do you have gangsters in your town?"

"I sincerely hope not," Mrs. Simpson said. "Baltimore is a refined and old city. Our hostess and I went to the ladies' seminary together there. The very same school that the Misses Hedley also attended. Isn't that right, Jensen honey?"

"Reagan and I attended the seminary," Jensen said. "Danika was educated at home, on account of her delicate health."

Reagan, Jensen, Danika, Wallis—was nobody in America called plain Jane or Mary?

"Such interesting names," I commented.

"We also have a brother, Homer," Jensen said.

"Ah, so you have a parent interested in the classics?" I asked.

She wrinkled that button of a nose, frowning. "No. Daddy likes baseball."

"So how is your dear mother?" Mrs. Simpson asked me. "Still keeping herself busy in Germany?"

"She comes and goes," I said. "I saw her recently in good health, thank you."

"She has staying power, I'll say that for her. Still, I suppose that tough upbringing on the streets has given her resilience."

"Surviving Castle Rannoch would have given her more resilience," I said, not willing to be drawn into a spat. "The rooms there are much colder and bleaker than my grandparents' house." I went to move away, then couldn't resist asking, "Are you here with Mr. Simpson?"

A frown crossed the perfectly made up face. "Regrettably, he has been called back to America on business."

"Dear me. What a pity." I gave her a sweet smile and realized that she no longer intimidated me. At least adversity does have some advantages.

Lemonade and sandwiches arrived. Jensen Hedley dragged off Gussie to play tennis. The baroness parked herself in one of the deck chairs and promptly tucked into the sandwiches. They looked so tempting—egg and cress, crab and cucumber and even smoked salmon, my favorite—that I was about to join her when a man in wrinkled cricket whites came sauntering across the lawns. He had a red, weathered face surrounded by a halo of wispy white hair and childishly innocent eyes. What's more, I recognized him. His was the face that had peered over the bush when we arrived.

$\mathcal{C}$hapter 25

The elderly man gave no indication of having recognized us, however, and came toward us with a big smile on his face. "Well, well. Here they are. Spendid. Splendid. Cromer-Strode." He shook our hands heartily. "And I met you when you were a little girl," he added to me. "At Hubert Anstruther's. I believe your mother was—"

"Married to him at the time," I finished for him, still not quite able to look him in the eye. I couldn't stop wondering who had provided those other pink arms and legs in the bushes and whether Lady Cromer-Strode knew anything about it.

"And this delightful young person is our visiting princess." Lord Cromer-Strode turned his attention to Hanni. "Is this your first experience of an English country house, Highness?" He took her hand, pressing it between his.

"Yes, it is my first visit to England," she said.

"Then you must let me give you a tour of the grounds," he went on. "Give you a feel for the place. Dippings is noted for its sublime landscapes and the rose garden is in all the guidebooks. We have trippers clamoring to take a look almost daily. Come along, drink up that lemonade and we'll have time for a turn before tea."

A turn at what? I wondered. A feel for which place? Did he make a habit of such behavior? I wondered if I was being invited along as chaperon.

"We'll leave my daughter and Lady Georgiana to catch up on news, shall we?" he went on, making it perfectly clear that I wasn't. "They have hardly seen each other since schooldays. Off we go then."

He put an arm around her waist and shepherded her away. I stood there in an agony of indecision. Could I come up with an excuse to go after them? Surely even the most randy of old men would not try anything with a visiting princess, would he? I could already hear the queen's voice ringing in my ears; *And you just sat there and allowed her to be deflowered in broad daylight? Germany will declare war and it will all be your fault.*

If I see them heading toward the rhododendron shrubbery, I'll go after them, I decided.

"Isn't it spiffing fun that we're together again, Georgie?" Fiona came to stand beside me. I remembered she always was on the hearty side.

"I'm not sure whether I should be letting the princess go off unchaperoned," I said as the two figures disappeared around the side of the house.

"Don't be silly, she's with Daddy. He'll take really, really good care of her," Fiona said. Like other members of our class, she didn't say her *r*'s properly. The words came out as "weely, weely." With her I suspected it was affectation. She slipped her arm through mine. "Why don't we go for a little walk too? We have some darling, darling little woolly lambs at the home farm. Well, they're rather fat and jolly now but they were absolutely darling a month or so ago."

Since the home farm was in the same general direction that the princess had taken I agreed to this.

"Isn't it too, too lovely to be together again?" Fiona said. "I know we're going to have such a jolly time. Mummy has invited lots of absolutely topping people and it's going to be splendid fun."

I managed a happy smile.

"Have you heard my news?" Fiona said. "Did you know I am engaged to be married?"

"No, I didn't. Congratulations. Who is the lucky man?"

"Why, it's dear Edward."

"Edward?"

"Surely you know him. Everybody does. Edward Fotheringay."

"Lunghi Fungy, you mean?" I blurted the words out.

"I don't like that silly nickname. I have forbidden Gussie to address him in that way. But I'm so glad you know him. Isn't he wonderful? Everybody adores him."

Including my mother, I thought. And from what I saw, he reciprocated the sentiments.

"And is Edward here at the moment?" I asked casually.

"Of course he is. We couldn't have a house party and not invite Edward, could we? He has driven my American cousins into Cambridge today, seeing that he was a student there and can show them around properly."

Given his behavior with my mother and his flirtation with Hanni, I wondered just what else he might be showing them during the course of the day.

"But they'll all be back in time for dinner," Fiona continued merrily. "Ah, here we are. This is the home farm. Isn't it absolutely sweet? Almost like a toy farm. I've always adored it. And Daddy loves it so much. He spends most of his time here, just talking to the pigs."

I snorted. I couldn't help it. I know a lady never snorts but it just came out. The pink image from the shrubbery was simply too strong. So his family thought that he spent all his time at the home farm, did they?

By the time we returned to the house our luggage and maids were installed in our bedrooms. I found that Hanni had come back, apparently unscathed, before me and was talking with the baroness in her room, while the silent, scowling Irmgardt scurried around, unpacking trunks.

"And how was your walk?" I asked cautiously.

"I enjoy very much," Hanni said. "He is very kind man. Very friendly. We had to climb over stool, is it called?"

"Stool?"

"Between fields."

"Stile," I said. "You mean steps over a wall?"

"Yes. We climb over stile and he was kind enough to lift me up and down."

And do a little incidental groping, I thought.

"The princess's room is most satisfactory," the baroness said. "I understand your room is next door. My room is not so pleasant, I regret to say. At the back of the house, facing north, up flights of very steep stairs."

"I'm sorry," I said. "Should we speak to Lady Cromer-Strode about it?"

The baroness sighed. "I am prepared to suffer," she said. "Obviously a German title means nothing to these people. I am treated like a maid."

"Perhaps they are not aware of your rank," I said. "The queen arranged this and she may not even have been aware that you would be accompanying us."

"That could be true," she said, "especially if you did not remind Her Majesty that I was staying with you."

So I was to be the guilty one. "I'll try and have your room changed for you."

"Please do not derange yourself. I shall suffer. The extra stairs shall be good for my fitness."

"I haven't even seen my own room yet," I said. "It may not be as pleasant as this one. I'll call for you when it's teatime, shall I?"

"Teatime? I thought we just ate on the lawn."

"That was a snack to keep us going until tea," I said.

"At least we are to be fed properly here," the baroness commented as I left Hanni's room. Mildred had already unpacked everything and was busy pressing out every crease. Truly she was a marvel. I couldn't think why I'd be so relieved to get rid of her again.

"What a delightful view from your window, my lady," she said excitedly. "I'm sure you are going to have such a happy time here. And I see there are some attractive young men. I passed one of them in the hall just now. Very handsome and quite flirtatious too. He actually winked at me." And she blushed.

At four o'clock we made our way down for tea, which was held in the long gallery. Lady Cromer-Strode was wafting around gushing and officiating. "Do try the Victoria sponge. It is Cook's specialty. And those little crunchy things. Divine. I don't know where my husband can have gotten to. Up at the farm again, I suspect. He puts in far too many hours on that farm. Absolutely dedicated, isn't he, Fiona, honey?"

Fiona agreed. I rather fancied I saw meaningful glances pass between some of the guests and wondered which ones of them had been taken on visits to the farm. We tucked in well even though it was only an hour since we'd eaten sandwiches. Isn't it remarkable what fresh air will do for the appetite? There were the most delicious scones with thick cream and homemade strawberry jam as well as brandy snaps and cream puffs that were so light they melted in the mouth. Obviously the baroness was going to be very happy here. One by one the other guests drifted in. Jensen and some other tennis players. A young man I thought I recognized came to sit beside me.

"Hello, I'm Felix," he said. "I don't think we've met."

"Georgiana," I replied. "And I think I saw you at Gussie's party the other night."

"The fateful one when poor old Tubby toppled?"

I nodded.

"That was a rum do, wasn't it? Who'd have thought poor old Tubby?"

"Does Gussie give a lot of these parties?"

"Oh, all the time, old bean. The host with the most is our Gussie."

"He must have a good allowance. The champagne and cocktails were positively flowing," I said awkwardly. One of the rules of our set was not to discuss money, but in my role as sleuth, I rather needed to know where Gussie acquired his.

"Well, I don't know about allowance, but he does all right by himself, old Gussie," Felix said guardedly. "One way and another." There was something in the way he said it that made me wonder about that cocaine. I had thought of Gussie as the genial host, but what if he supplemented his income by supplying his friends with drugs?

"You were at Cambridge with him, were you?" I asked.

His face lit up. "Oh, absolutely. All Trinity men. We rowed in those days. Not anymore. Gone to seed rather."

"So what do you do now?" I asked.

"Not much, really—to the despair of the pater. Haven't found my niche in life yet. Wasn't cut out for the army or the law or the church and there's not much else left, is there?"

I agreed that there wasn't.

"So how about you? Are you one of those fearsome bright girls who went to university?"

"I'm afraid not. Although I'd quite like to have gone, but it wasn't offered."

Felix nodded in sympathy. "Hard times, I know. Everybody penny pinching. So I suppose you were forced to go out and earn your own living?"

"I wasn't allowed to, actually. It was frowned upon."

"What do you mean?"

"Not considered suitable."

At this moment Gussie sauntered over. "So you've met Georgie, have you? Jolly good. So I hear the relatives have also arrived for a few days. Shall you be visiting?"

"Relatives?" Felix asked.

"King and queen, old chap. Don't be so dense. She's Binky's sister."

Felix turned bright pink. "Oh, I say. I've put my foot in it rather, haven't I? Talking about penny pinching and having to work for a living?"

I laughed. "We're penny pinching like everyone else, and I'd love to work for a living."

"There's a splendid girl staying here who's doing frightfully well in her own business. I'm terribly admiring," Felix said. "Oh, here she is now."

Belinda entered the room, deep in conversation with his lordship. From the chatty way that they parted, I found my suspicions running riot. She saw me and came straight over.

"Darling, what a lovely surprise. I had no idea you'd be part of this bun fight."

"Belinda, what are you doing here?" I asked.

"Darling, have you ever known me to turn down a free meal? I told you I was going to the country. One simply can't stay in London when the weather turns warm."

"How is it that you know absolutely everybody?" I asked.

"One works at it, darling. It's a matter of survival. With the amount I'm making from my fashion business at the moment, I'd starve, so it's a question of going where the food and wine are good. And after all, we were at school with Fiona."

"We loathed her," I said under my breath. "Remember when she first arrived and would follow us everywhere? You told her awful stories about the upstairs lavatory being haunted so that we could have some peace and quiet there."

Belinda laughed. "I remember." She looked around the room. "I say, it's rather a jolly party, isn't it? Quite a few people you know, including Lunghi Fungy."

"I've just heard he's engaged to Fiona."

"Been promised to each other since birth, darling. Nothing will come of it. Who could be married to someone who gushes about little woolly lambs?"

"She seems to think something will come of it. She even asked me to be a bridesmaid."

"Then perhaps Lunghi is doing the sensible thing. After all, Fiona is an only child and she'll inherit all this someday. Lunghi's own family situation is precarious."

"Aren't the Fotheringays an old family?"

"But flat broke, darling. Old man lost everything in America in the crash of '29, just like your father. Lunghi's been out in India working for some trading company like a common clerk, so one understands."

"I see." I wondered if my mother knew this. Usually her instincts were spot on. Maybe his youth and extreme good looks were too much of a temptation.

With tea over we went upstairs to change for dinner. It's funny how life at country houses is centered around one meal after another. And yet those who live such lives don't seem to become overly fat. Maybe it's all that tramping around the home farm, not to mention other energetic forms of activity around the estate. I let Mildred select a dress and jewelry for me and even attempt to make my hair look fashionable. The result was not displeasing. I came down again to find that the French doors in the drawing room were still open and Pimm's and cocktails were being served on the terrace. It was a balmy evening. Swallows were swooping wildly overhead. A peacock was calling from the copse nearby—that unearthly shriek that sounds like a soprano being killed with a saw. Groups of guests were already standing together, chatting. The three Misses Hedley were now talking with their cousin Fiona, all wearing almost identical green flowered dresses, which made them look like a living herbaceous border. Another group of younger guests, including Gussie and Belinda, were standing to one side, smoking and drinking cocktails, while the older set was clustered around Lord Cromer-Strode. I picked out Mrs. Simpson standing apart, hands on painfully thin hips, staring out across the park and looking displeased. Maybe she had expected a dinner partner who had been detained at Sandringham!

"Ah, here is the delightful young Lady Georgiana." Lord Cromer-Strode came to meet me and put an arm around my waist as he steered me toward the company. "I'm sure you know the young folk, but you may not have met Colonel and Mrs. Horsmonden, just back from India, and Sir William and Lady Stoke-Podges, also old friends from colonial days." He kept his arm firmly around my waist as he said this and, to my shock, his fingers strayed upward until they were definitely making contact with the underside of my breast. I didn't quite know how to react, so I stepped forward to shake hands, thus freeing myself. A glass of Pimm's was pressed upon me. We made pleasantries about the seasonably fine weather and the possibility of rain before the first Test match. Lord Cromer-Strode talked of getting together an eleven to play the village cricket team and there was heated discussion on who should be opening bat.

"Young Edward has a good eye and a straight bat," his lordship said. "Ah, here he is now. Wondered where you had got to, young man."

Edward Fotheringay came onto the terrace with Princess Hanni. He had a slightly guilty look on his face. She was looking pleased with herself. Baroness Rottenmeister was nowhere to be seen.

"So you've found our visiting princess, have you, my boy? Splendid. Splendid. Come along, everybody, drink up."

Fiona broke away from her cousins and rushed to greet him. "Edward, my sweet, sweet pet. You don't know how I have been pining for you all day. How was Cambridge? Terribly, terribly hot and nasty?"

"Quite pleasant, thank you, Fiona. It's finals week. The place is like a morgue. Everyone studying, you know."

Guests continued to arrive, most of them older people I didn't know. Baroness Rottenmeister appeared, head to toe in black as usual and with a face like thunder.

"I called for the princess, but she had already gone ahead without me," she said to me. "You have taught her bad habits."

After a while the first dinner gong sounded.

"Everyone know who they are escorting in to dinner?" Lady Cromer-Strode fluttered around us, ushering us toward the French doors like a persistent sheepdog.

Mrs. Simpson appeared at her shoulder. "It appears that my dinner partner isn't here, Cordelia. Do I take it that your husband will escort me to table?"

"My husband?" Lady Cromer-Strode looked flustered. "Why no, Wallis. That wouldn't be proper. Lord Cromer-Strode escorts the highest-ranking lady. And that would be Lady Georgiana, surely?"

"Her mother was a common tart," Mrs. Simpson said loudly enough for her voice to carry.

"A well-known actress, Wallis. Be fair," Lady Cromer-Strode muttered in answer. "And her father was first cousin to the king. You can't argue with that."

"I also happen to have royal connections," Mrs. Simpson said in a miffed voice.

"Yes, but not official ones, Wallis. You know very well that everything in England is done by the book. There are protocols to be followed. I'm sure that Sir William Stoke-Podges will be happy to escort you, won't you, William?"

She thrust them together before she fluttered over to me. "Lady Georgiana, I think that maybe you should go in to dinner with my husband."

"Oh no, Lady Cromer-Strode." I gave her an innocent smile. Mrs. Simpson paused, waiting for me to concede that she was indeed the ranking female. "Her Highness the princess outranks me. She should go in with your husband."

"Of course. How silly of me. Princess Hannelore, honey, over here." And she was off to grab Hanni while I was paired up with Colonel Horsmonden.

"And what about me?" The baroness appeared at my side, still looking seriously out of sorts. "I appear to have no escort."

"Oh, dear." Lady Cromer-Strode clearly hadn't put her into the starting lineup. "You see, nobody told us that the princess would be bringing a companion. I'm so sorry. Now let's see. Reverend Withers, can I ask you to do me a favor and escort this lady into dinner? What was your name again, honey?"

The baroness flushed almost purple. "I am Baroness Rottenmeister," she said.

"And this is Reverend Withers. Your wife isn't here, is she, vicar?"

"No, she is visiting her family in Skegness."

"Then you'll be kind enough to take this lady in to dinner, will you?"

"Delighted, my dear." He offered her his arm.

The baroness stared at him as if he was something a little higher up the evolutionary scale than a worm. "You have a wife? And you are priest?"

"Church of England clergyman, my dear. We're allowed to marry, y'know."

"A Protestant!"

"We are all children of God," he said, and steered her into the line. I went to take my own place beside the colonel.

"Now we seem to be one man short." Lady Cromer-Strode glanced down the line of couples. "Who could that be? Who is not here?"

As if on cue, Darcy O'Mara came up the steps onto the terrace. He looked dashing in his dinner jacket, his dark hair slightly tousled and his eyes flashing. My heart did a flip-flop as he fell into place with Belinda. What on earth was he doing here?

Before I could see if he was going to look my way there was a stir among the guests and the butler stepped out to announce, "His Royal Highness the Prince of Wales, my lady."

My cousin David, looking dapper as only he could look, came striding out with that jaunty air of his.

"So sorry I'm late, Lady C-S." He kissed her on the cheek, making her flutter all the more. "Got held up at Sandringham, you know. Hope I haven't put you out at all. Ah, Wallis, there you are." He made a beeline for her. Wallis Simpson shot me a triumphant smile as she slipped her arm through his and she pushed past me to the front of the line.

I hardly noticed the insult because David's speech had triggered some sort of memory. Those two big initials lying on a sheet of paper in Hanni's room at Rannoch House. C.P., wasn't it? Who had sent her a sheet of paper with only two letters on it, and what did they mean? And why did they have a big red *X* slashed through them the second time I saw them?

Chapter 26

The banqueting room was aglitter with chandeliers dangling from a ceiling painted with cherubs. Many-branched candelabras were set along a mahogany table that extended the full length of the room. Light sparkled from silver cutlery and reflected in the highly polished surface. I was seated near the head of the table, between Colonel Horsmonden and Edward Fotheringay. The Prince of Wales sat on one side of Lord Cromer-Strode and Hanni on the other. Mrs. Simpson was directly opposite me.

"Still no escort of your own, I see," she said. "Time is marching on, you know. You won't have that youthful bloom forever."

"I'm waiting for one who doesn't officially belong to someone else," I said, and gave her a sweet smile.

"You have a sharp tongue, young woman," she said and promptly turned her attention to the prince and Lord Cromer-Strode. On one side of me, I overheard Lord Cromer-Strode telling what was obviously a really bawdy anecdote. "So the farmer said, 'That's the biggest bloody great pair of . . .'" The end of this sentence was drowned out with Mrs. Simpson's shrill laughter and the prince's chuckle. Hanni looked bemused. I suspect she didn't get the double entendre, although Lord C-S's gesture had been plain enough to me. But then, as I watched, I saw that Hanni's attention was not directed to those directly around her. She was busy casting come-hither glances at first Edward and then Darcy.

I thought again about those strange letters. Had they been some kind of threat? If so, why hadn't she shared her fears with me? Who knew she was in London and where she was staying?

The meal began with lobster bisque and went from strength to strength from there. Colonel Horsmonden launched into accounts of his life in India—tiger shoots, maharajas' palaces, mutinies in the bazaars, each tale made boring as only an old colonel can make it, peppering them with names of people I had never heard of.

In the spirit of self-preservation I mentioned to him that Edward had also just come back from India and suddenly they were talking across me.

"I'm surprised we've never met, my boy," the colonel said. "I thought I prided myself in knowing everyone in the service over there."

"Ah, but I wasn't in the service," Edward said. "I was in trade, sir. Import-export."

"Stationed where?"

"All over the place. Never in one place for long, you know. And I also did a bit of mountain climbing in the Himalayas."

"Did you, by Jove. Then you must know old Beagle Bailey. Ever climbed with old Beagle Bailey?"

"I can't say that I have, sir."

"Don't know old Beagle? Institution in the Himalayas, is old Beagle. Mad as a hatter, of course. So who did you climb with?"

"Oh, just some chaps from Cambridge."

"And where did you pick up your sherpas?"

"We didn't use sherpas."

"Didn't use sherpas? How did you manage? Nobody climbs without sherpas. Dashed foolish. They know the country like the back of their hands."

"They were only small climbs that we undertook," Edward said quickly. "Just weekend stuff. A bit of fun, you know."

"Not much fun if a storm comes down in the Himalayas," Colonel Horsmonden said. "I remember once we were in Kashmir. Going up a glacier on Nanga Parbat. Do you know Nanga Parbat? Damned fine mountain. And within ten minutes the storm had come down and we almost got blown off the dashed mountain."

They talked on. I was conscious of Hanni's eyes moving from Edward to Darcy, and of Darcy eating unconcernedly. The Prince of Wales chatted with Lord Cromer-Strode but his eyes never left Wallis Simpson. So much for being captivated by Hanni, who looked as innocently voluptuous as anybody could possibly look. Certainly Lord Cromer-Strode was aware of her charms. He kept turning to pat her hand, stroke her arm, and, I suspect, grab her knee under the table, judging by the amount of time only one hand was visible. Hanni didn't seem to be objecting, whatever he was doing.

Gussie was also chatting away easily as he ate, regaling the American girls with tales of English boarding schools and making them shriek with laughter.

"A fag master? What on earth is a fag master?" one of them demanded. "It sounds just terrible."

And I found my thoughts straying to the events of the past week. If Gussie was indeed supplying his friends with cocaine, and if Tubby and Sidney Roberts had somehow fallen foul of him, how could he sit there behaving as if nothing had happened? Surely that was a stupid idea on my part. Gussie was one of those affable, not too bright young men I had danced with during my season. I could picture him trying drugs, even selling drugs to his friends, but not killing anyone. It just didn't make sense.

Dinner ended and Lady Cromer-Strode led the women into the drawing room while the men lit up cigars and passed around the port. Mrs. Simpson hogged the best armchair, and Belinda started chatting with the American girls. The baroness and Hanni had obviously had words. I heard the baroness say in English, "It is unpardonable insult. Tomorrow morning I shall telephone your father." Then she stalked to the far side of the room and sat down, away from the rest of the company.

I wandered across to the open French doors. The scent of roses and honeysuckle wafted in from the gardens. A full moon was reflected in the pond. A perfect night for romance and the man with whom I wanted to stroll in the moonlight was in the next room, only he was showing no interest in me. Maybe Mrs. Simpson was not wrong. Some of us just didn't flirt naturally. Perhaps my mother could give me some pointers, but I doubted it. She oozed sexuality. It came naturally from her pores. I had inherited the blood of Queen Victoria, who was not amused by much and, in spite of producing umpteen children, could never have been dubbed as sexy.

Hanni came to stand beside me. "It is real swell, *ja?*" she said. "Darcy is here. And Edward too. I can't decide which one I like better. They are both hot and sexy, don't you think?"

"They are both good looking," I said, "but one of them happens to be engaged to Fiona."

Hanni grinned. "I do not think he loves her very much. During dinner he looked at me and he winked. That must mean that he likes me, yes?"

"Hanni, you are to behave yourself. We are guests of Fiona's family."

"Too bad." She paused. "Her father is a real friendly guy too. But he pinched my bottom on the way in to dinner. Is that old English custom?"

"Certainly not," I said.

"And on our walk he asked me if I liked to roll in the hay. Hay is what you feed to animals, no? Why should I want to roll in it?"

"Lord Cromer-Strode is a little too friendly, I believe. Please watch out when you are alone with him. And especially if he suggests a roll in the hay."

"Why? Is this bad thing?"

"It is not the sort of thing that visiting princesses do." Again I found myself staring around the room, wondering just who had been with him in the rhododendrons earlier. Belinda saw me looking at her and beckoned me over. "So I see Darcy O'Mara is here," she said. "Do you think he was officially invited or is he party-crashing again?"

"Lady Cromer-Strode seemed to be expecting him." I tried to sound disinterested.

"I wonder what he is doing here. These people certainly aren't his usual crowd. I didn't even realize he knew the Cromer-Strodes. Which can only mean one thing." She gave me a knowing smile. "You see, he is still interested in you."

"I don't think I'm the one he's come for," I said as I watched the men drift into the room amid lingering clouds of smoke. Hanni looked up expectantly and then turned and walked deliberately out onto the terrace. Edward went to follow her, then thought better of it. Darcy gave me a look that I couldn't quite interpret, then did follow her. I stood watching them go, trying not to let my face betray any emotion.

"Maybe I should go after them," I said to Belinda.

"You shouldn't run after him," Belinda replied. "Not a wise move."

"Not for myself," I said. "For Hanni. I'm supposed to be keeping an eye on her and she is awfully eager for sexual experiences. I'm sure Darcy will be only too willing to oblige."

"He probably will," Belinda agreed. "No man would refuse what that innocent little miss is offering so obviously and freely, and Darcy is certainly more hot-blooded than most men."

I sighed. "I've wrecked my chances with him, haven't I? If I hadn't been so stupidly moral and correct, he wouldn't have looked elsewhere."

"You can't change the person you are," Belinda said. "All that history of family honor instilled into you—you'd have felt wretched if you'd gone to bed with Darcy and then he'd still dumped you."

"I feel pretty wretched now," I said. "I know he's completely unsuitable, but I can't help the way I feel about him."

"Nobody can choose when and where to fall in love. It just happens. You see somebody and . . ." She stopped, looking across the room. Edward Fotheringay was surrounded by Fiona and her American cousins, who were giggling at his every word, and he was staring straight at Belinda.

"It's a little hot in here, don't you think?" she said casually, putting one hand up to the back of her neck in a remarkably suggestive gesture. "I think I might also stroll on the terrace." And she moved gracefully toward the French doors. After a minute or so Edward followed her. So that was how it was done. She made it seem so easy. If I tried it, I'd probably trip over the door frame or fall off the terrace.

I stood alone, observing the Prince of Wales now making a beeline for Mrs. Simpson, who was patting the arm of her chair as if he were a pet dog. The older men clustered around the brandy decanter and murmured something about playing billiards. The older women sat together on the sofa and gossiped among themselves.

"You're awfully pensive tonight." A voice at my elbow made me jump. Gussie smiled at me. "Penny for your thoughts?"

"I'm rather impoverished at the moment," I said. "I'll share them for half a crown."

He laughed. "So you drive a hard bargain."

"Sheer desperation, I assure you. It's hard to live in London with absolutely no funds."

"Yes, I suppose it must be."

It had just struck me that I had an ideal opportunity to pump him for information. "It must be lovely to be you and to be able to give all those jolly parties and live in that beautiful flat," I said.

I thought he gave just a momentary frown. "I don't know if I like the flat quite so much anymore. Not since old Tubby fell off my balcony. I still can't get over it. I keep wondering if there was anything I could have done to save him—apart from stronger railings, of course."

"I feel the same way," I said. "It was like watching a film, wasn't it? Not quite real."

"My feelings exactly. Almost in slow motion."

I nodded.

"I say," he said after a pause, "do you fancy a turn about the garden? It's a lovely night. Full moon and all that."

"Thank you," I said. "That would be lovely."

He took my arm and steered me out onto the terrace. I was conscious of Darcy and Hanni standing close together, only a few feet beyond the French doors. She was looking up at him adoringly. Inside, somebody had started playing the piano—"Clair de Lune." There was no sign of either Belinda or Edward.

"It's a lovely night, isn't it?" Gussie said. "Quite balmy, still."

"It's a beautiful night." I slipped my hand into Gussie's and directed him down the steps from the terrace. My heart was beating very fast. We were stepping into unknown territory here. I wasn't sure where flirting ended and seduction began. I turned to Gussie and gave him an encouraging little smile. "I was waiting for someone to take me for a stroll in the moonlight," I said. "It's very romantic, isn't it?"

"Well, I suppose it is. I didn't think you'd be interested, you know."

"Why?"

"Well, because, I mean to say, you're Binky's sister. But you're a grand girl, Georgie. Not at all bad looking either. In fact I can't think why some fellow hasn't snapped you up before now. You'd make a splendid wife. Good breeding. Reliable."

"You make me sound like a spaniel," I said. "Safe, reliable. How about warm and sexy?"

He laughed nervously. "Dash it all, Georgie, you are Binky's sister."

"I'm also a woman." I nearly laughed as I said it. What a stupid line.

"Yes, you are." He fell for it. He was looking at me in a strange, speculative way.

We were now alone on the dark, moonlit lawn. I could hear the fountain splashing and the distant tones of the music. I turned to face him.

"Well, aren't you going to kiss me?"

"I say. Rather."

He brought his lips toward mine. They were surprisingly cold and moist. A little like kissing a cod. When I had kissed Darcy, I wasn't conscious of lips or tongues or anything. Just that wonderful sensation of tingling, surging desire, melting into him. Now I was horribly conscious of everything Gussie was doing or trying to do: his large, flabby tongue, for one thing. And his hands, which were reaching down inside the back of my dress to unhook my brassiere. But I kept my eyes closed and pretended that I was in rapture, making little moans of pleasure from time to time.

This seemed to egg him on. His breathing became louder. He tried to reach under my arm and grab my breasts. Then he half dragged me to a nearby stone bench. We sank down together. One hand slid down the low neck of my dress and fondled my right breast as if he were testing a ripe orange. Then a hand started sliding up my skirt until it made its way between my legs.

By now I was a little alarmed, and confused. Just how far did I want this to go? Wouldn't now be a good time to stop? Gussie was panting like a steam engine and wrestling with my knickers. It suddenly came to me that I didn't want to lose my virginity to Gussie Gormsley. If I had resisted Darcy when I had wanted him with all my being, then it was surely rather hypocritical to give in so easily to someone I didn't want.

Gussie was now inching down my panties.

Other thoughts tumbled into my consciousness: it was rumored that one bled the first time. In fact bloody sheets were carried out of the bedchamber as proof that the deed had been done. What on earth would people think if I staggered back into the drawing room bloody and disheveled? My cousin the prince and Mrs. Simpson were sitting there. Word might even get back to Her Majesty.

Gussie was now fumbling to undo his belt. He reached into his trousers and produced something I couldn't quite see, but he took my hand and placed it upon the thing. I recoiled in horror. The thing was twitching with a life of its own. It reminded me of a newt we'd once kept as children.

"I'm sorry," I said, trying to draw away, "but I should go back inside. They'll wonder where I've got to."

Gussie was still panting. "You can't leave me like this, Georgie," he said, pushing up my skirt with frantic gestures. "You can't egg a chap on and then want to stop. I've got to have a bit of the old rumpy-pumpy, you know. Now do be a good girl and give it to me."

He pushed me back quite roughly until I was lying on the cold stone of the bench. I hadn't realized until then how strong he was or how far we were from the house. He started kissing me again, lying on me with his full weight. I couldn't help thinking of one of Belinda's favorite maxims: If rape is inevitable, lie back and enjoy it.

Suddenly that didn't seem so amusing anymore. I didn't want to be another Belinda. I didn't want to turn into my mother. I shook my mouth free of him. "I said no, Gussie." I tried to force him off me. He was having trouble lifting my skirt high enough. Thank heavens there was rather a lot of material in the skirt, and a couple of layers of underskirt too. I tried to bring up my knee, but he was very persistent.

"I said let go of me." I pushed, wriggled and turned at the same time and we both rolled off the bench onto the damp grass. I tried to get up. Gussie tried to pull me back down.

"What's going on here?" a man's voice demanded. "Some damned animal in the bushes. Go and get my gun!"

Gussie scrambled to his feet and took off without waiting for me. I stood up, and was brushing myself down when I realized that the voice belonged to Darcy.

"He took off like a greyhound out of the gate, wouldn't you say?" Darcy said in an amused voice.

"What are you doing here?" I demanded.

"Just stretching my legs. Nice night for a walk. More to the point, what were you doing?"

"None of your business."

"Don't tell me you were enjoying it."

"Again, it's none of your business what I do."

"It's just that a month or so ago you gave me a long lecture about not wanting to turn out like your mother and saving yourself for the right man and the right time. Please don't tell me that you find Gussie Gormsley more irresistibly attractive than me. If you do, I really shall go and get my gun and shoot myself."

"I wasn't intending to let Gussie . . ."

"I see. That was not how it appeared to the outside observer."

He started to walk beside me back to the house.

"Anyway, I can take perfectly good care of myself," I said. "You always seem to be showing up and acting as if you have come to rescue me. But you really don't need to."

"My pleasure, your ladyship."

"Please don't let me keep you another second from the enchanting Princess Hanni. Who knows, maybe you'll end up in a fairy-tale castle and have to learn the goose step."

He actually smiled at this. "It's hard to resist when a woman literally throws herself at one," he said.

"I'm sure it is. She's just out of the convent. She is determined to find out what she's been missing."

"I'll say." He smiled again.

"And no doubt you'll be delighted to show her."

"I'm only human, after all. We chaps find it hard to say no to a warm body."

"I believe she's still waiting for you." I started to walk ahead of him.

He caught up with me and grabbed my arm. For a moment I thought he was going to embrace me, but then he said, "You can't go inside like that."

"Like what?"

"Well, for one thing you have grass stains on your back, and for another, you have bits of underwear sticking out from your dress. Ah yes, I see. Your brassiere has mysteriously become unlatched. Allow me to—"

"Absolutely not," I said. "I'll manage."

"You can't go back in there with bits sticking out. Stand still." I shivered involuntarily at the touch of his warm hands on my back. "There. Reasonably respectable again." His hand lingered on my bare shoulder.

"Thank you." I started to move away from him.

"Georgie," he said quietly, his hand still on my shoulder. "When I disappeared from London—I had to go away in a hurry."

"Evading the law?" I asked.

"I had to go home to Ireland. I got word that my father was selling the estate to Americans. I rushed home to try and make him change his mind. I was too late. The deed was done."

"I'm awfully sorry."

"I suppose it was inevitable. He was strapped for cash. They made him an offer he couldn't refuse. And the only good thing is that they want to resurrect the racing stable. They're keeping my father on as trainer / adviser / general dog's body. He's going to live in the gatehouse." I saw him wince as if in pain. "Lucky he couldn't sell the title along with it, or I'd be plain Mr. O'Mara for the rest of my life."

"I really am sorry, Darcy," I said.

"Well, there's nothing I can do, but now I really am homeless. I'm certainly not going to stay at the gatehouse and watch some millionaire from Texas living in my family home."

"Darcy, where did you go?" Hanni's voice floated toward us.

"Your lady love is waiting," I said as Hanni appeared from the darkness.

"Georgie—that woman you saw me with at the Savoy—"

"You really don't have to explain your women friends to me, Darcy." For some reason I felt that I might cry. I only wanted to escape to the safety of my own room.

"She wasn't a woman friend. She was my sister, Bridget. She felt the same way I did about losing the house. We were commiserating together."

Before I could say anything, Hanni spotted Darcy and came running toward us. "Darcy, where did you go? I lost you," she complained.

"Just doing a good deed," Darcy said. "I was a boy scout, you know. My lady." He gave a slight bow and then turned back to Hanni, and allowed himself to be led away by the hand, leaving me alone in the moonlight.

I TRIED TO slip back into the drawing room without anybody noticing. I had no idea if Gussie had returned before me, and in what state he had been. I expected all eyes to be on me, but the scene in the room was exactly as I had left it: the prince sitting obediently on the arm of Mrs. Simpson's chair, looking down at her as if she were the only woman in the room; the other women still chattering, heads together. I heard one of them say, "That can't possibly be true. Where did you hear that?"

"Anyone feel like a game of billiards?" Lord Cromer-Strode asked. "Colonel? What about Edward? Where has the damned boy got to now?"

Fiona was staring at the French doors, stony-faced. "He's taking a walk. It is rather hot in here," she said.

"How about whist?" Lady Cromer-Strode sensed tension in the atmosphere. "Anybody for whist, bridge if you'd rather, or what about pontoon?"

While tables were being set up, I took the opportunity to creep up to my room. Once there I stood staring out of the open window into the night, trying to come to terms with what had just happened. How could I have been so stupid to have encouraged Gussie? And why did Darcy take the trouble to explain his actions to me, only to run off after Hanni again? Nothing about men made sense. Why had we wasted time at school on deportment and French and piano when what they should have done was to give us lessons on understanding male behavior. Perhaps it was beyond comprehension.

A woman's laugh floated across the lawns, setting my imagination running riot again. How long did the queen expect me to stay here? I wondered. Could I now conclude that Hanni was well settled and flee back to London? At this moment I longed to be sitting in my grandfather's little kitchen while he made me a cup of tea so strong that the spoon almost stood up in it.

"Forget the lot of 'em, my love," he'd say. "They ain't worth tuppence."

"My lady, I am so sorry," said a voice behind me. I leaped a mile. It was Mildred of course. I had completely forgotten about her again. What was it about her that made her so unmemorable? Maybe that I was wishing she didn't exist? Now she came scuttling into the room, looking flustered and embarrassed. "I had no idea that you would wish to retire so early, my lady," she twittered. "I thought the young folk were still downstairs. I gathered there was a gramophone and dancing, so naturally I assumed—"

"It's quite all right, Mildred," I said. "I can't expect you to stand to attention waiting for me at all hours."

"Oh, but you can, my lady, and you should. What use is a lady's maid if she is not available and ready for service at all times? I was having a nice chat with Lady Cromer-Strode's personal maid. We knew so many people in common, you see, and then a footman came into the servants' hall and said that he'd seen you going upstairs. My heart nearly stopped, my lady." She put her hand to her chest in impressive fashion. "I ran upstairs as fast as my legs could carry me. Please say you'll forgive me."

"I do forgive you, Mildred. Now if you like, you can go back to the servants' hall and your nice little chat."

"Are you not feeling well, my lady? May I have some hot milk sent up? Some hot Bovril? Some iced lemonade?"

"I am perfectly well, thank you. Just tired, and I wish to be alone."

"Then let me help you out of your garments and you'll be ready for bed."

"No—thank you." I blurted out the words more fiercely than I intended, remembering the unhooked brassiere and those grass stains. Mildred wouldn't comment. Maids didn't, but she'd notice and she'd gossip. "I'd rather be alone tonight, thank you, Mildred. Please leave me."

It was the closest to my great-grandmother, Empress of all she surveyed, that I had ever come. It produced an immediate effect. Mildred actually curtsied and backed out of the room. Most satisfying, in fact the one satisfying thing in a long and annoying day. I undressed, feeling hot with shame as I wrestled off the remains of my brassiere and noted my crumpled dress. What would Mildred think?

I lay in bed, feeling very alone and empty. Darcy was now with another woman. He had come to my aid, but only because he pitied me. I lay for a long time, watching the moonlight stream in through the long windows. It shone full onto a painting on the far wall. It was a painting of the Alps and reminded me of my happy schooldays in Switzerland. What's more, I recognized the mountains. "Jungfrau, Mönch, Eiger," I murmured to myself and felt comforted having a familiar sight looking down on me. Then something nagged at my brain. I heard Hanni's voice saying something about her beloved Bavarian mountains. "The Zugspitze and the Jungfrau," she had said. But the Jungfrau was in Switzerland.

Chapter 28

I woke with early morning sun streaming in through my window and a dawn chorus of birds that was almost deafening. A cool, fresh breeze was blowing in through my open windows. I no longer felt sleepy so I got up. It would be hours before breakfast was served and even an hour or so before I could expect Mildred with the tea tray. I decided to go for a walk. I tiptoed down the main staircase and let myself out through the front door without encountering anybody. The lawns were heavy with dew. The rosebushes were strung with spiderwebs on which the dewdrops glistened like diamonds. A low strand of mist hung over the ornamental pond. As I started walking I began to feel better. I had been cooped up in London for too long. I was a country girl at heart. My ancestors had tramped those Scottish Highlands. I strode out, arms swinging, and started to hum a tune. Soon this whole Hanni business would be just a bad dream. She'd be back in Germany, breaking a succession of hearts. I would be back at Rannoch House. I might even go home to Scotland until I was summoned to Balmoral. I'd ride my horse every day, avoid Fig and visit Nanny.

I had crossed the lawn and moved into the shade of a stand of trees. Suddenly I froze. Someone was moving through the rhododendron bushes. My mind went instantly to his lordship's antics but surely even someone as lusty as he couldn't be at it at six in the morning. Then I caught a glimpse of a figure all in black. So at least he or she was fully clothed, whoever it was. That should have been a relief, but the way that figure was skulking immediately made me suspicious. A poacher, maybe? Perhaps it would be wise to reveal my presence and thus not startle the person.

I coughed loudly. The effect was instant. The figure spun around and I was amazed to see that it was Irmgardt, Hanni's maid.

"Irmgardt, what on earth are you doing?" I asked, before I remembered that she spoke no English.

"Die Prinzessin," she said, *"macht Spaziergang."*

This much German I could understand. So the princess was out walking early.

"Where is she?" I asked. *"Wo?"*

Before she could answer there was a tramping through the bracken and Hanni appeared, looking red cheeked and ridiculously healthy.

"Oh, Georgie, you are awake too. It is lovely day, is it not? The birds made so much noise that I could not sleep, so I go for walk. At home we walk much, up mountains. Here there are no mountains," she added regretfully then glanced at Irmgardt, who was still following us. "But my maid does not allow me to go alone. Go back, Irmgardt. I do not need you." She repeated this in German, shooing her away like a duck or a chicken. Irmgardt retreated reluctantly. "Old broad make her follow me," Hanni muttered to me. "She does not trust me to go out alone no more. Now I've got two pain in necks."

At that moment we heard the thud of hoofbeats and Edward Fotheringay came riding toward us on a fine bay.

"Morning, ladies," he called, reining in his mount. "Lovely day, isn't it? I've just been for a good gallop. Old Cromer-Strode keeps a fine stable. Where are you two off to?"

"We both woke early and are taking a stroll," I said.

"Why don't you come for a ride with me?" Edward said. "I'll go and see about some mounts while you go and change."

Actually I was dying to get on a horse again but Hanni said, "I do not like to ride horses. I do not like my clothes to smell of horse sweat. But I would like to go for a ride in your new car, like the American girls. That would be real swell. I never went out alone in a motorcar with a man."

"Oh, right-o," Edward said. "Always happy to put my new machine through its paces for a pretty girl. Give me a few minutes to take the horse back and change my clothes and then we'll be off."

He urged his horse to a canter, leaving us to walk back to the house together.

"Your baroness is not going to be happy about this, Hanni," I said. "She won't allow you to go out unchaperoned in a young man's car."

"I do not care what she thinks or says." Hanni tossed her head defiantly. "She is here as my companion, not as my mother. Besides, I do not wish to be with the baroness. She is in bad mood."

"Why is that?"

"She says she is treated like servant here. Her rank is higher than theirs but they make her stand at back of line and they seat her with not important people like a bad married priest."

"I expect they didn't realize who she is," I said. "They probably think of her as just your companion."

"She says I must tell them and demand that she is treated with respect," Hanni said. "But I do not wish to do this. It is rude, don't you think? It is not my fault that she is old and ugly."

"Hanni, you really mustn't talk like that, even when we are alone. You are a royal person. Whatever you say will be made public, you know."

"I know you won't tell anyone because you're my pal."

"But I really can't let you go out alone with a young man," I said.

"You can come with us. You can watch me."

Did I really want to watch Hanni and Edward making cow eyes at each other, and more to the point, would they want me sitting there in the back-seat watching them? But then a thought struck me. I was supposed to be doing a spot of sleuthing. In fact it was rather important that I begin sleuthing as soon as possible. Sometime within the next week there would be an inquest into the death of Sidney Roberts. Our involvement in that death would be made public. A royal scandal would ensue, Germany would react with horror, diplomatic messages would fly across the Channel and if we were really unlucky, a new world war would break out. I couldn't turn down such a perfect opportunity to question Edward, away from the bustle of Dippings.

"All right," I agreed, "I'll come along and play gooseberry."

"Play gooseberry?"

"Another silly English term," I said.

"English is very silly language," Hanni said.

I had to agree with her.

※

EDWARD DIDN'T SEEM to mind too much that I was being brought along. "The more the merrier," he said. "So where do you want to go? Anywhere in particular? We could make a day of it."

A brilliant idea came to me. Cambridge—it seemed to be the one link between Edward and Gussie and Sidney Roberts. I couldn't see how I'd find any clues there—no dropped note in the cloisters saying, *Meet me by the river. Drug shipment due at dawn,* but it would be interesting to observe Edward in his old habitat.

"I think the princess might enjoy seeing Cambridge," I suggested. "If it's not too far to drive."

"Not at all. Always glad to show off the old college," Edward said, smiling at Hanni.

We made our getaway from Dippings before the general populace had stirred. The butler kindly arranged for some tea and toast so that we didn't depart on an empty stomach, and the cook hastily made a hamper for the journey. It was all very civilized and a jolly day seemed to be ahead of us— if one didn't count poor Sidney Roberts. Hanni seemed to have completely forgotten about him. He hadn't come up once in conversation. Nor did she seem to have any worries about an upcoming inquest and the public attention that it would generate. Perhaps she wanted to be in the spotlight. It certainly went with her personality. She sat in the front seat of Edward's natty little sports car, occasionally glancing up at him with obvious delight that she was finally (almost) alone in a car with a boy.

"I bet your baroness wasn't too pleased about this." Edward turned to her with a wicked grin.

"I did not wake her," Hanni said. "She does not like to be awoken too early. Irmgardt will tell her where I have gone."

"You'll probably be sent straight back to the convent when you get home," Edward teased.

"I have proper English lady, relative of king, in the backseat," Hanni said. "She will make sure you behave well."

"Ah, but what about you?" Again Edward's grin was flirtatious. "Can she succeed in keeping tabs on you? Not an easy task, I fear." He glanced back at me and winked.

I smiled back. "I'm really looking forward to seeing Cambridge," I said. "I've never been there."

"Never seen Cambridge? Then you haven't lived. It's quite the most beautiful city in England. Far superior to Oxford, of course, which is nothing but a bustling country town."

"I detect prejudice."

He laughed. He had a most appealing laugh. I could see why the girls were drawn to him. I was a little drawn myself, but since I was clearly fourth in line after Fiona, Belinda and Hanni, not to mention my mother, there was no point in pursuing this. I wondered about Edward and Fiona. Did he know he was engaged to her, or was it one of those things that families arrange on the birth of their children? I could see the way he was looking at Hanni, and I had also seen him follow Belinda into the garden last night. Men who followed Belinda had only one thing on their minds.

The fifty-mile drive through leafy byways was delightful. Dappled sunlight, the cooing of pigeons, the sound of a cuckoo and the wind in my hair in the backseat of the open car. Hanni and Edward chatted from time to time but as we gathered speed I couldn't join in their conversation from the backseat, which gave me time to think. What had Sidney Roberts been doing at that party? He was clearly out of place, from the point of view of both class and views. Dedicated communists surely do not habitually frequent parties at which the sons and daughters of the decadent upper crust indulge in cocktails and cocaine—not unless he had come to convert us, which he didn't seem to be doing. Instead he seemed remote and ill at ease, lurking on the balcony.

I replayed that balcony scene in my mind, but Sidney had given no indication of why he was there—unless, like many of the lower classes, he was flattered to have been invited. Or, like Darcy, he simply wanted some good food and drink. But he didn't seem the type.

I remembered that Gussie had seemed surprised to see him at the party. He'd asked Edward what Roberts was doing there and Edward had implied that he had to invite him and he was a good enough chap in his way. What did he mean by "had to" invite him? Were they somehow beholden to him? Another suspicion came into my mind. Was Sidney the one who supplied their drugs? Was the earnest communist character merely a façade?

"So you were at Trinity College, were you, Edward?" I leaned forward from my backseat.

"That's right. Good old Trinity. One of the younger colleges, I'm afraid. Founded by Henry the Eighth. Those American girls yesterday laughed themselves silly when they heard that something founded in fifteen hundred and something was considered young. But it's definitely one of the loveliest colleges. I'm going to give you a tour and you'll have to agree."

We were entering the city of Cambridge. The view as we crossed the Cam and saw those golden stone buildings across spacious lawns almost took the breath away. On the river itself was a merry scene with students punting and sitting on the lawns, enjoying the sunshine. The occasional student cycled past, books under his arm and black gown flapping out behind him in the wind. A pair of female students, deep in heated discussion, strolled under the trees. I looked at them with interest, as one examines a new species in the zoo. I hadn't really considered that women would also attend the university and felt a pang of regret that I would never have that kind of opportunity.

We abandoned the car under the shade of a huge chestnut tree and started to walk. The glorious sound of boys' voices floated out from King's College Chapel, where it must have been time for matins. Edward played at dutiful tour guide, identifying each building that we passed until we came to an impressive arched gateway in a high wall.

"You see," he said, ushering us through the arch. "Quite the loveliest, don't you think?"

I followed them through the gate and into a vast courtyard bordered by richly carved yellow stone buildings. A lush green lawn covered most of the area and in the middle was an ornate roofed fountain.

"This is the great court, the largest of any at Oxford or Cambridge," Edward said. "They say the students used to wash in that fountain before there were proper bathrooms and of course this is the site of the famous great court run. The object is to run around the perimeter of the court before the clock finishes chiming noon. It's only been done a couple of times, I understand. Come on. Follow me."

I fancied I could still hear those sublime voices from King's College, until I realized that Trinity possessed a similar chapel, with its own choir. Sweet notes hung in the air. I almost began to believe that angels inhabited Cambridge.

"It's so peaceful here," I said as we crossed the court.

Edward laughed. "They're all holed up studying for final exams," he said. "You should see it on a normal Saturday night." He opened a door for us to step into the darkness of a building. "This is the hall, where we take our meals," he said, indicating a dark-paneled, high-ceilinged room to our left. "I probably shouldn't take you inside. The chaps wouldn't take kindly to visitors during exam time. And through here is another court, and you have to see the Wren library."

"Sir Christopher Wren?" I asked.

"The very same."

Just as we were about to leave the building a young man in a far more impressive gown than I had seen so far came sweeping in through the door. He went to pass us with a cursory nod then stopped. "I say, I know you, don't I?" he said to Edward. "Fotheringay, wasn't it? You were an apostle, if I'm not mistaken."

"And you are Saunders," Edward said. "So you've become a fellow, have you?"

"For my sins. Too lazy to move out, I suppose, and the food's good. What have you been doing with yourself?"

"Been abroad mostly," Edward said.

"Have you, by Jove. Good for you." He gave Edward a strange look that I couldn't quite interpret. "Wish I weren't so dashed lazy. Where did you go?"

"Oh, here and there. All over the place." Edward shifted from one foot to the other, clearly uncomfortable in the other man's presence.

"And who are these delectable creatures?" the gowned man asked, suddenly turning to us.

"Guests at a house party in Norfolk," Edward said. "Lady Georgiana Rannoch and Princess Hannelore of Bavaria."

The other man threw back his head and laughed. "Good one, Fotheringay."

Obviously he thought his leg was being pulled. But Edward did not attempt to assure him. "Well, we'd better be getting along," he said. "Good seeing you, Saunders."

"You'll probably run into a few other angels if you keep your eyes open," Saunders said, then nodded to us and went on his way.

We stepped out into bright sunlight and continued across a second court, not as large as the first, but just as charming.

"What are apostles?" I asked.

"Oh, just some undergraduate club we belonged to," Edward said carelessly.

"Was Gussie a member too?"

"Gussie? Good Lord, no." He laughed. "Not Gussie's cup of tea at all."

"How about Sidney Roberts?"

"Sidney Roberts?" He sounded surprised. "He may have been. Can't really remember. He was an unremarkable kind of chap, poor devil. Now that's the Wren library over here."

He strode out ahead of us to a truly beautiful building with delicate columns and large arched windows, then opened the door for us to step inside. That distinctive smell of old books, furniture polish and pipe tobacco permeated the air. It reminded me of some other place. I tried to identify the room at Castle Rannoch before I remembered the bookshop. Which gave me an idea. I waited until Edward led us upstairs, then I turned back and slipped into the library proper. An elderly man sitting at a desk looked up in horror as I came in.

"Young lady, what are you doing here?" he hissed at me, sotto voce. "Visitors are not permitted during finals week."

"I'm so sorry," I said, "but we were being shown around and I do so love old books that I had to get a glimpse of the place for myself."

His expression softened. "You are fond of old books then?"

"Passionately," I said. "I collect them."

"Most unusual for a young lady."

"I often visit a wonderful old bookshop in London. It's called Haslett's, in the East End, down by the river. Do you know it?"

He nodded. "A most eclectic collection. Have you made any major finds there?"

"One or two." I looked directly at him. "By the way, who are the apostles?"

"I take it you don't mean Matthew, Mark, Luke and John?"

"I heard some undergraduates discussing them."

"It's a sort of secret society, one gathers. Highly socialist in its leanings— rights for the workers and down with the old order. All that kind of bosh. Did you hear about them at the bookshop?"

"No, I overheard a couple of chaps saying something just now. And angels?"

"Ex-members become angels, so I'm told. I think it's all perfectly harmless. Young men become so passionate, don't they? Then they settle down, get married and turn out to be perfectly normal." He chuckled. "I would love to show you some of our rarest editions, but as I said, no visitors are allowed during finals week, so I regret . . ."

"That's quite all right. Thank you for your time," I replied and made a hurried exit.

"We thought we'd lost you," Edward said as I caught them coming down the stairs.

"Sorry, I was daydreaming and wandered off in the wrong direction." I gave him a winning smile. So Edward and Sidney Roberts had both been members of the same secret society—a society with strong leftist leanings. But how could that be significant?

Chapter 29

Clouds were gathering in the western sky as we drove home. The air had become muggy, with annoying little midges flying around and the promise of a thunderstorm brewing. Hanni dozed in the front seat beside Edward. I stared speculatively at the back of his well-cut hair. Edward Fotheringay, alias Lunghi Fungy, enigma. He studied modern languages yet chose to go to India, where he drifted around, not doing much of anything apart from a spot of disorganized climbing, from what one gathered. He had been a member of a secret society with socialist leanings and yet he dressed expensively and enjoyed a life of luxury. He was supposedly engaged to one girl but openly and shamelessly flirted with others. God knows what he did with Belinda—and I'd almost forgotten his involvement with my mother!

"So Edward," I said, leaning forward in my seat, "which modern languages did you study?"

"German and Russian."

"Interesting. Why those?"

"I'm a lazy bugger, actually. My mother was of Russian ancestry so I didn't have to work too hard."

"What did Gussie study?"

"Classics, stupid idiot. I mean to say, what use are classics? He had a hard time of it too. He wouldn't have got through Greek if that swat Roberts hadn't coached him and done his translations for him."

I gave a merry laugh. "So that's why he was beholden to Sidney Roberts. I wondered why he was invited to your party."

Did I detect a certain stiffening in his demeanor?

"And what made you go to India?" I went on, chatting away merrily. "Did you have some family connection there too?"

"Grandfather had been there in the police force in the Punjab, but that wasn't the reason. I just had the desire to travel and India is an easy place to move around if one is English. Those nice free bungalows to stay at, and dinners at the officers' mess and dances."

"It sounds like a fascinating place," I said.

"Oh, rather. Elephants and tigers and things. And primitive customs—burning their dead on the steps of the Ganges. Disgusting habit."

"So what will you do now, do you think?"

"Haven't decided yet."

"I understand that marriage is on the horizon, or so Fiona says."

"Fiona would." He glanced down at Hanni, who was now blissfully asleep. "It's one of those dashed annoying things—both sets of parents decided it would be a good idea when we were infants. Oh, don't get me wrong. Fiona's a nice enough girl, but . . ." He let the end of the sentence die away.

"She will inherit Dippings one day," I pointed out.

"That's true. And there's no shortage of cash there. Sorely tempting, but unfortunately not my cup of tea."

The first fat raindrops pattered onto the car.

"Blast and damn," Edward muttered. "Now we're going to get wet. I took off the hood. I'll just have to put my foot down and make a run for it."

The engine roared as the motor car positively flew down the lane, wheels screeching at each corner. For a while it was exhilarating, but suddenly I became scared. He was driving so fast that he'd have no chance if we met a vehicle like a hay cart coming in the other direction. I was flung from side to side as he took the sharp bends. And I caught a glimpse of his face. It was alight with a strange, fierce exhilaration.

The storm broke in earnest when we were about ten miles from our destination. Thunder rumbled overhead. We were soaked through by the time we pulled up in front of Dippings. Servants rushed out with big umbrellas. There was a flash followed by a great clap of thunder as we went up the steps. Lady Cromer-Strode came out of the long gallery to greet us. "We were just finishing tea," she said. "Oh, you poor dears, just look at you! You're soaked. I'll have the servants run baths for you immediately or you'll come down with a chill. Edward what on earth were you doing driving with the top down in such weather?" Then her gaze fell to Hanni and her expression changed. "Your Highness," she said, "I am so sorry. We had no idea how to contact you, you see, or we'd have brought you back at once. Such a tragedy."

"What is such a tragedy?" I asked.

"Her Highness's companion, the baroness. I'm afraid she's dead."

"Dead?" Hanni's voice trembled. "You tell me that Baroness Rottenmeister is dead? Was there an accident?"

"No, my dear. It was natural causes. The doctor says it was a heart attack, sometime this morning. It was after the maid brought in her morning tea. She was of advancing years, wasn't she?"

"But—but I had no idea." Hanni's bottom lip trembled like a child's. "And I was rude to her last night. I quarreled with her. Maybe I made her upset and this caused the heart attack."

I put an arm around Hanni's shoulder. "I'm sure it was nothing you did, Hanni. People have little arguments all the time."

"Yes, but now she has died and I can't ask her to forgive me. I shall go to hell." Hanni was trying hard not to cry.

"Come on," I said, my arm still around her shoulders. "We need to get you out of these wet clothes. Irmgardt will run you a nice hot bath and perhaps Lady Cromer-Strode will be good enough to have some hot chocolate sent up to your room. Then you can have a good rest."

"I do not wish to rest. I should have dreams. Old broad will come back to haunt me," she said.

I tried not to smile as I led her upstairs.

"Georgie, what will happen now?" she asked. "They will want me to come home immediately."

Oh, good Lord. I hadn't thought of that complication. Of course her parents wouldn't want her to stay on with no chaperon. I remembered that the queen was nearby at Sandringham House.

"I will visit Her Majesty," I said.

"Must we do this today?"

"I'm afraid we must. Her Majesty would want to know about it and she'll certainly need to contact your parents."

"Then I will come with you. I will talk to them myself."

"Oh no, I think it would be wiser if you stayed here. They would not wish to discuss your future in front of you."

"You treat me as if I was a pet dog." Hanni pouted. "I do not wish to go home." She sneezed suddenly.

"Your parents will be even more angry if you catch a chill."

I opened Hanni's bedroom door and firmly escorted her inside. Irmgardt was sitting mending in the window. She jumped up with a look of horror on her face when she saw the princess. "Hot bath, Irmgardt," I said. "*Heiss Bad.* Right away."

She scuttled out of the room, while I helped Hanni out of her wet things and put her into her bathrobe as if she were a small child. She gave me a watery smile. "You are kind person, Georgie." She was looking at me almost as if she felt sorry for me. She probably was sorry for me—the hopeless old maid at twenty-one!

"So did you know that the baroness had a weak heart?" I asked her.

She shook her head. "She always seems so healthy. She takes long walks. She has good appetite."

That was certainly true. It did cross my mind that too much rich food at Dippings, after rather lean offerings at Rannoch House, might have contributed to her demise. I was glad that her death had been ruled a heart attack. Because if it hadn't, it would have been the third suspicious death in a week.

Chapter 30

Mildred fussed over me when she saw the state I was in. By now I was feeling miserable and a little shaken and didn't mind being fussed over. Neither did I mind being tucked up in bed with a glass of hot chocolate and some nice biscuits. Mildred had instructed me to stay there until she came to dress me for dinner, but after half an hour I was restored and ready to tackle my next unpleasant task. I asked the butler to make a telephone call on my behalf to Sandringham. He did so and I was summoned to the royal presence right away. Lady Cromer-Strode was happy to provide a car, luckily with a roof on it, as it was still coming down in buckets. The drive was only ten miles but it seemed like an eternity as I rehearsed what I was going to tell the queen. Of course it wasn't my fault that the baroness had died, but I rather felt that she might see it that way. Too many unfortunate things had happened to the princess since she had been entrusted to my care.

Even under rainy skies the ornamental gardens of Sandringham at the height of summer are incredibly beautiful. The beds, laid out in their formal designs, were absolutely perfect. Not a bloom was out of place. The house was less perfect, in my opinion. It was one of those sprawling Victorian country homes that are a horrible mixture of styles, bits jutting out here and there, towers, turrets, cupolas, and a mixture of red brick, gray stone, white and brown decorative trim and seaside boardinghouse windows. But I knew that the king was particularly fond of the place, and that was all that mattered.

A footman bearing a large black umbrella whisked me inside. I was led through to a small sitting room and announced. I found the royal couple behaving like any other household on a Sunday afternoon. The king had his stamp collection spread out in front of him on a small table. The queen was in the middle of writing letters. She looked up and extended her hand to me.

"Georgiana, what a pleasant surprise," she said. "I'm afraid you're a little late for tea. Do sit down." I attempted the usual kiss and curtsy with the usual clumsy nose-bumping results.

"I'm just replying to a letter from my granddaughter Elizabeth. Her penmanship is very pleasing for her age, don't you think?" She held up a letter for me, written on lined paper in a neat, round childish hand.

"And what brings you here, my dear?" the king asked. "Surely not just to keep a couple of old fogies company?"

"I am so sorry to disturb you, ma'am, sir," I said, "but I felt I should let you know right away. A rather unfortunate thing has happened." And I related the news about the baroness.

"Good gracious. This is unfortunate," the queen replied, glancing across at her husband. "A heart attack, you say? I suppose they are sure of that?"

I stared at her in surprise. "What do you mean, ma'am?"

"It did just cross my mind that she might have taken her own life, out of guilt for letting the young person under her protection become involved in a murder investigation. These foreigners are known to have an exaggerated sense of duty."

"Oh, I don't think so, ma'am," I said hastily. "The baroness did not strike me as that kind of person. She thought a lot of herself, for one thing, and also she was a Catholic. Don't they consider suicide a mortal sin?"

"We all do," the queen said. "But in certain cases it is understandable. We must notify the girl's parents immediately. We haven't yet received a reply to the letter we wrote a few days ago. We could perhaps use the telephone, of course. Do you think a telephone call would be the right thing to do, my dear?"

The king frowned then shook his head. "It's not as if it's a national emergency, is it? Never did like telephones. Damned annoying things. All the shrill ringing and then you can't hear a blasted thing that's being said on the other end and you end up shouting. No, I think a letter should suffice, May."

"Then I will compose one immediately."

"And what should happen to Princess Hanni, ma'am? She probably shouldn't be sent home before the inquest, should she?"

The queen frowned. "No, that wouldn't be the right thing to do. And as to that, have you made any progress?"

"I have learned a few interesting facts, ma'am, but I wouldn't call it progress yet. I shall begin my investigation in earnest tomorrow."

"What are you having the girl do now, May?" The king looked up from his stamps.

"Just keep her eyes and ears open. We are trying to avoid any embarrassment, you know, and Georgiana has a good head on her shoulders."

The king snorted. "If we lived in a different sort of country, you'd be head of the secret police."

"What rubbish. I merely find our own solidly loyal police force a little on the plodding side, that's all. I don't see that asking Georgiana to assist them in their investigation is so wrong."

"They'll certainly think it is. Leave the investigating to professionals and let the young girl enjoy herself the way young girls are supposed to."

"If you think so, my dear." The queen gave me a knowing look that indicated I was to take no notice of the king.

"So what should be done with the princess?" I asked.

"We could bring her here, of course," the queen said, "although it's remarkably dull for a young person and I don't think I could prevail upon my son to entertain her. He's being extremely perverse these days."

"These days. He's been perverse since he was born," the king muttered.

"He was at Dippings last night, I take it?"

"Yes, ma'am."

"I thought so. And he had a chance to talk to the princess?"

"I don't think he noticed her, ma'am, even though he was seated at dinner opposite her."

"I take it the American woman was there."

"She was."

"With husband?"

"Minus husband this time. On business in America, so we are told."

"You see, it is becoming serious, just as I told you." The queen glanced over at her husband, then turned back to me. "And do you think my son is still smitten with her?"

"Like a puppy dog, rushing to her beck and call," I replied. "She bosses him around shamelessly. She even calls him by his first name in public."

The queen sighed. "Dear me. How utterly vexing. I had such hopes that the Prince of Wales might behave like any normal healthy male and show interest in such a charming young thing as Princess Hannelore. Tell me, Georgiana, is the princess happy at Dippings?"

"Very. There are lots of young people and she is having a good time."

"Then let us leave her safely where she is until we receive word from Germany. We'll give my little scheme one last chance before she has to go home."

I thought of Lord Cromer-Strode and his rolls in the hay and his pinching of bottoms and wondered just how safe Hanni would be. But I couldn't find a way to express this particular fear to someone as starchy as my austere relatives. Besides, the queen was still talking and one does not interrupt. "The Cromer-Strodes will be motoring up to London for our garden party on Wednesday so I will request that they bring Hannelore with them. She'll enjoy that. And Lady Cromer-Strode is a good sort. She'll make sure the girl is well looked after. Which will leave you free to pursue other things." And again she gave me that knowing, frank stare.

ON THE WAY back to Dippings I wondered if I should catch a train to London that night. I certainly had no wish to face Gussie or Darcy again, if they were still there. Actually I didn't want to endure another jolly evening in company. Then I realized that, of course, it would not be a jolly evening. There had been a death in the house, so presumably no dancing, cards or gramophone would be allowed. Oh, golly, would one be expected to wear black? I had only brought light colors with me. But then I suspected that was true of all the guests. It was midsummer, after all, and the only person wearing black had been the now deceased baroness.

The rain looked as if it might be easing up as we drove through Little Dippings. There was a definite brightening to the western sky, as if the setting sun were trying to break through.

"Do the trains run on Sunday evenings?" I asked the chauffeur.

"Oh no, your ladyship," he replied. "No trains at all on a Sunday from Dippings Halt. Tomorrow morning at eight is the first one."

So I was trapped whether I liked it or not. I shifted uneasily on the leather seat of the Rolls. I had felt as if I had been walking on eggshells ever since Hanni arrived, and now I felt that I might snap like an overwound watch spring any moment. I suppose the news of the baroness's death had been a final straw. Three deaths in one week—my grandfather would say that was too much of a coincidence. And yet the baroness's death had been ruled a heart attack—I presumed by a competent doctor. And anyway, who would want the baroness dead, apart from Hanni?

I almost smiled as I remembered Hanni's gangster talk of "taking out the old broad," then remembered how distraught she had been on receiving the news. She had found the baroness annoying, that much was obvious, but that didn't mean she wished her dead. And besides, she had been in a car with me when the baroness had died. Of course Irmgardt had still been in the house. . . . Ridiculous, I said to myself as we swung through the gates into Dippings.

The butler himself came out with a large umbrella to meet me.

"You are just in time for supper, my lady," he said. "Lady Cromer-Strode thought just a simple meal, given the distressing circumstances."

"The baroness's death, you mean?"

"Precisely, my lady."

"Very sad," I said. "I understand she was dead when the maid took her tea in this morning?"

"Oh no, my lady. She was alive and well when the maid delivered her morning tea."

"That would be Irmgardt, the princess's maid?"

"No, my lady. It was your own lady's maid, Mildred, who kindly volunteered to take up her tea, seeing that you had already left for the day. It was when the baroness did not appear for breakfast that our parlor maid, Mary Ann, went to summon her and found her dead. The poor child has been quite distraught all day. A very sensitive little thing."

"I take it a doctor was called?"

"Oh, indeed. Her ladyship's own physician, Doctor Harrison. But he was too late to do anything, of course. He said it was a massive heart attack and there was nothing anybody could have done, even if they had been with her. Very sad for the princess, to have lost her companion."

"Very sad indeed," I agreed as we stepped into the entrance hall and heard the sound of voices coming from the dining room. Among them I detected Hanni's light chatter. She sounded as if she'd recovered from her shock quite well. "Are we changing tonight for dinner, do you know?" I asked.

"Only if you have brought a more somber color with you, my lady."

I didn't think I had but I went up to my room to see what miracle Mildred could produce. Knowing her she had probably managed to dye one of my outfits black in time to wear. Then I froze, halfway up the stairs. Mildred! I had forgotten all about her. What on earth was I going to do with her if I went back to London? I couldn't bring her to an empty London house from which the cook and butler had mysteriously disappeared. Suddenly she felt like yet another millstone around my neck. Why on earth had I hired her in the first place? Trying to do the right thing, as usual. I wished I had been born more like my mother, whose one thought in life was to please herself and the rest of the world be damned.

She wasn't in my bedroom when I went in, but the butler must have alerted her because she came flying in breathlessly a minute after me.

"I'm sorry, my lady. I didn't know when you'd be returning or whether Their Majesties would ask you to dine with them."

"It was just a brief visit to inform them of the baroness's death," I said. "I understand that you were the last person to see her alive."

"I was, my lady. And I feel terrible now. Perhaps there was something I should have noticed, something I should have done."

"The doctor said it was a massive heart attack and nobody could have done anything," I said, "so please don't distress yourself."

"She was snoring, you see. I tapped her quietly and told her that her tea tray was on the bedside table. She muttered something in German, but I don't speak the language so I have no idea what she said, and given her temperament, I thought it wise not to startle her, so I tiptoed out again."

I nodded.

"But now I'm asking myself whether she was trying to tell me that she felt unwell or I should fetch a doctor, and of course I didn't understand."

"She was probably telling you to go away and let her sleep," I said. "There was nothing you could have done, Mildred. Honestly."

"You're too kind, my lady." She managed a watery smile. "I think maybe the blue dress for dinner, as it is the plainest."

"Mildred," I said carefully, as she took the dress from the wardrobe, "I'm going up to London in the morning. If my business takes too long I may have to stay overnight at Rannoch House, but there is no need for you to accompany me. I'll inform Lady Cromer-Strode that you'll be staying on here, awaiting my return."

"Very good, my lady," she said and gave a secret smirk. Obviously she was having a good time and being well fed at Dippings.

Chapter 31

Diary,

Two days in a row that I've been up at crack of dawn. I hope it isn't
   becoming a habit. Luckily rain has stopped. Looks like lovely fine
   day. Unfortunately I won't be enjoying it. I have places to go and
   people to see. I wish the queen didn't have such faith in me. I haven't
   a clue what I'm supposed to do!

I had the chauffeur drive me to Little Dippings Halt, the nearest railway
station, to catch the eight o'clock train to London. Then I had to change
twice before I caught the express from Peterborough to King's Cross. Frankly
it was a blessed relief to be away from people and it gave me time to do some
serious thinking. I went through the various events—Tubby tumbling from
the balcony, Hanni standing in front of Sidney Roberts's body with a bloody
knife in her hand and now this news that the baroness had died of a heart
attack. The three tragedies seemed completely unrelated—an accident, a
brutal, daring murder and a death by natural causes. Maybe they were just
that but three deaths within a week were a little over the norm, even for the
most violent of societies. And they had all happened since Hanni came into
my life.

   Which made me wonder whether the incidents were somehow actually
directed at her: was there some kind of plot against her? I knew her father

was no longer a reigning monarch, but he was no longer in favor with that funny little man Hitler, who seemed to be the rising star in German politics. And there was a move to restore him to his throne. Could this be some plan to discredit her father? I had heard that the German Nazi Party was ruthless and would stop at nothing to further its cause. . . . But if someone wanted to do away with Hanni, why not just stab her instead of a harmless young man like Sidney? Or was he so harmless? Why had he been invited to that party? Why had he come? They weren't his crowd at all. He was clearly ill at ease there.

I tossed these thoughts around but still had come to no great revelations as we puffed into King's Cross Station. I had intended to go to Rannoch House first, but then I remembered that my grandfather and Mrs. Huggins would probably not be there. So instead I caught the train east, out to the Essex suburbs. Granddad came to the front door, wearing an old apron, and looked astonished to see me.

"Well, blow me down with a feather," he said. "What are you doing here, my love? I thought you was living it up on a country estate."

"I told you the queen wanted me to try and solve this murder before the inquest, so I've left Hanni and come to see what you and I can do."

"And I thought I told you, in no uncertain terms, that you was to stay well away," he said with a frown, as he ushered me into his spotless little house.

"I can't. Queen's orders."

"Then let her come and ruddy well solve it herself," he said angrily. "Putting a young girl like you in harm's way."

He led me through into the kitchen, where he was obviously in the process of preparing his lunch. Runner beans, fresh from the garden, were being sliced on the kitchen table. He lit the gas under the kettle without waiting to see whether I wanted tea at this hour of the day.

"I won't do anything silly, I promise." I took a chair at his kitchen table. "Have you managed to find out anything yet?"

"Give us a chance, ducks. It's been the weekend, hasn't it? Mrs. Huggins and me, we had to pack up our stuff and scarper out of your posh house and get ourselves settled in at home. But I did ask a couple of questions of a bloke I know who's still on the force in the city. I see him sometimes down the Queen's 'ead. He couldn't help much, mind you, but he did say these communists—most of them are harmless enough. They want a world that can never exist—equality for everyone, money shared around equally, jobs for all. Sounds wonderful, but won't ever happen, will it? People are greedy, see. They don't want to share. And my pal did say that the communists over on the Continent aren't quite as idealistic and harmless. Russia's sending out agitators, trained to whip up crowds, stir up hatred for the ruling classes, and get the people mobilized in action. There's going to be civil war in Spain, he says. And that's Russia's aim. Topple governments one by one."

"That's obviously why there was so much fuss when Princess Hanni appeared to be involved in an incident at a communist meeting place, even though I'm sure Sidney was one of the harmless sort."

"There are some nasty pieces of work among them," Granddad said. "Look what they did when they took over Russia. Killed their own grandmothers without a second thought. Murdered your poor relatives, didn't they? Down to the smallest nipper. Lot of savages, if you ask me. Of course, you'd never get the British people to rise up like that. We're too sensible. We know when we're well off."

"I hope so," I said. "But I really don't think that this murder had anything to do with communism. It just happened in the wrong location. I suspect it was something quite different—someone with a grudge against Sidney Roberts, or it may be to do with drugs. Perhaps Sidney owed money for drugs and hadn't paid up."

Granddad smiled. "They wouldn't kill him for that, love. You don't kill the goose that lays the golden egg, do you? Threaten him, break his kneecaps, but keep him alive to find ways to get the money. That's what the drug peddlers would do."

I shuddered. "I was wondering whether Gussie Gormsley was peddling drugs. He lives awfully well and there were some hints that his money is ill gotten. But I can't see Gussie breaking anybody's kneecaps."

"Can you see him stabbing anybody?"

"Frankly, no. I don't think he'd have the skill, for one thing. And if the murderer could only have escaped through an attic window and across the rooftops—well, Gussie's a little heavy for that sort of acrobatics."

The kettle let out a shrill whistle and Granddad poured the boiling water into the teapot. "So what had you planned to do, now that you're here?"

"I've no real idea. Go and interview Sidney's parents, maybe have a chat with Chief Inspector Burnall and see what he has found out."

"You think he'd welcome that, do you? Poking your nose into his investigations?"

"I'll be subtle, I assure you. I'll visit on the pretense of asking whether a date for the inquest is set and letting him know that Hanni needs to return to Germany soon—oh, and I think I should attend one of the communist meetings—incognito, of course. Sidney did invite Hanni and me to come to one, so I'm sure they're quite safe. I could look around and see who is there and what is said."

Granddad shook his head and made a tutting sound.

"It will be all right, Granddad."

"Just as long as them blackshirts don't bust in on it and turn it into a right old punch-up. They like doing that sort of thing, you know. Another bunch of hooligans, if you ask me. And that Oswald Mosley—calls himself a gentleman? Well, no English gentleman I know behaves like that. Wants people to go around saluting him, like that Hitler!"

"What would you do?" I asked him. "You've helped to solve real cases, haven't you?"

"I was mostly just on the beat," he said. "But I did work with some good men, and I did learn a thing or two. I remember old Inspector Parks. He had some fine old sayings. For instance, he used to say, 'Start with what you know. Start with the obvious.'"

I frowned, thinking. "Well, the obvious is that three people have died in a remarkably short space of time, but only one of them was a murder, so that's the one we should be looking at."

"Another of his old sayings was 'If anything seems to be a coincidence, there's probably more to it.' So was anyone present at all three of these suspicious deaths?"

"Only Hanni and I. Oh, but wait, we were away when the baroness died, on a trip to Cambridge with Edward Fotheringay. Gussie was present when Tubby fell off the balcony and was in the house when the baroness died."

"And you say you suspect he might be making some money from supplying drugs to his friends?"

"It did cross my mind."

He nodded. "That's something I could look into for you. I know a couple of blokes who might know a thing or two about the drug trade. Go on, don't let your tea get cold."

I took a sip.

"So going back to the obvious—what exactly did you see with your own eyes?"

"Tubby falling. Not being pushed. Hanni standing with a knife in her hand . . ."

"So we have to consider the possibility that she was the one what stabbed him."

I laughed. "Oh no. That's impossible."

"Why is it?"

"She's a princess, Granddad. A young girl. Just out of the convent. Innocent and naïve."

"Not too naïve to try to swipe something from Harrods," he pointed out.

"But taking a handbag is one thing. Killing someone—I can't believe that. For one thing, she looked absolutely stunned, and I really don't see how she would have had time to do it, since I was only a few steps behind her, and for another, how did she come by the knife? It was quite long, you know. She couldn't have hidden it inside her little handbag. And then comes the question of why. Why would a German princess want to kill a harmless lower-class young man she'd only just met and whom she rather fancied?"

Granddad took a slurp of his own tea. "Another of old Inspector Parks's sayings was, 'In a murder case the first question should always be, Who benefits?' "

I thought about this. "In Tubby's case, we'd have to see who inherits the estate with him gone. In Sidney's case, nobody. I don't think he had anything to leave."

"Not just monetarily. Who would benefit from his being out of the way?"

I thought again. "Well, I did hear that he worked with labor unions, to help them organize strikes. Maybe one of the big factory owners wanted him out of the way because he was a nuisance. That might make sense because the police think the efficiency of the stabbing indicated a trained killer."

"And just how do you propose to find out who might have hired a trained killer?"

I put down my teacup. "I have absolutely no idea, Granddad. Frankly I don't know what I'm doing, but I have to give it a try, don't I? I really don't want to start a new world war."

Granddad put down his teacup and burst out laughing. "Oh, that's a good one, that is. You—starting a new world war because a young bloke gets himself stabbed?"

"Look how the last one started! With one silly archduke being assassinated in a little unimportant country. People seem to think an incident involving Hanni and the communists might be enough to unsettle things in Europe. I don't see how, personally, but . . ." My voice trailed off.

"You worry too much, love," Granddad said. "You take yourself too seriously. You're young. You should be enjoying yourself, not feeling responsible for other people."

"I can't help it. I was brought up with duty rammed down my throat."

He nodded. "Well, I'll see what I can do."

"And I wondered if you might come back to Rannoch House with me. Just for a day or so. I don't like the thought of being alone there."

"Of course I will, my love. As long as you don't expect me to dress up in that ridiculous butler's outfit. But I don't think you'll get Mrs. Huggins to join us this time. Had enough of that kitchen of yours, she has. Said it gave her the willies working underground like a mole."

"I quite understand. Of course she needn't come. It's just me. I've left my new maid at Dippings and Hanni's staying there until things are decided for her."

"So you and I best get working then." He picked up the beans. "But first we need a good lunch. I was going to do lamb chops and new potatoes, with beans from my garden. How does that sound?"

I smiled at him. "Perfect."

Chapter 32

After lunch we caught the train up to the Smoke, as my grandfather called it. Then we went our separate ways, he to Scotland Yard and I out to the western suburbs this time and to the address I had found for Mr. and Mrs. Roberts, Sidney's parents.

The Robertses lived in a humble semidetached house in Slough. Its red brick façade was coated with the grime of endless coal fires and its pocket handkerchief–sized front garden sported one brave little rosebush. On the journey there, I had thought out how I should approach Sidney's parents. I knocked and the door was opened by a thin little woman in a flowery pinny.

"Yes?" she said, eyes darting suspiciously.

"Mrs. Roberts, I'm here about your son," I said.

"You're not another of those reporters, are you?" She went to close the door again.

"No, I was a friend of his from Cambridge" (all right, so it was a small lie, but detectives are allowed a certain degree of subterfuge, aren't they?) "and I wanted just to pay my respects and tell you how very sorry I was."

I saw the wariness soften and crinkle into pure grief. "You're welcome to come inside, miss," she said. "What did you say your name was?"

I hadn't, of course. "It's Maggie," I said, reverting to my maid's name as I had done once before. Maggie MacDonald."

"Pleased to meet you, Miss MacDonald." She held out her hand. "The hubby's in the back parlor. He'd like to meet one of our Sidney's friends."

She led me down a dark hallway into a little room with the obligatory three-piece suite and piano, its top littered with Goss china pieces, little souvenirs from past day trips to Brighton or Margate. A man had been sitting in one of the armchairs, reading the paper. He jumped to his feet as I was ushered in. He was painfully thin and balding, wearing braces over his shirt. His face looked completely haggard.

"We've got a visitor, Father," Mrs. Roberts said. "This young lady used to know our Sidney at the university and she's come to pay her respects. Isn't that kind of her?"

"Much appreciated," he said and immediately I felt rotten about deceiving them. "Take a seat, please. And how about a cup of tea, Mother?"

"Oh no, please. I don't want to put you to any bother," I said.

"No bother, I'm sure." She scuttled out into the kitchen, leaving me to face Mr. Roberts.

"So you knew our Sidney at the university, did you?"

"Yes, but I lost touch with him when we graduated, so you can imagine what a shock it was to read about him in the newspaper. I couldn't believe it was the same Sidney Roberts that I had known. I just had to come to London and find out for myself what had happened."

"It happened, all right," he said. "Our bright, wonderful boy, his life snuffed out just like that. Doesn't seem fair, does it? I went through the whole Battle of the Somme and I came out without a scratch, but I tell you this, miss, I'd willingly have sacrificed my life in a second in exchange for his. He had so much to live for, so much promise."

Mrs. Roberts had come back in with a teapot under a crocheted cozy and three cups on a tray. Obviously this was one of those households where there is always tea ready. "Here we are then," she said with forced brightness. "Do you take milk and sugar?"

"Just milk, please," I said. She poured me a cup and the cup rattled against the saucer as she passed it to me with an unsteady hand.

"I was telling her how I wished I could have traded my life for his," Mr. Roberts said.

"Don't get yourself worked up again, Father," Mrs. Roberts said. "This has really been hard on him, miss. First losing his job and now this. I don't know how much more we can take."

I looked longingly at the door, fervently wishing that I hadn't come. I also wished I could help them with money, although I rather suspected that they wouldn't take it.

"I understand that Sidney still lived at home?" I asked.

"That's right. He came back to us after the university," Mr. Roberts said. "We were worried that he'd get a job far away and his mother was delighted when he said he'd be stopping in London, weren't you, old dear?"

She nodded, but put her hand to her mouth.

"The newspaper said that Sidney was killed in the docklands area of London? What was he doing there?"

Mr. Roberts glanced at his wife. "He worked in a bookshop. All that education and he ended up working behind a counter like any of the other young men from around here. I'll tell you, miss. We had such high hopes for our Sidney. He was such a bright boy, see. We scrimped and saved to send him to the grammar school and then he goes and gets a scholarship to Cambridge as well. He had the world at his feet, our Sidney did."

His voice cracked and he looked away from me.

"We thought he'd go into the law," his wife continued for him. "He had always talked about becoming a solicitor so we expected him to become articled to a good firm when he came down from the university. But no. He announces to us that he wants nothing to do with the bourgeois establishment, whatever that is."

"It seems he got in with a funny lot at his college," Mr. Roberts said confidentially. "You probably knew about them, if you was one of his friends there."

"The apostles? The secret society? Is that who you mean?"

"That would be the ones. You've heard of them then?"

"I did hear something about them. And I know that Sidney was—well, rather idealistic about things."

"Idealistic? Ruddy stupid, if you'll pardon the language, miss," Mr. Roberts said. "All this talk about power for the people and down with the ruling classes and everyone should govern themselves. It can never happen, I told him. The ruling classes are born to rule. They know how to do it. You take a person like you or me and you put us up there to run a country and we'd make a ruddy mess of it."

Mrs. Roberts hadn't taken her eyes off her husband's face. Now she looked at me as if willing me to understand. "His father tried to make him see sense, but it was no use. He started writing for that *Daily Worker* newspaper and hanging around with those communists."

"Bunch of layabouts the lot of them. Don't even shave properly," Mr. Roberts intervened.

"No good can come of this, we told him. When you want to get a proper job, this will come back to haunt you."

"His mother wanted to humor him to start with," Mr. Roberts said. "You know how mothers are, and he was her only boy, of course." He paused and cleared his throat. "She thought he'd grow out of it. Young people often do go to extremes, don't they? But then they find a nice girl, settle down and see sense. Only—only he never got a chance to grow out of it, did he?"

"Do you have any idea at all who might have done this awful thing?" I asked.

They stared at me blankly. "We think it had to be a mistake. The person who stabbed him mistook him for someone else. It was dark in that place, so we hear. Maybe the killer stabbed our poor Sidney by mistake. I can't think of any other explanation for it."

"Had anyone threatened him?" I asked.

Again they stared blankly. "We never heard he was in any kind of trouble," Mr. Roberts said. "Of course he would go to them communist rallies and sometimes there was a bit of a scuffle there. His mother didn't want him to go. But apart from that, we've no idea. It couldn't have been anybody trying to rob the till, because he was upstairs when they stabbed him."

"Have the police given you any idea at all of what they might suspect?" I asked.

"If they have any ideas, they certainly haven't shared them with us," Mr. Roberts said bitterly. "Asked a lot of stupid questions about whether Sidney was connected to any criminal activity. They thought it was done by a professional because of the way he was stabbed, I gather."

Mrs. Roberts shifted forward to the edge of her chair. "But we told them he'd always been a good boy. Never done a thing to make us ashamed of him. And if he was up to anything shady, we'd have known, wouldn't we, Father?"

"Was Sidney worried about anything recently?" I asked.

They glanced at each other.

"Funny you should say that, miss. I think something was upsetting him. He had a nightmare and we heard him moaning in his sleep and he said, 'No, it's wrong. You can't do it.' In the morning we asked him about it but he'd completely forgotten. So maybe he was in some kind of trouble and hadn't told us. They do have gangs working in that part of London, wouldn't you say? Perhaps they wanted to pressure our Sidney to take part in a robbery or something and he'd refused. He would refuse, you know. Very upright, was our Sidney."

"Or we wondered whether he'd overheard something not meant for his ears, and he was killed because he wanted to go to the police."

"That sounds possible," I agreed, wondering why it had never occurred to me before. "What about Sidney's current friends? I know who his friends were at university. Did he keep up with the old crowd?"

"Not very much," his mother said. "There was that young man with the silly name. Sounded like a mushroom."

"Edward Fotheringay, pronounced 'Fungy'?" I asked her.

She smiled. "That's the one. He came to the house a couple of times and picked up Sidney in his little sports car. 'I thought you said you was against the upper classes,' we said to him. His dad liked to tease him from time to time. But he said that this Edward was all right and cared about the masses too. Apart from that, he didn't bring anybody home. No girlfriend, as far as I could see. He didn't go out much, apart from those communist meetings. He always was rather serious, wasn't he, Father?"

"No girlfriend he ever told us about anyway," Mr. Roberts said. He was looking at me strangely, with his head cocked to one side, like a bird, and it suddenly came to me that he thought I might be Sidney's girlfriend. "If you'll pardon my saying so, miss, but you seem very concerned about him. More than the average acquaintance from university would be."

I gave what I hoped was a nervous laugh. "It's true. We were close friends once. That's why I was so angry to hear about this. I want to get to the bottom of it. I want his killer to be brought to justice."

"We're very grateful for any help, miss." The Robertses exchanged a look.

I decided to plunge ahead. "I was wondering . . . Sidney wasn't drinking or smoking too much recently, was he?"

"He'd take the odd pint and the odd cigarette, but no more than the average person, not as much actually, because our Sidney was always careful with his money, as you probably remember. He left quite a bit in his savings account, didn't he, Father?"

My ears pricked up—so quiet, well-behaved Sidney had been squirreling away quite a bit of money, had he?

"He did. Over fifty pounds," Mr. Roberts said proudly.

So much for the theory that Sidney was selling drugs. Fifty pounds wouldn't have begun to cover one of Gussie's parties.

I finished my tea and took my leave of the Robertses.

I was feeling tired and depressed by the time I arrived at Rannoch House and was relieved to find my grandfather already in residence and yet another cup of tea on the stove. This one, however, was most welcome.

"So did you learn anything?" my grandfather asked.

"Only things that I can now rule out. Sidney Roberts was a good boy, according to his parents. He lived simply at home. He had fifty pounds in a savings account. They had high hopes for him and were disappointed when he became a communist sympathizer. So we can assume that he was not profiting from selling drugs, nor was he a drug user. There was a suggestion that maybe he had fallen foul of some kind of criminal element—that some gang wanted him to carry out some kind of robbery for them and he had refused, or that he'd overheard something not meant for his ears."

Granddad nodded. "A possibility in that part of town. He worked in a bookshop that sold old books, you say. Were there rare books among them— books that could be sold for a bob or two? Maybe someone had asked him to nick a few."

I hadn't thought of this. The simplest of solutions. "You could find out about that kind of thing, couldn't you? Your friends on the force could come up with gangs who might deal in stolen art, antiques, that kind of thing."

He nodded. "Yes, that would be easy enough. But it seems rather extreme to me. You don't stab a bloke through the heart because he won't nick a book for you. However, if he was going to rat on them to the coppers . . . you say he was an upstanding young man . . . now that's another business. I'll see what my old pals have got to say on that."

"And tomorrow I'm going to Inspector Burnall," I said. "Their investigation might have turned up a thing or two by now."

"I wouldn't count on it, love," Granddad said. "Now, about our supper tonight. There ain't much food in the larder, seeing as how we thought you was going to be away. What do you say I go and get us a nice bit of fish and chips?"

I started to laugh. "Granddad, I don't think you'd find fish and chips in Belgravia," I said.

Chapter 33

RANNOCH HOUSE
TUESDAY, JUNE 21, 1932

Diary,
Going to be a hot day. Muggy and still, even at eight thirty. Not looking
   forward to what lies ahead. Not cut out to be sleuth.

The morning's post brought a letter from Buckingham Palace. I thought
this was strange, given that the royal couple was in Norfolk, but when I
opened it I found that it was merely an official invitation to the royal garden
party the next day. It concluded, *Please present this invitation to gain admission to the palace grounds.* So I was to be facing Her Majesty the next day.
She'd expect me to have something to tell her. I had better put in a good
day's work today.

   After breakfast Granddad set off for his old police station in the East
End and I headed for Scotland Yard. I was in luck. Chief Inspector Burnall
was in his office and I was ushered in. The chief inspector, dapperly dressed
as always, looked surprised to see me.

   "What brings you here, my lady? Come to give yourself up?"

   I gave him my best imitation of my great-grandmother's steely stare.
He wilted under it. "Just joking, my lady. Now, what can I do for you?"

   "I came to find out if a date for the inquest has been set. It appears that
Princess Hannelore may have to go home to Germany quite soon, so if you

think her testimony may be helpful, you should probably schedule the inquest before she leaves."

"She's intending to do a bunk, is she?"

"Her companion, the Baroness Rottenmeister, has just died. Naturally protocol would demand that she not stay on in this country unchaperoned."

"Another death? They seem to be falling like flies around your princess. Are you sure her last name isn't Borgia?" Again he gave a tentative chuckle.

"The baroness died of a heart attack while the princess and I were being shown around Cambridge," I said coldly. "And you can't seriously believe that the princess or I had anything to do with the murder of Sidney Roberts, other than coming upon his body."

"She was found with the knife in her hand."

"But you said yourself that the blow was delivered by a trained assassin. Do you really think that the nuns trained her to kill at the Holy Names convent?"

"I suppose not," he agreed.

"And you can't possibly suspect me."

He hesitated for a second, making me continue, "Really, Chief Inspector—what possible motive would either of us have had to want Mr. Roberts dead? I had only met the man twice before—once in a park and then a brief conversation at a party."

"Three times," he said. "You met him three times, not twice. At the British Museum, remember?"

"Ah. Well, actually I didn't meet him at the British Museum. Princess Hannelore did."

"Oh?"

"We became separated and when I found her again she told me excitedly that she'd met Sidney doing research there, and he had invited us to his bookshop."

He paused then said, "So you only have Her Highness's word that she had met this man there?"

"Yes, I suppose so."

"So if Her Highness had wanted an excuse to go to the bookshop, she could have concocted this story."

"I suppose she could. But why?" Even as I said the words I saw one possibility. Hanni was smitten with Sidney. She wanted a chance to meet him again. She had proven herself not above subterfuge when it suited her.

"You've thought of a reason?" he asked.

"Yes. I'm afraid the princess was rather boy mad, Chief Inspector. And I believe she was setting her cap at Sidney Roberts. I can't see why, because she certainly wouldn't have been allowed to continue a friendship with a penniless, lower-class man. Perhaps he appealed to her because he was forbidden fruit in her eyes."

The chief inspector nodded. "And an unknown assassin chose that exact moment to stab Mr. Roberts and then vanish into thin air. Very convenient, don't you think?"

"Not vanish into thin air. Didn't the shop owner say that there was a window in the attic and a way across the rooftops?"

Chief Inspector Burnall shook his head. "We examined that window. The dust on the sill had not been disturbed."

"He could just as easily have hidden among the bookshelves and then slipped out after we left the shop to call the police. He could have taken refuge in a nearby building and we probably wouldn't have seen him. But the point is, Chief Inspector, that we didn't kill Sidney Roberts, we had no motive for killing Sidney Roberts and we certainly did not have the expertise to kill him."

"I suppose I have to accept that," he said. "But maybe you can help me out by suggesting someone who might have had a motive."

"Why would I know that?"

"You were all at the same party a few nights previously, when another young man died. A party at which I gather cocaine was in use?"

"I told you, I personally witnessed that death. It was a horrible accident. Tubby was reeling drunk. He fell against the railings and they gave way. Nobody was near him."

"Not entirely thanks to being drunk, as it turns out," Burnall said slowly, not taking his eyes off my face. "An autopsy revealed that he had a considerable level of alcohol in his system, that's true. He also had a lethal amount of phenobarbital. Someone had slipped him what the Americans call a Mickey Finn."

"Poisoned him, you mean?"

"Knocked him out. Someone wanted to make sure he fell off that balcony, and to doubly guarantee this, they had also removed some of the screws that held the bars in place."

"Good heavens." I couldn't think of anything else to say.

"So I want you to think carefully, my lady. Do you have any reason to suspect that someone at that party wanted your pal Tubby out of the way? Or did you possibly see someone tampering with a drink?"

I shook my head. "It was dark and people were mixing cocktails all the time. An awful lot of drinking was going on and Tubby had a glass in his hand every time I saw him. As to who wanted him out of the way, I should have thought you'd have examined the line of inheritance by now."

"We have, my lady. No brothers, so the estate would pass to a cousin. Several cousins, including the young man who gave the party."

"Gussie Gormsley?" I asked in a shocked voice.

"As you say. Augustus Gormsley. Granted he's only a second cousin, but maybe he has similar intentions on those ahead of him in the line."

I laughed. "Oh, surely this is madness, Inspector. Gussie is—" I was about to say harmless and then I remembered how he would have forced himself upon me if Darcy hadn't shown up. Not entirely harmless then. But I pictured that scene on the balcony and saw Gussie handing Tubby the drink. "That drink wasn't even intended for Tubby," I said. "Gussie was offering it around. Tubby took it."

"Who was it intended for then?"

I froze as I remembered. Gussie was trying to press the drink upon Sidney Roberts. After Sidney had refused, Tubby had taken the drink and downed it. But could I really bring myself to mention this fact? After all, these were members of my set. We didn't go around killing people. And I had only seen what happened after Gussie came out onto the balcony. He could have offered the drink to any number of people inside first.

"I've no idea," I said. "Gussie was just being a good host and making sure that everyone was drinking."

"I see." Again he looked at me long and hard.

"So may one ask whether you have made any progress in the murder of Sidney Roberts?" I asked, changing the subject. "He wasn't mixed up with any kind of criminals, was he?"

"Why do you ask that?"

"Because I went to see his parents to express my condolences and his mother said he had been worried lately and in his sleep he muttered something about it being wrong and that they shouldn't do it. So I thought that maybe he'd been coerced into something illegal."

"Interesting." He nodded his head. "As of yet we haven't heard that kind of rumor, but we'll look into it. We'll be looking into every angle, I can assure you—unless there is any other tidbit of information you'd like to share with me right now."

"Had I any information, I would share it willingly," I said. "I take it you have been notified that the princess is staying near Sandringham at the moment, and I shall be at Rannoch House for the next day or so, so you'll know where to contact us about the inquest."

I rose to my feet. He did the same. "You people, you stick together, no matter what, don't you?" he said.

"What do you mean?"

"I believe you know more than you're telling me, but one of your lot is to blame and it will come out. And when it does and I find you've been withholding evidence, I'll come after you. I don't care who you are."

"I'm sure you don't," I said coldly. "You arrested my brother earlier this year when he was completely innocent. But I repeat what I just said: I know nothing about either of these strange events. I wish I could tell you more."

Then I made a grand exit.

Chapter 34

As I walked back to Rannoch House through St. James's Park, watching children playing, couples strolling hand in hand, office workers sitting on the grass enjoying the sunshine, it seemed to me that nobody had a care in the world but me. Of course this was fallacious thinking. At this very moment all over the city there were men lining up in the hopes of finding work, or getting a handout of soup or bread. But the depression couldn't spoil a summer day's fun in the park for these people. I, on the other hand, could not shake off my burden.

After my visit to Chief Inspector Burnall, I was more confused than ever. One of my lot. The words kept echoing through my head. One of my lot had definitely killed poor Tubby Tewkesbury and the person who had handed him the drink had been Gussie. But he had first tried to press the drink upon Sidney Roberts. Had Gussie known he was carrying a drink laced with phenobarbital? Had he intended to let Sidney fall through that railing? In which case why? Various possibilities went through my mind—upright Sidney had threatened to report the cocaine use to the police, or he had been some kind of go-between, ferrying drugs between the docklands and Mayfair, until his conscience got the better of him. But did one kill for what seemed so trivial a reason? And if Gussie hadn't known the drink was laced then who else at the party wanted Sidney dead and why? The partly unscrewed railings seemed to indicate Gussie—after all, it was his flat.

I glanced across at the simple white outline of the modern block, fronting the park. Maybe I should see for myself. Gussie was safely far away in the country. I should be able to persuade the doorman to let me in. I changed course and made for the block of flats. The uniformed doorman saluted and let me into the glass and marble entrance hall where a hall porter sat. I explained to him that I had been at the party.

"Oh, that party," he said, nodding with understanding.

"And everything was rather chaotic and we left in rather a hurry," I said. "And I'm afraid I might have left my little evening bag in the flat."

"I'm sorry, miss, but Mr. Gormsley is not in residence," he said.

"I know that. I was staying with him in the country until yesterday," I said. "I'm sure he wouldn't mind my taking a look around for my bag. You must have a pass key and I am awfully fond of it, you know."

I saw him wrinkle his forehead, debating. Then he got to his feet. "I suppose I could take you up there for a moment." He shuffled into his cubicle to fetch a set of keys and then escorted me up in the lift.

Gussie's flat smelled of stale smoke, and the afternoon sun streaming in through those huge windows made it rather unpleasantly warm. The porter stood in the doorway. He obviously had no intention of leaving me alone.

"I'm not sure which room I might have left it in," I said. "It all looks terribly neat and tidy, doesn't it?" It did. Gussie's man had done a splendid job. I went into the drawing room with its low modern furniture and ghastly modern art. There was a desk in the corner but I could hardly make the porter believe that I had opened it to stash my evening bag inside. And of course I had no idea what I might be looking for. A blotter with the imprint of a letter telling Sidney he had better deliver the drugs or else? Probably not. Or a letter from Sidney saying that he felt compelled to go to the police? The wastepaper basket was empty, the desk pristine.

"Maybe I left it in the bedroom," I said, making him raise an eyebrow. "We left our wraps on the bed, I remember. Perhaps it fell under the bed."

"I'll look for you, miss. I don't want you getting down on your hands and knees," he said. I waited until he went ahead into the bedroom, then I dashed back to that desk. It opened easily enough. It even contained a letter rack of unanswered mail. I flicked through it quickly, opened one drawer after another, then closed them as quietly as possible.

"Any luck?" I called.

"Nothing, miss."

"I'll just check the kitchen then." I moved away from the desk.

After ten minutes I had to admit that I had found nothing. Of course the police would probably have given the flat a thorough search by now and taken away anything incriminating. All I could surmise, as I rode the lift down with the hall porter, was that Gussie was living beyond his means. He had an awful lot of unpaid bills, some of them second and third demands, from his tailor, his wine merchant, from Fortnum's. So if he was peddling drugs, he wasn't getting rich from it.

"I'm sorry you didn't find what you were looking for," the porter said as he ushered me out.

It was now well after lunchtime and my stomach was growling in unladylike fashion. I continued through the park back to Rannoch House and found no sign of my grandfather. I grabbed some bread and cheese and changed my clothes before venturing out again. I was rather relieved that Granddad wasn't there, because my intention was to do a little snooping around in the area of the bookshop and possibly to attend a meeting at the communist headquarters. I didn't think he'd approve of either. I left him a note saying that I was meeting friends and probably wouldn't be home until after supper. I didn't want him to worry.

I found the bookshop with slightly less difficulty this time. The alleyway looked like a peaceful backwater, deep in late afternoon shadow while the sun painted the upper stories of the warehouses around it with a rosy glow. Even the Russian tearoom only contained two very old men, their heads sunk to their chests and half-drunk cups of tea in front of them. The beggar was no longer on the corner; in fact, nothing moved as I made my way toward the bookstore. A loud toot made me jump until I remembered that the river lay just beyond the bottom of the alleyway. A bell jangled as I let myself into the bookshop. I noticed that it hung at the top of the door on one of those little brackets. I had forgotten about the bell. We would have heard it jangling if anyone had tried to slip out of the bookshop behind us, wouldn't we?

Mr. Solomon appeared from the depths of the shop. "May I help you, miss?" He didn't seem to recognize me and I wondered if he had poor eyesight.

"I was one of the young ladies who found your assistant stabbed last week," I said. "I've felt awful about it ever since and I'm sure you have, too."

"Indeed I have, miss. Such a fine young man. So much promise."

"I just wondered whether the police are any closer to finding out who did this," I said.

"The police tell me nothing," he said. "I'm in the dark as much as you are, although my money is on those blackshirts."

"Blackshirts?"

"Yes, the thugs that that fascist Mosley surrounds himself with. You've heard about him and his New Party, have you? Now there's a troublemaker if ever there was one. Modeling himself on that horrible man Mussolini."

"I saw them in operation recently, causing a disruption at Speakers' Corner."

He sighed. "They came in here, you know, only a couple of weeks ago. They despise communists and of course they despise Jews. Nothing but thugs. They tipped over a tray of valuable rare books before they left."

"But why stab Mr. Roberts?"

"As a gesture of superiority, maybe, or they may have thought they were killing me, since I represent everything they hate."

"Have you suggested this to the police?"

"I rather get the impression that some policemen admire the fascist ideas and certainly despise socialism. They don't want to be equal. They like power."

I looked at his serious face with its sunken eyes and perpetual worried frown and wished I could do something useful.

"Sidney worked here and he also wrote for the *Daily Worker*, is that correct?"

"He did. He wrote very well. Had he lived, I believe he might have become a fine writer."

"And I also understand that he was involved in helping unions to voice their grievances."

"He did that too. He was a fine orator as well. The party needed people like him—men who truly wanted to make lives better. There aren't many of them around, I fear."

"So you didn't ever get an idea that he was mixed up with anything—well, illegal?"

"Illegal?" He looked shocked. "What are you suggesting, young lady?"

"I don't know—burglaries, drugs?"

"Our Mr. Roberts? He would have refused. He had the highest moral standards."

There was nothing more I could think of asking and I couldn't find an excuse to let me investigate the shop for myself, but I was reluctant to leave.

"Sidney invited me to come to one of his meetings," I said. "I didn't have a chance to, but I feel that I should, to honor his memory if nothing else."

Mr. Solomon stared at me critically. "That is a fine sentiment, young lady. It just happens that there is to be a lecture tonight at the church hall around the corner. I think you may find it very informative. Eight o'clock it starts. I look forward to seeing you there."

I came out into the deep shadow of the alleyway and stood looking back at the dusty paned windows, wondering if I might have a chance to slip back inside should Mr. Solomon leave for a moment. And if I did gain access, what then? The police had thoroughly searched the place and found nothing. Or if they had found anything, they were not willing to share the information with me. I lingered for a while until Mr. Solomon finally emerged. He closed the door behind him and turned the key. I flattened myself into a doorway as he passed me, then went to try the door. It was, of course, hopelessly locked.

I heard a nearby church clock chiming the hour. Five. Crowds were streaming past the end of the alleyway, dockhands and typists going home for the day. I had three hours to kill before the lecture but it hardly made sense for me to go home on one of those packed tube trains. By the time I found my way back to the nearest tube station and arrived home, I would have to turn around and leave again, and my grandfather would probably try to stop me. So all in all it made sense to stay in this part of town. I came out of the alleyway and located the hall where the meeting was to be held, just around the corner as Mr. Solomon had said. It even had a sign on the notice board outside: *Tonight: Mr. Bill Strutt, of the British Workers League, will give a talk on Vision for a New Britain. Come and hear his inspiring talk.*

I wandered back along Wapping High Street, taking in the sounds and smells of the docklands—the dank, rotting smell of river water competing with fish and chips from an open shop front, the mournful tooting of tugboats echoing over the clattering of shoes on cobblestones. I went into the fish and chip shop and bought myself ninepenceworth of cod and chips, then ate them from the newspaper as I walked along. Very satisfying until I noticed the grease staining the glove I had stupidly forgotten to remove. I kept walking until I made my way back to the Tower of London, with Tower Bridge framing the Thames. The white stonework of the tower was glowing pink in the evening sunlight. It presented a most attractive picture.

I found a bench and sat taking in the busy river scene. A cargo boat came upriver, causing the bridge to open and backing up traffic on either side. The river flowed past, dark and oily, with flotsam twirling in the turbid waters. The sun sank lower and a chill breeze swept up the river, making it no longer pleasant to sit there.

I still had more than an hour to go and although Wapping High Street was busy enough at this time, it wasn't the sort of area where one should draw attention to oneself. I wished I had a male escort so that I could go into one of the many pubs that were doing good business, in spite of the depression. Finally I remembered the Russian tearoom. I went back to the alleyway and went inside, causing stares all around. It was only when I was seated that I noticed that all the other people sitting at the tables were men.

"I remember you," the elderly waiter said in a strong accent. "You and the other girl. You came here when the poor young man was stabbed."

"That's right," I said.

"Why do you come back here again?" he demanded, in a voice heavy with a foreign accent.

"Sidney Roberts invited us to one of his meetings, so I felt I should attend in his memory."

He sniffed. "Not a good place for a young girl after dark. You should go home."

As the sun sank, it had occurred to me that it probably wasn't a good place to be after dark and that I somehow had to find my way back to the nearest tube station when the meeting was over. But I had seen buses. I'd take a bus to a better part of town, where I could find a taxicab. I ordered a cup of tea. It came up in a glass in a silver holder, and was pale and sweet with lemon floating in it. I sipped gratefully and made it last, while I listened to the conversation going on around me. I guessed it to be mainly in Russian, but I thought I heard some German too.

At about seven thirty I left and went back to the hall. The doors were open and one or two people were already seated inside—workingmen in cloth caps, and a middle-aged woman in black. They nodded to me and I returned the nod. Gradually the benches were filled, and the air became heavy with smoke (and coughing). The smell of unwashed bodies in the lingering warmth of the summer evening was not too pleasant either. The bench was already feeling hard and uncomfortable and I could sense eyes upon me. I was sure I stood out as not belonging, even though I had dressed as simply as possible. Many of these people were in threadbare clothes, their elbows and knees well patched. I was too clean, too civilized, too well dressed. I was seriously wishing I had followed Granddad's advice and not come. What could I hope to achieve by being here? These people were Sidney's friends. They would have wanted to protect him, not kill him.

"I haven't seen you here before." A young man in a bright red waistcoat sat down beside me.

"No. It's my first time. I was a friend of Sidney Roberts—you know the one who was killed last week?"

"Oh yes. I heard about it. Poor fellow." He was well-spoken and I noticed that he wore a signet ring. One of us, then. "Welcome," he said. "My name's Miles. I think you're in for a treat. Bill is a splendid speaker."

I wanted to ask this Miles if he was possibly at Cambridge with Sidney, but at that moment the door at the front of the hall opened and several men filed out onto the stage. The speaker was introduced. He was an unassuming little man, probably in his forties and not much better dressed than his audience. But when he started to speak, I could see what Miles had meant. He talked of a vision for a new society—wealth being shared, the workload being shared. "The empire has grown fat and strong on the backs of the workers," he said, thumping the table now as he warmed up. "And do we get any thanks? No, we get our pink slips instead when production drops. Who fought in the trenches in the war? The workers. We did. And where were the officers? Drinking Scotch behind the lines. And who is lining up for jobs or bread today while the bosses go home to a big roast dinner? You've got it, my friends. We have kept the empire running and nobody has ever thanked us.

"So what if we made it change? If we were the bosses? If we elected our own to run the coal mines and the wool mills and the docks and the country? We'd know how backbreaking the work was, wouldn't we? We'd see that every man got fair pay for his labor. We'd improve safety conditions. No more mine cave-ins, no more fingers lost to faulty machines. And it can happen in our time. All we need is to make our cause known and the people will rise up behind us. Elect us to parliament and it will be like an ever-growing stream."

"There's already a Labor Party, in case you haven't noticed," a heckler called from the back.

"Labor Party?" Bill Strutt laughed. "And what do they care about the workers? No more than the Tories, do they? Have they stopped the layoffs or supported the strikes and hunger marches? No, they bloody well haven't. It's time for a change, comrade. It's time for true socialism. It's time for us to take over what is rightfully ours."

"And what makes you think we'd be better off?" another heckling voice demanded. "Look at Russia. Are they better off under Joe Stalin? They're starving, mate. One wrong move and they're sent to Siberia, so I've heard."

"Ah, but Russia's different," Strutt said. "The Russian peasants—well, they were almost like serfs, weren't they? Not educated like our British workers. Not used to having a say in the running of things like our British workers. So Russia's still got a long way to go, but as for us—we're ready to take over, comrades. . . ."

There were halfhearted cheers and stamping of feet. I began to feel it was all rather silly. I looked around me. Many of the faces were focused on the speaker, enraptured. Then I froze. The lighting in the hall was poor but in a far corner I thought I had spotted a face I knew. It looked remarkably like Edward Fotheringay.

Chapter 35

I pulled my cloche hat more firmly down over one eye so that Edward couldn't spot me and waited for the speech to end. It did, amid heckles and hurled insults. It seemed an element of the crowd had been planted merely to stir things up. Finally Bill Strutt had had enough.

"Comrades, I see we have some present who don't want to listen or learn. In every society there are closed minds that we will never reach, and so I'll call it a day right here, before things turn violent. I ask you to remain calm and controlled as you leave here. Let's show that we are the better people, that we don't need violence to promote our cause. Hang on to the vision, comrades. To a better future for us all—a communist future!"

There was loud applause, and a few boos, as he stepped down from the stage. The crowd was on its feet, making for the front doors. I glanced over at Edward and saw that he was inching forward through the crowd, like a salmon swimming upstream, rather than joining the exodus. I too was being swept toward the exits. I dodged and moved aside, gradually working my way to the side aisle where I was out of the stream. The men who had been on the stage had now disappeared through the small door to which Edward was also heading. I moved forward painfully slowly, jostled by burly laborers and dockworkers.

"Exit's this way, love," one of them said. "Come on, I'll buy you half a pint." He attempted to put an arm around me.

"No, thanks. I'm waiting for someone," I said, dodging out of reach. I looked around but Edward too had now disappeared. There was a door to one side marked *Lavatory*. I went inside and locked the door behind me.

Finally the clatter of feet subsided. I came out to find the hall in darkness. There was still a modicum of daylight coming in through high windows, enough for me to see the layout of the hall and the fact that the big doors at the end were now shut. Everyone had gone home, except for those who had disappeared through the little door beside the stage. I made my way there, stumbling over a chair that had been left in a side aisle and then holding my breath in case anyone had heard. But nothing moved as I reached that doorway. I opened the door and went through.

Inside the narrow passage was complete darkness. I looked around for a light switch, then thought better of it. I shouldn't draw attention to my presence. I didn't know how safe I was—Edward, after all, had been the one who mixed the cocktails that evening. He had been the one with that strange, exhilarated look on his face as he drove very fast through the rain storm. There was definitely something about him that was not to be trusted.

I crept down the narrow passageway, inching along by feel. When I came to a half-open door on my right, I checked it out, only to find it was a broom cupboard. I counted paces from it, realizing that it would be a place to hide should the men return this way unexpectedly. The passage ended suddenly in what seemed to be a wall. My fingers searched over it but found no door or knob. Where could they have gone? And why hadn't I been sensible enough to carry a torch, as any good detective should?

At last my fingers located a crack in the wall, what felt like the side of a door, but I could still feel no knob, nor the top of the door. I put my ear to it and could hear faint voices beyond it.

"That girl was here this afternoon," I heard a man's voice say clearly. "She was planning to attend the meeting tonight."

"Yes, I thought I saw her in the hall." Was that Edward's voice? It was too muffled for me to be sure.

"Do you think she suspects anything?" The third voice appeared to be female, but deep and guttural, with a pronounced foreign accent.

"What does it matter? She'll be too late, won't she?" Edward's voice again?

"You still mean to go through with it, then?"

"I know what happened to Roberts—stupid little prig with his lower-class morals. If I were planning to back out, I'd be on my way to Australia as fast as my legs could carry me."

"I am still disturbed about Roberts. Was it really necessary to kill him?"

"He would have betrayed us." This was the foreign woman's guttural voice.

"And you still think this is a wise course of action? Given the situation?"

"What option do we have? The first attempts failed and time is definitely running out."

"It was stupid to kill the baroness."

"No choice, old boy. She was going to telephone the princess's father, and that would never have done, would it?"

So it seemed there were three speakers, two males, one female, all speaking softly as though they didn't want to be overheard.

"So everything's in place, then? Anything you need us to do?"

"Have the escape route ready, if either of us manages to get away."

"It's not the ideal situation. I've said that all along."

"It will have to do. Now or never, don't you agree?"

"I suppose I have to agree. I never thought this was a good idea in the beginning. What's it going to achieve, apart from turning half the population against us?"

"You're not going soft on us, are you, Solomon?"

"You know my views on violence. Only when absolutely necessary."

"Quite right. When absolutely necessary."

The voices were moving off. Something else was said but I couldn't catch it. I thought I heard some kind of thud. I felt my way back down the hall and into that broom cupboard in case they reappeared suddenly. But they didn't. I waited and waited until my legs were stiff and cramped from standing bent over among the mops and buckets. Finally I came out and listened. Nothing. There must have been another way out from the room in which they had been speaking.

I worked my way back to the main hall. It was dark outside by now with a streetlamp twinkling in through one of the windows. The hall had become a place of danger—with flickering shadows and strange shapes. A raucous burst of singing from a pub made me fully aware that I was in an area where there was not likely to be safety. Slowly and carefully I made my way down the aisle, until I had reached the front doors. I pushed hard, but they refused to give. I searched for a handle. There was none. From what I could tell, they were padlocked from the outside. I was trapped in here.

There had to be another way out. Those speakers had gone through what appeared to be a solid wall and had not returned. I made my way back again, conscious now of every small sound, the echo of my feet on a stone floor and mysterious rustles and creaks which were probably no more than an old building settling in the night air but which sounded horribly ominous to me. I couldn't make myself believe that I was completely alone. I saw moving shadows in every corner and jumped at a passing motorcar's horn.

"Buck up, Georgie, this isn't like you." I gave myself a stiff talking-to. I, who had dared to stay up on the ramparts to spot my grandfather's ghost; I, who had been lowered down the castle well by my brother and his friends—now I was scared to be alone in the dark? Well, this was a little different. I had just heard several people confessing to killing the baroness and Sidney Roberts, from what I could gather. That meant my life wasn't worth much if they discovered me here.

I made my way slowly back down that narrow passage and found the crack in the wall again. I felt around but couldn't come up with a corresponding crack for the other side of a door, nor could I find any kind of handle. I pushed. I poked. Then in frustration I kicked at the floorboard. I felt something give and part of the wall swung silently inward. I hesitated only a second before stepping through. I knew where I was instantly, of course. That characteristic smell of old books and pipe tobacco. I was back in the bookshop. So there had been another way out that the police hadn't discovered. Not very bright of them.

I wondered which floor I was on. There was almost no light. I wondered if I could find a light switch and if I dared to turn it on. I stood silently listening, just in case the speakers had not left but only moved to another part of the shop. I certainly didn't want to bump into anyone in the dark. To reassure myself, I reached back to touch the doorway through which I had come, and couldn't find it. I backed up, my heart beating faster now, and touched bookshelves on three sides of me. If it had been a secret entrance, it had swung back into place. I was now trapped in the bookshop.

After waiting what seemed like an eternity, listening for any sound or movement, I left the shelter of my side aisle, feeling my way along the bookshelf. Ahead of me I could see a faint glimmer of light, barely enough to outline the rows of bookshelves. Slowly I made my way forward, toward that light, until my foot stubbed against something soft. I bent down, then recoiled in horror. A person was lying there. Cautiously I reached out and touched, feeling down a sleeve until I located a hand. It was still warm. I held the wrist for a pulse, but I couldn't detect one. The faint glimmer of light outlined the glasses on a skeletal face. It had to be Mr. Solomon.

I should go for help. Maybe there was still a chance to save him. I inched around him and felt my way forward. The glimmer of light grew until I could see it was a streetlamp, shining in through the dusty panes of the front windows. I let out a huge sigh of relief. I'd be able to find the nearest policeman and tell him everything I knew. Whatever these people had planned, I'd be able to stop them. I grabbed the front door handle. It moved but the door wouldn't open. I shook it, jiggled, pushed with all my might, but apart from making the bell jangle peevishly, nothing happened. They had locked the door behind them. I was trapped in here with Mr. Solomon's body.

I looked at the windows and wondered if I could find anything strong enough to break them with, but the panes were so small that I'd never be able to get out that way.

I sank to the floor beside the window and rested my arms on the wide window ledge. At this moment I didn't want to be grown up and independent and on my own in a big city. I wanted more than anything to be home. I wanted to be with Nanny, and Binky, and even Fig at this moment, in a safe place far from here. And I wanted someone to rescue me: I peered out of the window, hoping that my grandfather would come and break down the door and take me away. But I had told him I was going out with friends and he had no idea who my friends were or how to contact them. And Darcy was far away in the country, taking moonlight strolls with Hanni—since Edward had left the field entirely open for him.

I'd just have to sit here until morning, when people came to work and I could break a window and shout for help. And then . . . then the police would come and I'd have to explain how I was trapped alone with Mr. Solomon's body. And they'd only have my word that I wasn't one of those who killed him. I could picture Harry Sugg's annoying grin. "Oh yes?" he'd say. "Got locked in by mistake, did you? And this man just happened to die by mistake, did he? Well, I don't see anyone else inside this locked building, so do you mind telling me who killed him if you didn't?"

Thoughts buzzed angrily around inside my head. These communists were planning something awful, something that Sidney had refused to take part in and Mr. Solomon had objected to: a violent demonstration of some kind—taking over the Houses of Parliament or even killing the prime minister maybe. And if one of them came back to the shop in the morning, perhaps with a van to take away the body, they would find me and I'd be disposed of too. I sat there in the lamplight as it shone on the books piled on the floor around me. Really this was the untidiest shop I'd ever seen. Close to me was a stack of children's books. I started looking through them, hoping to find a familiar and comforting friend from my nursery days. But they turned out to be foreign, with illustrations of evil witches and savage ogres. Not at all comforting. At the bottom of the pile there was one called *Let's Learn Russian.* The cover had a picture of two happy, smiling communist children, carrying a hammer and sickle. How appropriate, I thought. Perhaps they handed out a copy to everyone who attended those stupid meetings. I flicked it open.

The Russian alphabet is different from ours, I read. *You will need to master it before you can read Russian words.* My eye scanned down the page. Russian uses the letter *C* when we would use the letter *S.* My gaze moved further. The Russian letter *R* is written like our *P.* I found myself thinking of the two letters someone had sent to Hanni, the first time with a question mark, the second time with a cross through them. *C.P.* not C.P. but S.R.— Sidney Roberts?

Which meant it had to be Edward Fotheringay and his stupid Cambridge leftist secret society. He had studied modern languages, German and Russian. His mother had been Russian. He claimed he had been in India but Colonel Horsmonden had never met him there and Edward had been evasive in answering the colonel's questions. Which now made me suspect that he had never been in India. He'd been in Russia, training for the moment when he was sent back here to overthrow the government by force, as the communists had done there. Or maybe to create chaos and perhaps a new world war, out of which world communism would emerge triumphant. I should have picked up the signs earlier. He was the one who mixed the cocktails at the party and tried to kill Sidney there. And he had tried to involve Hanni. I didn't see how or why, unless he wanted to stir up trouble between England and Germany, or use her somehow to put the German communists in power. But she was naïve enough and he was handsome enough that she'd believe anything he told her.

So the next question was: had Edward persuaded her to help him kill Sidney? But it didn't make sense. We had been at the bookshop together.

She had gone up those stairs only moments before me and she certainly had no knife on her, and she certainly hadn't learned to kill at the convent.

I closed the book and put it back. This was absurd. The letters probably had nothing at all to do with Sidney Roberts or his death. The night dragged on. I must have dozed from time to time, because I sat up with a crick in my neck and noticed that the sky had taken on a grayish tinge. Daylight was coming. Poor Mr. Solomon was lying there, his mouth and eyes open, looking as if he was a wax dummy in Madame Tussauds.

I had to find a way out of here. I prowled as far from the light as I dared, examining side aisles and kicking walls for any sign of a hidden door. But by the time it was light, I had pushed and kicked at every bookshelf and still had found nothing. Of course, there was always the attic that Mr. Solomon had mentioned. It was certainly worth a try. I went upstairs and spotted a trapdoor in the ceiling. It had a cord attached. I pulled and a ladder hung down. I went up it cautiously because I am rather afraid of spiders and I hate cobwebs. It certainly was dusty up there. Piles of books were stacked next to old trunks and shapes hidden under dust sheets. In the half-light they looked ominous and I almost expected a sheet to fly off, revealing God knows what.

But I made it successfully to the small window at the far end. The sill was clean where the police had dusted for prints, and luckily they must have forced the window open because I didn't have to struggle too hard to do so. I dragged over a trunk, stood on it, and stuck my head out. The world outside was blanketed in thick mist so that it was impossible to see more than a few feet. What I could see was not encouraging. Oh, golly, the roof was steep and ended in a sheer drop. The slates were damp with the heavy mist. I didn't relish trying to climb out and if I started to slide, I'd have no way of stopping myself.

I climbed back down inside and piled books on top of the trunk until they were high enough for me to climb out of the window. I eased myself out, then pulled myself up until I was standing on the window ledge, holding on to the top of the window frame for support. The only way to go was up. I inched my way around the dormer window, clambering up the side of it until I could reach the top of the roof. I was thankful that I had worn my old lisle stockings and not my good silk ones, and my crepe-soled sandals rather than leather. Even so the slates were horribly slippery and I could hardly breathe because my heart was beating so fast. I straddled the roof apex, rather like riding a horse. In the direction I was facing I could make out that my roof ended against the blank wall of a taller building. No point in going that way, then. I couldn't see any drainpipe or way down at all.

So I turned around and moved in the other direction, inching forward with my heart hammering in my chest. It was an awfully long way down. I reached a cluster of chimney pots and managed to maneuver past them, then continued on as the roof turned at a right angle. I came to the end of the building and stopped, biting back tears of frustration. Between my roof and the next building was a gap. It wasn't particularly wide but there was no way I could lower myself down to the gutter and then turn to a position from which I could leap across, even if I had the nerve to leap across. And if I leaped, I had nothing to hold on to.

I had no idea what to do now. My muscles were trembling from the exertion and tension and I didn't want to go back to that attic window. If I shouted from up here, would anyone be able to hear me? Certainly not see me in this mist. Then the mist swirled and parted for a moment and I heard the lapping of water. Somewhere below me was the Thames. I waited patiently for the mist to part again. The river was a good way down but directly below me, and I had jumped off a tall rock into the loch at home many times. The question was, would it be deep enough? This was answered almost immediately by the deep sound of a ship's siren sounding eerie and mournful through the mist. Big cargo ships docked here, and it appeared to be high tide. Of course it would be deep enough. Anyway, I couldn't come up with a better plan after a night with little sleep and a lot of terror.

The sky became lighter and the mist swirled and broke apart. Every now and then I was treated to a clear view of the gray waters below. I could do this. I was going to do it. I swung my leg over and moved, crablike, down the steep surface. A slate came loose and slithered down the roof to plop into the water. A pair of pigeons took off, fluttering, from the roof nearby, almost making my heart stop and making me lose my balance. Through the mist behind me came sounds: the city was waking up.

I don't know how long I would have perched there, trying to pluck up courage, but I realized that my foot was going to sleep. That wouldn't do. I had to act now. I took a deep breath, stood up on the gutter, then jumped outward. I hit the water with a mighty splash. The cold took my breath away. I went under and kicked to the surface, spluttering, the taste of oily water in my mouth. Mist curled around the surface of the water and hid the banks, making me unsure in which direction I was facing. My skirt clung around my legs like some horrible type of sea creature as I fought to stay calm. The distant moan of a foghorn reminded me that big ships sailed here. I had no wish to be run down by a passing cargo boat. To my left I could make out the dark outline of the building from which I had just jumped and I struck out for it.

Now the only problem would be finding a way up from the river. A blank wall presented itself to me. Then I heard a shout and saw men standing on a high dock that jutted out to my right. Suddenly one of them peeled off his jacket and jumped in, swimming to me with powerful strokes.

"It's all right, love, I've got you," he said. He put an arm around my neck and dragged me back to the shore.

I wanted to tell him that I was perfectly capable of swimming to the steps by myself, but he was holding me so tightly I couldn't talk. We reached a ladder, extending up to a dock, and hands hauled me unceremoniously out of the water.

"Well done, Fred," voices said.

"You'll be all right now, love."

Then one said, "You shouldn't have done it. He's not worth it. There's always something to live for. You'll see." And I realized that they thought I'd been trying to kill myself. I didn't know whether to laugh or be indignant.

"No, you don't understand," I said. "I got locked in a building by some communists and the only way to escape was onto the roof, and the only way down from there was to jump."

"Of course it was, darling." They looked at each other, grinning knowingly. "Come on, we'll take you back to the hut and get you a cup of tea. No need to mention this to the police."

And I realized, of course, that suicide was a crime.

Chapter 36

An hour later I was safely back at Rannoch House, confronting an angry grandfather.

"Almost out of my mind with worry, I was," he was yelling. "I didn't know whether something had happened to you or you were just staying late at one of them fancy parties you go to."

"I'm so sorry," I said, and explained the whole thing to him.

"Ruddy silly thing to do," was all he could say afterward. "One of these days you'll go too far, my girl. If you was a cat, you'd have used up several of your nine lives already."

"I know," I said. "But it was really lucky that I took the chance because now I know. As soon as I've changed, I've got to see Chief Inspector Burnall and tell him what I've discovered," I said. "They are planning some kind of trouble, Granddad."

"You ain't going nowhere," he said firmly. "First of all I'm running you a hot bath, then you're going to eat a good breakfast and then we'll telephone Scotland Yard and Chief Inspector Burnall can come to you. He won't be in his office yet anyway, will he?"

One couldn't argue. It was like being with Nanny again. When she had that certain look, one just knew that all protests were futile. I allowed myself to be marched upstairs, then I lay luxuriating in hot water for a time before dressing and coming down to a boiled egg and fingers. Even this was like being in the nursery again and it gave me a lovely warm feeling of security.

Granddad made the call to Scotland Yard and Chief Inspector Burnall arrived in person about half an hour later.

"You have something important to tell me, my lady?" he asked.

I related the events of the previous evening. He listened attentively.

"And can you name any of these people?"

"There were two men and one woman, I think, although the woman's voice was deep and foreign, so it could have been another man. The dead man was Mr. Solomon. I'm sure of that, and I'm pretty sure that one of them was Edward Fotheringay."

"The same Edward Fotheringay who is currently sharing a London flat with Gormsley?"

I wanted to say "How many Edward Fotheringays can there be?" but I nodded politely instead. At this moment he was listening to me.

Then he smiled and broke the illusion. "This is all rather far-fetched, wouldn't you say, your ladyship? Are you sure you're not trying to lead me up the garden path, away from your pal Gormsley, for example?"

"I can prove it to you," I said. "You'll find Mr. Solomon's body in his bookshop. I believe they killed him because he wasn't willing to go along with their scheme, just as Sidney Roberts had objected to it."

Burnall was on his feet immediately and making for my front hall. I heard him barking orders into the telephone. He came back into the room.

"I have men on their way there now. So if you'd be good enough to put a statement in writing for us?"

I went to the desk in the morning room and tried to phrase my experience as succinctly as possible. I hadn't quite finished when our telephone jangled. Burnall beat my grandfather to it. He came back with a quizzical look on his face.

"Now do you mind telling me the truth, my lady?"

"What do you mean? I've just told you the truth."

"There was no body in the bookshop."

"But I was there. I touched it. It was a dead person. His skin was cold, and I'm sure it was Mr. Solomon's face."

"My lads had to break down the door and they found nothing suspicious inside."

"Then I was right. Those people must have come for the body after I left."

Burnall was staring at me as if he was trying to read my mind. "It's a serious offense lying to the police."

"I didn't lie!" I could hear myself shouting and I know that a lady never raises her voice. My governess would have been horrified at me. "Look, I might have died last night. Ask those men who fished me out of the Thames this morning if you want proof that I was there."

His look softened a little. "I don't doubt that you had some kind of frightening experience, and maybe you were locked in the bookshop by mistake, but I think you let your imagination run away with you, didn't you? Maybe you touched a cushion or a pile of rags?"

"A pile of rags that was wearing glasses and had teeth? I felt his face, Chief Inspector, and he was dead. If you'd like to take me there, I'll show you the exact spot where he was lying. If you look carefully enough you'll find traces of blood, I'm certain. But this isn't the important matter today. If these people are planning some kind of dramatic and violent act, you need to have men on the alert and in place."

"And where would you suggest that I place these men?" he asked.

"I have no idea. A first step would be to arrest Edward Fotheringay."

"I have already told my men to bring him in for questioning. If you're sure you can remember no more specifics, then I don't see what else I can do at this moment."

"You don't really believe me, do you?"

"I believe any threat should be taken seriously, but given the vanishing body and the general nature of the danger, I can't judge how much of this is girlish hysteria and how much truth. In fact, if it weren't for Sidney Roberts, I wouldn't be going any further with this. Since he was finished off by an accomplished assassin, I have to accept that there may be something to what you're saying."

He turned back to the door. "I should alert the home secretary, I suppose. If there is some kind of foreign criminal element involved here, then he needs to know. And I suggest you stay put, my lady. If everything you've told me about last night is true, then you're lucky to be alive."

Then he left. My grandfather appeared. "Toffee-nosed geezer, isn't he? Come on, then, up to bed with you. You need a good sleep."

I didn't argue with that. I was beginning to feel sick and hollow inside, as much from fear as from lack of sleep. I went upstairs and curled up under my eiderdown. I must have nodded off immediately because I was awoken by someone shaking me. I started and tried to sit up.

"Sorry to wake you, ducks"—my grandfather's face was peering at me—"but I just remembered you're supposed to be at that garden party."

"Oh, Lord, I'd completely forgotten." I scrambled out of bed. "What time is it?"

"It's almost one and the party starts at two."

"Goodness. I'd better get a move on, then, hadn't I? For once I wish Mildred was here. She'd know what I was supposed to wear."

I flung open my wardrobe and realized that my trunk, containing almost all my clothes, was still up at Dippings. I had nothing to wear. I couldn't go. Then a chilling thought struck me: royal garden party. The king and queen mingling with their subjects on the palace lawn. Could this have been the event those conspirators had planned for?

I rushed downstairs and telephoned Chief Inspector Burnall, only to be told that he was out on a case. The young woman on the switchboard asked if I wanted to be put through to another officer, but I didn't think anyone would take me seriously. Besides, there would be policemen on duty at the palace. I had to go to the garden party myself to alert them. Nothing for it but to use up the last of Binky's money. If the princess came to stay with me again, I'd ask the queen for a contribution. If my suspicion was correct, she'd owe me a little more than a new dress!

I still had the white feather hat I usually wore to weddings, so I put that on—looking rather ridiculous with a simple cotton dress—then I caught a taxi to Harrods. I pointed to the hat. "Something to go with this. Royal garden party. Hurry."

The saleswoman looked startled but she was brilliant. In a few minutes we'd settled on a white silk dress with navy stripes that looked really elegant on me. I put it on, wrote a check, left the cotton dress behind in the changing room and was on my way to Buck House, arriving just a little after two o'clock. I joined the line of people at the side entrance, waiting to be admitted to the grounds. For some of them it was clearly a first visit to royalty and they looked nervous and excited. I heard a man in front of me saying, "If they could see me now, eh, Mother?"

And she replied. "You've done right proud for yourself, Stanley."

The queue inched forward, each person handing in his or her invitation at the gate. When it was my turn I asked, "Can you tell me if someone called Edward Fotheringay was invited today?"

The harried young man shook his head. "Afraid I can't, off the top of my head. We have the master list inside in the palace but if someone presents an invitation we admit them."

"Could you send someone to check for me?"

"I'm afraid we're rather fully occupied at the moment," he replied stiffly.

"Then can you tell me where I would find the person in charge of security?"

The line behind me was murmuring at being held up. The young man looked around, wondering how to get rid of me. Then he gestured to a uniformed bobby, who came hurrying over. "What seems to be the trouble?" he asked.

I took him aside and told him that we had to find out whether Edward Fotheringay was at the garden party. A matter of national security. I needed to speak to someone in charge. I could tell he wasn't sure whether to believe me or not.

"National security, you say? And your name is, miss?" he asked.

"I am the king's cousin, Lady Georgiana Rannoch," I said, and saw his expression change.

"Very good, m'lady. And you think this young man might try something disruptive?"

"I'm very much afraid he will."

"Follow me, then, your ladyship." He set off at a brisk march, up a flight of steps and into the lower floor of the palace. "If you'll wait here, I'll go and find my superiors."

I waited. Outside in the hallway a grandfather clock was ticking off the minutes with a sonorous tock, tock. At last I couldn't stand it any longer. I stuck my head out the door. Complete silence. No sign of any activity. Had the constable actually believed me or had he dumped me in that room purposely to keep me out of the way? I couldn't wait another second. If Edward was in that crowd, he had to be stopped. The gardens were now overflowing with well-dressed people, top hats and morning coats, flowing silk gowns and Ascot-style hats. I almost got stabbed in the eye by many a protruding feather as I edged my way through the crowd. Some less genteel ladies thought I was trying to gain an advantageous position and blocked me with a threatening elbow.

Waiters were moving through the crowd carrying trays of Pimm's and champagne, canapés and petit fours. I moved into the wake of one of them and let him clear a path for me as my eyes searched left and right for any sign of Edward. But there were any number of dark and elegant young men in top hats, and plenty of bushes and statues to skulk behind. The whole thing was hopeless if that wretched bobby hadn't believed me. Then a voice called my name, and there was Lady Cromer-Strode, waving to me.

"We've been looking for you," she said. "Hanni was afraid you hadn't come."

Hanni was standing beside her, looking sulky in an unbecoming plain gray silk dress.

"Lady Cromer-Strode said I must wear this because I am in mourning for the baroness and my pink frock was not suitable," she said. "It belongs to Fiona. It is too big."

It was. Fiona was a healthy girl. She stood on the other side of her mother, looking resplendent in bright flowery turquoise.

I looked at Hanni, trying to reconcile my suspicions with the person I had entertained for the past week or so. "How are you faring at the Cromer-Strodes', apart from having to wear a dress you don't like? Having a good time?"

Hanni frowned. "It is boring," she said. "Most people went home. Only old people now."

"Darcy and Edward both left?" I asked in a low voice because I didn't want Fiona to hear.

She nodded.

Fiona must have heard her beloved's name. "Edward said he'd be joining us today," she said, "but I haven't seen him yet."

"There was a long line waiting to get in," I said. "He's probably held up outside."

Even as I said it, I realized that the men at the gate would probably not have been instructed to stop Edward from entering. I should go back and warn them. "I'll be back," I said. "Save me a spot."

As I fought my way back toward the gate, a murmur went through the crowd and the Guards band on the terrace struck up the national anthem. The royal couple must have emerged from the palace. An expectant hush fell upon the crowd as they parted to provide a pathway for the king and queen. As everyone was peering forward for that first glimpse of the royal couple, I was the only person hurrying in the wrong direction. I jumped when someone grabbed my arm.

"I didn't know you were coming to this bean feast." It was my mother, looking absolutely ravishing in black and white, a glass of champagne in her hand.

I wasn't usually glad to see her, but today I could have hugged her. "What are you doing here?" I asked.

"Max's idea. His motorcar company wants to go into some kind of partnership with an English company. He thought this would be a good way to meet the owner informally—set things off on the right foot, so to speak. He's probably standing in a corner, doing business even as we speak. I have to say, that man does know how to make money." She glanced at me critically. "Nice dress," she said, "but off the peg. You really should get yourself a good dressmaker."

"Question of money, mother. If you'd like to finance a wardrobe . . ."

"We'll go shopping, darling. . . ."

"Mother," I cut in, "you haven't seen Edward Fotheringay this afternoon, have you?"

She gave me a frosty stare. "Now why should I be looking for Edward Fotheringay?"

"Last time I saw you, I'd say you were rather chummy with him."

"That was just a mad, impetuous fling," she said. "A sudden yearning for someone nice and solid and British—oh, and young too. Good firm body. But it turned out to be quite wrong for me. The boy has no money and he can't keep his hands off other women. So please don't mention his name again, especially not when Max is around."

"But you haven't seen him today, have you? It's important."

"I haven't been looking for him, darling." She was glancing around, enjoying the admiring and envying stares she was getting. She always did like being the center of attention. I was about to move on when she grabbed my arm again. "I meant to ask you," she said, "who is the pretty little blond girl you brought with you to that party? She's over there now, wearing the most extraordinarily ugly dress."

"That's Princess Hannelore. Didn't I tell you she was staying with me?"

"Princess Hannelore?"

"Of Bavaria, you know."

My mother was staring at Hanni, who was now at the front of the pathway along which the king and queen would be coming. "Unless she has shrunk considerably in the last few weeks, that is definitely not Princess Hannelore." She looked amused at my stunned face. "Hannelore is taller than that, and thinner too, and from what I heard in Germany, she's been quite ill and is currently recuperating on her family's yacht on the Med."

"Then who is this?" I gasped.

"Never seen her before last week," my mother said. "Oh, there's Max now. Yoo-hoo, Max darling!" And she was gone.

Murmurs indicated that the royal couple was approaching. Hanni, or whoever she was, stood there, leaning forward to catch a glimpse with the rest of the crowd. Suspicions raced through my mind. Could Edward have persuaded her to do something for him? Set off a bomb? I studied her carefully. She was not carrying a purse and wore only a small straw hat. Nowhere to conceal a bomb then.

The king and queen had come into view, shaking hands and entering into conversation with those they passed. Still no sign of Edward. Then two things happened at the same moment. I spotted a familiar face. Darcy O'Mara was standing on the opposite side of the reception line. His dark unruly curls had been tamed for the occasion and he looked breathtakingly handsome in a morning suit. Before I could catch his eye I saw Hanni reach into the folds of that voluminous dress and pull out a small pistol.

The king and queen were almost upon them.

"Darcy!" I shouted. "She's got a—"

But I didn't have time to finish the sentence. Darcy rushed forward and threw himself upon Hanni as the gun went off, sounding no louder than a cap pistol. They fell to the ground together. There were screams and shouts, general chaos as policemen and palace servants came running.

"She has a gun!" I screamed. "She was trying to kill Their Majesties!"

"Stupid fools," Hanni spat out at the men who wrestled the gun away from her. "We shall succeed next time."

I waited for Darcy to get up. But he didn't. He was lying on the gravel and a trickle of blood was coming from under his right shoulder.

Chapter 37

"Darcy!" I screamed and fought my way toward him. "He's hurt. Get an ambulance. Do something!"

Hands were already turning him over. His face was ashen white and a big, ugly dark stain decorated his morning coat. "No!" I dropped to the ground beside him.

"He can't be dead. Darcy, please don't die. I'll do anything. Please." I took his hand. It was still warm.

Darcy's eyes fluttered open and focused on me. "Anything?" he whispered, then lapsed into unconsciousness again.

"Out of the way," a voice was saying. "I'm a doctor, let me through." And a portly man in a morning coat knelt beside me, huffing and puffing a little.

He opened Darcy's coat and shirt, took out his own handkerchief and pressed it onto the wound. "You men. Get him into the palace, quickly."

Several men picked up Darcy and the crowd parted for them as they carried him. I glimpsed Her Majesty's shocked face before she turned back to the crowd. "Everything is under control," she said in her clear voice. "We shall proceed with the party as if nothing had happened." And she began to move through the crowd, shaking hands again.

"Edward Fotheringay," I shouted as the police dragged Hanni away. "He must be here somewhere. Don't let him leave."

Then I stumbled up the steps after the procession. They placed Darcy on the floor in a serving area, below the *piano nobile*. The portly doctor had stripped off his coat, rolled up his sleeves and was examining Darcy's body.

I could stand it no longer. "Shouldn't we have called an ambulance? Shouldn't he be going to hospital instead of your wasting time examining him here?"

He looked up at me, his big, bearded face red with effort. "My dear young lady. I am considered by most to be the premier surgeon in England, although a young pup from St. Thomas's would no doubt dispute that fact. I just need to check whether—ah, good. Yes."

He looked up at the crowd that had now gathered around us. "My car and driver are waiting outside. Be good enough to summon them, my man." This to one of the palace staff who stood nearby, wide-eyed. "And you, bring towels. We need to stop the bleeding."

Then he stood up with some difficulty. "Westminster is closest, I suppose, but Thomas's is bigger and, as an old University College Hospital man, I regret to say probably better in an emergency situation. That's it then. Carry him out to my car. We'll go to Thomas's."

I touched his arm. "Is he going to be all right? Is he going to live?"

He looked down at me and smiled. "He's a lucky devil. The bullet went through his right shoulder, appears to have missed his lung, and came out the other side. So no need to dig around to locate it. All he needs is cleaning and sewing up, and I can do those myself. He's going to be devilishly sore for a while, of course, but unless he insists on throwing himself into the path of bullets on a regular basis, I can safely say that he'll lead a long and happy life."

Tears flooded into my eyes. I turned away and headed back to the gardens because I didn't want the staff to see me crying. Outside in the bright sunlight I was immediately accosted by plainclothes security men, who were now very interested to hear what I had to say. So I had to go through the story, from the arrival of the mock-princess to the episode after the communist rally the night before. They took notes, painfully slowly, and asked me the same questions over and over, while all the time all I wanted to do was be with Darcy.

At last they let me go. I took a taxi to St. Thomas's Hospital across the Thames. In usual infuriating hospital fashion they wouldn't let me see Darcy for what seemed like ages. I sat in that dismal waiting room with its brown linoleum and drab green walls plastered with cheerful notices, ranging from *Coughs and sneezes spread disease* to *You can't catch venereal disease from lavatory seats.*

When I had badgered a passing nurse for the umpteenth time I was finally permitted to see him. He was tucked into white starched sheets and his face looked as pale as the pillow behind him. His eyes were closed and I couldn't detect any breathing. I must have let out a little gasp because his eyes opened, then focused on me and he smiled.

"Hello," I said, feeling suddenly shy. "How are you feeling?"

"Floating, actually. I think they must have given me something. It's rather nice."

"You knew, didn't you?" I said, perching on the edge of his bed. "You knew she was going to do something like that?"

"Suspected it, yes. We were tipped off that they planned to send agents over here by someone within the party in Germany, so I kept a close eye on that young lady."

"That's why you were playing up to her and being so friendly?" Relief flooded through me.

"It wasn't exactly a hard assignment," he said. "Now if they'd asked me to shadow the baroness—well, the poor old thing might still be alive, but it would have been a harder job."

I looked at him until he said, "What?"

"Darcy—who are you?"

"You know who I am. The Honorable Darcy O'Mara, heir to the now landless Lord Kilhenny."

"I meant what are you?"

"A wild Irish boy who enjoys the occasional bit of fun and excitement," he said, with the ghost of his usual wicked grin.

"You're not going to tell me any more, are you?"

"They told me not to talk."

"You're infuriating, do you know that?" I said more vehemently than I intended, in the way that one does after a shock. "You scared the daylights out of me. Don't ever do something like that again."

"But if it takes something like this to get you to come willingly to my bed, then it was worth it. And I haven't forgotten your promise."

"What promise?"

"That you'd do anything if I didn't die."

"You just get yourself strong enough first," I said. I leaned forward and kissed his forehead.

"Oh, believe me, I fully intend to be strong enough." He reached up to touch my face.

"There will be no more of that," said the ward sister firmly. "In fact it's time you went."

Darcy's hand remained touching my cheek.

"Come back soon, won't you?" he whispered. "Don't leave me to the mercies of that dragon."

"I heard that," said the sister.

RANNOCH HOUSE
MONDAY, JUNE 27, 1932

Diary,
Eventful day ahead.
Mildred arrived back in London last night and announced her intention to leave me. It seems Lady Cromer-Strode has made her an offer she can't refuse. I tried not to smile when she imparted this sad news to me.
Darcy will be released from hospital later today.
Oh, and the queen has summoned me.

"What an extraordinary thing to have happened, wasn't it, Georgiana?" the queen said. It was several days later and order had been restored to Buckingham Palace. The press had had a field day with headlines about anarchists and assassins in our midst and the outpouring of love for the royal family had been most touching. So Hanni and her misguided friends had achieved quite the opposite of their objective.

"Most extraordinary, ma'am."

"That young woman duped all of us. I still can't imagine how she got away with it."

"She seized the opportunity, ma'am. From what we have been told, they had a communist agent working inside the Bavarian court. They were hoping to create instability in Germany and topple the current German government. When the real Princess Hannelore fell ill suddenly and the king wrote a letter to tell you that she could not accept your kind invitation after all, that letter was intercepted. The royal party departed for their yacht and a long cruise and the communists sent this girl in Hannelore's place. She's an actress, you know, and she has worked bit-parts in Hollywood. She realized that her English would sound American, hence she pretended to be a fan of American films. I must admit she played her part very well. She only slipped up once that I could tell."

"When was that?"

"She said the Jungfrau was in Bavaria. Of course it's in Switzerland. What Bavarian would not know the names of her own mountains?"

"She was really German?"

"Yes, but not Bavarian."

"So the girl was really the ringleader? She seemed so sweet and innocent."

"As I said, she played her part remarkably well. She's older than eighteen, of course, but she looks remarkably young for her age. But she wasn't the ringleader, as you put it. The maid—Irmgardt—she was the agent sent from Russia to oversee the whole thing. She was the one whose voice I heard that night in the bookshop. They caught her at Dover, trying to escape."

"And the baroness—was she part of their plot?"

"Absolutely not. She was a real baroness. She hadn't seen Hannelore for some time so she was easily deceived, but obviously her presence was becoming a threat to them. First they managed to banish her to the Dowager Countess Sophia's, but then, when they were together again, she threatened to telephone the princess's father. Of course that would have upset the whole apple cart. It was the maid Irmgardt who put the drug in her tea to produce a heart attack. Hanni and Edward Fotheringay had a perfect alibi, in a car with me."

"Horrible, utterly horrible." The queen shuddered. "And who did kill that poor young man at the bookshop?"

"Sidney Roberts? Hanni did it herself, of course. She was, after all, a trained assassin. One gathers that the knife had a folding blade, so she was able to hide it quite easily. You're very lucky to be alive, ma'am. She was constantly looking for opportunities to kill you. She kept pestering me to take her to the palace, then to take her to see you at Sandringham."

"Goodness." The queen had to take a sip of tea. "One doesn't expect such threats in the English countryside, does one?"

"Or from the English nobility," I added. "I'm so glad they finally caught Edward Fotheringay trying to flee the country."

"Of course that boy was only half English, so one understands," the queen said. "He had a Russian mother, didn't he?"

"An aristocrat, which makes it even more strange that he was seduced by communism."

"Young people are so strange," the queen said. "Except you, of course. You've done splendidly, Georgiana. The king and I are most grateful." She paused, looked at me and sighed.

"And all this leaves my son no nearer to making a good match, does it?"

"I'm afraid not, ma'am."

"I worry what will happen to the empire when the king dies, Georgiana, if the boy can't even choose a bride for the good of his country. There are so many suitable girls to choose from—you, for example."

"Oh no, ma'am," I said. "I could never compete with Mrs. Simpson." Besides, I thought but didn't say out loud, my interests lie elsewhere.

Royal Flush

This book is dedicated to Merion Webster Sauer and her son, Lee,
who have been temporarily elevated to the peerage.

My grateful thanks as always to John and Jane
for their wonderful insights and critiques,
and to Jackie Cantor and Meg Ruley
for making my writing life so easy, pleasant and fun.

Author's Note

Although real people walk across these pages, this book is purely fictional. Balmoral is portrayed just as it is, but if you try to find Castle Rannoch on the map, it only exists in my imagination. And I'm afraid I've taken liberties with the road from Balmoral to Castle Rannoch. There really is no serviceable direct route, but I've had one made through the mountains for the purposes of this book.

Chapter 1

RANNOCH HOUSE
BELGRAVE SQUARE
LONDON W.I.
AUGUST 12, 1932

It is my opinion that there is no place on earth more uncomfortable than London during a heat wave. I should probably qualify this by confessing that I have never gone up the Congo River into the Heart of Darkness with Conrad, nor have I crossed the Sahara by camel. But at least people venturing to those parts are prepared to be uncomfortable. London is so seldom even vaguely warm that we are always caught completely unprepared. The tube turns into a good imitation of the infamous Black Hole of Calcutta and the smell of unwashed armpits, strap-hanging inches from one's face, is overwhelming.

You may be wondering whether members of the royal family frequently ride on the underground. The answer, of course, is no. My austere relatives King George V and Queen Mary would have only the vaguest idea of what the tube train was. Of course, I am only thirty-fourth in line to the throne, and I am probably the only member of my family who was at that moment penniless and trying to survive on her own, in London, without servants. So let me introduce myself before we continue. My full name is Lady Victoria Georgiana Charlotte Eugenie of Glen Garry and Rannoch. My grandmother was the least attractive of Queen Victoria's many daughters, judging by those early photographs I've seen of her. But then those old photographs did tend to make most people look grouchy, didn't they? Anyway, no proposals from kaisers or kings were forthcoming for her, so she was hitched to a Scottish duke and lived at Castle Rannoch, in remotest Scotland, until she died of fresh air and boredom.

My brother, Binky, is the current duke. He's also pretty much penniless, our father having lost the last of the family fortune in the great crash of '29, before shooting himself on the moors and saddling Binky with horrendous death duties. At least Binky's got the estate with the home farm and the huntin', shootin' and fishin', as the landed gentry are wont to say, so he's not exactly starving. I've been living on baked beans, toast and tea. I was raised with no skills other than passable French, knowing how to walk with a book on my head and where to seat a bishop at a dinner table. Hardly enough to tempt a prospective employer, if getting an ordinary job were not frowned upon for someone in my position. I tried it once—the cosmetics counter at Harrods. I lasted all of four hours.

And of course England is in the midst of a most awful depression. You only have to look on any street corner at those tragic men standing with signs saying *Will accept any kind of work* to know that things are pretty grim for most people. Not for most of my social class, however. For most of them life goes on unchanged, with yachts on the Med and extravagant parties. They probably don't even know the country is in a bad way.

So now you know why there is no Bentley and chauffeur parked outside Rannoch House, our family's London home on Belgrave Square, and why I can't even afford to take a taxicab too often. I do usually try to avoid the tube, however. For a country-bred girl like myself the descent into that black hole has always been a cause for alarm—and more so since I was almost pushed under a train by a man who was trying to kill me.

But on this occasion I had no choice. Central London was so unbearably stifling that I decided to go and visit my grandfather, who lives on the fringes of London in Essex, and the District Line was the way to travel. Oh, and I suppose I should clarify that I'm not speaking about my grandfather the Scottish duke, whose ghost is still reputed to play the bagpipes on the battlements of our ancestral home, Castle Rannoch in Perthshire, Scotland. I'm speaking of my nonroyal grandfather, who lives just outside London in a modest semidetached with gnomes in the front garden. You see, my mother was an actress and the daughter of a Cockney policeman. She was also a notorious bolter. She left my father when I was only two and has subsequently worked her way from an Argentinian polo player, to a Monte Carlo rally driver and a Texan oil millionaire. Her romantic exploits have truly spanned the globe, unlike her daughter who has yet to have a romantic exploit.

After she bolted I was raised at Castle Rannoch. As you can imagine, I was kept well away from my mother's side of the family when I was growing up. So I have only just got to know my grandfather and frankly I adore him. He is the only person in the world with whom I can be myself. It's like having a real family for once!

To my intense disappointment my grandfather was not at home. Neither was the widow next door with whom he had developed a close friendship. If Granddad had been on the phone, I could have saved myself the trip. But the idea of telephone communication hadn't exactly reached darkest Essex yet. I was standing in Granddad's front garden, under the disapproving stare of those gnomes, not sure what to do next, when an elderly man walked past with an elderly dog on a leash. He looked at me then shook his head.

"He ain't there, love. He's gone." (He pronounced it "gawn.")

"Gone? Where?" I asked in alarm as visions of hospitals or worse swam into my head. Granddad's health had not been too brilliant recently.

"Down Clacton."

I had no idea what a Clacton was or how one went down it. "Down Clacton?" I repeated hopefully.

He nodded. "Yeah. Workingmen's club outing. In the charabanc. Her next door went with him." And he gave me a knowing wink. I let out a sigh of relief. An outing. In a coach. Probably to the seaside. So even my grandfather was managing to escape the heat. I had no choice but to take the train back to the city. All my friends had deserted London for their country estates, their yachts or the Continent, and here I was, feeling hot and increasingly despondent in a carriage full of sweaty bodies.

"What am I doing here?" I asked myself. I had no skills, no hope of employment and no idea where to turn next. Nobody with any sense and money stayed in London during the month of August. And as for Darcy, the wild son of an Irish peer whom I thought was my current boyfriend . . . I hadn't heard from him since he disappeared yet again, ostensibly to go home to Ireland to recover from his gunshot wound. This might be true, or it might not. With Darcy one never knew.

Of course I could go home to Scotland, I told myself, as the air in the tube train became stifling. The memory of the cold wind sweeping down the loch and the equally cold drafts sweeping down the corridors of Castle Rannoch was sorely tempting as I rode the escalator up from St. James's tube station, dabbing ineffectively at the beads of sweat trickling down my face. And yes, I know ladies don't sweat, but something was running down my face in great rivulets.

I was almost ready to rush home to Belgrave Square, pack a suitcase and catch the next train to Edinburgh, when I reminded myself why I had left home in the first place. The answer was Fig, my sister-in-law, the current duchess—mean-spirited, judgmental and utterly awful. Fig had made it very clear that I was a burden to them, no longer wanted at Castle Rannoch, and that she begrudged my eating their food. So when it came to enduring the heat and loneliness in London or enduring Fig, the heat won out.

Only two more weeks, I told myself as I walked home through Hyde Park. In two weeks' time I was invited to Scotland, not to my ancestral home, but to Balmoral. The king and queen had already gone up to their Scottish castle, just a few miles from our own, in time for the Glorious Twelfth, the day when the grouse shooting season officially begins. They would remain there, shooting and stalking anything with fur or feathers, for the next month and expected their various relatives to come and stay for at least part of this time. Most people tried to avoid this: they found the bagpipes at dawn, the wind moaning down the chimney, the Highland dances and the tartan wallpaper hard to endure. I was used to all this. It was just like Castle Rannoch.

Cheered by the prospect of good, fresh Highland air in the not-too-distant future, I picked my way past the bodies in Green Park. It looked like the aftermath of a particularly nasty battle—with half-naked corpses strewn everywhere. They were, in fact, London office workers making the most of the weather, sunbathing with their shirts off. A frightful sight—the bodies striped white and red depending on which parts of them had been exposed to the sun. I was halfway across the park when the bodies started to move. I noticed the sun had disappeared and at the very moment I looked up there was an ominous rumble of thunder.

The sky darkened quickly as storm clouds gathered. The sunbathers were hastily putting on their shirts and making for shelter. I began to hurry too. Not fast enough, however. Without warning the heavens opened and rain came down in a solid sheet. Girls ran screaming to the shelter of trees, which was probably not wise, given the approaching sounds of thunder. Hail bounced from the footpaths. There was no point in my seeking shelter. I was already soaked to the skin and home was only minutes away. So I ran, my hair plastered to my face, my summer frock clinging suggestively to my body, until I staggered up the steps of Rannoch House.

If I had felt depressed before, I was now well and truly in the dumps. What else could possibly go wrong? I had come to London full of hope and excitement, and nothing seemed to be working out. Then I caught sight of myself in the hall stand mirror and recoiled in horror. "Just look at you!" I said aloud. "You look like a drowned rat. If the queen could see you now." Then I started to laugh. I laughed all the way upstairs to the bathroom, where I took a long soak in the tub. By the time I had dried myself off I was feeling quite normal again. And I wasn't going to spend another dreary evening alone in Rannoch House with only the radio for company. Someone apart from me must be in London. And of course I immediately thought of Belinda. She was one of those people who never stayed in one place for long. When last seen she was flitting off to a villa in Italy but there was just a chance she might have tired of Italians and come home.

I sought out the least rumpled of my summer dresses (having had no maid to iron my clothes for a while now and very little idea how to iron them myself), hid my wet hair under a demure cloche hat and set off for Belinda's mews cottage, in nearby Knightsbridge. Unlike me, Belinda had come into an inheritance when she turned twenty-one. This had enabled her to buy a dinky little mews establishment and keep a maid. Also her living costs were practically nil, given the amount of time she spent in other people's homes, not to mention their beds.

The thunderstorm had passed over, leaving the evening air slightly cooler but still muggy. I picked my way past puddles and avoided the taxicabs that splashed through standing water on the street. I was at the entrance to the mews when I heard a loud roaring sound behind me. I was conscious of a sleek dark shape hurtling toward me and only just had time to fling myself aside as a motor bicycle came at me. It shot through the enormous puddle that had collected at the mews entrance, sending a great sheet of muddy water all over me.

"I say!" I tried to shout over the roar of the engine as it continued into the mews without slowing. I took off in pursuit, absolutely boiling with rage now, not pausing to consider whether the bike riders might be bank robbers or burglars fleeing from the police. The motorbike skidded to a halt farther down the mews and two men dressed in leather jackets, leather helmets and goggles were starting to dismount.

"What the devil do you think you were doing?" I demanded as I approached them, my anger still blinding me to the fact that I was alone in a backstreet with two distinctly antisocial characters. "Just look at what you did. I'm soaked."

"Yes, you do appear to have become a trifle wet," the first rider said, and to my extreme annoyance, he started to laugh.

"It's not funny!" I snapped. "You have ruined a perfectly good dress, and as for my hat . . ."

The person who had been riding pillion dismounted and was in the process of unbuckling a helmet. "Of course it's not funny, Paolo." The voice was female, and she pulled off her helmet and goggles with a flourish, shaking out a sleek head of dark bobbed hair.

"Belinda!" I exclaimed.

Chapter 2

BELINDA WARBURTON-STOKE'S MEWS COTTAGE
KNIGHTSBRIDGE
LONDON W.1.
AUGUST 12, 1932

Belinda's eyes opened wide with recognition. "Georgie! Oh, my goodness, you poor thing. Just look at you. Paolo, you've nearly drowned my best friend."

The other motorcycle rider had now removed his own helmet and was revealed to be an absolutely gorgeous man of the Latin type, with dark, flashing eyes and luxuriant black hair. "So sorry," he said. "I did not see you. The shadows, you know. And we were going rather fast." He spoke with a pronounced foreign accent, overlaid with an English education at some stage.

"Paolo just loves anything fast," Belinda said, gazing at him adoringly. The thought crossed my mind that she probably fit this criterion. Fast and loose, that was Belinda all right.

"We've just come from Brooklands," she went on. "Paolo's been practicing his motor racing. And he flies an aeroplane too. He's promised to take me up."

"You must introduce me, Belinda," Paolo said, "and then you must take your friend inside, give her a drink to calm her nerves and clean her up a little."

"Of course, darling," Belinda said. "Georgie, this is Paolo."

Paolo turned those incredible dark eyes on me. "Georgie? This is a name for a boy, no?"

"It's short for Georgiana," I said.

"Oh, very well, I suppose I had better introduce you formally," Belinda said. "May I present Count Paolo di Marola e Martini. Paolo, this is my dearest friend, Lady Georgiana of Glen Garry and Rannoch."

Paolo turned that devastating gaze onto me again. "You are Binky's sister?" he asked.

"I am. How do you know Binky?"

"We were at school together for one dreadful year," Paolo said. "My father wanted to turn me into a Civilized English Gentleman. He did not succeed. I loathed it. All those cold baths and hearty rugby games. Luckily I was asked to leave because I pinched the bottoms of the maids."

"Yes. That sounds like you," Belinda said. She opened her front door and ushered us in. "Florrie," she called, "I need a bath run straightaway." She turned to look at me. "I'd ask you to sit down but frankly you'd make an awful mess of my sofa. But you can mix her a drink, Paolo. A good strong one."

"I'm afraid I have to be on my way, *cara mia*," Paolo said. "I will leave you two girls to your gossip. But tonight we will go dancing, *si*? Or I take you to Crockford's for a little gambling, and then to a nightclub if you like."

"I'd adore it," Belinda said, "but unfortunately I'm busy this evening."

"Nonsense," Paolo said. "Telephone whoever it is and say your long-lost cousin just came into town, or your sister has had a baby, or you've come down with chicken pox."

"I must admit it's very tempting," Belinda said. "But I really can't back out now. The poor dear would be devastated."

"Another man?" Paolo demanded, eyes flashing.

"Keep your hair on," Belinda said.

"My hair? What has this to do with my hair?"

Belinda chuckled. "It's an expression, darling. It means don't get upset over nothing."

"These English expressions are very silly," Paolo said. "Why should I not get upset if you have a date with another man?"

"Don't be silly. Of course I don't have a date with another man," Belinda said. "I'm doing my brother a favor and entertaining an old American who wants to buy one of his racehorses."

"And you could not cancel that for me?" Paolo moved dangerously close to her and ran his fingertips across her cheek. I could see her weakening.

"No, I couldn't let my brother down," Belinda said.

"I shall be devastated," Paolo moaned. "Absolutely brokenhearted. I shall think that you don't truly love me."

Why did men never say things like this to me, I wondered.

"You know, I've just had a brilliant idea." Belinda swiveled around to look at me. "Georgie could go instead of me, couldn't you, darling?"

"Oh yes," I said bitterly. "I'm certainly dressed for entertaining visiting Americans."

"It's not until eight thirty, darling," Belinda said, "and you can have a bath here and wear whatever you like from my wardrobe. My maid will help you dress, won't you, Florrie?" She turned to the maid, who was hovering at the foot of the stairs.

Nobody waited for the maid to reply.

"Splendid," Paolo said, clapping his hands. "Then I bid you ladies *arrivederci* and I will call for you at nine, *cara mia.*"

"Not on your motorcycle, Paolo," Belinda said. "I refuse to perch on the pillion in my evening togs."

"Dogs? You wish to bring dogs?"

"Togs, darling. Another word for clothes."

"English is such a silly language," Paolo said again. He bowed to me. "*Arrivederci.* Until we meet again, Lady Georgiana." And he was gone.

"Belinda," I said as she turned to face me with a big smile on her face. "You have a frightful nerve. How can I entertain this visiting American? I know very little about racehorses, and he'll expect to be meeting with you."

"Don't be silly, darling." Belinda put a comforting hand on my arm and steered me toward the stairs. "He's not really here to buy racehorses. He's in oil or something. I met him at Crockford's when I was having a little flutter last night, and I agreed to go to dinner with him because the poor lamb is in town on business and he hates to dine alone. But of course I couldn't tell Paolo that. He's madly jealous."

"So you've stuck me with an unknown American, who is going to be disappointed that I'm not you and is probably expecting more than dinner."

"Of course not." We had reached the bathroom, from which steam was now billowing. "He's from the Midwest and the only thing that's likely to happen to you is that you'll die of boredom. He'll be so impressed when he finds out that he's dining with the king's cousin. And you'll get a lovely dinner and good wines. I'm doing you a favor, really."

I laughed. "Belinda, when have you ever done anybody a favor? You are one of the world's great manipulators."

"You're probably right." She sighed. "But you will do it for me?" She almost dragged me up the last of the stairs.

I sighed. "I suppose so. What have I got to lose?"

"I don't know. What have you?" She regarded me quizzically. I blushed. "Don't tell me you haven't done it yet! Georgiana, I despair of you. Last time I saw you and Darcy, you appeared to be very chummy."

"The last time I saw him I thought we were chummy too," I said, feeling a black cloud of gloom settling over me. "But he was in hospital at the time, remember. Weak and recovering from a gunshot wound. The moment he came out of hospital he went home to Ireland to recuperate and that's the last I've seen of him. Not even a postcard."

"I don't think he's the postcard-writing type," Belinda said. "Don't worry, he'll turn up again, like the proverbial bad penny. Darcy's as much an opportunist as I am. He's probably found someone to host him on a yacht off the French Riviera."

I chewed on my lip, a bad habit that my governess, Miss MacAlister, had tried to break but never fully succeeded. "The problem is that I'm due up in Scotland soon. That means I won't be seeing him all summer."

"You should have leaped into bed with him when you first had the chance," Belinda said. "Men like Darcy won't wait around forever."

"I know," I said. "It's that Castle Rannoch upbringing. All those ancestors who did the right thing. I kept thinking of Robert Bruce Rannoch, who stood his ground at the battle of Culloden and fought on alone until he was hacked to pieces."

"I fail to see what that has to do with your losing your virginity, darling."

"Duty, I suppose. A Rannoch never shirks her duty."

"And you feel it's your duty to remain a virgin until you either wed or die, do you?"

"Not really," I said. "In fact it seems rather silly when you put it that way. I just had this vision of my mother, leaping from one bed to the next all her life, and I didn't want to turn out like that."

"But think of the fun she's had doing it. And all those lovely clothes she's acquired along the way."

"I'm not like that," I said. "I'm afraid I must take after my great-grandmother, Queen Victoria. I want to find one man to love and to marry. And I really don't care about the clothes."

"I can see that." Belinda eyed me critically. She turned to her maid, who was standing patiently with arms full of towels. "Help Lady Georgiana out of those disgusting wet clothes, Florrie. And then take them away and wash them and bring her a robe."

I allowed myself to be undressed and then lowered myself into the bathtub while Belinda perched on the tub rim.

"So what do you think of Paolo?" she asked. "Isn't he divine?"

"Very divine. Did you meet him in Italy?"

"He came to the villa where I was staying"—she paused for effect—"with his fiancée."

"His fiancée? Belinda, how could you?"

"Don't worry, darling. It's not the same over there. They are Catholic, you know. He's been engaged to this girl for at least ten years. She's very proper and spends half her time on her knees, praying her rosary, but it keeps his family happy, knowing he'll eventually marry someone like that. In the meantime . . ." She gave me a wicked grin.

I felt rather odd, lying in a tub of hot water while Belinda perched on the rim, but she seemed to feel this was quite normal. "This is like old times, isn't it, darling?" she commented. "Remember the chats we used to have in the bathroom at school?"

I smiled. "I do remember. It was the only place we could go where we couldn't be overheard."

"So what have you been doing with yourself?" she asked. "How is your char lady business going?"

"It's not a char lady business, Belinda. It is a domestic service agency. I prepare people's London houses for their arrival. I don't scrub floors or anything like that."

"And the relatives at the palace still haven't found out about it?"

"No, thank God. But in answer to your first question, it's not going at all. I haven't had a job in weeks."

"Well, you wouldn't, would you?" Belinda stretched out her long legs.

"Nobody comes to London in the summer. Anybody who can escape from it does so."

I nodded. "I've begun to feel that I'm the only person still here. Even my grandfather has gone to Clacton-on-Sea on an outing."

"So how have you been surviving?"

"Not very well," I said. "I'm pretty much down to tea and toast. I'll have to do something soon, or I'll be joining the lines at the soup kitchens."

"Don't be silly, darling. You could get yourself invited to any number of country houses if you wanted to. You probably are the most eligible spinster in the country, you know."

"I don't know people the way you do, Belinda. And I wouldn't know how to invite myself to someone's house."

"I'll do the inviting, if you like."

I smiled at her. "The fact is that I just don't enjoy sponging off people."

"Well, you could always go home to Castle Rannoch."

"I considered that, which shows you how desperate I've been feeling. But if it was a choice between Fig and starvation, then I think starvation would win."

She looked at me with concern. "My poor, sweet Georgie: no work, no friends and no sex. No wonder you're looking gloomy. We must cheer you up. You'll get a good meal tonight, of course, and tomorrow you can come with me to Croydon."

"Croydon? That's supposed to cheer me up?"

"The aerodrome, darling. I'm going to see Paolo's new plane. He may even take us up."

Having seen the reckless abandon with which Paolo drove a motorcycle, I wasn't too keen to go up in his plane, but I managed a smile. "Spiffing," I said. At least it would be better than sitting at home.

Chapter 3

RANNOCH HOUSE
AUGUST 13, 1932

Weather still muggy.

At ten o'clock the next morning Belinda showed up on my doorstep, looking fresh and stunning in white linen trousers and a black-and-white-striped blouse. The ensemble was topped off with a jaunty little black pillbox hat. One would never have guessed that she had probably been out all night.

"Ready?" she asked, casting a critical eye over my summer dress and the cloche, from which most of the mud had been removed. "Are you sure that outfit will be suitable for flying upside down?"

"I think I'll leave the flying upside down to you," I said, "and I don't possess any trousers other than the ones I wear around the estate at home, and they smell of horse."

"We'll have to do something about your wardrobe, darling." She attempted to smooth the creases from my cotton skirt. "What a pity your mother is so petite, or you could have all her castoffs."

"She's offered to buy me new clothes on several occasions, but you know my mother. She always forgets and flits away again. Besides, I don't think I'd feel comfortable accepting money that comes from her German boyfriend."

"She's still with her beefy industrialist, then?"

"The last time I heard. But that was a month ago. Who knows."

Belinda chuckled. I closed the front door and followed her to a waiting taxicab.

"So do tell, I'm dying to hear about last night," she said as the cab drove off. "How was your dinner with Mr. Hamburger?"

"Schlossberger," I corrected. "Hiram Schlossberger, from Kansas City. It went exactly as you predicted. He was completely overawed by my royal connections and he would keep calling me 'Your Highness' even though I told him I was only 'my lady' and that we didn't have to be so formal. He was rather a dear, actually, but I'm afraid he was rather boring. He produced snapshots of his wife and children and dog and even the cows on his ranch."

"But you did get a good meal out of it?"

"Delicious. Although Mr. Schlossberger wasn't happy with it. He turned his nose up at the foie gras and the lobster bisque and said all he wanted was a good steak. Then he complained about the size of it. Apparently at home he eats steaks that are so large they hang over the sides of the plate."

"Heavens, that's half a cow. But you had some decent bubbly, I hope?"

I shook my head. "He doesn't drink. Prohibition, you know."

"How ridiculous. Everybody knows that prohibition exists, but everybody drinks anyway. Except him, apparently. So what did you drink?"

I made a face. "Lemonade. He ordered it for both of us."

Belinda touched my arm. "My darling, I am so sorry. Next time I foist off one of my men on you, I'll make sure he doesn't drink lemonade."

"Next time?" I asked. "Do you make a habit of this sort of thing?"

"Oh, absolutely, darling. How else does one get a decent meal occasionally? And one is doing a public service, actually. These poor men come to London to do business and they don't know anybody so they are delighted to be seen with a young society woman who can show them how to behave. Your Mr. Hamburger will be bragging about you for years, I'm sure."

We alighted from our taxicab at Victoria Station and soon our train was huffing and puffing through the drearier parts of south London on our way to Croydon. Belinda had launched into a long description of the villa in Italy. I was half listening as I stared out of the window at those pathetic back gardens with lines of washing strung across them. Because an idea was germinating in my mind. All those men Belinda had mentioned—in London alone on business and having to eat without companionship. What if I started a service to supply each of them with a charming dinner companion of impeccable social pedigree—in other words, *moi*. It would be better than cleaning houses and at the very least would keep the wolf from the door. At best it might prove to be highly successful and I'd be able to buy myself a decent wardrobe and mingle in society a little more frequently.

I HAD NEVER been to Croydon Aerodrome before and I was surprised at the hustle and bustle and brand-new buildings. As our taxi approached along a leafy lane, a large biplane roared over our heads and landed on the runway. I had never even seen a real airliner land before at close quarters and it was an impressive sight as the great bird touched down on the tarmac, bounced a few times and then went rolling along as an earthbound machine. To me it was quite remarkable that anything so large and clumsy-looking could actually fly.

As we were walking over to the new white terminal building in the art deco style, the airliner came roaring toward us, propellers whirling, making a terrible din. I paused to watch as steps were wheeled up to it and one by one the passengers disembarked.

"That's an Imperial Airways Heracles, just in from Paris," someone behind me remarked.

It all seemed so glamorous and improbable. I tried to picture stepping into that little capsule and being whisked across the globe, above the clouds. My only trips abroad had been across the Channel to Switzerland, thence by uncomfortable train.

"The weather doesn't look too promising, does it?" Belinda said, brushing away the midges that danced in front of our faces. "It feels like thunder again."

It did indeed feel extremely muggy and unpleasant. "Where are we to meet Paolo?" I asked.

"He'll be over by the hangars." Belinda started off for the more ramshackle part of the airport, dotted with huts and bigger buildings that actually housed aeroplanes. We located Paolo standing beside a shiny new aeroplane that looked incredibly flimsy, so I was relieved when he greeted us with, "Sorry about the weather. We will not be going up this afternoon, I fear. The Met boys have warned us of another storm."

"Oh, that's too bad, after we've come all this way," Belinda said. "And I was so looking forward to it."

"You would not enjoy being shaken like a cocktail, *cara mia*, and besides, you would see nothing flying through cloud, and you might get struck by lightning."

"In that case"—Belinda was still pouting—"you had better take us for a good lunch to make up for our disappointment. We're starving."

"There is a restaurant in the passenger terminal," Paolo said. "I cannot vouch for the quality of the food, but you can eat and watch the airliners come in from around the world. It's quite a spectacle."

"All right. It will have to do, I suppose." Belinda slipped her arm through his and then her other arm through mine. "Come on, Georgie. We'll make this man pay for not arranging for good weather, shall we?"

"But I have no control over your British weather," Paolo complained. "If we were in Italy, I could guarantee that the weather would be good. In England it always rains."

"Not always. Two days ago you were complaining it was too hot and sunny," Belinda said.

We passed through the sparkling new building, our feet tapping on the marble floor. I looked up in fascination at the mural that decorated the wall. It depicted the time zones around the world. It was already night in Australia. I experienced a pang of longing. So much of the world waiting to be explored, and the farthest I had been was Switzerland—all very safe and clean.

The lunch was surprisingly good with a well-cooked fillet of plaice and strawberries and cream to follow it. As we lingered over our coffee I stared out of the window with rapt attention, while trying not to notice Belinda and Paolo sharing bites of a strawberry in a most erotic fashion. I had seen the storm clouds building in a great bank of darkness, so I wasn't really surprised by the first clap of thunder immediately over our heads. People who had been standing on the tarmac rushed for shelter as the rains began. Chauffeurs hastily put covers on open motorcars.

"Well, that's put an end to any more flying today," Paolo said. "I hope it stops before I have to ride back to London. Riding a motorcycle in a storm is simply not fun."

"You could get struck by lightning," Belinda said. "I thought you loved danger."

"Danger, *sì*. Getting soaking wet, no."

"You'll have to leave the motorcycle here and come back on the train with us," Belinda said.

"But I could not reach the house where I am staying without my motor-cycle," he said. "Where could I spend the night, do you think?"

Of course he knew the answer perfectly well.

"Let me think," Belinda said.

I turned away, wishing I were not the wallflower again. Then somebody shouted, "Look! There's an aeroplane attempting to land."

I peered into the downpour and thought I could make out a blacker speck against the dark clouds.

"He must be crazy to try and land in this," someone else said. "He'll get himself killed."

Everybody rushed to the windows to watch the spectacle. We could see the tiny machine bobbing around, disappearing into cloud one minute and reappearing the next. Then it went into a great bank of darkness. Lightning flashed. Thunder roared. There was no sign of the plane. Suddenly a cheer went up. The little craft came out of the cloud, only a few feet above the runway, and touched down, sending out a sheet of spray behind it.

Everyone streamed out of the restaurant. We followed, caught up in the excitement, and stood under the canopy as the small craft came toward us. It was a biplane, no bigger than a child's toy.

"It's a Gypsy Moth," Paolo said. "Open cockpit, you know. I don't think I'd be brave enough to land a Moth in this kind of storm."

The aeroplane came to a halt. The pilot swung himself out of the rear cockpit and climbed down to applause and cheers. Then he took off his helmet and a gasp went up from the crowd. The pilot was a woman with striking red hair.

"It's Ronny!" Paolo exclaimed, pushing forward through the crowd.

"Ronny? It looks like a girl to me," I said.

"Veronica Padgett, darling." Belinda was following Paolo through the crowd. "You know, the famous aviatrix. She just set the solo record from London to Cape Town."

The pilot was now making her way into the building, graciously accepting the cheers and congratulations as she moved through the crowd.

"Ronny, well done," Paolo called out as she passed us.

She looked up, saw him and gave him a big smile. "What-ho, Paolo. Bet you couldn't do that."

"Nobody in his right mind would have attempted that, Ronny. You're quite mad, you know."

She laughed. She had a rich, deep laugh. "Possibly. I told myself so many times during the last half hour."

"Where have you come from?" Paolo asked.

"Not far. Only over from France. I knew I probably shouldn't have taken off, but I didn't want to miss a party this evening. But the whole thing was utterly bloody. Couldn't see the blasted railway lines in France and then there was fog over the Channel and then I flew into this bank of filthy weather. Bucketed around all over the place. I almost lost my lunch, and my compass was playing up too. No idea where the damned runway was. My God, it was fun."

I looked at her in amazement. Her face was positively glowing with excitement.

"Come on, let's get out of this infernal weather," she said, turning up her flight jacket collar as another clap of thunder sounded overhead and the wind whipped across the aerodrome. As we fell into place behind her, Belinda tapped Paolo on the shoulder. "Are you planning to introduce us or are you keeping her all to yourself?" she asked.

Paolo laughed, a trifle nervously. "I'm sorry, I should have introduced you. Ronny, these are my friends Belinda Warburton-Stoke and Georgiana Rannoch. Girls, this is Ronny Padgett."

I saw Ronny's eyes widen. "Rannoch? Any relation to the dukes of?"

"The last one was my father; the current one is my brother," I said.

"Good God. Then we're almost neighbors. My family place is not too far from you on the Dee."

"Really? It's amazing we've never run into each other before."

"I don't go up there often," she said. "Too damned quiet for my taste. And I'm a good bit older than you. When I was shipped off to boarding school you were probably still crawling around in nappies. And I left home for good when I was sixteen. Didn't want any part of being presented and all that bosh. Since then I've never stayed in one place for long. Born with wanderlust, I suppose. Are you up there much yourself?"

"I have to go up to Scotland in a couple of weeks," I said. "But not to Castle Rannoch if I can avoid it. It's not the liveliest of places these days. I'm due at Balmoral for the grouse shoot."

"Murdering all the poor defenseless little birds," Ronny said. "Barbaric when you come to think of it. But by God it's fun, isn't it? I suppose it must be in the blood, don't you think?"

"I think it must," I said. "I adore hunting but I always feel jolly sorry for the poor fox when it's torn to pieces. I'm not a particularly good shot, so I don't feel sorry for the grouse in the same way. And they are awfully silly birds."

Ronny laughed again. "They certainly are. Maybe we'll bump into each other sometime. If I'm there you can come and shoot with me on the estate."

Belinda, I noticed, was pouting. She was used to being the center of attention.

She tugged at Paolo's arm. "After what Ronny has just achieved, the very least you can do is to fete her with champagne," she said.

"Belinda, I sometimes think you believe that all I am good for is keeping you supplied with champagne and caviar," Paolo said.

"Not at all, you do have other uses." She gave him her cat-with-the-cream smile.

I saw the lingering glance that passed between them. Then he turned to Ronny. "I'm instructed to buy you champagne if they stock a decent bottle at the bar here. Coming?"

She looked around, then laughed again. "Why not? You only live once, don't you? And I've never yet said no to a decent champers." She strode ahead of us, through the crowd and into the main hall of the building. "I don't suppose you've seen my maid, have you?" she asked, her eyes searching the crowd. "Timid little thing. Looks as if she expects everyone to bite her. I told her to meet me here with the dress I plan to wear tonight. She damned well better show up or I'm sunk. I can't go to a party dressed like this."

We made our way toward the bar but there was no sign of a maid. "Probably waiting for me at the hangar, which is where I left the motorcar, thank God. At least it will be dry."

"You have a motorcar, do you?" Paolo asked, eyeing her with interest. "Any chance of a ride into town?"

"Sorry, old thing. I'm heading for deepest Sussex. No use at all."

"Too bad," Paolo said. "I came on my motorcycle and I do so hate getting wet. Now I have no choice but to leave the wretched thing here and go back to London by train."

"What a hardship for you," Belinda said in a clipped voice.

He put an arm around her shoulder. "I didn't mean it like that, *mi amore*. I just meant that once I am in London I will have no means of transport except for those horrible taxicabs that creep around slower than beetles. I'm sure Ronny drives deliciously fast."

"I certainly do, old bean," she said, and laughed again.

We were just entering the bar when a young woman called out, "Miss Padgett!" and came toward us, staggering under a large suitcase. She looked red faced and distinctly flustered. "Oh, Miss Padgett, I'm so sorry I'm late," she gasped. "It started to thunder when I was halfway from the station and I had to take shelter. I'm mortally afraid of thunder, you know. I hope I haven't inconvenienced you."

"Of course you bloody well have," Ronny said. "You can't seem to get anywhere on time. But you're lucky this once. I've been waylaid to drink champagne, so run along to the motorcar and wait for me there."

"The motorcar?"

"It's in the hangar. You know. Number 23? You've been there before. Where I keep the Moth." She turned to us. "Heavens, it's like talking to a brick wall. I take it you have efficient maids, Lady Georgiana?"

"Please call me Georgie, everyone does," I said. "And at the moment I have no servants at all. I've recently moved to London and frankly I'm still slumming it."

"Splendid idea," Ronny said. "You see, Mavis, Lady Georgiana is the daughter of a duke and she can make do without servants. So you'd better shape up or I may have to follow suit. A new age is dawning, you know."

Paolo had been conferring with the barman, and there was a satisfying pop as the cork flew off a bottle of Bollinger.

"Well, go on then," Ronny said to the long-suffering Mavis, who was now staring at me in fascination. "Take my suitcase and put it in the car, then wait for me there. Oh, and see if you can put the top up. We don't want to get wet."

Mavis attempted a curtsy then staggered off. As she went, Ronny's clear voice echoed across the marble foyer. "I'd sack her in a moment but frankly I know I'd find things like washing and ironing too tiresome."

Chapter 4

RANNOCH HOUSE
AUGUST 13, 14 AND 15, 1932

Wet.

"So what did you think of Ronny?" Belinda asked me on the way home.

"Interesting. Different."

"She's certainly her own person, isn't she?" Belinda said. "Heart of a lion, but she doesn't care what she says or whom she insults." She turned to Paolo, who was slumped in the window seat. "I saw you were rather taken with her."

"She amazes me and amuses me," he said, "but as to anything more, she has about as much sex appeal as a plate of spaghetti Bolognese."

"I don't know, spaghetti can be quite sexy, if eaten in the nude." Belinda gave him the most provocative look.

Paolo laughed. "Belinda, you are quite the most shameless girl I know. Angelina would go and say a dozen Hail Marys if a thought like that even crossed her mind."

"That's why I'm more fun than Angelina," Belinda said. "Go on, admit that you have more fun when you are with me."

"Of course I do, but I do not think you will make anybody a suitable wife."

I watched them as the train chuffed toward Victoria. Belinda was going to wind up like my mother, leaping from bed to bed with gay abandon, I decided. The thought seemed to worry me more than it did her.

They dropped me off at Rannoch House then disappeared, presumably for a night of sin. I didn't sleep much either. The thunderstorm had left the air sticky, and even with the windows open it was too hot to sleep. I lay awake, listening to the sounds of the city, and found myself thinking about Belinda and Paolo. What would it be like to spend the night in the arms of a man? Then of course my thoughts turned to a particular man. What was he doing at this moment? Was he really still recuperating at his family's place in Ireland or was he somewhere else, with someone else? One never knew with Darcy.

When I first met him I had thought him a wild Irish playboy opportunist, living by his charm and his wits. But now I suspected he was more than he had told me. In fact I thought he might be some kind of spy. For whom I couldn't say, but definitely not for the communists. He had taken a bullet that almost cost him his life to save the king and queen.

I just wished I knew where he was. I wished I had the nerve to show up on his doorstep. But I was rather afraid of what I might find there. When it came to men, I seriously lacked confidence—probably because the only male I knew until the age of eighteen was my brother.

I fell asleep eventually and woke to the sound of the milkman's horse and the rattle of bottles. The air had cooled overnight and the sweet smell of roses and honeysuckle wafted across from the gardens in the middle of the square. I got out of bed feeling energized and renewed, the black mood of the day before having vanished with the night air. My nature is such that I can never stay down in the dumps for long. And today I had a task ahead of me, one that might set me up with a splendid income for the foreseeable future.

I sat at my desk and composed an advertisement for the *Times*. When I had finished I was rather pleased with myself and wanted to show it to Belinda. But I knew better than to disturb her before eleven o'clock and especially when she was probably not alone. So I printed it out neatly and delivered it to the *Times* office. I thought the girl who wrote the receipt for it looked at me strangely and I wondered if she recognized me. I do appear in the odd photograph in the *Tattler*, since the press thinks of me as an eligible young woman of good pedigree. (Little do they know the state of the Rannoch bank accounts.)

"Are you sure this is what you want it to say, miss?" she asked.

"Yes, quite sure, thank you."

"Very well." She took my money. "So this will appear for the first time in tomorrow's paper and run until you tell us to stop it."

"That's correct," I said. She was still staring at me as I left the office.

I came home full of anticipation and went through my wardrobe for garments suitable for evenings on the town. Luckily I had had a maid for one whole week earlier in the summer, and during that time she had cleaned and pressed my good clothes, so that my evening dresses were not as crumpled as my everyday wear. I sat in front of the mirror and experimented with putting my hair up. (Disaster. I looked like Medusa.) Then I got the scissors and snipped at the ends in the hope of turning it into the kind of sleek bob Belinda wore. Again not too successful. Now all I had to do was wait.

The next morning I ran out to buy the *Times* as soon as the newsagent was open and there it was on the front page in the middle of the other advertisements. *Alone in town on business? Let Coronet Escort Service enhance your evening's entertainment. Our high-class girls make ideal companions to grace your dining and dancing.* I had had to supply a phone number, naturally, and had no choice but to give the Rannoch House number. I just hoped that nobody recognized it and told Binky or Fig. But then I reasoned I wasn't doing anything wrong. That Mr. Hiram Schlossberger had enjoyed every minute of my company the other evening. So why shouldn't similar gentlemen pay for the privilege?

Clearly the idea was not a silly one, because that afternoon I received my first telephone call. The man had a pronounced North Country accent, but I couldn't hold that against him. I thought of all those rich mill owners and people who said things like "Where there's muck, there's brass." Even if his conversation and manners were boorish, he'd pay well. He asked me my price, which no man of breeding would do, and stammered a little when I told him five guineas.

"That's an awful lot," he said. "She'd better be good."

"The very best," I said. "A high-class girl from a good family. You'll be enchanted with her."

"I bloody hope so," he said. "Have her meet me at the Rendezvous Club behind Leicester Square. That's close to where I'm staying."

"Very well," I said. "And what time shall I tell her?"

"Ten o'clock?"

I put down the mouthpiece. It wasn't going to be dinner then, at that hour. Nor a theater. A late supper at a nightclub, maybe? Then dancing, gambling, a cabaret? My heart raced in anticipation. This was the sort of life I'd dreamed of living—out late with the bright young things, coming home at dawn.

I spent a ridiculously long time getting ready, soaking in a hot bath and then actually trying to apply makeup, something I've never really learned to do well. But when I looked in the mirror, I was satisfied with the luscious red lips, even if black mascara on my eyelashes didn't really go with my red-blond hair and coloring and the cocktail dress was not as slinky as I would have liked. It was one that the gamekeeper's wife had run up on her sewing machine for my season. It was a copy of something I'd admired in a magazine, but somehow the combination of Mrs. MacTavish's sewing skills and my taffeta didn't make me quite look the same as the softly draped girl with the cigarette holder in *Harper's Bazaar*. But it was the best I could do and I looked clean and respectable.

My heart thumped wildly all the way in the taxicab. We passed the bright lights of Leicester Square with its theater marquees and bustling crowds and finally pulled up on a dark side street.

"Are you sure this is it, miss?" The taxi driver asked in a concerned voice.

I wasn't sure. It looked awfully dark and lonely. But then I saw a blinking sign over an entrance. Club Rendezvous. "Yes, this is it," I said. "Thank you very much."

"You are meeting somebody, I hope," he said as I paid him.

"Yes, I'm meeting a young man. Don't worry, I'll be fine." I gave what I hoped was a confident smile.

The taxi sped away, leaving me alone in the deserted street. It had rained again and the flashing red sign was reflected in the puddles as I crossed the road. I pushed open the door and found myself facing a flight of steps going down to a basement. Music spilled up to greet me—the wail of a saxophone and a heavy drumbeat. I held on to the rail as I went down the steps. This then was a real nightclub. I had never been in a place like this. The stairs were steep with worn carpet on them. And I was wearing my one pair of high-heeled shoes, in my attempt to look glamorous. I haven't mentioned yet that I am apt to be clumsy in moments of stress. Halfway down, my heel caught in a threadbare patch in the carpet. I pitched forward, grasped at the railing and ended up slithering down the last of the stairs, arriving at the bottom in a most undignified way as I cannoned into a potted palm. I hastened to pick myself up before anyone observed this unorthodox entry. I was in a sort of dark anteroom with an antique writing desk and chair, mercifully unoccupied. The area was separated from the main area by a row of potted palms, one of which now had a frond hanging down, thanks to me. A man had just been emerging from the club beyond the palms. He was staggering slightly as if drunk and started in alarm when I came hurtling down the stairs toward him.

"Let me give you a word of advice, girlie," he said in slurred tones, wagging a finger at me. "Don't drink any more tonight. You've already had enough. Trust me, I know." Then he staggered past me up the stairs.

I collected myself and smoothed down my skirt and my hair before I went through into the club itself. It was dimly lit, with candles on small tables and the only real light coming from the stage, where a girl was dancing.

"Can I help you, miss?" A swarthy man in a dinner jacket appeared at my side. He didn't seem to possess a razor.

"I'm meeting someone here," I said. "A Mr. Crump."

"Ah. I see." He gave me something between a grin and a leer. "He's expecting you. At that table on the far right."

The man looked up as I approached him and he rose to his feet.

"Mr. Crump?" I said, holding out my hand to him. "My agency sent me. Coronet Escorts?"

He was a ruddy, bloated sort of fellow with what he probably thought was a jaunty mustache but which looked more like a hedgehog perched on his upper lip. What's more, he was wearing an ordinary day suit and a rather loud tie. I saw him giving me a long once-over.

"You're younger than I expected," he said. "And you're wearing more clothes too."

"I assure you I'm old enough to be a perfect companion for you," I said. "I'm educated and well traveled."

He smirked. "I'm not planning to quiz you on your knowledge of geography." Then he became aware that we were both still standing. "I suppose you'd like a drink before we go?" he said.

"That would be nice. I'd like champagne if they have it." I took a seat at the table.

"Bloody 'ell," he muttered. "You London girls certainly have expensive tastes." I noticed that he had a beer in front of him. He beckoned to a waiter and a bottle of champagne was brought to the table.

"I hope you'll join me," I said, feeling embarrassed now that he'd had to buy a whole bottle when all I'd wanted was a glass.

"Why not? Help us both to loosen up, won't it?" he said and gave me a wink.

The bottle was opened with a satisfying pop. Two glasses were poured. I took a sip then held up my glass to him. "Cheers," I said. "Here's to a lovely evening for both of us."

I noticed he swallowed hard. In fact it almost looked as if he was sweating. "So I expect you want paying up front, do you?"

"Oh, I don't think that will be necessary," I said. "But I shall expect cash at the end of the evening."

"So what's the plan then? Do we go back to my hotel, or do you have a place where you take clients nearby? I know I should have asked on the telephone but this was all rather last minute, wasn't it? In fact I'd never have thought of it if I hadn't seen your advert this morning. I don't usually do this sort of thing."

I was just trying to digest what he had said when the music picked up in tempo. There were whoops and catcalls coming from the front of the room. I looked up at the stage. The girl was still dancing, but I was suddenly aware that she wore almost no clothing. As I stared in fascinated horror, she opened an ostrich feather fan which she held in front of her, then, to a final drumroll, she produced her brassiere and tossed it into the front rows of the audience.

Suddenly the penny dropped. *My hotel or your place?*

"Wait," I said. "What were you expecting from me?"

"Only the usual, darling," he said. "Same as you do with all the men. Nothing too kinky."

"I think there must be some mistake," I said. "We are a respectable escort service. We provide girls as dinner companions, theater companions, not the sort of thing you obviously have in mind."

"Don't play coy with me, sweetheart," he said. The words were slurred enough to tell me that he had been drinking for some time. He reached across and grabbed my arm. "What are you trying to do, push up the price? I wasn't born yesterday, you know. Come on, drink up your bubbly and we'll go back to my hotel, or you'll be charging me by the hour."

I attempted to stand up. "I'm afraid there's been a horrible misunderstanding here. I think I'd better go."

His grip on my arm tightened. "What's the matter, girlie, don't you fancy me, or what? Isn't my brass good enough for you?" The smile had disappeared from his face. He was blowing beery breath in my face. "Now you come with me like a good girl or you know what I'll do? I'll have you arrested for soliciting."

He stood up and attempted to drag me with him.

"Let go of me, please," I said. I sensed people at the tables around us watching. "Just let me go and we'll forget the whole thing."

"No, we bloody won't," he said. "I've had to pay for a bottle of champagne. And we made an agreement, me and your agency. We struck a bargain and Harold Crump doesn't take kindly to people who try to back out of business deals. Now stop playing the prissy little miss and get moving."

"Didn't you hear the young lady? She will not be coming with you," said a voice behind me.

I recognized that voice and spun around to see Darcy O'Mara standing there, looking amazingly dashing in a white dinner jacket and bow tie, his unruly black hair combed into submission, apart from a wayward curl that fell onto his forehead. It was all I could do not to throw myself into his arms.

"And who are you, butting in like this?" Mr. Crump demanded, blustering up to Darcy only to find he was several inches shorter.

"Let's just say that I'm her manager," Darcy said.

"Her pimp, you mean."

"Call it what you like," Darcy said, "but there's been a mistake. She should never have been sent out tonight. Our agency only deals with clients of the highest social echelon. We have a new girl answering the telephone and she omitted to put you through our normal vetting process. And now I've seen your behavior, I am afraid there is no way I could allow one of our girls to go anywhere with you. You simply don't pass muster, sir. You are, to put it bluntly, too common."

"Well, I never did," Mr. Crump said.

"And you're not going to now," Darcy replied. "Come, Arabella. We're leaving."

"Here, what about my champagne?" Mr. Crump demanded.

Darcy reached into his pocket and threw down a pound note on the table. Then he took my arm and half dragged me up the steps.

"What the hell do you think you were doing?" he demanded as we stepped out into the night. His eyes were blazing and I thought for one awful moment that he might hit me.

"That stupid man got it wrong." I was near to tears now. "I advertised my services as an escort. He must have misunderstood. He thought I was—you know—a call girl."

"You advertised your services as an escort?" Darcy's fingers were still digging into my upper arm.

"Yes, I put an advertisement in the *Times* and called myself Coronet Escorts."

Darcy spluttered. "My dear naïve little girl, surely even you must have realized that the words 'escort service' are a polite way of advertising something a little more seedy? Of course he thought he was getting a call girl. He had every right to think so."

"I had no idea," I snapped. "How was I to know?"

"Surely you must have had your suspicions when you saw that club. Nice girls do not go to places like that, Georgiana."

"Then what were you doing in it?" I demanded, my relief now turning to anger. "You walk out of my life. You don't bother to write. And now I find you slumming it in a place like that. No wonder you're not interested in me. I don't take my clothes off in front of a group of men."

"As to what I was doing there . . ." he said. I thought I detected the twitch of a smile on his lips. "I had to meet a man about a dog. And I can assure you that I didn't bother to look at what was taking place on the stage. I've seen far better and had it offered for free. And as to why I disappeared and didn't get in touch—I'm sorry. I had to go abroad in something of a hurry. I just got back yesterday. And you're damned lucky I did, or you'd still be trying to fight off that troglodyte."

"I would have managed," I said huffily. "You don't always have to step in and rescue me, you know."

"It seems that I do. You're simply not safe to be allowed out alone in the city," he said. "Come on. We're going to Leicester Square where we can pick up a taxicab, and I'm sending you home."

"What if I don't want to go home?"

"You have no choice, my lady. Exactly what would your family think if you were snapped by a passing newspaperman, coming out of a seedy London gentlemen's strip club? Now walk."

He propelled me along the pavement until he flagged down a taxicab. "Take this young lady back to Belgrave Square," he said in an authoritative voice I had never heard from him before. He bundled me into the cab. "And you remove that advertisement from the *Times* the first thing tomorrow morning, do you hear?"

"It's my life. You can't dictate to me," I snapped because I thought I might cry any moment. "You don't own me, you know."

"No," he said, looking at me long and hard. "But I do care about you, in spite of everything. Now go home, have a cup of cocoa and go to bed— alone."

"Aren't you coming with me?" My voice quivered a little.

"Is that an invitation?" he asked, the scowl vanishing for a second before it resumed, and he said, "Regrettably I still have business to conclude. But I expect we'll run into each other on some future occasion in a place that is more suitable." Then he leaned into the cab, grasped my chin, drew me toward him and kissed me hard on the mouth. Then he slammed the taxi-cab door, and I was driven off into the night.

Chapter 5

Cooler, more normal weather.
Internal turmoil not cooler at all.

I managed to make it all the way home without crying. But as soon as I shut the big front door behind me, the tears started to roll down my cheeks. It wasn't just the fright and embarrassment of what happened and what might have happened, it was the knowledge that I had now definitely lost Darcy. I went up to bed and curled into a tight little ball, wishing I were somewhere safe, with someone who loved me, and coming to the realization that I actually had nobody, apart from my grandfather, that I could count on.

I awoke to the sound of distant knocking. It took me a moment to realize that someone was hammering on my front door. It was only nine o'clock and I pulled on my robe and went downstairs cautiously, wondering who it could be at this hour. Certainly not Belinda. Hope rose for an instant that it might be Darcy, coming to apologize for his boorish behavior last night. But when I opened the door a young policeman was standing there.

"I've been sent from Scotland Yard to speak to Lady Georgiana Rannoch," he said, eyeing my night attire and wild hair. "Is she available, please?"

"I am Lady Georgiana," I said. "May I ask who has sent you from Scotland Yard and what this is about?"

"Sir William Rollins would like to have a word with you, my lady."

"Sir William Rollins?"

He nodded. "Deputy commissioner."

"And why does Sir William wish to speak with me?"

"I couldn't tell you, my lady. He doesn't confide in ordinary coppers. I'm told to go and fetch you, and I go. Now if you could hurry and get dressed, he doesn't like to be kept waiting."

I tried to think of a crushing retort. He was, after all, speaking to the daughter of a duke and second cousin to the king. I opened my mouth to say that if Sir William Rollins wished to speak to me, he could present himself at Rannoch House. But I couldn't make the words come out. In fact my legs were a trifle shaky as I went back upstairs. What could Scotland Yard possibly want with me? And not just Scotland Yard, but somebody frightfully high up there? In my past dealings with the Metropolitan Police I had had to contend with a truly obnoxious inspector and a rather smarmy chief inspector. Clearly this was something more serious, then, but I couldn't for the life of me think what. . . . Unless . . . Surely they couldn't have found out about last night? And even if they had, I had done nothing against the law—had I?

I grabbed the first dress I could find in my wardrobe that looked vaguely presentable, ran a brush through my hair, cleaned my teeth and splashed water on my face. Then I came downstairs again to face whatever I had coming to me. I found it hard to breathe as the squad car whisked me toward Whitehall and entered into the forecourt of Scotland Yard. The door was held open for me and I tried to enter with my head held high, only to trip over the doormat and come flying into the foyer at a full stagger. (That tendency to clumsiness in moments of stress again, I'm afraid.)

Even more humiliating for me, a young, fresh-faced bobby grabbed me and saved me from crashing into a glass partition. "Keen to be arrested, are you, miss?" he said, giving me a cheeky grin.

I tried to give him a look that would have done my great-grandmother credit when she pronounced the words "We are not amused," but somehow I couldn't make my face obey me either.

"This way, your ladyship," my original escort said, and ushered me into a lift. It seemed to take an eternity to go up. I found I was holding my breath, but by the time we reached the fifth floor, I had to gasp. At last it juddered to a halt. The constable pulled back the concertina door and I stepped out into a deserted hallway. At the end of the hall he pressed a button. A door opened and we were admitted to an outer office where two young women were busy typing. This was different from my previous experience of Scotland Yard. The floor was carpeted, for one thing, and the rich, herby smell of pipe tobacco hung in the air.

"Lady Georgiana to see Sir William," the young policeman said.

One of the young women got up from her desk.

"This way, please. Follow me." She looked and sounded the epitome of efficiency. I bet she'd never tripped over a rug in her life.

She led me down another hallway and tapped at a door.

"Come in!" a voice boomed.

"Lady Georgiana, Sir William," the woman said in her efficient voice.

I stepped inside. The door closed behind me. The pipe smell was revealed as coming from a big, florid man who sat behind the desk. He spilled over the sides of a large leather chair, the meerschaum clenched between his teeth. As I entered, he removed it from his mouth and held it poised in one hand. If I had summed up the typist as efficient, I could sum him up in one word too: powerful. He had fierce eyebrows, for one thing, and the sort of expression that indicated he didn't like to be crossed, and rarely was.

"Lady Georgiana. Good of you to come so quickly." He held out a meaty hand.

"Did I have a choice?" I asked, and he laughed heartily, as if I had made a good joke.

"I'm not arresting you, you know. Please. Take a seat." I sat.

"Then would you like to tell me what I'm doing here?" I asked.

"You don't have an inkling?"

"No. Why should I?"

He leaned back, eyeing me across his large mahogany desk. "Some disturbing news has just come to light," he said. "Our vice squad keeps an eye on the newspapers for potentially illegal and antisocial activities. When an advertisement showed up in no less than the *Times* yesterday, they checked on the telephone number given in the advert. They couldn't have been more surprised to find out that the number was that of your London residence—a telephone owned in the name of the Duke of Glen Garry and Rannoch. So we immediately came to the conclusion that there had been a misprint in the newspaper and we contacted the Times to tell them so. We were then informed that there was no misprint."

He paused. Those alarming eyebrows twitched with a life of their own, like two prawns. "So I thought you and I had better have a little chat and settle this matter before it goes any further. Would you like to clarify things for me?"

I was currently staring in fascination at the eyebrows, while wishing that the floor would open up and swallow me.

"It was all a hideous mistake," I said. "I merely intended to start a small escort service."

"Escort service?" The eyebrows shot up.

"Not what you're thinking. Well-bred girls who would be available as dinner or theater partners for men who didn't like to dine alone. Nothing more. Perhaps my wording was inept?"

He shook his head, chuckling now. "Oh dear, oh dear me. Your wording couldn't have been more obvious if you'd written 'Call Fifi for a good time.' But I must say I'm relieved that you haven't actually joined the oldest profession yet."

I could feel my face positively glowing with the heat of embarrassment.

"Absolutely not. And I assure you I will be withdrawing the advertisement this morning."

"Already done, my dear," he said. "But in future I must warn you to be a little more prudent if you desire to go into business. Check with someone older and more worldly wise so that you don't make any more embarrassing blunders, eh?"

"I will," I said. "I'm sorry. It really was innocently intended. I'm a young woman trying to earn a living like everybody else in this city, you know. I thought I had found a niche and leaped in to fill it."

"I'd stick to the more acceptable professions in future. All I can say is you're lucky our man happened to pick up on that advert so quickly. Can you imagine what a field day the gutter press would have had if they'd come upon it first? The tart with the tiara? The Buck House brothel?"

He watched me wince at each of these epithets. I could tell he was rather enjoying himself.

"I've told you it won't happen again," I said. "And fortunately the press has not found me out."

"All the same," he went on slowly, "I think it might be wise if you left the city immediately. Take the next train to your home in Scotland, eh?

Then if by any chance any nosy parker did stumble upon yesterday's paper and called the number, they would realize that Rannoch House was empty and closed up for the summer and that there had been a mistake. We'll brief the *Times* to verify that the telephone number was their error."

He looked at me inquiringly. I couldn't do anything but nod in agreement. He obviously had no idea that going home to Scotland meant facing a dragon of a sister-in-law who would want to know what I was doing landing on their doorstep with no warning. But I did see his point. I went to stand up, presuming the interview was at an end. Sir William put his pipe to his lip and took a long draw on it.

"One other small thing," he said. "Do you happen to know a woman by the name of Mavis Pugh?"

"Never heard of her."

"I see. Only yesterday evening a young woman was found dead on a byway close to Croydon Aerodrome. It appeared that she had been run over by a fast-moving vehicle—a motorcycle by the looks of it. We assume it was just a tragic accident. The lane was leafy and shady, and it was just after a sharp bend. Maybe she stepped out at the last minute and he didn't see her. But he didn't stop to report it either. And we've turned up no witnesses."

I tried to keep my face interested but detached. I tried not to let Paolo come into my mind. "I'm very sorry for the woman, but I don't see what this has to do with me," I said. "I can assure you that I've never ridden a motorcycle in my life and was nowhere near Croydon Aerodrome last night, as the owner of a seedy nightclub can verify."

"Nobody is suggesting you were," he said. "I asked because her handbag was thrown across the road by the impact. Some of the contents wound up in the ditch. Among them was a half-finished letter, apparently to you. The writer was using a cheap ink and most of it had washed away but we could read 'Lady Georgiana' and the words 'Older brother, the Duke of . . .' "

"How extraordinary," I said.

"So if you don't know this woman, we wondered why she was writing to you." His eyes didn't leave mine for an instant. In spite of his age, and he must have been over fifty, his eyes were extraordinarily bright and alive. "We wondered, for example, whether she might have been thinking of blackmailing you."

"For what? My brother and I are virtually penniless. He at least owns the property. I own nothing."

"The lower classes don't think like that. To them all aristocrats are wealthy."

"I can assure you that I am not being blackmailed by anybody. Was this woman known to be of the criminal classes?"

"No," he said. "She was a lady's maid."

Then a memory stirred within my brain as I put together the words "Mavis" and "lady's maid." "Wait," I said. "Was she by any chance in the service of Veronica Padgett, the famous lady pilot?"

"Aha." He gave a smug smile. "Then you do know her?"

"I encountered her once, a few days ago at Croydon Aerodrome. She had come to meet her mistress and bring clothes for a party. Miss Padgett was cross with her because she was late. She pointed me out and said that Lady Georgiana could manage without a lady's maid and she was thinking of following suit, so this young woman would have known who I was. But I didn't have any direct communication with her."

"You say her mistress was cross with her? Maybe she was writing to you to apply for a job."

"Possibly," I said. "But I got the feeling that Miss Padgett was just needling her, not really threatening to dismiss her. What does she say about it?"

"She was quite upset, actually. She was down at a house party in Sussex and she had left her maid in London. She had no idea what the maid would have been doing near the aerodrome when her mistress wasn't planning to return to London for several days and had given her maid no instructions to leave the residence."

"I wish I could help you, Sir William," I said, "but as I just told you, I had no dealings with this person."

"You're a friend of this Miss Padgett, are you?"

"Not at all. I only met her once and then by chance. She happened to land her aeroplane at Croydon Aerodrome when I was visiting with friends. She knew one of our party and we went to drink a glass of champagne with her while she waited for her maid."

"I see," he said. There was a long pause. "Just an unfortunate coincidence," he went on, "but it's lucky that you're leaving London, or this might turn into another whiff of scandal that we simply can't allow."

"Is that all?" I asked. I felt as if my nerves were close to snapping. Honestly, I'd done nothing wrong and I was beginning to feel as if I were a prisoner in the dock and the black cap might be produced at any minute.

He nodded. "Well, that seems to be that, then." He glanced at his watch. "If we made a dash for King's Cross, we might still catch today's Flying Scotsman. It leaves at ten o'clock, doesn't it?"

"Today's Flying Scotsman?" I stared at him, openmouthed. "I will need some time to pack, you know. I can't just up and go to Scotland."

"Have your maid do it for you, and she can follow on a later train. Surely you have the bulk of your clothing at Castle Rannoch?"

Now I was feeling both angry and flustered. "Contrary to popular belief, all aristocrats are not rich enough to own a vast wardrobe. The few items of clothing I possess are with me in London."

"But you can do without them until tonight. I'll have my man drive you via Belgrave Square so that you can give your maid instructions and pick up the odd toiletry."

"I have no maid at the moment," I reminded him.

"No maid? You've been living in Rannoch House alone?" His manner implied that I had indeed been operating the suspected house of ill repute.

"I can't afford a maid," I said. "Which is why I've been trying to find work."

"Dear me." He gave an embarrassed sort of cough and tapped his pipe into the ashtray. "And I suppose I can't expect you to travel by a slow train to Edinburgh, and the overnight Pullman into Glasgow won't work then?"

"I can't make an easy connection from Glasgow, nor expect our chauffeur to meet me there," I said.

"Very well, it had better be tomorrow then. I'll have my girl book your seat. And I can't urge you strongly enough to talk to nobody in the meantime."

"I presume you want me to telephone my brother to let him know I'm coming?" I said.

"Don't worry, that's been taken care of," he said.

I felt myself flushing red again, wondering just what had been said. Would it be clear to all that I had been sent home in disgrace like a naughty schoolgirl? Sir William rose to his feet. "Very well, you'd better get going. Don't answer the telephone whatever you do, and if you can draw the blinds and make the house appear to be unoccupied, so much the better. My man will call for you in the morning."

Annoyance was gradually overtaking fear. This man was ordering me around as if he was my superior in the army.

"And if I choose not to go?" I demanded.

"I should have no alternative but to bring the matter to the attention of Their Majesties. I should hope you'd wish to spare them any embarrassment. Besides, I understand you are expected at Balmoral in the near future anyway. You are merely putting forward your arrival by a few days. Simple as that. Off you go then. Enjoy the grouse shooting, you lucky devil. Wish I could be up there instead of stuck behind this desk."

And he gave me a hearty laugh, playing the benevolent uncle now that I was following his wishes. I nodded coldly and left the room with as much dignity as I could muster.

Chapter 6

I felt as if I was about to explode as I let myself into Rannoch House under the watchful eye of the young constable. In truth I suspect that the anger I felt was a result of my embarrassment and humiliation. I just prayed that Sir William hadn't revealed my gaffe to Binky and Fig. Binky would think it was a huge joke, but I could just picture Fig giving me that withering look and going on about how I'd let the family down and suggesting it was my mother's inferior blood coming out again. This of course turned my thoughts to my grandfather. He was the one person I would dearly have loved to see at this moment because I needed a good hug. Belinda would be no use, even if she wasn't currently in Paolo's arms. She'd think the whole thing was screamingly funny. "You of all people pretending to be a call girl, darling," she'd say. "The one remaining virgin in London!"

But my grandfather was not on the telephone and I didn't think Sir William would take kindly to my gadding around on a tube train. So I packed the sort of clothes one needs in Scotland, then sat in the gloomy kitchen below stairs, sipping a cup of tea. At that moment the telephone rang. I jumped up but remembered the instruction not to answer it. A little later it rang again. Now my nerves were seriously rattled. Had the press twigged to me after all? Or was it a potential client who had discovered my advertisement in yesterday's newspaper? I moved uneasily about the house, occasionally peeping through the closed blinds of the front bedroom to see if any reporters had stationed themselves in the square.

Then at about five o'clock there was a loud knock at the front door. I rushed to the bedroom window and tried to see who was there, but the front door is under a covered portico. It could have been Belinda of course, but the knock had somehow sounded mannish and demanding. It came again. I held my breath. If it was someone from Scotland Yard, then it was their own silly fault that I wasn't answering the door. I was obeying instructions. I watched and waited and eventually I saw a man walking away from the house. An oldish man, not too well dressed. Then suddenly there was something about the walk I recognized. Forgetting all instructions, I rushed down the stairs, flung open the front door and sprinted down the street after the retreating figure.

"Granddad!" I shouted.

He turned around and his face broke into a big smile. "Well, there you are after all, ducks. You had me worried for a moment there. Did I wake you from a little nap?"

"Not at all," I said. "I was instructed not to open the door. Come inside and I'll tell you all about it."

I almost dragged him back inside Rannoch House, glancing around for reporters lurking in the bushes inside the gardens. I know the gardens are private and require a resident's key to enter, but reporters are notoriously resourceful and can leap iron railings when required.

"What's this all about, my love?" he asked as I shut the front door behind us with a sigh of relief. "Are you in some kind of trouble? I suspected as much when that bloke told me you'd been to my house—the one day I was away, of course. Went on the annual outing to Clacton."

"How was it?" I asked.

"Smashing. All that fresh sea air did a power of good to these old lungs. I felt like a new man by the time we came home."

I looked at him critically. I knew his health hadn't been good for some time and he didn't look well. A stab of worry shot through me that I might lose the one rock in my life, coupled with a pang of regret that I wasn't in a position to do more for him. I wished I could send him to the seaside for the summer.

"So what's up, ducks?" he asked me. "Come and make a cup of tea and you can tell your old granddad all about it."

We went down to the kitchen and put on the kettle while I told him the whole story. "Blimey," he said, trying not to grin, "you do get yourself into a right pickle, don't you? Escort service? High-class girls?"

"How was I to know?" I demanded hotly.

"You weren't. Brought up too sheltered, that's your trouble. But next time you have any bright ideas, you run them past your old granddad first."

"All right." I had to smile.

"Anyway, no harm done," he said. "You're lucky you got out of it as easily as you did."

"I wouldn't have if Darcy hadn't been at the nightclub," I confessed. "He stepped in and rescued me. And the bad thing is that somehow Scotland Yard got wind of this and they are shipping me off to Scotland posthaste, just in case any reporters stumble upon it."

"That's going overboard, isn't it? What if a reporter did stumble upon it? You'd just say it was a poorly worded advertisement."

"Scotland Yard is getting the *Times* to say the telephone number was an error. They think I'd be embarrassing the Crown."

"No more than their own son is embarrassing them," Granddad said. "Has he still got that married American woman in tow?"

"As far as I know. I must say the press is being wonderfully discreet about it. It hasn't made the papers at all."

"Because Their Majesties have requested it be kept hush-hush."

The kettle boiled and I made tea while Granddad perched on a hard kitchen chair, watching me. "So you're to be shipped back to Scotland, are you? To Balmoral or to your brother?"

"Castle Rannoch. My Balmoral invitation is not for over another week."

"I can't see your sister-in-law throwing out the red carpet for you."

"Neither can I," I said. "In fact I'm rather dreading it, much as I adore being in Scotland at this time of year."

"Don't you let her push you around," Granddad said. "It's your home. You were born in it. Your father was a duke, and the grandson of the old queen; hers was just a baronet who got his title for lending Charles the Second money to pay his gambling debts. Remind her of that."

I laughed. "Granddad, you're awful. And I believe you're a bit of a snob at heart."

"I know my place and I don't claim to be what I'm not," he said. "I don't have no time for people who give themselves airs about their station."

I gazed at him wistfully. "I wish you were coming with me," I said.

"Now can you see me huntin' and shootin' and hobnobbing with the gentry?" He chuckled, and the chuckle turned into a wheezing cough. "Like I said, I know my place, my love. You live in your world and I live in mine. You go home and have a lovely time up there. I'll see you when you get back."

Chapter 7

THE FLYING SCOTSMAN, TRAVELING NORTH
AUGUST 17, 1932

**Going home. Excited and dreading it at the same time. Lovely day. Bright
and warm.**

The next morning I sat in a first-class compartment on the Flying Scotsman
as the countryside flashed past, bathed in sunlight. It was all very pleasant
and rural, but my head was swimming with conflicting emotions. I was
going home—back to a place I loved. Nanny still lived in a cottage on the
estate, my horse was waiting for me in the stable, and my brother would be
pleased to see me, even if Fig wasn't. The thought of Fig clutched at my
stomach. I wasn't afraid of her, but it is never pleasant to know that one is
not wanted. I wondered what Sir William had said to her. Would she know
that I'd been sent home in disgrace?

Outside in the corridor I was conscious of a bell ringing and a voice
announcing the first sitting for luncheon. Luncheon in the dining car was
something I would not normally have allowed myself in my present impe-
cunious state, but today I felt I deserved it. After all, for the foreseeable
future I'd not be fending for myself, and someone at Scotland Yard had paid
for my train ticket. I got up, glanced in the mirror to make sure I looked
respectable then came out of my compartment into the corridor, almost
colliding with a person emerging from the next compartment. He was a

rather good-looking young man, tall, with blond hair, brilliantined into a set of pretentious waves, and wearing a sporty-looking blazer and slacks.

"Frightfully sorry," he muttered, then he appeared to really notice me. His eyes traveled over me in the way that eyes usually traveled over Belinda. "Well, hello there," he said in what I suppose was a slow, sexy drawl. "I say, what a lucky coincidence to find someone like you in the next compartment. Here was I, steeling myself for eight hours of boredom and the crossword puzzle. Instead I bump into a frightfully pretty girl, and what's more, a pretty girl who appears to be alone." He glanced up and down the empty corridor. "Look here, I was on my way to the cocktail lounge. Care to accompany me for a drink, old bean? One simply can't survive without a gin and tonic at this time of day."

Part of me was tempted to go with him; the other part was affronted at the way he had been mentally undressing me. This didn't happen to me often and I wasn't sure whether I should enjoy it or not. As always in moments of stress, I reverted to type. "It's frightfully kind of you, but I was on my way to the dining car."

"It's only the first sitting. Nobody goes to the first sitting except for aged spinsters and vicars. Come on, be a sport. Come and keep me company with a cocktail. It's a train, you know. The rules of society are bent when traveling."

"All right," I said.

"Jolly good. Off we go then." He took my elbow and steered me in the direction of the cocktail bar. "Are you going up to Scotland for the grouse shoot?" he asked as we maneuvered unsteadily forward against the rocking of the train.

"I'm going to visit family," I said over my shoulder, "but I expect I'll do a little shooting. How about you?"

"I may do a little shooting myself but I'm particularly going to watch a chum of mine try out his new boat. He's designed this fiendish contraption with which he plans to break the world water speed record. He's going to be trying it out on some ghastly Scottish lake, so a group of us decided to come along as a cheering section."

"Really?" I said. "Where shall you be staying?"

"I've managed to wheedle a sort of invitation to a place nearby called Castle Rannoch," he said. "I was at school with the duke, y'know. I must say the old school tie works wonders everywhere. But I can't say I'm looking forward to the castle with great anticipation. Positively medieval by the sound of it. No decent plumbing or heating and family ghosts on the battlements. And the live occupants sound equally dreary, but it really will be dashed convenient for all the excitement so I expect I'll be able to stomach it for a few days. How about you? Where are you staying?"

"At Castle Rannoch," I said smoothly. "It's my family home."

"Oh, blast it." He flushed bright pink. "Don't tell me you're Binky's sister. I really have bally well put my foot in it, haven't I?"

"Yes, you do seem to have," I said. "Now, please excuse me. I don't want to miss the first sitting at luncheon with the vicars and spinsters." I spun away from him and stalked off fast in the opposite direction.

The dining room was quite full by the time I arrived, and not just with the threatened spinsters and vicars, but I was found an empty table and handed a menu. I noticed a man seated opposite me staring with interest. He was an older military type—slim, upright bearing and neat little mustache, and I wondered if he made a habit of picking up young women on trains. In fact he half rose to his feet, as if to come in my direction, when he was beaten to it by another man.

"I'm frightfully sorry," the latter said in high, breathless tones, "but the whole wretched place appears to be occupied so I wondered if you'd mind frightfully if I joined you. I promise that I don't slurp my soup or drink my tea from the saucer."

He was the complete physical opposite of the other man—short, chubby and pink, with a dapper little mustache and a carnation in his buttonhole. His dark hair was carefully combed to cover a bald spot. Completely inoffensive in any case and he was giving me a hopeful smile. He could even have been one of the aforementioned vicars, traveling minus dog collar.

"Of course," I said. "Do sit down."

"Splendid. Splendid," he said, beaming at me now. He took out a crisp white handkerchief and mopped his brow. "Warm on this train, isn't it? They'll all get a frightful shock when they reach Scotland and the usual howling gale is blowing."

"Do you live in Scotland?" I asked.

"Good lord, no. I'm a cosmopolitan bird myself. London and Paris, that's me." Then he extended a pink, chubby hand. "I should introduce myself. I'm Godfrey Beverley. I write a little column for the *Morning Post.*

It's called 'Tittle Tattle.' All the juicy gossip about what's going on around town. You've probably heard of me."

A small alarm bell was going off in my head. This man was part of the press. Was he ingratiating himself to me so that he could get the inside scoop on my current rapid departure from London?

"I'm sorry," I said smoothly, "but we take the *Times*, and I pay no attention to gossip."

"But my dear young lady, you must be one in a million if you don't find gossip utterly delicious," he said, looking up expectantly as soup plates were delivered to our table.

"Ah, vichyssoise—my favorite," he said, beaming again. "I've heard they do a decent meal on this train these days. So much better than when they used to stop for lunch at York and we all had to cram down awful sausage rolls in twenty minutes. And I didn't get a chance to ask you your name, my dear."

I tried to come up with an innocuous name and was just about to say Maggie McGregor, which was the name of my maid at home, when the maitre d' appeared at our table. "Some wine for you, your ladyship?" he asked.

"Uh, no, thank you," I stammered.

"Your ladyship?" My table companion was gazing at me in eager anticipation. He put a hand to his mouth like a naughty child caught at the biscuit barrel. "Oh, heavens above, how silly of me. Of course. I recognize you now from your pictures in the *Tattler*. You're Lady Georgiana, aren't you? The king's cousin. How absolutely crass of me not to recognize you. And here I was thinking you were an ordinary wholesome young girl going home from boarding school or university. You must have thought me frightfully presumptuous, trying to sit at your table. And how gracious you were about it too. Please do forgive my boorishness." He half rose to his feet.

"Not at all," I said, smiling to calm his fluster. "And please do stay. I hate to eat alone."

"You are too, too kind, your ladyship." He was positively bowing now.

"And I am an ordinary wholesome young woman," I said. "I am going home to visit my family."

"To Castle Rannoch? How delightful. I shall be staying at my favorite inn, not far from you. I always like to go up to Scotland during the season. Everybody who is anybody is there, of course, and there is always the chance that your esteemed family members will appear from Balmoral and mingle with humble commoners like myself from time to time." He paused to work his way through the soup. "I presume you have been invited to Balmoral?"

"Yes, one is always expected to put in an appearance each season," I said, "but I plan to spend a few days at home on the family estate first."

"They must all miss you so much when you are away," he said. "Have you been traveling in Europe?"

"No, I've been in London for most of the time," I said, then I remembered that he was Mr. Tittle Tattle. "Of course one visits friends frequently at their country houses. I'm a country girl at heart. I can't stay in the city for too long."

"How true, how true," he said. "So do tell me with whom you have stayed recently. Any juicy scandals?"

"Not since the German princess," I said, knowing he would be fully conversant with that one.

"My dear, wasn't that awful? You are so lucky to have escaped with your life, from what one hears."

The empty soup plates were whisked away to be replaced with roast pheasant, new potatoes and peas. Godfrey Beverley beamed again. "I have to confess that I do adore pheasant," he said, and tucked in with relish.

"So tell me," he asked after he had demolished most of the food on his plate, "what is this we hear about your esteemed cousin the Prince of Wales and his new companion? Is it true what they are saying, that she is a married woman? Twice married, in fact? And an American to boot?"

"I'm afraid the Prince of Wales does not confide in me about his lady friends," I said. "He still sees me as a schoolgirl."

"How shortsighted when you have blossomed into such a lovely young woman."

I was about to remind him that he had also taken me for a schoolgirl, and he must have remembered at the same moment because he became flustered again and started playing with his bread roll. The plates were removed and a delicious-looking queen pudding was placed in front of us.

"I wonder if *she* will be up in Scotland?" he asked in conspiratorial undertones.

"She?"

"The mysterious American woman about whom the rumors are flying," he whispered. "She certainly wouldn't be invited to Balmoral, but I do hope to catch a glimpse of her. They say she is the height of fashion—which reminds me, have you seen much of your dear mother lately? I am inordinately fond of your dear mama."

"Are you?" My hostility toward him melted a little.

"Of course. I adore that woman. I worship the ground she treads upon. She has provided me with more material for my columns than any other human being. Such a deliciously naughty life she has led."

The hostility returned. "I see very little of her these days," I said. "I believe she is still in Germany."

"Oh no, my dear. She's been in England for the past couple of weeks at least. I spotted her at the Café Royal the other evening. And she sang with Noel Coward at the Café de Paris the other night. There is a rumor he's writing a play for her. You wouldn't happen to know if that's true, would you?"

"You obviously know more about her than I do," I said, feeling ridiculously hurt that she had been in London and hadn't contacted me once. Not that she had contacted me for months on end when I was growing up or away at school. The maternal instinct never ran strongly through her veins, I suspect.

I managed to eat my meringue without shattering white bits all over me and also managed a couple of polite answers to Mr. Beverley's persistent questions over coffee. With great relief I drained my cup and called over the steward to pay my bill.

"Already taken care of, your ladyship," the steward said.

I looked around the car, a little flustered over who might have been treating me to lunch. It certainly wasn't Mr. Beverley. He was counting out his money onto the tablecloth. Then I decided that perhaps Sir William might have arranged this, trying to soften the blow of my having to leave London in disgrace, I suppose.

I rose and nodded to Mr. Beverley, who also staggered to his feet. "My lady, I can't tell you what a pleasure it was to make your acquaintance," he said. "And I do hope that this will be the first of many meetings. Who knows, perhaps you will be free to take tea with me one day while I am at the inn. There is a delightful little teahouse nearby. The Copper Kettle. Do you know it?"

"I usually take tea with the family when I am home," I said, "but I'm sure we'll bump into each other at some stage, if you are planning to stay in Scotland long. Maybe at one of the shoots?"

At this he turned pale. "Oh, deary me, no. I do not relish killing things, Lady Georgiana. Such a barbaric custom."

I almost reminded him that he had tucked into the pheasant with obvious relish and that somebody had had to kill it at some stage, but I was more anxious to make an exit while I could.

"Please excuse me," I said. "I was up very early this morning and I think I need to rest after lunch." I gave him the gracious royal nod and retreated to my compartment. Really this had been a most tiresome two days. It was with great expectation that I thought of home.

Chapter 8

STILL ON THE TRAIN
AUGUST 17

The compartment was warm with afternoon sun and I was replete with a good lunch. I must have dozed off because a small sound woke me. The slightest of clicks, but enough to make me open my eyes. When I did, I sat up in alarm. A man was in my compartment. What's more, he was in the process of closing the curtains to the corridor. It was the military-looking man who had been eyeing me closely in the dining car.

"What do you think you are doing?" I demanded, leaping to my feet. "Please leave this compartment at once, or I shall be obliged to pull the communication cord and stop this train."

At that he chuckled. "I've always wanted to see that done," he said. "I wonder how long it takes to stop an express going at seventy miles an hour? A good half mile, I'd guess."

"If you've come to rob me, I have to warn you that I am traveling with nothing of value," I said haughtily, "and if you've come to assault me, I can assure you that I am blessed with a good punch and a loud scream."

At this he laughed. "Oh yes, I see what they mean. I think you'll do very well." He sat down without being asked. "I assure you that I mean you no harm, my lady, and I ask you to forgive the unorthodox method of introduction. I tried to introduce myself to you in the dining car but that odious little man beat me to it." He leaned closer to me. "Allow me to introduce myself now. I am Sir Jeremy Danville. I work for the Home Office."

Oh, golly, I thought. Someone else from the government making sure I got home safely and caused no royal scandal. He probably wanted to know what I'd told Godfrey Beverley.

"I caught this train deliberately," he said, "knowing that we could talk without danger of being overheard. First I want your word that what I am going to say to you will never be repeated to anyone, not even to a family member."

This was unexpected and I was still in the process of waking up from my doze. "I don't see how I can agree to something when I have no idea what it is," I said.

"If I told you it concerns the safety of the monarchy?" He looked at me long and hard.

"Very well, I suppose," I said.

I began to feel a little as Anne Boleyn must have done when she was summoned to the Tower and discovered it wasn't for a quiet dinner party. It crossed my mind that someone might have telephoned the queen over my little gaffe and I was about to be dispatched posthaste to be lady-in-waiting to a distant relative in the Outer Hebrides.

Sir Jeremy cleared his throat. "Lady Georgiana, we at the Home Office are not unaware of the part you played in uncovering a plot against Their Majesties," he said. "You showed considerable spunk and resourcefulness. So we decided you might be the ideal person for a little task involving the royal family."

He paused. I waited. He seemed to expect me to say something but I couldn't think of anything to say as I had no idea as to what might come next.

"Lady Geogiana," he resumed, "the Prince of Wales has recently had a series of unfortunate accidents—a wheel that came loose on his car, a saddle girth that broke on his polo pony. Fortunately he was unharmed on both occasions. These could, of course, be deemed unlucky coincidences, but as we looked at them more closely, we found that the Duke of York and his other brothers had also experienced similar unlucky accidents. We have come to the conclusion that someone is trying to harm or even kill members of the royal family, or more accurately heirs to the throne."

"Golly," I exclaimed. "Do you think it's the communists at work again?"

"We did consider that possibility," Sir Jeremy said gravely. "Some outside power trying to destabilize the country. However, the situation and nature of some of these accidents draw us to a rather startling conclusion: they appear to be what one might call 'an inside job.' "

I went to say "golly" again and swallowed it down at the last moment. It did sound a trifle schoolgirlish. "You mean someone has infiltrated the palace?" I said. "I suppose that's not completely impossible. After all, one of the communists managed it in Bavaria."

"We don't think it is the communists this time," Sir Jeffrey said bluntly. "We think it's closer to home."

"Someone connected to the family?"

He nodded. "Which makes our surveillance rather difficult. Naturally we have our special branch men protecting the Prince of Wales and his brothers to the best of our ability, but there are times and places when we can't be present. That's where you come in. They're all currently at Balmoral for the grouse shooting."

"Well, that's all right then, isn't it?" I looked up at Sir Jeremy. "They'll be safely out of harm's way up there."

"On the contrary. The Prince of Wales had a near miss while out driving only yesterday when the steering locked on the shooting brake he was driving."

"Gol—gosh," I stammered.

"So you see we were glad to know that you were on your way home. You are part of their inner circle. You can move freely among them. You'll be the ideal person to keep your eyes and ears open for us."

"I'm not actually invited to Balmoral for another week," I said.

"That's no problem. Castle Rannoch is close enough, and several members of the Balmoral shooting party are currently staying with your brother. We'll let Their Majesties know that you will be arriving early and will be joining the shoot as part of your brother's house party."

House party! That certainly didn't sound like Fig. Surely no guests would stay long enough at Castle Rannoch to shoot anything, particularly if Fig displayed her usual meanness and allowed only half a slice of toast each for breakfast and two inches of hot water in the bathtub. Another thought struck me.

"Do Their Majesties know about this?"

"Nobody knows except for a handful of our men," Sir Jeremy said. "Not even the Prince of Wales or his brothers suspect that these are anything more than accidents. In fact the Prince of Wales made a joke that he should probably check his horoscope before venturing out. And nobody is to know. Not the slightest hint, you understand. If this is true, then we are dealing with a cunning and ruthless person, and I want to make sure that we nab him before he manages to do some real damage."

"And you have no idea who this person might be?"

"None at all. We've conducted a thorough check into the backgrounds of all the royal staff, in fact into all those who might have access to the Prince of Wales and his brothers. And we've come up empty."

"I see. So you weren't exaggerating when you said it was one of us. You really meant one of our inner circle."

"As you say, your inner circle." Sir Jeremy nodded gravely. "All we ask of you is to keep your eyes and ears open. Our man on the spot will make himself known to you and you can report anything suspicious to him. Naturally we do not expect you to place yourself in any kind of danger. We can count on you, can't we?"

It was hard to make my tongue obey me. "Yes. Of course." It came out as a squeak.

$Chapter\ 9$

Castle Rannoch
Perthshire, Scotland
August 17

Night had not quite fallen as our aged Bentley turned into the driveway leading to Castle Rannoch. The sun sets very late in summer in Scotland and although I could see the lights from the castle winking through the Scots pine trees, the horizon behind the mountains still glowed pink and gold. It was a rare glorious evening and my heart leaped at the familiar surroundings. How often had I ridden my pony along that track. There was the rock from which Binky dared me to dive into the loch, and there was the crag that I alone had managed to climb. Beyond the fence our Highland cattle looked at the motorcar with curiosity, turning their big, shaggy heads to follow our progress.

All the way home my spirits had been rising as we left the city of Edinburgh and climbed through wooded countryside before emerging onto the bleak, windswept expanse of the Highlands, with peaks rising around us and burns dancing in cascades beside the road. Whatever might happen next, I was home. As to what might happen next, I decided to put it from my mind tonight. It was all too worrying, and what's more I was starting to smell a rat. I had a distinct impression that I was being used. The convenient way I was summoned to Sir William, shamed into agreeing to retreat to Scotland immediately, only to find Sir Jeremy on the train—it was all too pat. Did the police really scan the advertisement page in the *Times* every day? Did they really check on every suspicious telephone number? And was it really such a sin to run an escort service? Then something occurred to me that made me go hot all over: Darcy. I knew he did something secret, which he wouldn't discuss. In fact I suspected he was some kind of spy. Had he tipped off the Home Office about my little gaffe, thus giving them a brilliant excuse to pack me off to Scotland without alarming me unduly?

They could have just summoned me to the Home Office and told me what they wanted me to do, but then I suppose I could have refused. Under this little scheme I was a sitting duck for their plans, with no way of wriggling out of the journey. And it seemed more and more likely, as I played everything over in my head, that Darcy was the one who had instigated the whole thing. Some friend, I thought. Betraying me and then setting me up for a difficult and maybe dangerous assignment. I am well rid of him.

The tires of the Bentley scrunched on the gravel as the car came to a halt outside the front door. The chauffeur jumped out to open my door but before it was fully open the castle door opened, light streamed out and our butler, Hamilton, appeared.

"Welcome home, my lady," he said. "It is so good to have you back."

So far, so good. At least someone was pleased to see me.

"It's good to be back, Hamilton," I replied and went up the worn steps and in through the big front door. After a small anteroom lined with stags' heads, one steps into the great hall, the center of life at Castle Rannoch. It rises two stories high with a gallery running around it. On one side is a giant stone fireplace big enough to roast an ox. On the wood-paneled walls hang swords, shields, tattered banners carried into long-ago battles, more stags' heads. A wide staircase sweeps up one side, lined with portraits of Rannoch ancestors, each generation hairier as one went back in time. The floor is stone, making the hall feel doubly cold and drafty, and there are various sofas and armchairs grouped around the fire, which is never lit in summer, however cold the weather.

To outsiders the first impression is horribly cold, gloomy and warlike, but to me at this moment it represented home. I was just looking around with satisfaction when Fig appeared in the gallery above.

"Georgiana, you're back. Thank God," she said, her voice echoing from the high ceiling. She actually ran down the stairs to meet me.

This was not the reception I had expected and I stared at her blankly as she ran toward me, arms open, and actually embraced me. She'd called me by my name so she couldn't have mistaken me for anyone else. Besides, Fig doesn't make anyone welcome, ever.

"How are you, Fig?" I asked.

"Awful. I can't tell you how frightful it's been. That's why I'm glad you're here, Georgiana."

"What's wrong?" I asked.

"Everything. Let's go into Binky's den, shall we?" she said, slipping her arm through mine. "We are not likely to be disturbed there. You'd like something to eat, I suspect. Hamilton, could you have the drinks tray and a plate of those smoked salmon sandwiches brought through for Lady Georgiana?"

All right. This was Scotland, after all. My sister-in-law had been bewitched, or taken by the fairies and a changeling left in her place. But since she was offering me smoked salmon and the drinks tray, who was I to refuse? She steered me across the great hall, down the narrow passage to the right and in through an oak-paneled door. The room had the familiar smell of pipe smoke and polished wood and old books: a very masculine sort of smell. Fig indicated a leather armchair for me and pulled up another one beside me.

"Thank God," she said again. "I don't think I could have endured it for another day alone."

"Alone? What's happened to Binky?"

"You didn't hear about his dreadful accident then?"

"No. What happened?"

"He stepped on a trap."

"An animal trap?"

"Of course an animal trap."

"When did MacTavish start using animal traps on the estate? I thought he was always so softhearted."

"He doesn't. He swears he never laid the trap, but he must have done, of course. Who else would put a bally great trap on one of our paths, and especially a path that Binky always walks in the morning?"

"Crikey. Is Binky all right?"

"Of course he's not all right," she snapped, reverting to type for the first time. "He's laid up with a dashed great dressing over his ankle. In fact he was extremely lucky he was wearing those old boots that belonged to his grandfather. I kept telling him to throw them away but now I'm glad he didn't listen to me. Anything less stout and the trap would have had his foot off. As it was the trap wouldn't close completely and he got away with nasty gashes down to the bone and a cut tendon."

"Poor old Binky. How terrible for him."

"Terrible for him? What about terrible for me with all these awful people in the house?"

"What awful people?"

"My dear, we have a house full of disgusting Americans."

"Paying guests?"

"Of course not paying guests. What on earth gave you that idea? Since when did a duke take in paying guests? No, these are friends of the Prince of Wales, or rather a certain woman among them is a friend of the Prince of Wales."

"Oh, I see. Her."

"As you say, 'Her.' The prince is at Balmoral, of course, and his woman friend would certainly not be welcome there, so the prince asked Binky if he could offer her hospitality so she'd be close enough to visit. And you know Binky—always too softhearted. Can't say no to anybody. And he looks up to the prince, always has done. So of course he said yes."

I nodded with sympathy.

"And the prince suggested that maybe we build a little house party around her and her husband—oh, did I mention that she still has a husband in tow? Mooches around like a lost sheep, poor fellow. Spends his time playing billiards. Can't even shoot. So Binky goes ahead and invites some people to make up a house party—the cousins, of all people, to start with."

"Which cousins?"

"On the Scottish side. You know that dreadful hairy pair, Lachan and Murdoch."

"Oh yes. I remember well." Lachan and Murdoch had always rather terrified me with their wild Highland appearance and behavior. I remember Murdoch demonstrating how to toss the caber with a fallen pine tree and hurling it through a window.

"Well, my dear, they haven't improved with age, and you have no idea how much they eat and drink."

I had a pretty good idea, if Murdoch's caber tossing was any indication. We broke off as there was a discreet tap at the door and Hamilton entered, bearing a tray with a neat pile of sandwiches decorated with watercress, a decanter containing Scotch, and two glasses.

"Thank you, Hamilton," I said.

"My lady." He nodded, smiling at me with obvious pleasure. "May I pour you a little sustenance?" and without waiting for the go-ahead, he poured a liberal amount into one of the tumblers. "And for you, Your Grace?"

"Why not?" Fig said. This was also unusual. She normally drank nothing stronger than the occasional Pimm's on summer outings. But she took hers instantly and had a jolly good swig. I tucked into a sandwich. Local smoked salmon. Mrs. McPherson's freshly baked bread. I couldn't remember tasting anything more divine. Hamilton retreated.

"But that's not the worst part of it," Fig said, putting her empty glass back on the tray with a loud bang.

"It's not?" I wondered what was coming next.

"The dreadful American woman arrived and guess what? She's brought her own house party with her. The place is positively crawling with Americans. They are eating us out of house and home, Georgiana, and you have no idea how demanding they are. They want showers instead of baths, for one thing. They told me that baths are quite unhygienic. What can be unhygienic about a bath, for heaven's sake? It's full of water, isn't it? Anyway, they had the servants rig up a shower contraption in the second-floor bathroom, and then it fell on some woman's head and she was screaming that she'd been scalded and got a concussion."

I gave a sympathetic grin.

"And what's more, they are always taking showers and baths. They want them every day, can you imagine? And at all times of the day and night. I told them that nobody can possibly get that dirty in so short a time, but they bathe every time they come in from a walk, before dinner, after dinner. It's a wonder they're not completely washed away. And as for drinking . . . my dear, they want cocktails, and they're always experimenting with new cocktails. They used Binky's twenty-year-old single-malt Scotch to make some drink with orange juice and maraschino cherries. I'm only glad that Binky was lying in agony upstairs and didn't see them. I tell you it would have finished him off on the spot."

For the first time in my life I looked at my sister-in-law with some sympathy. She was definitely looking frazzled. Her short, almost mannishly bobbed hair was usually perfectly in place and it currently looked as if she'd come in from a gale. What's more she had spilled something down the front of her gray silk dinner gown. Tomato soup, I'd gather.

"It must have been terribly trying for you," I said. "And as for poor Binky . . ."

"Binky?" she shrieked. "Binky is lying up there being fussed over by Nanny and Mrs. MacTavish. All he has is a mangled ankle. I have Americans."

"Chin up. It can't be for too much longer," I said. "Nobody stays in Scotland for more than a week or so."

"By the end of a week or so we shall be destitute," she said, her voice dangerously near to tears. "Eaten out of house and home, literally. I'll have to take in paying guests to make ends meet. Binky will have to sell off the rest of the family silver."

I put out a tentative hand and rested it over hers. I believe it was the first time I had willingly touched her. "Don't worry, Fig. We'll think of something," I said.

She looked up at me and beamed. "I knew I could rely on you, Georgiana. I am so glad you're here."

Chapter 10

CASTLE RANNOCH
AUGUST 17

Late.

As we emerged from Binky's den and came down the corridor to the great hall, a noisy party was coming out of the drawing room, at the far end of the opposite hallway.

"And so I said to him, 'You simply don't have the equipment, honey,' and he said, 'I've got a bloody great big one, and what's more, when it's revved up, it goes like a ramrod.' He thought we were still talking about the boat."

There was a roar of laughter. Even though they were still a good distance away and bathed in shadow, I recognized the speaker before I could get a good look at her. It was, of course, the dreaded American woman, Mrs. Wallis Simpson. As she came closer I noticed that she was looking rather thin, angular and masculine in a metallic pewter-gray evening dress and matching metallic helmet. And old. She was definitely beginning to look her age, I thought with satisfaction.

"Wallis, honey, you are shameless." The speaker was an older woman, dressed in sober black. She was statuesque in build and towered over Mrs. Simpson, but she carried herself well with a regal air, rather like a larger version of Queen Mary. "How you can tell tales like that in public I don't know. Thank heavens Rudi is not still alive to hear."

"Oh, don't come the countess with me, Merion," Wallis Simpson said. "I remember you when you were plain old Miss Webster, remember? You took me for root beer floats at Mr. Hinkle's soda fountain in Baltimore when I was just a toddler, and you flirted with that young guy behind the counter!"

"Who is that?" I murmured to Fig, indicating the older woman.

"Oh, she's the Countess Von Sauer."

"I thought you said they were all Americans."

"They are. She's part of the Simpson woman's party. She was originally called something perfectly ordinary like Webster but she did her tour of Europe and snagged herself an Austrian count. I don't think the Simpson woman has forgiven her for one-upping her on the social scale."

"She's trying hard enough to remedy that now," I muttered to Fig.

"She certainly is. The Prince of Wales has been over here to visit almost every evening. I told him I didn't approve and he said I was a prude. When have I ever been a prude, Georgiana? I consider myself as broad-minded as anybody. After all, I did grow up on a farm."

"Fritzi, honey, I left my wrap. Be an angel and fetch it for me or I shall freeze." The countess turned to a large, pink young man who was trailing at the back of the party. "It's positively frigid in here. It makes our Austrian castle feel like the Côte d'Azur."

"Mama, you're always forgetting things. I shall be worn to a rail if you keep me running around like this. Do you know how far it is to your room from here? And all those horrible stairs?"

I turned to Fig again.

"She's also brought her reprobate son with her," she muttered. "He piles his plate with all the good sandwiches at tea and he pinches the maids' bottoms."

"Hasn't the keep-fit movement reached Austria yet?" one of the men in the party asked. "Babe can't start the day without her gymnastics and dumbbells, can you, Babe, honey?"

"I sure can't," a petite, bony woman replied.

At that moment they emerged into the great hall and Wallis Simpson noticed me. "Why, it's the actress's daughter," she said. "What a surprise. When did you get here?"

I was still feeling angry on behalf of Fig and Binky and wasn't about to take any of her cutting remarks. "Actually it's the duke's daughter," I said, "and the current duke's sister, and the king's cousin and great-granddaughter to Queen Victoria, and you are currently a guest in my ancestral home."

"Ouch," said a man who had been lingering at the back of the party. I recognized him as Mr. Simpson, the invisible and until now silent husband. "I reckon you've met your match there, Wallis."

"Nonsense," she said with a guttural chuckle. "It's lack of sex. It makes people touchy. We should do the kind thing and get her hitched up with a gamekeeper while she's up here. Think of Lady Chatterley."

And they went into peals of laughter again.

"Who is Lady Chatterley?" Fig whispered to me.

"A character in a book, by D. H. Lawrence. It's banned over here. He had it printed in Italy, and there are smuggled copies all over the place."

"And what's so terrible about it?"

"The lady and the gamekeeper have a continuous roll in the hay together and describe it with four-letter farm words."

"How disgusting," Fig said. "I bet the writer has never seen a real gamekeeper, or he'd never have thought they had sex appeal. They smell of dead rabbits, for one thing."

"One of these days you'll go too far, Wallis," Mr. Simpson said sharply.

She glanced up at him, then put a hand up to his cheek and chuckled again. "I don't think so. I believe I know exactly how far I can go."

The big man in the party now came over to me, his hand extended. "So you're the young lady of the family, are you? Glad to meet you. I'm Earl Sanders. This is my wife, Babe."

I shook hands all around. I noticed Mrs. Simpson didn't offer hers.

"So who is up for whist or bridge?" Wallis Simpson asked. "Or shall we be devils and play roulette?"

"I'm afraid we don't possess a roulette wheel," Fig said frostily. "If we choose to gamble, we go to Monte Carlo."

"Don't worry, Earl's brought his own," Mrs. Simpson said. "He can't go more than a day without gambling, can you, Earl honey?"

"The question is where are we going to play without freezing to death and without having the cards blown away by a howling gale?" the Countess Von Sauer asked. "Surely not in here."

"I was sensible enough to bring my mink," Babe said. Her morning keep-fit regimen was certainly paying off. She hadn't an ounce of spare flesh on her and made the angular Mrs. Simpson look positively feminine. No wonder she was cold. She turned to her husband and retrieved the fur from him, wrapping it snugly around her shoulders. "I even wore it in bed last night. My dears, the draft from that window. It wouldn't close properly and there was a hurricane blowing."

"Will the drawing room not do?" Fig asked. "I can have the servants move back the sofas and set up tables."

"There are some rather loud young men in there, smoking up a storm and working their way through the whiskey decanter," Mrs. Simpson said.

"See, what did I tell you?" Fig muttered.

"Then it will have to be in here," Fig said out loud. "I'll call the servants."

"How about that nice little room that looks out on the lake?" Babe suggested. "The one where we had coffee this morning."

"But that's the morning room." Fig sounded horrified.

"So is it a crime to go in there after noon?" Wallis Simpson asked with amusement. "Really, I find all these British rules too, too fascinating."

"I suppose you can use it if you insist upon it," Fig said. "It's just that we never do. Not after luncheon."

"It's probably haunted," the big man chuckled. "The ghost only appears after the stroke of twelve midday. Babe swears she saw a white figure floating down the corridor upstairs."

"That would be the White Lady of Rannoch," I said. "Did you hear her moaning? She often moans."

"Moans?" Babe looked apprehensive.

"Frightfully," I said. "She was thrown in the loch with a great stone tied to her for being a witch. The locals also say that they see bubbles coming up from the loch and that could be the White Lady returning. Of course, it could be just the monster."

"Monster?" The countess sounded alarmed now.

"Oh yes. Didn't you hear we have a famous monster in the loch? It's been there for hundreds of years."

"Mercy me," the countess said. "I think I might skip the cards tonight and go straight to bed. Fritzi, would you pop up ahead of me and make sure there's a hot water bottle in the bed and that my nightdress is wrapped around it?"

"Of course, Mama." He nodded dutifully and went.

"Well, I need my nightly gamble," the big man said. "You guys go take a look at that morning room place and I'll go fetch the roulette wheel."

They disappeared. Fig looked at me. "Now you can see for yourself," she said. "Torment, utter torment. Did you ever hear of anyone wanting to use the morning room after luncheon?"

"Never," I agreed.

"You'd think the one who became a countess would know better, wouldn't you? She does have a castle in Austria."

"And the other man is an earl, isn't he?" I commented, watching his large retreating rear.

Fig broke into tense laughter. "No, that's just his Christian name. I made the same mistake and called his wife 'countess' and she thought it was a hoot." She went to walk ahead then turned back to me. "But tell me, what was all that about the White Lady of Rannoch? I've never heard of her."

"I made her up," I said. "It occurred to me that if you want the Americans to leave, you should make them want to leave. The occasional night-time haunting by the family ghost might help to do the trick."

"Georgiana, you are wicked," Fig said, but she was beaming at me with admiration.

"And we can institute some other measures to make them uncomfortable," I said. "Turn down the boiler, for one thing. We did that at Rannoch House when we wanted the German baroness to move. They won't stay if they can't get their hot showers."

"Brilliant!" Fig was still beaming.

"And does Fergus still play the pipes?" I asked, referring to one of our grooms who led the local pipe band.

"He does."

"Have him play them on the battlements at dawn, like they used to do in the old days. Oh, and serve them haggis for breakfast. . . ."

"Georgiana, I—I mean, we couldn't. Word would get back to the Prince of Wales and he'd be angry with Binky."

"What for?" I asked. "We're just carrying on our normal family traditions to make them feel welcome."

She stared at me hopefully. "Do you really think we dare?"

"Let me put it this way: how long do you want them to stay here?"

"We'll do it," she exclaimed. "We'll turn it into a castle of horrors!"

The sound of laughter erupted down the hallway from the direction of the drawing room. "And I should go and remove the whiskey decanter from those two cousins of yours," she said. "They break things when they get drunk."

"I suppose I should come and say hello," I said hesitantly.

"You should." Fig strode ahead. She pushed open the drawing room door. Two young men in kilts looked up as we came in. The room was in a fog of cigar smoke—Binky's cigars, I suspected.

"Och, hello, Cousin Fig. Come and join us," one of them said. "We're just celebrating the removal of the American terror."

"And finishing Binky's good Scotch, I notice," Fig said, holding up an almost empty decanter. "When it's gone there isn't any more, you know. We're absolutely paupers, Murdoch."

Murdoch's eyes drifted past her to see me standing in the doorway. "And who's yon bonnie wee lassie?"

"This is your cousin Georgiana," Fig said. "Georgiana, these are your cousins Lachan and Murdoch. I don't believe you've met for many years."

Two giants with sandy hair rose to their feet. They were both wearing kilts. One had a red beard and looked like the Rannoch ancestors come to life. Then I looked at the other. He was clean shaven and was—well, rather good-looking. Tall, muscled, rugged. Like a Greek god, in fact. He held out his hand to me. "No, this is never little Georgie. Remember when you used to make me play at being your horse and carry you around the estate on my back?"

"Oh, that was you." I smiled, the memory returning. "I do remember when Murdoch threw that tree trunk through the window."

"Och, he does things like that," Lachan said, still smiling down at me and still holding my hand. "So come and sit down, have a wee dram, and tell us what you've been doing."

"I've just had a drink with Fig," I said, in case she thought I might be joining the enemy. "And I've been leading a blameless life in London. How about the two of you?"

"Running the estate, mainly," Murdoch said. "We can't afford the manpower any longer so we both have to work like dogs to make a go of it."

"Apart from the times you're away at your Highland Games," Lachan pointed out.

"I win prizes at those Highland Games. Didn't I win us a pig last year? And a barrel of whiskey?"

"You did. But then you also went down to Aintree for the races and then to St. Andrew's for the golf," Lachan said with a grin.

"Well, that's business, isn't it?" Murdoch replied. "I have to go to Aintree to watch our racehorses."

"While I'm stuck at home dipping the sheep."

"Of course, I'm the elder."

"But I'm the smarter."

"You are not. Whatever put such an idea into your thick head?"

They had half risen to their feet again. Fig looked at me nervously, suspecting this might come to blows. "Georgiana, you really should look in on your brother before he goes to sleep."

"Of course," I said. "Excuse me, won't you?"

"Come back when you're done," Lachan said. As I went out I heard him say, "Whoever thought that wee Georgie would turn out so nicely?"

And for the first time in ages I smiled to myself.

Chapter 11

CASTLE RANNOCH

AUGUST 17

Now very late in the evening.

"So that's the sum total of your house party?" I asked Fig as we started to climb the staircase to Binky's room. "Two wild cousins? In which case it's lucky Mrs. Simpson brought her own friends."

"Of course that's not the sum total," Fig said. "We have two more young men staying here. I don't know where they've disappeared to."

"No other women?"

"It is a shooting party, after all," Fig said. "I believe Binky did ask a couple of females but they were busy."

I grinned to myself. It would indeed take a brave young woman to endure Castle Rannoch. "Not too many women are interested in shooting, I suppose," I said kindly.

"I can't see why not," Fig said. "I absolutely adore it."

"So who are these young men?" I asked, feeling suddenly hopeful at being the only unattached female in the group. "Anyone I know?"

"Well, you must know Prince George."

"The king's youngest son?" I asked. "Oh yes, I know him well enough." As I said it I remembered a rather disreputable party at which His Highness had begged me not to mention to anyone that I'd seen him there.

"An ex–navy officer and quite handsome," Fig went on. "A good catch for you, Georgiana."

Again I kept quiet about the look that had passed between him and the performer Noel Coward, and the fact that I'd seen him slip into the kitchen at that party, where I later found cocaine being used. Not such a good catch, in fact. But quite pleasant, as relatives went.

"I expect the king and queen have someone of higher rank than me in mind for their son," I said tactfully. "A European alliance at this unsettled time."

"Speaking of which," Fig said, and stopped short. Voices were coming down the upper corridor toward us. Male voices. One of them had a strong foreign accent.

"Shall we attempt to ascend that mountain tomorrow, do you think?"

I froze on the stairs. "No, not him!" I hissed as I recognized that voice. It was my nemesis Prince Siegfried, of the house of Hohenzollen-Sigmaringen, whom everyone expected me to marry. Since I referred to him as Fishface and knew that he preferred boys, I was less than enthusiastic about this. A horrible thought crossed my mind that this whole thing was a plot. I'd been whisked back to Scotland not to solve any crime but to be thrust together with the man I so vehemently avoided. If I spotted a priest while I was in the same room as Siegfried, I resolved to run.

"Prince Siegfried, you mean?" She looked innocently at me. "You don't like him? He has beautiful manners and he's connected to all the great houses of Europe. He might even be king someday. If anything happens to his brother."

"Like being assassinated, you mean?"

"Well, yes, but . . ." She stopped, as the speakers had come into view. They were chatting merrily and stopped in surprise when they saw us.

"Good heavens, it's Cousin Georgie," Prince George said. "When did you get here?"

"Just arrived, sir, " I said.

"I didn't know you were expected. How jolly," my cousin went on. "And look here, you don't have to call me 'sir' when we're alone. I know my father expects it at all times. Mother even makes the granddaughters curtsy to her each morning. They just can't see that all these stuffy rules are obsolete. This is the jazz age. People should be free, shouldn't they, Siegfried?"

"Not too free," Siegfried said. "Within our class, maybe. But as for encouraging the lower classes to be too familiar, I am afraid I am against it." He bowed to me and clicked his heels. "Lady Georgiana. We meet again. How delightful." He sounded about as delighted as one who has been presented with a plate of rice pudding.

"Your Highness." I nodded in return with an equal amount of enthusiasm. "What a pleasant surprise to find you here."

"So you've come to join the shooting party, have you?" Prince George asked.

"I have. Is Binky still arranging a shoot here or are you going over to Balmoral to join theirs?"

"We've been over to Balmoral a couple of times. Binky's a bit out of commission at the moment, as you've probably heard. We've just been cheering him up, haven't we, Siegfried?"

"What? Oh *ja*, absolutely."

"So why aren't you staying at Balmoral?" I asked the prince.

"Too impossibly stuffy, and Mummy going on at me to hurry up and get married. And then all the tension with David. They've heard that the Simpson woman is here, of course, and, like our great-grandmother, they are not amused." He grinned.

"Well, would you be?" I said. "The Prince of Wales will be king someday. Can you imagine a Queen Wallis, if she ever casts off her current husband?"

The prince chuckled. "I do get your point. David simply doesn't take the job seriously. He's a good enough chap, kind and generous, y'know, but he finds the affairs of state too boring and I can't say I blame him."

"You're lucky," I said. "The job won't come to you unless there is another huge flu epidemic or a massacre." I had been exchanging banter but as I said it I felt a cold shiver pass over me. Could it be true that somebody was trying to eliminate those who stood between him and the throne? I'd have to look at the succession list in the morning and see who that could possibly be. Certainly not Prince George. Being king would put an end to his current lifestyle.

"You're looking awfully pensive," he said. "Come down and have a nightcap with us. Are your fearsome cousins still ensconced in the drawing room?"

"They are."

"My God, what brutes. Throwbacks to the stone age, didn't we agree, Siegfried?"

"Oh yes, absolute brutes. We risk our lives every time we encounter them."

I stifled a giggle, as they both seemed rather enchanted with this.

"I'm on my way up to see Binky," I said, "but I'll no doubt see you in the morning. Your Highnesses." I inclined my head again.

Siegfried clicked his heels and we passed on the stairs.

"You see, Georgiana, two charming young men and you hardly say two words to them, much less flirt," Fig admonished. "You have to learn to flirt, my dear, or you'll wind up an old maid."

I stole a quick glance at her solid, angular face. I was dying to ask if she had ever flirted with Binky and if she had, why he hadn't run screaming in the opposite direction. Apart from her pedigree she didn't seem to have much going for her.

We continued along the hallway. Cold drafts swept past us, stirring the tapestries and making me think that I could easily do more with this White Lady of Rannoch idea. From outside the castle came the sound of a screech owl. Definitely a place that lent itself beautifully to ghosts and ghoulies and long-legged beasties and things that go bump in the night. At the far end Fig opened the door cautiously. "Binky, are you awake?" she whispered. "I've brought someone to see you."

My brother raised himself from his pillows and turned to look in our direction. "Georgie," he exclaimed with delight, and held out his hand to me. "What a lovely surprise. And how good of you to come. You heard about your poor brother's accident and rushed to his side, did you? I call that splendid family loyalty."

Whatever Fig had been told of the reason for my sudden arrival, she had kept wisely silent. I went over and kissed his forehead. He looked rather pale, and there was an improvised cage over his left ankle that was swathed in white linens.

"I'll leave you two to chat then," Fig said. "I'm off to bed. Those Americans have completely worn me out."

"Sleep well, old thing," Binky called after her. He looked back at me. "She's been having a beastly time of it. Glad you're here to keep her company."

"How about you? I hear you've turned poacher," I said. "Messing around with traps."

"I like that. I nearly lose my foot and my sister makes jokes about it."

"Only because I'm worried about you," I said. I perched on the bed beside him. "What a rum thing to happen, Binky."

"It most certainly was. I still can't fathom it. I mean, if someone wanted to come and poach on our estate, they wouldn't bother to walk a couple of miles from the boundary, would they? They'd nip under the fence and lay their traps in the woods where they wouldn't be noticed. This was left out among the heather on that little path up the mountain that I like to take in the mornings. You know, the one that gives the good view over the estate and the loch."

I nodded. "I used to ride up there sometimes. Lucky you weren't on horseback or it would have snapped the horse's leg."

"It damned near snapped mine," Binky said. "In fact if I hadn't been wearing what grandfather used to call his 'good stout brogues,' I'd have lost my foot, I'm sure of it. As it is, I have to keep soaking it and having revolting poultices to prevent infection, but luckily no bones were broken."

"Have you any idea who'd want to do a thing like this?" I asked.

"Some idiot who thought that the animal he was trying to trap habitually used that particular path," Binky suggested. "But as to what animal that could be, I've no idea. We've a couple of grand stags on the property at the moment but nobody could be crass enough to bring down a stag in a trap, could they?"

"If they were hungry enough and poor enough, I suppose."

"But the risk of being seen when he went to collect the stag would be enormous. Besides, how could he drag it off the property? He'd be almost in full view of the castle all the way."

"It does seem strange," I agreed. "You don't think . . ." I paused, weighing whether to say this. "You don't think the trap was meant for you?"

"For me?"

"Everyone knows you like to take that walk in the mornings."

"For me?" he repeated. "Someone wanting to harm me? But why? I'm a harmless sort of chap. No enemies that I can think of."

"Perhaps someone wants to inherit Castle Rannoch," I said, but my voice trailed off at the end. "So who would inherit Castle Rannoch if you died?"

"Why, Podge, of course," he said.

Oh, golly, Podge, his son. Was he in danger too, and how could I warn his nanny without alarming her too much?

"And after Podge?"

"That pair who are working their way through my whiskey. Murdoch's the elder and then Lachan." He looked at me and laughed. "But you're not suggesting that they had something to do with this? Murdoch and Lachan? We've played together since we were boys."

"Perhaps it was just a horrible practical joke that went too far," I said.

"A practical joke? To set a trap that could take someone's leg off? Not my idea of a joke."

"I agree," I said, "but they do seem like a wild pair. Perhaps they didn't think the trap was very strong."

"They know all about traps," Binky said. "They had trouble with poachers a while back and they told me they were thinking of setting mantraps. I talked them out of it."

"So this wasn't a mantrap."

"Oh no. Definitely meant for an animal." He looked up at me sharply and then laughed. "What on earth put that into your head, Georgie? I mean to say, we're no longer in the times of the clan wars. I can't see any brazen Campbell sneaking onto the estate to have off my leg, nor any member of the Clan Rannoch trying to take over the castle. Who'd want it, for God's sake? There's no income from it. We had to sell off a good part of the land to pay the death duties, and all that's left just produces enough for our daily needs. And as for living in the castle—well, I can understand those Americans complaining like billy-o. Of course the plumbing needs updating, and of course it would be a good idea to have central heating put in, but we've simply no money to do it."

"Perhaps somebody wants the title," I suggested. "It's rather fun to be Your Grace, isn't it?"

"If you want to know the truth, it's damned embarrassing to be a penniless duke," Binky said. "I'd rather be just a plain farmer on a prosperous farm, like our cousins."

I left him soon after and went to bed. I had always thought of my room as friendly and cozy, but as I lay there and listened to the moan of the wind around the castle walls, I decided I was downright chilly. I'd have given anything for a hot water bottle, but of course it would be letting the family down to admit to being cold and asking for one. Four months of London living had made me soft.

So I curled into a tight little ball and pulled the quilt over my head. But sleep wouldn't come. I had forgotten the country could be so noisy. The lapping of the loch, the creak of the pine trees in the night wind, the shriek of a rabbit as it was taken by a fox, the baying of a distant hound all kept me from slumber. Those and my racing brain. Somebody had wanted to kill or maim Binky, that was obvious. And he was an heir to the throne— albeit only thirty-second in line. Which would rule out both Murdoch and Lachan. They came from the nonroyal side of our family and all they'd inherit was the dukedom. But they'd have to finish off little Podge first. I shivered. If I did anything at all, it would be to protect him.

Chapter 12

I woke with first light. Dawn comes early in the Highlands and the slanting rays of sun were painting a bright stripe on my wall. The dawn chorus in the forest was deafening. Falling back to sleep was impossible. Besides, such a morning made one want to be up and out, and I wanted to see for myself where that trap had been set.

I washed and put on my jodhpurs and hacking jacket. Nobody else was stirring in the house, apart from the occasional maid who bobbed a curtsy and shyly whispered, "Welcome home, my lady," as she went about her early duties. I made my way to the stables and a great surge of happiness shot through me as I saw my horse, Rob Roy, his face poking over the door of the loose box. He gave a whicker of surprise at seeing me. I'd always thought he was particularly intelligent. When I tried to put on his saddle, however, it became obvious that he hadn't been ridden for some time. He was incredibly skittish and I had to calm him down before he'd let me tighten the girths.

When I mounted he danced like a medieval charger until I gave him his head and then he took off like a rocket. For a while I let him run, feeling the exhilaration of speed as we shot across the parkland behind the castle. When the manicured lawns turned to springy turf and a path wound through pine forest, I reined in Rob Roy and we slowed to a walk. I didn't want him stepping on another trap! As we emerged from the woodland and the path started to climb through the heather and bracken, I looked down at the castle and grounds below me. The loch was hidden in early morning mist, which curled up the shoreline, making the castle look as if it was floating on a cloud. Then through the mist I saw a movement and heard the soft thud of hooves on a dirt trail and the clink of bit and harness. Another rider was out early. I noted the graceful movement of horse and rider, fluid as if they were one being. Who could it be? The rider, a young man with dark hair, resembled nobody staying at the castle. Then of course my suspicions were roused. Was this the trap setter, returning to inflict more damage?

I swung Rob Roy around and plunged down through the heather to cut him off. He was moving too fast and had passed by the time I reached the path on which he was traveling. I spurred Rob Roy into a flat-out gallop, trying not to lose the other rider in the mist that now swirled around us.

"Hey," I shouted. "You there. Hold up a minute."

He reined in and spun the horse around so that it danced like a medieval charger, rising on its back legs.

"This is private land," I shouted as I closed in on him. "What do you think you are doing here?"

"As to that, I might ask you the same question," he said. "Last time I saw you it was in a sleazy London nightclub."

"Darcy!" I exclaimed, recognizing him as the mist parted. He was wearing a white shirt, open at the neck, and his dark hair was windblown even wilder than usual. On that dancing horse, against the backdrop of heather and mountains, he looked like a Brontë hero and I felt my heart hammering. "Don't tell me you're staying at the castle and nobody told me."

"I'm not actually." He urged his horse toward mine. "I'm staying with a group of friends a couple of miles away. They're renting a house on Lord Angus's estate. They're testing a new speedboat. They want to break the water speed record. And I didn't realize that I'd strayed off Lord Angus's land, so for that I apologize. I was just enjoying the speed of a good horse after all that time cooped up in the city."

"I know, it feels glorious, doesn't it?" We exchanged a smile. I couldn't help noticing how Darcy's dark eyes lit up when he smiled and I felt a little flutter in my heart.

"But what about you?" he asked. "When did you get here?"

"I arrived last night," I said. "I decided to come and help Fig with her party of Americans."

"I see. I must say that was noble of you." He looked amused and suddenly I remembered what I had deduced on the drive from the train. He knew why I was here. Someone must have tipped off Scotland Yard or the Home Office or the special branch or whoever they were to my misdeeds at the nightclub. That constable had come too early in the morning for this to have been reported in a normal fashion during normal office hours. So it had to have been a late night or early morning telephone call. Who else but Darcy himself could have made that call? If he was, as I suspected, a spy of some sort, he'd be chummy with those shadowy people in the special branch.

"It was you, wasn't it?" I blurted out.

"What was me?"

"You tipped off Scotland Yard about my embarrassing evening at the nightclub. You betrayed me. You tricked me into coming up here so that I could be a spy for Sir Jeremy Whatever-His-Name-Is."

"I have no idea what you're talking about, my dear."

"I'm not your dear," I said, feeling my cheeks burning now with anger. "Obviously you don't care a damn about me. You only show up when I'm useful to somebody in the government. I'm fed up with being used."

"I'd volunteer to use you more often, but you don't give me the chance," he said, that wicked smile spreading across his face and his eyes flirting.

"Oh, most amusing," I snapped.

"Just trying to make you see that you are upsetting yourself over nothing," he said.

"Over nothing? I like that. You pretend to be interested in me one minute, then you disappear for weeks on end with no communication whatsoever, then you betray me to Scotland Yard. Well, I've had enough. I can't trust you, Darcy O'Mara. I don't want to see you again."

I spun Rob Roy around and urged him into a gallop. I knew we were going too fast for the twists and turns of the path, but I didn't care. I just wanted to go fast enough to obliterate all thoughts and feelings.

I didn't once look back, so I don't know if he attempted to follow me or not. Probably not. What was one girl less to a man like Darcy? As I neared the castle I decided to pay a call on Nanny. She had now retired to a little cottage on the estate and I was pretty sure she'd be up at this early hour. Of course she was, and she greeted me with a beaming smile and open arms.

"I had no word that you'd be coming, my dove," she said in her soft

Scottish voice, hugging me to her ample bosom. "Well, this is a lovely surprise."

She had shrunk, I noticed. I'd always thought of her as a big woman but she now only came up to my shoulder. She bustled about, pouring me a cup of tea and ladling out a big bowl of porridge.

"You came because of your poor brother, I suppose," she said. "We were all stunned to hear it. Who could have done such a wicked thing?"

"Who indeed," I said.

"Some lad on the estate trying to make an extra shilling or two by catching the occasional rabbit, maybe," she suggested.

"Rather a big trap if he was after rabbits," I pointed out.

"I'd hate to think it was someone who bore a grudge against His Grace," she said.

I looked up sharply. "Do you know of anybody who bore a grudge?" I asked.

She shook her head. "He's well liked around here."

"Has anyone been dismissed recently?"

She thought. "The head gillie did have to let a boy go for helping himself to shot," she said. "Young Willie McDonald. Always was a nasty piece of work, that one."

Willie McDonald, a nasty piece of work, I thought. Of course, that made much more sense then any conspiracy theory against the royal family. I should have a chat with Constable Herries at the local police station and suggest he put the fear of God into young Willie to get him to confess.

"So how is your poor brother faring?" Nanny asked, as I tucked into the porridge.

"He seemed cheerful enough last night. Of course I haven't taken a look at the wound."

"The gamekeeper's wife has been dressing it for him. She said it looked verra nasty." (She rolled her *r*'s in the true Scottish manner.) "We're just praying it doesn't turn septic. And your poor brother, laid up when he's got a houseful of people he should be entertaining."

"I think he's rather glad to avoid some of them," I said and she chuckled.

"I saw that American lady going off with the prince the other morning," she continued. "My, but she gives herself airs and graces, doesn't she?"

"Some people are already worrying that she sees herself as queen someday."

"But she already has one husband, doesn't she? And to think that the British people would stand by and let a woman like that be queen. They'd never allow it."

"Let's hope it never comes to that. I'm sure the Prince of Wales will do his duty in the end and not let us down. He's been raised to be king, after all."

She nodded and sat, staring into the fire.

"So how have you been keeping?" I asked her.

"Not too bad, thank you. A touch of rheumatics now and then. And lonely sometimes, stuck away out here. Your brother visits me, but apart from that . . ."

"What about your neighbors?"

"Gone," she said. "The cottages on either side of me both stand empty now. They've cut back on estate workers since all that land was sold off, you know. And your brother only employs a handful of gillies on the estate too. The old men are retiring and there's no young men to fill their shoes. They don't want this type of hard work anymore. They're off to the cities. Not that there *are* many young men now. Not since the Great War took them away."

While she was speaking my brain was racing. Empty cottages on either side of her. Suddenly I had a good idea about who could fill one of those cottages, at least for a while. My grandfather could come up here to get the fresh air he needed and he could help me with my current assignment. I resolved to write to him immediately.

As soon as I left Nanny I checked out those empty cottages and decided that one of them would do very nicely. It appeared to be fully furnished and not too dusty. It also had a pleasant little kitchen that looked out over the lake. I could picture my grandfather sitting there with his cup of tea. I closed the door carefully then mounted and rode back to the castle. I left Rob Roy in the hands of the groom and went in to see about breakfast. All that Highland air had given me a marvelous appetite. There was only one occupant in the dining room—a young man sitting at the long table, tucking into a large helping of kedgeree and scrambled eggs. He rose as I came in, then his eyes lit up.

"Well, hello there," he said. "We meet again, I see."

It was the objectionable young man from the train.

"What are you doing here?" I asked.

"I think I mentioned that I had an invitation to stay," he said.

"You also mentioned that the castle was positively medieval and the hosts boring, if I remember correctly," I said coldly.

"Yes, well, that was rather crass of me, wasn't it?" he said. "I'm sorry that we got off on the wrong foot. You see, it never occurred to me that you were Binky's sister. I mean, dash it all, he'd always talked of you as a skinny, mousy little thing. So I never dreamed that this gorgeous creature could be associated with Castle Rannoch."

"Flattery will get you nowhere with me," I said.

"Really? It usually works rather well, I find. But I should introduce myself. I'm Hugo. Hugo Beasley-Bottome."

"Dear me," I said. "I bet you were teased about that name at school, weren't you?"

"Beaten to a pulp, constantly. Your brother was one of the house prefects when I first arrived and he was rather kind to me, so I've always, y'know, looked up to him." He gave what he hoped was a winning smile. "And I only know you as Binky's sister."

"I'm Georgiana," I said, not prepared to give him the more familiar form of my name.

He held out his hand. "Delighted to meet you, old bean. I understand poor Binky is laid up with a mangled foot. Rotten luck, what? But I look forward to being shown around by you."

"You wouldn't like it," I said. "It's positively medieval."

His fair skin flushed at this. "Oh, look here. Couldn't we forget that disastrous first meeting and start all over?"

I had taken an instant dislike to him but upbringing won out and forced me to say graciously, "Of course."

"You've been out riding already." He looked me up and down again in that frankly appraising way I found disturbing. He was mentally undressing me again.

"No, I always sleep in my jodhpurs," I said.

He laughed. "Oh, *très* droll. I like a girl with wit. I say, do have some breakfast and join me. I hate eating alone."

I remembered how those words had brought nothing but trouble to me. It was because Belinda had told me that men who came to London hated eating alone that I had come up with my stupid idea of an escort service in the first place. I was tempted to say I wasn't hungry and leave him to it, but the thought of a good breakfast, after months of austerity, toast and tea, was too enticing.

"Please do sit down," I said. "Your kedgeree is getting cold."

I went over to the sideboard and helped myself to kidneys, bacon and fried eggs. If this was economizing, then Binky and Fig weren't doing too badly.

"So where do you live, Mr. Bottomly-Beasley?" I asked.

"It's Beasley-Bottome," he corrected. "And my family has a place in Sussex. I have a pied-à-terre in London."

"And do you work?"

"Oh, rather. Boring desk job, actually. Pencil pusher. My older brother will inherit the estate and there's not much money in the family, so I was cast out upon the cruel world."

We actually had a lot in common and he was attractive in a film-starrish sort of way, so why couldn't I warm to him? After all, he had been to the right sort of school. He was one of us and I did need a husband. But there was just something about him—the exaggerated cut of his jacket, maybe, and the brilliantine in his hair, and those bedroom eyes, and the way he called me gorgeous when I wasn't. Healthy or "not bad looking" at best.

Fortunately before I had to make more polite conversation with Hugo Beasley-Bottome animated voices down the hall heralded the arrival of the Americans.

"And I had just got myself lathered up nicely when the hot water gave out," came a voice. I think it must have been Babe's. "I had to finish my shower in freezing cold water. My dears, it was not a pleasant experience, I can tell you."

"Positively primitive," Mrs. Simpson said, "but I understand from a certain person that Balmoral is even more so. And they have a bagpiper at dawn there every morning—can you imagine?"

"Bagpiper at dawn?" I said brightly as they came into the breakfast room. "Oh, we do that here, as well. In fact, it's done at all the Scottish great houses."

"Well, I've never heard him."

"No, I gather he's been laid up with bronchitis and hasn't had the wind to play the pipes for the past week. We really miss him."

They stopped as Hugo rose to his feet yet again and introductions were made all around. Hugo was almost oozing charm and the Americans were easily won over.

"How nice that you've joined us, Mr. Beasley-Bottome," Babe said. "You'll liven up our little party no end." And her eyes held his for longer than was socially acceptable. I began to think that bed hopping might well be a national sport across the Atlantic, until I remembered my very correct man from Kansas.

"So what do we have planned for today, Wallis honey?" Countess Von Sauer asked.

"I believe I'm going on a little jaunt in an automobile. You'll just have to amuse yourselves," Wallis said.

"I tell you what," Hugo announced brightly. "Why don't you come with me down to the loch? My friends are testing a new speedboat and may be going to have a go at the world water speed record. It should be ripping fun."

"That does sound like a good idea, doesn't it, Earl?" Babe said. Anything to be with Hugo, I suspected. "We could take a picnic. I just adore picnics. It looks as if it's going to be a fine day."

"Lady Georgiana, why don't you ask your cook if she could pack a picnic for us," the countess suggested.

"And should we take our bathing things?" Babe asked.

"The loch is freezing and there is the monster," I said, giving her an encouraging smile.

"Does this monster actually appear in broad daylight?" Fritzi, the countess's wayward son, asked. "I mean, is it an established phenomenon? Have they been sacrificing virgins to it for generations?"

"Oh, absolutely," I said.

"Lucky it wasn't in Baltimore," Wallis Simpson muttered. "They'd have run out of virgins too quickly."

Again the group tittered.

"In which case I'll bring my gun along," Earl said. "I've always wanted to bag a monster. It will look great stuffed on the wall beside that marlin."

I left them making noisy preparations and bumped into Fig. She was pleased to hear about the picnic and the prospect of a day free from Americans. "And sandwiches cost so much less than a proper lunch," she said. "Maybe Mrs. McPherson can make pasties. She's such a dab hand with pastry, isn't she?"

"And I notice the hot water boiler has already been turned down," I added in a low voice. "It was commented on. Babe had to finish showering in cold water."

She gave me a conspiratorial smile. "And I'm just about to go and see Fergus about playing the pipes in the morning. He'll love it that we've reintroduced that old custom. And I must remember to suggest the haggis for dinner tonight. I wonder if Cook will have time to make it. What goes into it exactly?"

"It's a sheep's stomach with the rest of the intestines minced up with oatmeal and sewn into it."

"Is it? How disgusting. I know it's always served on Burns Night and New Year's Eve but I only eat the required mouthful myself. I don't suppose Cook has the odd sheep's stomach on hand."

"And it has to boil for hours," I pointed out.

Fig made a face again. "Well, let's hope she can procure one by tomorrow. The mere description ought to drive them away." She went to walk away then looked back at me. "This has to work, doesn't it, Georgiana?"

"One hopes so," I said.

Chapter 13

Calm and pleasant weather to begin with . . .

I weighed up whether to join the picnic party. Frankly a day in the company of Earl and Babe was not exactly enticing, but it would give me an excuse to find Constable Herries and have a little chat with him about Binky's accident. Before we left I had a couple of tasks to complete. One was the letter to my grandfather and the other was a visit to Podge. I found him playing in my old nursery, surrounded by toy soldiers and a fort, while his nanny sat mending an item of clothing.

He jumped up when he saw me, scattering soldiers underfoot. "Aunt Georgie!" he cried and flung himself into my arms. "Look at my toy soldiers. They used to belong to Papa. And the fort. He's letting me use them because I'm old enough now. Come and play with me."

We played a pleasant game while I tried to think what I could say to warn his nanny without being too dramatic. I did point out to her that there might be more illegal traps on the estate, so that Podge should never be allowed to stray far from the house and that she should keep a good eye on him at all times.

"I always do, my lady," she said in a shocked voice. "He's not allowed to run wild, you know. If he goes out, he goes out in his pram."

Podge looked wistfully toward me as I left. I remembered how lonely nursery life had been and how I'd longed for a little sister or brother. Of course I hadn't realized in those days that my mother was just not the breeding kind, and besides, by the time I was old enough to think about a brother or sister, she had already bolted to another man. I went up and dressed for the picnic.

After much preparation and many last-minute forays for forgotten items, we loaded into the shooting brakes and headed for the lochside. The two princes had decided to go off climbing together. There was still no sign of the wild cousins, so it was just Hugo and I with the remaining Americans. Countess Von Sauer and her son went in the first car with Earl, so I found myself stuck with Hugo and Babe.

"Well, this is cozy, isn't it?" Hugo said, pressing his knee rather too closely against mine and slipping an arm around my shoulder as the car drove away. I gave him a frosty stare and was glad that the ride would be a short one. It was easy to locate where the action was on the loch as the speedboat had attracted quite a crowd of local spectators. As we pulled up at the jetty and got out, we could see the long, thin boat, painted bright blue, being towed back to shore by a rather more sturdy vessel, full of people.

"What happened?" Hugo shouted, going onto the dock to meet the approaching vessel.

"Damn thing became airborne at one twenty," someone shouted back. "He was lucky it didn't flip over."

"What the hell are you doing back here?" someone shouted from the boat. "I thought you'd gone."

"Couldn't keep away, old chap," Hugo shouted back. "Missed your delightful wit."

The boat docked and the party came ashore. Suddenly there was an excited squeal and someone was running down the dock toward me.

"Georgie, it is you!" she exclaimed, arms open. It was Belinda.

"Good heavens, what are you doing here?" I asked in amazement.

"I was about to ask you the same question," she said, enveloping me in a cloud of Chanel perfume as she hugged me. I hadn't recognized her earlier as she was wearing a most un-Belinda-like outfit of beige twill trousers and open-necked shirt with a brown pullover, but her face was still perfectly made up.

"I arrived last night," I said. "I came to help Fig." This had now become the obvious excuse.

"Darling, I never thought I'd hear you say those particular words," she said. "I thought you loathed Fig."

"I do, but she's in a bit of a pickle at the moment. Binky's laid up and the house is full of Americans, including the dreaded You-Know-Who."

"Is she here?" Belinda looked around. "Well, I never."

"Not at this moment. She's gone off driving with a certain prince. Mr. Simpson is over there—the one with the sulky expression on his face."

"I'm not surprised. Wouldn't you be sulky if your wife only dragged you around for respectability and then kicked you out of the bedroom at night to dally with a prince?"

"I'm not sure he actually comes to her bedroom at night, but I wouldn't want to be an object of pity like poor old Simpson. So what are you doing up here?" I saw the answer to that question making his way down the dock toward us.

Belinda looked up at Paolo adoringly. "I'm here because of Paolo, silly. He's the one who's driving the boat. He's going to break the world speed record. Isn't it too, too thrilling?"

"It sounds rather dangerous to me," I said.

"Of course it is. Paolo's only happy doing something dangerous," she said.

The rest of the boaters now came down the dock toward us, deep in discussion, and words like "thrust" and "velocity ratio" floated in the clear Highland air.

"I think you know almost everybody, don't you?" Belinda waved in their general direction. "Paolo, look who it is. It's Georgie."

"Well, that's not too surprising, seeing that it's her family home on the other side of the loch," Paolo said, and kissed my hand. "You arrived just too late to see my impression of a waterbird. I was airborne for several seconds, you know. Quite exhilarating."

"It's supposed to stay in the water, or rather on it," an American voice said behind him. The speaker looked ridiculously young and terribly earnest, peering owlishly through round spectacles.

"That's the designer, Digby Flute," Belinda muttered to me. "Father owns film studios in Hollywood. Pots of money. He's tried breaking the record himself twice and nearly killed himself each time."

"So now he wants Paolo to kill himself instead? That's nice of him."

Belinda smiled. "He's improved his design and it has a new engine, built in Germany. In fact, speaking of Germany, guess who's designed and supplied the engine."

She gestured to a big, blond and very Germanic-looking man who was picking his way toward us from the shore.

"Max!" I exclaimed. "Does that mean my mother is somewhere in the vicinity?"

I hadn't quite finished this sentence when I saw her. She was standing deep in conversation with two other people I recognized and one I didn't. The first was a large, pink and frightfully rich young man called Augustus Gormsley, usually known by his nickname of Gussie. The second was Darcy. And with them was a girl I had never met before: darkly exotic looking, slim, petite and at this moment regarding Darcy with smoldering brown eyes. My first temptation was to duck behind a pine tree and disappear, but I was too late. Gussie spotted me.

"I say, it's your daughter, old bean," he said to my mother and then beckoned me over. "What-ho, Georgie."

I had no alternative but to join them. "Hello, Gussie. Darcy. Hello, Mummy." I managed to sound calm and civil. "What a surprise to see you here."

"Hello, darling." My mother and I exchanged the usual air kisses. "You're looking rather pale," she said. "Aren't you well?"

"It's been a trying summer so far," I said. "I didn't expect to see you here. Where are you staying?"

"At Balmoral, darling, where else?"

I couldn't have been more surprised if she had told me a hermit's cave on the mountain. "Balmoral? I didn't realize you were pally with Their Majesties these days."

"Not me, Max. He took the Prince of Wales shooting at his lodge in the Bohemian Forest last winter and the prince is returning the favor. Besides, it's all in the family, you know. Max is connected through his Saxe-Coburg-Gotha line."

"Goodness, I didn't realize he had royal blood. So should I have been calling him Your Highness all this time?"

It occurred to me that I hadn't really called him anything because his English was very limited, so it probably hadn't mattered.

"No, darling. The Saxe-Coburg-Gotha lot were on his mother's side, so he's just plain Herr, more's the pity. I do rather miss being a duchess. One got such good service in Paris, where such things matter."

"I'm sure there are plenty of dukes floating around for you to snag," I said.

"The trouble is that I've become rather attached to Max," she said. "He does have his faults—like not being able to speak English and preferring to live in Germany with all those dumplings. But he is rather sweet and cuddly, isn't he?"

It was like asking if a grizzly bear was sweet and cuddly. I refrained from commenting. "So you've come to join the royal shooting party?"

"And of course Max is interested in seeing how his engine is performing." She giggled. "Frankly, between the two of us, his engine performs remarkably well for his age."

She smiled coyly and held out her hand as Max came toward her. "You remember my daughter Georgiana, don't you, Max darling?"

Max clicked his heels and gave me a nodding bow.

"I hear you've come to shoot with the prince," I said, pronouncing each word slowly.

"*Ja*. Shoot wiz prince. Is *gut*."

"And he came to your hunting lodge last winter?"

"*Ja*. Vee shoot vild boar. Big tooths."

"Tusks, Max. Boars have tusks," my mother corrected. She patted his hand. "His English is improving wonderfully, don't you think?"

"Definitely," I said.

Paolo and the young American descended on us and started talking about engines and thrust again.

"This is the part I find horribly boring," my mother said. "I think I shall go back for a lie-down, if one is allowed to lie down at Balmoral. It's all horribly hearty and outdoorsy, isn't it?"

I felt a ridiculous wave of disappointment that my mother hadn't seen me for months and now had no wish to spend any time with me. I should have become used to it by now, but I hadn't. "You could go and cheer up poor Binky," I said and related the saga of his accident.

"If I can sneak in without encountering the dreaded wife," she said, "maybe I'll do that. I've always had a soft spot for your brother." And off she went. He wasn't her son, of course, but she had briefly been his stepmother and I knew he was fond of her.

I stood watching her go with that strange hollow longing that always came over me when I met my mother. And then I realized that she had left me with three people I had no wish to talk to: two men who had behaved badly and a dark, sultry girl who was far too beautiful and sexy. Was she now my replacement in the girlfriend stakes? I could feel Darcy's eyes on me, and forced myself not to look around. I was trying to move away, giving the impression that there was somebody I simply had to speak to, when I was snagged by Gussie.

"Long time no see, Georgie," he said. "How have you been?"

"Well enough, thank you, Gussie," I replied coolly. He seemed to have forgotten that the last time we met, I had had to fight him off, while he tried to remove my knickers.

He moved closer to me. "You know I was hoping we could maybe pick up where we left off last," he said, proving that he hadn't forgotten at all.

"You mean when I was saying 'Get off me, you brute' and you weren't listening?"

He chuckled. "All the girls say no, but they don't really mean it. It's just to appease their consciences. Afterward they can say 'I tried to fight him off but he was just too strong for me.' "

"I really meant it."

"Oh, come on, Georgie," he said, turning slightly pinker. "Everyone likes a bit of the old rumpy-pumpy from time to time, surely. I mean, it's awfully good fun, isn't it?" He looked at my face. "You mean you don't? You haven't?"

"Frankly that's none of your business," I said haughtily. "But if you really must know, I intend to wait until I meet someone I can love and respect," I said.

"Good God." He studied me as if I were some kind of exotic species of unknown animal. "Oh, well, let me know if you find such a being. And if not, I'm always available if you change your mind."

Darcy and the dark girl were moving off. My gaze followed them.

"Now there's someone who doesn't follow your rules," Gussie said.

"Who is she?"

"Name's Conchita. Spanish, I believe, or is it Brazilian? Father owns plantations. Oodles of money. Paolo persuaded her to invest in this latest madness. She and the Yank are funding it, and Paolo's driving it."

"And what about you?"

"Oh, I've just come along for the excitement," he said. "And I promised Father I'd write him up a column for one of his daily newspapers. Oh, there's Hugo come back," he added. "I knew he couldn't stay away long."

I spotted Hugo Beasley-Bottome, moving through the crowd as if looking for someone. "He's been up here before, has he?"

"Oh yes. Pops up and down all the time. He was staying with us at the house until a few days ago. I didn't realize he'd come back."

"He's staying at Castle Rannoch now," I said.

"I say, is he? I wonder why he decided to change his abode. I don't think anyone in our party upset him and the food's halfway decent and there's plenty of booze."

"He inveigled an invitation out of my brother, so he said. Even though he was damned rude about the place. Called it positively medieval."

"Well, it is, isn't it?"

"I suppose so, but then why go out of his way to stay with us?"

Gussie followed Hugo's progress through the crowd. "Of course we all know what he's doing here and where he'd like to stay, but he hasn't received an invitation."

"Where's that?" I asked, immediately thinking of Balmoral.

"The Padgetts', of course."

"Padgetts?"

"Yes, you know. Major and Mrs. Padgett. They live on the edge of the Balmoral grounds. He's the master of the estate or whatever the official title is. He's been in the royal service for donkey's years. He used to be rather important at one stage, one of the favorites of Queen Victoria and then King Edward. Now he's more or less retired—they only bring him out on rare ceremonial occasions."

"Oh yes. I believe I have met him. But why would Hugo want to stay there?"

"Because of Ronny of course, old thing. He has what the Americans call 'hot pants' for her. She's not shown any interest in him but he doesn't give up."

"Oh, of course. Ronny Padgett," I said, finally putting two and two together. "I met her at the aerodrome. She said her family lived up here, but I had never connected her with the major at Balmoral."

"Well, she's up here now. She comes and goes in that little plane of hers. Lands on the lakes, so hold on to your hat if you're picnicking on the shore. She comes in awfully low."

I laughed. At least Gussie was one of my social set. He was amusing. One knew where one stood with him. It was unfortunate that I wasn't attracted to him. He'd have made a good catch and I might have enjoyed a luxuriously decadent lifestyle with him. I looked around. Darcy and the dark lady had now completely disappeared. But I did spot Constable Herries keeping an eye on things from the road above. I excused myself and made my way up to him.

"How are you, Constable?" I asked.

He touched his helmet. "Well enough, my lady. I'm sorry to hear about His Grace's accident."

"Nasty business," I said. "I wondered whether you had made any inquiries about it?"

"Inquiries, my lady?"

"Into who might have set such a trap on Castle Rannoch land?"

He leaned his red, whiskered face closer to me. "I suspected it was someone from the estate who just wanted to snare the odd rabbit and now dare not come forward and own up."

"What if it was deliberately set by someone with a grudge against us?"

He gave me a startled look. "Now who would ever do a thing like that?"

"I understand that a boy called Willie McDonald was let go recently. Have you spoken with him?"

"You'd have a job speaking with him, my lady. He went off and joined the Royal Navy. He said that leaving the estate was the best thing that ever happened to him and now he was free to see the world."

"Good for him," I said. Back to square one.

Chapter 14

Weather brisk (which is Scottish terminology
for blowing a howling gale).

We ate our picnic in the shade of a large Scots pine tree. My mother returned
from visiting Binky up at Castle Rannoch and came to join us as the picnic
was being set up.

"How utterly beastly for poor Binky," she said. "He looks awfully pale. I
suggested he go to my little pied-à-terre on the Riviera to recuperate but he
claims he has no money to travel."

"That's true. He doesn't," I said. "Father saddled him with enormous
death duties."

"Typical of your father," she said. "Utterly useless and never thought
about anyone but himself. If he'd truly adored me, I would have stayed, but
he preferred all those horrible outdoor sports, like shooting and fishing, to
staying home and amusing me." She broke off and touched my arm. "Who
is the rather divine-looking blond boy?"

"That? His name is Hugo Beasley-Bottome."

My mother burst out laughing. "What an unfortunate name. So tell
me about him."

"He seems to be a sponger. He was with the motorboat party and now
he's invited himself to Castle Rannoch."

"So no money then?"

"Not your type at all," I said. "Decades too young and penniless, I suspect."

"But darling as one ages, one likes them young. So good for the ego, even though they've no staying power at that age."

"What do you mean?"

She looked at me strangely. "They go off like rockets, darling. Really, didn't I manage to give you the slightest hint of the facts of life when you were growing up?"

"You were never there," I said. "My education was hopelessly lacking. I didn't even manage to find a friendly gamekeeper."

She laughed again. "You'd better make up for lost time, hadn't you? Isn't there a likely male in the picture?"

"Not at the moment," I said, glancing around to see if Darcy was still anywhere around, but he and the señorita had disappeared.

"Too bad. I expect you'll find one soon," my mother said languidly, her gaze moving to Hugo as she spoke. "I might as well join you for lunch."

"You can't afford to make Max jealous, can you?" I said. "Think of all those lovely Parisian gowns."

"When Max is talking about engines, he wouldn't notice if a zeppelin dropped on his head." She lowered herself onto the best rug and stretched out luxuriantly. "So what are we eating?" she said. "Don't tell me that Mrs. McPherson has made pasties."

The Americans eyed her with suspicion.

"Don't mind little *moi*," she said, waving a gracious hand in their direction. "I eat like a sparrow."

"Pardon me, but I don't think we've met." Babe lowered herself to the rug beside my mother.

"My mother, the former Duchess of Rannoch," I said hastily, and saw Mummy frown. She hated to admit she had a daughter of my age.

"And you were the famous actress Claire Daniels, weren't you?" Countess Von Sauer exclaimed.

"Once upon a time I suppose I had my modicum of fame," Mother said with brilliantly pretended humility.

Of course, after that she was the center of attention.

Unfortunately the wind had come up and was blowing dust and pine needles onto the food, while the speed racers were testing their engine, emitting the occasional loud roar that jangled all our nerves and made conversation difficult. Mother, of course, made herself the center of attention instantly. She turned the full force of her dazzling charm onto Hugo so that he was transformed into her lapdog. I even began to feel a little sorry for him. As for the Americans, it was as if they were in the presence of a visiting goddess, which I suppose she was.

I sat on the two inches of blanket my mother was not occupying, staring out across the lake, simply not able to get into the swing of their conversation. Too many worrying thoughts were buzzing around my head. These thoughts ranged from Sir Jeremy's mandate to Binky's trap to Darcy and the mysterious dark woman. What was I supposed to do about any of the above? And why was I supposed to step in and rescue other people when nobody seemed to show any interest in me whatsoever? I was looking along the edge of the lake—I suppose that subconsciously I was trying to catch a glimpse of Darcy and see if he'd actually gone off with that Conchita woman—when I sat up, suddenly alert. Someone was creeping through the stand of fir trees on the point behind us. I watched as the figure darted from tree to tree, obviously not wanting to be seen. And he was coming closer. Thoughts of the trap and the reported accidents to the royal heirs instantly flashed across my mind.

Suddenly I'd had enough. If this person was cowardly enough to plan horrid little accidents and set a trap for my brother, then I was going to put a stop to him right now. I stood up and started to wander apparently aimlessly, bending to pick a sprig of heather here and there, but all the time making my way closer to those trees. When I was close enough, I darted behind the nearest pine then moved from tree to tree, just as our stalker was doing. I caught sight of him again as he crept through deep shadow to the next large pine.

Right, my lad, I thought. He was making quite a bit of noise. He would have been useless stalking a deer. I, in contrast, moved silently. He had no idea I was behind him until I leaped out and pounced.

"Got you!" I shouted, grabbing at the collar of his jacket. "All right. Let's take a look at you then, you miserable specimen." In truth I was rather relieved to find that he was a miserable specimen. I don't know what I would have done if I'd leaped out on a hulking six-footer armed with a gun or knife. As it was he gave a little squeak, tried to flee and was yanked backward by me, almost sitting down in the process.

"The constable's just up there on the bank," I said. "He'll be here in two seconds if I call him, so you'd better confess."

"My dear young lady, I've done nothing wrong. Unhand me, I beg you," he said. I recognized the voice at the same moment I staggered with him into a patch of sunlight.

"Mr. Beverley!" I said in a shocked tone. "What were you up to?"

"Your ladyship! Nothing, I assure you nothing at all," he said, most flustered now as I released my hold on him. "I was just trying to—well, you know, it's silly really, but I have always had a crush, as it were, on your dear mother. I couldn't believe my luck when I saw she was here. So I was seizing the chance to get a little closer to her, that's all."

"You were spying on her. You were going to eavesdrop and then reveal all in your column. I know how you newspapermen work."

"Oh no, I assure you."

"You do run a gossip column, don't you?"

"Yes, but . . ."

"So you were just doing your job and going to report gossip."

He looked red faced and crestfallen now, like a deflated balloon. "Well, I do have to confess . . ."

"You're very lucky I don't turn you in to our police constable," I said. "I could, you know. Someone has been setting traps on our estate. You could well be a prime suspect."

"Oh no. I'd never do anything violent," he said, fluttering his hands in distress. "You know I abhor violence."

"Very well," I said. "I'll let it go, just this once, but if I catch you spying on us again, then I will have no qualms about turning you over to our constable."

"I don't suppose there is any chance, is there, that I might just be allowed to greet your divine mama? I've worshipped her from afar for so long now." He gazed at me hopefully, like a dog begging to be taken on a walk.

I looked over at the rugs where my mother was still holding court. "Why not?" I said. I took him by the hand and led him across to our group.

"Mother, I'd like you to meet one of your biggest fans," I said. She deserved a little punishment for the way she ignored her only daughter.

Godfrey Beverley stepped forward, bowing like a medieval vassal. "Such an honor, Your Grace—well, I know it's not really 'Your Grace' any longer, but I still think of you as nobility, you know."

"Indeed." Mother's mouth was set in a firm line. "How do you do? Mr. Beverley, isn't it?"

"You remembered. How flattering."

"How could I forget? All those witty little columns . . ."

I moved off, leaving them to it. A few moments later Mummy showed up at my side again, looking absolutely furious. "How could you desert me and leave me with that odious little man?" she demanded.

"Oh, Mummy, I'm sure he's harmless. He said he was completely infatuated with you. So I thought I'd make his day and bring him to meet you."

"Oh, you've made his day, all right," she said. "And as for harmless, he's one of the most vicious little serpents I've ever come across. He just loves to unearth nasty snippets of gossip about me to put in his column. And you know what the next one will be, don't you?"

When I didn't respond she went on. "He had somehow found out that we were staying at Balmoral and he said wasn't it amazing how broadminded and modern the royal couple had become, allowing us to live in sin under their roof, as it were? Insufferable little smarmy prig. I could kill him."

I should point out that under moments of extreme stress my mother reverts to type, and she did have a grandmother who sold fish in the market.

"He's probably watching from the bushes," I said, trying not to smile. "Don't let him see that he's upset you."

"That's probably what he does for sexual thrills—watches from the bushes," she snapped. "He's certainly never been near a woman in his life, or a man either. I bet he does needlepoint in his spare time."

I could see that she was really riled. "Why don't you come back to the castle for some tea?" I asked.

She shook her head. "I'm sure I'm getting a migraine after that encounter. I really do need to lie down or I'll look like an old hag by dinner." She returned to our party to announce her departure, but it seemed that everyone was restless by this time and wanted to go back to the castle. Maybe the strength of the wind and the blowing dust had become too much for them. The mechanics working on the boat were busy covering it in a tarpaulin, and Gussie came down the dock to us.

"They can't do any more today with this gale blowing," he said. "They might end up with dirt in the engine."

I didn't like to tell him that this wasn't a gale, just a normal afternoon breeze for our part of Scotland, where the strong westerlies from the

Hebrides are funneled through a gap in the Grampians. I wondered why they had picked our particular loch for their speed trials. It wasn't calm at the best of times.

"I tell you what," my mother said, looking around at her adoring fan club, which by now included Hugo. "Why don't we all come up to Castle Rannoch to join you for dinner tonight? I'm sure there will be plenty of food. There always is and I know it would cheer up Binky to see old friends. Maybe we can have him carried down to dinner."

Everyone seemed to think this was a good idea. I was just trying to picture Fig's face when she found that at least half a dozen more people would be descending on us. I dragged Mother aside. "Why on earth did you suggest this? You know what Fig's like. She'll have hysterics."

Mummy smiled. "Precisely. That will teach her to be rude to me," she said.

"When?"

"Earlier today. When I arrived at the castle I met her coming down the stairs and she asked me in extremely uncivil tones what I wanted. I reminded her I used to be Binky's mother and do you know what she said? 'Yes, but not for long, was it?' What a spiteful tongue that woman has. She deserves an unexpected dinner party."

"It's all right for you," I said. "You're not the one who has to break the news to her."

She chuckled. "Think of poor Binky. He desperately needs cheering up."

"I don't know if the sight of more people eating his food will do the trick," I had begun to say, when the sound of an engine made us turn around.

"I thought they'd finished with that bloody boat," my mother said, then realized that the sound was not coming from there. Suddenly a small plane appeared, approaching low through the gap in the mountains. It roared over our heads, almost clipped the top of the tallest pines, skimmed over the surface of the lake, bounced a few times then touched down, sending out a sheet of spray behind it.

"Good-o. Ronny's here," Hugo exclaimed, my mother clearly having been discarded for the moment.

I was amazed to see that Ronny's aeroplane, if it was indeed the same one, now had floats instead of wheels.

As we watched Ronny's plane come to a halt, the countess gave a sudden scream. "Look. The monster!"

Excitement broke out on the shore as great black ripples came toward us. People tried to flee, knocking others out of their way in their fear. Then Constable Herries's voice came loud and clear.

"That's no monster. It's just the way the wind comes down from the pass and creates a particular series of waves. It's blowing extra hard this afternoon. We've seen it before and I expect we'll see it again. Now everyone calm down and go home. Monster indeed. There's no monster in this loch."

The crowd dispersed, muttering excitedly. Some were convinced they'd seen a head rise from that wave. I wasn't sure I hadn't seen something myself. Babe and the countess twittered as they were herded back to the cars.

"What if it comes on land? What if it swallows up that boat?" the countess said. "Fritzi darling, I expect you to protect me."

Her son didn't look as if he relished the prospect of fending off a large monster.

"I think we should sacrifice Lady Georgiana to appease it," Hugo said. The laugh broke the tension, but I sat in the car with my cheeks bright red. Was it so obvious to the world that I was still a virgin?

Chapter 15

BACK AT CASTLE RANNOCH
AUGUST 18

Late afternoon.

As I had predicted, Fig did not take the news of the extra dinner guests with great enthusiasm.

"How many people, did you say?" she demanded, her voice close to a shriek. Clearly she had never had a governess to constantly remind her that a lady never raises her voice. "Coming here? Tonight? Why in God's name didn't you stop them?"

"How could I stop them without looking terribly petty or telling them we currently had the Black Death?" I said. "They decided among themselves that they were enjoying each other's company so much that they'd all like to dine together."

"Then let them all dine together somewhere else," she snapped.

"But they wanted to cheer up Binky," I said. "They suggested he be carried down to join us."

"It's those blasted Americans, isn't it?" (I had tactfully forgotten to mention that the idea was entirely my mother's.) "They act as if they own the place. That Babe creature actually gave Hamilton a lecture about the lack of hot water this morning. She said it wasn't good enough. Not good enough? I ask you. The nerve of it. That woman spends all too much time in the bathroom, if you ask me. It's not healthy."

Fig was clearly in a state now.

"It will be all right," I said. "I'm sure Cook can whip up a big hearty soup or something as a first course to fill them up."

"Would you go and tell her, Georgiana? I really don't think that I can face her at the moment."

"If you like," I said, having been a real favorite of Cook's during my childhood.

"I'm so glad you're here," she said yet again. Wonders would never cease.

As I had suspected, Cook took the news more calmly than my sister-in-law had done, but she clearly wasn't pleased. "Eight more for dinner, you say? What does Her Grace think I am, a miracle worker? A conjurer? I'm supposed to produce a few rabbits out of a hat?"

I gave a sympathetic smile.

"She barely gives me enough money to feed the regular household and now I'm supposed to whip up banquets out of thin air?"

"Just do your best, Mrs. McPherson," I said. "They'll realize that this is all very last minute and they can't expect haute cuisine."

"It would never have been haute cuisine at the best of times," she said dourly. "Good plain food, that's what I do. None of this fancy French muck—snails covered in garlic." She made a disgusted face. "What's wrong with good local beef and Scottish salmon fresh from the stream?"

"Nothing at all," I said. "You're a wonderful cook, Mrs. McPherson. Everybody says so."

"Och, get away with you." She gave an embarrassed chuckle. "Well, it will have to be neeps and tatties for them tonight. I've nothing else."

"Neeps and tatties?" I asked. She was referring to the Scottish peasant dish made with potatoes and turnips. Filling but not exactly elegant.

"Aye. Like I said, I'm no miracle worker. That roast should be big enough for a slice or two each but we'll need to fill them up somehow. Do them good. They can sample our traditional Scottish fare. And lucky for you I made a nice rich broth with that leftover lamb from the other night. I can thicken that up into a soup. I don't know about the fish course, though. It's too late for the fishmonger to deliver anything. I can't divide loaves and fishes meant for twelve and make enough for twenty."

"I'm sure they won't necessarily expect a fish course, Mrs. McPherson," I said.

"They'd be getting one at Balmoral, wouldn't they?"

"It's only my mother and Herr Von Strohheim who are currently staying at Balmoral. The rest of them are in a house on Lord Angus's estate. I don't suppose they've a decent cook there, which is why they all jumped at the chance to come here and sample your cooking."

Mrs. McPherson was softening. "Maybe I'll see if we've enough smoked trout to go around," she said. "I was keeping it for a luncheon salad, but no doubt we can obtain more. And the boys have brought in a bushel basket of berries to make a crumble, so we'll get by, I suppose. We usually do."

"You're very kind, Mrs. McPherson," I said. "Her Grace will be so impressed."

She sniffed. "That one is only impressed when I cut corners and save her a penny or two," she muttered. "In the old duke's time there would have been none of this penny pinching."

"He did go bankrupt," I pointed out.

"Her Grace also requested a haggis when she came to see me today," Cook said. "Is that another of her economy ideas?"

I laughed. "No, she's hoping to scare away the Americans. She says they're eating her out of house and home."

"Och, so that's it?" She started to laugh, her ample bosoms shaking up and down like a jelly. "Well, you can tell her that I make the best haggis in this part of Scotland so they're liable to like it and ask for more. I've the sheep's stomach already boiling away ready to stuff tomorrow."

I left her and returned upstairs quite cheered. It was good to be home again. The whole party assembled in the great hall for tea, the cousins and the princes having returned from their various outdoor pursuits. The wind that had picked up at lunchtime had heralded the arrival of bad weather and was now howling down the chimneys while rain peppered the windows. Our guests were clearly feeling the cold and gazed hopefully at the empty fireplace. Fig was pretending that she was comfortably warm and didn't need to light the fire, proving that she was as good an actress as my mother. It really was awfully dismal in the great hall. I was longing to go upstairs for a second cardigan but I couldn't let the side down. In truth I was glad one of the dogs was leaning against my leg.

I was quite enjoying studying Fig. I could see that she was considerably put out watching Earl spreading heaps of her special Fortnum & Mason jam with gay abandon on his scone. Suddenly there were raised voices in the entrance hall and Mrs. Simpson swept in, looking less amused than my austere great-grandmother had done. Her usually immaculate coiffure was windswept and her silk outfit was streaked with rain.

"Wallis honey, you look terrible." The countess rose to greet her.

Obviously Wallis didn't appreciate the remark. She already knew she looked terrible and didn't need anybody to point this out.

"Come and have a cup of tea to warm you up before you go change." The countess took her arm and led her over to us.

"We've had an absolutely beastly day," Wallis said. "And the storm was the least of it. My dears, something terrible happened. We were lucky to escape with our lives."

"What on earth do you mean?" Babe asked.

"We were on our way back here, driving down the pass, when a damned great boulder came flying out of nowhere and struck us. Luckily it landed on the bonnet. A couple of feet in the wrong direction and David and I should both have been crushed. I tell you, my heart has only just started beating again. David was wonderfully calm. He said these things happen in the Highlands. 'Then I can't think why you choose to spend any time up here,' I said. 'I've never seen a more godforsaken place to begin with.' He wasn't thrilled with that remark and we had words. So all in all a most trying day."

She took the teacup that was offered her and sipped gratefully. The other Americans made a terrific fuss of her. Even her husband was nice to her. But my thoughts were racing again. Another accident that could have killed the Prince of Wales. Then a new thought struck me. Maybe we had got it wrong: maybe it wasn't the prince who was the target. Maybe someone was trying to eliminate Mrs. Simpson. I had seen enough American gangster films to know that people paid other people to take out an enemy. What if someone in the royal circle wanted to remove her permanently from the prince's life? Or on the other hand, what if her husband was angry enough with the way he was being cheated to want to get rid of her without paying alimony?

I decided I should make discreet inquiries to find out if Mrs. Simpson had been present when the other accidents happened to the prince. I noticed Lachan and Murdoch exchange an amused glance as she swept from the room. Then they too got up and excused themselves. One by one the party dispersed to go and rest before dinner or, in the case of Babe, to have yet another bath before dinner. I resolved to go and see exactly where this boulder fell onto the car and if it was possible that someone could have given it a convenient push. It was not unheard of for rocks to fall down mountainsides, but the chances of timing a rock to fall on a car would be slim, I should have thought. But I couldn't deny that it was yet another accident.

I went up to change for dinner. I was in the upstairs bathroom when I heard voices. I should probably clarify that I am not in the habit of hearing voices. The plumbing system at Castle Rannoch is eccentric, to say the least. It was added a few hundred years after the castle was built, of course. One of the features of the plumbing is that voices are carried by the pipes from one part of the castle to another. Two men were talking in low tones, in what sounded like Scottish accents.

"So are you going to tell her?" I heard one voice whisper.

"Are you mad? We'd be chucked out on our ear. She'd see to that. And I can't afford anything to come between me and my goals right now. This place is ideal for it. You must see that."

"What if somebody saw?"

"Then we plead ignorance. We didn't mean it, did we?"

And the sound of chuckling reverberated in the pipes.

Chapter 16

Evening.

I stood there, not noticing the rain and wind blowing in on me. (Oh, didn't I mention that it's a Castle Rannoch tradition to keep bathroom windows open at all times? Guests find this somewhat startling and hard to endure—especially when coupled with the tartan wallpaper and the groans and creaks emitted by the pipes.) A conspiracy then. It had never occurred to me before that maybe there could be Scottish nationalists at work in the castle—men who wanted home rule, like Ireland, or maybe wanted to replace the primarily German strain of monarchy with the old Stuart dynasty. Rannoch seemed an odd place to be harboring such feelings, as our family traced its ancestry back to the Stuarts on the old duke's side as well as to the currently reigning monarch through my grandmother.

I went back to my bedroom deep in thought. When my maid, Maggie, came to dress me for dinner and was anxious to chatter about castle gossip, I was happy to oblige her.

"So is anyone new on the staff since I went away?" I asked.

"Why, you've only been gone a few months, your ladyship," she said, chuckling. "Nothing's changed here, you know."

"So how many men actually work in the house these days?" I asked.

"Hamilton and His Grace's valet and Frederick and the under footman. Is that it?"

She looked at me strangely. "Yes, that would be it, apart from the gardener's boy who comes in to help with the boots and bringing up the heavy stuff from the cellar."

"And what about on the whole estate, how many men would you say there were?"

She laughed. "Are you thinking of taking yourself a local husband, my lady?"

"No, just trying to work something out," I said. "There would be the grooms, and the gardeners and the gillies, wouldn't there?"

"And don't forget the gamekeeper and field hands and the shepherd, and old Tom."

Quite a few then, but only four who would be allowed in the castle. Except that some of them did come into the castle from time to time. Fergus came in to play the pipes on special occasions. The gardeners brought in firewood; the gamekeeper and the gillies delivered fish and birds. But would any of them dare to meet in a castle bathroom? Hardly likely.

"So do you think that anybody here would have home rule feelings?"

"What do you mean, my lady?"

"Wanting to do away with the king and queen and turn Scotland into a separate state."

"Why would anyone want to do that?" She looked perplexed.

"Some people feel that way."

"Not anybody around here. We think the world of the king and queen. In fact, everyone in these parts knows someone or has a relative who works on the Balmoral estate and they can't speak highly enough of Their Majesties."

WHEN I CAME down to dinner, I found Binky had been carried down and was now reclining in an ancient bath chair that looked as if it once transported our venerable great-grandmother the queen. He was holding court, chatting to our visitors who had already arrived. I was uneasy to see that Darcy was among them, as was the dark and sultry Conchita, dressed in a slinky scarlet gown with a black fringed Spanish shawl over it. So was Ronny Padgett, looking remarkably civilized and feminine in a long bottle-green dinner dress with a white silk wrap and white elbow-length gloves. I went over to talk to her immediately so that I didn't find myself in a group with Darcy. I told myself it shouldn't matter that Señorita Conchita was making cow eyes at him, but it did. I suppose it's not that easy to fall out of love so quickly.

"I saw you land on the loch this afternoon," I said. "I didn't realize your plane could land on water."

"I had fins made for the Moth so that I can fly up here," she said. "The lochs are the only places nearby flat enough to put down a plane."

"It must be a wonderful feeling to fly," I said.

"I'll take you up sometime if you like," she said. "Just let me know when. I'm here for a while. At least until they put that boat through its paces." She leaned closer to me. "Between ourselves I'm hoping to be given a chance to break the record myself. I'm sure I'd do a damned sight better than that foreign idiot Paolo. But then, he's got the money and we Padgetts are as poor as church mice."

"Really?" I looked surprised.

"Yes, Father has a grace-and-favor position at Balmoral these days. There were times when he was in the thick of things. He had been promised a knighthood at least for services to Queen Victoria and King Edward, but he suffered some kind of ill health and was sent up here to recuperate. And here he's stayed. It's rather lonely for my mother. We really are in a godforsaken spot in the middle of nowhere."

"Don't they come down to London?"

"Not often. We no longer have a London house and my little matchbox is too small to accommodate them properly."

A memory stirred in my head at the mention of her London flat. "By the way, I was awfully sorry to hear about your maid."

She nodded. "Yes, it was a rum do, wasn't it? Poor little thing. She was still a country girl at heart. Hadn't a clue about traffic. Always wandering across the road without looking, even in London. Although what she was doing at Croydon Aerodrome on that particular evening I simply can't fathom. I'd told her to wait at the flat in London for my instructions and I wasn't planning to return for several days." She broke off and looked at me with interest. "So how did you come to hear about her accident?"

"The police mentioned it to me," I said. "It seems that there was a half-finished letter to me in her purse when she was killed."

"A letter to you? How extraordinary—what did she want?"

"I've no idea," I said. "It had fallen into a ditch and most of the ink had washed away, but it was clearly addressed to Lady Georgiana and I suspect I'm the only person with that name in London. The police thought that maybe she was asking me for a job."

"A job—with you? Why would she be doing that?"

"I thought perhaps because you were threatening to dismiss her."

"Dismiss her?"

"You told her to watch her step when I saw you together."

She looked at me and laughed. "That's the way I always spoke to her. She knew that. It's just the way I am. And I was actually quite fond of her, clueless though she was. I tell you, I'd like to catch the blighter that mowed her down. I'd strangle him with my bare hands."

"If she'd wandered out into the road, as you say, he probably couldn't have avoided hitting her."

"But then why bugger off and leave her there to die? Why not summon the police and admit to it like a man?"

"Frightened to, maybe? Maybe he had black marks against him for reckless driving before and feared his license would be taken from him."

She nodded. "Poor old Mavis." She sighed. "And dashed inconvenient for me. Now I'm up here with no maid, only an idiot local girl who tried to iron my leather jacket."

Hugo moved in on us. "I watched you land that plane this afternoon, Ronny. I must say you are magnificent. So when are you going to take me up?"

"If you're not careful, Hugo, I might just tip you out," she said, laughing. "I do love barrel rolls, you know. They are a great way to get rid of unwanted suitors."

So the attraction was not mutual.

"How can you afford to run a plane?" I blurted out before I remembered that a lady never mentions money.

She shrugged. "I have sponsors. And one of the reasons that I enter all these damned air races is that they come with very nice cash prizes. I'm going to try solo to Australia this autumn. It's never been done by a woman and the *Daily Mail* is coming up with a fat check if I succeed."

"Do you have a good chance of succeeding?"

"Fair to middling, I'd say. There's a lot of desert to be flown over. You come down in the middle of the Arabian Desert and that's pretty much it. Nobody's likely to find you before you run out of water." She looked around the room. "Speaking of which, I'm dying of thirst. Isn't there anything stronger than sherry around here?"

And she wandered off, leaving me alone. I wondered if I actually envied her or pitied her. It would be wonderful to be so daring and independent, of course, but then I pictured the loneliness and the likelihood of dying in the desert and was glad that I didn't have her nerve.

Hugo was still lingering nearby. He sidled up to me. "I say," he said, "this old place is rather fascinating, isn't it? Awfully rich in history. So tell me, does it have a laird's lug? I've heard about them but I've never actually seen one."

"Yes, it does, actually."

"And what exactly is it? A place where the laird could spy on his guests, isn't it?"

"Exactly. A little secret room built into the walls, where the laird could listen through slots to hear if anyone was plotting against him."

"Dashed interesting. You wouldn't like to take me to see it, would you?"

I gave him an exasperated look. "I thought you were supposed to be keen on Ronny, Hugo. And now you're trying to lure me off somewhere secret? I'd stick to one girl if I were you."

"No, I really am interested in Scottish history," he said.

I laughed. "I'll have one of the servants show you the laird's lug tomorrow if you're keen on Scottish history." Then I moved to join Belinda and Paolo, who were talking with Max and Digby Flute, the young American.

Belinda intercepted me halfway across the floor. "Darling, talk to me about something normal," she said. "I shall scream if I hear the words 'torque' and 'thrust' again. Strangely enough I found the use of the word 'thrust' quite titillating until now, but not when it so clearly applies to a boat engine."

"They're still at it, are they?"

"Nonstop." She sighed. "And speaking of that—what is up between you and Darcy? You're not exactly acting like dearest chums, are you?"

"Absolutely not," I said. "He did something—well, for which I can't forgive him."

"The lovely señorita, you mean? My dear, he hasn't been near her, and it's not for want of trying on her part."

"No, it was something in London. He—" I stopped, unable to talk about it. "Let's just say that he is not my favorite person at the moment."

"Such a pity when you're both in the same place for once and the atmosphere is so romantic up here. Oh, and talking of romance, take a look at the dreaded Mrs. Simpson. I think she was expecting another dinner guest and he hasn't turned up."

I followed her gaze to the group around Binky. Mrs. Simpson was standing close to him, only half paying attention to a story he was telling. She kept glancing up nervously, or was it impatiently? Lachan and Murdoch had now joined us, looking resplendent in full Highland dress. They stood a little apart, deep in conversation, and suddenly it dawned on me that they were two men with slight Scottish accents. Could they have been the ones I overheard in the bathroom? Surely they weren't Scottish nationalists out to kill the heir to the throne? But then they did have Stuart blood in them. I went over to join them.

"We didn't see you all day," I said brightly. "Where did you disappear to?"

"We were after a damned fine stag that your brother told us about," Lachan said, smiling down at me. "We didn't mention it to the others because they'd have ruined everything, tramping through the bracken like a herd of elephants and alerting every creature within miles."

"So did you find the stag?"

"We did," Murdoch replied. "Up on the flanks of Ben Alder. But it's a canny beast. It never let us get close enough for a good shot."

The flanks of Ben Alder, I thought. A perfect location to spy on the road down the pass and give a signal to someone that a car was approaching. . . . I looked up at Lachan's jolly, weathered face and twinkling blue eyes and tried to picture him calmly eliminating the heirs to the British throne. It seemed impossible, but then I'd been taken in before. I knew enough to realize that criminals do not look guilty.

Hamilton was approaching with the drinks tray. Lachan and Murdoch made a beeline for it. I was still watching them when Darcy appeared at my side.

"So are you going to sulk and ignore me forever?" he asked in a low voice. "Aren't you being rather childish?"

"I'm just tired of never knowing where I stand with you," I replied. "You disappear for weeks at a time. You flirt with other women. You probably do much more than flirt."

I saw the smile twitch at his lips. "You have to take me the way I am."

"I need someone I can rely on," I said.

Lachan had poured himself a generous Scotch and turned back to me. "What can I get for you, Cousin Georgie?" he asked.

"That's very kind of you, Lachan," I said. "A sherry would be nice."

"Sherry? That's for old ladies. Come and let me pour you a dram of Binky's single malt." He put a big arm around my shoulder. I let myself be led away from Darcy. Luckily an interruption occurred at that moment with the announcement of the Prince of Wales. So that's why Mrs. Simpson had been so jumpy earlier.

Now she's in a pickle, I thought. Her husband is here. Fig was moving through the crowd like a sheepdog, trying to line us up to go in to dinner. "We won't process in until the piper gets here," she said, "but here's how the order of procession should go. Since Binky can't be part of it, His Royal Highness should escort me, Prince George should escort Lady Georgiana, Prince Siegfried with Countess Von Sauer, Herr Von Strohheim with—" She broke off as she looked at my mother, obviously trying to remember what her current name was. It was still Mrs. Clegg, as her Texan millionaire husband did not believe in divorce, but Fig wasn't to know that. She moved on hastily down the rest of the line. Mrs. Simpson was paired with Darcy and did not look pleased.

"These customs are so quaintly old-fashioned, aren't they?" she said to her lady friends, loud enough for those around her to hear. "So backward. No wonder Britain is being left behind in terms of world progress."

"They do rule half the globe, Wallis honey," Babe pointed out.

"One wonders how, with all these inbred families and their stupid customs. It really irks me to see that woman go ahead of me." She leaned out of the line to glare at my mother. "I mean, she's no longer a duchess, is she?"

She had meant my mother to hear. Mummy turned around to her and gave her a sweet smile. "Ah, but I usually try to discard mine before I move on to the next one. You are planning to discard this one, aren't you? Or are you worried he'll want too much alimony?"

There was the hint of a twitter from the other women but Mrs. S looked daggers at my mother as she turned back serenely to Max and slipped her dainty hand through his arm. Darcy caught my eye and gave me a wink. I had returned the smile before I remembered that I wasn't speaking to him.

$\mathscr{C}hapter\ 17$

CASTLE RANNOCH
AUGUST 18

Evening. Blowing a gale outside. Not much warmer in.

Suddenly the most awful wail echoed through the house. The countess grabbed at Siegfried's arm. "What is it? Is it the ghost? The White Lady of Rannoch?"

"Och, it's only the piper," Murdoch said. "Come to pipe us in to dinner."

And it was. Old Fergus looking very grand in his kilt and bonnet. We lined up behind him and marched down the hall to the banqueting room. The room, with its rough stone walls and high arched windows, can be austere at times but tonight it was ablaze with candles. Their light sparkled from the silverwear and highlighted the starched white tablecloth, stretching down the length of the room. Fig had certainly pulled out all the stops. I sat in the middle of the table, between Lachan and Prince Siegfried. Babe sat opposite and was clearly fascinated by Lachan's Highland dress.

"So is it true what they are saying, that Scotsmen wear nothing under their kilts?" she asked.

"If you care to reach under the table you can feel for yourself," Lachan said. Babe shrieked with laughter.

"I was hoping to serve you our traditional haggis tonight," Fig said. "But unfortunately—"

"Unfortunately we weren't able to catch any today during our hunting expedition," Murdoch interrupted.

"Catch them? I thought haggis was a type of sausage thing," Hugo said.

"Oh aye, it is. That's how you serve it after you've caught it," Lachan said earnestly. "You mince it up and make a sausage of it, but before that it's a canny wee beast. Ferocious for its size."

"Mercy me," said the countess. "And what does it look like?"

"Verra hairy," Lachan said. "With pointy little teeth, and it lurks in the heather and goes for the ankles of bigger prey. In fact if I hadn't seen Binky's trap with my own eyes, I'd have thought he'd been attacked by a band of haggis."

Those of us in the know were trying not to laugh, but Babe and the countess were gazing at Lachan, quite fascinated.

"We could take you on a haggis hunt tomorrow if you like," he suggested. "We saw haggis tracks today when we were out on the moor."

"That would be just fascinating, wouldn't it, Earl?" Babe said.

I waited for someone to burst out laughing and tell them the joke, but nobody did.

"So how was the climbing today, young fellows?" the Prince of Wales asked. I noted he had been seated nowhere near Mrs. Simpson and she, as a result, was sulking. "Did you plant the flag on any summits and claim them for England?"

"That would hardly be wise, seeing that we're in Scotland," Prince George replied. "But alas we reached no summit. We stupidly left the ropes and climbing paraphernalia behind. Didn't think we'd need it, you see, until we came to this great overhang. Well, we weren't prepared to tackle that with no ropes and pitons so we had to retreat."

"You should take Georgiana with you," Binky said. "She knows these munros better than anyone."

"Munros?" Gussie asked. "What the deuce is a munro?"

"Local name for a peak over three thousand feet," Binky said. "Georgie used to be up and down these munros like a bally mountain goat, didn't you, old bean?"

I felt all those eyes on me, staring at me as an object of curiosity.

"You make me sound like the wild woman of the glen," I said.

I noticed Mrs. Simpson give Earl a dig in the side and mutter something.

"We would be honored if you would accompany us tomorrow, Lady

Georgiana," Siegfried said. "Your expertise would be most welcome. And we shall bring ropes this time and by the grace of God we shall conquer the summit."

He made it sound as if he was talking about Mont Blanc and not a Scottish hill only three thousand feet high, most of which involved simple scrambling.

Dinner passed pleasantly enough. The soup was delicious, there was enough beef to go around and even the neeps and tatties were commented upon as tasty. Talk turned to the speedboat and the monster. Binky's opinion was that someone had resurrected the old legend to drive tourist trade up here.

"I've lived here all my life and never heard it mentioned until recently," he said, "and I've certainly never seen it."

"But you have to agree that the way the water in that lake moved suddenly, looked awfully like a big creature swimming," the countess exclaimed. "What about that wake? Something had to have made those ripples."

"A plane had just landed," I pointed out, "and the loch goes from shallow to very deep just about there, so the waves do behave strangely with the right wind conditions."

"I'm sure I saw a head," the countess said. "A very large head."

"Maybe it's a submarine, spying on your speedboat," the Prince of Wales said, turning to Digby and Paolo. "A rival for the world speed record, maybe."

Dinner concluded with berry crumble and fresh cream followed by Welsh rarebit. We women followed Fig dutifully from the room to the drawing room, where coffee was waiting. Conchita came over to join me.

"We have not yet been introduced," she said, those dark eyes flashing. "You are the daughter of this house?"

"I'm the sister of the current duke," I said. "I'm Georgiana Rannoch."

"And I am Conchita da Gama. From Brazil."

"What are you doing in Scotland?"

"I make friends with Paolo in Italy. He needs money to pay for racing boat. I have much money," she said. "My father, he own rubber plantations in Brazil and now he find oil on his land. Very lucky, no?"

No wonder Darcy was interested, I thought. He was penniless like me. She'd be a very desirable catch.

It was as if she was reading my thoughts. "This Mr. Darcy O'Mara," she said, her eyes straying to the door, "he is handsome, do you not think? And the son of a lord, and Catholic."

I could see where this line of thought was going. "And penniless, I'm afraid," I said.

"No problem." She waved her hand. "I have enough money to do what I want. But I do not understand. He tells me there is already a lady he admire."

Irrationally a great surge of hope rose in my heart. Then, of course, I wondered if I was the lady to whom he was referring. Obviously not, judging by the way he had treated me in London. The men soon joined us, or at least some of them did. Mr. Simpson was nowhere in evidence. The Prince of Wales headed straight for the arm of Wallis Simpson's chair when she patted it as if summoning a dog. Dancing was suggested. The rugs were rolled back in the great hall, someone set up the gramophone and we started, as always, with the Gay Gordons. I don't suppose the person who suggested the dancing had realized what she was in for. Lachan came to claim me and I was delighted to be able to shine for once. Scottish dances are one thing I do know how to do well.

After that Lachan grabbed Ronny to join us for the Dashing White Sergeant, which requires one man and two women. Murdoch attempted to drag Belinda and Fig onto the floor but most of the others looked on this time, Highland dances being unfamiliar to them. I was conscious of Darcy watching me from the shadows. Was I the lady he was talking about, I wondered, or had he just said that to dissuade the affectionate Señorita Conchita? From what I had seen, he hadn't been pushing her away too hard. Did I want him to like me? I wondered. He was in every way unsuitable husband material. I'd probably not even be allowed to marry him, since he was Catholic—forbidden to those in line to the throne of England.

The dance ended. A Paul Jones was suggested and everyone was urged onto the floor. We ladies moved in a clockwise direction while the men circled around us counterclockwise. The music stopped and I found myself with Lachan again. This time it was a waltz. He held me tightly. Darcy passed us, dancing with Conchita who was flirting shamelessly. I looked up at Lachan and gave him an encouraging smile. His grip on me tightened, almost crushing me.

"You've turned out quite nicely, Cousin Georgie. A nice trim wee waist, good sturdy limbs and not a bad figure. And you're not my first cousin, are you?"

"No, our grandfathers were brothers, I believe, which would make me a second cousin."

"Well, that's good to know." He spun me around dizzily.

"I believe you judge women like heifers," I said, and he laughed loudly.

The music summoned us back to the Paul Jones. The men and women circled each other again until I found myself opposite Earl. He was about to put his arm around my waist when Darcy stepped in rapidly. "My dance, I think," he said, and snatched me from under Earl's astonished nose.

"That's not quite cricket," I said. His tight hold on me was quite unnerving.

"Cricket is a very boring game, don't you think?" he whispered, his lips inches away from mine. "I much prefer other, more energetic sports." He swept me across the floor in a slow fox-trot. "So you're talking to me again now, are you?"

"I forgot." I turned my head away.

He was holding me very close. I could feel the beat of his heart against mine and the warmth of him against my cheek.

"Are you going to stay angry at me forever?" he asked.

"I don't know. Did you tell Conchita that I was your girlfriend?"

"Well, I had to say something. She was all over me."

"So I was just an excuse again. I seem to be part of your life when it's convenient." I tried to lean away from him but his hand on the middle of my back was unrelenting. And he was laughing. "So you've decided that your hairy cousin is a better catch?"

"He may be."

"Don't be ridiculous. You're too damned sensitive, you know."

"Sensitive? I like that. You come and go as you please. You tell me—" I broke off. Had he ever actually told me he loved me? I wasn't sure.

"I can't be around all the time, Georgie. You should realize that," he said softly into my ear. His lips were brushing my cheek as he spoke and all the time he was steering me toward the edge of the dance floor. Then he fox-trotted me down the nearest hallway, in which, due to Fig's economy measures, no lamp was burning.

"There, that's more like it, isn't it?" he said. He pulled me to him and his lips searched for mine. I wanted to kiss him but I kept reminding myself why I was angry with him in the first place.

"First I want you to admit that it was you who telephoned that frightful priggish man at Scotland Yard about my embarrassing evening," I managed to say, turning my face to avoid his lips.

"Oh, God, not now, Georgie. Don't you want to kiss me?"

"Not until . . ." I said, weakening as his lips were now nuzzling at my ear and continuing down my throat.

"Not now?" he whispered as his lips moved across my chin and brushed my own lips with a featherlight kiss.

"This isn't fair," I said.

"Don't you know that all's fair in love and war?" he said, whispering the words one at a time, in between imprisoning my lips between his own. I felt the warmth of his body, pressing hard against me. Oh, God, I wanted him.

"Now, do you want me to kiss you or not?"

"All right, just shut up and kiss me," I said and turned my face to him.

I was no longer conscious of time or space. When we broke apart we were both breathing very hard.

"Georgie," he whispered, "is there somewhere we could go that's a little more comfortable than a cold and drafty hallway?"

"There's nowhere exactly comfortable in Castle Rannoch," I said, "and the only place that could be described as warm is the linen cupboard. I used to curl up there with a book and a torch when I was a child."

"The linen cupboard. Now that sounds intriguing." He gave me what could be described as a challenging grin. "Do you think it's large enough for two people?"

"Darcy!" I was half shocked, half excited.

"You could show me," he whispered, pulling me close to him and nuzzling at my neck again. "Or surely Castle Rannoch must possess a famous bedroom in which Mary, Queen of Scots, was born or Saint Margaret died."

I laughed uneasily, my sense of propriety fighting with my rising passion. "Neither. If you want to know, Castle Rannoch possesses the most uncomfortable beds in Scotland—probably in the civilized world."

"It's amazing that any Rannoch offspring were ever conceived then."

"I was conceived in Monte Carlo," I said. "I don't know about Binky. I think Rannochs always go away to get that sort of thing done."

"Then you'll just have to show me the linen cupboard." He slipped an arm around my waist, holding me very close to him as he steered me to the back stairs. We went up one flight, pausing for a couple of kisses along the way. My heart was really racing now. Darcy and I, alone together just as I had pictured it. I was not going to get cold feet this time!

We were just starting on the second flight of stairs when a piercing scream echoed through the castle. Then another. The screams were coming from the floor above us. We broke apart and rushed up the next flight of stairs, Darcy leading the way and taking the steps two at a time. Feet echoed below us as people came up the main staircase.

We were halfway up the second flight when we met the countess, staggering toward us, her face a mask of pure terror. "I saw her," she gulped. "The White Lady of Rannoch! She came wafting down that hallway."

We piled into the hallway but of course there was nothing to be seen. Ghosts don't usually wait around for an audience. The men opened doors, one by one, but there was no sign of a ghost.

As we turned to come back down, Fig drew me aside. "Well done, Georgiana," she said. "Brilliant, positively brilliant."

"It would have been brilliant," I whispered back, "but it wasn't me."

Chapter 18

It was a subdued group that assembled downstairs in the drawing room. Countess Von Sauer was sipping brandy and recounting her horror to anyone who would listen.

"It was coming down the hall toward me—a white disembodied face and light hair and hands, that's all I saw—and it was sort of wafting. Then I suppose I screamed and it just—melted away. Vanished. I won't feel safe sleeping here again, I can tell you that. Fritzi, you'll just have to find us a hotel."

"At this time of night, in the middle of nowhere, Mama?" Fritzi looked worried. "I tell you what. I'll sleep on a mattress on the floor of your room and we'll look for a hotel in the morning."

"I'm sure you're quite safe, Countess," Binky said. "Georgiana and I have lived here all our lives and have never met a hostile ghost yet."

"But that's because you're family members," the countess wailed. "Everyone knows that family ghosts are only hostile to strangers."

"If you ask me, it was someone playing a practical joke," the Prince of Wales said, looking around at the assembled group. "And if it was someone here, it would be the honorable thing to own up right now."

Our guests looked at each other but nobody spoke.

"Then let us think back to see if anyone was missing from the room when the countess screamed," the prince went on.

"Mr. Simpson, for one," my mother couldn't resist saying.

"Well, honey, he had a headache and went up to bed," Mrs. Simpson said, smiling serenely. "And I don't think he could be mistaken for a white lady, even in the poorest light. He's rather tall, you know. And he has dark hair." Her gaze fell on me. "But I did notice Lady Georgiana leaving the room . . . with Mr. O'Mara."

"I can assure you we had other things on our mind than playing at ghosts," Darcy said. I felt myself blushing like a schoolgirl.

I looked around the room. "And where's Hugo?" I asked.

"Yes, where is he?" someone else said. "He was dancing in the Paul Jones a little while ago."

We looked up as footsteps were heard coming down the stairs. All eyes watched as Hugo came down. He did have very light hair, worn rather long.

"Where have you been?" Earl demanded.

Hugo looked suitably confused. "Can't a chap bally well go to take a leak without having to get permission first?"

"Which bathroom did you use?" Fig demanded.

"Why this interest in my call of nature?" Hugo grinned. "In answer to that, the closest one, just off that hall to the left."

"It was a real ghost, I know it," the countess insisted. "Real people can't just vanish."

I watched Hugo as he took his place among the guests, chatting easily as if nothing had happened. He did have light hair, and he wasn't that tall. Was this his idea of a joke or something more serious? I resolved to keep a closer eye on him. The party broke up soon after. The mood had been broken and nobody showed any interest in dancing again. Off they went and we were left with our houseguests plus the Prince of Wales, who showed no intention of leaving in the near future. One by one they went off to bed, with Fritzi promising faithfully to stand guard at his mother's bedside all night.

"Well, that was a rum do, wasn't it?" the prince said, when the Americans and Hugo had also gone to their rooms, leaving only essentially family members. "It's been a rum day altogether—what with that dashed great rock crashing onto my car and now this."

"And don't forget Binky's foot getting caught in a trap," Fig said, looking with concern at her husband. "One might almost think that someone is out to do us harm."

There, she had expressed it out loud. I looked from one prince to the other, and then at the two Scottish cousins. The Prince of Wales laughed. "I don't believe that any communist or anarchist would go to the trouble of setting traps and arranging for rocks to land on cars," he said. "One good bullet would do the trick much more cleanly."

He was right about that, of course. If someone did want to do away with the prince, or with the heirs in general, then these were petty accidents with small chance of success, when a bullet or bomb could be guaranteed to kill. It was being done with monotonous frequency to one European royal family after another.

"Maybe it's all someone's idea of a joke," Binky suggested.

"It would have to be someone with a rather twisted sense of humor," Fig said bitterly.

I just happened to glance across at the cousins and I saw a smirk pass between them. Was this really their idea of a joke? I worried about this later as I lay in bed. They were poor, by their own admission, so I could understand if they wanted to do away with Binky and get their hands on this estate. But they had no connection to the Prince of Wales, and why would anyone want to frighten the countess? The latter was the most easily explained, of course. She had proved herself to be of a nervous disposition. It was she who had seen the monster in the lake. Maybe she had caught sight of Hugo heading for a bathroom and decided she was seeing a ghost.

Of course then my thoughts turned to Hugo. Why had he decided to invite himself to Castle Rannoch when I'm sure the rented house was more pleasant and full of young people like himself. Was he really so besotted with Ronny Padgett that he followed her everywhere? Could he be the one with a grudge against our family? The whole thing was too ridiculous. Then I remembered the feel of Darcy's lips on mine and the delicious anticipation of the linen cupboard, and fell asleep with a smile on my face.

I was woken by the most ungodly sound—a half-strangled scream, an unearthly wail. I leaped out of bed and ran to the window because the sound seemed to be coming from outside. It was still only half light. Then the sound came closer and of course I realized what it was. It was old Fergus piping in the day around the castle, as had been done for the past six hundred years. I slipped on my dressing gown and went out into the hallway. I could hear voices coming from the other side of the stairwell, where the Americans were housed. Animated voices in considerable distress.

"You heard it too, did you? Unearthly, that's what it was. A soul in torment. I knew this place was haunted from the moment we came here."

I crossed the landing and found Babe and Earl, the countess and Fritzi huddled together in their nightclothes. The countess looked up, saw me and screamed. "It's the White Lady!" she exclaimed, clutching at Earl.

"It's only me, Countess."

"It's young Lady Georgiana," Earl said. "You heard it too, did you? Confounded noise woke me up. What was it, some kind of animal in distress?"

"No, it was only our piper, resuming his morning round of the castle. He's been off sick but now it sounds as if he's back in fine form."

"Bagpipes, you mean?"

"Of course. You are in Scotland, you know."

"But it's not even light yet."

"Precisely. Bagpipes at dawn. That's the tradition here."

"You mean every morning from now on?" Babe looked shocked.

"Every morning. And I expect he'll entertain us at dinner too, now he's back."

"Oh, my God." Babe put her hand to her head. "Where are my headache powders, Earl? And I need an ice pack."

"An ice pack?" I asked. "It's summer. You won't find any ice."

"Is there no ice in the whole of Scotland?" Earl demanded.

"Pretty much."

"Earl, I don't know how much longer I can take this," Babe said. "I mean, Wallis knows I'd do anything for her, but this is beyond human endurance."

"I agree," the countess said. "You could all come and stay with me at Castle Adlerstein. It's on a lake in Austria; it really is much more agreeable."

"It really does sound like a better idea," Babe agreed. "What do you think, Poopsie?" I tiptoed away and went back to bed. The plan seemed to be working splendidly!

$\mathcal{C}$hapter 19

Morning.

When I next awoke it was to Maggie bringing in the tea tray. "A glorious morning, your ladyship," she said. "I hope you'll be taking advantage of it."

Oh, golly, I thought. I had been coerced into taking the two princes climbing. Another wicked thought went through my head. The munro they wished to tackle could be ascended by no more than what we might describe as a brisk ramble. Of course there was a rather tricky ascent that involved the crag, if one went directly up from the lake. I could take them up that. They'd be terribly impressed. I just hoped I was still up to it and could remember the route.

When I appeared for breakfast, dressed for climbing in trews, shirt and Windbreaker, I met Siegfried, looking as if he was about to tackle Mount Everest.

"So we attempt the climb today, Lady Georgiana?" he asked, somewhat nervously. "We go for the summit?"

"Absolutely."

"I have all prepared. Ropes. Pitons."

"Ice axes?" I suggested with a grin.

He shook his head seriously. "I do not believe one needs ice axes in summer. I saw no ice yesterday."

Honestly the man had no sense of humor. I was tempted to say that we could easily manage without any equipment, but then, it rather amused me to think of Siegfried and Prince George going up our little crag, roped together.

"So we set off after breakfast, then?" I said.

"Unfortunately His Highness will not be joining us," Siegfried said. "He was summoned to Balmoral."

"Nothing's wrong, I hope?"

"His father wished to speak to him. Something about gambling debts, I believe."

So Prince George's sins were gradually coming to light, were they? Did I really want to be stuck alone on a mountain with Siegfried? "Should we not postpone our climb until he is able to join us?" I asked.

"He fears he may be sent back to London," Siegfried said. "And if he is able to join us once more, then I shall have learned the correct route and be able to lead. I have great experience, you know. I have tackled the Alps and the Dolomites. I know no fear."

"Jolly good," I said. "Then we may well attempt the part with the overhang."

He blanched, making his already pale face even paler. "But it seemed impossible."

"Not with a good rope and pitons," I said. "What is a thousand-foot drop if you are securely anchored? Until after breakfast, then."

I thought he looked a trifle green. I was beginning to enjoy myself for the first time in ages.

The Americans were also not looking at their best. Babe looked particularly haggard. So did Mrs. Simpson. "How am I expected to get my beauty sleep if we're awoken in the middle of the night?" she demanded.

"I'm sorry," I said. "I realize you must need quite a bit of it these days."

I saw Mr. Simpson smirk. Again I felt sorry for the man. At least he had a sense of humor.

Lachan and Murdoch entered while we were in the middle of breakfast. I was tucking into the usual bacon, eggs and smoked haddock, while watching Babe and Mrs. Simpson having half a grapefruit and a slice of toast each.

"So are we all ready?" Lachan asked, helping himself to everything that was going.

"What for?"

"Did you no say you wanted to go on a haggis hunt?" Lachan asked.

"Not for me. Nothing fierce," the countess said quickly.

"Well, I think that might be fun," Babe said, eyeing Lachan's broad shoulders. "Let's do it, okay, Earl?"

"Whatever you want, baby."

"And where is that delightful young man Hugo?" Babe asked. "Maybe he'd like to join us."

"I think I saw him going out a while back," Mrs. Simpson said. "I expect he's gone back to his friends with the speedboat. Oh, and I gather from sources in the know that a shoot is being planned tomorrow at Balmoral, for any of you who enjoy such things. I may just go shopping in the nearest town, if there is a nearest town. I'm running low on nail polish."

"We have to stay and go shooting, Babe," Earl said. "You know I love shooting things. I've been looking forward to it. Wallis promised us shooting here every day and there has been none so far."

"My brother was not intending to step on a trap and nearly lose his foot," I said coldly. I was a trifle vexed by the way they discussed my family and my home as if we didn't exist.

"Of course not, poor sap," Earl said. "So should I take my gun on your little expedition today, young man?"

"Maybe not," Lachan said. "You might miss and that would enrage them."

I kept waiting for Lachan to burst out laughing, or for someone to let them in on the secret. But no one did and I wasn't going to. After all, it was rather fun and they had been rather annoying. I left them preparing for their quest and set off with Siegfried. The walk across the estate to the foot of Bein Breoil took some time, owing to the amount of equipment Siegfried was carrying and the fact that his new climbing boots pinched his toes.

As we walked I looked back at the road snaking over the pass and tried to imagine where one could roll a boulder down onto a car with any degree of success. It seemed impossible. Close to the estate, which was where they said they had been struck, the area beside the road was tree lined and reasonably flat. Surely any boulder would hit a tree first. Up at the top, where the pass narrowed, there would have been greater chance of success, but that wasn't apparently where the prince's car was struck. Interesting.

At last we reached the base of the crag. I had to admit that from down here it did look rather formidable, rising some two hundred feet of sheer granite.

"Right. Off we go then," I said. "Do you want me to lead first or will you?"

"Ladies first," Siegfried said. He was already sweating from carrying all that equipment.

I began to climb the rock face, my fingers and toes remembering the old tried-and-true route. When you knew where the handholds were, it wasn't too alarming. When I reached a suitable point for Siegfried to pass me, I drove in a piton and signaled for him to come up. He did, passing me with much heavy breathing and sweat on his brow. In this fashion we made it almost to the top and I showed him how to skirt around the overhang. At last we hauled ourselves up to the top of the crag and rested, sitting on a large boulder while we admired the view. A fresh wind blew in our faces and the loch below reflected the mountains. I breathed deeply, savoring everything about the scene, except for the person sitting beside me.

"So we achieved it with no problem, you see." Siegfried was looking very pleased with himself. I could see this story would be embellished and retold among the courts of Europe.

"Well done, Your Highness," I said.

"Please, call me Siegfried," he said, "and I shall call you Georgiana when we are alone."

I hoped that wouldn't be too often.

"You know, Georgiana," he said, "I have been thinking. It would not be such a bad idea if we were to get married."

I'm glad I had a firm seat on that boulder or I might have plunged to my death.

"But Your Hi—I mean, Siegfried—I believe you are as little attracted to me as I am to you," I said tactfully. This actually meant *I know you prefer boys,* and it was better than shouting "Not if you were the last man in the universe" for all of Scotland to hear.

"That has nothing to do with it," he said. "We of noble birth do not marry for love, we marry to cement alliances among the great houses of Europe. It is important that I choose the right wife. I may be king someday."

"If your brother and your father are assassinated, you mean?"

"Possibly."

"And what makes you think you won't follow suit?"

"I shall be a just and popular king, unlike my brother and my father. And you will make a suitable consort for me. I know that your family is in favor of this match and do not think you could do better."

The local gamekeeper would be better, I longed to say.

"I shall make few demands on you," he went on, waving a hand expansively. "Once you have produced me an heir, you will be free to take lovers, as long as you are discreet at all times."

"And you will also take lovers, and be equally discreet?"

"Naturally. That is how things are done."

"Not for me, Siegfried," I said. "I intend to marry for love. I may be naïve, but I believe that I will find true happiness with the right man for me someday."

He looked extremely put out. "But your family wishes this alliance."

"I'm sorry. My family doesn't contribute a penny toward my sustenance. They don't have a say in my happiness. I wish you well in finding a suitable princess."

"Very well." He got to his feet. "We shall now make the descent. After you, my lady."

"We can belay down past the overhang," I said. "Do you want me to go first, while you play out the rope for me?"

"If you wish." He was cold, remote and correct, obviously not used to being rejected. I adjusted my harness and walked out backward over the cliff. I had only gone down a few feet, past the worst part of the overhang, when I heard a sound I associated with sailing ships at sea. It was the creak and groan of a rope under stress. While my brain was still processing the thought that the rope was about to break, it did and I fell.

I made a grab at the rock face but my fingers were torn from their handholds as I plummeted down. I had an impression of rock wall flashing past me, and the words formed themselves in my brain, *I am about to die. Bother.* And for some reason I was remarkably annoyed at being about to die a virgin.

It was almost as if I was descending in slow motion. I steeled myself for the inevitable crunch when I crashed into the scree at the bottom of the rock face. Then suddenly I was jerked upward and tipped upside down. I swung dizzily in my harness with the sky beneath my feet and the ground twirling above me. I didn't know how I'd been saved from certain death, but I presumed the rope must have snagged itself on some outcropping. In which case it could give way again any second. I continued to twirl, upside down. I tried, ineffectually, to right myself, but I was scared of putting any sudden pressure on the rope.

So I hung there, swaying in the breeze, just praying that Siegfried had the sense to find the easy route down and go for help. If not, I wasn't sure how long I could hang here. I could already feel the blood rushing to my head and singing in my ears. I was going to pass out if I stayed in this position much longer. Wind whistled past me, swinging me around. Clouds were rushing in, already blotting out the higher peaks. Soon I'd be hidden from sight.

"Help," I yelled into nowhere. "Somebody come and help me."

The singing in my head had become a roaring. Spots were dancing in front of my eyes. Gradually the world slipped away.

Chapter 20

A MOUNTAINSIDE NEAR CASTLE RANNOCH
AUGUST 19

When I opened my eyes two pale beings hovered over me, looking down at me with concern. For a moment I wondered whether this was heaven and that angels were actually blond. Then I noticed that one of them had fish lips and the other said, "She's coming round, thank God." I realized that one face belonged to Siegfried, the other to Hugo Beasley-Bottome.

"Where am I?" I asked. "Did I fall?"

"You, old fruit, are the luckiest girl in Scotland, I'd say," Hugo said. "I heard yelling and went to investigate, and there was the prince here, gesturing like a madman at the cliff. Then I noticed that you were dangling in midair. The bally rope was caught on a small tree that was jutting out from the rock. It was dashed impossible to get at you, you know."

"Then how did you get at me?" I tried to sit up. The world swung around alarmingly and I lay back again.

"Your cousin Lachan arrived to join us. He climbed up and attached a second rope, which was held by a piton, then with him bracing, we were able to break the branch that held you and lower you down. Dashed tricky maneuver, I can tell you."

"Thank you, very much," I said. "I don't know where you got the ropes from, Siegfried, but they must have been old. We should have tested them first."

"The rope was not old," Siegfried said. "Prince George brought it over himself from Balmoral. We laid it out to measure it and it was in fine form. Nothing wrong with it."

"Obviously something was wrong with it or it wouldn't have broken," I said.

Then I noticed Hugo's face. It had a strange, wary look to it. What was he doing up here in the first place? Or Lachan, for that matter? This was rather out of the way for a good haggis hunt, surely, and I thought I remembered someone saying that Hugo had gone down to be with his friends on the loch.

Lachan himself appeared at that moment. "Och, she's awake and talking. That is good news. Well, let's carry you back to the castle, wee Georgie, and get some brandy down you for shock. Your Highness, why don't you run on ahead and tell them we're coming so that they can have a bed with a hot water bottle ready."

"Very well," Siegfried said. "If you are sure the two of you can carry her between you."

"Between us?" Lachan laughed. "Why, she weighs no more than a feather." Then he swept me up into his arms.

"I'll bring the rest of their equipment, then," Hugo said.

Lachan strode down the steep path as if I weighed nothing at all.

I was beginning to recover. "So what happened to your haggis hunt, then?" I asked. "Surely you didn't bring them up here to do their hunting?"

He grinned. "It was canceled. They made the mistake of telling one of the groundsmen about it and he laughed himself silly. Now they're right put out about our little joke."

"I thought it was rather a good joke, personally," I said.

"So did I, but your brother has given Murdoch and me a stern warning. No more silly tricks or we're on our way home."

"Have you played any other silly tricks, then?" I asked.

"What? Oh no. Nothing at all." I was sure from his face that he was lying. Had he confessed to Binky that he was responsible for setting the trap? Surely he wasn't the White Lady. Nobody could have mistaken anything as large, red and obviously male for a ghostly woman.

As we approached the castle, servants ran out to meet us. Siegfried must have embellished the story or told it with great drama because they were looking terrified.

"Oh, my lady, thank goodness you're safe," Hamilton said. "And thank you, Mr. Lachan, for saving her for us. Your room is ready, my lady, and I've taken the liberty of having some hot tea and brandy sent up."

"Thank you." I smiled, feeling for a moment safe and cared for. Lachan carried me up the stairs and placed me on my bed. "Well, you'll be all right now, I expect," he said. Fig appeared at that moment in a frightful fluster. "They say you nearly died, Georgiana. I thought no good could come of climbing."

"The climb was no problem," I said. "The rope snapped on the way down."

"Who is in charge of ropes here? I'll see he's fired immediately."

"Fig, the rope came from Balmoral with Prince George," I said. "And Siegfried said it looked just fine when they laid it out."

"Then I suppose a sharp rock must have cut through it." She pushed Maggie aside and placed the hot water bottle beside me. This was a good idea as I was now feeling decidedly shivery. The tea tray arrived and Fig poured a generous helping of brandy into my cup. I drank, gasping at the combination of alcohol and heat, then I lay back.

"Have a good rest now, and then we'll send up some lunch," she said. "And by the way, have you heard? The Americans came back in a frightful temper. It seems your dreadful cousin had spun them a yarn about hunting for haggis. Really those men are too much."

"That's rich, coming from someone who made the piper play at dawn," I said with a grin. "You're just as bad as they are."

"Well, I suppose if it helps to drive them away, I can't complain."

"I think it was jolly funny," I said. "You should have heard Lachan describing how ferocious the haggis were and how they went for your ankles."

"I suppose that is rather amusing." Fig's face actually cracked into a smile. "I wonder what they'll say when we have haggis for dinner tonight. Cook has it all prepared, you know."

"Excellent." I closed my eyes. Fig shushed Maggie out of the room and I lay there alone. All in all it had been a surreal morning, with Siegfried asking me to marry him and then the fall. It did cross my mind that the two could be related. Had he cut the rope in a fit of pique because I had turned him down? Foreigners were known to be so emotional and he did come from a part of the world where vengeance was a daily occurrence.

I must have drifted off to sleep because I awoke to hear the sound of a door creaking open. All Castle Rannoch doors creak, as do the floorboards. It's positively a requirement in a castle to have creaking doors. My eyes opened in time to see Hugo Beasley-Bottome creeping into the room.

"Hugo!" I exclaimed. "What are you doing here?"

He started, as if he had expected me to be asleep. "Sorry. I just thought—well, I thought that you and I might have a little chat."

"I'm not in a chatting mood at the moment," I said warily. "I've just woken up."

"I wanted to get you to myself," he said, "and now seems like a good time. There are always so many bally people around."

He came over toward my bed. I sat up hastily, drawing my covers around me in a good display of maidenly effrontery. "Mr. Beasley-Bottome, this is my bedroom and I certainly didn't invite you in."

At that a smile flashed across his face. "A chap has to take whatever opportunity he can in this life. That's what they taught us at school, don't y'know?"

"Please leave," I said.

"Hold on a jiffy, old bean. I said I only wanted a chat. I'm not intending to ravish you on the spot, although I must say the idea is tempting. . . ." He paused. "I don't quite know how to put this but I think you'd want to know . . ."

At that moment the door burst open and Lachan stood there, giving a good imitation of an avenging relative. "What do you think you're doing in here?" he demanded. "Out, this minute. Can't you see the wee lassie needs her rest and quiet?"

"I only wanted a few words with her," Hugo said.

"Do you want a few words with yon boy?" Lachan demanded.

"I really don't at the moment," I said.

"Then out." He made a grab for Hugo, who took the hint and headed for the door.

"And just in case there are any more interruptions, I think I'll set up camp outside your door tonight," he said.

"Lachan, you really don't have to guard my honor." I didn't know whether to laugh or not.

He went across to the door and closed it. "It's not that. I took a good look at yon rope. It didn't seem to have broken because it was worn. It looked more like a clean cut to me. Someone had cut almost through it and left the last strands to break."

"I see." I took a deep breath. "And how do I know that you weren't that person, playing one of your famous jokes?"

"Some joke, wee Georgie. You'd have fallen on your head from a great height and we'd currently be holding your wake." He leaned closer. "That's why I've been keeping an eye on yon Hugo person. How did he arrive so quickly on the scene, that's what I'd like to know. He was no climbing with you, was he?"

"No, I hadn't seen him all morning."

"Then what was he doing in such a convenient spot as to be offering help when you were stuck up there, unless he knew what was going to happen to you?"

"Oh, dear," I said. "I did feel awfully uneasy when he came creeping in a few minutes ago. I'm glad you turned up when you did."

He patted my leg under the blankets. "Don't you worry now. I'll be outside the door and it would take a strapping man to get past me."

"Thank you, Lachan," I said.

He went to go, then turned back. "Georgie, about my wee jokes—you know about the rock that landed on the Prince of Wales and Mrs. Simpson?"

"That was you?"

"Not me. Murdoch. And it was an accident, I can assure you. He decided he might as well get in some practice for the Braemar Games. It's a good spot here, away from the competition. He was up to throwing the hammer and he didn't have a hammer on the spot, so to speak, so he had improvised by tying some rope around a large rock. Well, somehow it came loose as he was twirling it around his head and it went flying off in the wrong direction. We heard the awful clunk and the yells, and when we saw it was the Simpson woman, we made ourselves scarce."

"Well, that's good news," I said, trying not to smile. "At least it wasn't deliberate. And you didn't accidentally put out the trap for Binky to step on, did you?"

"Good God, no. I'd never hurt a kinsman. I might be tempted to do it for a Campbell, maybe, but who'd want to hurt Binky? He can't have an enemy in the world. A bit soft, maybe, and not overly endowed with brains, but there's not a mean bone in him."

"That's true," I said.

He leaned over and gave me a kiss on the forehead, then patted my shoulder. "Sweet dreams, young lady," he said. "I thought you did a fine job today. No silly hysterics. Just what one would expect from a Rannoch."

He left me then, with several thoughts to consider. Was he seriously considering marrying me? He and Murdoch had described themselves as penniless, but Binky had referred to their farm as prosperous. But Lachan was the younger brother. He wouldn't inherit anything.

"This is ridiculous," I said out loud. Of course I wasn't considering marrying him. I could have had a prince, a possible heir to a throne. I could always have someone like Gussie if I wanted, but I didn't want. I knew who I wanted and he had nothing to offer me in the material sense. Ah, well, two men who were interested in me in one day. That wasn't bad. Things were looking up in some ways.

They were looking down in others, of course, because it was apparent that someone had tried to kill me today. Or rather not to kill me, but to kill one of us. I thought that Siegfried's brutish countrymen would probably go more directly for a bomb through the window. Then, of course, I realized what should have been obvious all along: the rope had come from Balmoral. It had been intended for Prince George. Once again someone was targeting an heir to the throne—and this time somebody sixth in line. It was about time I stopped lying here and started working, before it was too late and one of the accidents took its toll.

Chapter 21

I must have dozed off for quite a while because when I awoke the room was bathed in pink twilight and there were sounds of commotion outside my door. Raised voices. A man shouting. I got up and opened the door cautiously. The first person I saw was Earl, standing at the top of the stairs. "She's nowhere to be found, I tell you," he was saying.

I came out onto the landing. "What's wrong?" I asked.

"It's Babe. She's disappeared," he said. "I can't find her anywhere."

"Maybe she went out for a walk before dinner," I suggested.

"We went out for a walk earlier," he said. "We came back and she said she wanted to take a bath before dinner. She'd never go out walking again after she'd taken a bath. I did other things. Wrote a letter. Tried to make a telephone call to London—without success, I might add. Then when I went back to the room, she wasn't there. I just don't understand it."

Fig had now come up the stairs to join us and together we went up the second flight to Earl and Babe's bedroom.

"There, you see," he said. Her dinner dress was laid out, ready to wear, on her bed. "She went to the bathroom in her robe. And her toilet bag is missing."

"Have you checked the bathroom?" I asked. "She could have fallen asleep in the bath, or even passed out."

"That was my first thought," Earl said. "But the bathroom is unoccupied."

We walked down the hallway to the nearest bathroom. It was, indeed, unoccupied and there was no sign that Babe had ever been there. No lingering steam on the mirror to indicate that a bath had been taken recently. (Of course, steam does not tend to linger long at Castle Rannoch, owing to the gale coming in through the open windows.)

"Is it possible she used another bathroom?" Fig suggested. "She might have found this one occupied and decided to look elsewhere."

We crossed the landing to the hallway on the other side where the Simpsons and the Von Sauers were currently staying. That bathroom was occupied, but the annoyed voice coming from it was that of Mrs. Simpson, who told us in no uncertain terms to go away.

"Would she have gone downstairs and used one of our bathrooms?" I asked. There was one on my landing and another on Fig and Binky's side.

"I don't think Babe would want to be seen going down the staircase in her robe," Earl said. "I didn't think of checking another floor, but I'm willing to give anything a try right now."

We went downstairs and examined my bathroom. Also empty. Lastly we went across to the grandest hallway, the one that contained the bedrooms of Fig and Binky, Prince Siegfried and also that of Prince George. The bathroom door was closed. We tapped on it. No answer. Earl rapped on it loudly. "Babe, are you in there?" Still no answer. "Oh, God," he exclaimed. "What if she's drowned in the bathtub? We must break down the door."

"Nobody is breaking down a door," Fig said. "We'll get a key."

I was dispatched to summon Hamilton, who arrived with the pass keys. We tried several and at last the bathroom door opened. The window faced the back of the castle and this part of the house had already descended into darkness. But we could make out a white shape lying on the floor.

"Oh, my God!" Earl sprang forward, while Fig turned on the light.

The harsh glare of the bulb revealed Babe, lying sprawled next to the lavatory in a pool of water and blood, while around her lay shattered pieces of what had been the lavatory tank. One could see where it had come away from the wall, high above the loo, revealing a brighter patch of tartan wallpaper. Most embarrassingly, she had obviously been sitting on the throne when she was struck. She was wearing nothing but a short kind of negligee and her little white bottom stuck up piteously.

Pandemonium ensued. Hamilton was sent to telephone for our doctor and an ambulance. Earl was on his knees pleading for Babe not to die, having first covered her posterior with his jacket to prevent further embarrassment. The countess appeared at that moment, started to have hysterics and had to be led away by her son, moaning, "A house of horrors, I knew it. What did I tell you? Somebody get me out of here before doom befalls us all."

No sooner had she disappeared than Prince Siegfried arrived in a silk dressing gown with a black sleeping mask pushed up on his forehead, wanting to know what all the infernal row was about when he was trying to take forty winks. Fig and I were the only ones staying calm and sensible. Fig had always boasted about her Girl Guide training and I must say her first aid badge came in rather useful. She was down on her knees among the muck, feeling for a pulse. She looked up eventually and nodded.

"She's still alive. Get towels to mop up this mess and blankets to put around her. We shouldn't move her until a doctor examines her. She could have a fractured skull."

I attempted to move the pieces of shattered lavatory tank from her.

"It must have toppled onto her when she pulled the chain," I said.

"How extraordinary. I've never heard of that happening in my life," Fig said. "She must have pulled the chain jolly hard."

"You've no business having guests to stay in a house that is falling to pieces," Earl said angrily. "This place is a positive death trap. I said so to Babe only this morning."

"What an extraordinary day," Fig muttered as we moved out of the way to make room for the maids who had arrived with piles of towels and blankets, and had begun to mop up the floor. "First you fall off a mountain and nearly kill yourself, and now this. Anyone would think there was a curse on the castle or something. You've never heard of any curses on the Rannoch family, have you?"

"There was that witch who was thrown into the lake," I suggested. "But she's had six centuries to curse us so I expect she would have done it by now."

Fig sighed. "I don't suppose we'll hear the last of it. That man Earl will want to sue us or something. That's what they do in America, isn't it? We'll be bankrupted. Destitute. We'll have to go and live in one of the cottages. . . ."

"Don't you start getting hysterical," I said, putting a calming hand on her shoulder. "Remember, a Rannoch never loses his nerve."

"Blast the stupid Rannochs," she said. "This place has brought me nothing but grief. I should have married the nice young vicar at St. Stephen's in our village, but I wanted to be a duchess." She really was closer to hysterics than I had ever seen her.

Fortunately the doctor arrived at the same time as the ambulance, causing Fig to put on a brave face and resume her role as duchess. His face was grim as he examined her. "A nasty business," he said. "I don't see any signs of a fractured skull, but to have been knocked out this long would indicate a severe concussion at the very least. We must try and transport her to hospital without disturbing her. Lift her very carefully, men. I'll come with you."

They put her onto a stretcher and off they went. Earl went with them, as did the countess and Fritzi. The nearest hospital was in Perth and they announced that they'd take a hotel room nearby. Mrs. Simpson, on the other hand, did not go with them.

"Of course I want to offer support to dear Babe," she said, "but I see no point in sitting in dreary waiting rooms or hotels, waiting until she is well enough to receive visitors. In fact I rather think it wouldn't be wise for me to be spotted in a Scottish hotel room. It might give rise to gossip, you know."

So the prince won out over her dearest friend. Mr. Simpson looked fed up. I wondered how much longer she'd keep him around for respectability's sake. But they did go out to dine, as did Hugo Beasley-Bottome, so it was essentially only family plus Siegfried who were at dinner when the haggis was ceremonially piped in. Then, of course, we had to pretend that we enjoyed it. It wasn't awful or anything, just not, as Fig had put it, our cup of tea. But after all the trouble we'd forced poor Cook to go to, we simply couldn't send any back. So we struggled with it manfully, except for Siegfried, who pushed his portion away, declaring that he never ate anything when he couldn't identify what part of the animal it came from.

Only Murdoch and Lachan tucked into it with glee, with much chomping and smacking of lips. I glanced across at Lachan. Oh, dear, I could never marry a man who smacked his lips over haggis.

There was no suggestion of any kind of evening jollity tonight. I went up to bed almost immediately after coffee. I was feeling completely exhausted, I suspect by the shock of two alarming events in one day. I lay there, listening to the sigh of the wind while I tried to blot images from my mind—the world swinging crazily as I hung upside down, and then Babe, lying in the midst of all that blood and water with the lavatory cistern broken around her and her little white bottom exposed for all to see. Someone was at loose in our midst who had evil, if not murder, on his mind. I had been charged with trying to find out who it was and I hadn't done anything so far. I had better get a move on with my investigation. This had to be stopped.

Chapter 22

CASTLE RANNOCH

AUGUST 20, 1932

Promising to be a lovely day.

I was woken by the sound of tapping on my door. It was already misty daylight. I must have slept through the piper, if indeed he had played again this morning. Maggie came in with my morning tea, followed by Hamilton, with a perplexed look on his face.

"I'm sorry to wake you, my lady, but . . ."

"What is it, Hamilton?"

"There is a person in the front hall, wishing to speak to you."

"What kind of person?"

"A person from the lower classes, my lady."

"And what does he want with me?"

"He says to tell you that he came 'as quick as he could, and Bob's your uncle, he's here.' But I don't think that Bob is your uncle, is he, my lady?"

I sat up in bed, laughing. "It's a Cockney expression, Hamilton. And it's not a person, it's my grandfather."

"Your—grandfather, my lady?" There was a distinct gulp.

"My mother's father, Hamilton."

"Am I to understand that he will be staying here, at the castle?" He must have been rattled. He forgot to add "my lady."

"Oh no. Not at all. He's going to stay in one of the empty cottages on the estate. The one next to Nanny looked quite nice, I thought."

I saw the relief sweep over his face. "Very suitable, my lady. And what should I do with him until you come down?"

"Put him in the morning room with a cup of tea and the paper," I said. "He is house-trained, you know."

"My lady, I wasn't implying . . ." he stammered.

"Tell him I'll be down immediately," I said and jumped out of bed. Hamilton backed out and I instructed Maggie to hand me the first items of clothing she could find. I was so excited, I wriggled impatiently as she did up my buttons. If Granddad was here, then everything would be all right. I could stop worrying because he'd know what to do. As I came down the stairs, a sticky problem presented itself. If my grandfather had taken the night train, he'd want breakfast, and I wasn't quite sure how to handle introducing him to the breakfast room. I couldn't risk letting him come into contact with Fig. Not that I didn't think he could give as good as he got, but Fig could be crushingly snobby and he didn't deserve that. Maybe if it was early enough, we could have the room to ourselves.

I positively ran down the stairs. Granddad was in the morning room, perched on the edge of a brocade and gilt chair, a cup of tea in his hand, looking uneasy. He stood up as he heard my approaching feet and a big smile spread across his face. "Well, look at you." He put down the teacup and opened his arms wide. "Don't you look a treat. Blimey, some gloomy great place you've got here, haven't you?"

"You've never been to Castle Rannoch before?"

"Never been invited, my love. And never had the desire to come this far north, if you want to know. We in the Smoke have the belief that civilization ends south of Birmingham. I only came because I got the feeling you wanted me here."

"I do," I said, hugging him fiercely. Fig would never have approved of such a wanton display of affection. She and her parents only ever shook hands. I wondered how little Podge was ever conceived, but then I supposed she had been instructed to close her eyes and think of England. "It was good of you to come so quickly," I went on. "I really didn't expect to see you for days."

"It's all right, my turning up now, isn't it? I mean, there is a place for me?"

"Of course. The cottage is unoccupied. I looked at it the other day."

"So let's take a look at this cottage, shall we?" Granddad asked. "This place is giving me the willies."

We were just crossing the great hall when Fig appeared, looking worried. "They're all off to Balmoral. A day to ourselves, thank heavens," she said, and then noticed my grandfather. "Oh, I didn't realize . . ."

"This is my grandfather, Fig," I said. "He's come up to Scotland for a while."

"Your grandfather? You mean your mother's father?"

"I don't think he's the old duke's ghost, the one who plays the bagpipes on the ramparts at midnight." I grinned. "Of course he's my mother's father."

Fig held out her hand and said, "How do you do?" in the frosty manner she employed with anyone not of her class.

Granddad took the hand and pumped it heartily. "Pleased to meet yer," he said.

"Are you just passing through the area?" Fig asked, still plum-in-mouth frosty.

"No, he's going to be staying for a while." I watched her face. "If that's all right," I added.

I could see Fig trying to picture my Cockney grandfather at table with a prince or two. She opened her mouth several times then shut it again.

"In one of the empty cottages," I said. "He'll be able to keep Nanny company."

Relief spread across her face. "One of the cottages. Of course. Of course." And she gave an almost hysterical laugh.

"I'm taking him there now," I said. "Please excuse us."

I led him out of the front door and down the steps.

"Blimey," he said. "That's your sister-in-law?"

I nodded.

"Looks like she's got a bad smell under her nose, don't she?" he said.

"She does rather."

"No wonder you wanted to get away."

We crossed the forecourt. I noticed one of the shooting brakes being loaded up with guns and bags in readiness for the shoot at Balmoral. Poor Earl—he had been looking forward to a shoot. Now the party from here would be reduced to Prince Siegfried, the cousins, and Hugo Beasley-Bottome. I wondered if the Simpsons were included in the invitation. Hardly.

"So what did your friend Mrs. Huggins say about leaving her to travel up here?"

"It worked out nicely because her daughter's taken a cottage down in Littlestone on the Kentish coast and she wants 'Ettie to go with them. 'You go and enjoy yourself, Albert,' she said to me. 'It will do you a world of good.' So here I am."

"I'm so glad." I beamed at him.

It was a misty morning and rooks were cawing madly from the big elms. The cottages loomed as indistinct shapes through the mist. We opened the one I had in mind and I set to work taking dust covers off furniture and then locating a broom to give the place a good sweep.

"Cor blimey, look at you wielding that broom." Granddad laughed. "Don't let that lot up at the castle see you doing that. They'll have a fit."

"It's what I do for a living these days," I said. "I'm actually getting rather good at it, don't you think?"

"Oh yes. Smashing," he said, coughing through my cloud of dust.

"Now, we need to make you up a bed. . . ." I found a linen closet and we made the bed between us. "And I'll have supplies sent down from the kitchen. I'd invite you to come up to the castle and eat with us, but I'm afraid . . ."

"Don't get your knickers in a twist, ducks," he said. "I wouldn't feel right among all those toffy noses. I shall be right as rain in this snug little place, if you don't mind coming down to visit occasionally."

"Of course I will," I said. "In fact I'm going to need your help."

"What's up?" he asked, looking at me with concern. "Something's wrong, I can tell."

I knew I was sworn to secrecy but I felt that I could tell my grandfather anything. So I did. I recounted the whole story from the encounter on the train to the various accidents that had happened since.

"I can only conclude that the rope was meant for Prince George," I said, "and that the cistern that came down on that poor woman was also designed for the prince, although Binky and Fig also use that bathroom."

"Are you sure you're not reading too much into this? Accidents do happen. Back when I was on the force, we used to say that bad luck came in threes. Maybe what you've told me was bad luck, no more: a rope that broke, an old lavatory that collapsed?"

"That rope was cut, Granddad. I'm sure of it. And what about the ghost that the countess saw? And the trap that caught Binky's foot? It's too much at once, especially after what Sir Jeremy told me. A whole string of accidents, all aimed at the royal family."

He nodded. "Supposing you're right, do you have anything to go on?"

"Nothing at all," I said.

"Back when I was working for the Met, my old inspector would have said the first question to ask is 'Who benefits?' "

"I can't think," I said. "Someone next in line of succession? But then nobody here fits that bill."

"Are you sure?" Granddad asked. "What about that Siegfried fellow you went climbing with?"

I laughed. "He's an heir to his own country's throne, if they don't assassinate everyone in the near future, and I don't think he's related to us at all. Besides, why would Siegfried lure me up onto a mountain and then have a rope break? There are plenty of ways to bump somebody off at Castle Rannoch without that long trek."

"So anyone else staying here who might see himself with a crown on his head someday?"

I laughed nervously. "Granddad, I'm thirty-fourth in line and I believe I know everybody ahead of me. So it would have to be somebody who wanted to bump off at least thirty-four people, which simply doesn't make sense."

"Maybe it's someone with a grudge against the royal family, then," he said.

"Like the communists, you mean? But Sir Jeremy said that they'd checked that possibility and it couldn't be an outsider."

"Then maybe someone who's staying in the area isn't what he claims to be. What about that whole nasty affair with your foreign princess? The communists managed to fool you all then, didn't they? And almost bumped off Their Majesties."

My thoughts went straight to Hugo. I remembered how he had miraculously appeared to rescue me the previous day and then how he'd tried to sneak into my bedroom when I was resting. Had he been coming to finish me off? I wondered.

"It seems to me that the first thing I should do today is to take a look at that line of succession," I said. "And to have a talk with Binky about one of our guests, called Hugo Beasley-Bottome."

"Blimey, what a name," Granddad said. "So you think he might be suspicious, do you?"

"Well, he was right there on the spot when I had to be rescued from that rope. What was he doing hanging about on a mountainside? And I know nothing about him. He just invited himself to stay at the castle and appeared out of nowhere."

"How did he manage to invite himself?"

"He was at school with Binky, apparently."

"Then ask your brother about him. And if that rope was tampered with, find out who had a chance to tamper with it. Where was it kept?"

"It came from Balmoral with Prince George, so Siegfried said."

"Now that's a thought," Granddad said. "Which one is Prince George?"

"He's the king's youngest son. Sixth in line."

"He's 'ere, is he?" Granddad asked.

"He was. He was called back to Balmoral."

"So either someone could be working to get rid of him or"—he paused and looked up at me, his bright little Cockney eyes twinkling—"or he set up the accidents himself to make it look as if they were aimed at him."

"Why would he do that?"

"I can't tell you that. But why wasn't he climbing if he'd brought the rope?"

"He was summoned back to Balmoral, apparently," I said, my voice trailing off at the end of this.

"Which is why he didn't use his lav either, I suppose."

I nodded, then I shook my head vehemently. "That's silly. He'd have no motive for playing these tricks on other people. For one thing, nobody here is ahead of him in the line of succession. And anyway, he said how glad he was that he wouldn't have to be king one day and how he didn't envy his oldest brother."

"All the same, I'd check into that rope if you feel you must do something. So is there anything I can do to help you?"

"Nothing at the moment. Why don't you get yourself settled and I'll introduce you to Nanny. She bakes wonderful scones. Then you might want to take a walk around the estate. See the lay of the land."

He put a hand on my shoulder. "Look, you take care of yourself, my love. I don't want you putting yourself in harm's way and if you ask me it's ruddy cheek of this Sir What's-His-Name to ask you to get involved."

"But I am involved, Granddad, whether I like it or not. I was the one dangling on that rope yesterday and my brother has a crushed ankle. This person has to be stopped before he kills one of us."

Granddad made a tsk-tsk noise with his tongue. "Then you leave the stopping to the trained professionals—those blokes in the special branch. Why aren't they up here, doing their job?"

"I expect they are," I said. "Or at least one of them is. I was told that someone was in position at Balmoral and would introduce himself to me." My mind immediately jumped one stage ahead as I said this. Was it possible that Darcy was that person? Why else would he be up here?

"Well, the sooner you pop over to Balmoral and find this bloke, the better," he said. "I don't want you sticking your neck out again. This sounds to me like a spiteful, twisted kind of person—the sort of person who gets his pleasure out of other people's suffering. That trap, for example—just downright nasty."

"Don't worry about me. I'll be extra careful," I said, as breezily as I could manage, but as I walked back to the house I began to wonder. How could I be extra careful when danger could be lurking anywhere around me and I didn't know whom to trust?

Chapter 23

When I returned to the castle, after having made sure Granddad was comfortable in the cottage, I noticed that the shooting brake had already left for the day's grouse shoot at Balmoral. I also remembered that I hadn't yet had breakfast. I found the breakfast room empty, so I tucked into a plate of bacon, kidneys and fried bread, plus a couple of slices of toast and Cooper's Oxford marmalade. It's amazing what country air does for the appetite.

Then I went into the library and sat down with paper and pencil. First I made a list of everyone who had been staying here, or in the area, then I checked what connection they might have to the British throne. I was half expecting to discover that Babe was a long-lost relative, but she wasn't. Gussie had distant connections, as did Darcy, through his mother. But I couldn't come up with anybody in the direct line in the top hundred or so.

Maybe we've got this wrong, I thought. Maybe this is some kind of personal grudge. I knew that Prince George, for example, ran with quite a wild crowd. What if he was involved in drugs or some kind of underworld pursuit? Both of the accidents yesterday seemed to have been aimed at him. But then, there were the previous ones—the broken saddle girth on the Prince of Wales's polo pony, the wheel that came loose on his car . . .

I broke off and shook my head. If there really was one person causing these accidents then he certainly didn't mind taking frightful risks. How could an outsider have been able to tamper with the girth on the prince's pony or with the wheel of his car? The answer, of course, was what Sir Jeremy suspected—not an outsider. One of us. As improbable as it seemed, someone staying at Castle Rannoch must have tampered with that loo. I went upstairs and examined it. Unfortunately there was now nothing to see. The maids had done a good job of cleaning up, and apart from the lack of a tank, the room looked perfectly ordinary. In any case it wouldn't have been hard to have made the tank unstable enough so that a good yank on the chain would have brought it down.

I went along the hall to Binky's bedroom. Fig was sitting with him, watching him while he ate a boiled egg. He looked up as I came in.

"Dashed funny business, Georgie," he said. "Have you ever heard of a lavatory tank falling off the wall onto anybody?"

"Never," I said, "but then I don't think it was an accident that it fell. I think that maybe someone tampered with it."

"Why would anyone do that?"

"I have no idea. But why would you step on a trap? Why would the rope snap when I was climbing?"

"Are you trying to say that these were all deliberate?" Fig demanded. "How utterly beastly. Who would do such a thing?"

"I don't know," I said. "I'm as much in the dark as you are. None of it makes sense."

"You don't think those cousins of yours think that this kind of thing is funny, do you?" Fig demanded. "Remember the time they took that pig dressed up as a baby, into church, and tried to have it christened?"

"There's a difference between high spirits and mean-spiritedness," Binky said. "Any of these accidents could have killed someone. They may have killed someone. Have we heard any news on the American woman this morning?"

"Improving, thank God. She woke up before the ambulance reached the hospital, but they are keeping her there for observation."

"Well, that's good news, isn't it? Will they be coming back here?"

"I believe they have decided it is safer to stay in a hotel," Fig said with what could only be taken as a triumphant look. It did cross my mind to wonder whether she might have tampered with the lavatory tank in her desperation to get rid of unwanted guests.

"So our little house party is dwindling," Binky said. "Is the Simpson woman going to stay on?"

"As long as the Prince of Wales is within driving distance," I said.

Binky grinned. "And how about you, old bean? I hear you had quite an ordeal yesterday. Fully recovered?"

"Oh yes, thank you. It was rather frightening at the time. I thought I'd had it."

"I should speak to Harris about not checking those ropes." Harris was the head gillie. "After all, it's his job to make sure they are sound."

"But Prince George brought the rope with him from Balmoral," I said. "I'm going over there today, if I can have a car."

"Don't see why not, do you, Fig?"

She tried to come up with a good reason why I couldn't use her petrol, but in the end she had to nod. "No, by all means. Go and join the shoot. It will do you good. I'd go too if I weren't stuck here as hostess."

"And Binky, there's one other thing." I paused near the doorway. "This Hugo Beasley-Bottome. Tell me about him."

"Not much to tell," Binky said. "He was a new boy in my house at school when I was prefect. A skinny little runt at the time. Got bullied a lot so I stepped in. He was dashed grateful. But I haven't seen anything of him since I left school. I was surprised when he wrote and asked to come and stay, but one can't say no to a fellow old boy."

I went back to my room to change into something suitable for Balmoral. A skirt in the Rannoch tartan (rather disgusting mixture of red, yellow and brown) and white blouse. On my way to the garages I sought out Harris, our head gillie. He was an old man with a shock of white hair and skin like brown leather, and he was busy sorting out fishing tackle.

"Would you take a look at this," he said, holding up a reel of twisted line to me. "The mess they make of things. You'd think they'd never fished in their lives before."

"They probably haven't," I said. "I wanted to ask you about the rope that broke on the climb yesterday."

"Aye, I heard about that," he said, nodding seriously. "Verra nasty business, my lady."

"It was. Did you have the rope stored here overnight?"

"No rope ever went out from this place," he said. "I don't know who put together the equipment for yon climb, but it was not I."

I thanked him and went to find a car. Our chauffeur had gone with the shooting brake so I helped myself to the estate car rather than the Bentley.

I hadn't driven in months and I relished the freedom of sitting behind the wheel, driving along the familiar lanes with the windows down and the fresh breeze blowing in my face. There was no sign of activity at the dock today. It was still misty in places and I assumed that some of the group had been invited to take part in the shoot. Max, for one. When I came to a straighter piece of road at the far end of the loch, I put my foot down and felt the rush of excitement as the car picked up speed.

Obviously I was going a little too fast, but as I came around a sharp bend, I encountered a car going even faster. I was only conscious of a long, sleek shape hurtling directly at me. I swung the wheel. My car went up the bank, teetered, almost tipped over then righted itself again. I came to a stop with my heart pounding only to see the sports car speeding away in my rearview mirror.

"Bloody fool," I shouted after him as he disappeared into a patch of mist. Yes, I know a lady never uses the word "bloody" but this was a moment of extreme stress. Besides, only the Highland cattle were around to hear me and they'd never tell. Then the mist swirled and I got a good look at the driver as he sped away along the lochside. It was Paolo, driving alone.

Of course my thoughts now ran riot: had he come at me deliberately, or was he just driving too fast in his usual reckless manner? I couldn't come up with any good reason for Paolo wanting to kill me, but I found my thoughts straying to Ronny's maid, who had been run down by a motorcycle at Croydon Aerodrome. Was that also Paolo and had he not even bothered to stop then? And of course it did occur to me that Paolo was just the kind of risk-taker who could have carried out the various things that had happened to us. But why would a rich Italian count wish harm on the British royal family?

I wondered whether I should say anything to Belinda. She was my best friend and Paolo seemed in every way unsuitable—not only was he a reckless driver with an obsession for speed, but he was also engaged to someone else. I didn't want her to be hurt, but then, women in love don't want to hear anything bad about the object of their affection, do they? If I said anything I'd have to be careful.

I drove on, considerably more cautiously than before, until I came to the main gate of Balmoral. The gatekeeper came out of his funny little octagonal lodge, then recognized me and saluted as he opened the gate. I nodded graciously as I passed. The driveway took me through lush woodland, so much in contrast to the starkness of the bleak moorland around Castle Rannoch. Then the road emerged again and there was Balmoral Castle across its broad expanse of lawn. It looks like any other old and distinguished Scottish castle, with its dramatic towers and ivy covering, but of course, it's a complete fake, having been built in the 1850s for Queen Victoria. If I'd built something, I would have gone more for comfort and elegance and less for authentic castle feeling.

I drove around to the back of the castle and under the arch that led to the stables and various outbuildings. I parked inconspicuously and went to look for one of their gillies. Of course, I realized instantly that all the available men would be out acting as beaters for the shoot, so I took the opportunity to do some snooping around. I discovered various tack rooms and saw other ropes hanging in neat coils. From the ease with which I had gained entry, it became clear that almost anyone could have wandered in without being seen—if they had gained admittance to the estate, of course. But then if someone had come on foot over the hills, as opposed to the road, he could probably have found a way onto the estate, again without being spotted.

I checked some of the other ropes and they all seemed to be in perfect condition, and I remembered that Siegfried had said that he and Prince George had also laid out the rope to see how long it was, and hadn't seen any defects. Wouldn't they have noticed if someone had almost cut it through at one point? Did this then indicate that the damage had been done after the rope reached Castle Rannoch, the night before the climb, in fact?

I had no way of finding out. I gave up and went to pay my respects to Their Majesties, King George and Queen Mary. As I came out into the stable yard I heard the sound of children's voices, and there were the two little princesses, holding hands with a woman I supposed to be their governess. They looked up in surprise and then the older princess's face broke into an enchanting smile. "I remember you," she said. "You're our cousin Georgiana, aren't you?"

"I am. And you are Lilibet and this is Margaret." I smiled back at them.

"You have to say Princess Margaret," the three-year-old said, wrinkling her little nose, "because I'm a princess."

"In which case you have to call me Lady Georgiana," I replied, trying not to smile.

She looked perplexed at this. "Is a lady better than a princess?" she asked her governess.

"One hopes a princess will grow up to be a lady someday," the governess replied solemnly.

"Oh," Margaret said and fell silent.

"We've been to visit our ponies," Elizabeth said. "We take them treats." Suddenly her face lit up. "I know. We can go riding together. When I'm with the groom he won't let go of my bridle and we have to walk slowly, but now that you're here I can go out with you and we can gallop."

"I don't mind," I said. "If your parents agree."

"I'm sure they'll agree. You're our cousin. So when can we go?"

"Not today," I said. "I have to pay a visit to your royal grandmamma."

"Everyone's gone out shooting," Elizabeth said, "but I don't think Grandmamma went with them. She doesn't like all that noise. I feel sorry for the dogs, don't you? I bet they don't like the sound of the shooting. Dogs have very sensitive hearing, you know."

"I'm sure they get used to it," I said.

"You have to come and see our new corgi puppy. He's beautiful." The princess's eyes were shining.

"I will, I promise."

"And now we must go and wash our hands before lunch," the governess said, nodding to me. "And we mustn't hold up Lady Georgiana any longer."

The girls looked back wistfully as I parted from them. I watched their progress, wondering if they could be in any kind of danger and whether anyone was watching over them. Whom could I tell? Where would I find Sir Jeremy's man?

I found the castle bathed in sleepy silence. The chiming of a clock in a distant room was the only sound as I stood on the tartan-carpeted floor and wondered where to go next. Then I thought I heard the murmur of voices coming from a hallway to my left and I headed in that direction, past the watchful gaze of black marble sculptures—Balmoral being more ornate in its decoration than Castle Rannoch. The voices were coming from an open doorway to my left and I knocked before going in. Her Majesty was seated at a table in a big bay window, apparently writing letters. Several older women sat in a group around the empty fireplace, chatting. Their conversation broke off as I came in.

"Georgiana!" The queen sounded surprised. "I had no idea you had arrived. We weren't expecting you until next week." She sounded a trifle vexed. She was a person who did not like to be taken off guard.

"I came up to Castle Rannoch because of my brother's accident, ma'am," I said. "I couldn't leave my sister-in-law to entertain a house party alone." I went over to her and attempted the usual combination of kiss on the cheek and curtsy, as usual getting this wrong and bumping my nose against the royal cheek. "So I felt I should come over and pay my respects as soon as I settled in."

"I'm glad you did, my dear." She patted my hand. "You will stay for luncheon, I hope. It's not the most stimulating of gatherings, I'm afraid. Everybody's gone off to shoot except for us elderly females."

"Thank you, ma'am. I'd be delighted to stay."

The queen looked over at her ladies. "You know young Georgiana, don't you? Henry Rannoch's girl? Lady Peebles, Lady Marchmont, Lady Ainslie and Lady Verian."

Four serene and elderly faces smiled at me.

The queen patted the seat next to her. "And how is your poor brother faring? What an extraordinary thing to have happened. My son George told us all about it."

"He seems to be improving, thank you, ma'am."

"That is good news. Such a strange summer. The king hasn't been at all well. He's looking so much better since he's been up here in the fresh air. I just hope the shoot won't be too much for him."

A gong summoned us to luncheon. I followed the queen and her ladies into the dining room. As we walked down the hallway, I wondered how I could find out exactly who was staying at Balmoral. The servants would know, if I could slip off unobserved for a chat.

Luncheon was, as usual in royal circles, a rather heavy meal. The king was fond of good solid English food, so we had mulligatawny soup, followed by steak and kidney pudding, followed by a rather grand version of bread pudding with custard. Feeling somewhat replete, I went with the ladies back to the sitting room.

"I think we might drive up to see how the shoot is progressing, don't you?" the queen suggested. "I want to make sure that the king is not over-taxing himself."

A shooting brake was ordered. We bumped along a track through some leafy woodland and then up a steep hillside until the vehicle could go no farther through the rocks and heather. Then we got out and walked, following a narrow track through the bracken. It was still misty and the grouse moor ahead loomed like a ghostly shape as the breeze parted the mist then drove it in again.

"They can't have been too successful today," the queen said, turning back to us. "How do they expect to see birds through this mist? I don't hear any shooting going on, do you? I hope everything's all right." She strode ahead with Lady Ainslie while the rest of us followed.

"It's touching to see how concerned she is about the king, isn't it?" Lady Marchmont muttered, drawing closer to Lady Peebles. "Did you ever see a couple so attached to each other?"

"Especially since she was supposed to marry his brother," Lady Peebles replied. "I must say she changed her allegiance rather rapidly."

"Well, wouldn't you, given the choice?" Lady Marchmont retorted.

I was close enough to overhear this little exchange, and turned back to them. "I remember hearing about that," I said. "The Duke of Clarence, wasn't it? What exactly happened? He died, didn't he?"

"Right before the wedding."

"How tragic."

"Oh no, my dear," Lady Peebles said. "It was a great blessing for everyone. A great blessing for England. He would have made an awful king—so lacking in moral fiber. He was a completely dissolute person, an embarrassment to the family."

Lady Marchmont nodded. "There was that scandal with the homosexual club, wasn't there?"

Lady Peebles shot her a glance, warning that such matters probably shouldn't be discussed in front of my delicate ears.

"She probably doesn't know anything about that kind of thing," Lady Marchmont said, dismissing me with a wave of her hand. "I know I didn't at her age. No idea such creatures existed. I remember someone saying that one of my suitors was a 'pansy boy' and I thought that meant he was keen on gardening."

I laughed with them.

"So was the Duke of Clarence really a homosexual?" I asked.

"I suspect he was AC/DC," Lady Marchmont said. "They say he couldn't keep his hands off the maids, and there were rumors of visits to prostitutes. . . ."

"I've even heard it suggested that he was Jack the Ripper," Lady Peebles said with a disparaging sniff, "although that's simply out of the question."

"But I suspect the rumors about prostitutes are true enough. And there were enough tales of drugs and drink. No, I think Her Majesty had a lucky escape. He would have led her a frightful dance. King George may be a boring old stick, but at least he's dependable. And he clearly adores her. And England is in good hands."

"How did the Duke of Clarence die?" I asked.

"Flu epidemic," Lady Peebles said shortly. "Almost as bad as the big one of 1918. I remember clearly because I was a young girl" (she pronounced it "gell") "at the time, and due to be presented at court that year, but my parents put it off until the next season because they didn't want to risk bringing the family up from the country. I was most disappointed. I couldn't understand what all the fuss was about with a simple influenza. Of course we now know that influenza isn't always that simple."

"I heard a rumor that he didn't die at all," Lady Marchmont said in a low voice. "The story went around that he was being kept a prisoner in an insane asylum."

"What utter rot," Lady Peebles said hotly. "My father attended the funeral himself. And don't ever let Her Majesty hear you repeating that kind of street gossip."

She stopped talking as we heard the sound of dogs barking up ahead.

"Ah, there they are." The queen turned back to us with a nod of satisfaction. She quickened her pace. For an older woman she could certainly stride out wonderfully. "I expect they've seen us," she added because someone was coming toward us. He was running very fast and the way he almost barreled into us made it clear that he hadn't seen us until then nor was he expecting to meet anyone on the path.

"Oh, Your Majesty," he gasped, his face red with exertion and embarrassment, "I had no idea. I wasn't expecting . . ."

"It's all right, Jack," she said. "Why such a hurry?"

"They've sent me down to fetch a doctor and the police," he said, the words still coming out between gasps. "There's been a horrible accident. Someone's been shot."

Chapter 24

Lady Peebles took charge.

"We must take Her Majesty back to the castle immediately," she said.

"I'm not likely to faint at the sight of a little blood, Blanche," Her Majesty said, "but what happened? Who is it?"

"I couldn't tell you that, Your Majesty. One of the young gentlemen."

"Is he badly hurt?"

"Looks nasty from what I saw, Your Majesty."

"Should we not transport him back to the house in the motorcar?" Her Majesty suggested. "It's close by."

"I don't think he can be moved, ma'am," the servant said. "They'd have taken him to the shooting brakes, wouldn't they? But they told me to go for the doctor, and the police."

"Then you must ride back in the motorcar with us," the queen said. "I suppose we'd only be in the way if we stayed and we don't want to find that our motor is blocking the way for an ambulance, do we?" She nodded to her ladies. Lady Peebles went to take her arm, then thought better of it.

I slipped away from them and continued up the track, into the mist. I felt an absurd sense of panic. A young gentleman had been shot. I didn't know whether Darcy was part of that shoot or not, but I found myself praying "Please not Darcy, please not Darcy" as I broke into a run, stumbling over tussocks of heather, rocks and rabbit holes. Figures loomed ahead through the mist but there was an eerie silence. I could hear a lark singing somewhere above the gloom. Then the mist parted and I came upon them. They were standing still, almost posed as a tableau: the king, still holding his gun, at the middle of the scene; three of his sons, the Prince of Wales, the Duke of York and Prince George; plus his daughter-in-law, the Duchess of York, standing around him in a protective knot; with the lesser players off to one side. Farther off were the servants, holding the bags of game, the spare guns and the dogs, who strained at their leads as they saw me coming and began barking again. There was a look of bewildered shock on all the faces. And out beyond the tableau I could make out something lying on the ground with two people on their knees beside it.

"Who's that coming now?" The king's voice carried through the clear air.

"Looks like young Georgie," someone said, probably the Prince of Wales by the voice.

"Georgie?"

"Binky's sister, from Castle Rannoch."

I reached them, a little out of breath from having run uphill.

"Hello, sir." I nodded to the king. "Her Majesty was coming to see how you were doing, but now she's gone back in the motorcar with your man to fetch a doctor."

"I'm afraid it's a little too late for a doctor," the king said, in a clipped voice that was fighting to show no emotion. "Poor fellow's had it."

"Who is it?" My heart was thumping so loudly I could hardly breathe.

"Some young chap staying with you, I gather," the Prince of Wales said. "Beastley something. I wouldn't look if I were you. Not a pretty sight."

My gaze moved past the group to the smaller tableau on the ground. As I moved toward it I spotted my mother. She had been clinging to Max's arm, but now she broke away and ran up to me. "Isn't it too, too horrible?" she said. "That poor boy. So handsome too. What a ghastly thing to have happened. I feel quite weak and nobody thought to bring a flask of brandy. I just hope they take us back to the house soon. I might faint any moment."

"Mummy, you're as strong as an ox," I said. "I'm sure you'll hold out splendidly."

"Such an unfeeling daughter," she said with a dramatic sigh. "Max, you will catch me if I faint, won't you?"

"What must I do, *Liebchen*?" he asked, the word "faint" being beyond his English vocabulary. Probably also the word "catch."

I moved past her to see for myself. Hugo Beasley-Bottome was lying, staring up at the sky with a look of utter surprise on his face. There was a considerable amount of blood splashed around him. Kneeling beside him were Darcy and an older man with a neat little gray mustache. Darcy stood up quickly as he saw me.

"What are you doing here?" he asked.

"I came over to visit the queen," I said. "What happened?"

The older man stood up a little stiffly, as if he'd been kneeling too long. He was tall and of a military bearing. "I said we should not have gone out in this kind of weather," he said. "Too risky with the mist coming and going. Young fool must have wandered ahead and got into the line of fire. That's what happens when you introduce newcomers who don't know the damned rules. Did you know the fellow?"

"He was staying at Castle Rannoch," I said, staring down at him with pity and revulsion, "but I'd never met him before."

"I'd never come across him until a few weeks ago either. He showed up at the house a couple of times," the man said. "Believe he was rather keen on my daughter." He came across to me. "I'm Major Padgett, by the way. We have met before. I've known your family for years. We're neighbors."

"Yes, of course. Georgiana Rannoch. How do you do?"

"And you know this young man?" He indicated Darcy.

"Yes, I do." Darcy's eyes met mine. "Hello, Darcy."

"I was friendly with his father at one time," Major Padgett said. "Owned a dashed fine stable of racehorses."

"Not anymore," Darcy said. "Joined the ranks of the paupers, I'm afraid."

"Haven't we all?" Padgett said, and there was bitterness in his voice. "Haven't we all? Forced to live on the proverbial crust these days. Bad times, what?"

"Look, I don't think Georgie should be up here," Darcy said. "Not a suitable place for a woman. Why don't I take her back to the castle?"

I was about to protest that I could stand the sight of a dead body as well as anybody else, but I saw Darcy's look. He was trying to tell me something.

"Good idea," Major Padgett said. "Take all the women back in the first of the motorcars, but we chaps should probably stick around until the local constable gets here. I don't know what he'll be able to do—decent fellow, but not the brightest—but one must do the right thing and there has been a death that needs to be officially ruled accidental."

It was just beginning to sink in that there had finally been a death. Several near misses over the course of a couple of days and now someone had actually died. It could, of course, have been an accident. With this kind of weather conditions someone could have been shot accidentally if he'd wandered off from the main group, lost his bearings in the mist and moved into the line of fire. But it was just one accident too many. And why Hugo, was completely beyond me. Not one of our set. Not someone I had even met before.

"All right," I said. "I don't suppose I can be of use up here anyway. I'll do more good making sure that tea is ready by the time the rest of you get back."

Darcy took my arm and led me away. "There's something funny going on here," he muttered to me. "Hugo Beasley-Bottome wasn't out ahead of the group. I saw him standing over to one side, next to the Prince of Wales."

I must have turned white and opened my mouth in surprise. "Well, that explains it, then, doesn't it?" I whispered. "Someone was aiming at the prince and missed and got Hugo by mistake. Or they thought that Hugo was the prince. They both have blond hair and are similarly dressed."

Darcy looked at me strangely. "You don't seem unduly surprised."

"I think one was expecting it to happen eventually." I stopped walking and turned to look at him. "I take it you are my contact here."

"Contact? Sweetheart, you know I'm all too willing to make any kind of contact with you at any time, but I really don't know what you're talking about."

"Then if you're not, who is?" I blurted out. I'd probably have made a rotten spy. I tend to say the wrong thing under duress.

"Do you mind clarifying before I decide you have gone potty?"

"Do you mean to tell me that you weren't sent here by Sir Jeremy?"

He looked at me warily. "I came up here because I thought you were going to be up here, if you want to know. And I had a chance for some free board and lodging with Paolo and friends. And you know I never turn down a free meal. Or the offer of a bed." He gave me a wicked grin. "And the only Sir Jeremy I know is head of some boring department of the Home Office." He was reading my face. "That's the one? You think I might be a pencil pusher for a civil servant?" He reached out and touched me lightly on the arm. The effect on me was unnerving, even in these circumstances. "Look here, Georgie, what's all this about? Did you know that someone was trying to kill the Prince of Wales?"

"I'm sorry, I can't tell you," I said. "I'm sworn to secrecy."

"You don't trust me?" He withdrew his hand from my arm. "I took a bullet for the king and queen, and you still don't trust me?"

"Of course I trust you," I said. "Only, Sir Jeremy told me that nobody was to know and that I'd find a contact working undercover at Balmoral."

"You thought that contact might be me?"

I nodded.

"Sorry to disappoint you," he said. "And this Sir Jeremy asked you to protect the Prince of Wales from a mad assassin, did he? Exactly what training do you have in that department?"

"No, he asked me to keep my eyes and ears open. And it's not just the Prince of Wales, Darcy. He suspects that someone is trying to kill the heirs to the throne. And now I've seen for myself, I have to agree with him."

"But why ask you?"

"Because he thinks it has to be one of us, not an outsider. And I can observe from the inside, so to speak."

"Interesting. So what have you observed so far?"

"Until now it's all been apparent accidents, nothing you could say was deliberate. There was Binky's foot caught in a trap. The lavatory cistern that crashed down on Babe . . ."

"I heard about that from her husband. Frightfully miffed, he was."

"Well, wouldn't you be if your wife was nearly killed by a flying lavatory tank?"

"Not the prettiest way to die. But I gather she survived to flush another day."

"It's not funny, Darcy," I said, going to slap his hand and then thinking better of it. "It fits the pattern of these accidents."

"So what other accidents have there been?"

"There was the rope that broke when I was climbing with Prince Siegfried—"

"What?" Darcy demanded.

I related the details of the incident. "And you think the rope was deliberately sabotaged?" Darcy demanded. He was no longer flippant. His face was grim.

"I haven't had a chance to look at it since the accident and I don't know if I could tell if a rope had been deliberately cut, but Siegfried said the rope had come over from Balmoral with Prince George and they'd laid it out to measure it and it was in fine condition."

"So do you think someone was trying to get rid of you or Prince Siegfried? I know which I'd choose," he added, making me smile.

"I was wondering whether it was Prince George that was the target. After all, he brought the rope, and that lavatory tank that fell on Babe—it was in the bathroom he used."

"I see." Darcy and I walked side by side in silence. "So I wonder who this contact of yours really is," he said at last. "And obviously your Sir Jeremy is not quite the boring cove I took him for."

"So tell me who exactly took part in this shoot."

"The king and three of his sons. The Duchess of York. Your mother and her fat German friend. Prince Siegfried. Major Padgett and a couple of older men who I believe are His Majesty's equerries. Then there were the outsiders: Gussie, myself, Hugo, your two hairy cousins—oh, and the American, Earl, turned up with a young Austrian count."

"That would be Fritzi," I said. "I'm surprised Earl is here. You'd have thought he'd be sitting at Babe's bedside."

"He said he couldn't turn down the chance to shoot with the king. He'll be able to dine on that story forever back in America."

"Yes, I suppose he will." My mind was already working overtime. Earl so keen to be part of the shoot, with Babe lying in hospital. That didn't sound like the devoted husband. Was it possible something quite different was going on here? What if Earl had rigged up that cistern to fall on his wife's head, and Hugo had seen him? I didn't think that Hugo would be beyond a bit of blackmail. Hugo's death might have nothing whatever to do with the royal line of succession.

The first of a line of shooting brakes appeared below us at the edge of the moor. Darcy put his hand on my arm and turned me to face him. "Look, Georgie. I don't like the sound of this at all. I don't want you involved in it in any way. I hope you weren't the intended target when that rope broke, but we can't rule out the possibility that you were. You are also part of the line of succession."

"Thirty-fourth, Darcy. If someone wanted to be king, he'd have to kill off an awful lot of people ahead of me. Somebody would catch him before he got to number one."

Darcy was still frowning. "I wonder what motive anyone would have. Surely nobody could believe that he'd wind up as king if he killed off everyone between him and the throne! Maybe it's a particular grudge against the Windsor family or royalty in general? Somebody the king could have pardoned and didn't?"

"That's a thought," I said, "but it rules out one element: it had to be somebody who was part of our set. An outsider would have been spotted creeping through Castle Rannoch, and how could an outsider have got to today's shoot? There's a wall around the estate to start with, isn't there, and he would certainly have been spotted."

"Not necessarily," Darcy said. "As for finding a way onto the estate, that's not hard. And there's plenty of woodland cover below the grouse moor and with today's mist I believe that someone could have crept close enough to shoot somebody."

"Did you see where he was shot?" I asked.

"In the back and neck. I got there a little late but that's what Padgett said."

"I wonder if you can kill somebody with a grouse gun," I said. "Surely those little pellets couldn't kill a person, could they?"

"If one of them hit the right spot, it could. If it struck an artery in the neck, for example. There was a lot of blood around."

"So could you tell if it was pellets or a single bullet hole?"

Darcy shook his head. "When we saw that he was already dead we left him where he was. Didn't want to tamper with evidence until the police got here."

"So we should know pretty soon whether it was one of the party with his grouse gun, or an outsider with a different type of weapon."

"Are you thinking of joining the police force?" he asked, looking amused for a moment. "A nice, well-bred girl like you is not supposed to discuss weapons without feeling faint."

"That's rubbish and you know it," I said. "Think of all the nice, well-bred girls who volunteered as nurses in the Great War and saw the most unimaginable horrors without fainting."

"That's true enough, I suppose," he said, "but I'd be much happier if you didn't stick your nose into this any further and you stayed safely at home. At least now there will be a police investigation, we hope. Something might come out that we hadn't suspected: perhaps one of the beaters with a good motive?"

"If it was a beater then Hugo would have been shot in the chest, not the back," I pointed out.

"You know what I'm getting at—someone who works his way into royal service with the goal of harming the family."

"Sir Jeremy said they had done extensive background checks and come up empty. He said it had to be one of us."

Darcy shook his head. "We were standing in little groups, but pretty much in a line. And we had a line of beaters out in front of us. And gillies behind us with the dogs. And when you think about it, who the deuce among us would want to kill? The only people I know nothing about are the American and the Austrian count."

"Would you have noticed if anyone had dropped back?"

Darcy shook his head. "Can't say I would. When you're intent on waiting for the next grouse to be flushed you don't look around."

We had reached the cars. Darcy took my hands in his. "You go on back to the house. I should stay with the shooting party until the police arrive. And Georgie, don't go off on your own. Stay with the queen and the ladies, understand? The police will be coming now. This is in their hands."

We stood there for a moment, holding hands, just looking at each other.

"I owe you an apology," I said. "I felt sure you were the one who tipped off Sir William to my stupid blunder."

He actually blushed. "Ah well, I'm afraid that was me."

"See. I knew it." I tried to snatch my hands away. He held on tightly.

"Listen, Georgie, the only reason I called him was to tell him there had been a horrible mistake and if the press got wind of anything, he was to tell them not to print. I was protecting you, nothing more."

"I see. Then you weren't part of their nefarious scheme to trick me into coming to Scotland and do their dirty work for them?"

"I promise you I wasn't."

We looked at each other again. "And did you really come to Scotland just to be near me?"

He grinned. "I knew you were due at Balmoral soon, so I thought I'd take my chances."

I couldn't help thinking how wonderful he looked standing there with the breeze ruffling his untidy dark curls. I longed to run my hands through them. I longed to—I wrenched my thoughts back to the current problem.

"You'd better get going," he said. "I shouldn't leave them up there alone. They'll mess everything up. Take care, won't you?" He leaned forward to kiss me.

"Oh, good, there they are." A woman's voice rang out. We looked up to see the Duchess of York hurrying down the hillside with my mother in tow. "Don't leave without us," she called.

We waited patiently until they reached us. "You're about to go back to the house, are you?" the duchess continued. "Jolly good. Your poor mama was feeling quite faint and I felt that I should get back to my daughters. This is the sort of thing they should hear directly from me, not from palace gossip. Elizabeth is very sensitive, you know. I don't want them upset."

I nodded. "I saw them a little while ago, ma'am. Elizabeth wants me to go riding with her."

"Oh, she'd love that, if you have the time. She gets so frustrated at having to go slowly beside Margaret and the groom, and she really is turning into a splendid little horsewoman."

"I'll come over tomorrow, if you like. It may be better if she's away from the castle if the police are going to be there again."

The duchess looked surprised. "The police? Why would they be at the castle?"

"There has been a death," I said.

"Yes, I know, but an accidental shooting. It's unfortunate and very sad for the poor young man but hardly a matter for the police."

I was going to remark that grouse are usually shot in the air so unless Hugo had the power of levitation he was unlikely to be in the line of fire, but then I saw Darcy's warning glance and kept quiet. The chauffeur had come around and helped the duchess into the backseat. My mother hopped in beside her. I looked back at Darcy as I climbed in.

"Take care of yourself," he said.

Chapter 25

We were a subdued little group who took tea in the sitting room at Balmoral later that afternoon. The men had arrived back, grumbling about the day's shoot being ruined and who had invited a boy like that who had no idea of the rules of shooting etiquette. I noticed that Darcy was no longer among them. Neither was Major Padgett, nor were Earl and Fritzi. I looked around the assembled company: the king and queen, their older companions, their sons, my cousins, Siegfried, Gussie, my mother and Max. Surely nobody here could have shot Hugo, and certainly none of the above was my contact from the special branch.

I noticed the tragedy hadn't put them off their tea. There was the usual delightful assortment of teatime favorites on the low tables—hot buttered crumpets, warm scones with cream and jam, freshly baked shortbread, slices of Dundee cake, a Victoria sponge. Maids went among us, refilling teacups. The men were tucking in with relish. Much as I adored such things and had been deprived of them recently, I couldn't bring myself to eat more than a couple of bites. I hoped Darcy made the local constabulary see the possibility that this was murder and not an accident and that extra precautions should be taken around the royal family.

I waited around for a while to see if Darcy would join us or if there were any developments with the police. I rather feared that the local constabulary would be so in awe of the participants in this drama that they would be quick to write it off as an accidental death. And maybe it was. I hoped that Darcy would at least suggest to the police that they bring in an inspector from Aberdeen. Suddenly I wanted to be away from the stifling atmosphere of that sitting room. I took my leave and drove back to Castle Rannoch—more slowly this time. I didn't want to risk running into Paolo, the racing maniac, again. As I turned onto the stretch of road that ran beside the loch I saw there was activity at the landing stage and I pulled off to see what was happening. The blue speedboat was in the water, a few yards offshore, with several people working on it. Belinda was sitting with Conchita on the dock, the latter sporting a rather daring halter top and shorts. Belinda was also wearing shorts and their bare toes dangled in the water. It was a delightfully innocent scene. I got out and went over to join them.

"Having fun?" I asked.

"Oh, oodles of fun, buckets of fun," Belinda said, rolling her eyes. "Conchita and I were just agreeing we can't remember when we had a more scintillating day."

"Is there anything more boring than men who talk about nothing but machines?" Conchita agreed. "First Darcy and Augustus go off and leave us, in order to shoot poor little birds, and then Paolo and the American and Ronny do nothing but talk about motors and propellers and equally boring things. We were so glad when the weather improved and at least Belinda and I could sunbathe, but the boys forgot to bring any deck chairs."

"An altogether annoying day," Belinda said. "Were you part of the shoot at Balmoral?"

"I was over there, paying my respects to the queen, but I didn't shoot with them. And I'm rather glad I didn't join them because there was a horrible tragedy. You remember Hugo Beasley-Bottome? He was shot and killed."

"*Madre de Dios,*" Conchita said, and crossed herself.

"How utterly awful," Belinda said. "Frankly I thought he was a frightful bore and a little too greasy, but he didn't deserve to die. Who shot him?"

"They don't know. The theory is that he wandered ahead in the mist and into the line of fire."

"Horrible." Belinda shuddered. "What a dope he was. You'd think someone would have basic common sense about staying with the group, wouldn't you?"

I nodded. Belinda looked at Conchita. "I don't suppose Ronny's heard yet," she said.

"She'll probably be relieved," Conchita replied callously. "She didn't like that he make cow eyes at her all the time. And he was too young for her. Almost cradle snatching, she said."

"Where is Ronny?" I asked.

Belinda nodded. "In the boat. Where else. Honestly, she enjoys tinkering with motors like a man. And she's trying to persuade Paolo to let her have a go at driving the wretched thing."

"She'd probably be very good at it," I said. "We've watched her land planes."

"I'm sure she'd be fabulous, but you know Paolo. He's not about to share his new toy, even if he's not paying for it."

Conchita stood up, stretching luxuriantly like a cat. "I have had enough of this. I go back to the house to take a nap. I thought racing motorboats would be exciting, but it is very boring. And no interesting men around."

"There's that little American in the boat," Belinda said with a smirk.

"Him? He would not know what to do with a real woman if he found her in his bed. Darcy—he would know, but I do not think I interest him."

"There's always Gussie," I said, cheered by the knowledge that Darcy had not taken advantage of Conchita's being ready, willing and very able. "He's rich and available."

"Then you have him," Conchita snapped. "Englishmen make the most hopeless lovers. They make love as if they are playing rugby, with horrible grunting noises. And they do not even consider that a woman likes to enjoy it too." She ran her hands over her swimsuit in a very suggestive gesture, then turned her back on us and started to walk away down the lakeside.

"She's sulking because Darcy turned her down," Belinda said. "I hope you're not going to let him slip through your fingers this time, Georgie. He really is keen on you, you know. He has to be. Not many men would turn down such an open invitation from someone like Conchita—especially since she is so filthy rich."

"I don't want to let him slip through my fingers, believe me," I said. I took Conchita's place on the dock beside her. "So are you still madly in love with Paolo?"

She shrugged and kicked her feet up and down in the water. "I don't think I was ever madly in love. Madly in lust, maybe. And I have to confess the sex is heavenly, and I love the excitement of all that speed."

I hesitated, wondering if I should share my suspicions. After all, he had been driving away from Balmoral in an awful hurry. "You should be careful about all that speed," I said at last. "He nearly ran me off the road this morning."

"I know. He doesn't think anybody has the right to be on the road but him. Completely selfish, like most men. And he has these odd moments of Catholic guilt—mumbles about needing to go to confession and worries about spending hundreds of years in purgatory. They are a funny lot, aren't they?"

"So the bloom has gone off the rose, has it?" I smiled.

"To tell you the truth, I don't quite like playing second fiddle to a boat. I mean, darling, since we've been up here he has hardly noticed I'm alive. Except for at night, of course, but then he's been working so hard all day that he doesn't have the energy to do it more than once. And he's talking about needing to go back to his fiancée for her birthday."

"I'm glad," I said.

"Glad he's going back to his fiancée?"

"Glad you haven't fallen for him in a big way. I wouldn't want to see you get hurt."

"Don't worry about me." She patted my knee. "I'm a survivor, Georgie. I'm like a cat. I always land on my feet like your mama."

"I don't want you to end up like my mama."

She shrugged. "It's not such a bad life she's had. At least she's never been bored, and boredom is what I dread more than anything. I'm terrified if I got married that I'd be stuck on some dreary country estate and my main excitement of the day would be picking roses and hearing the children recite their party pieces at teatime."

"You obviously need to marry someone rich," I said, "then you can have houses all over the place and flit from one to the other."

"And keep a lover in each place." Her eyes positively twinkled. Then she frowned, staring past me at the road. "I didn't know the local policeman had a car," she said. "I thought they were only issued bikes."

"He does only have a bike," I said, turning to follow her gaze. "I expect that's the plainclothes boys from Aberdeen coming to examine the scene of the shooting at Balmoral."

"In which case, why are they driving away from Balmoral?" she asked.

"Good point. Perhaps they are heading toward Castle Rannoch to talk to me. I should let them know I'm here."

But as I stood up, the police car had already come off the tarmacadam and was crunching over the gravel toward the dock. Two men got out, both of them plainclothes detectives, wearing macks and trilby hats in the time-honored tradition. I didn't recognize either of them—not that I've had much to do with local police. I was about to say, "Can I help you?" when one of them called out, "We're looking for Count Paolo di Martini. Either of you girls know if he's around here?"

My hackles rose a trifle at being addressed as "you girls."

"You'll find him out in that blue boat," I said coldly.

"What do you want him for?" Belinda asked, but they walked past her as if she didn't exist. Out at the end of the dock they shouted Paolo's name and gestured that he should come to shore.

"Go away," Paolo called. "Can't you see that I'm busy?"

"Detective Inspector Manson, Metropolitan Police," one of them shouted, and held up his warrant card. "We'd like to speak to you imme-diately, if you don't mind, sir."

"I do mind," Paolo said.

"Then let me rephrase it. Signor di Martini, we would like you to help us with our inquiries."

"Go to hell," Paolo said.

"In which case you leave me no alternative. Paolo di Martini, you are under arrest."

"What? What are you talking about?"

I don't know how long the shouting might have gone on if Ronny hadn't got the motor started and brought the boat to the dock.

"What nonsense is this?" Paolo demanded as he scrambled ashore.

"Paolo di Martini, I arrest you in the name of the law for the man-slaughter of Mavis Pugh."

Paolo looked almost amused. "Who in God's name is Mavis Pugh? I have never heard of her."

Ronny gave a little cry and leaped ashore after him. "It was you, Paolo. You ran her down. You horrid, callous beast. How could you do such a thing?" She flung herself at him as if she was about to strike him.

Paolo put up his arms to defend himself. "But I do not know this per-son." He looked bewildered and scared now. "What is this? I am innocent. Belinda, tell them I am innocent. You say I have killed someone? Is not possible."

"You own a motorcycle, do you not? A motorcycle that we found in your hangar at Croydon Aerodrome?"

"Yes, but . . ."

"On that motorcycle we found conclusive evidence linking you to the hit-and-run death of a young woman. We found traces of her hair and fiber from her jacket on your tires and frame. Now I should warn you that you have the right to remain silent, and anything you say can be used as evidence against you. So if you'll just come with us without a fuss." He put a big hand on Paolo's arm.

"No. There is a mistake. I never run down a person. Never in my life."

"If you're indeed innocent I'm sure it will all be sorted out quite easily, sir." He steered Paolo toward the waiting car and opened the back door for him. "In you go, sir."

"Belinda, don't let them take me away!" Paolo shot Belinda a frightened look as the car door closed on him.

Belinda looked utterly stunned. "Oh, God, Georgie. This is awful. I should do something. You know about things like this. What can I do?"

"Belinda, you've seen the way he drives. Don't you think it's possible that he's guilty? Remember he almost ran me down at your mews."

"But he didn't run you down, did he? That's the point. He drives fast but he has a racing driver's reflexes. And I'm sure he'd never hit somebody and then drive off without stopping. He's not like that. He's a gentleman." I could see she was fighting back tears. It was the first time I had ever seen Belinda not composed and in control of herself.

"Come up to the castle and have some tea," I said gently. She shook her head.

"No, I have to get back to the house so I can be there in case he telephones for me."

"Come on, I'll take you back to where you're staying," Ronny said. "I have my car here. I'm sure Digby can put the covers on the boat, can't you, old thing?" She smiled at the young American, who was standing beside her, staring openmouthed with shock.

"Do you want me to come with you?" I asked.

Before she could answer we heard the sound of running footsteps and a figure could be seen racing up the road toward us. As it neared it revealed itself to be a figure not cut out for such activity: round, short, stubby little legs. It was Godfrey Beverley.

"My dears, such excitement," he said. "Was that really a police motorcar? I thought I could spot policemen a mile away. They call it plainclothes but they all wear identical macks, don't they? And that was never that handsome Italian count they were dragging away, was it? I presume it was to do with the shooting accident."

"Shooting, what shooting?" Ronny asked sharply.

"My dears, haven't you heard? Someone was accidentally shot at Balmoral today. I was up there, tramping around a little myself, and now the place is absolutely crawling with police."

"Who was shot?" Ronny snapped.

"Some young man, I gather. Nobody I had heard of before. Rumor has it that he was staying with you at Castle Rannoch, Lady Georgiana. Hugo something?"

"Oh no." Ronny put her hand to her mouth. "Not Hugo. How awful. I was so horrid to him and he was so potty about me. Now I feel like a rat."

"And they've arrested the count for it, have they?" Godfrey's eyes were positively bulging. "And I was on the spot. My dears, what a coup."

"They haven't arrested the count for it," I said coldly. "They want him to help them with something quite different. A little matter in London. They weren't even local police."

"Oh, I see. Well, no matter."

Ronny put an arm around Belinda. "Let's go, shall we? I can't bear it here another second."

"And I must get back to the castle," I said. "Please excuse me."

Godfrey was staring down the road in the direction of Balmoral as Ronny and Belinda walked up to Ronny's weathered old Morris Cowley. "Now that was strange," he said.

"What was?"

"Two guns," he said. "Why would one need two guns?"

$\mathcal{C}hapter$ 26

A COTTAGE AND THEN A LOCHSIDE
AUGUST 20

As soon as I arrived back at the castle I put the estate car away and was
going up the front steps when I decided instead to find Granddad. I needed
someone solid and unflappable at this moment. The last few days had all
been too much excitement. Perhaps Granddad and I could even have a
simple dinner together at the cottage, away from the hustle and bustle and
the Simpsons and the cousins and Fig. I almost broke into a run as the cottages came into sight on the other side of the walled kitchen garden.

Granddad was sitting outside with a cup of tea beside him. He stood
up as I came toward him. "This is the life, ain't it? Nice fresh air, good cup
of tea. I can just feel these old lungs getting better already."

"I'm glad," I said.

"The pot's still warm," he said. "Fancy a cuppa yourself, love?"

"Yes, I would, actually."

He looked at me critically. "You're looking decidedly peaky. Don't tell
me something went wrong today?"

"Horribly wrong." I recounted the whole thing. "So it seems to me that
someone was aiming at the Prince of Wales," I said. "They were standing
quite close to each other and they would have looked awfully similar from
behind. Because nobody would have wanted to kill Hugo. He's nothing to
do with the royal family."

"And you are sure this really wasn't an accident?" He looked up from pouring hot tea into a coarse earthenware cup decorated in blue and white stripes.

"How could anyone mistake Hugo for a grouse? It was misty, but surely anyone could have made out the shape of a person through the mist. And after everything else that has happened, I can only conclude the shooting was quite deliberate. Darcy thinks so too."

"Oh, so he's here, is he?" Granddad gave me one of his cheeky Cockney smiles. "Well, that should make you perk up."

"It would if I weren't so horribly afraid. I was supposed to keep my eyes and ears open, and so far I've done nothing except almost get killed. And if the special branch sent up a man of their own, then he's lying really low." I took a long drink of tea. It was sweeter, stronger and milkier than I usually have it but it felt most reassuring.

"Maybe he's among the servants and just hasn't found a way to talk to you yet," Granddad said. "And anyway, I presume the police have been called in?"

I nodded.

"Well, unless they are complete fools up here in Scotland, they'll be able to tell if foul play has taken place. And it's now out of your hands, thank God. Since it's Balmoral, they'll no doubt send up some bigwig in the police force, so you could always have a word with him—let him know what's been going on. Then they'll conduct their inquiry and you stay out of it."

"Yes," I said. "That will be wonderful."

"How about a freshly baked scone, ducks?" Granddad asked.

"Wonderful. Did they send some down from the kitchen?"

"No. They sent down enough stuff to feed an army but the scones came from my next-door neighbor, your old nanny."

"Did they? How sweet of her."

"Apparently she's a really good cook, and what's more, she loves to cook. In fact she's making me a meat pie tonight. I can see I'm going to be fatter than a pig if I don't get out and walk." Then he made a face. "I suppose you're thinking that you brought me up here to help you, but frankly I don't see what help I could be."

"You could talk to servants," I said. "You could get pally with the gun bearers."

He chuckled sadly. "I stick out like a sore thumb up here, my love. No Scottish gun bearer is going to get pally with a bloke from the Smoke."

I realized this was probably true, but he added, "Besides, like I told you, you're off the hook. It's now in the hands of the police, and about time too."

Then his face lit up. "Tell yer what. Why don't you join us for a bite of supper?"

"I wasn't invited," I said.

"The more the merrier."

"Perhaps Nanny has set her cap at you and won't welcome the intrusion."

"Listen, ducks." He grinned. "Mrs. 'Uggins next door set her cap at me long ago and I ain't got snared yet, 'ave I? You come along and join us. Your old nanny will be thrilled to pieces. You mark my words."

Of course he was right. Nanny positively beamed throughout the meal. I had sent word back to the castle that I wouldn't be joining the family for dinner, then I'd changed out of my trousers into a simple silk dress. At least I thought it was a simple silk dress until I saw their faces.

"Blimey, this ain't Buckingham Palace, you know," Granddad said, looking at Nanny and laughing.

"We don't usually dress for dinner in the cottages, but we're very flattered that you've done so," Nanny said. "At least I know I brought you up with good manners."

"I only changed out of dirty old trousers," I said. "And whatever you are cooking smells heavenly."

I returned to the castle just as the last of the daylight was fading, feeling replete and content. I don't think I had ever been in a room with two people who loved me before. As soon as I stepped into the front hall, Hamilton appeared. "Oh, my lady, you've just had a visitor. The Honorable Darcy O'Mara."

"Where is he?" I looked around expecting him to emerge from the shadows.

"He left again. We told him that you were dining out and he said that he couldn't stay."

"How long ago was this?" I asked.

"About half an hour, my lady."

I thanked him as patiently as I could, kicking myself for not mentioning that I was dining at the cottage with Nanny. Then I ran back out into the night. I realized I had little hope of catching him, but I roused the chauffeur and had him bring out the estate car for me. Then I drove into the night.

"This is ridiculous," I said to myself. "I shouldn't be chasing a man. Besides, he'll be back at the house across the loch by now."

Then, just as I reached the loch, I spotted someone going down to the jetty. I parked the car and jumped out.

"Darcy?" I called.

My voice echoed back from the hills, unnaturally loud in the evening stillness. He started at the sound of his name, then came toward me, a big smile on his face.

"They said you'd gone out. Were they just keeping me away because I didn't look suitable? I had to mention that I was the son of a peer to stop your butler from looking down his nose at me."

I laughed. "Yes, he can be awfully snooty at times. I was having supper with my old nanny and my grandfather in one of the cottages."

We stood there, looking at each other.

"What are you doing on the dock?" I asked.

"I have no car and I couldn't seem to borrow one tonight. So I rowed across and then walked."

"That's a long walk."

"I just wanted to make sure you were all right."

"I'm very well, thank you."

"That's good. Look, Georgie, I want you to be careful because I may have to go away for a while."

"Oh." My voice obviously conveyed my disappointment.

"I don't think the local police are going to investigate Hugo's death," he said. "Major Padgett has persuaded them to treat it as an accidental shooting, so that the royal party is not upset any further. His thought is that they can't risk embarrassing a member of the royal family, in case one of them was accidentally responsible for the fatal shot. The police agreed that nothing could be gained by trying to find out who pulled the trigger."

"I see. So we're back to square one."

"So I'm going to have a word with those who might be persuaded to take this further, including your Sir Jeremy." He saw me about to speak. "Oh, don't worry, I won't divulge that you spilled the beans to me."

"I'm glad you're doing that. Someone has to. So what has happened to Hugo's body? Won't there be a medical examination to determine how he died?"

"There will. But if it just shows that an unlucky pellet struck an artery, then it will only affirm that the shooting was a horrible accident, won't it?"

"Yes, I suppose it will."

"Anyway, let's hope someone will risk rocking the boat and start a proper investigation." He reached out and touched my cheek. "And in the meantime, please don't do anything to put yourself in harm's way. No climbing or shooting or any unsafe pursuit, do you hear?"

"Very good, sir," I said.

He laughed and ran his hand down my cheek. "I have to go. I've a taxi coming to take me to the station. I'll be back as soon as I can."

I nodded. His touch on my cheek made me feel as if I was going to cry. Then he pulled me toward him and kissed me, full and hard on the mouth.

"That's a first installment," he said, breaking away rapidly. "More to come later."

Then he ran down the dock and lowered himself into a rowing boat. I heard the splash of oars as he pulled away.

Chapter 27

The piper must have been told that he need no longer pipe in the day because it was fully daylight when I awoke to a tap on my bedroom door. I expected it to be Maggie with the tea tray and looked up, bleary eyed. Instead of Maggie's sturdy figure in a white apron, I focused on a frock coat and sat up. It was Hamilton.

"I'm sorry to wake you, my lady, but there is a gentleman to see you."

"A gentleman?" I remembered that he had referred to Granddad as "a person." So this was someone from the upper class then.

"Yes, my lady. He presented his card. Sir Jeremy Danville from London. He said it was urgent."

"Thank you, Hamilton. Please put him in the morning room and tell him that I'll be down as soon as I can."

"Very good, my lady." He gave a slight bow and went to back away, then turned to me again. "Strange men turning up at the crack of dawn. Will this be an ongoing occurrence, do you think, my lady?"

"Let's hope not," I said, laughing.

I washed, dressed and went downstairs. Sir Jeremy looked as if he was suffering from the effects of taking the night train. There were bags under his eyes and his hair wasn't quite as perfectly groomed as the last time I had seen him. He stood up smartly as I came in.

"Lady Georgiana. I'm so sorry to disturb you at this early hour, but I took the night train as soon as I heard the news."

"I'm so glad you're here," I said. "Would you like some breakfast or should we go somewhere where we can talk privately?"

"A cup of coffee would be most welcome, but I think we should talk as soon as possible. Time may be of the essence."

I ordered a pot of coffee and some toast to be sent to Binky's study then ushered Sir Jeremy inside.

"You heard about the unfortunate shooting death, of course."

"I arrived on the scene just after it had happened," I said. "Well, now we have conclusive proof of your suspicions, don't we? Somebody was obviously trying to kill the Prince of Wales and mistook Hugo Beasley-Bottome for him from behind."

"Is that what you think?" Sir Jeremy asked, looking at me strangely.

"What else should I think?"

"Did BB get a chance to speak with you? Did he share any suspicions? Because it's my feeling that someone shot him deliberately because he had found out something important."

"Hugo, something important?"

"So he didn't have a chance to share his suspicions with you? I thought it would be easier if he were staying at Castle Rannoch."

"Oh no," I said as light dawned. "Are you trying to tell me that Hugo was the contact you placed up here?"

"Of course. I assumed he would have had a chance to speak with you by now."

"Oh, dear," I said. "He did try, several times, but I thought, you know, he was just being fresh. He came across as a young man with an eye for the ladies. I thought he was just trying to get me alone for—entirely different reasons." I could feel my face turning red.

Sir Jeremy sighed. "As you say, 'oh, dear.' He did tend to play up the young wastrel image, didn't he? He thought it was the perfect cover. 'Everyone thinks I'm a harmless, spoiled idiot,' he used to say."

"And you think that he had made an important discovery so someone had to silence him?" I felt a shiver running through my body. If someone had killed Hugo then he would have no compunction about killing me, if he thought Hugo had told me anything. Did he know I had been sent here to spy? Then of course it came to me that the broken rope on the climb might not have been intended for Prince George or someone else at all. It might have been intended for me. And if it hadn't snagged on that little tree on the outcropping, I'd have been dead by now.

There was a knock at the door and one of the maids came in with a tray of coffee and freshly baked toasted buns. "Cook says she'd just got them out of the oven so she thought you'd like them better than toast," she said, placing the tray on a side table. "She remembered you were always fond of her buns."

"Thank you." I felt tears threatening to come. It was the ridiculous contrast of normality—a home where I should feel safe and the knowledge that nothing was safe anymore.

I poured coffee and Sir Jeremy sighed with pleasure as he took his first bite of the toasted bun. "One misses so much living in a service apartment in London," he said. "My man is adequate in the cooking department but if I want more than a boiled egg I have to go to my club."

"To get back to Hugo," I said. "Do you have any idea what he might have discovered? Had he shared any suspicions at all?"

He shook his head. "Nothing. He'd been up and down between London and Scotland several times this summer but gave me no indication he was onto anything at all."

"That's too bad," I said. "As I say, I arrived on the scene not long after he had been shot. I saw the members of that shoot. There was nobody present who could possibly have shot Hugo. Apart from an American and an Austrian count, I know everybody."

Sir Jeremy wiped his mouth fastidiously. "In my long career one thing I have learned is that murderers are remarkably good at concealing their true personalities. I can tell you of several brutal serial murderers who were described as good family men, even by their wives. However, I have been supplied with the list of those present and we will be trying to match guns and fingerprints. I fear it will be a thankless task, however."

"Surely you can't match bird shot to any particular shotgun," I said.

"Quite right," he said. "Only BB wasn't actually killed by bird shot."

"He wasn't?"

"No. The killer was crafty, Lady Georgiana. He fired a single shot, from a rifle, we suspect, to bring down his quarry, then he fired his shotgun at close range to finish him off and make it seem as if it was this that struck an artery and killed BB."

"Goodness," I said. "That's interesting. So that's what Godfrey Beverley meant."

"Godfrey Beverley? The gossip chappy?"

"Yes, he's staying in the area. He mentioned something about why anyone would need two guns. Do you think he might have seen something important?"

"I'll check him out. Do you know where he's staying?"

"At a nearby inn. That's all I know. It shouldn't be too hard. There aren't many inns around here."

"I'll put men onto it, then."

"And all you have to do is look for a rifle that's been fired recently."

"As you say, 'all we have to do,' " he echoed dryly. "I doubt that the killer will just leave the rifle out for inspection, and it won't be easy to gain permission to search the rooms of certain royal personages."

I stared at him, coffee cup poised in midair. "Surely you can't think that a member of the royal family could have done this?"

"I have to consider everybody on the scene as a possible suspect," he said. "Regardless of birth."

"Golly," I said, before I remembered that it made me sound like a schoolgirl. Note to self: Work on developing more sophisticated means of exclamation.

Sir Jeremy put down his own cup and stood up. "What I would like to do now, if you don't mind, my lady, is to take a look at BB's room."

"Certainly," I said. "If you'll come this way. I'm not sure which one it was but one of the servants can tell us."

I led him up the central staircase. He nodded in satisfaction at the swords, shields, banners and stags' heads on the walls. "None of this namby-pamby stuff," he commented.

"No, we Rannochs have been killing people very successfully for generations," I said.

He gave me a quizzical half smile. "So am I to consider that a relative of yours might be an ideal suspect?"

"Nothing to gain," I said. "Binky's thirty-second in line. I don't think he's up to bumping off thirty-one people. Besides, he's laid up with a mangled ankle." And I related the details.

Sir Jeremy frowned. "And you think this could be related to our investigation?"

"I'm almost sure of it," I said. "I don't know if you've met my brother, but he's a harmless, likeable chap. I'm sure he has no enemies. The only thing that differentiates him from the man in the street is that he happens to be a duke and cousin to the king."

"But not close enough to the throne to make any difference," Sir Jeremy said. "So someone who has a grudge against those with any amount of royal blood—is that what we should be looking for?"

"Possibly," I said.

I led him to the end of a long hallway and opened the door. As in all rooms at Castle Rannoch, the wind was swirling from an open window. It was a brisk morning and clouds were racing across the sky. Either Hugo was a tidy person or the maid had been in. His dressing gown lay across his eiderdown; his slippers were at the foot of his bed. His silver-backed brushes and shaving things were on the chest of drawers. But there was no hint as to the personality of the man who occupied the room. Sir Jeremy opened drawers, then closed them again.

"Nothing," he said. Then he bent and looked under the bed. "Aha." He pulled out a briefcase and tipped the contents onto the bed. There was a copy of *Horse and Hound*, train tickets and a small notebook. Sir Jeremy opened it expectantly, then he groaned. "Look at this," he said.

Several pages that had clearly been written on had been ripped from the book. The remaining pages were blank.

"Someone got here first," he said.

I stared at him. "You don't think someone came into this room and tore pages from his notebook?"

"That's exactly what I think."

"But that's impossible. There's nobody in the castle at the moment except for the Simpsons, Prince Siegfried and my two cousins, and it wouldn't be them."

"Prince Siegfried? Of Romania?"

I nodded.

"A friend of the family?"

"I rather think the queen is matchmaking," I said. "She wants me to marry him."

"But you're not keen?"

"Absolutely not."

"And why should Prince Siegfried not be on our list of suspects?"

"He's wet and harmless, I'm sure," I said. But even as I said it I remembered the climbing accident. Siegfried was on the spot. But why tamper with a rope he was using himself?

Sir Jeremy walked over to the window and looked out. "We're a long way up," he said, "but it wouldn't be impossible for someone to reach this room from the outside. He could climb up the ivy with very little risk of being seen."

I stood behind him and looked out. "A long climb," I said, "and a risky one."

"We've seen this as a person who takes risks," he said. "It took an enormous amount of gall to wait for the perfect moment to shoot someone, then calmly walk up to him and deliver the second shot."

"Yes," I said, and shivered again.

We continued to search the room but there was nothing more of interest, apart from a postcard Hugo had written to his mother. *Having a fine time in Scotland. See you soon, I hope.*

I put it back on the dressing table.

Chapter 28

Sir Jeremy took his leave soon after, saying that he had an appointment with the Aberdeenshire police at Balmoral. He'd be taking a room at the inn in Braemar, to be on hand, and I could always leave a message for him there.

"But this is in the hands of the police now," he added as I escorted him down to the front door. "They'll take fingerprints and with any luck the right guns will turn up. And we're putting extra men to guard the members of the royal family."

I watched him drive away, feeling empty and frightened. I wished that Darcy hadn't gone. My grandfather was in a cottage nearby but this case was out of his league. He couldn't barge into Balmoral and find a member of my social set who was trying to kill members of the royal family.

Then I stopped to think about this. Had I witnessed, actually witnessed personally, anyone trying to kill members of the royal family? The tumbling lavatory, the broken rope were not necessarily meant for Prince George. Hugo had possibly been shot quite deliberately because of what he had found out. So who had done something he needed to keep concealed? Of course my thoughts went straight to Paolo. He loved anything risky. He was currently under arrest for running down a helpless servant girl. I remembered how fast he was driving away from Balmoral yesterday. Had he shot Hugo and then gone to Castle Rannoch to retrieve Hugo's notes before showing up at the boat, as cool as a cucumber?

I went out of the front door and started to walk across the park. A herd of fallow deer stood in dappled shadows. At the sound of my footsteps they looked up and darted away. I watched them bounding away and wondered how it would be if one always had to live on the lookout for predators. I identified with them at this moment. My thoughts moved on, replaying everything that had happened since I came to Scotland. I cringed with embarrassment as I remembered Hugo trying to talk to me. He had tried to get me into the laird's lug—the one place where we had no chance of being overheard.

I froze on the spot. The laird's lug—was it possible that he had left something there for me to find? I ran back to the house and through the great hall, then pushed aside a tapestry in the darkened hallway beyond. The small door in the wall opened and I felt my way up the steps into the small round chamber. It was only when the door closed behind me, plunging me into complete darkness, that I realized that of course there was no electric light. I was seized by a sudden and irrational fear that the killer would be waiting for me and I half stumbled, half slithered back down the stairs. I couldn't find the doorknob for a moment and was about to hammer on the door when my fingers closed around it. I pushed out past the tapestry, nearly giving one of the maids a heart attack.

"Oh, my lady, you gave me such a fright," she gasped. "I had no idea there was a door there. Oh, my goodness." And she had to lean against the wall with her hand over her heart.

"Go and have a cup of tea, Jinty," I said. "I'm sorry. I didn't mean to startle you."

Off she went and I went to find a candle and matches. Luckily they were not hard to locate in a place where frequent power cuts were the norm during bad weather. I also brought with me a doorstop and propped the door open. The candlelight flickered from the stone walls as I went into the chamber. Of course it was quite empty. It most resembled a prison cell, with a stone bench running around the wall and the ceiling tapering to a vault just above my head. Set into the wall were narrow slits that allowed past lairds to listen in to conversations in the rooms on the other side— presumably to see if anyone was plotting to assassinate him.

I felt silly about my panic and was about to leave when I noticed the map, lying on the bench in the far corner. I picked it up. It was a road map of central Scotland, put out by the RAC. Someone had drawn a circle extending about twenty miles out around the Balmoral area and written the words: *CastleCraig? Gleneagles? Dofc?* The last looked as if he had left a word unfinished.

I stood staring at it in the flickering candlelight. Had this map lain in the laird's lug for ages, left by someone who wanted to do a bit of rambling through the glens, or had Hugo left it for me to find? The latter seemed a bit far-fetched until I looked down at the floor and noticed that it hadn't been swept for some time and that there were signs of fresh footprints from a shoe bigger than mine. A man had been in here recently.

Leaving, I shut the door behind me and smoothed the tapestry into place, and encountered Hamilton coming out of the servants' quarters. I asked him about the names.

"Castle Craig? Gleneagles? Dof-something? No, I can't say I've heard of any of those places."

"So you don't think they are around here?"

"They are not any towns with which I'm familiar, my lady," he repeated.

I wasn't sure what to do next. Pass on the information to Sir Jeremy, I supposed. I also wondered what Fig would say if I requested the use of a car again. All that petrol to and from Balmoral would be beginning to add up. As I came into the great hall, I heard the sound of voices coming from the breakfast room.

"And I rather think they've gone out riding." It was Fig's voice, sounding annoyed.

But her words triggered a memory: I had promised Princess Elizabeth that I would take her out riding today. I had a perfect excuse to return to Balmoral and to pass on my information to Sir Jeremy. I went upstairs to change into my jodhpurs and hacking jacket, then I grabbed the remaining bun from the plate in Binky's study and went out to find a motorcar.

"I am most happy to drive you, my lady," our chauffeur said in a peeved voice when I asked for the keys.

"I really think you should be available in case Their Graces require you," I said diplomatically. "Besides, it's a rare treat for me to be able to drive myself."

"I understand, my lady." He handed me the keys and I climbed into the estate car. The moment I turned out of the carriage court I remembered that I hadn't visited my grandfather yet. I should at least pop in to see him before I left. He'd be happy to know I was doing something harmless like going out riding with a princess. I pulled off the drive and left the estate car under the shade of a horse chestnut tree, then crossed the kitchen garden to the cottage.

I was just passing the runner beans when I had a brilliant idea: I broke into a run and arrived at Granddad's cottage out of breath.

"Where's the fire?" he asked.

"What fire?"

"You came bursting in here like all the 'ounds of 'ell were after you," he said. "Don't tell me something else 'as 'appened."

"No, but I've just had a wonderful idea. I'm about to motor over to Balmoral. I wondered if you'd like to come along, as my chauffeur."

He looked at me then burst out laughing. "As your chauffeur? I wouldn't be no ruddy good at that, ducks. I can't drive. I never learned. Never had no need either, what with living in the Smoke."

"Come anyway. I can drive. Lots of my sort of people drive themselves and bring their chauffeur along to watch the motor when they leave it. I'll find you a peaked cap, and bob's your uncle, as you would say."

He looked at me, head to one side like a Cockney sparrow, then laughed again. "You're a card, I'll say that for you. Now, can you see a bloke like me at Balmoral, hobnobbing with royalty and gentry?"

"You'd only be hobnobbing with their servants and that might be a great help to me. You might be able to worm some information out of them about the shooting yesterday. Servants love to gossip. And how often would you have a chance to visit a royal palace?"

His smile had faded. "You really want me to come along, don't you?"

"Yes, I'd like it very much. I feel more secure with you around."

He frowned. "You don't anticipate any more funny business, do you? Because if so, I don't want you going near that place."

"I'm going out riding with Princess Elizabeth. I'm sure we'll be quite safe," I said.

"All right, then. What are we waiting for? Where's me titfer?"

"Your what?"

"Tit for tat. Hat. Rhyming slang. Ain't I taught you nothing yet?"

Five minutes later we were breezing down the side of the loch. There was no sign of activity at the jetty. For one thing it was clearly too windy to attempt any trials of the speedboat; besides, its driver was under arrest and presumably facing charges in London. Poor Belinda, I thought. Then I changed my mind. From our last conversation it sounded as if she was growing tired of him. Besides, Belinda always landed on her feet. She'd be off to new pastures without a second glance back.

I left the loch behind and concentrated as the road climbed and wound through the mountains. The gatekeeper at Balmoral looked weary as he opened the gate for me. "So much coming and going, your ladyship," he said with a dignified bow. "It's been like Waverley Station at the rush hour. The police are here again. There's men tramping all over the place." And indeed I noticed a man standing not far from the driveway, watching us. Sir Jeremy and Darcy had already produced results, I thought with a sigh of relief. At least some investigation was being done.

At the castle I left Granddad guarding the estate car in the back stable yard, then was shown up to the princesses' nursery where the two girls were busy playing with toy horses. Elizabeth leaped up with delight. "You've come!" she exclaimed, eyes glowing. "I was hoping and hoping that you would." She turned to her governess. "Now may I go riding, Crawfie?"

The Duchess of York was consulted and it was agreed that it would be fine for the princess to go out with me, providing we didn't venture too far afield. Elizabeth changed into her riding togs and we left the nursery to Margaret's wailed protests that she was a good rider too. Ponies were saddled up and off we went. It was a glorious day for riding and we set out at a brisk trot.

"Could we go a bit faster?" Elizabeth asked after a while. "Trotting is so boring, isn't it?"

"All right. But don't fall off, or I'll be in trouble."

"I never fall off," she said scornfully and urged her pony into a fast canter. I let her ride ahead of me. She really was a splendid little rider. Up a broad path we went, through the woods and then out onto the moor.

"Hey, Lilibet, slow down," I called. "We shouldn't go too far from the house, remember."

She brought her pony to a halt and waited for me.

"Isn't it heavenly up here?" Elizabeth said, looking around at the vast sweep of hills and glens. "I love the way we can be free to be ordinary at Balmoral, don't you?"

"I'm usually ordinary," I said, "but I do understand."

We walked on.

"Mummy even takes us down to the village shop and I can spend my pocket money," Elizabeth went on. "I wish we could stay up here all year long."

"Your daddy has important work to do for the country," I said.

"I'm glad Uncle David will be king," she said. "Daddy would hate it. So would I. When I grow up, I want to marry a farmer and have lots of animals—horses and dogs and cows and chickens." She looked at me. "Who do you want to marry?"

"Oh, I don't know."

"You're blushing," she said. "I bet you do know who you'd like to marry. Is he handsome?"

"Very."

"Are you going to tell me his name? I promise I can keep a secret. Then I'll tell you the name of a handsome boy I know."

She broke off as we heard a strange humming, whooshing sound. Something whizzed past us. At first I thought it was a bee. Then, when the second one came, followed by a metallic ping as something hit an outcropping of rock, I realized what it was.

"Someone is shooting at us," I said. "Ride as fast as you can."

"But surely—" she began.

"Go on. Ride. Go!" I slapped her pony's rear and it took off like a rocket. I let her get a head start before I followed. Her pony was going as fast as it could but it was small and our progress seemed painfully slow. At any moment I kept expecting to feel a bullet hit me in the back. Then the path dipped into a stand of trees and swung around some rocks. Only then did I realize that we were probably out of range and slowed to a trot.

"Are you sure someone was shooting at us?" Elizabeth asked, wide-eyed.

"Pretty sure. The speed those things went past, they had to be bullets. And I heard a sort of ping when one struck a rock."

"But who would want to shoot at us?"

"I've no idea. But somebody was shot yesterday."

"I know. Mummy told me. She said he was silly to have wandered off, and the other shooters couldn't see him in the mist, but it's not misty today, is it, and we're not near the grouse moor."

"There are supposed to be policemen all over the estate, looking after us," I said. "Let's hope we run into some of them soon, because we can't risk going back the way we came."

"There's a house over there." Elizabeth pointed to a large gray stone building nestled in a dip in the landscape and half hidden by large pine trees.

"Good idea. Let's go and they can presumably telephone the castle."

We urged on our horses again and dismounted outside a white gate.

"Do you know who lives here?" I asked.

Elizabeth shook her head. "Someone who works for Grandpapa, I suppose."

We tied the horses to the front fence.

"We should loosen the girth straps if we're going to be here long," Elizabeth said. "We don't want my pony to be uncomfortable."

"I'm sure he'll be fine. And we shouldn't be here long."

We left the horses and walked up a short gravel path to the front door. I was about to rap on it when I saw the name. Gleneagles.

Chapter 29

The door was opened by a tall thin woman wearing a rather shapeless green silk dress. Her iron gray hair was drawn back into a bun, making her narrow face look even longer. She looked at me warily.

"Yes? Can I help you?"

Then she looked past me and saw the princess. "Your Royal Highness!" she exclaimed, and bobbed a curtsy. She frowned at me, trying to remember, then smiled. "And it's Lady Georgiana, isn't it? I haven't seen you for a long while. How very kind of you to pay us a visit."

"I'm afraid we weren't intending to visit anybody," I said. "We were out riding and came here because someone was shooting at us."

"Shooting at you? You mean with a gun? Are you sure? You didn't wander into the path of a shoot like that poor man yesterday?"

"No," I said. "We were nowhere near a shoot and I have to conclude that someone was actually aiming at us."

"Goodness gracious," she gasped. "Please come inside." She peered out past us as if expecting to see a hooded figure with guns standing there. She shut the door hurriedly behind us. "Won't you come through to the sitting room?"

"I should telephone the castle first and let them know what has happened," I said. "You do have a telephone, don't you?"

"Usually yes." She frowned. "But the line came down when an oak fell in a big storm and I've been waiting for the men to reconnect us. And I'm afraid my husband and daughter have taken both of our vehicles. But you're quite safe here. My husband should be back soon and he can drive you back to the castle."

She ushered us through to a spacious but rather dark sitting room. The furniture was good quality but with a faded air to it. "Please take a seat. I'll have the girl make you some tea, or you'd probably prefer milk, wouldn't you, Your Royal Highness?"

"Thank you very much. Milk would be lovely." Even in moments of stress, Elizabeth didn't forget her manners.

The woman went back into the hallway again, calling out to a servant. I leaned close to Elizabeth. "Who is that? Do you know?"

She nodded. "I think her husband is in charge of the estate for Grandpapa."

"Major Padgett, do you mean?"

"That's right. He's nice, isn't he? He helped me with my riding last summer."

We stopped talking as Mrs. Padgett came back in.

"Tea will be ready in a moment," she said. "What a horrible ordeal. I trust that neither of you was hurt?"

"No. Luckily Princess Elizabeth is a good horsewoman. We rode out of range quickly."

"Extraordinary. Quite extraordinary." She shook her head. "On the estate too. Who could possibly get onto the estate without being noticed?"

"I suppose it's not hard if one is determined," I said.

"Do you think it could be foreign anarchists? One reads of such things in other countries but surely Britain is safe." She stared at me. I noticed she had mournful brown eyes, like a cocker spaniel's, but not as bright.

"I would hope so," I said.

Tea was brought in, plus a glass of milk for Elizabeth. Mrs. Padgett poured and handed around a plate of oatcakes. "Our cook is a dab hand with the local cooking," she said. "Her oatcakes are famous."

I tried to eat but in truth I was still too upset. I kept hearing the strange whoosh of that bullet passing close to me and then imagining it thudding into Elizabeth's back. The thought of it made me quite sick.

I looked around the room, trying to make light conversation, and my gaze fell on a collection of silver-framed photographs on the little writing desk in the corner. I recognized a much younger Major Padgett, with resplendent mustache and a chest full of medals, standing beside Queen Victoria. Another one with King Edward VII. Yet another on a polo pony. He had been a dashing man in his time. Then there were pictures of Ronny: standing beside her plane, holding up a trophy, as a young girl in her swimming suit, laughing amid the waves.

"Is Ronny your only child?" I asked.

"Yes," she said. "She came to us rather late in life. We couldn't have children, you see. And then we were offered her. It seemed like a miracle at the time."

"She's certainly gone on to wonderful feats," I said.

A smile flashed across the sad, tired face. "Yes, hasn't she? And we've been so happy to see so much of her this summer. Usually she finds Scotland too boring, but this year she's been coming and going all summer. I realize it is the speedboat trials and not her parents that entice her, but it's very nice all the same. We are rather cut off here for most of the year." And her expression reverted to sadness again.

"Hester, old thing, any chance of a cup of tea?" came a booming voice down the hallway, and Major Padgett came in. He started visibly as he noticed us. "Good gracious," he said. "Your Royal Highness. Lady Georgiana. What on earth are you doing here?"

"They were shot at," Mrs. Padgett said. "They took refuge here and of course we still have no telephone so I couldn't let anyone at the castle know."

"Shot at? Are you sure?" He frowned. "But there is no shooting going on today. In fact we've had the place full of blasted policemen, tramping over everything and asking damned fool questions. Well, I hope my wife has kept you entertained?"

I noticed a look that I couldn't interpret pass between them.

"Very well, thank you."

"Then we'd better get you back to the castle, hadn't we?" he said. "Your parents will start to worry about you if you don't show up soon, Your Highness."

"We have our ponies," Elizabeth said firmly. "We can't leave them here."

"Princess Elizabeth can ride in your motorcar with you, and I'll follow with the horses," I said.

"Splendid." He smiled at me. He was still a handsome man when he smiled.

We arrived back at the castle without incident. Sir Jeremy was not in evidence but Major Padgett brought me to Chief Inspector Campbell, who listened with a disbelieving scowl. "Are you sure this wasn't just an overactive imagination?" he said. "After hearing about yesterday's little incident, maybe?"

"Quite sure," I replied coldly. "If you'd care to send out some men, I'll accompany you and show you where the bullet struck the rock. Then you'd know this wasn't girlish hysteria. And you could retrieve the bullet and see if it matched the gun used in yesterday's murder."

"Good God," he said, looking at me as if I was a sweet puppy that had suddenly revealed itself to be a dangerous wolf. "Very well. I'll arrange for men and a car."

We retraced our steps and I was delighted when I was able to locate the rock, point out the scar where the bullet bounced off, and finally see them find the bullet. They were suitably somber as we drove back. So was the chief inspector. Deferential, almost. And he remembered to call me "my lady" this time.

Sometimes it's nice to be right.

Nobody seemed to know where I might find Sir Jeremy, which was annoying. He had told me I could leave messages for him at the inn in Braemar where he was staying, so I decided I'd have to do this. As I was crossing the hallway the gong sounded for luncheon. I was definitely hungry by this time, but I couldn't face polite conversation with the queen and her ladies, so I slipped out of the front door. There was nothing else that could be accomplished at Balmoral. I was just on my way to find my grandfather and the car when I encountered Lady Peebles, coming up to the front door with a basket on her arm.

"Hello, my dear," she said. "Was that the luncheon gong I heard already?"

"Yes, it was."

"Dear me. How time flies." She brushed back a wayward strand of gray hair. "What a shocking business yesterday, wasn't it? I hope you've recovered."

"Thank you. I'm very well."

"That poor boy," she said. "Not one of us, of course. What was he doing here, anyway? Who invited him, do you know?"

"He came as part of the house party from Castle Rannoch," I said, "but I had never met him before. A school friend of Binky's, I understand."

"Then that's not so bad, is it?" She smiled easily. "I mean, it's easier to take if it is not someone with whom one is intimately acquainted."

"Of course," I said. I looked down at her basket. "You've been picking flowers."

"Yes. Aren't they lovely roses? The queen is so fond of the white ones, so I enjoy bringing her some when they're just opening up. And where are you off to?"

"I've been out riding with Princess Elizabeth," I said. "Now I'm going home again."

She smiled. "She needs the company of some younger people like yourself. It's not good to be stuck with us old dinosaurs all the time. She deserves a normal childhood, I feel."

We were about to go our separate ways when a thought struck me. "Lady Peebles. Tell me about Major Padgett," I said.

"Major Padgett? What do you want to know about him?"

"How he comes to be in his current position, I suppose."

"What is there to tell? Been in royal service most of his life. Army man, of course. Distinguished military career before he went into the old queen's household. Pally with King Edward when he was the Prince of Wales."

"And what happened to him?"

"I don't exactly know. I was not at court myself at the time. In fact I was preparing to be presented. But I gather there was some kind of scandal. All very hush-hush. I heard from someone that he'd had a nervous breakdown. Anyway, he was sent up here to recuperate and here he's stayed. I must say he runs the estate most efficiently, but perhaps he's the kind of man who can't take any strain."

I left her then and went to find Granddad. He was sitting on a wall in the shade and got up when he saw me, hastily putting his peaked cap back on his bald pate.

"Ah, there you are, love—I mean, yer ladyship. All finished, then?"

"Yes, we can head for home."

"That's good. This place gives me the willies."

"You said Castle Rannoch gave you the willies."

"So it does. I ain't used to this kind of thing. Even the servants here are a toffy-nosed bunch. One of them asked me why her ladyship had brought a chauffeur up from London when there were perfectly good men wanting employment up here."

"I suppose he has a point," I said. "So what did you tell him?"

"I said her ladyship was being specially kind and giving me a chance for some fresh air, because I've had a bad chest. Which is true," he added.

"So did you learn anything?"

"They were all talking about it," he said. "Rumors flying like crazy in the tack room where we went for a cup of tea. Most people thought it was an accident, but someone thought the young man was a Russian spy or a German spy and that someone working for our government had finished him off. No suggestion as to who might have done the shooting. But one thing was clear: he wasn't out in front of the group. Several of the beaters were there and they swore they always kept an eye out for shooters who wandered into potential danger."

We left the estate and drove along the River Dee toward Braemar. I decided to keep quiet about today's shooting incident. There was no sense in worrying my grandfather unduly. But I found that I couldn't put it out of my mind. I kept hearing the whooshing noise of those bullets flying past me. Who would want to shoot at us?

I went over the scene in the Padgetts' dreary living room and my head started buzzing with strange thoughts. Someone with a grudge against the royal family? Someone who was not entirely mentally stable? Someone with unlimited access to the royal lifestyle? Didn't all these add up to Major Padgett, who had seen a promising career and royal favor shrink to a dreary house tucked away in the back of beyond?

Chapter 30

CASTLE CRAIG, BRAEMAR
AUGUST 21

As I drove I worked out what I should say in a note to Sir Jeremy. I was, after all, making a preposterous accusation. But it seemed the only concrete lead so far. I remembered Mrs. Padgett's anxious, guarded face. Had she had to shield a husband with mental problems all these years? Did she suspect that he had anything to do with the shooting? If she did, she was a good actress, I decided. She had looked genuinely startled. So had the major himself. Tread carefully, therefore.

The road ran along the side of the river through a dramatic valley framed by soaring hills. In places the valley narrowed and the river flowed swiftly, dancing merrily over stones on its way to the coast. In other places it was more sedate, with meadows on either side. Fly fishermen in waders stood in the shallows flicking their lines in and out of the water. After a pleasant drive the old granite tower of the Braemar church was visible through the trees and we came into the village. There was nobody at the inn except for a daft-seeming young girl who giggled as she spoke in such broad Scottish that I had trouble understanding her. Something "she'd no ken and she'd whist but she was oot the noo." Although who "she" was and where she had gone were beyond my comprehension. I presumed this girl was not the normal receptionist or it would have been extremely bad for trade.

Given the circumstances I wrote a simple note. *I need to speak to you urgently. Georgiana Rannoch.*

I was just leaving when a large woman came in, panting with exertion. "Och, I'm sorry, my dear," she said. "I was out delivering a meal to old Jamie. He canna cook for himself these days and yon girl is too daft to be trusted not to spill it—aren't you, you daft ha'porth? What can I do for you?"

I told her I had left a note for Sir Jeremy and please make sure he got it immediately. As soon as I opened my mouth she turned pale and bobbed a curtsy. "Och, I didna recognize you at first, my lady. How is your dear brother, the duke? Keeping well, I hope."

"Yes, thank you." I didn't really wish to go into the details of the trap. I left her and was walking back to the car but those words continued bouncing around my head. "Your dear brother, the duke."

And I found myself thinking of a recent time when that same phrase had been used, in a letter to me from Mavis Pugh. *Older brother, the Duke of . . .* What had she wanted with my brother? What had she wanted to tell me, or ask me? And of course now a nagging doubt crept into my mind. Had she found out something important and was she killed because of it?

Then I remembered that Lady Peebles had also uttered a similar phrasing as we walked up the path toward the grouse moor. *She was engaged to the king's older brother, the Duke of Clarence . . .*

The Duke of Clarence, I thought. The eldest son who was so unsuitable, so morally unsound, and who had conveniently died, leaving the throne to the more reliable younger son. And I remembered how Lady Peebles had jumped on Lady Marchmont for mentioning the stupid rumor that he hadn't actually died, but that he was shut away somewhere. Absurd, of course. Someone in the country would have had to know about this and something would have leaked out by now. It was forty years ago, after all. The Duke of Clarence would now be an old man, almost seventy.

"Right," I said. "We've done all we can do. Let's go home." I began the long, winding drive that would take us over the pass and then down to Castle Rannoch. About a mile outside Braemar we passed a tall wrought-iron gate on our left. I had half noticed it before, but not given it a second thought. My mind associated it with some kind of hospital. Now I slowed and noticed there was a plate on the brick wall beside the gate. It said *Castle Craig Sanitarium*.

I brought the car to a halt and jumped out. "I'll be right back," I called.

Beyond the gate a driveway disappeared into trees. I caught just a glimpse of a building beyond. I tried to open the gate, but it was locked.

"You'll no get in there," a voice behind me said, and I turned to see an old man with a grinning sheepdog beside him.

"Is it under quarantine because it's for TB patients?"

He shook his head, a slow smile spreading across his lips. "That's what they'd like you to think, but it's for those who are wrong in the head."

"An insane asylum, you mean?"

"They don't like to call it that. Nervous breakdowns—that's what they say these days, don't they? It's where rich folk put the relatives who've gone a wee bit funny. You know, think they are Napoleon or something." He chuckled. "What did you want in there anyway?"

"I was just curious."

"You need an appointment before they'll let you in," he said. "Terrible strict on security they are, ever since one of their patients escaped and killed his mother with an ax. You must have read about it."

"Oh, I see. Thank you."

He nodded and went on his way. I walked slowly back to the car. I was thinking of the three names written on that map. I'd now found two of them. And the third: Dofc . . . "Oh no," I said out loud. Could those letters possibly stand for the Duke of Clarence? And that rumor that he hadn't died at all, but had been locked away somewhere so that his more suitable younger brother could take the throne. I remembered how quickly and firmly Lady Peebles had squashed this thought. Did she know something? Was it possible that he was here and that someone was trying to kill heirs to the throne on his behalf? It seemed almost too preposterous for words. . . .

"What's up now?" Granddad asked as I returned to the car.

"Granddad," I said cautiously, "how good are you at acting?"

"Acting? We left that to your mother. A proper little show-off she was from the word go."

"I was wondering if you could possibly play my loony old uncle for a few minutes? You don't have to do much, or say much, because I don't want them to hear your London accent. But you could look vacant and smile a lot, couldn't you?"

"What's this in aid of, then?"

"This place is a posh insane asylum," I said. "I need a reason to go and visit and you'd be the prefect reason."

" 'Ere, you ain't thinking of leaving me in there, are you?"

I patted his knee. "Of course not. But I need to find out if a certain person is locked away in there, so I need an excuse to go inside."

"I suppose I can manage it," he said. "Yer grandma always said I must be twins because one person couldn't be so daft." He smiled, wistfully.

"Super. We'll drive back into the village to find the nearest telephone box."

Soon I was standing outside the Cock 'o the North pub, asking the operator to connect me with Castle Craig. A refined voice that sounded as if it belonged on Princes Street in Edinburgh came on the line.

"Castle Craig Sanitarium."

All I had to do was to pull rank. "Good afternoon, this is Lady Georgiana Rannoch," I said, switching into full royal mode. "I would like to come and speak to your matron about my great-uncle. He has been acting, well, a little strangely lately and we in the family feel that—he needs a place where he would be looked after."

"I quite understand, my lady," she said. "And we would be just the place you are looking for. When would you like to come and visit us?"

"The thing is that I have Uncle in the car at this moment, so I wondered if I could bring him to see you in a few minutes. He goes back to his own house in the far north tomorrow and frankly he shouldn't be going there alone."

"This is most irregular." She sounded flustered now. "Matron never lets anybody visit without an appointment."

"I rather hoped you'd make an exception," I said, "seeing that this property is on land originally purchased from the Rannoch estate, and that we are neighbors of long standing." It was completely untrue that Rannoch land extended this far east, but she wasn't to know that.

"One moment, please. Let me go and talk to Matron," she said. "Please hold the line."

There was a long silence, then I heard the sound of footsteps and the voice said, a trifle breathlessly, "Matron says she'd be willing to make an exception in your case."

"Splendid," I said. "You may expect us in a few minutes."

"Do you mind telling me what this is all about?" Granddad asked as we drove back to the sanitarium. "Exactly why do we need to get inside a loony bin?"

"Because its name was written on a map that was left for me, and the person who wrote it was subsequently murdered," I said.

"You think it's one of the inmates who is running around causing mischief?"

I thought about this. If by some ridiculous chance the Duke of Clarence was shut away there, a virtual prisoner, then it wouldn't be likely that he'd have the ability to influence actions in the outside world. His captors would see that he had no contact with anybody.

I shook my head. Too ridiculous for words. "I'm not quite sure why we're going there," I said, "but I just know it has to be important. We'll keep our eyes open—especially for an old man, about your age."

"What kind of old man?"

I shook my head. "I have no idea. One who looks like King George?"

By the time we reached the gate it was open and a man in a dark uniform with brass buttons was standing beside it. He saluted me as I drove through. I noticed in my rearview mirror that he was locking the gate behind me. A shiver of apprehension shot through me. Was I recklessly driving into a lion's den? The driveway led through parklike grounds until it reached an elegant redbrick house, built in the shape of an E. A woman in a crisply starched white uniform was standing on the steps in the middle part of the E.

"This is a pleasant surprise, my lady," she said in her cultured voice. "Do come inside. And this must be your dear uncle."

"That's right. This is Mr. Angus MacTavish Hume. Uncle Angus, we're going to have a short visit at this nice place."

"Hospital?" He said the word in a stage whisper.

I laughed, gaily. "No, it's not a hospital. It's like a hotel. You'll see."

The woman in white ushered us in to a black-and-white-tiled entrance hall and offered us a seat on a leather sofa. "If you'd be good enough to wait here, I'll let Matron know that you have arrived."

Her heels tapped away on the tiled floor. As soon as she turned the corner I leaped up. "Keep guard for me," I whispered and I started to try the doors on either side of the hall. The first was a closet; the second opened into an office. There were filing cabinets against the walls but I didn't think I'd have time to go through them, not knowing what I was looking for. I didn't for one minute think there would be a file labeled *Duke of Clarence. Top secret.* If he was here, it would be under an assumed name.

But on the desk was a large visitors book, open at today's date. No visitors so far today. I turned back to the day before, and the one before that. Not many people came to visit their loony relatives, I noted. Then I saw a name I recognized: V. Padgett. And under the patient's name: Maisie McPhee.

"Someone's comin'," Granddad hissed through the door. I sprinted back to the sofa, just as a hatchet-faced older woman in a blue uniform appeared. "I understand you have brought your uncle to see over our institution, my lady," she said in disapproving tones. "This is highly irregular. We like to do things by appointment here."

"I understand, but it seemed so opportune that we were passing when I had Uncle with me in the car. Naturally he has to be comfortable with any arrangements made for him." I glanced at him and he gave his best imitation of an inane smile. I helped him to his feet.

"How exactly did you hear about us?" she asked.

I gave her a rather patronizing smile. "We are almost neighbors," I said. "I've lived here since I was born. One knows what happens on estates that border our own."

"I see." Did I detect a slight hardening of her expression? "Our fees are not paltry," she said, "but of course that should be of no concern to someone like yourself."

"My uncle is not without his own funds," I said, taking his hand in mine. "But we have to make sure this place is right for him."

Granddad grinned inanely, as instructed.

"He has certain definite requirements," I went on. "He likes morning sunlight, you see, and a good view, and plenty of lawns for strolling, and some good conversation with his fellow guests. So I wonder if we could be shown around and see some rooms?"

"We didn't know you were coming." She sounded slightly flustered. "We're not prepared . . ."

"Oh, come now"—I was now giving a good imitation of my austere great-grandmother, Queen Victoria—"if your place is so substandard that it has to be prepared to be seen by an outside visitor, then it's hardly a suitable spot for my great-uncle."

"My lady, we adhere to the highest standards," she said frostily. "It's just that I don't know which rooms are available for viewing. Some of our residents are easily startled by outsiders. Some can even be violent and I wouldn't like you to witness anything unpleasant."

"I think it is important that I see the place as it really is, don't you? If I'm to trust you with my dear uncle, I have to know what I'm doing."

"I see." A ghost of a smile touched her lips but not her eyes. "Well, I suppose I can give you some idea of what we have to offer. As it happens we do have a couple of vacancies at present. If you'd please follow me."

As she walked ahead I grabbed Granddad. "See if you can find a Maisie McPhee," I whispered. He shot me an inquiring look.

Matron looked back. "Come along. This way," she said briskly. She led us down a long, well-lit hallway. The doors on either side had small windows in them and nameplates on them. I tried to glance in each.

"So do you have many men of my uncle's age?" I asked. "He is a very sociable chap. He'd like to be able to play chess and talk to other old codgers."

She gave me a warning look, glancing back at Granddad, who was deliberately trailing. "Most of our residents are no longer able to play chess and chat. Are you sure your relative wouldn't be happier in a residential facility for the elderly?"

"But he wanders," I whispered. "He tries to escape all the time. The staff found him standing by the road, trying to hitchhike, wearing only his combinations."

"Ah. I see." She turned into a light, open area with armchairs and low tables. There was a piano in the corner and a radio on a side table. "Our more—uh, sociable residents usually meet in the common room."

A few of the chairs were occupied. One old man was wearing what looked like a nightcap and had a tumbler of what seemed to be whiskey on the table beside him. He looked up as we came in.

"Lunchtime yet?" he asked.

"You've just had lunch, Mr. Soames. It was grilled plaice, remember?"

A hollow-eyed woman looked up. "I want lunch too," she said. "They try to starve us here, you know. No food for weeks."

"Rubbish, Lady Wharton. You do tell awful stories." Matron attempted a laugh.

"Could we have a tour of the kitchen and dining room?" I asked. "Uncle is very particular about his food."

"Our food is of the highest quality, my lady," Matron said, "and the kitchen staff will just be washing up after luncheon, but I can show you the dining room." She led us through the common room and into a pleasant room set with small tables. It had windows on either side, opening onto a view of the hills, and the ceiling was half timbered.

"You see. Pleasant views. Just what your uncle ordered," she said with a smile to him.

"So how many other elderly men do you have in residence at the moment?" I asked.

Did I detect a slight hesitation? "Let me see. Colonel Farquar, Mr. Soames . . . I believe there are ten of them. And we have fifteen ladies in residence. Ladies always seem to live longer than men for some reason, don't they?" Another attempt at a smile.

"And if I could just peek at the kitchen," I said. "Is it through here?" I went through the doorway without waiting for permission. Startled kitchen staff looked up as I came in. It was all perfectly all right—spotless, in fact—and the smells were not unpleasant. In fact if I really had a senile uncle, it would not have been a bad place for him.

"My lady, I really don't think—" Matron actually grabbed my arm. "We shouldn't disturb them now. Carry on, everyone."

She almost dragged me out of the kitchen, then looked around. "Where has your uncle gone?"

Granddad had done a bolt. Good for him!

"Oh no," I said. "You see what I mean? He's always trying to run away. He can't have gone far."

Matron was already running, her heels tapping on the bare floor. "James, Frederick, there's an old man loose in the building," she called and two young men set off in pursuit.

"Don't let him get out. We'll never find him in all that shrubbery," I called after them. One changed course and ran for the front door. I followed the other one up the stairs. We ran along one hallway, then out to the side of the E. I slowed and tried to read nameplates on the doors, and to glance inside each room. Then I heard shouts and sounds of a scuffle. I sprinted around the corner, to see two young men in white coats wrestling Granddad into submission. They appeared to be using what I deemed to be considerable force.

"Let go of him!" I shouted.

Matron appeared, breathing hard, behind us. "He's not one of ours yet, Sims," she called. The young men dropped Granddad's arms. He stood there giving a good imitation of being terrified. I went up to him. "You are naughty, Uncle," I said, taking his hand. "You promised not to run away, remember? Come along."

Matron caught up with us, breathing heavily. "That was silly, Mr. Hume," she said. "You don't need to run away. You are among friends. You'll be well taken care of here." She drew me to one side. "I see that he is a handful," she whispered. "If you'd like to leave him with us now, perhaps?"

"No, I think he'd like to go home and have a chance to say good-bye to his staff and set his affairs in order first," I said hastily, drawing him closer to me. "And we haven't yet had a chance to see a vacant room?"

"Oh yes. We were interrupted, weren't we? I believe the one in Sunshine wing is the closest, and you said it was important for your uncle to receive morning sunlight. James, would you run ahead and make sure the room is ready to receive visitors?"

The young man ran ahead while we walked slowly back to the spine of the E and then along its length to the other wing. As we walked along this wing I spotted the nameplate *M. McPhee*. I tried to peer in through the window but all I could see was a lump in a bed.

"Ah, here we are," Matron said, and opened the door to an empty room. It was spartan, to say the least. "We encourage our guests to bring their own furniture. It makes the transition from home easier for them."

"Very nice," I said. "Quite suitable, in fact. I think he'll resist the idea at first, but he'd be quite happy here." I turned to smile at him again. Matron was standing behind him this time, blocking any chance of escape. "I will talk this over with my brother, the duke, and we will contact you as soon as possible with our decision."

"We look forward to your uncle joining us, my lady," she said with a groveling smile now.

As we came back along the hall I appeared to notice the nameplate for the first time. "Good heavens. That wouldn't be Maisie McPhee, would it?" I asked.

"Yes. Did you know her?"

"If it's the same one, she used to work for us years ago, when I was a small child," I said.

"I don't believe it could be the same person," the matron said.

"I'd recognize her right away," I said, "and perhaps she'd still remember me. She was very kind. Very nice."

I had my hand on the doorknob, attempting to open the door.

"I don't think she'd know you, my lady," the matron said, hastily removing my hand from the door. "She doesn't know anybody any longer."

The noise outside her door had roused Maisie McPhee. She sat up in bed and stared anxiously. I was surprised to see a young-looking, unlined face, light blue eyes and hair that had once been red, but was now faded and streaked with white.

"It's all right, dear," Matron called through the closed door. "You're quite safe here. Go back to sleep."

"But she's so young to be here," I said. "What a shame."

Matron nodded. "Advanced syphilis, I'm afraid," she said in a low whisper. "Nothing can be done." She took my arm and led us away.

Chapter 31

I heaved a big sigh of relief as we drove out of those gates and turned onto the road again. Granddad beside me gave a similar sigh. "Blimey, ducks, what I do for you. I thought I'd had me chips then. I thought they were going to drag me away and lock me up on the spot. Talk about giving you the willies. That place certainly did."

"Yes, it did, didn't it? Although it was all very nice and clean and bright. You were brilliant, by the way. Absolutely perfect. Now I can see where Mummy got her acting ability from."

"Go on." He almost blushed. "I just had to stand there and look stupid."

"But you ran away and gave us a chance to see more of the building. We'd probably never have gone upstairs if you hadn't done that. And I'd never have seen Maisie McPhee."

"Who's she when she's at home, anyway?"

"I don't know," I said. "But Veronica Padgett goes to visit her regularly, and she doesn't strike me as the philanthropic type who would visit an old servant."

"What makes you think she's an old servant? I thought they were all posh types in there."

"Maisie McPhee is the sort of name servants around here would have," I said. "But why would they pay to put an old servant in a place like Castle Craig?"

Then suddenly it hit me. "Unless—she's Ronny's real mother. Mrs. Padgett said Ronny was adopted. What if one of their servants got into trouble and they did the kind thing and adopted the baby?" After all, she had remarkably similar coloring to Ronny's. But why would they have continued to support her all these years, and end up by keeping her at a very expensive institution—unless Major Padgett was the father, of course.

Everything started to fit into place. Major Padgett who had had what was described as a scandal or a breakdown and been shipped off to a cottage on the estate. What if it had come out that he had contracted syphilis, then fathered a child of a maid? Queen Victoria could stand no kind of immorality. Had she done the kind thing and kept him in her service but effectively banished him? And syphilis often led to insanity, didn't it? Was Major Padgett really insane?

"You're awfully quiet," Granddad said.

"Just thinking things through and they are beginning to make sense," I said. "I hope Sir Jeremy turns up soon. I suppose I'd better put everything in a letter and leave it for him at the Braemar inn if he doesn't come by tonight."

As we had been talking the clouds had come in, blotting out the mountains and covering the road ahead in wet mist. I gripped the steering wheel tightly as the road snaked down a series of hairpin bends.

"I'm starving," I said after a while. "I missed lunch."

"Don't talk about food now, please," Granddad said.

I glanced at him. He did look rather green. "I'm sorry, I didn't know you got sick in motorcars," I said.

"I didn't know until now, did I? I ain't ridden in too many cars in my life, you know, and never on roads like this, and never with someone driving the way you drive."

"I drive jolly well," I said.

"I'm not disputing it, ducks, but you drive ruddy fast, and all these bends too."

"Sorry." I smiled and slowed to a crawl around the next bend. "Not too much farther now, I promise. See. There's a glimpse of the loch down below."

We came around another bend and there was the loch, stretching black and gloomy before us. The clouds were darker now and it looked as if it might rain any second. As we approached the jetty, Granddad said, " 'Ere, what's going on over there?"

A small crowd had gathered and I saw that the blue speedboat was in the water again, in the process of being tied up at the dock. I pulled off the road and we got out, pushing our way through the crowd.

"What's happening?" I asked. "Is everyone watching the speedboat?"

"No, my lady. Someone's just seen the monster," a young boy said. I recognized him as the son of one of our estate workers.

"Seen the monster? What rubbish. Who saw it?"

"Ellie Cameron," he said, pointing to a slightly older girl, now standing gripping the arm of a friend.

"What's this about a monster, Ellie?" I asked.

She dropped a hasty curtsy. "I saw it, I really did, my lady. I was watching yon boat and then these strange waves started and I thought it was just, you know, the wake and the wind to begin with, but then I saw this monstrous head come out above the wave, and I screamed."

"A monstrous head?" I smiled. "I think you've a good imagination, Ellie."

"Och no, your ladyship. I know what I saw. A great big whitish thing it was, in the middle of the lake."

"Well, there's nothing there now," I said. "See, it's quite calm."

The boat crew were climbing onto the dock, when suddenly someone shouted, "Look there! What's that?"

Bubbles were rising from the black water. Then something broke the surface—something large and white. Someone screamed. Then someone else shouted, "It's a body!"

The boat's crew scrambled down into the boat again and were in the process of starting the engine when someone shouted, "Don't worry. I'll get it. Stay where you are."

I knew that voice. It was Darcy, the last person I expected to see here. I spotted him just in time to watch him strip off his jacket and dive from the dock, swimming out to the body with masterful strokes. We watched as he grabbed hold of a leg and then towed it in to shore.

"Stand back, please," he said, breathing heavily as he reached the shallows and stood up. "And somebody go and get the police."

Several boys ran off while the rest of the crowd watched in fascinated silence to see what would happen next. It was a strange picture: Darcy standing in the shallows dripping wet, his shirt and trousers clinging to him like a second skin, looking so very much alive, while behind him, bobbing in the waves, was the bloated body of Godfrey Beverley, clad only in his undergarments.

At that moment Darcy spotted me. "Georgie." I watched his eyes light up, much to my satisfaction. "Do you have a car here? Could you go home and telephone the police?"

"It's all right, mister," one of the boys said. "Freddie MacLain is already off away on his bicycle to the public telephone box."

"Do you want help with . . ." I couldn't finish the sentence properly, staring with fascination at the bloated, bobbing thing in the water.

"Only in keeping everyone away," he said. "I'm going to drag him up on dry land and then we'll try not to disturb him until the police are here."

"You think it might be foul play?"

"What else could it be?" he muttered, grunting with exertion as he dragged Godfrey's body ashore.

"He was always creeping around at the water's edge, trying to listen to other people's conversation," I said. "He could have slipped, fallen and knocked his head on a rock."

"Possibly. But why was he spying on other people?"

"He's Godfrey Beverley, the gossip columnist. Trying to find the next scoop."

"Then I say he found it and paid for it with his life," Darcy said grimly. "If there had been no other death around here, then I'd be prepared to call it an accident, but after what we are learning . . ."

He broke off as the boating party made their way down the jetty toward us and we heard a clear voice exclaiming, "Oh no. I simply can't go past that thing! I can't even look. Somebody come and give me a hand."

It was, of course, my mother, looking ridiculous stage-nautical in a navy and white sailor suit and matching hat. Several male hands obliged to help her down from the jetty. She started tottering over the stony beach in high-heeled platform-soled shoes until she saw me.

"Darling," she called, rushing to my arms, "isn't it too, too terrible? It is Godfrey, isn't it? That poor little man. I still can't believe it."

"You loathed him," I reminded her.

"Yes, but I certainly didn't push him into the water and drown him," she said. "Much as I'd like to have done. He really does look more disgusting in death than in life, doesn't he? Like a malformed balloon. Do you think he'd pop if one stuck a pin in him?"

"Mummy, don't be awful," I said.

"I'm just trying to make light of the situation because it's so horrible," she said. "God, I feel quite faint. I need a brandy. I do wish Max would leave that stupid boat alone and hurry up."

"Come on, old girl. Come and sit in the car," Granddad said, appearing suddenly from the motorcar.

"Good lord, Father—what on earth are you doing here?"

"What's this with the 'Father' nonsense? I always used to be plain old Dad and that's good enough for me. Always did give yourself airs and graces, didn't you?"

"Don't forget I used to be a duchess, Father," Mummy said, glancing around in case this conversation was being overheard. "And you didn't answer my question."

"Keeping an eye on your daughter, which is more than you've ever done."

"Now don't start that again," she said. "Some of us were just not cut out for motherhood. I did my best and she's turned out all right, hasn't she?"

"She's turned out a treat, but that's beside the point. Anyway, let's not argue now. Come and sit in the car. You look like you've had a nasty turn."

"Yes, I think perhaps I should sit down until Max gets here." She allowed herself to be led to my estate car and collapsed with great drama into the front seat. I turned my attention back to the dock to see if Max was anywhere in view and was amazed to see Paolo was coming toward me, with Belinda clutching his arm.

"Oh, Georgie," Belinda cried, letting go of Paolo's arm and rushing up to me. "What a horrid thing to have happened. I was looking out of the back of the boat and it just sort of bobbed to the surface and I couldn't think what it was to start with."

I put a comforting hand on her shoulder. "It is rather beastly, isn't it?"

She nodded. "So lucky Paolo didn't strike the body when he was going really fast. He'd have killed himself for sure."

"But what is Paolo doing back here?" I asked. "The last I saw of him he was being bundled into a police car."

"They had to let him go," she said, with a triumphant toss of the head. "He proved to them that he was actually dining with people on the other side of London when the poor girl was run down. Of course I knew he couldn't possibly have done anything like that."

Paolo took her arm. "Come, *cara*. I do not wish to be here when the police arrive. I have had enough of English police."

"These are Scottish police," I said.

He shrugged. "English, Scottish, all the same. All very stupid and cannot see past the end of their noses. I kept telling them they make a mistake and somebody steals my motorbike, but they do not listen."

"I'll see you later, Georgie," Belinda said, as Paolo dragged her away.

Max arrived with Digby Flute, and my mother extricated herself from the car to fly to his side. "Max, darling. It's been such a horrible shock. Take me away from here," she said, giving a fabulous rendition of a tragic heroine about to expire.

"Do not worry, *Liebchen*. We go," he said.

The crowd had dwindled. A few of the boys still lingered, watching wide-eyed. Darcy was bending over the body, covering it with his jacket.

"Someone's done a good job of giving him a nasty bash on the back of his head," he said, straightening up. "I suppose it was okay to let all the witnesses go. We know where they are staying if the police need statements."

I nodded. I was starving and I really wanted to go home, but I didn't want to leave Darcy alone to this unpleasant task. I just didn't want to leave Darcy.

"I thought you said you had to go away," I said.

"I changed my mind."

"I'm glad."

"Anything else happen that I should know about?"

"Nothing, apart from someone shooting at me when we were out riding this morning."

"Georgie—I thought I told you to stay put and be careful."

"I was with Princess Elizabeth on the Balmoral estate. And there were policemen on the property."

"Whoever is doing this is getting desperate," he said.

"Yes, well, I have some idea now about who that person might be," I said. "I tried to find Sir Jeremy but I couldn't locate him."

"You say you have an idea who is doing all this?"

"Only an idea," I said, "but I believe it might be Major Padgett."

"Padgett, who works on the royal estate? Ronny's father?"

I nodded. "It does seem strange, doesn't it, but he fits the picture and he had the opportunity."

"But he's been with the royal family for years," Darcy said. "Why would he want to harm anybody?"

"I thought that he might be, you know, insane? There was some scandal about him and someone said he'd had a nervous breakdown, which was why he was sent up to Scotland. And he was there on the shoot, wasn't he? And he did try to persuade the police not to investigate further."

"Yes, but—" He broke off, then nodded. "All right. I'll pass along the information if I get a chance."

"Oh, and Darcy," I said, "can you find out about someone called Maisie McPhee?"

"What about her? Accomplice?"

"No. She's in an insane asylum, but she's linked somehow, I'm sure. She's probably in her late forties. Can you find out if she had a child about thirty years ago? Can you find out if she married?"

"That's a tall order," he said, "but someone will know how to check through the records in Edinburgh, I suppose."

"You should get home. You're shivering," I said.

"I'll have to stay until the police get here," he said.

"Looks like there's a bobby on a bike coming this way now," Granddad called from the car. It was Constable Herries, red faced and peddling furiously. It turned out he had already summoned an ambulance and was going to stand guard until it arrived.

"Have you notified your superiors?" Darcy asked.

"No sir, we don't usually bother them about a drowning," Constable Herries said. I saw Darcy frown. "The boy told me that the body just bobbed up in the middle of the loch."

"It did. We both observed it," I said. "Mr. O'Mara swam out and dragged him into shore."

"Poor fellow. I wonder how long ago he fell in and drowned?"

"I saw him alive yesterday," I said.

Constable Herries frowned. "That's unusual, that is. Usually they lie on the bottom until their stomach contents start fermenting and that takes days."

"I don't think he drowned," Darcy said. "There didn't appear to be water in his lungs."

"What do you mean, sir?"

"I think somebody killed him and then dumped him into the lake."

"Murder, you mean?"

"That would be my guess."

"Dear me." Constable Herries pushed back his helmet and scratched his head. "Someone should be told about this."

"Don't worry, Constable. We'll telephone from Castle Rannoch and report it," I said.

"If you're sure, my lady."

"I am." I turned back to Darcy. His dark curls were plastered to his face and he was still dripping. "And I should probably take Mr. O'Mara home and let him change into dry clothes, if you don't mind."

"Of course, my lady. You do what you think is best."

I turned to Darcy. "You'd better come up to the house and get out of those wet clothes. We can supply blankets and have someone dry your clothes for you," I said.

"Thank you for the offer," he said. "I think that's the first time you've actually invited me to take off my clothes, but I'm afraid I should go straight back to where I'm staying and then get to work if you want me to notify people about your suspicions."

"Thank you," I said. "I'm very grateful."

"Just doing my job, ma'am." He touched his head in mock salute.

"Jump in the car, I'll run you home."

"I'd make the seats wet."

"We'll risk it," I said. "How else were you going to get there?"

"Well, I didn't fancy rowing in this wind," he admitted and walked toward the car, leaving a trail of drips behind him.

Granddad opened the door and Darcy climbed into the backseat. Then Granddad took the passenger seat beside me.

"You bring your chauffeur and then you drive?" Darcy sounded amused.

"This isn't my chauffeur, it's my grandfather." I laughed. "I'm sorry, I forgot you two hadn't met before."

"Holy Mother of God. You're full of surprises, aren't you?" He held out his hand. "How do you do, sir. Darcy O'Mara. A pleasure to meet you."

"Likewise, I'm sure. I take it this is your young man," Granddad said.

"Granddad—" I began, my cheeks turning red, but Darcy interrupted. "You take it correctly," he said.

$\mathcal{C}hapter$ 32

I don't even remember driving home. I only came down off my cloud when I walked into Castle Rannoch to be met by an irate Fig.

"Where on earth have you been?" she demanded. "We've not seen hide nor hair of you for ages. You simply don't turn up for meals and I'm left to entertain and make conversation on my own."

"I'm sorry," I said. "I've been at Balmoral again. Princess Elizabeth wanted me to go riding with her."

"Well, in that case, I suppose you couldn't turn it down, could you?" she muttered, looking annoyed. It always made her cross that I was related to the royal family by birth while she was only related by marriage.

"Am I too late for tea? I'm starving," I said.

"I took tea with Podge in the nursery today," she said. "With all these people here I've been neglecting him fearfully. And there was nobody in for tea, except Binky. Siegfried's out somewhere. The Simpsons have finally gone, by the way."

"Have they really? Hooray."

"As you say, hooray. I thought we'd never get rid of them, especially when they elected to stay on after the other Americans went. But I think your cousins finally proved too much to endure. They are a trifle primitive, aren't they?"

"What happened?"

"We were in the middle of the meat course last night when Murdoch described how he'd dismembered a deer he'd shot. It would be venison, of course. Quite put them off their meal, I could see that."

I grinned. "Well, you finally have your way. They've all gone."

"Except for those awful cousins of yours. The amount they eat and drink. I've asked Binky to give them the boot, but you know how soft he is. We'll be reduced to tea and toast for the rest of the year." She eyed me critically. "What is wrong with you?"

"Nothing. Why?"

"You've had a silly grin on your face all the time I've been talking."

☰

We passed an uneventful evening. I was tense and uneasy all through dinner, at which Fig, myself and the two cousins were positioned along the full length of the huge banquet table, making conversation almost impossible without shouting. I was waiting for Sir Jeremy to telephone or appear in person at any moment, but he hadn't contacted me by the time I was ready for bed. This probably meant that he had not returned to the inn yet, or that the idiot girl was manning the shop and had forgotten to give him the message. Either that or her accent was so broad that he hadn't understood what she was saying. I wasn't sure what to do about this. Apart from telephoning the inn again, to see if he'd come back, I had no way of getting in touch with him and I worried that something else might happen at Balmoral the longer Major Padgett was on the loose. I just hoped that Darcy had managed to contact the appropriate people and that all would be well. Anyway, there was nothing more I could or should do now. I would be acting foolishly to attempt to go back to Balmoral again. Instead I'd attempt to enjoy myself. I'd take Granddad for some of my favorite walks. I might even teach him to fish.

The next morning I slept late and awoke to glorious sun streaming in through my open window. I breakfasted well and was on my way to visit Granddad when I heard a voice calling across the parkland: "Hector. Come out this minute, wherever you are. This is no longer funny."

And Podge's nanny came into view, looking around anxiously.

"What's the matter?" I asked.

"That naughty boy, he's hiding from me," she said. "I let him out of his pram because he does so love to run across the grass and now I can't find him." She sounded close to tears.

"Don't worry, he can't have gone far," I said, but my insides clenched themselves into a tight knot. I kept telling myself this was a simple case of a naughty three-year-old, but my mind was whispering other, darker possibilities.

"Get Graham to round up the gardeners and gillies to help you look," I said, indicating one of our groundsmen, who was working in the kitchen garden. "Tell him I said so."

"Yes, my lady."

"And I'll start looking too. Where exactly did you lose him?"

"Not far from here. He was playing with his ball on that lawn, running around quite happily. I went to sit on the bench and when I turned back, he was gone. Of course I thought he was just playing a silly trick on Nanny, then I called him and he didn't answer. Oh, what can have happened to him, my lady?"

"Don't worry. We'll find him. You didn't hear the sound of a motor, did you?"

"What do you mean, my lady?"

No sense in alarming her unduly. "Not important. Go and get Graham now. Go on." I pushed her in the direction of the kitchen garden and I started to hurry toward the spot she had indicated. If he really had run off, or was hiding, he couldn't have gone too far. He only had little legs. And if his nanny hadn't heard or noticed a motorcar then it wasn't likely that someone had driven away with him.

I searched through the shrubbery, calling his name, telling him that Auntie Georgie wanted to play with him, then that his papa wanted to see him—Papa being the most important person in his life. Nothing stirred among the bushes. Perhaps I am overreacting, I told myself. Perhaps he went back to the house to fetch a toy. Perhaps he's safely in his nursery at this very moment. But I couldn't shake off the feeling of dread.

I had just reached the driveway when I heard someone calling my name and saw my grandfather waving. "What's the big hurry, ducks?" he said. "Are you training to run a race?"

"No, Granddad. It's little Podge, my nephew. He's missing and I'm worried that—" I let the rest of the sentence drift off into silence.

"Are you sure he hasn't just wandered off? Kiddies do that, you know."

"I know. But we've called and called and he's not anywhere."

He put an arm around me. "Don't worry, ducks. He'll turn up. You get on with your searching and I'll help. But he wouldn't have got this far from the house on his own, would he?"

"I wouldn't have thought so, but . . . wait! What's that down there?" I had spotted the glint of something red, lying on the light gravel not far from the gates. I ran toward it and bent to pick it up. "It's one of Podge's toy soldiers," I shouted. "Go and tell them."

I started to run as fast as I could until I reached the castle gate. I looked up and down the road. I heard no sound of a retreating motorcar. There was silence apart from the sigh of the wind in the pine trees and the gentle splash of waves on the shore of the loch. I stood, hesitant, at the side of the road, not knowing what to do next. I had no way of knowing in which direction he might have gone if he had, in fact, come out of the gate by himself. Someone should alert the police, of course. I hoped Granddad would do just that.

At that moment I heard the sound of an approaching vehicle. It was a small motorcar, a Morris, by the look of it. I stepped out into the road, waved it down as it approached and wrenched open the passenger door. "You haven't seen a small boy, by any chance, have you?" I asked. Then I realized that I recognized the driver. "Oh, Ronny, it's you."

"Oh, hello, Georgie," she said pleasantly. "A small boy? About how old? There were a couple of boys fishing about a mile back."

"He's only three. My nephew, Podge. He's run off. His nurse is beside herself."

"He can't have run far if he's only three. He's probably hiding somewhere." She grinned. "I used to hide when I was that age. I used to scare the daylights out of my parents. Once I got up in the attic and couldn't get down."

I held up the toy soldier. "I found this on the driveway, not far from the gate, so he must have come this way."

"In that case, hop in," she said. "I can help you look if you like."

"Thanks awfully." I climbed in and we started off slowly, scanning the lochside and hedgerow as we drove, windows open and constantly calling his name. It suddenly struck me how ironic this situation was, if her father was indeed the kidnapper and she was helping me to chase him down.

We had gone about half a mile when something caught my eye. "Wait. What's that over there?"

Ronny jammed on the brakes. I jumped out before the motorcar came to a complete stop and ran across to an old boathouse, perched on the edge of the loch. Outside the boathouse I had spotted another glimpse of red. It was a second toy soldier. Ronny had come to join me. I held it up for her.

"Do you think he's gone in there?" she asked. She started to open the rotting door with great caution. "He must be an adventurous little chap."

"Maybe someone's taken him in there," I said, my voice literally shaking with terror by now.

"The door wasn't properly shut," she said, pulling it wide open now. "It's awfully dark in here." She glanced back at me. "Podge? Is that his name?" she asked, then called, "Podge, are you in here?" Then she turned back. "I think I might have a torch in the car."

I stepped inside, dreading what I might be about to find. The only light came from the reflection on the water that lapped a long way below me. A walkway ran along three sides. Up here it was shrouded in gloom and smelled overpoweringly damp and mildewy. I started to poke around amid old sacks and rotting cartons, my heart thumping every time I touched something soft or wet. I was conscious of Ronny standing behind me.

"He doesn't seem to be in here," I said, looking up at her.

"No," she replied. "He's not."

"You've found him?"

"Let's just say I know where he is."

"Where is he?"

"Safe. For the moment."

"What do you mean?" I stared at her, trying to take this in. "Your father took him?"

"My father? My father is dead."

"Major Padgett is dead?"

"He's not my real father, but then you know that, don't you? Hugo must have told you. Why else did you visit Castle Craig yesterday? You know all about my real parents."

"Maisie McPhee is your real mother, I presume," I said.

"Well done. My real mother. She's gone insane. She doesn't even know me, but I still go to see her. I feel I owe it to her."

She looked at me and started to laugh. "You really are terribly naïve and trusting, aren't you? I planted the soldiers along the way and you, my dear, took the bait so easily . . . and now I've reeled you in."

That's when I realized that what she was holding was not a torch at all. It was a pistol.

"You kidnapped him? It was you?"

"Yes," she said in a matter-of-fact voice.

"Why? Why do that to a small boy who has done you no harm?"

"Security, my sweet. I might need a bargaining chip to get me safely out of the country. And you"—she paused as if examining me—"you were becoming a blasted nuisance. Hugo told you everything, didn't he?"

I was still trying to take this in. "It was you who shot at me yesterday? Who killed Hugo?"

She laughed again. "Poor old Hugo. Too smart for his own good. And too soft too. He had it figured out but then he made the mistake of telling me. He wanted me to do the honorable thing and turn myself in. How silly can you be?"

"I was too slow," I said. "I should have realized. I knew there was something worrying me. You gave yourself away when we spoke together after Hugo had died. Godfrey Beverley told you that someone had been shot. He didn't say he was dead, but you spoke of him in the past tense."

"As you say, you were too slow."

"And Godfrey Beverley," I said, as pieces fell into place in my head. "He was looking directly at you when he asked why anyone would need two guns."

"Stupid little man," she said. "Always poking his nose where it wasn't wanted. I realized he must have seen me."

"And your maid? You borrowed the motorbike and ran her over?"

"She snooped. She had to go."

I stared at her, noting the easy way she dismissed these murders.

"What have you done with Podge?" I demanded.

"He's quite safe. You don't have to worry about him."

"Of course I worry about him. Take me to him."

"He's on my Gypsy Moth, right here on the lake. Climb down into the boat and you can row us out to him." She indicated a small rowing boat tied at the bottom of the steps and motioned with the pistol that I should go down them.

I was trying to control my racing thoughts, wondering what chance I stood if I dove into the water and went for help. There was nothing nearer than Castle Rannoch and by that time she could have killed Podge or taken off with him. I wondered if I could reach the plane first if I dove in and swam to it. I was a strong swimmer and she would have to climb down the ladder then untie the rowing boat, which would give me a good head start. It was worth a try and it was better than doing nothing. She was obviously going to kill me and probably Podge too. What did I have to lose?

I took a deep breath and launched myself into the black water. I heard the shot echoing around the boathouse. At any second I expected to feel the sting of a bullet but I hit the surface and went under. I gasped at the cold and had to stop myself from coming up to take an immediate breath. Instead I kicked out underwater, praying I was heading in the right direction. I kept swimming underwater until I could see brighter daylight ahead of me. I held my breath until my lungs were on fire and I came up, gasping for air. No sign of the rowing boat yet. I struck out for the plane with powerful strokes, swimming faster than I had ever done before. I hadn't worked out what I'd do when I reached the aeroplane. She still had the pistol and I was still a sitting target, but I'd work that part out when I came to it.

The aeroplane bobbed on its floats tied to a buoy, within easy swimming distance now. I reached it, hauled myself onto the fin and stood up, holding on to the lower of the double wings. It felt flimsy and insecure. I hadn't realized before that aeroplanes were made of wood and fabric and wires, like large kites. The rowing boat was now clear of the boathouse and she was rowing hard toward me. This was good news, in that she couldn't shoot and row at the same time. If I could grab Podge and get him into the water with me, we might just be able to evade Ronny in her rowing boat.

As I stood up and looked into the aeroplane, I could see it had two open cockpits, one behind the other. I looked into the backseat first. No sign of Podge. There were a couple of what looked like rucksacks, half pushed under the seat, but they were too small to hold a child.

I maneuvered my way along the fin to the forward seat and couldn't see him there, either. I swung my leg over and climbed inside, reaching around on the floor to see if there might be a secret compartment where he could be hidden. But there was nothing.

I didn't have any time to decide what to do next. The plane started shaking, indicating that Ronny had reached it and was climbing on board. I'd better start swimming again. I swung one leg over the side.

"I wouldn't do that if I were you," Ronny said. She was standing only a foot or so away and the pistol was now pointed at my head.

"He's not here," I said lamely.

"No. He's not."

"But you said . . ."

"Georgie, you really must stop believing what people tell you. It's such a pathetic trait."

"Where is he?" I was really angry now, even though I knew she had the gun and she was probably going to shoot me. "What have you done with him?"

"I told you he was safe, and he is, for the time being. He's tied up in the boot of my car. He was there, behind you, all the time." She laughed as if this was a good joke as she moved nimbly along the float and untied the craft from its buoy.

"Then why take the trouble to bring me out here? You could have shot me in the boathouse and tossed my body into the water."

"I could have, but I decided that you'd do just as well as a hostage. You swam here under your own steam and I don't have to go to the trouble of carrying your nephew from the motorcar and risk being seen. Please sit down. I promised to take you up, didn't I? Well, now you're getting your chance."

I noticed, really for the first time, that she was wearing a leather flight jacket. She had come prepared. I was already soaking wet. It was quite likely I was going to freeze to death before she shot me or tipped me out.

"Sit," she commanded again, indicating the front seat. I had no choice. I sat.

She rummaged in one of the bags in the backseat and threw something at me. "Here." It was a pair of goggles. "Now strap yourself in."

"Why are you doing this?" I demanded. "What have we ever done to you?"

"Robbed me of my birthright," she said. "You know who my father was, don't you? He was the heir to the throne. The Duke of Clarence."

"The Duke of Clarence? He was your father? But he died long before you were born."

"He didn't die. It was a monstrous conspiracy," she said. "They kidnapped him and had him shut away up here. He never recovered his health and died when I was a baby, so I've been told. So when you look at it that way, I'm the rightful heir to the throne."

"Even if this is true, I'm sure he didn't marry your mother, so you're not the rightful heir to anything."

"He did marry her," she said angrily. "He did. She told me."

"No one would ever believe you," I said.

"No. That's why this was the only way to get back at the stupid royal family. And I must say I've enjoyed it. I never intended to kill anyone, you know. Just frighten them. Just make them feel they were never safe. And I succeeded."

"But why? Why waste your energy on that when you have so much to live for? You're a famous woman. You've set records. You'll go down in the history books."

"It's never enough," she said simply. "There is never enough to fill the void."

She climbed into the rear seat. "Hold tight!" she shouted. The machine roared to life. The whole contraption started to shake.

Then without warning it started to move, faster and faster, bouncing over the water until suddenly it was airborne. Loch and mountains fell away beneath us. There was Castle Rannoch, nestled among the trees. There was the boathouse and the car parked beside it, looking like a child's toy. Scotland stretched beneath us—the bleak expanse of Rannoch Moor and beyond it the glittering of the sea and the Western Isles.

"Where are we going?" I turned to shout. It suddenly occurred to me that she was attempting to fly to America and that we'd never make it and come down somewhere in the middle of the Atlantic. I was shivering badly now, both from the cold wind and from the fear. She was sitting behind me so I couldn't see what she was doing. Not that I could take any action anyway. I was strapped into a seat, up in the air.

Then I felt the plane shake. I swiveled in my seat to look at her and saw, to my dismay, that she was standing up.

"What are you doing?" I yelled.

"I've always wanted to fly," she shouted back. "Now seems like a good time to try it." Then she laughed again. "Oh, don't worry about me. I have a parachute on my back. You're the one who needs to worry. You'll be up here alone. It's perfect really. Much simpler than a hostage. Either you'll go down into the Atlantic or you'll eventually crash. If you do, the plane is full of fuel. It will explode and you'll be burned beyond recognition. Everyone will think it's me. Poor Ronny Padgett. So sad. Give her a state funeral. And I will be making a new life in America! Land of opportunity, they say."

I was trying to unbuckle my harness to stop her, but I wasn't quick enough. She launched herself over the side. I watched her falling, spread-eagled, toward the earth.

Chapter 33

For a long moment I just sat there, too stunned to do anything.

"I am alone in an aeroplane, thousands of feet up in the air," I said out loud, and added, since there was nobody within miles to hear me, "Bugger." (I thought the occasion warranted a swearword. I only wished I knew some stronger ones. I'd have used them all. Loudly.)

Frankly I was finding it hard to breathe and it wasn't just the wind in my face. Even if I knew how to fly an aeroplane, there were no instruments in my compartment. And I didn't know how to fly an aeroplane anyway. Let's face it—I had never even been in one before. But I wasn't just going to sit there and accept my fate. "Do something," I commanded myself.

For the moment we were flying smoothly forward, out toward the Atlantic Ocean. I forced my freezing, trembling fingers to unbuckle the harness, then I turned and knelt on the seat. The wind was so strong I could hardly move. I grasped the struts that held up the overhead wing and pulled myself into a kneeling position on the space between the two seats. There was a windshield, making forward progress difficult. I had to inch one leg around, holding on to that windshield for dear life. The plane reacted to my weight as I slithered hastily into the backseat.

"So far, so good," I said to encourage myself. Then I took stock of the cockpit. I stared at the instrument panel in front of me, hoping for a glimmer of inspiration. Needles were moving on dials but I had no idea what any of them meant. There was also a metal handle coming out of the floor between my legs. I moved it tentatively to one side and the machine started to bank. Hastily I restored it to its previous position. So I could turn the machine if I wanted but what use would that be? I presumed that pushing the stick forward might therefore make it go down, but I had no idea how I would slow it down enough to land on water. We were heading due west. Soon we would be out over the Atlantic and then destruction was inevitable. Come to think of it, it was inevitable anyway. I've always been an optimistic sort of person and I do have the blood of all those impossibly brave Rannochs coursing through my veins, but I was finding it awfully hard to be brave.

I wondered if I dared experiment in trying to turn the aeroplane before it was actually over the Atlantic. Then I wondered what chance of survival I would have if I brought the plane very low over the water and then jumped out. That made me wonder if the other rucksack contained a second parachute. I opened it and it contained a change of clothing and a bar of Cadbury's chocolate. I started to eat it. I was halfway through when I became aware of a noise—a loud droning sound. I turned around and found that I was being followed by another aeroplane. Hope sprung up. They had come to rescue me! Then of course I realized that they thought this was Ronny's machine and they had no idea I was in it.

I waited until the other machine was very close, then I stood up, waving my arms.

"It's me. Help!" I shouted. Not very informative, but the best I could do in the circumstances.

The other aeroplane signaled to me, a thumbs-up, which I took to be a good thing. I could see two flyers in helmets and goggles staring at me before their machine rose and began to fly over me. It was hovering over me like a giant dragonfly, its shape blotting out the sun, then something snaked down beside me, almost whacked me on the head then swung out again. I realized that it was a rope ladder. Surely they weren't expecting me to grab it and climb up? On second thought this was a better choice than crashing into the ocean.

As I was leaning out, trying to catch it as it bobbed and danced in the wind, I realized that someone was climbing down it. Soon this person had hold of the upper wing and was standing on the wooden fuselage right in front of me.

"Can you climb up the ladder, do you think?" he shouted.

"I don't know." I looked up at the other plane. "My hands are freezing."

At that moment the decision was taken from me. A large cloud loomed in front of us.

"Too late," the man snapped and released the ladder. "Quick. Move up front. I need to fly this thing." I didn't really have time to think as we were swallowed up in cloud. "Careful now," he said, as I stood up and he stepped down into the cockpit beside me. He held on to me firmly as I reversed my previous maneuver, inching around the windshield and into the front seat.

"Good girl," he shouted. "Strap yourself in."

We came out of cloud into bright sunshine. There was no sign of the other plane.

"I don't want to do that again in a hurry," my visitor shouted. Finally I recognized the voice. I turned to look at him. It was Darcy.

"What are you doing up here?" I yelled back to him.

"How about 'Thank you for coming to rescue me'?"

"Do you know how to fly one of these things?"

"No, but I've got the instruction book here. You can read it to me." He reached into his jacket and then looked at my face and laughed. "Actually I have flown a plane before. I'll get us down safely."

Suddenly I felt my stomach drop as the plane swung to the right. We were circling, dropping lower and lower. There was a large sea loch ahead of us. We were skimming over bright water. Then we were bumping crazily until we came to a stop a few yards short of a rocky outcropping.

Darcy unbuttoned his helmet and took off his goggles. "Phew, that was close," he said, standing up. "I've never landed on water before."

"This is a stupid time to tell me that," I snapped and promptly burst into tears.

"Georgie." He reached forward and dragged me into his arms while the aeroplane rocked dangerously. "It's all right. We made it. You're safe now."

"I know," I said. I tried to stop crying, but I couldn't. I knelt on the seat with my cheek against his leather jacket and sobbed. "I feel such a fool," I said at last. "And I've made your leather jacket all wet."

"That's okay. Cows get wet from time to time, don't they?" He smiled and stroked my hair, which by now resembled a haystack. "But the rest of you is already wet. How did that happen?"

"I swam to the aeroplane. She tricked me. I thought that Podge was in it, but he wasn't."

"You've had quite a morning so far." He was still smiling. "At least you can't say it was dull."

"I thought you'd gone away again."

"Well, fortunately I got in touch with your Sir Jeremy and it turned out we had a few friends in common, so the need to go somewhere was avoided."

"How did you find me?" I asked, at last.

"Pure luck. We were sitting outside the house and we actually watched the plane take off. Next moment I received a telephone call to say that the rifle that killed Hugo Beasley-Bottome had been found at the Padgetts' house and that your nephew was missing. Then someone said they'd seen two people in the plane, so we assumed the worst. Luckily Paolo had come back from London in his own floatplane this time, so we were up in the air shortly after you. And Paolo's machine is a lot faster, so we caught you quite quickly. I take it Ronny *was* in the plane at some point? You didn't actually take off by yourself?"

"Of course she was in the plane."

"What happened to her?"

"She jumped out," I said. "She said she was wearing a parachute but I didn't see it opening. I think she just fell."

"A suitable ending for her." Darcy nodded gravely. "I would have hated to see someone like that be hanged or put into an insane asylum."

"Her mother is in one," I said. I was about to say that she had contracted syphilis, but I couldn't discuss such an unmentionable subject with Darcy.

"Maisie McPhee, right? Sir Jeremy's men looked her up at the New Register House in Edinburgh, you'll be pleased to know. She did have a child—unnamed baby girl about the right age for Ronny."

"And the father?"

"Someone named Eddy Axton, although it looks as if the birth certificate has been tampered with."

"Eddy Axton. That sounds very ordinary. And she didn't marry him or have any other children?"

"No."

"Poor Ronny, all those grand illusions for nothing."

"As you say, poor Ronny." He ran his hand down my cheek. "You are freezing. We should get you home as quickly as possible."

"Yes, we must get back to Rannoch immediately," I said, remembering, "I know where my nephew is hidden. We have to save him." I looked around us. Nothing but hills and moorland, lapping water and seagulls circling overhead. "Why on earth did you choose to land here? We're miles from anywhere."

"I have no idea where we are, but I wasn't taking any chances with a plane I'd never flown before. I chose the first open area of water I saw, where I wasn't likely to bump into a mountain."

"Well, come on. Let's not waste any more time. We have to get to shore and telephone the police."

"Your wish is my command, my lady. Now I suppose you'd like me to swim to shore."

"It's shallow. You can wade," I said. Then as he went to climb out of the aeroplane, I touched his hand. "Darcy. Thank you for coming to my rescue. You were very brave, and you landed it jolly well too, considering."

He laughed and lowered himself into the water.

"It's absolutely freezing," he shouted up to me. "The things I have to do for you!"

Chapter 34

Soon Darcy had found a telephone, rounded up a local policeman and borrowed a car. As we were driving back to Castle Rannoch, I sat beside him, snuggling up to him for warmth, for once in a glow of happiness. As we came over the pass to Castle Rannoch, we spotted Paolo and the American standing on the jetty, jumping up and down, waving their arms and pointing.

"What's going on there?" Darcy asked. He had the driver stop the car and we both got out. "What's happening?" Darcy shouted, running toward Paolo.

"She's taken my boat, without my permission," Paolo shouted back.

"Who?"

"Ronny, of course."

"Ronny? But I thought she was dead. She jumped out of a plane," I said.

"She must have had a parachute then," Paolo said, "because suddenly I heard my boat engine start and she was in it."

"Where is she now?" Darcy asked.

"Look, there, at the far end of the loch. You know what she's going to do, don't you? She's going to make a run at the speed record, but the boat isn't ready yet. Damned fool. She'll ruin everything."

"She hasn't got Podge with her, has she?" I shouted. "We must stop her."

Before I could get the words out, a blue shape came hurtling down the loch, motor screaming. Faster and faster it went until it shot past us as a blue blur. Then someone yelled, "Look out!"

And someone else screamed, "It's the monster!"

The wind was ruffling the water, driving it into a great wave that curled up along the middle of the lake, looking for anything like the coils of a giant serpent. The boat hit the wave full-on. It became airborne. For what seemed like an eternity it soared, flying over the surface of the water, then it rose straight up, flipped, bounced and broke apart, with pieces flying in all directions. The wave subsided. There was silence. Small pieces of blue floated on the oily surface of the lake.

I found I was running along the shoreline, yelling, "Podge. Not Podge."

Darcy caught up with me. "Georgie. Come on, I'll take you home. There's nothing you can do here."

"But he might still be alive."

"If he was in that boat, he won't be. But you told them where to find him. I'm sure he's safe."

I found I was holding my breath all the way up the drive to Castle Rannoch. As the car came to a halt outside the front steps, the door opened and Fig came running out to meet me, with Binky behind her, hobbling on crutches.

"Georgiana, thank God you're safe," she said.

"Never mind about me. What about Podge?"

"In his bed, sleeping," she said.

"They found him in time, then?"

"Thanks to your wonderful grandfather. He saw you driving off in a car and he was sensible enough to note the license plate number. The police found the car right away and discovered my little boy in the boot. Imagine doing that to a child. That woman is a monster. I hope they catch her."

"She's dead," I said.

※

"SHE ALWAYS WAS reckless." Major Padgett looked across at his wife, who sat silent and grieving in their cold, dreary drawing room. "Even when she was a small child she took risks and didn't respect boundaries. Too much like her father, I'm afraid."

"She claimed her father was the Duke of Clarence," I said.

"Did she tell you that?"

I nodded. "But her birth certificate gives her father's name as Eddy Axton. Not royal at all."

"Eddy Avon," he said. "I tried to alter it."

"Why? Who is Eddy Avon?"

"The Duke of Clarence was also known as the Earl of Avonlea and among the family he was always known as Eddy." Major Padgett sighed. "I knew it would come out eventually. How can such a monstrous secret remain hidden? It has eaten into me all these years."

"Then it really was true that he was kidnapped and kept alive? He didn't die of influenza?"

He sighed. "I'm afraid so."

"You were one of the people who kidnapped him? Who held him prisoner in a mental institution?" I looked at him with undisguised revulsion.

"I was, God forgive me." He stared down at his highly polished shoes. "I was removed from a promising military career to act as equerry to His Royal Highness the Duke of Clarence, the heir to the throne. Everything I learned about him distressed me and disgusted me. His depraved sexual behavior with both men and women, his use of drugs, his errors of judgment . . . I hoped that he would never come to the throne. He would have been the ruin of the monarchy. When his doctor confided to me that he had contracted syphilis from a prostitute, I thought I should die of shame.

"Then a miracle happened: a most virulent strain of influenza swept the country. It felled the prince. He was at death's door, lying in a coma. There were certain powerful personages at court who saw this as a chance to make sure he never recovered. They wanted me to finish him off, but I would not be party to deliberate killing.

"However, a second miracle occurred. On that very day a young footman succumbed to the disease. He was not unlike the prince in stature and coloring. A small group of conspirators managed to replace the comatose prince with the dead footman. The royal family was kept at a distance because of the risk of contracting the disease. The footman was buried with royal pomp, while the footman's coffin contained several large rocks."

He looked up at us with hopeless eyes. "The Duke of Clarence was whisked away to the country estate of one of the conspirators. Against all odds he recovered, at least partially. The high fever had damaged his brain and his heart and also sped up the progression of syphilis. He remained bedridden, sometimes violent and not always coherent. A doctor told us he was not expected to live long, so it was decided to secret him far, far away, up here in Scotland."

"Did members of the royal family know about this?" Darcy asked.

Padgett shook his head. "Of course not. And they must never know. Nobody must ever know. Has it already gone beyond this room?"

"Sir Jeremy Danville knows what I suspected," I said.

"But he is head of the special branch," Darcy said quickly. "They do not divulge secrets. And you can rely on Georgie and me."

Major Padgett nodded. "It has been such a burden, all these years. I was assigned the task of being his keeper, you see. I can't tell you how I despised that task—how I felt the whole thing was morally wrong."

"Why did you accept if it was so repugnant to you?" Darcy asked.

"I am a military man," Padgett said. "I obey orders, I put my country before myself and my word is my badge of honor. I was present at the first meeting of the conspirators when a vow of silence was made. I do not break vows, whatever the consequences, but I have regretted it every day since. It meant the end of my career. It banished my poor wife to a life of loneliness and social withdrawal."

"I didn't mind, dear," she said from across the room. "I married you for better or worse, you know. Watching you sink into despair has been hardest. And we did have Ronny for a short while."

"So he recovered enough to father a daughter?" I asked.

Major Padgett nodded. "Even in his incapacitated state, he couldn't keep his hands off the maids. We watched him closely, but young Maisie McPhee was his night nurse and he didn't always sleep. My wife had always wanted a child so we decided to adopt this one and make sure it was raised in a good home. And the Duke of Clarence's heart finally gave out soon after Veronica was born. We raised her as our own. It was like two guinea hens trying to raise an eagle chick."

"You told her about her real parents then?" I asked.

"Of course not. Only a handful of prominent men were party to that secret. We thought it only right to tell Veronica she was adopted when she was old enough. As I said, she always sought danger and the forbidden. She went into my office, which was off-limits to her. She snooped through my private files and she found regular payments to Maisie McPhee. She went to visit that woman, who was already slipping into insanity. Apparently Maisie spun our daughter a grandiose tale about her royal parentage and claimed they had actually married, which wasn't true. Veronica blackmailed and coerced me into confirming who her father was.

"After that she started having grand ideas about being a member of the royal family. We tried to make her see sense. We were glad when she took up flying and started to make a name for herself as an aviatrix. But obviously it wasn't enough for her."

"She told me before she jumped from the aeroplane that nothing was enough to fill the void."

"God rest her soul," Mrs. Padgett said. Darcy crossed himself.

DAYLIGHT WAS FADING when Darcy and I finally drove down the winding road to Castle Rannoch. The sky was glowing pink and gold. A flight of wild duck circled the loch. It felt as if the world was finally at peace.

"Darcy," I said after a long silence, "why haven't you given up on me? What do you see in me? I'm not your sort of girl at all. I'm penniless, for one thing. I'm not glamorous. I'm not sexy. I'm not beautiful."

"True enough," he said with that horrible Irish candor. "I have to confess, to start with it was the challenge. You were so impossibly haughty and virginal, and it was intriguing to see if I could bed a granddaughter of Queen Victoria."

"Great-granddaughter," I corrected.

"Great-granddaughter, then. And after a while I started thinking, 'You know, I think one could have a good roll in the hay with her, once she'd been warmed up a bit.' "

He looked at me and I blushed.

"And now?" I said.

I suppose I was hoping he'd tell me that he loved me.

"I never like to give up on a challenge," he said breezily, "especially when the goal is in sight."

Not the answer I was looking for. We drove on for a while in silence.

"Is that the only reason?" I said. "I'm a challenge to you? And when you've finally achieved your goal, you'll lose interest instantly?"

"Not exactly," he said. "The problem is, Georgie, that I can't seem to get you out of my head. I know I should be going after a rich heiress who will keep me in the style to which I'd like to be accustomed. But I keep coming back to you. I don't know why."

He reached across and covered my hand with his own. "But here I am," he said. "And here you are. Let's just take it from here and see where it goes, shall we?"

"Yes, let's." I turned my face up to him to be kissed. Then I yelled, "Look out!" as several sheep wandered across the road.

Historical Note

Ronny Padgett is modeled on famous aviatrix Amy Johnson who broke many records in the 1930s, including flying solo to Australia in her Gypsy Moth. She was killed in WWII.

Prince Albert Victor, Duke of Clarence and Avondale, 1864–1892, has long been a subject of rumor and speculation. He was the oldest son of King Edward VII and thus heir to the throne. Although there is little firm evidence, his reputation was one of dissolute behavior. He is reputed to have frequented both male and female prostitutes, to have been whisked away from a raid on a homosexual brothel, and even to have been Jack the Ripper. So when he died of influenza at the age of twenty-eight, leaving the path to the throne open for his solid and reliable younger brother, who later became George V, rumors flew that his death had been aided or even that he had been kidnapped and was kept prisoner in an insane asylum.

None of these rumors has ever been substantiated, but they certainly make for a good story!

His future bride, Princess May of Teck, later married his brother George and the royal couple were reported to be extremely happy.

The activity on the Scottish loch—both the speedboat and the monster are quite correct for the time. Attempts were being made on the water speed record, some with fatal results, and the Loch Ness Monster was about to capture headlines and enthrall readers throughout the world.

Printed in the United States
by Baker & Taylor Publisher Services